THREE ENTHRALLING GALACTIC SAGAS IN A DISTANT, DAZZLING FUTURE

Mistworld
On this fog-shrouded sanctuary for outlaws and rebels, a lethal menace is about to strike with devastating ferocity. Only Investigator Topaz, expert assassin and high-level esper, has any chance of stopping it . . .

Ghostworld
Base Thirteen was a mining colony on a lonely planet of bizarre beauty. But it was abandoned long ago, and nothing alive remains. Or so the Empire thinks . . .

Hellworld
The Hell Squads are sent to new planets on one-way missions of exploration. Such assignments are fraught with countless dangers even under the best conditions. And the Squad that lands on Wolf IV is presented with anything but the best conditions. In fact, what they find is beyond imagination . . .

Also by Simon R. Green in paperback

DEATHSTALKER

DEATHSTALKER REBELLION

DEATHSTALKER WAR

DEATHSTALKER HONOUR

BLUE MOON RISING

BLOOD AND HONOUR

DOWN AMONG THE DEAD MEN

SHADOWS FALL

SIMON R. GREEN

DEATHSTALKER PRELUDE

VISTA

Mistworld first published 1992 by Victor Gollancz Ltd
Ghostworld first published 1993 and *Hellworld* 1995
by Victor Gollancz

First published as one volume in the USA 1997
under the title *Twilight of Empire*
by Roc, an imprint of Dutton Signet, a division of
Penguin Books USA Inc.

First published as one volume in Great Britain 1998
as a Vista paperback original
Vista is an imprint of the Cassell Group
Wellington House, 125 Strand, London WC2R 0BB

A catalogue record for this book is
available from the British Library.

ISBN 0 575 60330 5

Typeset by SetSystems Ltd, Saffron Walden, Essex
Printed and bound in Great Britain by
Cox & Wyman Ltd, Reading, Berks

98 99 10 9 8 7 6 5 4 3 2 1

Contents

MISTWORLD

Call her Mary. When she sang she could break your heart or mend it, but that was before the Empire found and used her. Now she's just another refugee running for her life. Deep within her, madness stirs. Her name is Mary. Typhoid Mary. And nobody in Mistport will ever forget her.

CHAPTER ONE

A Ghost in the Night

A low gusting wind came moaning out of the North, unsettling the snow-flecked mists that filled the narrow Mistport streets. Lamps and lanterns hung at every door, burning yellow and red and orange against the endless sea of grey. The mists were always at their thickest in the early hours of the morning, before the rising of Mistworld's pale sun.

A dim figure padded confidently across a slippery slate roof, his slender frame barely visible amidst the swirling snow flurries. The pure white of his thermal suit blended harmoniously into the snow and the mists, whilst its heating elements insulated him from the wind's cutting edge. The man called Cat crouched down by an outjutting attic window and pushed back his suit's cowl, revealing pale youthful features dominated by dark watchful eyes and the pockmarks that tattooed both cheeks. He winced as the freezing air seared his bare face, and then he slid carefully down the snow-smeared tiles to bump into a gently smoking chimneystack. He took a firm hold on the uneven brickwork and leaned out from the roof to stare about him.

From his high vantage point there lay stretched out before him all the tiled and gabled rooftops of Mistport, his hunting ground and private kingdom. Cat had spent most of his twenty years learning his trade and refining his craft to become one of the finest burglars Thieves' Quarter had ever produced. The ornately carved and curlicued wood and ironwork of Mistport's buildings were hand and footholds to him; the cornices and gables his landmarks and resting places.

Cat was a roof runner.

Light from the huge half moon shone clearly through the curling mists, reflecting brightly from the snow-covered roofs and streets and setting out the scene below in eerie starkness. To Cat's left lay the scattered glow of Thieves' Quarter, sprawled in a tangle of shabby streets, where outleaning timbered buildings huddled together as though for warmth in the cold night. Its occasional lights shone crimson against the dark, like rubies set on velvet. To his right lay Tech Quarter and the starport.

Sensor spikes blazed in the night, blue stormfire shivering up and down the slender crystal lances. Oil lamps and torches burned in regular patterns across the starport grounds, marking out the huge landing pads, each of them half a mile wide. Of all the port's buildings only the steelglass control tower, last remnant of the Empire's original Base, still boasted bright electric lights. Less than a dozen ships lay on the landing pads, mostly abandoned hulks stripped down for the high tech they possessed. A handful of smugglers' ships lay scattered across one pad; five silver needles glowing ruddy from the flickering torches. Beacons suddenly flared into life around the largest pad, like corpsefires on a newly built cairn, and Cat realized with a thrill of excitement that there was a ship coming in. Ships of any kind were growing rare these days, so any new arrival was good news. Cat turned reluctantly away, and looked down at the streets below him.

Nobody moved in the empty alleyways, and the pale blanket of freshly fallen snow remained unbroken. Only thieves and spies braved the bitter cold of Mistport's night, and they never left tracks.

Cat pulled his cowl back down to shield his face, and releasing his hold on the chimneystack he slipped carefully over the roof's edge. He took a firm grip on the narrow drainpipe and slowly eased himself head first over the edge until he was hanging upside down, his feet hooked securely under the guttering. The rusty ironwork groaned under his weight, but held firm as he thoughtfully studied the small steel-latticed window before him. The window was less than two feet square, and the grille was cast from stainless steel. *How very inhospitable*, thought Cat. *Anyone would think they were afraid of being burgled.* He looked more closely at the windowframe, smiling complacently as he spotted two slender wires attached to the upper right-hand corner of the grille that disappeared into the brickwork to no apparent purpose. Obviously an alarm of some kind. Cat drew a pair of miniature cutters from inside his left boot, reached out to cut the wires, and then hesitated. They were too obvious. He checked again, and grinned wryly as he discovered a small electronic sensor fitted flush into the grille's ironwood frame. Touch the grille or the frame, and the sensor would set off an alarm. Cat slipped the cutters into his glove, and drawing a slender steel probe from his right boot he delicately shorted out the sensor with the casual skill of long practice. He slipped the probe back into his boot, and then took the cutters and carefully snipped both of the wires, just in case. He put the cutters back in his left boot, took out a small screwdriver, and calmly set about undoing the four simple screws that held the grille in place.

Blood pounded in his head from being upside down so long, but he ignored it as best he could and refused to be hurried. He dropped three of the screws one by one into the white leather pouch at his belt, and then put away the screwdriver and tugged cautiously at the steel grille. It came away easily in his hands and hung loosely by the one remaining screw. Cat grinned. So far, everything was going as planned. He pushed aside the grille and slipped an arm through the window. His head followed, and he breathed gently as his chest and back scraped against the unyielding ironwood frame. He took a firm grip on the inner frame with his hand, and then, taking a deep breath, he worked his feet loose from under the guttering. His body jerked violently in the windowframe as his legs fell free, but the jolt wasn't enough to pull him back out the window. He waited a moment while his breathing steadied, then released his grip on the inner frame. Inch by inch he worked his upper torso through the narrow gap until his waist and hips followed easily. Only someone as wiry and limber as he could have managed it. Which was one of the reasons why even Cat's rivals acknowledged him as the finest roof runner in Mistport.

He swung lithely down from the window, and crouched motionless in the shadows while his eyes adjusted to the gloom. The narrow landing stretched away before him, with a stairway to his left and two closed doors to his right. Moonlight spilled through the open window behind him, but even Cat's experienced eyes were hard put to make out details in the darkness beyond the shimmering light. He took off his gloves and tucked them into his belt, and flexed his long slender fingers through a quick series of exercises. To a good burglar, the hands were just as important as the tools they used. Cat always looked after his hands. He gingerly pressed the tips of his fingers against the floor, closed his eyes and concentrated on the feel of the polished wood. Faint vibrations tingled under his fingertips, and Cat frowned thoughtfully. There were sensor panels hidden in the floor, no doubt designed to set off all kinds of alarms if a man's weight triggered them. Still without opening his eyes, Cat leaned slowly forward and swept his fingers back and forth across the floor in a series of widening arcs, judging by the rise and fall of the vibrations where it was safe and where it was not. He slowly worked his way along, inch by inch, until he was sure he'd located the main pattern, and then he opened his eyes, stood up, and padded confidently down the landing, easily avoiding the treacherous areas.

Just like the old game, he thought dryly. *Step on a crack, break your mother's back* . . . He frowned, remembering how long it had been since Mistport could afford to maintain paved sidewalks. The times were not what they were. Cat shrugged, and moved quickly on to the lower of the two doors. The sooner this part of the job was over, the better; the same white suit that hid him in the snow and the mists was wildly conspicuous on a dark deserted landing.

He stopped before the closed lower door and studied it warily. His fence had briefed him as thoroughly as possible on the house's exterior, but hadn't been able to tell him much about the interior. The door had to be booby-trapped in some way; it was what Cat would have done. He ran his fingers gently over the harsh-grained wood, but couldn't detect anything out of the ordinary. He took a pencil torch from inside his right boot, thumbed it on, and leaning closer he ran his gaze over the doorframe, inch by inch. Sure enough there was a small, slightly raised button high up on the frame; a simple catch that was released when the door opened. Cat shook his head dolefully at such a meagre testing of his talents, and taking out the steel probe he slipped it quickly past the button to turn it off. And then Cat frowned and pulled back the probe. The alarm button was already in the off position; they must have forgotten to set it before going to bed. Cat rolled his eyes heavenwards. This was becoming ridiculously easy. He snapped off the torch, put it away with the probe and, taking a firm grip on the door handle, slowly eased the door open. He checked quickly for back-up alarms, and then peered cautiously into the bedroom.

A sparse light filtered past the bolted shutters to show him a dim form huddled under thick blankets in the canopied bed that took up most of the small bedroom. A few glowing coals burned redly in the fireplace to his right, taking the chill off the air. Cat slipped into the room, closed the door behind him and moved over to the bed, silent as the ghost he seemed. He paused briefly as the sleeper stirred and then lay still again. Cat didn't carry any weapons; he didn't believe in them. He was a roof runner and an artist in his craft, not some bully-boy vandal or heartless thief in the night. Cat had his standards. He stood motionless beside the bed until he was sure it was safe to move again, then leaned forward over the sleeping shape and reached out his hand. Judging his moment nicely, he eased it under the pillow and drew out a small brass-bound casket. The bed's occupant slept on, undisturbed. Cat stepped back from the bed, drew a small key from the pouch at his belt, and tried it cautiously in the casket's lock. The key turned easily, and Cat grinned broadly as he pushed back the lid and the crystal in the casket blazed light into the room.

As an Outlaw planet, Mistworld was cut off from Empire trade, and high tech was limited to what the smugglers could bring in on their infrequent visits. A computer's memory crystal thus became far more tempting loot than any diamond or ruby. Cat didn't know what information the crystal held, and didn't care. His fence said she had a buyer for the jewel, and that was all that mattered. Cat reached into the pouch at his belt and brought out a blank crystal, glowing twin to the jewel in the casket. He carefully substituted one crystal for the other, closed the lid and locked it. He dropped the key back into his pouch, leaned forward and deftly replaced the casket where he'd found it. His hand had barely left the pillow when the bedroom door suddenly flew open. Light flooded the room, and a tall figure with a lantern filled the doorway.

Cat pulled the blankets from the bed and with one desperate heave threw them over the newcomer's head. The bed's occupant sat up sharply, pulling a silk nightdress about her, and Cat paused to drop her an appreciative wink. The newcomer struggled furiously on the floor, helplessly entangled in the bedclothes. The dropped lantern lay on its side in the doorway, filling the room with a flickering light. Cat decided it was time he was going. He stepped carefully around the pile of heaving blankets and made for the open door. The woman in the canopied bed opened her mouth and sang.

Cat sank to his knees as the song washed over him, scrambling his nervous system. *A Siren!* he thought wildly. *They set a Siren to guard the crystal!* The song screamed through his body, shaking in his muscles. He lurched to his feet, considered punching the woman out, decided this was no time to be heroic, and plunged for the doorway. The Siren's song washed over him in waves, numbing his hands and feet and blurring his eyesight.

Cat staggered out of the door and down the landing, paying no attention to the pressure alarms in the floor, just concentrating all his will on not giving in to the Siren song that was trying to batter him unconscious. He finally reached the end window, and pulled himself up into the narrow opening. He wriggled through the window with frantic speed, and then his heart missed a beat as a hand closed around his ankle, bringing him lurching to a halt. He kicked and struggled wildly, and the hand lost its grip and fell away. Cat pulled himself out the window, grabbed the drainpipe, and hauled himself up towards the roof. He scrambled over the guttering and then collapsed to lie flat on the snow-covered tiles. He lay there a while, shaking in every limb, slowly relaxing as he realized he'd left the Siren's song behind. A woman whose voice and esp could combine to scramble a man's thoughts was an impressive guard. Unless, of course, the burglar happens to be a deaf mute . . .

Cat grinned, and rising quickly to his feet, he padded away into the mists. For the first time in years, he was glad not to have heard something.

CHAPTER TWO

A Gathering of Traitors

Leon Vertue's main reception office was warm, comfortable and desperately civilized, and Jamie Royal hated it. Much as he appreciated good living and luxury, he resented having his nose rubbed in it. There was something decidedly smug in the office's ostentatious display of wealth. The sign over the modestly plain front door had simply said BLACKSMITH, but Jamie doubted that anyone who worked in this luxurious office would know an anvil if they fell over it. He sighed, leaned back in his recliner chair, and tried to look as though he was used to such comforts. He surreptitiously trailed his fingers across the slick shining surface of the chair's arms. Plastic. Now that was real luxury. Jamie could count the number of times he'd seen plastic before on the fingers of one hand. More and more, he felt that he was very much out of his depth.

He crossed one leg over the other, doing his best to look relaxed. He glanced casually about the office, hoping to find a lapse in taste so he could sneer at it. The wooden wall panels gleamed dully in the light of the banked fire, and the single great window was closed and shuttered against the night cold. The main light came from a single overhead lightsphere, set into the ceiling. Jamie didn't care much for the electric light. It was brighter than he was used to, and he didn't like its unwavering intensity. There was something cold about electric light, cold and . . . unnatural. Jamie put the thought firmly from his mind and concentrated his attention on the gorgeous redheaded secretary sitting behind her desk. Her flawless skin had a rich peaches-and-cream glow, even under the harsh light, and her features had a sharp, classical perfection. Her figure was simply spectacular. Jamie cleared his throat loudly, and gave her his most charming smile. She didn't look particularly impressed. Jamie sighed and went back to look around the office.

Papers and magazines lay scattered across the coffee table before him, but they were all at least a week old, well past the date when they should have been handed in for recycling. The headlines were mainly concerned with the discovery of the wrecked starship *Darkwind*, and a few vague allegations of corruption within the Communications Guild. Stale news, not yet old enough to be interesting again through hindsight. Jamie Royal leaned back in his luxurious chair and let his mind wander. Ever since he'd split up with his last partner, his luck had gone from bad to worse. Madelaine Skye had been an excellent partner, but unfortunately she turned out to be somewhat over-burdened with scruples. Partly her sister's fault. Dear Jessica. A nice-looking girl, much like Madelaine, but about as much use as a chocolate kettle. How a warrior like Madelaine had ended up with such a wet blanket for a sister was beyond him. Jamie smiled slightly, remembering. Jessica hadn't exactly been impressed with him, either.

Looking back, it was a wonder he and Madelaine had stayed together as long as they had. Much as he hated to admit it, Jamie missed her. If nothing else, she'd had enough sense to keep him away from people like this. Jamie smiled fondly. Sweet Madelaine; a good fighter and a better partner. If only things had been different . . . Jamie shook his head firmly. What was past was past, and should be forgotten.

He looked about him, bored. The receptionist was buffing her nails with great thoroughness and intense concentration, but Jamie wasn't fooled. He'd spotted the throwing knife strapped to her shapely calf. He sighed regretfully, and then shifted uneasily in his recliner chair. There was such a thing as too much comfort. Get used to living in luxury and all too soon you started getting soft; and in Jamie's business growing soft could get you killed. Jamie Royal had enemies. He also had debts, which was why he'd come to Leon Vertue's body bank.

'Mr Royal? Dr Vertue will see you now.'

'Very kind of him,' murmured Jamie. The receptionist gestured languidly at the door to her left, and went back to working on her nails. She didn't look up as Jamie walked past her desk, and he sighed resignedly. You can't win them all.

The door led into a long narrow corridor, brightly lit by a dozen lightspheres set into the ceiling at regular intervals. Jamie tore his eyes away from the lights and swallowed dryly. He'd known Vertue was rich, but such a conspicuous use of electricity impressed the hell out of him. Jamie could have lived in extreme comfort for over a year on what it must have cost Vertue just to have the lightspheres installed. He pulled himself together and hurried down the corridor. It wouldn't do to keep Vertue waiting. He was said to be touchy about such things.

The corridor turned a sharp corner halfway along, and finally ended in a single great door of polished steel. Jamie looked for a door handle, but there wasn't one. He waited patiently before the door, studying himself in the bright shining mirror. He looked more confident than he felt, but that wasn't saying much. He pulled his jacket straight and adjusted his cloak so that it hung in a more flattering manner. The old grey cloak was showing its age, but it still kept out most of the cold and the snow, and that was all Jamie had ever asked of a cloak. He scowled at his reflection, trying hard to look tough and intimidating, but his mirror image remained stubbornly unimpressive. Jamie Royal was tall, thin and, despite being only in his mid-twenties, well on his way to being prematurely bald. His chin was weak, his stance was awkward, and if he had any muscles he kept them well hidden. It would have been easy to dismiss him as harmless, if it hadn't been for his eyes. Jamie's eyes were dark and intense and very much alive. They could express everything from camaraderie to staunch support to heartfelt sympathy without meaning any of them. They were a conman's eyes, and Jamie was very proud of them.

He shifted uncomfortably from foot to foot before the great steel door, his hands moving restlessly at his sides. He felt naked without his sword and dagger, but he'd had to leave them at reception. Vertue was possibly the most universally despised man in Mistport, and he didn't take chances. In certain quarters the reward for delivering his head, preferably unattached to the body, continued to rise. Jamie looked up at the security camera overhead and smiled ingratiatingly. There was a faintly threatening hiss of compressed air and the door swung slowly open. Jamie drew himself up to his full height and walked into Dr Vertue's chamber as though he owned the place.

The walls of the vast chamber were lined with shining crystal. The glow from a single overhead sphere reflected brightly from the walls, filling the chamber with a sharp silver light. Jamie came to a sudden halt as the door slammed shut behind him. Dozens of bulky steel units took up most of the floor, and though Jamie had never seen them before he knew exactly what they were; reclamation tanks. The means whereby a body could be broken down into its respective parts . . .

Each of the units was covered with a thick haze of frost, and Jamie shuddered as he looked about him. Cold as Mistport's streets were, this place was colder. The presence of death hung heavily on the freezing air, like the final echoes of a despairing scream. Jamie pulled his cloak tightly about him, and walked reluctantly forward to meet the two men who stood waiting for him beside the nearest reclamation tank.

The overly tall, stooped man on the left was Dr Leon Vertue. Wrapped in thick furs of grubby white, he had the appearance and bearing of a hungry wolf. His long white hair hung in thick greasy strands, accentuating his gaunt features. His hands were large and powerful, but immaculately manicured. Surgeon's hands. Jamie recognised him immediately, though they'd never met before. Most people had heard of Dr Vertue, but no one associated with him by choice. Vertue was the owner-manager of Mistport's main body bank. They were all illegal, of course, but a man who needs an organ transplant to save his life isn't going to be too fussy about where the other organ comes from. And there were always men and women from the back streets and alleyways who would never be missed . . .

The man standing beside Vertue was a stranger to Jamie, but he recognised the type. He looked hard, vicious and competent, and he wore his long jet black hair pulled back in a mercenary's scalplock. The sharply defined lines in his face showed him to be in his early forties at least, but there was nothing soft or tired about the corded muscles that stirred restlessly as he moved lightly from one foot to the other. He wore a plain black thermal suit and a black fur half-cloak. There was a sword on his left hip, and a gun on his right. His face and forehead bore the ritual scars of the Hawke Clan, which meant that he was one of the Empire's finest professional fighting men. It also meant he was very expensive. Jamie wondered how many men the mercenary had killed in his long career, and then quickly decided that he didn't want to know. Even when standing perfectly still and relaxed there was something . . . dangerous about the man. Jamie looked away, and wished fiercely that he was somewhere else. Anywhere else.

He glanced uneasily through the glass top of the reclamation tank before him. Curling blue mists seethed and roiled continuously in the unit, as though struggling to escape. Jamie wondered briefly if the tank contained a body, and if so, whose. He told himself firmly that it was none of his business, and looked back at Dr Vertue and his mercenary. Jamie coughed politely to show he was waiting for them to open the conversation, and Vertue smiled lazily at him. The doctor's pale eyes and long white hair gave him an anaemic, washed-out look, but Jamie wasn't fooled. Vertue's smile showed him for the predator he was.

'Dear Jamie,' said Vertue silkily. 'So nice of you to come and see me at such short notice. Not that you had any choice in the matter, of course.'

'Of course,' said Jamie. 'Now what the hell do you want?'

The mercenary stiffened slightly, but Jamie carefully kept his eyes fixed on Vertue. He couldn't afford to sound cowed, or they'd walk all over him. He knew and they knew he was going to end up doing whatever Vertue wanted, but if he behaved like a servant he'd get treated like one. His only chance of getting out of this with his hide intact was to act as though he still had an ace or two hidden up his sleeve. Though given his present situation, he'd have settled for a Jack or a ten.

'I want you to do me a favour, Jamie,' said Vertue, still smiling. 'And in return, I'll do you a favour. What could be more simple?'

'What indeed?' said Jamie easily. 'Suppose you get a little more specific, and I'll tell you whether or not I'm interested.'

'Would you like me to break one of his arms?' asked the mercenary. His voice was low, calm, pleasant; he might have been asking the time or making polite conversation.

'Maybe later,' said Dr Vertue. 'You have to make allowances for Jamie, my dear Blackjack. He has hidden qualities.'

'I don't have to make allowances for anyone,' said Blackjack. 'But you're the boss.'

Jamie felt a few beads of sweat appear on his forehead, despite the cold. He had no doubt the mercenary had meant what he said.

'Forgive me for seeing you in this intemperate climate,' said Vertue, 'but I have a job here that really can't wait much longer. You understand how it is; I wouldn't want the merchandise to spoil . . .'

'Anyone I know?' asked Jamie flippantly.

'I believe so,' said Dr Vertue. 'Her name was Skye. Madelaine Skye.'

Jamie fought to keep his face calm. *No . . . Oh no; not Madelaine . . .* They'd been partners for almost three years. They'd never been lovers, but they could have been. Madelaine Skye; a good woman to have at your back in a fight, or at your side in a bar. They'd worked together on a hundred different jobs, on both sides of the law. He'd always admired her guts and her expertise. The best damned partner he'd ever had. Jamie Royal had many acquaintances, but few friends. And now he had one less.

You bastards . . .

His hands curled into fists, and then he glanced at Blackjack and saw immediately that the mercenary was just waiting for him to try and start something. Jamie fought down his anger, feeling it burn cold and fierce in his gut. There'd be time for revenge later.

'Who killed her?' he said quietly.

'Who do you think?' said Dr Vertue.

Jamie carefully didn't look at the smiling mercenary. 'So Madelaine's dead,' he said finally. 'Am I supposed to be impressed by this?'

'I'll settle for intimidated,' said Dr Vertue. 'Are you ready to discuss business now?'

Jamie Royal took a deep breath, and let it out slowly. The cold air seared his lungs and the pain helped to calm him. Not for the first time he swore to give up dice altogether. His winnings never lasted long, and when he lost he ended up in situations like this. Jamie had worked with all sorts in his time, but Dr Leon Vertue represented an all-time low. There were those who said he'd been a clonelegger before coming to Mistport, and Jamie could well believe it.

'I'm always ready to discuss business,' said Jamie steadily. 'What did you have in mind?'

'Nothing too difficult,' purred Dr Vertue. 'You are familiar with the Blackthorn tavern?'

'Sure,' said Jamie. 'Cyder's place. The most stony hearted fence in Mistport, but her prices are fair. More or less.'

Vertue took a slim package from under his furs and handed it to Jamie. He hefted it once, raising an eyebrow at its weight.

'Cyder is holding a package for me,' said Vertue. 'I want you to go to the Blackthorn tavern tomorrow evening, pick up that package, and give her yours in return. I'm entrusting you with a great deal of money, Jamie; be careful not to lose it on your way to the Blackthorn.'

Jamie nodded, and slipped the slim package into an inner pocket. 'This package I'm picking up; what's in it?'

'A memory crystal. Do handle it with care, Jamie; as far as I and my associates are concerned, that crystal's safety is far more important than your own. Should the crystal prove to be damaged in any way, I would be most upset with you. Bring the crystal to me and place it in my hands, and your service to me will be complete. In return, I will take care of your debts. All of them.'

'That's it?' said Jamie, frowning. 'You must be crazy, Vertue. There are any number of couriers who could handle this for you, for a tenth of what it'll cost you to pay off all my debts. Why bother with me?'

'I need someone who is both discreet and reliable,' said Vertue amiably. 'Not to mention desperate. As I'm sure you're aware, the theft of memory crystals carries the death penalty in Mistport. You will do this little task for me, won't you, Jamie?'

'What makes you so sure you can trust me?'

'Your word is said to be good,' said Vertue, smiling faintly as though the idea amused him. 'And you and Cyder know each other well. Too well for either of you to even think of trying a double-cross.'

'But just supposing I did?' said Jamie. 'What could . . . ?'

Blackjack leaned forward suddenly, and one scarred hand shot out to wrap itself around Jamie's throat. The mercenary bent Jamie back over the reclamation tank, and then grabbed his belt and lifted him up and out over the unit. Dr Vertue opened the tank's lid, and Blackjack started to lower Jamie towards the blue mists. He kicked and struggled, gasping and choking for air, but he couldn't break the mercenary's grip. Jamie looked down into the mists with bulging eyes. They swirled eagerly, hungrily, and beyond them he could see light glinting on the many saws and scalpels that stood ready to pare him down to his essential elements; so much skin, so much bone and cartilage, various organs and, of course, the eyes. There was always a demand for eyes. Blackjack lowered him into the curling mists, and only the mercenary's choking hand kept Jamie from screaming.

'Enough,' said Dr Vertue, and Blackjack swung Jamie away from the tank and placed him carefully on his feet again. He let go and Jamie sagged against the side of the unit, gasping for breath and not even trying to hide the unsteadiness in his legs. To be placed alive into the reclamation tank, to die inch by bloody inch as the scalpels and saws cut into you . . .

I'm sorry, Madelaine . . . I can't even avenge you. I'm too scared.

Jamie realized he was leaning on the reclamation tank to support himself. He quickly pulled his hand away and stood up straight. Vertue chuckled quietly. Blackjack didn't even smile.

'You won't betray me, Jamie,' said Dr Vertue. 'Who else can afford to pay off all your debts? And besides, if you should even contemplate such a thing, I'll send Blackjack to fetch you. You have very lovely skin, my dear Jamie. I could get five thousand credits for two square feet of your skin. Go to the Blackthorn tavern tomorrow evening. Collect the package from Cyder. Pay for it. Hurry back here. Got it?'

'Got it,' said Jamie. 'Can I go now?'

'By all means,' said Dr Vertue.

Jamie Royal turned and walked unsteadily out of the freezing cold chamber. His hands were trembling and his legs shook, but he had enough self-respect left that he wouldn't allow himself to hurry. They could scare him, but they couldn't make him run. The door swung open before him and he stepped out into the corridor. He waited until the door closed behind him, and then he leaned back against the cold metal and wiped at his face with a shaking hand. Sweat was pouring down his face, as though he'd just come out of a furnace rather than an icebox. Vertue and Blackjack were probably watching him on the security camera, but he didn't care any more. Vertue hadn't said what he wanted the memory crystal for, but then he hadn't had to. There was only one place willing to pay that badly for a Mistport memory crystal. Only one place that could regularly supply Vertue with the kind of high tech he needed to run his business and maintain his lifestyle. Only one place that would supply a mercenary like Blackjack for a bodyguard. The Empire. Dr Leon Vertue was an Imperial agent. And now, so was Jamie Royal.

If I didn't have so many debts . . .

Jamie shook his head bitterly, and walked away down the corridor. Memories of Madelaine Skye pressed close around him, but he wouldn't look at them. He didn't dare. It was her own fault; she should have chosen her partners more wisely.

Leon Vertue watched the monitor thoughtfully until Jamie disappeared around the corner in the corridor.

'Can he be trusted?' said Blackjack quietly.

Vertue shrugged. 'He's reliable enough, in his fashion, and you frightened him quite convincingly.'

'And when he's finished his work for us?'

'We can't leave any witnesses,' said Vertue, smiling gently. 'And there's always room in my units for one more body. There's so much demand these days.'

Blackjack looked at him calmly. 'That's a hell of a bedside manner you've got there, Doctor. Now if you'll excuse me, the *Balefire* will be landing soon, and I have a few security guards to bribe first.'

'There's no rush,' said Vertue. 'The *Balefire* will be placed under quarantine until Port Director Steel returns from his Council meeting. And that won't be for some time. Meanwhile, I have another job for you. I want you to kill someone.'

'When and where?'

'Tonight, at the city boundary; Merchants' Quarter. The . . . target we discussed earlier.'

'Good,' said Blackjack, smiling slightly. 'I've been looking forward to that.'

He turned and left without waiting for Vertue's reply, and the door opened before him and shut after him. Vertue scowled at the monitor screen as Blackjack strolled unconcernedly down the corridor. Leon Vertue had seen things and done things that would have sickened any normal man, but still he was scared of the black-clad mercenary. Vertue pouted angrily. He didn't like to be scared; it upset him. Vertue had many ways of dealing with those who upset him, all of them thoroughly unpleasant. He smiled reluctantly as his memories calmed him, but still his frown remained.

He looked back at the monitor, but Blackjack had already disappeared from sight. Vertue licked his dry lips, a little of his tension draining out of him. Even though they currently worked for the same masters, Vertue had never felt comfortable in the mercenary's presence. Under the polite phrases and stoic calm, he'd seen a deep contempt burning in Blackjack's eyes; a contempt for everything and everyone who wasn't strong.

Vertue scowled thoughtfully. He wouldn't always need the mercenary . . . and there was always room in the reclamation tanks for one more body. He smiled suddenly and laughed softly to himself. Leon Vertue turned his attention to the reclamation tank before him, and ran his hand caressingly over the moisture-beaded lid. He thumbed a control and the blue mists parted briefly, allowing him a glimpse of the cold white face below. Frost covered her staring eyes. She was very pretty. So very pretty. And her flesh would be so cold and inviting and helpful to his touch . . .

CHAPTER THREE

Decisions in Council

The Council chamber was surprisingly wide and roomy, but its timbered ceiling was as low as in any other dwelling in Mistport. The howling Spring gales made tall structures a risky business to live in, without high-tech support. Oil lamps and blazing torches lent the chamber a comforting golden glow, and a battered old heating unit murmured quietly to itself as it supplied a slow, steady warmth. Faded portraits of past Councillors lined the panelled walls, the familiar brooding faces staring down on the present Council with a stern watchfulness. A great circular table dominated the room. Almost thirty feet in diameter and carved from a single huge block of ironwood, it had been commissioned by the original Mistport Council over ninety years ago. Port Director Gideon Steel ran his plump fingers caressingly over the polished wood of the tabletop, and tried not to yawn as the arguments around him droned on and on.

His chair creaked complainingly as his two hundred pounds of weight stirred restlessly. Steel was beginning to think the meeting would never end. He'd been here six hours already, to no damned purpose he could see. As far as he could tell it was just business as usual, and they hardly needed him for that. Unless it concerned the starport itself, he was quite content to let the other Councillors go their own way and do what they wanted. Steel had no interest in politics or government, and was only a Councillor because his position as Port Director demanded it. Unfortunately, there was one item on the present agenda that did affect the starport; the installation of the one hundred and fifty disrupter cannon from the recently discovered wreck of the *Darkwind*.

Steel laced his podgy fingers together across his vast stomach and glanced around the Council table, not bothering to hide his boredom. Gideon Steel was a short, fat man with calm, thoughtful eyes and a disturbingly cynical smile. He'd just turned forty and resented it. He had little tolerance for fools or people who wasted his time, which was why he avoided Council meetings as often as he could get away with it. He sighed quietly, and tried to concentrate on the matter at hand. Eileen Darkstrom was still speaking, her harsh staccato voice echoing sharply back from the low ceiling. Steel sometimes wondered if she made such long speeches on purpose, so that when she finally finished everyone would be so grateful they'd vote for anything she proposed, just to stop her from starting up again. Steel grinned. He wouldn't put it past her. Darkstrom had only been a Councillor for five years, but she'd already got more done in that time than all the other Councillors put together. She was a great one for getting things done, was Eileen Darkstrom.

She was a short, stocky woman in her late thirties, with a thick bush of bright red hair that burned like glowing copper in the lamplight. Her skin was pale and freckled, but what would have been pleasant enough features were marred by her constant scowl. Darkstrom was a fighter, and didn't care who knew it. Her green eyes blazed fiercely as she hammered on the table with her fist, and Steel winced in sympathy for the table. As one of Mistport's leading blacksmiths, Darkstrom's muscular arm was enough to frighten anyone, let alone a table fast approaching its century.

She was finally getting around to the matter of the *Darkwind*'s disrupters, but Steel had given up trying to follow her tortuous argument. He looked away, and his gaze fell on the tall brooding man sitting to Darkstrom's left. He looked up, and their eyes met for a moment. Steel kept his features carefully impassive. Count Stefan Bloodhawk nodded curtly, and then turned his attention back to Darkstrom, his long elegant fingers laced together to provide a platform for his sharply pointed chin to rest on. The Bloodhawk was known to be well into his forties, but his aristocratic features were clear and unlined, and he had the lean musculature of a man half his age. His shoulder-length jet black hair had been pulled back and tied with a scarlet ribbon, showing off his prominent widow's peak. There were those who said he dyed his hair, but never to his face. The Bloodhawk's dark eyes were hooded and unrelenting, like those of the ancient bird from which his Clan took its name, and his great beak of a nose and high-boned features only added to the resemblance. Steel frowned slightly, and lowered his eyes. There were many things he hated about having to attend Council meetings, and having to talk politely with the Bloodhawk was right at the top of the list.

Count Stefan Bloodhawk was a paragon of virtue. Everybody said so, including him. He was head of a dozen uncontroversial charities, ostentatiously supported the right causes, and was Chief Commander of the city Watch. He was constantly bringing cases of injustice to the Council's attention, and then demanding to know what they intended to do about it. He belonged to the proper associations, moved in all the right circles, and practised a cold courtesy that was somehow more infuriating than any open insult could ever be. Steel was not alone in wondering just what such a paragon of virtue could have done to end up outlawed on Mistworld. The Bloodhawk kept himself to himself and offered no clues.

Steel glanced at him, and then at Eileen Darkstrom. She and the Bloodhawk had been friends for years and were rumoured to be lovers, though what the hell they saw in each other was quite beyond Steel. In his opinion, the Bloodhawk wouldn't know an honest emotion if it ran up and bit him on the arse. But then, Steel was just a little biased when it came to Count Stefan Bloodhawk. Over the years, Steel had made a great deal of money from his position as Port Director. He regarded it as a legitimate perquisite. He was careful not to be too greedy, and made sure his little extra ventures never interfered with his work as starport Director. Reasonable enough behaviour, he would have thought. Unfortunately, the Bloodhawk thought differently. More than once he'd used his position in the Watch to try and trap Steel into situations where he could be impeached. So far he hadn't succeeded, but of late Steel had had to be more than usually careful to hide his tracks. If Steel hadn't known better, he would have sworn the Bloodhawk was out to get him. The sanctimonious creep.

Steel looked across the table at Donald Royal, sitting slumped in his Chairman's seat, half-asleep as usual. His wispy white hair hung uncombed in long feathery strands, and his face held more wrinkles than Mistport had streets. He'd been a huge and muscular man in his day but, although his frame was just as large, the muscles had slowly drifted away over the years until now little remained of the giant he had once been. No one doubted his right to sit at Council; he'd earned that right through blood and sacrifice. His past deeds as both warrior and politician were legendary. But these days his mind tended to wander and, since he slept through most meetings anyway, Steel wasn't alone in wondering why the man couldn't just retire gracefully with honour and doze by his own damned fire.

Steel looked up sharply as he realized Darkstrom had finally stopped talking, and quickly joined in the polite applause as she sat down. Experience had shown that if Darkstrom felt she hadn't had enough applause, she was quite capable of getting up and starting all over again. Not for the first time, Steel hadn't a clue as to what the hell she'd been talking about, but since she'd always been solidly pro-tech, he had no doubt that she'd finally ended up backing his position over the disrupter cannon.

There was a quiet scraping of wood on wood as Suzanne du Wolfe pushed back her chair and rose to her feet. Steel sighed quietly and braced himself. Du Wolfe meant well, but as an esper herself it was only natural that she should support the esper cause. Steel just wished she'd be a little less open and a lot less long-winded about it. Du Wolfe glanced quickly around the table, tucking a curl of her long auburn hair behind her left ear. Tall, lithe and elegant, she was barely into her twenties and already heartstoppingly lovely. At first glance she seemed too young and innocent to be a part of Mistport's ruling Council, but there was a harsh strength in her dark, even eyes, and her beauty was marred by an old whiplash scar that lay redly across her broken right cheekbone. The scar gave her face an odd, twisted look and pulled up the right side of her mouth into a constant bitter half-smile.

The Empire distrusted its espers, and so kept them under a harsh and brutal discipline. Which was why so many of them ended up on Mistworld.

'Disrupters,' said Suzanne du Wolfe quietly, her hands resting

30

lightly on the tabletop as she leaned forward. 'No one doubts their worth as weapons, but we all know their limitations. Cannon have a faster recharge time than hand guns, but it still takes their energy crystals a good minute and more to recharge between each shot. With all respect, Councillor Darkstrom, there's nothing these disrupters can do that the esper shield can't do just as well and much more efficiently.'

She stopped, and raised her left hand. She frowned slightly, and a pale blue flame sprang into being, licking lazily around her hand without harming it. Du Wolfe smiled slowly, and the flame blazed up into a stream of bright burning fire, leaping and flaring like a glowing fountain. The other Councillors leaned back in their chairs, flinching away from the searing heat. And then the flame was gone, with nothing left to show it had ever been there, save for the unnatural warmth that still permeated the Council chamber. Suzanne du Wolfe was a Pyro.

'The psionic shield has kept Mistworld safe from the Empire for almost two centuries. Working together, espers can hex a ship's tech and mindwipe its crew in less time than it takes a computer to bring its guns to bear. And espers don't have to stop to recharge. Disrupters are all very well in their way, but an esper will always be far more dangerous than any man-made weapon.'

Suzanne du Wolfe sat down again, and looked around to see if anyone dared disagree.

'You may well be right,' said Darkstrom. 'But in the end espers are only human, and humans can make mistakes. Disrupter cannon just do as the fire computers tell them, and technology doesn't grow tired or irritable or make mistakes under pressure. A computer simply carries out its orders. No one here doubts that the psionic shield has proved itself to be an invaluable defence; I merely suggest that the time has come to augment that shield with a high-tech system of high-class weaponry. You've never seen what disrupter cannon can do to a starship, Councillor du Wolfe. I have.'

'We're all familiar with your history as a starship Captain,' said Suzanne du Wolfe sweetly, 'but that was a long time ago. No doubt the Empire have improved their force shields since then. If we try to match their technology with ours, we're always going to be at a disadvantage. They have vast sources of high tech to draw on, while ours are already running out. Our only hope is the psionic shield; the Empire will never come up with a defence against espers.'

'I'm not suggesting the psionic shield should be disbanded,' said Darkstrom with noticeably heavy patience. 'The shield will still be there, but as a back-up provision, in case the tech system should somehow fail. This would free your fellow espers from the need to spend long arduous hours on shield duty, and enable them to take on other tasks where their skills are more needed. At any given time, there are two hundred espers sitting in a trance at the command centre, waiting on the off-chance that the Empire might decide to launch an attack. Meanwhile, Mistport is falling apart around us because we don't have the technology or the espers to keep it running smoothly.'

'Right,' growled Steel. 'We can always use more espers. The psionic shield has always had one major drawback; it takes a minimum of two hundred espers working together to raise an effective shield. To fight off an attack by the entire Fleet, we'd need five times that number. What happens if for any reason we couldn't raise that many?'

'There are over two thousand espers in Mistport alone,' said du Wolfe sharply. 'And another fifteen hundred scattered among the outlying farms.'

'There are now,' said Darkstrom. 'But only half of them are experienced enough for shield duty. And can we be sure there'll always be that many? Esp doesn't always breed true.'

'Right,' said Steel. 'Finding the wreck of the *Darkwind* has been a stroke of immense good fortune, and we'd be fools not to make the most of it. In case you've all forgotten, it's getting harder all the time for smugglers to break through the Empire blockade. We're running out of high tech, and it's getting damn near impossible to maintain what technology we have. Even the best-tended machinery will break down in time, and we're nowhere near being able to build our own high tech. The *Darkwind* has provided enough systems and spares to maintain us for a few more years, but the disrupter cannon are the main jewels in the treasure chest. For the first time, we have a chance to make Mistworld completely safe from Imperial attack.

'Now with respect, fellow Councillors, I must insist on a decision. I've been away from the command centre too long as it is. The technicians are standing by, ready to install the disrupters. I must insist on an answer.'

'For once it seems we are in agreement, Director.' The Bloodhawk's quiet voice was cold but impartial. 'I see no point in further discussion. Since the disrupters are intended to work with the esper shield, rather than replace it, I see no reason why they shouldn't be installed. The future of the psionic shield can be discussed at a later date. Now, since we all have other duties compelling our attention, I call for a vote. I vote Aye.'

'I vote Nay,' said Suzanne du Wolfe quickly.

'Aye,' said Eileen Darkstrom.

'Aye,' said Gideon Steel.

Everyone looked to Donald Royal, who sat up a little straighter in his chair, blinking vaguely.

'We are voting on the installation of disrupter cannon at the command centre,' said Count Stefan Bloodhawk.

'I know,' snapped Donald. 'I'm not senile yet, Bloodhawk. Now we've got cannon, it's only sensible we make use of them. I vote Aye.'

'Well,' said Steel, rising ponderously to his feet. 'If there's no further business . . .'

'Sit down, Gideon,' said Donald Royal, smiling slightly. 'Your precious command centre can manage without you for a little while longer yet.'

Steel sank wearily back into his chair, which complained loudly on receiving his weight again. 'All right, Donald,' he said patiently. 'What is it this time? If it's about the sewers again, we can't afford the time or the technology or the engineers. I know we need sewers, I had to walk through the same streets to get here, but for the time being we'll just have to go on managing without them.'

'Mind you, the smell is getting worse,' said Darkstrom.

'How can you tell?' asked du Wolfe.

'It takes longer to scrape off my boots.'

'Desperate though our need for sewers is,' said Donald Royal heavily, 'we have something more important to discuss. Hob hounds have appeared at the city boundaries. The beasts are at our gates once again.'

For a moment nobody said anything. Steel frowned, and found himself reaching automatically for the gun on his hip.

'Have there been any actual sightings?' asked Eileen Darkstrom.

'Several,' said Donald grimly. 'And three deaths, all in the Merchants' Quarter. One of the victims was a little girl. She was only five years old.'

Steel shook his head disgustedly. The Winter had barely begun, and already the cold was worse than at any time since Mistport records began. As the temperatures fell lower and lower, and game became increasingly scarce, it was only to be expected that the Hob hounds would leave their bleak mountain passes and open tundras, and come sweeping down to raid the outlying farms and settlements, and then the city. The hounds were always hungry.

'What's being done?' asked the Bloodhawk.

'I'm sending Investigator Topaz and a company of the Watch into the Merchants' Quarter to check conditions,' said Donald Royal slowly. 'They'll make a start first thing tomorrow. It's not much of a response, but with the weather as it is I daren't send any men out at night. Still, if there are any answers to be found, I dare say Investigator Topaz will find them.'

That she will, thought Steel grimly. He'd had dealings with Topaz himself and wasn't in a hurry to repeat the experience. The last time the Bloodhawk had tried to nail Steel, he'd sent Topaz to look for evidence. If it hadn't been for some extremely fast footwork on Steel's part, she'd have found it. Still, it had to be said that the Investigator was a good choice when it came to hunting down Hob hounds. Even the hounds had enough sense to be scared of Topaz.

'What about the outlying farms?' he asked suddenly. 'Any news from them on the hounds?'

'Communications are still out because of the blizzards,' said du Wolfe, just a little smugly. 'The Espers' Guild are keeping essential news passing, but so far there've only been a few vague references to the hounds. A handful of people have gone missing in the storms, but we've had no killings reported.'

'That's odd,' said Darkstrom slowly. 'The hounds don't usually bypass the farms. And surely there should have been some reports of approaching hounds before this.'

'Yes,' said Donald Royal. 'There should have been. It's as though the damn animals just appeared out of nowhere.' He stopped short, and glanced worriedly at Suzanne du Wolfe. 'You said the blizzards had hit the farms; how will that affect our food supplies here in the city?'

Du Wolfe shrugged. 'Shouldn't affect us much. Bloodhawk; that's more your department, isn't it?'

'There'll be some shortages,' said the Bloodhawk calmly, 'but nothing to worry about. Most of our supplies come from underground hydroponics these days. We're in no danger of going hungry. Not in the short term, anyway.'

'I don't see what else we can do at this time,' said Darkstrom, getting to her feet. 'I move we adjourn until the Investigator returns with more up-to-date information.'

'Seconded,' said Steel quickly.

Donald Royal shrugged and sank back into his chair, the fire already fading from his eyes as the tiredness returned. Steel got to his feet as du Wolfe and the Bloodhawk pushed back their chairs, and as quickly as that the meeting was over. Steel made polite goodbyes to his fellow Councillors, then hesitated as he saw Donald Royal had made no move to rise from his seat. The others paid no attention, but Steel could tell something was wrong. Royal was usually a stickler for politeness and courtesy. Steel waited till they had left, and then moved back to pull up a chair and sit down facing the old Chairman.

'Donald,' he said quietly, 'it's me; Gideon.'

'I'm glad you stayed,' said Donald slowly, his voice firm and unwavering though his eyes remained weary. 'I need to talk to you, Gideon. Private business, not Council.'

'Of course,' said Steel. 'I'll help if I can. You know that.'

'It's about my grandson,' said Donald Royal.

'Jamie,' said Steel ruefully. 'I might have guessed. What's he been up to this time?'

'What do you think?' said Donald. 'Gambling, of course. He owes money. I've had to help him out on occasion before, but those were always small loans, and he always repaid them. From what I've heard, this time his debts are a great deal larger, and he owes them to some rather unpleasant people. So far, he hasn't dared come to see me, but no doubt he will eventually. You're his friend, Gideon; see if you can talk some sense into him. He can't go on like this. He can't afford it, and neither can I.'

'If I can find him, I'll do what I can,' Steel promised. 'But you know Jamie; he only hears what he wants to.'

'Yes,' said Donald Royal quietly, bitterly. 'I know.'

Steel shifted uncomfortably in his chair. He knew it couldn't be easy for a living legend like Donald Royal to have a grandson like Jamie, but the lad had been in tight spots before and always got out of them in the end. If nothing else, Jamie Royal was a survivor.

'I'll get in touch with you as soon as I hear anything,' Steel said finally, and Donald nodded slowly, his old eyes vague and far away. Steel got up and crossed quietly to the door. He looked back once, but Royal was still sitting in his chair, lost in his yesterdays. Steel left, closing the door quietly behind him.

He hurried down the bare wooden stairs to the Lobby. It had been more than six hours since dinner and he was starving. He could have eaten a horse and gnawed on the hoofs. He tempted himself with thoughts of sweetmeats and fresh cream pastries, and took the stairs as quickly as his bulk would allow. He paused in the lobby to tap his personal code into a monitor console, on the off-chance there was a message waiting for him, and the screen immediately cleared to show him the duty esper at the starport command centre.

'Director, I've been trying to contact you for hours.'

'Sorry,' said Steel. 'The Council meeting dragged on longer than any of us expected. But we've got the go ahead for the disrupters; you can tell the technicians to start installation immediately.'

'Director, we've had a refugee ship arrive from Tannim; the *Balefire*. A medium-size ship, around five million tons. She had to crash land on the main pad, but she came through it well enough. I've placed her under strict quarantine and put the centre on Yellow Alert. The *Balefire*'s Captain says that Tannim's . . . gone. I really think you should get back here as soon as as possible.'

Steel shook his head sickly. 'So, the rumours were true. Tannim has been Outlawed. The whole damned planet.'

'Yes, Director. According to the *Balefire*'s Captain, the Imperial Fleet just dropped out of hyperspace, took up orbit around Tannim, and then scorched the planet lifeless. There's no telling how many millions died. There was no warning given. None at all.'

'There never is,' said Steel. 'Dear God, a whole planet . . . Follow standard procedures, duty esper. I'll be with you as soon as I can. Any problems with the *Balefire*?'

'I'm not sure, Director. I've had the port espers scanning the ship, and apparently they've been getting some rather . . . unusual readings.'

Steel frowned. 'How do you mean, unusual?'

The duty esper shrugged unhappily. 'It's not easy to explain, sir, I think you'd better come and take a look for yourself.'

'If I must, I must,' said Steel. 'Maintain Yellow Alert, and contact the city Watch, just in case anyone tries to break quarantine. Any other problems can wait till I get there.'

He blanked the monitor and thought wistfully about sweetmeats and pastries. The esper scan was probably just a false alarm, but he didn't feel like risking it. In his own way, Director Steel took his duties seriously.

CHAPTER FOUR

Killer in the Mists

The sun had just begun its slow crawl up the sky as Investigator Topaz and Sergeant Michael Gunn led their company of Watchmen through the Merchants' Quarter. The early morning light filtered unevenly past the thick curling mists, and the sun was little more than a pale red circle glimpsed dimly through the fog. The night's bitter cold was falling reluctantly away, and the icicles hanging from roofs and gutterings and window sills had all developed their own persistent drip of icy water.

The winding narrow streets were still mostly deserted, but already the first few beggars and street traders had begun to appear from dark back-alleys and sheltered lean-tos. And here and there, lying half-buried in the snow, were the stiff unmoving bodies of whose who'd been unable to find shelter from the cold. All too many of them were children, left to wander alone in the bitter night, bereft of family or shelter or hope. The Watch passed the bodies by, paying the pathetic heaps of rags no real attention; it was too common a sight to be worth a second glance. One of Mistworld's first lessons was the futility of mourning over things that could not be changed, or even eased. The Outlaw planet was a harsh world, and cared little for the life it reluctantly sustained.

A lone horse moved slowly towards the Watch, its rider huddled inside a thick black cloak. Horse and rider moved with an eerie silence over the snow-covered cobbles, forming slowly out of the fog like some shadowy phantom. Investigator Topaz kept a wary eye on them as they passed by and disappeared back into the mists. The cloaked and hooded rider had paid the Watch no attention, but in this kind of area it was wise to trust nothing and nobody.

Topaz strode on through the thick snow, one hand resting lightly on the butt of the holstered gun at her side. Her eyes flickered at every alleyway and side-street she passed, but nobody challenged her and the shadows remained just shadows. It seemed the threat of the Hob hounds had been enough to keep the human vermin off the streets, for a time at least. Topaz frowned. The city boundary wasn't far now, and Topaz hadn't much experience of Hob hounds. She knew what everybody knew, that they were quick and they were deadly and there was no defence against them except to attack first, but that was all she knew for sure. She had a strong feeling that might not be enough.

She glanced at her husband, walking quietly beside her. Sergeant Michael Gunn was an inch or so taller than her five foot six, but his broad shoulders and muscular frame made him seem shorter. He was in his mid-thirties but, as yet, his face and body had made no concessions to either his hard life or the passing of time. His long brown hair was pulled back in a scalplock; the sign of the mercenary. Gunn had been a Sergeant of the city Watch for over five years, but he liked to keep his options open. His dark laughing eyes were fixed on the street ahead, and his stride was loose and easy almost as though he was looking forward to his encounter with the Hob hounds. Topaz smiled slightly. Maybe he was; Michael Gunn needed excitement the way most men needed food and drink.

The boundary wall loomed out of the thickening mists before them; a huge twenty-foot barrier of stone and mortar that marked the outer limit of the Merchants' Quarter, and the edge of the city. The stonework was scarred and pitted from the unrelenting weather, but the four-foot-thick wall was still strong enough to keep out most of Mistworld's predators. Unfortunately, a twenty-foot leap was nothing to a Hob hound. Topaz glared thoughtfully about her as Gunn spread out the Watchmen in a defensive pattern. They moved silently and cautiously into the surrounding warren of side-streets and alleyways, checking the snow for recent tracks. Gunn came back to join Topaz, and took his gun from his holster to check the energy charge. It was almost full. Gunn put the disrupter away and looked gloomily about him.

'Hob hounds in the city . . . if you ask me, the Council's gone daft. Everyone knows the hounds don't get this far South until midwinter at the earliest. Do you think this could be some kind of drill?'

Topaz shrugged. 'Could be, I suppose. But then, you never can tell what the damned hounds are going to do from one year to the next.'

Gunn grunted an acknowledgement, and glanced dubiously at the boundary wall. There could be half a hundred hounds gathered on the other side of that wall, and he'd never know it until they came scrabbling over the top. Should have built some eyeslits into the damned thing. Gunn sniffed disgustedly, and looked back at his men. The Watchmen had trampled the surrounding snow into slush, and half of them were so far away they were little more than shadows moving in the mists. The fog muffled most sounds, and even the slow gusting wind had been reduced to a dull, far away keening. At least it had finally stopped snowing. Gunn sniffed heavily and wiped his nose on the back of his glove. Ever since he'd first come to Mistworld six years ago, he'd had one damned cold after another. He was beginning to forget what it was like to have a sense of smell. He stamped his feet hard against the packed snow, trying to drive out some of the cold that was already gnawing at his bones. He should have brought his cloak. He glanced at Topaz, standing quietly beside him, and smiled fondly. She never seemed to feel the cold or, if she did, she refused to give in to it. There were those who mistook her poise and elegance for coldness, but Gunn knew better. Topaz prided herself on her control; that was what made her such a deadly fighter. Not for the first time, Gunn looked admiringly at his wife and wondered what he'd done right to deserve her.

Investigator Topaz was of medium height, a slim, handsome woman in her late twenties, who wore her sword and her gun with a casual competence that was both disturbing and intimidating. Her close-cropped dark hair gave her classical features a calm, aesthetic air. Her face was always composed and her stance was relaxed but unyielding. Michael Gunn had always admired her poise. Topaz had her fires and her needs, but she shared

40

them only with him – perhaps because he was the only man who'd ever earned her trust.

The fog seemed to be growing thicker and the sun was lost to sight. Lanterns glowed bravely on the surrounding walls, their light the only landmarks in the endless sea of grey. The mists pressed close about Topaz, leaving a sheen of moisture on her hair and cloak. The Investigator frowned thoughtfully. The Hob hounds preferred a heavy fog to do their hunting in. She thought about drawing her gun, but immediately decided against it. To do so this early might be misinterpreted by her men as a sign of weakness, and Topaz had sworn never to be weak again. She tried not to think about her past with the Empire, but her memories were always with her. Memories of the things she'd done, the things the Empire had made her do; all the many deaths . . . Topaz closed her eyes a moment, forcing back the past by concentrating on her assignment. There was always work, to bury the memories. Topaz had a lot she needed to forget, but sometimes it seemed to her that even on Mistworld there was no escape from the Empire; the spectre at the feast, the wolf at the gate. Topaz opened her eyes and glared coldly at the mists around her. She was free and she would stay free, even from her own memories. Her hand closed tightly around the pommel of her sword, and her heavy Investigator's cloak of navy blue settled about her shoulders like the weight of past sins.

'Chasing Hob hounds,' growled Michael Gunn. 'We should be tracking down last night's burglar, not wasting our time with this nonsense.'

'We have our orders.'

Gunn muttered something under his breath, and Topaz smiled slightly. 'What's the matter, my husband? Pride hurt?'

'Something like that. I would have sworn an oath our security could keep out anyone but a Poltergeist, but that flaming roof runner just walked right in like our defences weren't even there. And it's more than that; it's knowing that someone else was in our house, our home, invading our privacy . . .'

'He didn't get the crystal. You came back in time to stop him.'

'There is that. Though if I hadn't had to go to the toilet, maybe the sensor on the bedroom door would have caught him.' Gunn shook his head unhappily. 'At least the crystal is safely at

41

the command centre now and out of our hands. Anything that happens to it from now on is their responsibility.'

'Exactly,' said Topaz calmly. 'The Hob hounds are our responsibility.'

'All right, all right.' Gunn leaned against the boundary wall, the harsh uneven stone pressing uncomfortably into his back. His broad, stocky body was full of a nervous energy that gave him an edgy, restless look even when standing still. His right hand rested on his gunbelt, not far from his disrupter, while his dark darting eyes probed the shadows of the nearby alleys. The rest of the Watch were methodically searching the alleyways and side-streets for traces of the hounds, poking their swords and pikes into the darker doorways and openings. So far all they'd found had been half a dozen cats and one rather startled drunk.

Topaz rested her hand on her holstered gun, but knew that if the hounds were here, they'd have to be fought with cold steel in the end. Out of the whole company, only she and Gunn had disrupters. Energy guns were rare on Mistworld. Still, a reliance on energy weapons just made you soft in the long run, and Mistworld had its own ways of dealing with the weak. Gunn shivered suddenly. Topaz frowned.

'You're cold,' she said brusquely. 'I told you to wear your heavy cloak.'

'I don't like cloaks. They get in the way when you're fighting.'

'They keep you warm when it's cold. Here.' She took off her own cloak and draped it round her husband's shoulders, ignoring his protests. 'Don't argue with me, Michael. I don't feel the cold like you. I've been trained to survive much worse extremes of temperature than this.'

'You and your Investigator's training,' muttered Gunn, pulling the cloak about him none the less and fiddling with the clasp. 'Even a Hadenman couldn't do half the things you claim.'

'Wear the cloak,' said Topaz firmly, but her eyes were full of fondness. Topaz had spent many years as an Investigator, a paid murderer in the service of the Empire. She'd been very successful in her work, until she met the mercenary called Michael Gunn. He'd taught her to feel human again. Not long after, they'd both been Outlawed, and they had come, as so many before them, to Mistworld, the rebel planet. The only surviving rebel planet.

42

Now Topaz and Gunn were both Sergeants in the city Watch, guardians of law and order, a fact that never failed to tickle Gunn's sense of irony.

Topaz still kept the title of Investigator. Even she wasn't sure why.

'You ever seen a Hob hound close up?' asked Gunn.

Topaz shook her head. 'You have, haven't you?'

'Yeah. I led the raid up at Hardcastle's Rock this time last year. The place was crawling with the ugly beasts. The hounds had killed every man, woman and child in the town, far more than they could ever have hoped to eat. They killed just for the joy of it. Most of what's written about the hounds is rubbish. The largest I ever saw was barely ten feet long, and they're not poisonous. They don't need to be. They run on all fours, they're covered in fur, and the head is long and wolfish, but that's all they have in common with a hound. They're always hungry, and they move so fast they seem like a blur. Their fur is white and their hearts are dark. They delight in slaughter and the torturing of prey.'

'They should feel right at home in Mistport,' said Topaz, and Gunn cracked up. He loved Topaz's dry sense of humour, mostly because it was so rare.

Topaz suddenly became very still, and Gunn froze in place beside her. The Investigator's face had formed into harsh, unyielding lines, and her eyes were hunter's eyes.

'What is it?' asked Gunn quietly.

'There's something out there,' said Topaz, her voice little more than a murmur. 'Something moving, deep in the mists.'

'Here in the Quarter with us?' Gunn looked casually about him, but all he could see were the shifting shadows of the nearby Watchmen. 'Is it a hound?'

'I don't think so. It feels more like a man. About four o'clock, I'd say.'

Gunn glanced in the indicated direction. All he could see was the swirling mists, but suddenly his skin was crawling beneath his scalplock as all his old mercenary's instincts kicked in. The feeling of being watched and studied was all at once so overpowering he wondered how he could have missed it for so long. Assuming, of course, that his clash with the burglar hadn't suddenly turned him paranoid. Gunn whistled quietly, and three Watchmen appeared out of the mists before him.

'Anything to report?' he asked casually, but his hands moved surreptitiously in the mercenary's hand signals he and Topaz had carefully taught their men. His voice was routine, but his hands said, *We're being watched. One man. Four o'clock. Find him.*

'Haven't seen anything, Sergeant,' said the most senior of the Watchmen, nodding slightly.

'Okay,' said Gunn. 'Keep looking.'

The Watchmen faded back into the fog, and were gone. Topaz looked at Gunn.

'Do you think they'll find him?'

'I doubt it,' Gunn admitted. 'Whoever's out there has to be bloody good to have got this close without either of us catching on earlier. But who the hell would be that interested in us?'

'Empire agents?'

Gunn shook his head slowly. 'There'll always be some Empire spies in Mistport, but we were never important enough to justify any of them coming after us here.'

Topaz looked at Gunn thoughtfully. 'So why is there somebody out there watching us?'

'Hounds! 'Ware the hounds!'

Topaz and Gunn drew their disrupters at the Watchman's shout, and moved quickly to stand back to back. Watchmen boiled out of their hiding places and peered quickly about them, swords and pikes at the ready. Somewhere out in the fog a man screamed shrilly, and the sound was cut suddenly short. And out of the thickening mists the Hob hounds came howling.

Their white fur blended into the fog so that it was hard to tell where the one ended and the other began. Only their bright emerald eyes showed clearly against the grey of the mists, together with the steaming scarlet maws that gaped wide to show long, vicious teeth. The hounds moved like wild, demonic ghosts, and their cry was full of an endless hunger and an endless hate. They leaped among the Watchmen, rending and tearing, and blood flew on the freezing air. Men and hounds rolled together on the hard-packed snow, sword and fang searching for a dropped guard or a bared throat. One Watchman thrust his pike deep into a hound's side, spiking it to a sturdy wooden

44

door. The hound screamed and struggled, refusing to die until the Watchman cut its throat with his dagger. Two hounds pulled down a Watchman and tore him to pieces almost before he had time to scream. Gunn took careful aim with his disrupter, and the searing energy beam shot out to burn clean through a lunging hound. It fell silently to the snow and lay still, its fur blazing fiercely. Gunn slipped the disrupter back into its holster and drew his sword. The gun was useless until its energy crystal had recharged, and that would take at least two minutes. A lot could happen in two minutes. Gunn hefted his sword eagerly and headed for the nearest hound.

The snow and slush were stained with crimson and littered with the dead and the dying, and still the Hob hounds leapt and tore among the milling Watchmen. Steel flashed in the lantern-light, and the air reverberated to the savage howling of the hounds. Gunn and Topaz moved with deadly skill through the thick of the fray, guarding each other's back. Topaz shot a hound as it leaped for her throat, and then threw herself to one side as the burning body crashed past her to slam against the boundary wall. Another hound came flying out of the concealing mists towards her, and Topaz knew there was no time to draw her sword. She opened her mouth and sang a single, piercing note. The tightly focused beam of esper-backed sound smashed the hound into the snow. It quivered once and then lay still, blood seeping from its ears and muzzle.

Topaz holstered her gun and drew her sword. She looked quickly about her, and her heart missed a beat as she realized Michael Gunn had become separated from her in the fighting. She relaxed a little as she saw his navy blue cloak moving among the purple-cloaked Watchmen, and forced herself to concentrate on the matter in hand. Gunn had been a mercenary for over ten years; he could look after himself. Her sword sheared clean through a hound's rib cage, the keen-edged New Damascus steel barely jarring on the splintering bones. The hound collapsed, and scrabbled helplessly on the bloody snow. Topaz killed it quickly, and then a heavy weight slammed into her from behind, and she and the Hob hound fell together in a clawing, struggling heap. Topaz swore viciously as a flailing paw raked across her thigh. She pushed the pain to the back of her mind, and thrust her sword deep into the hound's guts even as its jaws reached for her face. The hound howled with rage and pain, and then fell limply across her, soaking her furs with its steaming blood.

Topaz pulled herself out from under the dead weight, and staggered to her feet. Her wounded leg ached fiercely. She looked down, and saw her left thigh was slick with blood, only some of it the hound's. Topaz shrugged and looked away. The muscle was still intact, and the leg still held her weight. That was all that mattered. She looked down at the dead hound, and shivered in spite of herself. Nine foot long, if it was an inch. The eyes were already glazing over, but its paws still twitched, as though searching for the enemy that had killed it.

Topaz hefted her sword and looked about her, but the fight was over. The Watchmen were finishing off the last few wounded hounds with their pikes, and the air no longer echoed to their howls. The only sounds now were the ragged breathing and occasional moans of pain from the surviving Watchmen. Topaz did a quick head count and found that, although they'd been facing a full dozen Hob hounds, she'd only lost nine Watchmen from her company of twenty-five. She grinned harshly. The Hob hounds were certainly impressive, but muscles and claws and fangs were no match for hand guns and cold steel. She looked round for Michael, to share her triumph with him, but he was nowhere to be seen. A sudden chill wrapped itself around Topaz's heart.

'Michael? Michael?'

There was no reply. Topaz gestured quickly to the Watchmen, and they spread out through the surrounding backstreets and alleyways, calling their Sergeant's name. It didn't take long to find him. Topaz saw the answer in the Watchman's face as he came to tell her. She followed him into a narrow alleyway, and stared silently at the unmoving body of her husband. Michael Gunn lay face down in the blood-soaked snow, his sword still in his hand. A dead hound lay only a few feet away. Topaz knelt beside her husband, her face as cold and composed as ever. She reached out to take his shoulder and turn him over, and then stopped when she saw the ragged hole burned through the navy blue cloak. A cold and deadly rage surged through her as she

46

realized the Hob hound hadn't killed her husband. Michael Gunn had been shot in the back with an energy gun.

There's someone out in the mists, watching us . . .

Topaz placed her hand gently on Gunn's shoulder, and squeezed it once. 'Rest easy, my husband. I swear upon my heart and upon my honour that I will avenge you. I promise you blood and terror, Michael; blood and terror to our enemies.'

She paused a moment, almost expecting him to repeat the mercenary's curse after her, but the only sound in the alleyway was the distant moaning of the wind. Topaz patted Gunn's shoulder once more, as though to apologise for leaving him, and then she rose slowly to her feet and walked out of the alley to rejoin the silently waiting Watchmen.

'The Sergeant is dead,' she said quietly. 'Carry him back to his home. I will notify the Council that the Hob hounds have been dealt with.'

Her voice was calm and perfectly composed, and, if she cried any tears, they stayed locked inside her. Topaz was an Investigator.

CHAPTER FIVE

Balefire

Steel sighed and put down his cup. They'd forgotten the sugar again. Eleven years as Director of Mistworld's only starport, and they still couldn't remember to put sugar in his coffee. It wasn't even real coffee. He leaned back in his specially reinforced chair and stared sourly about him. Computer banks and monitor screens lay spread out to every side of him, piled one on top of the other as often as not. Less than half of them still worked at any given time. The heavy wooden desk before him was overflowing with reports and schedules and inventories, but for the moment he couldn't work up the energy to deal with them. Steel felt tired and sluggish and irritable, and the *Balefire* worried at his nerves like a nagging tooth.

All around his soundproofed glass cubicle, the starport control tower worked on with its usual air of grim urgency. There was always more to be done than there was time to cope with, and everybody knew it. The technology broke down faster than it could be repaired, work piled up as deadlines were constantly shortened, and every year the damned winter blizzards arrived out of nowhere and buried the landing pads under seven foot of snow. The command centre carried on as best it could, and prayed for better days.

Gideon Steel sat slumped in his chair and gnawed thoughtfully at the last piece of sweetmeat. He reached for the console keyboard built into his desk, and tapped in a code. The command monitor screen lit up and, after a moment, the swirling colours slowly formed into a clear image. Looming out of the mists like a great steel mountain, the *Balefire* lay brooding on the main landing pad; the last ship out of Tannim before the Imperial Fleet scorched the planet lifeless. Steel's chair creaked complainingly as his two hundred pounds stirred uneasily. As Port Director, Steel was personally responsible for every ship that landed at the port, and the *Balefire* was a mystery. Steel disliked mysteries. He scowled at the screen and scratched absently at his bald patch, as if to stir his thoughts into action. As the only surviving planet to break free of Empire rule, Mistworld was the end of the line for those the Empire Outlawed; you either made your way to Mistport or your scalp hung from a bounty hunter's belt. Normally, when the Iron Empress Outlawed a whole planet there were thousands of refugees caught offworld. Strange that no other ships had come calling . . .

The monitor screen flickered, and the picture broke up into a mass of swirling colours. Steel cursed wearily, and heaved himself up out of his chair. He moved quickly over to the command monitor, and slammed a meaty fist down on to the top of the set. The screen flickered again, and then cleared reluctantly to show the *Balefire*. Steel shook his head slowly and returned to his chair. The sooner the first assignment of spare parts arrived from the *Darkwind*, the better. The command centre's systems were becoming increasingly jury-rigged and improvised, and therefore, not surprisingly, increasingly unreliable. The whole damn place was falling to pieces around him, and there was nothing he could do about it. Steel picked up the latest smuggler manifests from his desk and leafed disgustedly through the flimsy papers. Typical. He needed memory crystals and solar-energy converters, and what had the smugglers brought him? Lightspheres, heating units and flush toilets. Steel threw the manifests down and squeezed his eyes shut a moment. He had no right to complain. The smugglers risked their lives every time they braved the Empire blockade; it was only to be expected they'd concentrate on goods they knew they could get a good price for. And anyway, as the smugglers so often pointed out; beggars can't be choosers.

Steel opened his eyes and looked out of his glass cubicle at the surrounding command centre. Technicians and espers moved purposefully back and forth from level to level, tending the machinery and keeping alive the complex beast that the starport had become. Thick fog pressed close against the vast steelglass windows of the control tower, isolating it from the rest of the landing field. Only the espers and the monitor screens kept Mistport functioning, and there were never enough of either. To Steel's left lay the navigation systems, and to his right, the communications net. Directly before him, where the main computer banks had once been, there was now a row of camp beds. Lying on those beds were fifty men and women with blank faces and empty eyes. Each one of them had an intravenous drip strapped to their arm feeding them nutrients. Steel flinched at the sight of them, but didn't look away. They were his responsibility, like every other part of Mistport. In a sense, they were his children; a fact that never ceased to torment him. When the computers had first started to break down, he had sought out and gathered together the only kind of people who could replace a computer; lightning calculators and idiot savants, all of them with just enough esp to link up with a telepath. Take enough of these people and put them together with a handful of espers, and you ended up with a rough equivalent of a computer. A thinking machine. It was a poor substitute at best, and every now and again one of the units would have to be replaced. The weaker minds tended to burn out.

'Director.'

Steel looked back at his command monitor. The *Balefire*'s image had disappeared from the screen, and in its place was the worried face of the duty esper. He was barely into his twenties, but already his face showed deep-etched lines of care and worry. *We're starting them too young*, thought Steel. *And asking too much of them. How long before we're reduced to breaking in children, as long as they've got the esp we need?* He sighed, and shook his head wearily.

'Yes, lad; what is it?'

'The Captain of the *Balefire* has given us access to his flight computers, Director. Apparently, just before his ship dropped into hyperspace his onboard cameras were able to catch the last few moments of Tannim's Outlawing. I thought you might want to see the recording.'

'Of course. Run it.'

Steel keyed his command monitor into the main system, and

watched impassively as the screen showed him the death of a planet.

Hundreds of Empire ships surrounded Tannim, pouring down destruction. Refugee ships trying to flee the planet were blown out of space almost before they left the atmosphere. The searing disrupter beams showed stark and bright against the dark of space, and the planet writhed beneath them like an insect transfixed on a pin. The oceans boiled, and volcanoes and earthquakes ripped apart the land. The ice poles melted, and the air was churned into an endless maelstrom of storms and hurricanes. And still the Imperial Fleet grew larger as more and more ships dropped out of hyperspace and into orbit, and still the disrupter beams stabbed down, scorching the planet lifeless.

How many millions dead, how many millions . . . ?

The monitor screen went blank, and Steel sat for a long while in silence, staring at nothing. It was one thing to know that a planet's entire population had been destroyed, it was quite another to watch it happening. And yet he couldn't let it affect his judgement. He daren't. He had to be true to his duty; the protection of Mistport. He reached out and slowly tapped a code into his console. The command monitor lit up again.

'Duty esper.'

'Yes, Director?'

'Have you any more information on those strange readings your people picked up from the *Balefire*?'

'Nothing definite, sir. Our sensors detected a concentration of energy levels that suggest most of the ship's passengers are being carried in cryogenic units, but even so our espers are still picking up some very unusual life signs. There's something strange aboard the *Balefire*, Director. Something cold and powerful and . . . alien.'

'Alien? You mean an alien life form?'

'I don't know, Director. None of us have ever come across anything like this before. Whatever it is the *Balefire*'s carrying, it's well shielded. It could be anywhere aboard the ship.'

'Do you think this creature's dangerous?'

'I couldn't say, Director. But it is disturbing.'

Steel pursed his lips thoughtfully, and tapped them with an index finger. 'Get me the *Balefire*'s Captain.'

'Yes, Director.'

There was a pause as the screen went blank, and then a slow grim voice issued from the monitor's speakers.

'This is Captain Starlight of the *Balefire*.'

'Welcome to Mistport, Captain,' said Steel.

'Never mind the bedamned amenities; my hull's breached in a dozen places, my ship's systems are falling apart, and my cargo hold's full of refugees. How long before I can unload and get a repair crew in here?'

'I'm sorry, Captain. Until the *Balefire*'s been fully inspected and cleared, no one will be allowed to leave your ship for any reason. My security people are armed and have been given orders to shoot on sight.'

'What?'

'Mistport's already suffered one Empire plague ship, Captain. We don't take chances any more.'

There was a long silence.

'How are your crew, Captain?' asked Steel politely. 'What condition are they in?'

'Pretty bad. Most of them are dead, back on Tannim. I had to raise ship while I had the chance; I couldn't wait for them . . . The few I have with me are exhausted. They've each had to do a dozen men's work. They need medical attention, Director. I take it you will at least allow a doctor to come on board?'

'I'm sorry,' said Steel.

'You can't be serious, damn you! My crew needs a doctor. They could die!'

'Then they die.'

The words seemed to echo endlessly on the silence.

'If just one of my men dies needlessly . . . '

'Save your threats, Captain. I've heard them all before.'

'Aye; I'm sure you have.'

'My espers did a thorough scan on your ship, Captain. They picked up some . . . interesting readings.'

'Is that it? Is that the reason you're keeping us cooped up in this death ship? Just because a few bloody freaks have a bad feeling about us? I'll have your head for this!'

'I doubt it,' said Steel calmly. 'But I may have to take yours. We'll talk again later, Captain.'

He broke the connection without waiting for an answer. Everyone on Mistworld understood the concept of the Trojan horse. For those with short memories, Mistport's cemeteries were full of reminders. There was a sudden blast of noise behind him, and Steel winced as he turned quickly round to find Jamie Royal leaning nonchalantly against the open cubicle door. The young esper grinned at Steel, and trimmed an immaculate fingernail with a wicked-looking dirk.

'Gideon; how are you doing?'

'Close the door!' Steel roared. 'Can't hear myself think with all that noise!'

Jamie nodded casually, put away his knife, and pushed the door shut with his elbow. The uproar of voices and machinery cut off instantly. Steel leaned back in his chair and hid a smile behind his hand. He liked Jamie, though he often wondered why; the man drank too much, lived beyond his means, and would come to a bad end. If an outraged husband didn't kill him first.

'Hello, Jamie; what are you doing here?'

'I've been helping install your new cannon.'

Steel raised an eyebrow. 'Since when did you develop a taste for honest work?'

Jamie smiled sheepishly. 'My creditors were becoming insistent.'

'I'm surprised they could find you.'

'So was I. I must be slipping.'

Steel had to laugh. 'So, Jamie; how did you come to be involved with our disrupters? What you know about high tech could probably be engraved on your thumbnail without undue difficulty.'

'I've been acting as an interface between the technicians and your living computer.' The young esper shuddered suddenly. 'You can't imagine what that's like, Gideon. Those poor bastards have just enough mind left to realize what's been done to them. Neither man nor machine, but something caught horribly between the two. Inside, they're screaming all the time.'

'You think I like using that monstrosity? I don't have any choice, Jamie. We've less than half the computers we used to have, and those still on line are all linked into vital areas of port machinery. We need those people, Jamie; the port can't function without them.'

'That doesn't make it right.'

'No. It doesn't.'

Jamie smiled suddenly. 'Hark at me, preaching to you. What is the world coming to?'

'I sometimes wonder,' growled Steel. 'What do you think of the new defence systems?'

'They're all right, if you like that sort of thing.'

'You might try and sound a little more impressed, Jamie. Those cannon are strong enough to punch through an Imperial cruiser's shields.'

Jamie laughed and seated himself elegantly on the edge of Steel's desk, one leg idly swinging. 'Still putting your faith in technology rather than people, Gideon? The psionic shield has kept Mistworld safe for almost two hundred years, and no damned machinery is ever going to replace us. We're better and faster than any gun you ever saw.'

Steel groaned theatrically. 'Not you as well, Jamie. I've already spent hours arguing this out with the damned Council.' He broke off suddenly, and looked sternly at the young esper. 'I had time for a little chat with your grandfather. He's worried about you.'

'He's always worried about me.'

'Usually with good reason. Are you in trouble again, Jamie?'

'No more than usual.'

'Jamie . . .'

'Don't worry, Gideon, I know what I'm doing. I owe a few people money, that's all. I'm taking care of it.'

Steel knew better than to push for an answer once Jamie's face took on that bland, innocent look. In his own way, Jamie had his pride. He got himself into messes, so he had to get himself out. If it had been anyone else, Steel would have called it a matter of honour . . .

'So; what can I do for you, Jamie?'

'It seems I need your permission to leave the centre, and right at this moment a rather delightful blonde is waiting impatiently for me to join her.'

'Is she married?'

54

'How would I know?'

'I thought you were still seeing Madelaine Skye; or has she been arrested for tech running again?'

Jamie's face froze suddenly. 'I couldn't say. I won't be seeing her again.'

'But I thought you and she . . . ?'

'Not any more.'

Steel decided not to ask; he didn't think he really wanted to know. His life was complicated enough without getting himself involved in the never-ending intrigues of Jamie Royal's love life. 'All right,' he said finally, smiling in spite of himself. 'I'll fix it so you can leave early. We can manage without you, I suppose.'

Jamie grinned, snapped off a salute and left the cubicle, carefully shutting the door behind him. Steel watched him walk jauntily away, and shook his head ruefully. Jamie would never change. Steel turned his attention back to his command monitor, and for a long time sat quietly, studying the mist-shrouded hulk of the starship *Balefire*. After a while he leaned forward and tapped a code into his console.

'Yes, Director?'

'Call Investigator Topaz of the city Watch and tell her . . . tell her she's needed.'

Steel signed off without waiting for his order to be acknowledged and sank back in his chair, his fat hands clasped loosely across his ample stomach. It had been almost three years since he'd last seen Topaz; he'd hoped the gap would be a great deal longer. Out of all the people the Bloodhawk had sent after him, only Topaz had come close to actually proving anything against him. But with a strange refugee ship on the main landing pad, and the disrupter cannon still being installed . . . Steel smiled sourly. Whatever else you could say about her, Topaz was very good at finding answers.

Steel's hand strayed to his bald patch again, and he pulled it back. *I worry too much*, he thought irritably. *Getting soft*. He picked up his cup of unsugared coffee and sipped at it. The coffee had gone cold.

Topaz moved slowly about her living room, picking things up and putting them down again. A log stirred in the open fire and the flames jumped higher a moment before the wood settled again. The crackling flames were very loud in the quiet. A single lamp shed a warm comfortable glow across the room, but the shadows were still very dark. Topaz moved slowly among her possessions as though searching for a lifeline, but they gave her no comfort. She looked at her padded armchair beside the fire, but didn't sit down. She was too restless to settle yet. The room seemed too big and empty with just her in it. She and Michael Gunn had lived together as man and wife for almost seven years, and in all that time they'd never been separated from each other for more than a few days at a time, and then only rarely. She looked at his chair, on the other side of the fireplace, and realized with something like shock that he'd never sit in it again. She looked away, but everywhere reminded her of Michael.

And Michael Gunn was dead.

It hurts . . .

She'd made the arrangements for his funeral. Everything had been taken care of. Michael had wanted to be cremated; he didn't believe in graves or cemeteries, and he had a quiet horror of the bodysnatchers. No flowers, by request. Michael always said that flowers were for the living. So Topaz had accompanied her husband's body to the crematorium and watched impassively as his coffin was given to the flames. A small choir sang something tasteful in the background. Afterwards, the manager gave her an urn full of ashes he said were Michael's, and Topaz took it home with her. It didn't weigh much. She put the urn in a cupboard under the stairs and left it there.

Died in the morning, cremated in the afternoon. Ashes to ashes, dust to dust.

It hurts . . . like somebody hit me.

She wandered slowly, listlessly, through the living room, her mind far away as she searched for some kind of reason for Michael's death. He had his share of enemies, all mercenaries did, but few of them had the money or the resources to reach him on Mistworld. And assassins with energy guns were very expensive. Lord Raven had sworn vengeance over the affair of Shadrach's Burning. *Gunn and Topaz running sword in hand through the blazing courtyard while a hundred warriors in jet and silver murdered each other in a mindless frenzy. Behind and above them, the ancient castle blazed against the moonless night.* But the old Lord had been mad and dying even then, and his son had shown no interest in feud and vendetta.

Tobias Skinner still carried a grudge from the time Topaz and Gunn had murdered his brother. *The crowd roared as the slavemaster died and Topaz held up the severed head to show it to the crowd.* But Skinner no longer had the guts or the money for this kind of vengeance. Topaz shook her head slowly, and finally sank into her armchair. None of it made any sense. She'd already thought of a dozen old enemies and dismissed them all. If any of them had arrived at Mistport, now or in the past, she'd have known. She still had her contacts.

She sat brooding in her chair, her muscles aching from the continuous strain of being unable to relax. Her wounded thigh still troubled her with a dull persistent ache. Her head was pounding and her hands shook. She folded her hands together in her lap and stared into the fire. The day was slowly wearing on but, tired as she was, she still hadn't gone to bed. She had tried, but found on entering the bedroom that she couldn't stand the thought of sleeping alone in the empty bed. She didn't feel like sleeping anyway. She leaned her head back against the chair and stared unseeingly up at the ceiling. Thoughts moved sluggishly through her mind, drifting here and there, unable to rest. Memories, plans for revenge, theories of guilt and murder . . . none of them made any sense. The memories cut at her like so many knives, but she couldn't get away from them. Everywhere she looked brought back another memory. And anyway, she wouldn't give them up even if she could. They were all she had left of Michael now. Emotions roared within her like great consuming flames, but still her face remained calm and composed. She'd worn her mask a long time and knew that without it she'd break down completely. And she didn't have time for that now. She'd do her mourning later, after she'd tracked down Michael's killer. She had no faith in the Watch finding the murderer. Mistport was full of murderers. And besides; the Watch dealt only in justice. Topaz wanted revenge.

She reached out to the table beside her chair and picked up a small wooden casket. She held it before her for a long moment, just looking at it, remembering, and then she snapped open the

57

catch and raised the lid. Inside the casket was an ornately fashioned steel bracelet. Topaz took it out and hefted it in her hand, then slipped it round her left wrist and locked it firmly in position. It was a personal force shield. They were rare on Mistworld, even more so than energy guns. Topaz had brought it with her when she and Gunn had escaped from Darkmoon's Standing. She hadn't worn it in Mistport; with Gunn and the Watch to guard her back, she'd never felt the need. Now he was gone and she had a killer to find, alone. The bracelet weighed heavy on her wrist. Michael had been working on it for the past few months, trying out an idea he'd had. Michael loved to tinker.

Topaz stirred restlessly, needing to be going somewhere, doing something . . . But as yet she had no clues or leads to follow. Her mind was still too shocked to work logically, and she knew it. Until the shock passed, she was in no condition to begin her search. She sighed quietly. In the meantime, she needed something to do; to occupy her and keep her from thinking. She knew she ought to be collecting up Michael's things and sorting through his . . . effects, to decide what she was keeping, and what would have to go. But she couldn't do that yet. That was too final; too much like saying goodbye forever.

The monitor screen on the far wall chimed politely and Topaz jumped at the sudden noise. She waited a moment to be sure she had control of herself again, then got up and walked unhurriedly over to the monitor. She entered her code and the screen lit up to show her a familiar face; John Silver, the duty esper at Mistport command centre.

'Hello, John.'

'Hello, Topaz. I heard about Michael. I'm so sorry.'

'Thank you.'

'Have the Watch come up with any leads?'

'Not yet.'

Silver hesitated. 'Topaz . . . are you all right?'

'I'm fine, John. What was it you wanted?'

'Port Director Steel asked me to call you. We have a problem with a refugee ship that landed here earlier today. Steel wants you to come and take a look at it.'

Topaz smiled coldly. 'He must really be in a panic if he asked for me.'

'Topaz; if you don't want to do this, I quite understand. We can always find somebody else.'

'No; I have no other commitments. I'm free to take the assignment.'

'If you're sure . . . '

'I'm sure.'

'Very well. The Director will meet you on the main landing pad in two hours' time. The ship is the *Balefire*, out of Tannim. I'll tell the Director you're on your way.'

'Thank you, John. And thank you for your sympathy. You were always a good friend to Michael and to me.'

'You're welcome, Topaz. If you need anything, you know you can always call me.'

'Yes.'

'Goodbye, Topaz.'

'Goodbye, John.'

The monitor screen cleared, and Topaz turned it off. She stared at the blank screen for a while, and then turned abruptly away. If nothing else, the *Balefire* would give her something to do until she found the lead that would put her on the trail of Michael's killer. She smiled slowly as a thought came to her. She'd find Michael's killer, but not as a Sergeant of the city Watch. The Watch was limited by rules and regulations. Topaz would hunt her prey as an Investigator. Her smile became cold and grim, and her eyes held a dark humour that had no mercy in it. She left the living room and went upstairs to her bedroom to change her clothes. She still had her old Investigator's gown. She'd sworn never to wear it again, but that was a long time ago when Michael was still alive.

Topaz was an Investigator, and Mistport was going to learn what that meant.

CHAPTER SIX

Partners in Crime

Blackjack waited patiently by the bare stone wall that marked the starport perimeter. The landing pads lay hidden in the fog. The sun was sliding quickly down the sky towards evening, and the mists were growing steadily thicker as the temperature fell. Blackjack glanced casually about him, but so far no one had challenged his right to be inside the perimeter wall. At first glance Mistport security seemed extremely lax, with nothing to prevent anyone from just walking out on to the landing field, but Blackjack knew better. His trained mercenary's eyes had already identified the concealed proximity mines that lay between the pads and the perimeter. Mistworld as a whole might be lacking in high tech, but the starport had its fair share and more. Blackjack stared thoughtfully at the brightly glowing control tower, on the far side of the port. The glaring electric lights blazed through the mists with undiminished fury, the glowing windows like so many watchful accusing eyes.

Blackjack pulled his cloak about him, and tried not to think about the port sensors. They were supposed to have been taken care of, but the first rule of a mercenary was to trust no one, especially your allies. The second rule was not to worry about things beyond your control. Either he was safe or he wasn't, and he would deal with each situation as it arose. His gaze moved away from the tower and fell on the newly installed disrupter cannon, spread out in a semi-circle on the eastern perimeter, their shining silver barrels aimed proudly up at the fog-shrouded skies. The mercenary eyed the huge guns with respect. He'd seen what disrupter cannon could do, even in inexperienced hands. Enough cannon could destroy an entire planet, leaving nothing on its surface but vast oceans of slowly cooling ashes. Blackjack had never been to Tannim, but he had still shuddered when he heard the planet had been Outlawed. He turned to look at the vast, battered hull of the *Balefire*, standing alone on the main landing pad. The starship was a wreck, and the mercenary felt a quiet admiration for the Captain who had brought that ship down safely.

Blackjack glanced about him, but there wasn't much else to look at. The only other ships on the pads were the dozen or so assorted vessels belonging to the few smugglers still brave enough to crash the Empire blockade. A few dim figures moved quietly through the freezing mists, mostly security Watchmen and field technicians. The whole port had an air of desertion and desolation. Mistport had been designed to handle a hundred ships, everything from skimmers to starcruisers, but that was long ago, in the days of Empire. Mistport had won its freedom from the tyranny of Imperial rule, but only by paying a very heavy price. Technology was the lifeblood of a starport, and Mistport was running dangerously low. The landing pads hadn't been repaired or extended since the Empire first built them, almost three centuries ago. The high-impact crystal that could withstand the blast of a starship's engines and sustain its million tons of weight was now cracked and dull, worn slowly away by the unrelenting storms and cold.

Blackjack looked around sharply as two figures moved slowly out of the mists towards him. He let one hand rest on the butt of his gun, hidden from sight by his cloak, and then relaxed a little as one of the men lifted his hand in the pre-arranged recognition signal. A moue of distaste pulled at the mercenary's mouth. Paying bribes to traitors was hardly his idea of a day's work, but Vertue gave the orders and Blackjack had no choice but to obey them. For as long as the contract lasted. Afterwards . . . Blackjack smiled suddenly, though his eyes remained cold.

The two men followed a tortuous, invisible path through the hidden pressure fields and proximity mines. The location of the safe paths was a closely guarded secret, revealed only to those Watchmen responsible for starport security. Unfortunately for the starport, Watchmen were only human and every man has his price. Or his breaking point. Blackjack didn't know why Vertue should want a map of the safe routes and didn't much care. He had his orders.

The two security Watchmen finally came to a halt before him, and Blackjack bowed politely. The Watchmen nodded their heads briefly in return, and for a moment the three men stared silently at each other. The security men were tall and lean, and at least partly anonymous in their thick purple cloaks and padded helmets. They both carried pikes, the heavy steel heads gleaming dully in the light from the control tower. Yet for all their similarities, Blackjack had no difficulty in telling them apart. The one with the scarred face was Sterling; the one with the golden eyes was Taylor.

Blackjack's hand tightened on his gun butt. He'd heard a lot about Taylor, none of it good. Word was that Taylor was a Hadenman, and one look at those madly glowing eyes was enough to convince Blackjack that he was indeed facing one of the rare and legendary augmented men of lost Haden. Taylor's face was pleasant enough, almost handsome in its way, but the glaring golden eyes gave his features a wild, inhuman look. Even standing still, he gave an impression of strength and speed, and a savagery barely held in check. Blackjack was tempted to draw his gun and shoot Taylor where he stood; the man was dangerous. But he had his orders. And besides; the mercenary had an uneasy feeling he might not be fast enough . . .

The man at Taylor's side had to be Sterling, the ex-gladiator from Golgotha. Which was also fairly impressive; there were reputed to be even fewer survivors of the Golgotha Arenas than there were survivors from Haden. Blackjack decided that Vertue had known what he was doing after all, in sending a mercenary on a simple pay-off job. These two were both hard, experienced fighters. Blackjack smiled slightly. When all was said and done they were still amateurs, while he was a professional.

'You're Blackjack,' said Taylor suddenly. His voice had a harsh, rasping buzz; alien and subtly disturbing. It had no place in a human throat. 'I was expecting Vertue himself. Where is he?'

'The doctor is busy,' said Blackjack easily. 'He sent me in his place.'

'Prove it.'

Blackjack pulled off the thick leather glove on his left hand, and showed the two Watchmen the heavy gold ring on his finger carrying Vertue's seal. Taylor nodded, and Blackjack pulled the glove back on. His hand had only been exposed to the evening air a few moments, but already his fingers were numb.

'I was told to ask about the memory crystal,' he said evenly. 'Has it been installed?'

'Not yet,' said Sterling. His voice was light and pleasant, in stark contrast to the ugly scars that marred his face. And yet, bad as the scars were, they could easily have been repaired by a competent surgeon. Blackjack assumed Sterling wore them as a reminder of his past. Or possibly as a kind of boast. *Look at my scars; all this I endured, and still I survived.* Blackjack listened closely as the ex-gladiator spoke, searching the pleasant, civilized voice for clues to the man's character.

'The crystal hasn't been delivered yet,' said Sterling. 'When it has, I'll lock it into the computer systems myself. Once the computer's on line, no one will bother to check the crystal; they'll assume it's already been checked.'

'You'll have the crystal some time this evening,' said Blackjack. 'I'll see to it.'

'After this evening it'll be too late,' said Sterling.

'I said I'll see to it,' said Blackjack. 'Now have you got the map?'

'Have you got the money?' asked the ex-gladiator, his right hand moving casually to his belt.

Blackjack pushed back his cloak, careful to let both the security men see the holstered disrupter on his hip. Hanging from his belt, next to the gun, was a large leather pouch that clinked musically as Blackjack hefted it in one hand. 'Fifty in gold, as agreed. Where is the map?'

Sterling took his hand away from his belt and pulled a folded wad of paper from inside his sleeve. He handed it to Blackjack, who gave him the leather pouch in return. Both of them moved slowly and deliberately, careful to make no moves that might be misinterpreted. The transaction completed, they both stepped back a pace. Sterling opened the pouch, glanced inside, pulled the drawstrings shut again and nodded quickly to Taylor. The two Watchmen relaxed a little. Blackjack tucked the thick wad of folded paper into an inside pocket without even bothering to look at it.

Taylor raised an eyebrow. 'Don't you want to check the plans?'

'If they're not right, and you've cheated me, I'll have to kill you both,' said Blackjack calmly. 'Do you think I ought to check them?'

Sterling smiled slowly, and the scars on his face flexed and writhed as though they were alive. 'You're very free with your threats, mercenary. I spent seven years in the Arenas, and graduated undefeated. What makes you think you'd stand a chance against me?'

Blackjack's hand slammed forward in a straight-finger jab that sank deep into the ex-gladiator's gut, just below the sternum. Sterling's breath shot out in an agonised gasp and he sank slowly to his knees, his face horribly contorted. Blackjack turned unhurriedly to face Taylor, who hadn't moved an inch.

'He talks too much,' said Blackjack. 'Even worse, he's out of condition. I'm not.'

Taylor looked at him steadily with his disconcerting golden eyes. 'Neither am I,' he said quietly, in his harsh, rasping voice. 'Don't push your luck, mercenary.'

'Not unless I have to,' said Blackjack. 'Now pick up your friend and get him out of here. I don't think we should be seen talking together. I wouldn't want anyone to think I associated with the likes of you by choice.'

Taylor smiled suddenly. 'I'm going to remember you, mercenary.'

He bent down and picked Sterling up with one hand. The ex-gladiator must have weighed all of two hundred and fifty pounds, but the Hadenman lifted him easily. There was a disquieting strength hidden somewhere in Taylor's wiry frame. Hadenman. An *augmented* man. He settled Sterling comfortably over his shoulder, nodded once to Blackjack, and then walked off into the mists. Blackjack took his hand away from his gun. He'd never fought a Hadenman before and wasn't sure he wanted to.

Still, he thought calmly as he watched Taylor disappear into the mists, *It might be interesting someday to discover just how good a fighter an augmented man is . . .*

The Blackthorn tavern had known better days. Grubby silks hung at the blue-tinted windows and a small fire crackled dully in the large fireplace. Most of the tables and cubicles were occupied, but the customers ordered only the cheapest wines and made their ale last. The air was full of songs and laughter, but the gaiety had the forced, almost desperate sound of people determined to enjoy themselves while they still had the chance. Not for the first time in Mistport's short history, money was in short supply. A slow-moving cadaverous barman supplied drinks of dubious quality to the regular patrons scattered the length of the long wooden bar. The ancient oil lamps hanging from the overhead beams gave the smoky air a comfortable golden haze, like a fading photograph or a half-forgotten memory. The unpolished walls were stained with old wine and recent blood. The Blackthorn was a lively place on occasion. Sawdust on the floor hadn't been changed in weeks, but nobody complained. The Blackthorn had known better days.

Cyder sat in her private booth at the rear of the tavern, and shared wine with Jamie Royal. A tall and willowy platinum blonde who would admit to thirty years if pressed, Cyder was popularly regarded as the most stony hearted fence in Mistport. She never argued a price and she never gave credit. She had few friends and her enemies were dead. She toyed with a loop of her long silvery hair and smiled prettily at her companion. Jamie sipped cautiously at his wine. He glanced at the heavy brass-bound clock over the bar, put down his goblet and gazed reproachfully at Cyder.

'You said he'd be here by now.'

'Cat goes his own way,' said Cyder calmly. 'What do you want with a memory crystal, Jamie?'

'I've a buyer.'

'I'd guessed that, my sweet. The last time you were here, you were so desperate you even begged me for a loan.'

Jamie winced at the memory. 'You're right, I should have known better. There were . . . debts to be paid.'

'You never could throw dice worth a damn, Jamie.'

He laughed, and looked around the tavern. Two Wampyr had started a fight and the bartender was taking bets.

'So; how's business, Cyder?'

'It's been better.'

'Money's scarce all round.'

'That it is. Where did you find a buyer for a memory crystal?'

'Does it matter?'

'I'm curious.'

'Don't be.' Jamie sipped at his wine, pulled a face, and put his goblet down, pushing it firmly to one side. Cyder didn't blame him. She wasn't wasting a good vintage on Jamie Royal.

'Are you sure this Cat can be trusted?' he asked, checking the time again.

'He's the best roof runner I've ever worked with,' Cyder said mildly. 'You can trust him as you trust me.'

They shared a sardonic smile.

'Maybe he ran into some trouble,' said Jamie.

'He'll manage,' said Cyder. 'He always does.'

'Even against a Siren?'

Cyder looked at him sharply, her bright blue eyes suddenly cold and forbidding. 'No one said anything to me about a Siren.'

'They wouldn't. But I've been doing a little checking, on my own behalf.' Jamie smiled grimly. 'I don't go into anything blind. It wasn't difficult finding out the address you'd been given. Turns out that particular house is the home of Investigator Topaz. I take it you've heard of her?'

'Everybody's heard of her.'

'Right. Do you still think he'll be here this evening?'

Cyder thought for a moment, and then smiled brilliantly, all the worry gone from her face. 'He'll be here.'

'And the Siren?'

'I don't think she'll bother him much.'

'Cold bitch, aren't you?' said Jamie Royal. Cyder smiled sweetly.

'Harsh words, dear Jamie, from an Empire agent.'

Jamie pushed back his chair and was quickly on his feet, a throwing knife poised in his hand. Cyder kept herself carefully relaxed. Anywhere else in the tavern, the bartender would have shot Jamie dead the moment he drew a weapon on her, but here in her private booth there was no one to help her. Cyder wasn't particularly worried. It would take a lot more than Jamie Royal to worry her. She reached casually for her goblet, and even managed a small chuckle.

'Come on, Jamie; you're not the only one who can work things out. Who else would take care of all your debts in return for one memory crystal? Put the knife away; you're in Thieves' Quarter, remember? I don't give a damn who anyone works for, as long as their money's good.'

She sipped slowly at her wine, studying Jamie warily over the goblet's rim. He nodded abruptly and his knife disappeared back into his sleeve. He pulled his threadbare cloak about him and tried for some kind of dignity.

'We all do what we have to,' he said flatly. 'I'll be back in an hour for the crystal. Don't waste my time with a duplicate.'

Cyder nodded, and Jamie left without saying goodbye. Cyder finished the wine in her goblet, her lips thinning away from the dregs. With fewer ships than ever touching down at Mistport, good wine was scarce, along with everything else. Cyder had run the Blackthorn well since she won the tavern in a poker game, but unless things improved soon she'd probably lose it to her creditors. With so little around worth stealing, she barely made enough from her fencing to pay the bills as it was. Which was why Cyder dealt with Empire agents. Hard times breed hard people.

She rose gracefully to her feet, and swept out of her private booth. The fight between the two Wampyr was over, and the loser was being dragged away. Cyder smiled and nodded as she made her way through the crowded bar, bestowing a cheerful word here, a merry wave there, her long silvery hair tossing from side to side. It was a long way to her private stairway at the back of the tavern, but somehow she kept on smiling. *Keep the customers happy, love, keep the customers happy.*

Cat ran swiftly across the tiled and gabled roofs, jumping casually from level to level over drops that would have turned the stomach of any observer. More than once he climbed easily up sheer walls where the untrained eye would have sworn there were no foot or handholds to be had, and his white-clad figure became nothing more than a dim blur in the eddying mists as he drove himself unrelentingly on. He was late and he knew it. After escaping from the Siren, he'd followed his normal routine and found himself a safe hole to hide in while the immediate hue and cry blew over. He'd slept through the day and awakened to find it already evening. Throwing off the Siren's attack must have taken more out of him than he'd realized. He'd checked the time by the Main Square clock, winced, and then headed for the Blackthorn as fast as he could. Cyder didn't like him to be late.

He ran nimbly across a slanting, snow-covered roof and threw himself out into space across a dark, narrow alleyway. The ground was a long way down, but Cat didn't care. Heights had never bothered him. He landed easily on the steep tiled roof opposite, and padded carefully down to the edge. He sank down on his haunches, glanced quickly about him, and then slithered over the edge of the roof to hang by his heels from a precarious outcrop of guttering. The thick wooden shutters below him were closed and bolted. Cat hammered on them with his fist, waited impatiently, and then hammered again. There was a long pause. Cat had just drawn back his fist to try again when they suddenly flew open, almost taking his head with them. Cat took a firm hold on the two solid steel hoops set specially into the stonework and swung lithely down and in through the window. Cyder helped him in, and then leaned out the window to look quickly around. The street below was deserted, and all the nearby windows were still securely shuttered. Cyder pulled her shutters together, and slammed the bolts home.

Inside, a blazing fire warmed the tiny, low-roofed room. Cat darted over to stand before it, throwing aside his gloves to warm his numb hands at the dancing flames. The gloves' heating elements didn't work properly, which was why he'd been able to buy the thermal suit relatively cheaply. He grimaced as feeling slowly returned to his fingers, and then shook his head back and forth as the pain gradually died away. A hand tapped him on the shoulder, and Cat looked around to find Cyder glaring at him.

'You're late. Where's the crystal?'

Cat unlaced the leather pouch from his belt and Cyder snatched it from him, spilling the glowing memory crystal out on to her palm. She favoured Cat with a quick smile from her generous mouth before hurrying over to a nearby table to examine the crystal under a technician's loupe. Cat smiled fondly at Cyder as he pulled off his boots and then stripped off his thermal suit and draped it carefully over the back of a handy chair. He crouched naked in front of the open fire, savouring the heat on his bare skin. He grinned broadly as the cold seeped slowly out of his bones, and then he straightened up and indulged in a long, satisfying stretch. He turned away, and put on the simple woollen tunic set out to warm before the fire. He looked at Cyder, still totally immersed in the crystal, and wondered, not for the first time, what he'd done right to find her.

Beautiful as an Arcturan firebat, and about as deadly, Cyder was the best fence he'd ever worked with. She knew her business, and she always got him a good price. Of course, she cheated him shamefully on occasion, but that was only to be expected. Cat didn't care. Cyder set up his targets, gave him a haven from the night's cold, and owned his heart, though he'd never tell her that. She might use it against him.

Cat could feel a faint vibration coming up through the thinly carpeted boards beneath his feet. He smiled slightly. It must be getting quite noisy down below. A room directly over a tavern wasn't the most peaceful of places, but for a deaf mute it raised no problems at all. There was a glazed pot simmering over the fire, and Cat's stomach rumbled as there came to him the smell of his favourite stew. Taking the ladle and bowl set out for him, he served himself a generous portion and carried it over to the nearby table, where thick slices of fresh bread and a mug of steaming ale lay waiting.

Cyder put down her eyeglass as he sat down opposite her, and leaned across the table to kiss him thoroughly. 'Well done, my darling; the crystal's everything my contact said it was. Your cut will keep you in spending money for some time to come. Did you have any trouble?'

Cat shrugged, and shook his head innocently. Cyder laughed. 'Someday I'll stop asking. You only lie anyway.'

Cat grinned and got stuck into his stew, shovelling it down as though afraid it might disappear at any moment. He chewed and swallowed with an almost frantic speed, pausing only to take great mouthfuls of the chewy, thick-crusted bread. Cat had gone hungry too often in the past to take any food for granted. In all the time Cyder had fenced for him, he'd never once missed a meal, but old habits die hard. He caught Cyder watching him reproachfully, and slowed down a little.

He ate his second helping at an almost leisurely pace, watching Cyder's lips carefully as they told him the day's news. Such pretty lips . . . Cat hadn't heard a voice or spoken a word since the Empire smuggled a mutated virus into Mistport when he was a child. Hundreds had died; he was one of the lucky ones. He could read lips and talk clumsily with his fingers, and had a gift for insulting mimicry, but he couldn't even hear an esper; his natural shields were too strong. Cat didn't mind. For him, silence was a way of life.

On the roofs it made no difference at all.

He leaned back in his chair as Cyder carried on talking. His bowl was empty and his belly was comfortably full. He sipped appreciatively at his mulled ale, and watched happily as Cyder told him of her day and its happenings. Cat slept most of the day so as to be fresh for the night. He didn't like the day much anyway. The sun was too bright and there were too many people about.

'There's a starship on the pads,' said Cyder. 'The *Balefire*, with refugees from Tannim. All no doubt carrying a few trinkets of great sentimental value which they'll sell fast enough when they get a little hungry.'

Cat nodded, mopped the last traces of stew from his bowl with the last piece of bread, and popped it into his mouth. Only the rich could afford to buy passage as refugees, which meant good pickings for the likes of him. Cat smiled comfortably. Things were looking up.

CHAPTER SEVEN

Bitter Vengeance

Blackjack stood at his ease in Leon Vertue's luxuriously equipped office, and listened calmly while Vertue shouted at him. The mercenary was tempted to look away, and run his gaze over the fine paintings and tapestries that adorned the walls, but he didn't. That would have been rude. Instead, he stared politely at the doctor, his face calm and impassive, until Vertue finally ran out of insults and began to calm down a little. Blackjack had served many masters in his time as a mercenary, and gave each of them the respect and attention they deserved, but even masters like Vertue were entitled to politeness. The doctor finally fell silent and leaned back in his padded chair, breathing harshly. He ran his fingers through his tangled hair, and glared at the reports on his desk before him. Blackjack glanced at the visitor's chair, but didn't sit down. He hadn't been invited to. He stood at parade rest, staring straight ahead of him, and waited patiently for Vertue to get to the point. Vertue finally pushed the papers aside, and transferred his gaze to the mercenary.

'Damn you, Blackjack, you've ruined everything. According to these reports, Investigator Topaz is already on our trail. It's only a matter of time before she finds someone who can lead her to us.'

'None of our people will talk,' said Blackjack. 'They're too scared. I've seen to that.'

'You don't know Topaz.'

'I can still kill her.'

'Not now you can't,' snapped Vertue irritably. 'If you'd killed her when you were supposed to, instead of hitting her damned husband by mistake, we'd have got away with it. As it is, we don't dare touch her.'

Blackjack said nothing. He could have defended himself by pointing out he had no way of knowing Michael Gunn could be wearing his wife's distinctive cloak. He might have mentioned the appalling conditions, with the fog and the hounds. But he chose not to. He had no interest in excuses, whether from others or from himself.

Vertue rose from his chair and moved away from his desk to stare out of the window. Outside the wide pane of steel glass, the evening mists lay still and heavy, enveloping the city in a featureless grey haze. Vague silhouettes of surrounding buildings showed dimly through the haze. Street lights glowed amber and gold and crimson; islands of light in an ocean of uncertainty. *She's out there somewhere*, thought Vertue grimly. *She's out there, looking for me.* He remembered Topaz's cold implacable face, and couldn't repress a shiver. Topaz was an Investigator, and knew nothing of pity or honour or mercy. Vertue turned away from the window to face the politely waiting mercenary, and fought to keep his face calm and his voice steady.

'We can't afford any more contact with the Investigator,' he said quietly. 'Any further attempts on her life, successful or not, would only draw attention to her. For the time being, you leave her strictly alone.'

'That's what I have been doing,' said Blackjack. 'Did you bring me all the way here, just to tell me that?'

'Hardly,' said Vertue coldly. 'I have another assignment for you. You remember Taylor and Sterling?'

'Of course. The two Watchmen who provided us with information on the starport's internal security. Is there some problem with them?'

Vertue smiled grimly. 'It seems they feel they haven't been paid enough for their services. Either we come up with more money, or they'll feel it their duty to turn us in.'

'Leave it to me,' said Blackjack. 'I'll handle it. Do you mind if I kill those two?'

'Not at all,' said Leon Vertue. 'But if you do . . . I want the bodies. Particularly the Hadenman.'

Blackjack nodded politely, waited a moment to see if there was anything more, and then turned and left. Vertue watched him go, and shook his head slowly as the office door closed

72

quietly after the mercenary. The man was too cool, too controlled . . . and far too dangerous. Vertue knew Blackjack was no threat to him for as long as their contract stood, but no contract lasts for ever. Vertue nibbled at a fingernail, and then snatched his hand away. He frowned and reluctantly made a decision. He leaned forward and tapped a memorised code into the comm unit built into his desk. The monitor on the wall opposite turned itself on, but the screen remained blank. After a moment, a cold distorted voice issued from the speakers.

'Yes, Vertue. What is it?'

'I've given the mercenary his orders. He'll take care of Taylor and Sterling for us. I've warned him to stay away from Topaz.'

'Good. We're nearing a delicate stage in our plans, and Blackjack is becoming too conspicuous. As soon as he's dealt with Taylor and Sterling, I think it would be best if he was removed from the picture.'

'You mean kill him?'

'Certainly not, you damned fool! Do you want the whole Mercenaries' Guild on our backs? I mean pay him off, get him a berth on a smuggler's ship, and get him the hell off Mistworld as quickly as possible. Is that clear?'

'Yes, sir. I'll see to it. About the Investigator . . . '

'Forget her. Once Taylor and Sterling are dead, and Blackjack is safely offworld, there'll be no trail left for her to follow. Don't contact me again, Vertue. Your part in this is over. I'll call you in future, should it prove necessary.'

The speakers fell silent. Vertue pulled a face at the blank screen and turned it off. He wasn't some underling or servant to be spoken to in such a manner. And it was unthinkable that the mercenary should just pick up his money and walk away unscathed, after all the trouble he'd caused. Especially since the body bank was so short of raw materials.

Investigator Topaz picked up Marcus Rhine by his shirt front and slammed him back against his office wall. The cheap plaster cracked under the impact. Rhine clawed feebly at Topaz's hands, his feet kicking a good six inches above the floor. Both his eyes were puffed nearly shut, but he could still see clearly enough to flinch away when Topaz drew back her fist to hit him again.

'The name,' said Topaz. 'I want the name of the man who murdered my husband.'

Rhine nodded agreement as best he could, and Topaz dropped him in a heap on the floor. She stepped back and seated herself gracefully on Rhine's desk. Papers that had once lain in neat piles on the highly polished desk now lay scattered across the floor. Some of the papers were spotted with blood. Rhine's two bodyguards lay dead by the open door. For a man who made his living by threats, extortion and violence, Rhine should have paid more attention to his defences. He should also have known better than to refuse to speak to Investigator Topaz. Rhine sat up painfully, and leaned back against the wall as he slowly got his breathing under control again. He was a rangy man of medium height with square blocky hands and a great leonine head of tawny hair. He wore smart clothes in a sloppy manner and, though his face was painted in the latest fashion, his teeth were black and rotting. All in all, he looked very much like a rat with delusions of grandeur. His face bore the ritual scars of the Rhine Clan, but most of those scars were now hidden or distorted by blood and bruises.

'Talk to me,' said Topaz, and Rhine flinched.

'You must be mad,' he said thickly, blood trickling down his chin as his broken lips split open again. 'When you attack one Rhine, you attack us all. My family will have your head for this.'

'To hell with them and to hell with you,' said Topaz calmly. 'You've got a name, and I want it. You always know names, Marcus. And don't threaten me with Clan vengeance; you're not that important. You Rhines only exist because the Watch is usually too busy to waste time cleaning you out. You're just a cheap little bone-breaker, Marcus, and that's all you'll ever be. Now give me the name.'

'Sterling,' said Rhine sullenly. 'He's a Watchman, part of starport security. Used to be a gladiator a few years back. He didn't point the gun at your husband, but the word is he might know who did. You'll find him at the Redlance.'

He flinched back against the wall as Topaz got to her feet, but she just overturned his desk with a casual flip of her hand, and then walked past him to the door without even looking at him.

'You'd better be right about this, Marcus,' she said quietly, and closed the door behind her. She walked unhurriedly through the wrecked reception area, ignoring the damage she'd caused. A buxom secretary sat slumped in a corner, groaning quietly as she felt cautiously at her broken nose. She'd made the mistake of drawing a knife on the Investigator. Topaz ignored her too, and made her way out on to the street.

She paused outside and breathed deeply, as though trying to rid herself of a foul smell. The freezing air burned in her lungs, but she barely noticed. Topaz had been trained to withstand far worse. Evening had fallen, the light fading fast. It had just begun to snow again, and the mists were growing thicker. The wind had dropped to a bare murmur, and the fog lay heavily across the city. Topaz could barely make out the far side of the street she stood in. A typical Winter's night in Mistport. Topaz settled her sword comfortably on her hip, and drew her hand gun to check the energy level. The crystal was barely half-charged, but it was enough. She holstered the gun and strode off down the street. She'd never visited the Redlance tavern before, but she knew of its reputation. All the Watch did. If it was for sale, you could buy it at the Redlance. Drugs, whores, children, secrets . . . everything had its price.

The snow on the ground had been trampled into slush by the crowds that still filled the narrow streets. Most of them were workmen hurrying to get home before the real cold began, but there were still hordes of beggars and street traders trying for one last coin while the temperature permitted. The mists curled sluggishly as the bitter wind murmured among the stone and timbered buildings, and thick icicles hung unmelting from every guttering and window ledge. The passers-by were all huddled in thick furs and heavy cloaks, and Topaz drew more than one startled glance as she strode through the streets in her formal Investigator's uniform. Her thick navy blue cloak covered only a long robe of silvercloth, and her face and hands were bare. Topaz took no harm from the cold, and within her heart she was warmed by her own unrelenting fury. Michael was dead. Her husband, the only human being she'd ever cared for, was dead; murdered. And she would have a vengeance for that death.

*

The Redlance lay deep in the rotten heart of Thieves' Quarter. There were those who saw the Quarter as a single sprawling slum, infested with all the worst kinds of villains, but in reality it was no worse than any other part of the city. It was just a little poorer than most and a lot more obvious. The Watch Commanders kept saying they were going to clear out Thieves' Quarter once and for all, but somehow there were always other, more important things for the Watch to be doing. And besides, when all was said and done, Mistworld was a planet full of criminals, for only the Outlawed ever came to Mistworld. As long as you didn't rock the boat too much, nobody cared. For those who got out of hand, the Watch enforced the law, and the law knew no mercy. But there are always those who think themselves above the law, and they need their own private places to do business. Places like the Redlance.

Topaz strode grimly on through grimy streets and filthy backalleys until finally she came to the Redlance tavern. It looked like any other tavern in any other street; a small, nondescript building with a single flickering oil lamp to mark the swinging sign above its door. The stonework was discoloured and pitted from long exposure to snow and fog, and the two small windows were both securely shuttered. Just another tavern . . . but the door gave it away. Seven feet tall and four feet wide, the huge slab of ironwood was studded with intricate patterns of brightly polished steel. The Redlance's door was designed to keep people out, and it did so very efficiently. Topaz stood before it a moment, and then struck it once with her fist. There was a barely perceptible hum as the minicamera over the door swivelled to look down at her.

'You know who I am,' said Topaz. 'Open the door.'

There was a long pause, and then the door swung slowly open and Topaz entered the tavern. A deafening roar hit her like a fist as she stepped inside and the stale air was thick with smoke and sweat. Topaz stood at the top of the narrow stairway leading down into the tavern, and looked out over the packed crowd in search of the man she'd come to see.

The constant noise broke against the bare stone walls, which threw it back again. Laughter, insults, and the cries of bravoes nerving themselves to fight mixed one with the other into an unrelenting assault on the hearing. Men and women from all ranks and stations stood side by side, drinking too much and laughing too loudly. An average night for the Redlance. Topaz moved slowly down the stairway, keeping one hand on the butt of her gun under cover of her cloak. No one paid her any attention beyond a brief sideways glance; in a place like the Redlance, everyone was careful to mind their own business. Topaz stopped halfway down the stairs and frowned thoughtfully. There was no trace of Sterling. Topaz considered searching through the crowd for him, but immediately discarded the idea. She wasn't in the mood for a slow, polite line of inquiry. She made her way with careful grace down the remaining stone steps, worn and polished by countless booted feet, and headed through the milling crowd to the bar at the rear of the tavern. Everyone made way for her without having to be asked. They knew who she was. A few men looked as though they might object to her presence, but one look at her cold, determined face was enough to convince them not to press the point.

On reaching the bar, Topaz glanced unhurriedly about her until she spotted Pieter Gaunt, the owner of the Redlance. Gaunt was tall and muscular, with a shock of dark curls surrounding a bland, amiable face. His clothes tried hard to be fashionable, and almost made it. He was at least fifty, but looked thirty from a distance. He was known to have murdered seven men, three with his bare hands, and rumours put the count much higher. He made some of his money from drugs and prostitution, for old time's sake, but most of his income came from the acquiring and selling of information. Topaz's mouth twitched. Gaunt was about to undergo a new experience; the giving away of information for free. She loosened her sword in its scabbard and made her way through the crowd towards him. At the last moment, a large and extremely muscular bodyguard stepped out of the crowd to block her way. His right hand hovered over a sheathed short sword, and his left hand held a spiked knuckle-duster.

'I'm here to see Gaunt,' said Topaz, raising her voice to be heard over the din.

The bodyguard shook his head, and lifted the knuckle-duster to hold it in front of her face. He grinned suddenly, and slowly brought the spikes closer to her skin. Topaz kneed him in the groin, waited for him to bend forward, and then rabbit-punched him. The bodyguard collapsed on the floor and lay very still. A woman nearby screamed suddenly, but Topaz was already turning to face the second bodyguard. If anything he was even bigger than the first, and he carried his sword like he knew how to use it. Topaz drew her disrupter and shot him through the chest. The vivid energy beam ripped through him in a split second, and rushed on to blast a wide crater in the wall behind him. The bodyguard fell dead to the floor, smoke rising gently from the charred wound in his chest. The Redlance was suddenly quiet, the only sound a low whisper that ran swiftly through the watching crowd.

Energy gun . . . energy gun . . .

Topaz looked at Gaunt and smiled slowly. It wasn't a pleasant sight, but Gaunt didn't flinch. He stepped forward to join her, being careful to keep his hands away from his sides and not make any sudden movements. Close up, his bland and amiable features fooled no one. His eyes were dark and cunning, and a feeling of open menace hung about him, like the scent of freshly spilled blood.

'That's two good men you've just killed,' he said quietly, his voice pleasant and assured. 'They'll be expensive to replace. I trust you had a good reason for killing them.'

'I had to get your attention,' said Topaz. 'I'm looking for someone. You know where he is.'

Gaunt shook his head. 'I don't betray people to the Watch. It's bad for business.'

'I don't want him for the Watch. I want him for myself.'

Gaunt studied her thoughtfully, taking in her Investigator's robe and cloak, and then shrugged. 'Give me the name.'

'Sterling. Starport security. Ex-gladiator.'

'I know him. Wait here and I'll bring him to you.'

Topaz nodded curtly, her eyes colder than the Mistport night. Gaunt turned and walked away, and the crowd silently made way for him. He finally disappeared through a door behind the bar, and Topaz was left alone with the packed, unmoving crowd. She swept her gaze across them, and they stared warily back, their eyes dark with barely suppressed hate and fear and suspicion. Someone stirred to Topaz's left, and she lifted her right hand slightly to bring her gun into clear view. The stirring subsided and the long silence continued. Topaz had the feeling of being alone in a strange forest, surrounded by angry and dangerous animals. A slight smile touched her mouth at the aptness of the thought; and then she thought of Sterling and the smile vanished. The door behind the bar swung open and Gaunt came out, followed by Sterling. Topaz nodded calmly when she saw the scarred face, and switched the gun to her left hand. Sterling and Gaunt came out from behind the bar, and Topaz drew her sword.

'Sterling,' she said harshly, her voice ringing in the quiet. 'I have come for you.'

Sterling stopped a good ten feet away and studied her warily. 'So you're Topaz,' he said finally. 'I always thought you'd be taller.'

Topaz just looked at him and said nothing. Sterling glanced around the watching crowd as though looking for sympathy or support, but whatever he found in their faces didn't seem to reassure him. He looked quickly at Pieter Gaunt.

'Are you going to let her do this? Just walk into your place and take one of your people away?'

'You're not one of mine,' said Gaunt calmly. 'If you don't want to go with her, that's up to you. Make some room.'

The crowd fell back at his quiet command, forming a wide circle around Topaz and Sterling. Gaunt stepped quickly back into the crowd as Topaz moved slowly forward. Sterling backed cautiously away. He drew a long gleaming scimitar from the scabbard on his hip, and then produced a disrupter from a concealed shoulder holster. He slapped the inside of his left wrist against his hip and a yard-wide square of glowing light appeared on his left arm; a force shield. Topaz smiled, and activated her own force shield. The two shields hummed quietly in the silence as the two combatants slowly circled each other. Topaz moved gracefully, confidently, running the simple rules of combat through her mind. A gun takes at least two minutes to recharge between each shot. A force shield is only good for ten minutes' continuous use; after that, the crystal needs half an hour to recharge before it can be used again. A shield will stop a sword, but reflects the beam from a gun. A sword never needs recharging.

Sterling cut at Topaz's throat with his scimitar, but she caught it easily on her shield. She swept her sword out in a long arc for his gut, and he brought his shield down just in time to block it. Their swords flashed crimson and gold in the lamplight as they circled each other, searching out strengths and weaknesses, looking always for the opening that would let them use their guns. Hit the shield at the wrong angle and the energy beam would come right back at you. And if you found an opening and missed, the odds were you'd never get a second chance. Unfortunately, a moving target is very hard to hit when you have to watch out for a sword as well.

Topaz and Sterling cut and parried, thrust and recovered, their swords meeting and flying apart in a flurry of sparks. The two shields slammed together again and again, static sparking between them where the two energy fields met. Sterling used all his old gladiator's tricks, plus a few new ones he'd picked up in Mistport, but to no avail. Topaz might not be his better with the sword, but she was strong, fast and tireless, driven by some inner demon, while he . . . had got soft. His breathing grew harsh and ragged and sweat ran down his forehead to sting his eyes. His sword grew heavier with every blow, his arms and back ached unmercifully. *I should have shot her from cover when I had the chance*, he thought bitterly. *Who would have thought the bitch would be this good a fighter?* And still they circled each other, swords probing, cutting and thrusting in a never-ending rhythm. Sterling glared at the face before him, cold and savage and pitiless, and a slow fear ate at his heart.

Finally he made a mistake, his first and his last. He leaned too far forward in a lunge, and couldn't pull back in time. Topaz's sword flashed down to sink deep into his thigh, cutting clean through to the bone and flying out again in a flurry of blood. Sterling screamed and fell full length on the floor as his leg collapsed beneath him. His shield flickered, and went out. He lifted his gun for a last desperate shot, and Topaz leaned quickly forward and slammed down her force shield. The razor-sharp edge of the energy field cut cleanly through his wrist, severing his hand and cauterising the stump in the same moment. Sterling screamed again, and fainted. Topaz stepped back and looked about her to see if anyone cared to dispute her win. Nobody did. She turned back to Sterling, quickly lifting her gun to cover Gaunt as he reached for the disrupter Sterling had dropped.

'Don't try it,' said Topaz. 'Don't even think about it.'

'Of course,' said Gaunt. 'The spoils of war.' He nodded courteously and stepped back into the crowd. Topaz sheathed her sword, bent warily down to retrieve the gun and shoved it into her belt. Straightening up, she glared coldly at the unconscious ex-gladiator.

'Wake him up,' she said curtly.

Gaunt nodded to his bartender, who produced a bucket of soapy water from behind the bar. Gaunt took the bucket, and emptied it over Sterling. He came to in a rush, coughing and spluttering. Topaz turned off her force shield and holstered her gun, and taking the front of Sterling's tunic in one hand she hauled him to his feet and slammed him back against the bar. She pinned his legs with her body and then slowly increased the pressure of her arm, pushing his chest steadily back until Sterling thought his spine would break. He lifted his arms to try and stop her, and then nearly passed out again when he saw the blackened stump that ended his left arm. Topaz pushed her face close to his, and Sterling trembled at the cold implacable anger he saw there.

'Who killed my husand, Sterling? Tell me his name.'

'I don't know his name,' Sterling muttered, and then he gasped as Topaz increased the pressure on his chest. 'My back! You're breaking my back!'

'Tell me his name. Tell me who murdered my husband.'

'Taylor knows! Ask him! He was my partner, he knows all the names. I just followed his orders.'

'And where do I find this Taylor?' asked Topaz. She smiled humourlessly as Sterling hesitated, the muscles in her arm bunching and cording as she bent him back a little further. Sterling's face contorted in agony.

'Taylor's a Hadenman. Works for Mistport security, like me. He knows who killed your husband. Ask him!'

'And there's nothing more you can tell me?'

'Nothing! I swear it!'

'I think I believe you,' said Topaz. 'Which is unfortunate for you.'

Her arm muscles suddenly swelled, and Sterling screamed once as his spine snapped. Topaz drew her sword and cut his throat in one swift motion, stepping quickly back to avoid the jetting blood. Sterling fell limply to the floor and lay still.

'That's one for you, my husband,' said Topaz quietly. She looked slowly around her, and the surrounding crowd fell back, unable to meet her burning gaze. Even Gaunt looked away. Topaz smiled briefly, and made her way undisputed out of the Redlance tavern.

The silence held while she climbed the stairs and opened the door, but the moment the door closed behind her, the crowd returned to its original noisy and boisterous mood, only slightly muted by what had been witnessed. Gaunt gestured to two of his men and they dragged away Sterling's body, then returned for the two bodyguards. A serving wench set about cleaning up the blood with a bucket and mop. Blackjack emerged from the door behind the bar and made his way over to join Gaunt.

'Thanks for not telling her I was here.'

'She didn't ask me,' said Gaunt.

'If she had, would you have told her?'

Gaunt shrugged. 'Right now, I don't think there's anyone in this city who could deny that woman anything.'

Blackjack nodded slowly. 'I think you may be right, Gaunt. You may well be right.'

A dozen city Watch were waiting for Topaz when she left the Redlance tavern. She stopped outside the door, and glanced quickly about her. The Watchmen had fanned out to cut off all the exits. Topaz looked at their leader, and nodded resignedly.

'Hello, John. Looking for someone?'

'Port Director Steel needs you,' said John Silver, the starport duty esper. 'In fact, he needs you urgently.'

'That fat old thief can wait,' said Topaz shortly.

'No, he can't; he's running out of time.'

'Then get somebody else.'

'It has to be you, Investigator.'

Topaz scowled and searched Silver's face for some sign of

weakness. Instead, she saw only a weariness and a calm sense of duty that sat oddly on his youthful features. He wore a set of thick, superbly cut furs topped by the scarlet cloak of the esper, but they couldn't disguise his lean, muscular frame. He wore a simple short sword on his hip in a well-worn scabbard. Silver had been a pirate before coming to Mistworld, and Topaz knew that if it came to a fight she'd have to kill him to stop him. And she wasn't sure she could do that. Silver had brought both her and Gunn into the city Watch, had given them both a reason for living when they needed one badly. He was the nearest thing Topaz had to a friend.

'How did you find me?' she asked finally, more for something to say than because she really cared.

'You left quite a trail,' said Silver. 'Including four wrecked taverns and more than sixty injured people. They're still trying to get one man down from a chandelier in the Green Man.'

'I'm close, John,' said Topaz urgently. 'I'm so close to finding the man who killed Michael. I can't let you stop me. I daren't let the trail get cold.'

'You're needed at the starport, Investigator. There's something strange aboard the *Balefire*. Steel thinks it could be a threat to the whole of Mistport, and you know he doesn't panic easily. You must come back with us, Topaz.'

'Or?'

'There's a warrant for your arrest. You've upset several prominent people in the course of this evening, and they all want your head. As yet the warrant isn't signed. If you agree to help Steel, it won't be.'

'You think I give a damn about your warrant?'

'Don't throw your life away for no good reason, Topaz. Michael wouldn't have wanted that.'

'I swore him the oath of vengeance. The mercenary's oath.'

'This job shouldn't take you long, Topaz. A few hours, at most. In the meantime, if you'll tell me your lead I'll have these men track it down for you.'

Topaz looked around at the silent Watchmen. 'And if I don't go back willingly, you'll have me dragged. Is that it?'

'Pretty much,' said John Silver. 'That's why I came with them.

You just might be able to take out all these Watchmen, but you wouldn't kill me.'

'Are you sure of that?'

'No. But then, where's the fun in being sure?'

He laughed cheerfully, and after a moment Topaz smiled in reply.

'I'm looking for a starport security man called Taylor,' she said finally. 'He's a Hadenman, and he knows who killed Michael.'

'Shouldn't take us long to find him,' said Silver confidently. 'By the time you're finished with Steel, we'll have him waiting for you.'

'I hope so,' said Topaz. 'Because if you let him slip through your fingers, John, I may kill you, friend or no.'

She walked away into the thickening mists, and after a moment Silver and the Watch followed her back to the starport.

CHAPTER EIGHT

Starlight

Director Steel waited impatiently by the main landing pad, scowling at the night's cold and gnawing hungrily at a sweet-meat. The sun had been down a good hour and more, and the night chill was growing steadily worse. It was going to be a hard winter. Steel chewed slowly, savouring the rich flavour of the meat, and stamped his feet on the snow to keep them warm. He always felt the cold worst in his feet. The *Balefire* towered high above him, a mountain of shimmering steel beside which the slender control tower with its bright electric lights seemed nothing more than a garish toy. There was no wind, and the mists hung heavily across the landing field, muffling everything in a featureless grey blanket. And out of the mists came Investigator Topaz.

Her face was grim and brooding, and she came stalking out of the fog with a long impatient stride that was all the more intimidating because it was entirely unselfconscious. Steel studied her thoughtfully as she approached him. They'd met occasionally before, but never by choice, and Steel began to wonder if perhaps he'd made the wrong decision. He respected and he feared Topaz, but he hadn't a single clue as to what went on behind those cold, implacable eyes. From what he'd been hearing, she'd spent most of the day and evening blazing a bloody trail through the seamier side of Thieves' Quarter, in search of the man who killed her husband. Steel admired her for it; he wouldn't have entered that part of Thieves' Quarter without a disrupter in each hand and an army of Watchmen to back him up. And yet the Topaz he remembered had always been cold and unemotional, letting nothing get between her and her work, and it was that impartial Investigator's skill he needed now.

He frowned slightly as he watched her draw near. She was supposed to have been wounded fighting the Hob hounds, but you couldn't tell from looking at her. If she felt any trace of pain or weakness, it didn't show in her face or in her bearing. Part of her Investigator's training, Steel supposed. He looked again at her face and smiled slightly. Topaz didn't look at all happy about being called away from her vengeance. Steel felt no regrets. He needed her help, her Investigator's cunning. He bowed politely to Topaz as she finally came to a halt before him, and she nodded curtly in return before turning away to stare up at the *Balefire*.

The massive starship brooded sullenly on its pad, the vast burnished hull glowing ruddy from the surrounding torches before disappearing into the fog. Jagged holes pockmarked the stem and stern, and one whole section lay broken open to the mercy of the bitter cold. A central vane had been stripped of its covering, the naked steel struts pitted and corroded like ancient bones. It was a wonder the *Balefire* had held together long enough to reach Mistworld. Steel scowled, and took another bite of sweetmeat. He distrusted wonders.

'How long before we can go aboard, Director?'

The dry, harsh voice startled him, and Steel had to swallow quickly to empty his mouth before answering.

'Depends on the Captain. He knows we're here.'

'Why send for me, Steel? There must be others in the Watch with more experience than me.'

'You're different,' said Steel flatly. 'You used to be an Investigator.'

Topaz looked at him sharply. 'What makes you so sure you need an Investigator?'

'My espers have scanned this ship a dozen times, and the results are never the same twice, There's something unusual aboard this ship, something . . . strange.'

'Alien?'

'Possibly. Whatever it is, it's dangerous. That's the one thing my espers do agree on. It's dangerous, it's powerful, and it's hiding somewhere on the *Balefire*. I need you to help me find out what it is, and how best to deal with it. That's what an Investigator is for, isn't it?'

Topaz laughed suddenly, and Steel stirred uncomfortably at the bitter, unforgiving sound. 'Shall I tell you what an Investigator is for, Steel? The Empire takes us when we're still children and destroys what makes us human. We're not allowed emotions; they might weaken us. We're not allowed conscience, or empathy, or compassion; they might interfere with our training. The Empire shapes our bodies and moulds our minds, and when they've taught us all they know about killing and deception and the uncovering of hidden truths, they send us out among the stars, to the frontiers of Empire. We investigate new alien cultures as they are discovered, and determine whether they pose any threat to the Empire. If they do, or if we think they might, we have to advise the Empire on how best to subjugate or destroy the aliens. Enslavement or genocide; there's not much difference in the end. They call us ambassadors, but really we're just highly skilled assassins. And that, Steel, is what an Investigator is for.'

Steel shifted from foot to foot uncertainly and searched for something to say. 'Right now, all I care about is whatever's hiding in the *Balefire*. Are you going to help me or not?'

Topaz shrugged. 'The sooner this is over with, the sooner I can get back to my own business. If there is an alien aboard this ship I'll find it.'

'Thanks.'

Topaz looked at him suspiciously. 'Why are you here in person, Steel? Afraid the refugees might try to smuggle some valuables past you?'

'I know my duty,' said Steel coldly. 'I carry it out.'

'For a price.'

Steel looked away, unable to meet Topaz's sardonic gaze. 'I hear you had a little trouble delivering our memory crystal, Investigator.'

'Bad news travels fast. A burglar tried to steal the crystal one night; apparently no one had told him I was a Siren.'

Steel smiled slightly. 'How very unfortunate for him. Has he been identified yet?'

'Not yet,' said Topaz. 'Somehow he got away from me.'

Steel raised an eyebrow.

'The crystal was still locked securely within its casket,' said Topaz evenly. 'And it was still there when I delivered it to your security people, as you are no doubt happy to hear, Director.'

'Of course, Investigator, of course.'

Steel took another bite at his sweetmeat, pulled his cloak tightly about him, and glanced curiously at Topaz's choice of outfit. He'd noticed immediately that she was wearing her old Investigator's uniform again, but thought it best not to comment on it if she chose not to. As he watched, Topaz turned slightly away to look at the *Balefire*'s main airlock, and Steel saw a charred hole in the back of the thick navy blue cloak. He realized he was looking at the hole left by the energy beam that had killed her husband. Steel shivered suddenly, not entirely from the cold. How could she bear to wear the damned thing? He shrugged slightly, and looked away. The moon shone palely through the mists, and a light snow was falling. Steel wolfed down the last of the sweetmeat, and wiped his greasy fingers on his furs. He quickly pulled his glove back on, and beat his hands together to drive out the cold. If Topaz thought her presence was going to be enough to stop him collecting his usual tithe from whatever loot the refugees had brought with them, she could damn well think again. He'd just have to be a little more careful, that was all.

Captain Starlight sat in his command chair, staring out over the smoke-blackened bridge. His flight computers were silent, their lights dimming as the power levels fell. The main viewscreen was dead, and only static whispered from the speakers. Empty seats that should have held crew members stared accusingly back at him. When he slept, which wasn't often, Starlight heard his dead crew calling to him. Another light snapped out as the ship's main computers continued shutting down any system that wasn't essential to the ship's integrity. Starlight wondered why they bothered. He'd seen the damage reports; the *Balefire* wasn't going anywhere without a major re-fit. Darkness gathered on the bridge, and accusing shadows waited at the corners of his eyes.

Starlight stirred slowly in his chair, tiredness dragging at his limbs like chains. Two-thirds of his crew lay dead on Tannim, burned to ashes and less than ashes by the Empire hellships. His ship was a wreck, and he was an Outlaw. Starlight grinned mirthlessly. Poetic justice? Hardly. He'd broken his fair share of laws and regulations, what starship Captain hadn't, but he'd done nothing to deserve this.

And my poor crew . . .

He remembered their voices, screaming from the comm units as the *Balefire* fought her way through the outer atmosphere, her shields shuddering under constant fire from the Empire's ships. He would have waited for his crew if there'd been time, but there was no time, no warning, and he hadn't dared wait. It had been close enough as it was. Ten of his remaining crew were dead. Twice as many more were injured. And his passengers . . . his passengers. They'd known the risks when they came to him, when the Outlawing of Tannim was only the barest rumour. They'd known what might happen if things went wrong. They'd known all the risks and accepted them, but neither they nor he could possibly have predicted what had happened; the terrible thing he'd had to do to save his ship . . .

Captain Starlight stared around his empty bridge. His surviving crew were sleeping in their quarters, or trying to. There was nothing left for them to do now. Nothing left for anyone to do. Starlight rose slowly to his feet, weariness surging through him in a slow, familiar tide. The Port Director was waiting to see him, and Starlight had put if off long enough. He had his duties to perform, while he was still Captain.

They might have taken everything else from him, but he still had that.

Steel glanced surreptitiously at Topaz as she stared grimly into the surrounding fog. He wondered what she was seeing, deep in her own thoughts. In the space of a day and an evening, she'd lost her husband to an unknown killer and cut a bloody trail through the black heart of Thieves' Quarter, but still her face remained calm and controlled, her poise never faltered. There was no sign of tears in the dark brooding eyes, no trace of weakness in the firm unyielding mouth. Steel looked away, disturbed. It was said that those trained to deal with aliens became inhuman themselves. In Topaz's case, he could well believe it. If there was anything in her of grief or sorrow for the husband she'd lost, she showed none of it to the watching world. Even her revenge was a cold and determined affair.

A sudden hum of straining machinery brought Steel's attention back to the *Balefire*, as the main airlock irised slowly open, metal grating on metal amid an outrush of stinking air. Steel scowled, and tried to breathe only through his mouth. He stepped forward, and peered warily into the open airlock. The great ribbed-steel chamber was fully a hundred feet across, and dimly lit by a single glowing lightsphere set just inside the door. The ceiling and the far wall were lost in shadows. The foul smell slowly cleared as Mistport's freezing air entered the chamber, and Steel stepped cautiously in through the open door. He'd never liked iris doors. He was always afraid they were going to slam shut suddenly before he could get out of the way. He moved slowly forwards, and a dim figure stirred in the shadows at the rear of the chamber. Steel stopped where he was, and frowned uncertainly.

'Captain Starlight?'

The figure moved unhurriedly into the light. A tall, grey-haired man with hooded eyes, his cloak hung about him like a dirty shroud. His silver uniform was torn and blood-stained. His face was drawn and haggard, and his deep-sunk eyes were full of a weary bitterness.

'I'm Starlight.'

Steel nodded briskly as Starlight finally came to a halt before him. 'Port Director Gideon Steel, at your service, Captain. This is Investigator Topaz.'

Starlight looked steadily at Steel. 'My passengers are all refugees from Tannim. Their planet is dead; they have nowhere else to go. Will they be safe here?'

Steel shrugged. 'As safe as anywhere. Mistworld is a poor world and a harsh one. Your passengers will have to fend for themselves, or starve. And we'll have to check them out first, of course.'

'Of course.' Starlight smiled wearily. 'We might all be Empire spies.'

'Yes,' said Topaz. 'You might.'

Starlight looked at her, and Steel coughed discreetly.

'How many refugees have you brought us, Captain?'

'There were fifteen thousand. Most are dead now.'

'What happened?' asked Topaz.

'I killed them,' said Captain Starlight.

The *Balefire* was full of sound as Starlight led Steel and Topaz through an endless maze of steel corridors. There were constant creaks and groans as metals contracted and expanded under Mistport's varying cold; the brief furtive sounds like so many unseen mice. From time to time a sudden sputtering noise would make Steel jump, as one or another piece of machinery would give up the ghost and cease to function. Starlight and Topaz paid no attention to anything they heard, their faces equally cold and distant. Steel muttered under his breath and did his best to keep up with them. Though he was damned if he could see what all the hurrying was for; the cargo bay would still be there when they got there.

The overhead lights flickered uncertainly, and faded out one by one as the ship's computers slowly fell apart, their memory crystals gradually wiping clean as the power levels dropped. The air was breathable, but thick with the unpleasant fumes of burning insulation and spilled coolant, suggesting that the circulating pumps were already breaking down. The heating elements were out, and Mistport's cold was already permeating the ship. The *Balefire* was dying.

'Why you?' said Starlight suddenly, looking curiously at Topaz. His voice echoed on the still air. 'Why an Investigator?'

'That was my idea, actually,' said Steel quickly. 'My espers discovered something rather unusual aboard your ship.'

'Yes, I remember,' said Starlight. 'But there are no aliens aboard the *Balefire*.'

'My espers quite definitely detected something . . . '

'I don't give a sweet damn what your espers detected! I know my own ship. There's me, my crew, and the refugees. Nobody else.'

'No aliens among the refugees?' asked Topaz.

'None.'

'You won't mind if I inspect the ship for myself.'

'Do I have a choice?'

'No.'

They walked a while in silence.

'You said you killed most of the refugees,' Steel said carefully. 'What happened, Captain?'

'You'll see,' said Starlight. 'We're almost there.'

He led the way through a narrow tunnel and out on to an equally narrow walkway, and there they stopped. All around them there was nothing but darkness. Light from the tunnel didn't extend beyond the walkway. Steel glanced uncertainly about him. Although he couldn't see more than a yard in any direction, he was none the less disturbed by the faint echo that accompanied even the smallest sound. And then huge lights flared overhead as Starlight fumbled at a wall control, and Steel shrank back against the wall as the main cargo bay sprang into being before him. The bay was a single vast chamber of ribbed steel a hundred thousand yards square. Golden light shimmered on the walls and reflected back from the thousands of suspended animation units that filled the cargo bay. The refugees from Tannim slept soundly, undisturbed. Stacked one upon the other from wall to wall and from floor to ceiling, the sleep cylinders lay waiting like so many crystal coffins.

'Tannim was already under attack when I raised ship,' said Starlight, moving slowly along the narrow walkway, which now showed itself to be set high up on the cargo bay wall. Steel and Topaz followed close behind him. Within the nearest cylinders, they could just make out a few of the refugees, floating like shadows in ice. 'The Imperial Fleet was dropping out of hyperspace in its hundreds. Refugee ships were being blasted out of the sky all around me. The *Balefire* was under attack, and my shields were giving out. I needed more power, so I took it from the sleep cylinder support systems. I had no choice.'

Steel frowned thoughtfully. Even with the extra power, the *Balefire* shouldn't have survived long enough to drop into hyperspace. He shrugged; maybe she just got lucky. It happened. And then the significance of what Starlight had said came home to him, and he looked at the Captain of the *Balefire* with a slow horror.

'How much power did you take from the cylinders, Captain? How much?'

Starlight leaned out over the walkway's reinforced barrier, and tried for a life support read-out on the nearest sleep cylinder. None of the lights came on. Starlight dropped his hand, and turned back to face Steel and Topaz.

'The ship needed the power. I couldn't return it until the *Balefire* was safely into hyper. By then it was too late.'

'How many?' asked Topaz. 'How many of your refugees survived the power loss?'

'Two hundred and ten,' said Captain Starlight softly, bitterly. 'Out of fifteen thousand, two hundred and ten.'

CHAPTER NINE

Darkstrom and the Bloodhawk

The wreck of the *Darkwind* lay half-buried in the snow fifteen miles due north of Mistport, in the shadow of the Deathshead Mountains. Between the city and the mountains lay a huge raised plateau covered with hundreds of feet of accumulated snow and ice. The curving mountain range channelled the roaring winds so that they swept across the plateau in a single broad front, bludgeoning the snow utterly smooth and level, and wiping it clean of all forms of life. Even the Hob hounds avoided the plateau. The snows stretched unbroken and undisturbed for over twenty miles in every direction, and the temperature never rose above freezing, even in what passed for Mistworld's Summer. It was a bleak and desolate place, and it kept its secrets to itself. It had no name; it needed none. Everyone knew of the plateau and its dangers. There were stories of the few brave souls who'd tried to cross it, both alone and in teams, but in all of Mistport's short history, no one had ever succeeded. You either took the long route around the plateau, or you didn't make it.

Things might have stayed that way for some time, if it hadn't been for Arne Saknussen's attempt to cross the plateau. He had only been out on the snow five days when they made their discovery. Like many great discoveries, it happened entirely by accident. The wind had been blowing constantly for the last three days, and the snow was like a solid wall. The compasses were useless so close to the mountains, and Saknussen's party crept along at a snail's pace for fear of losing direction. And then the wind turned into a blizzard, and Saknussen called a halt. His men set thermite charges to clear out a hollow in which they could shelter from the storm, but in the panic of the moment they miscalculated the strength of the charges. The blast killed ten men and injured as many more, but, when the wind finally died down, Saknussen and the other survivors found themselves looking down into a hollow half a mile deep, at the bottom of which lay the wreck of the *Darkwind*.

That part of the plateau looked very different now. The sides of the hollow had been carefully sculptured and reinforced to provide easy access to the wreck. A series of windbreaks had been set up to protect the small town of fortified shelters that had grown up around the site. And down in the hollow, more than half the *Darkwind*'s length had been painstakingly cleared of snow. The long stretch of burnished hull showed stark and alien against the packed snow, like the hide of some immense metallic snake. Great derricks and cranes stood bunched together before the only opening in the hull, ready to winch out the various pieces of technology as they were brought to the airlock. Seen from the distance the derricks and cranes looked like nothing so much as awkward matchstick men, bending and straightening endlessly against the blinding white of the snow.

Eileen Darkstrom clambered awkwardly down from the power sledge that had carried her across the plateau, and stretched her aching muscles. The glare from the snow was painfully bright despite her dark glasses, and the bitter wind cut at her like a knife. She pulled her cloak tightly about her thick furs, and stamped her boots experimentally on the hard-packed snow. It seemed firm enough, but she didn't like knowing there was nothing under her feet but hundreds of feet of snow. Darkstrom decided firmly that she wasn't going to think about it, and moved forward to the rim of the crater to look down at the wreck of the *Darkwind*. Her gaze drifted hungrily along the length of the gleaming steel. Councillor Darkstrom had been Mistport's leading blacksmith for almost twelve years, but she'd never forgotten her time as a starship Captain. And then she smiled wistfully as she realized her main concern now was how quickly the ship could be gutted for its technology. How are the mighty fallen.

She looked away, and glanced around her as she waited for the Bloodhawk's sledge to catch up with her. All across the wide plateau the mists were so thin as to be nearly transparent. The midday sun shone brightly overhead, and no clouds moved in the clear blue sky. Almost beautiful, if you could forget how deadly it was. The Deathshead Mountains loomed up to her left and right: great blue-black crags topped with snow. They were supposed to be volcanic, and occasionally rumbled menacingly to prove it. Hot sulphur springs bubbled up out of their cracked sides, raising the temperature of the mountain slopes just enough to make them habitable. But so far, there were only a few human settlements on the slopes; the Hob hounds saw to that.

Darkstrom looked back into the crater and scowled. Earlier this year she'd pulled every string she could think of to try and get herself assigned to the plateau. The machinery coming out of the *Darkwind* made it a technician's dream, and she'd been determined to be a part of the project. But the Council wouldn't let her go. They said she was too valuable where she was; in Mistport. Now, finally, she was right where she'd wanted to be, and she couldn't stay. The only reason she was here on this Godforsaken plateau was to find out why communications were down between the farms and settlements and the city.

The coughing roar of an engine caught her attention, and she looked around to watch the Bloodhawk's sledge glide quickly over the snow towards her. The low, squat machine slid to a halt beside her, and then shuddered into silence as the Bloodhawk shut it off. He climbed gracefully down and stretched elegantly. Even after several hours spent hunched over the sledge's controls, Count Stefan Bloodhawk still looked every inch an aristocrat and a gentleman. His furs were of the finest quality, and his cloak hung in a becoming manner. His slim frame and gracious bearing were more suited to a debating chamber than this desolate plateau. But the Bloodhawk had always shown a strong sense of duty, and let nothing stand in his way, least of all his own preferences – which was perhaps one of the reasons why Darkstrom loved him so very much. He came over to join her, and they hugged each other awkwardly through their furs. The Bloodhawk then stood beside her, one arm still around her shoulders, and looked down into the crater. The cranes and the derricks were still hard at work, the roar of their engines little more than a distant murmur.

'Stefan,' said Darkstrom finally, 'what are we doing here? Grief knows I can use a rest from the sledge, but we can't afford too many stops if we're to reach Hardcastle's Rock before nightfall.'

'The Rock can wait a while,' said the Bloodhawk calmly. 'I've been talking to Councillor du Wolfe on the comm unit. It seems some of the technology leaving the *Darkwind* hasn't been arriving in Mistport. Since we had to pass this site on our way to Hardcastle's Rock, I said we'd stop and take a look at what's been happening here. It shouldn't take long. And besides, I know how much you've wanted to have a good look around the *Darkwind*.'

Eileen Darkstrom shook her head ruefully, a slow smile tugging at her mouth. Sometimes she thought he knew her better than she knew herself. Saknussen's crater was actually some way off their route, but she hadn't been able to resist at least taking a quick look at the *Darkwind*. Once the Bloodhawk had realized where she was leading him, he must have contacted Mistport and looked for some excuse that would let them stop at the site a while. Bless the man.

'All right, Stefan,' she said gruffly. 'I suppose we can spare the time for a brief visit. What kind of tech has been going missing?'

The Bloodhawk shrugged and led the way along the rim of the crater towards the nearest set of steps leading down to the *Darkwind*. 'It's hard to say, exactly. Most of the technology seems innocuous enough in itself; it's only when you put the various pieces together and see what they have in common that the losses become rather . . . disturbing. They're all the kind of thing that would be very useful to a clonelegger or a body bank.'

Darkstrom swore viciously. She'd take an oath there were no cloneleggers on Mistworld, but there were several illegal body banks. The Council and the city Watch spent a lot of their time trying to find the evidence that would close the evil places down. She ran the various names through her mind, trying to pick out those with enough money or influence to stage something like this. 'Vertue,' she said finally. 'Leon Vertue; it has to be.'

'He's a possibility, certainly,' said the Bloodhawk. 'But there are others. Let's take this one step at a time. First we'll check with the on-site security and see exactly what technology has gone missing. Then we'll check which personnel had access to that technology. And then . . . '

'We play it by ear.'

'Exactly, my dear. We ask questions, poke into corners, and generally make ourselves obnoxious. I can be rather good at that when I put my mind to it.'

'Indeed you can,' said Darkstrom solemnly.

The Bloodhawk smiled. 'So can you,' he said generously.

They laughed together and started down the wide snow steps cut into the side of the crater.

Inside the *Darkwind*, it was comfortably warm. Darkstrom pushed back her hood and pulled off her dark glasses, glad to be out of the cutting wind and away from the endless glare of the snow. She looked curiously about her as the Bloodhawk stepped out of the airlock to join her. It had been twelve years and more since she had last set foot in a starship, but the dull steel corridor brought memories flooding back. It was almost like coming home again. The walls were smooth and featureless, unrelieved by any ornament or decoration. The Empire didn't want its crews distracted from their duties. The overhead lightspheres glowed brightly, probably powered by a site generator, but the gentle, almost inaudible hum was just as she remembered. The first time you joined a ship, the never-ending hum from the lights drove you crazy, but after a week or so you just didn't hear it any more.

Darkstrom walked slowly down the wide, spacious corridor, the Bloodhawk at her side. He said nothing, recognizing that she was caught up in old memories, but stayed close at hand in case she needed him. Without looking around, Darkstrom reached out and took his hand in hers. She felt in need of some support. She'd forgotten how much she missed being Captain of her own ship. No, she corrected herself, that wasn't quite true. She hadn't just forgotten; she'd forced herself to forget. It was the only way to stay sane. She walked a little more quickly, as though trying to leave her memories behind her.

Captain Darkstrom of the *Daemon*. Five years of unblemished service. Not one unsuccessful mission on her record. One of the best Captains in the Fleet and headed for higher things. And then one of her cousins was Outlawed for keeping the wrong sort of company, and Eileen Darkstrom was politely reminded that regulations clearly stated no relative of an Outlaw could be allowed to command a starship. They told her she would have to resign her commission, or face being cashiered.

At first she couldn't believe they meant it. Surely the regulation couldn't apply to someone like her with her record. When she finally realized they did mean it, despite all she'd done for the Empire, Darkstrom took her ship and her crew out into the stars, and turned pirate. She did well enough for a year or two, but took little pleasure in it. She had no taste for the endless blood and destruction. Eventually she made one raid too many, and the Empire was waiting for her. The *Daemon* went down, and she had to run for her life in a battered ship's pinnace. Some time later, having fled from ship to ship and planet to planet, she ended up on Mistworld and started a new life, first as a blacksmith and then as a Councillor. Sometimes she wondered which of the two positions was the most important. Darkstrom shook her head suddenly. Things hadn't been all bad since she came to Mistworld. She had her freedom, something she'd never known in the Empire, and, more importantly, she'd met and fallen in love with Count Stefan Bloodhawk. She squeezed his hand gently, and smiled as he squeezed it back.

The corridors slowly filled with people as Darkstrom and the Bloodhawk made their way deeper into the ship. Technicians had broken into the corridor walls and were checking through the systems to see what was worth salvaging. Darkstrom was impressed by how well the *Darkwind* had stood up to its crash landing. According to the reports she'd seen, the stern was cracked open and the lower decks were nothing more than a mass of crumpled metal, but here amidships everything seemed more or less intact. Presumably the packed snow had absorbed some of the impact. Certainly the technicians seemed busy enough. Darkstrom moved casually among them, asking questions about the work, the technology; getting the feel of things. Most of the technicians relaxed a little once they realized she talked their language, and the Bloodhawk was careful to keep well in the background. He could be rather intimidating in situations like this, and he knew it.

On the whole, the men seemed happy enough with the way things were going. There were the usual complaints about the living conditions, but nothing serious. They understood the realities of life out here on the plateau. Slowly, carefully, Darkstrom began to drop a few questions about the missing technology. Most of the men didn't know what she meant, or claimed not to, but there were enough grim faces and sudden silences for her to be sure that some of them knew more than they were telling. Darkstrom took a few of these to one side and pressed them for details, using all her charm and her Councillor's influence. And finally somebody whispered a name. Joshua Crane.

'There's nothing definite on him,' Darkstrom said thoughtfully to the Bloodhawk, as the two of them made their way deeper into the heart of the ship. 'But he's our best bet. He's been in the right place at the right time just a little too often. From the sound of it, this operation's fairly small scale; it could be a one-man job at this end.'

'It's the man at the other end I want,' said the Bloodhawk. 'The man who gives the orders. I detest techrunners. When bloodsuckers like Vertue start hoarding machinery for themselves, it brings the whole of Mistport that much closer to collapse.'

'Just remember we want this Joshua Crane alive,' said Darkstrom, and smiled as the Bloodhawk reluctantly took his hand away from his sword hilt. 'A dead technician might stop the looting for now, but, without the name of his master, it'll only start up again later. I hope it does turn out to be Leon Vertue. I think I'd enjoy watching him hang. There's hardly a family in Mistport that hasn't lost someone to his damned bodysnatchers.'

'He'll get what's coming to him,' said the Bloodhawk.

Darkstrom smiled in spite of herself. The Bloodhawk was always so sure of himself.

The overhead lights grew fewer and far between as the two of them headed down to the main Engineering Bays. Few of the between-deck elevators were working, and Darkstrom had to rely on her old memories of the ladders and walkways. She was surprised how much of the ship's layout she still remembered after all the years but, even so, she had to stop every now and again to make sure she was on the right track. The *Darkwind* was the same class and type of ship as her *Daemon*, but she'd rarely had occasion to visit her own Engineering Bays in person. It was on one of her brief stops to get her bearings that she first got the feeling she was being watched. A few corridors and several sharp turns later, she was sure of it. She glanced at the Bloodhawk to see if he'd noticed it too, and almost smiled as she saw his hand was back near his sword hilt again. He met her eyes and nodded slightly. They stopped at the next intersection and looked casually about them, as though checking their route.

'He's behind us,' said the Bloodhawk quietly, his lips barely moving. 'About seven o'clock.'

'Got him,' said Darkstrom softly. 'Do you think he's got a gun?'

'No. If he had, he'd have used it by now. I think it would be best if we were to split up. I'll go back the way we've come, as though I'm heading back to the main section. Then, when he goes after you, I'll circle round and take him from behind.'

'Sounds fine to me.'

'You don't mind being used as bait?'

'Stefan; I can take care of myself in a fight. I wear a sword and I know how to use it. You really must stop worrying about me. Now on your way. And remember; we want him alive.'

'I'll remember.'

He turned and walked unhurriedly back down the corridor, while Darkstrom strode off towards Engineering. The hairs on the back of her neck prickled uncomfortably, and she was hard pressed to keep her hand away from her sword. Her unseen watcher was very close now; she could all but feel his presence. She wanted to stop and look around to reassure herself, but she didn't. Her instincts told her he was there, and they'd never played her false before. She kept her hand away from the sword on her hip and tried hard to look harmless. And yet despite all her instincts and anticipation, the arm that snaked suddenly around her throat from behind caught her completely by surprise. She started to struggle, and then stopped as her attacker held up a vicious barbed dirk before her eyes.

'Shout out and I'll kill you,' rasped a quiet voice beside her ear. 'Who are you?'

'I'm Councillor Darkstrom.'

'You picked the wrong place to go looking for trouble,

Councillor,' said the quiet voice. 'And you really shouldn't have sent your friend away.'

'He'll be back.'

'Not in time.'

'Are you Joshua Crane?'

There was a slight pause. 'You just said the wrong thing, Councillor,' said the quiet voice. 'Anything else, and I might have let you go, but now you know my name . . . '

'I'm not the only one who knows.'

'Then I'll just have to take care of your friend as well. It's too late now for the Council to send anybody else. The last consignment's already gone, and I'll be following it as soon as I've taken care of this final bit of business. There's a lot of money waiting for me in Mistport, and neither you nor anyone else is going to stop me.'

'You can't kill a Councillor and get away with it.' Darkstrom kept her voice calm and even, trying hard to sound confident. Crane just laughed.

'You'd be surprised what you can get away with, Councillor. You really shouldn't have let your friend go. Now I don't have to hurry this. I can have a little . . . fun first. Fun for me, that is. I don't think you're going to enjoy it much, Councillor.'

The dirk shone dully in the dim light as Crane turned it slowly back and forth. The barbed steel edge moved gradually closer to Darkstrom's face, and she tried to pull her head away. Crane tightened his stranglehold, and she couldn't move at all. The point of the dirk bit into her face, just above the right cheekbone, and a thin stream of blood rilled down her face. Crane slowly pulled the knife down, lengthening the cut he'd made. Even above the pain, Darkstrom could feel the faint tug of her flesh parting under the keen edge, and the fresh blood that dribbled down her face. She groaned once, and then slammed her elbow back into Crane's ribs. Twelve years as a blacksmith had given Darkstrom a good set of muscles, and Crane grunted loudly as the sudden blow drove the air from his lungs. The dirk stopped moving and Darkstrom back-elbowed him again, putting all her strength into it. Crane's stranglehold loosened. She stamped down hard on his left instep, and felt a bone crack under her boot. The dirk fell away from her face as Crane moaned with pain, and she threw herself forward out of his reach. She hit the floor rolling and was quickly back on her feet, reaching for her sword. And then she stopped and watched grimly as Crane fell heavily to the floor, clutching with desperate hands at the great crimson wound in his neck. Blood streamed through his fingers as he lay twitching on the floor, and then his hands fell away from his neck and he lay still. After a moment, he stopped breathing. The Bloodhawk stepped out of the shadows, stared briefly at the unmoving body, and nodded, satisfied. He set about cleaning his sword with a piece of cloth. Darkstrom shook her head angrily.

'Damnit, Stefan, we wanted him alive!'

'I couldn't risk it. He might have killed you.'

'I could have handled him.'

'Perhaps. But he had steel in his hand and you didn't, and I didn't like the odds. There's blood on your face. Use this.'

Darkstrom scowled at him, and then took the cloth he was holding out to her. She knew a peace offering when she saw one. She pressed the cloth to her face and dabbed gingerly at the narrow cut. It wasn't a bad cut, as cuts go.

'Are you all right, my dear?'

'I'm fine, Stefan. It's only a scratch.'

'I was worried about you.'

'Yes, I know. Let's get out of here. We can send some men back to clean up this mess.'

'Did Crane mention any names to you; like Leon Vertue?'

'No. Just that there was money waiting for him in Mistport.'

The Bloodhawk frowned thoughtfully. 'Without a name, I don't think we can justify turning back. Our mission to restore communications with the city is too important.'

'You're right; unfortunately. But it would have been nice to finally nail Leon Vertue.'

'Yes,' said the Bloodhawk, as he guided her back down the dimly lit steel corridor. 'But don't worry, my dear; I promise you, he'll get what's coming to him.'

CHAPTER TEN

Mary

Night lay heavily over Mistport, and the full moon shone dimly through the thick mists that curled across the landing pads. Jamie Royal huddled inside his threadbare grey cloak and peered about him from the safety of the perimeter shadows. The landing field was deserted, and even the marker torches were burning low. He pulled a map from inside his cloak and studied it carefully by the light of a pencil torch. The small spot of light danced across the unsteady map as his hands shook violently from the freezing cold. Jamie swore under his breath, and fought to keep his hands still. The night was cold, and getting colder. Every breath seared his lungs, and he couldn't stop his teeth from chattering. Jamie put the cold out of his mind as best he could, and concentrated on the map. The sooner he was finished with this, the quicker he could get out of the killing cold. Only a fool or a madman would linger out in the open during Mistport's night. Only the foolish, the mad . . . and the desperate. Jamie scowled, and studied his map.

The starport perimeter was dotted with pressure fields and proximity mines, but the safe paths through them seemed straightforward enough. Jamie put away his torch, carefully refolded the map and tucked it into his pocket. He'd already spent most of the evening memorising the safe routes, but he liked to be sure. He glowered into the thick fog and swore to himself that this was the last job he'd do for Leon Vertue, threats or no threats. He'd thought his job was over once he'd delivered that damned crystal to the Hadenman, but Vertue had insisted on this one last service. Blackjack had stood silently beside the doctor, smiling coldly, waiting for Jamie to try and refuse. Jamie wouldn't give him the satisfaction.

But I'll get you for this, thought Jamie fiercely. *I'll make you both pay for what you've done to me, and to Madelaine. My sweet Madelaine . . .*

He smiled sourly and shook his head. He was going to have enough trouble getting out of this with his skin intact as it was, without hatching wild schemes to get back at Vertue and Blackjack. Revenge would have to wait for another time, assuming he ever came up with a plan worth a damn. Jamie glanced about him, listening carefully. No shadows moved in the mists, and no sounds disturbed the silence. According to his information, the Watch patrolled the perimeter at half-hour intervals. Plenty of time to sneak through the port defences and hide himself in the mists. Assuming nothing went wrong. He took a deep breath, and moved cautiously forward out on to the landing field.

The proximity mines were easy enough to spot, now that he knew what he was looking for, but the pressure fields were undetectable to the naked eye. The first you knew about tripping one was when the Watchmen came charging out of nowhere to grab you. Jamie gritted his teeth and plunged on into the mists. Either the map was right, or it wasn't, and if it wasn't it was too late to worry about it now. The smugglers' ships loomed out of the fog to either side of him; long silver needles glowing ruddy from the flickering marker torches. The other pads were bare and empty, and Jamie felt horribly exposed and vulnerable as he padded silently on. His imagination filled the endless grey haze with watching eyes and armed guards, and he could feel his heart hammering wildly in his chest. He stumbled to a halt as a huge dark shape formed suddenly out of the mists, and then he relaxed a little as he recognized the hull of the *Balefire*. He was in the right place. He padded quickly over to the reception-area compound, and hid himself in the shadows of the outer wall.

He crouched on his haunches in the comforting gloom, and waited impatiently for his breathing to slow and his heartbeat to return to normal. *I'd make a lousy spy,* he thought ruefully. He shook his head and turned his attention to the straggling line of refugees emerging from the *Balefire*'s main airlock. They moved slowly, listlessly across the landing pad, dressed in silks and fineries totally unsuitable for the bitter cold of a Mistport night, but they didn't seem to notice, or even care. Their faces were blank and their eyes were empty, and none of them looked back at the ship they were leaving. Lost and alone, hoping against hope, they came to Mistport as so many had before. Because there was nowhere else.

Jamie hugged himself fiercely inside his cloak, and, straightening up, he stamped his feet hard to try and drive out the cold. He'd lost all feeling in his feet and hands despite his boots and gloves, and frost was forming in his hair and crackling on his face. Vertue or no Vertue, he couldn't stand this cold for long. If he couldn't find the refugee he was looking for quickly he'd have to leave and take his chances with the damned mercenary. He snapped alert as he heard footsteps nearby. He quickly glanced round, and winced as he saw John Silver standing in the doorway of the reception compound. What the hell was the duty esper doing here? Jamie shrank back against the wall, trusting to the shadows to hide him. His mental shield was as tight as he could make it and, as far as Silver's esp was concerned, he should be invisible.

Silver moved away from the door, hesitated, and then walked slowly towards Jamie. The duty esper was frowning, but his attention seemed fixed wholly on the refugees. Jamie reached down and carefully eased the dirk out of his boot. The slender knife seemed heavy in his hand. He didn't want to kill Silver, but he couldn't afford to be caught. They hanged traitors in Mistport. Silver drew steadily nearer. Jamie pulled back his arm for the killing thrust, and waited for the duty esper to come in range. And then someone called from inside the compound, and Silver stopped and looked back. Jamie froze in position, hardly daring to breath. Silver turned and walked back into the compound. Jamie relaxed, letting his breath out in a great sigh of relief. He put away his knife, shaking all over with the relief from tension. The sooner this job was over, the better; it wasn't doing his nerves any good at all.

He raised his esp and cautiously probed inside the reception compound, careful to keep his own mind shielded. It seemed he'd arrived just in time; the first few refugees were just being processed. Jamie frowned. There were two other espers apart from Silver, and they seemed to be scanning the new arrivals very thoroughly, as though searching for something. He couldn't tell exactly what they were up to without dropping his shields and alerting the other espers to his presence, but he could guess. They were looking for the same refugee he'd been sent to find. Jamie grinned. Unfortunately for them, he was there to make sure they never got the chance to find her. He chose his moment carefully, and then delicately mindprobed the refugees in the compound. There were only four and Jamie quickly dismissed them. Vertue had said she wouldn't be in the first few, and it looked like he was right. Jamie turned his esp on the refugees trudging slowly out of the fog, and probed them one by one as they approached the reception area. It was a long and wearying task, but Jamie stuck to it. He soon lost count of the refugees as they passed, but he didn't really give a damn. It was starting to look like he was wasting his time, and in a way he rather hoped he was. Treachery paid well enough, but his heart wasn't in it. He sighed quietly. There were still debts to be paid . . .

And then a tall blonde woman emerged silently from out of the mists. She wore the long gaudy robes of Tannim's patrician class, now torn and grimy and spotted with dried blood. She couldn't have been more than twenty, but pain and sorrow had etched deep lines in her face. She was still good looking, but she'd never be pretty again. She walked slowly and gracefully across the pad, staring straight ahead with a disquieting fixed smile. Jamie reached out to her with his mind, and a single word answered him. *Mary*. Jamie smiled almost regretfully, and darted out of the shadows to intercept her.

'Hello, Mary. I'm Shadow; your contact.'

She smiled at him, and Jamie shivered. Her eyes were cold and dark and very empty.

'Hello, Shadow. Mary has been programmed.'

Jamie glanced quickly around to make sure no one had noticed them and then, taking Mary's arm, he led her off into the swirling mists. He shot quick glances at her as he carefully retraced his path to the perimeter wall. She came with him unresistingly, not saying a word. Jamie was just as happy for her to stay that way. Her voice had been cold and unfeeling and somehow inhuman. What the hell had those Empire bastards done to her? And what did she mean, she'd been programmed? Jamie tried another mindprobe, but she had excellent shields,

107

either her own or implanted by Empire mindtechs. Jamie shrugged and hurried her on through the thickening fog. Vertue's contacts were supposed to have fixed it so that the control tower's sensors wouldn't pick them up, but Jamie didn't feel inclined to risk it any longer than he had to. He was beginning to get a very bad feeling about this whole operation. He glanced quickly at Mary. She was still smiling.

They reached the perimeter without being challenged, and Mary allowed Jamie to help her over the low stone wall. He quickly joined her in the narrow street, and then glared hurriedly about him. The mists were growing steadily thicker, and a light snow had begun to fall. Jamie shivered inside his thin cloak, and looked dubiously at Mary's flimsy robes. The night was cold, and getting colder. He was supposed to take her straight to Vertue's place, but the odds were she'd freeze to death on the way. Particularly if he had to waste time dodging the city Watch. Dressed as she was, Mary stuck out like a nun in a brothel. He had to get her some warm clothes, somewhere where they wouldn't ask awkward questions . . . Jamie smiled suddenly. The Blackthorn. Cyder was already connected with Vertue in some way via the energy crystal, so she wouldn't talk out of turn. And the tavern wasn't far off. Jamie took Mary's arm and hurried her along the dimly lit street. Cyder would be bound to have some clothes Mary could borrow. She might also have a few ideas as to what the hell was going on.

The Blackthorn was moderately busy when Jamie peered cautiously in through the open door. Most of the tables were full, and the bar was lined from one end to the other. The air was thick with smoke and the unrelenting chatter of people determined to have a good time while their money lasted. Jamie kept a firm hold on Mary's arm and led her into the tavern. He wasn't sure how the crowd would affect her in her present state. For the moment she was looking straight ahead, ignoring everything and everybody, and Jamie tried to relax a little. He made his way to the bar, looking around for Cyder, but she was nowhere to be seen. A bravo in greasy furs reached out a hand to grab at Mary. She didn't react, but the bravo froze in place as he found Jamie's knife hovering before his left eyeball. He swallowed dryly.

'Uh . . . no offence meant.'

'None taken,' said Jamie courteously, and pulled Mary on towards the bar. The bravo turned back to his jeering companions and did his best to pretend nothing had happened.

Jamie found an open place at the long wooden bar, and quickly filled it with Mary and himself. He waited impatiently for the tall cadaverous barman to get to them, and glanced warily round the packed tables. He hadn't thought the tavern would be so full at this hour of the night. Mary's arrival in Mistport was supposed to be a secret, and here he was bringing her into a crowd of people who'd sell her out in a minute if they thought they could make half a credit on the deal. Jamie scowled. He couldn't take her to Vertue dressed as she was. She'd never make it. And anyway, Jamie felt badly in need of some advice. Things were getting out of hand. He looked up as the bartender finally approached, and tried for a relaxed and confident smile. It didn't feel at all convincing.

'I'm looking for Cyder.'

'She's out on business, Mr Royal.'

'I've got to see her; it's urgent.'

'I'm sorry, Mr Royal, but she's not here. If you'd like to wait, she should be back any time now.'

'Okay. Thanks.'

Jamie took Mary's arm again and led her over to one of the private booths at the rear of the tavern. He sat down on one of the chairs, and then had to get up again and make Mary sit down. She stayed where he put her, still smiling gently to herself. Jamie collapsed on to his chair, and stretched out his legs. It felt good to be back in the warm again. He flexed his numb fingers, trying to work some feeling back into them, and wondered what the hell he was going to do. He couldn't afford to wait long, but, on the other hand, he couldn't leave with Mary dressed as she was. He growled disgustedly, and silently damned Vertue to hell and back. It was all his fault, whichever way you looked at it. Jamie studied Mary thoughtfully. As far as he could tell, she hadn't moved an inch since he'd sat her in her chair. Her face was still calm and cold, and her eyes were far away. It was as though she was . . . waiting for something. Jamie scowled at her.

She was still smiling. He looked away. The smile was starting to get on his nerves.

'Well, Jamie Royal; I didn't expect to find you here.'

Jamie looked up sharply, his hand dropping to the knife in his boot, and then he relaxed slightly. 'I might say the same about you, Suzanne. What is one of Mistport's leading Councillors doing in a dive like this?'

Suzanne du Wolfe shrugged, and pulled up a chair next to Jamie. 'Passing through. Who's your friend?'

'Just someone I'm minding; a business deal. Look, Suzanne, I need a favour. I've got to take her somewhere in a hurry, and she can't go out in the night dressed like this. Have you got a spare cloak or something you could lend her? I was going to ask Cyder, but she isn't here.'

Suzanne frowned. 'Are you in trouble again, Jamie?'

'Aren't I always? These days, everything I touch turns to dross.'

'Jamie . . . I heard about you splitting up with Madelaine. I'm sorry.'

'Thanks.' Jamie hesitated, and then looked steadily at Suzanne. 'Suze, I'm in trouble. Real trouble. I need your help.'

She smiled cynically and leaned back in her chair. 'All right; how much do you want to borrow this time?'

'No, Suze, it's not money I need. Or at least, not just money. It's your influence I need, your protection.'

'Jamie, there's not a lot I can do for you. As a Councillor, I might be able to turn a blind eye to a few things, but . . . '

'You're not just a Councillor,' said Jamie slowly. 'You're also a Wolfe.'

Suzanne's face hardened suddenly. 'Du Wolfe, Jamie. I'm only a Wolfe by marriage, and Jonathon's been dead almost three years now.'

'I know,' said Jamie. 'I helped hunt down the man who killed him, remember?'

'Yes. I remember.'

'I'm asking you as a friend, Suze. Once you're made part of a Clan, you're always a part of it. They'll help, if you ask them. And they're the only ones who can give me the kind of protection I need.'

'Come on, Jamie; who could you possibly have upset that you'd need that much protection?'

'Leon Vertue,' said Jamie quietly. 'He's an Empire agent. He owns all my debts, and he had Madelaine killed.'

'Oh Jamie, no . . . '

'I've been working for Vertue these past few days; a mercenary called Blackjack made it clear that I didn't have any choice in the matter. Vertue's planning something, Suze; something big. I want out, but if I try to run he'll send that damned mercenary after me. I've got to have protection, or I'm a dead man.'

'Jamie . . . '

'Please, Suze. I don't know what's going on, but it's got a real nasty feel to it.'

'All right,' said Suzanne du Wolfe. 'I'll talk to the Clan, and see what they say. In the meantime, you'd better stick close to me. They won't dare attack you while I'm around. Now; what are we going to do about your lady friend here?'

Jamie Royal and Suzanne du Wolfe both looked at Mary, and then froze in their seats. Mary was smiling at them, and her eyes were darker than the night. Her time of waiting was over.

Cat hung by his heels from the roof's guttering, and pounded angrily on the closed shutters with his fist, but they remained firmly shut. Cat scowled, and pulled himself back up on to the roof. Cyder should have been back by now. He crouched motionless on the snow-covered slates, lost in thought. The wind whirled the falling snow around him, and he shivered even inside his thermal suit. Finally he shrugged, and padded along the edge of the roof. He swung easily over the edge and slid down the drainpipe to his emergency entrance; a narrow window that opened on to the landing of the Blackthorn's upper floor. The shutter was always left unbolted and slightly ajar, as nobody but Cat was wiry and supple enough to clamber through it. Even so, he had a hard time of it when he tried, and Cat wondered if he was putting on weight. That was what eating regular meals did for you.

He wriggled free of the windowframe, and dropped silently to the landing floor. He looked quickly about him, but there was no one there. The lamps burned brightly in their holders, but still there was a strange coldness to the air. He started down the landing, and then paused as a door swung open to his right. All of Cat's warning instincts suddenly kicked in, and he faded quickly back into the shadows of an alcove. The moment he'd done it he felt ridiculous. There was nothing threatening about a door swinging open. It probably hadn't been shut properly. But still he didn't move from the shadows of the alcove. Cat trusted his instincts. He studied the open door carefully. No light spilled out into the landing, and Cat realized that the room beyond the door was completely dark.

Nobody came out and, after a moment, the door slammed shut. Cat waited, watching curiously, and then the door opened and slammed shut again. Cat felt his hackles rise as he watched the door open and shut time and again, time and again. There was a controlled deliberate violence to the slamming door that disturbed him deeply. He chose his moment carefully, and then darted out of his alcove and on down the landing while the door remained shut. The door flew open as he passed, and Cat flattened himself against the wall on the far side of the door. There was a pause before the door slammed shut again, but he didn't try to see what was waiting in the darkness beyond the door. He didn't want to know.

He padded softly down the landing, frowning as he began to be seriously worried. The slamming door had to be making a hell of a noise, but nobody had come to investigate it. He headed for the stairs at the end of the landing, and then hesitated as he realized he'd have to pass another door. It was shut, and it seemed just an ordinary door. Cat approached it warily, but it remained closed. He studied the door thoughtfully, and then glanced at the stairs. More and more he was getting the feeling that something bad had happened in the Blackthorn. His instincts were telling him to get the hell off the landing, but the closed door intrigued him. He glanced back, and saw that the other door was still opening and shutting, opening and shutting. He looked back at the closed door and worried his lower lip between his teeth. Finally he took off one of his gloves, tucked it into his belt, and placed his bare palm flat against the wood of the door. If there was anyone moving about inside the room, he should be able to pick up the vibrations. But no sooner had he put his hand to the door than he snatched it away again. The door was shuddering. Cat licked his dry lips nervously, and forced himself to try again. Gradually he realized that what he could feel was the continuous thudding of somebody beating against the inside of the door with their fists. Cat backed away, and then hurried to the stairs that led down to the bar.

What the hell had happened in the Blackthorn? And where was Cyder?

Cat hesitated at the foot of the stairs, facing the heavy wooden door that led into the bar. He never went into the bar during opening hours; it wasn't safe. If the Watch ever found out he made his home at the Blackthorn, they'd never leave him or Cyder in peace again. And besides, after the two doors up on the landing, he wasn't sure he wanted to see what was behind this door. But he had to find some answers. Cat braced himself, and pushed the door open.

Furniture lay scattered across the tavern floor like kindling. Deep gouges stretched across the walls like claw marks. All the mirrors were cracked and shattered; broken glass was everywhere. Cat stood unmoving in the doorway, frozen in place by horror and disbelief. He looked slowly about him, trying to take it all in. The long wooden bar was cracked from end to end. Tables and chairs lay overturned, as though a strong wind had blown through the tavern. Wine and ale lay pooled on the floor like spilt blood. All the windows were broken, and the lamps and lanterns had blown out. The only light came from the smouldering fires that burned sluggishly here and there among the wreckage. And all around, moving in strange ways, were shadows that had once been men and women. Some sat listlessly propped up against walls or overturned tables. Their mouths gaped open, and their eyes saw nothing. Others lay on their backs, staring unseeingly at the ceiling, their heels drumming against the floor. Still more lay huddled under improvised shelters, their eyes tightly shut, their mouths stretched wide by raw, rasping screams that Cat couldn't hear. A few men and women lay dead among the wreckage, though no wounds showed.

Cat moved slowly forward. He glanced behind the bar and winced. The bartender had died screaming, his hands pressed to his ears. Cat glimpsed a movement out of the corner of his eye

113

and spun round, poised to run or fight as necessary. Cyder stood just inside the main door, looking around in shocked amazement. Cat quickly made his way across the room to join her, stepping carefully around the various bodies. He took her in his arms, and for a moment she clung to him, her face buried in his shoulder. Then she straightened up and pushed him away. She looked around her wrecked tavern, and though her face was cold and hard, her shoulders were slumped in defeat.

'I'm finished,' she said quietly. 'There's no way I can raise enough money to put right this kind of damage. What the hell happened while I was gone? It looks like a bomb went off in here. A bomb, or a Poltergeist. Damn. Damn! Cat; you watch over the place while I go for a doctor. Maybe some of these poor souls can tell us what happened.'

Cat nodded unhappily, not liking the idea of being left in the Blackthorn on his own but, before he could protest, Cyder was already gone. Cat shrugged, looked uneasily about him, and sat down by the open door to wait.

In a fire-blackened booth at the rear of the tavern, Jamie Royal and Suzanne du Wolfe lay sprawled across the table, quite dead.

Typhoid Mary had come to Mistport.

CHAPTER ELEVEN

Two Warriors

Donald Royal's house stood near the inner boundary of Merchants' Quarter, not far from the starport. When he and his wife had first moved in their new home had been part of one of Mistport's most desirable areas, but that was many years ago. Now the house was old and crumbling and somewhat in need of repair as was the surrounding area. The great households had become lodging houses and tenements, and the old Playhouse was now a covered market. The well-off and the socially ambitious had long ago moved on to other, more reputable areas, but Donald had never moved. His wife had always loved their house and, since her death, there was nowhere else he wanted to be. Besides; it was his house, and he wasn't going to leave it just to fit in with the vagaries of fashion.

Donald Royal had always been a very stubborn man.

He sat in his chair, in his study, and glowered unseeingly at his low-burning fire. Jamie had been dead for nearly three days now, and the Watch were still no nearer finding out who killed him. They couldn't even agree on the manner of his death. His body had been badly burned, but the coroner's report had simply said heart failure. Donald shook his head slowly. He'd always said Jamie would die young, but he'd never really believed it. He hadn't wanted to believe it. Jamie had been his only living relative, the last of the Royal line. Donald had had such plans for Jamie, such hopes . . . All gone now. One of the comforts of growing old was watching your children and grandchildren grow up, and helping to guide them past the traps and pitfalls, all the mistakes you made. There was a real satisfaction in knowing you'd done your best for them, and they were the better because of it. And now it was all over. He'd outlived both his children and his only grandchild, and for what? To walk alone through an empty house and spend the evenings sitting by the fire to keep the cold from his bones.

Donald sank back in his padded armchair, and let his eyes drift over the accumulated possessions of his life. Every painting and ornament, every piece of tech and stick of furniture held its own special memory. Young Jack Random had sat in that chair opposite, when he first came to Mistworld to gather warriors for a rebellion on Lyonesse. That was more than twenty years ago, but Donald could still hear the fire of conviction in Random's voice as he spoke on the need for men everywhere to make a stand against the tyrannies of Empire. Donald had tried to explain that it wasn't as simple as that, but Random wouldn't listen. He'd gathered his little army, held them together with grand rhetoric and promises of loot and glory, and led them back to Lyonesse to face the waiting Empire. Some time later, Donald heard that the rebellion had been put down. Random's army had been cut to ribbons and the survivors hanged for treason, but Random himself had escaped, vowing revenge. Since then, Jack Random had led many rebellions on many worlds, but still the Empire stood. He hadn't yet learned what Donald Royal had learned long ago; that it would take more than force of arms to overthrow the Empire. The people still believed in the Empire, even while it betrayed and murdered them, and until they could be given something else to believe in the Empire would continue its bloody rule.

Donald stirred uncomfortably in his chair as other memories came back to him. Lord Durandal had stood beneath that portrait as he expounded his mad scheme to enter the Darkvoid in search of the legendary Wolfling World. If he found it, he never returned to tell of it. And that ornate china vase had been given to Donald by Count Ironhand of the Marches, to commemorate the time they stood together with a single company of Watchmen and fought back over a hundred Hob hounds. Donald couldn't stand the ugly little vase, but he kept it so as not to upset the Count. Donald had always liked Ironhand. He frowned suddenly, as he remembered Count Ironhand had been dead for over fifteen years. Drowned, saving a child who'd fallen in the River Autumn. Brave and chivalrous, Ironhand, even to the end.

They were all dead now; all the old heroes and warriors who'd held Mistport together and made it strong. Dead and gone down the many years, with only him to remember them and the glorious deeds they'd done.

And who'll remember me, when I'm gone? he thought slowly. *Who'll remember Donald Royal, except as a footnote in some dusty history book.*

And now Jamie was dead.

Donald shook his head slowly, a cold harsh anger building within him. He was old and he was tired, and he hadn't drawn a sword in anger in more than twelve years, but he was damned if he'd let his kinsman's death go unavenged. He levered himself up out of his chair and paced up and down before his fire, thinking furiously. Where to start, that was the problem. There was a time, not that long ago, when he could have just summoned a company of the Watch and demanded access to the investigation, but these days he had little real power. He'd lost interest in politics when his last opponent died, and since then he'd let things slip. He only stayed on with the Council out of a sense of duty. Besides, the Watch weren't getting anywhere. Going about it all wrong, as usual. Instead of concentrating on what happened to Jamie at the Blackthorn, they should have been asking what brought him there in the first place. There was also the question of what he was doing sharing a private booth with Councillor du Wolfe. They didn't have a damn thing in common. All right, they might have been lovers, but Donald would have sworn du Wolfe had better taste than that.

Donald scowled thoughtfully as he paced up and down, slowly grinding his right fist into his left palm. He'd have to go back further, try and discover what Jamie had been up to prior to his death. And that wasn't going to be easy. Jamie never kept books or records on his various dealings, for fear they'd be used against him in a court of law. But who else would know? Donald stopped suddenly as the answer came to him. Jamie might not have trusted anything to paper, but his old partner might have. It hadn't been that long since they split up. And, even if she hadn't kept any records, the chances were she might know something about why Jamie had gone to the Blackthorn on that particular night.

Yes; all he had to do was find Jamie's old partner, Madelaine Skye.

Donald stalked out of his study and hurried down the gloomy hallway to an old familiar cupboard. He fumbled with the key in his eagerness, but finally hauled the door open. Inside lay all his old swords and daggers, still lovingly oiled and cared for and wrapped in specially treated rags to protect the metal. He chose his favourite sword and carefully unwrapped it. The long and heavy weight of it felt good in his hand, as though it belonged there. He smiled, remembering, and then slipped the sword into its scabbard, buckling the belt around his waist. He unwrapped a knife, and slipped it into the top of his boot. He hefted his old throwing axe in his hand, but reluctantly decided against it. He hadn't practised in so long his eye was bound to be out. He put the axe back and, instead, gathered up a few useful odds and ends and distributed them about his person. Just in case.

He closed the cupboard door, and locked it. The sword at his hip seemed heavier than he remembered, but then he wasn't as young as he used to be. He grinned at the understatement. Luckily, he'd always relied on skill as much as muscle. He pulled on a pair of thick leather gloves and wrapped his heaviest cloak about him. If he remembered correctly, Jamie had said Madelaine Skye had an office in the old Bluegelt building in Guilds' Quarter. About an hour's walk, if he hurried. Donald Royal smiled. It felt good to be doing something again, after all the many years.

Guilds' Quarter wasn't quite as impressive as Tech Quarter, but it was certainly just as prosperous. The squat stone-and-timber buildings had a smug, self-satisfied air of solidity and respectability. The streets were well-lit and reasonably clean, and beggars were firmly discouraged from loitering. Powerful men lived in Guilds' Quarter, men on the way up. Or on the way down. It was that sort of place.

But Guilds' Quarter, like every other Quarter, had its good areas and its bad areas. Madelaine Skye's office was in one of the worst areas; a shambling clutter of streets so close to the inner boundary that it was only just a part of the Quarter. The Bluegelt building was the tallest in its street, with three floors in

118

all, but the brickwork was old and pitted, the façade was decidedly shabby, and the whole place exuded a distinct air of genteel poverty. Donald could remember when the Bluegelt had been one of the major merchant houses, but of late it had obviously come down in the world. He stood in the street outside, staring glumly at the dark empty windows, trying to get his breath back. When he was younger he could have made the walk with no problem, but at his age nothing came easily any more. He moved wearily over to the great front door and leaned against it for a moment while he waited for his second wind. The lantern over the door shed a dirty yellow glow that illuminated very little outside its pool of light. Donald didn't care. There was little enough in this street worth looking at.

His breathing finally evened out again, and he stepped away from the door, pulling his cloak tightly about him. The evening was fast turning into night, and he had to get inside soon before the real cold began. He tried the door handle, and it turned easily in his hand. The door wasn't locked. Donald shook his head unhappily. The Bluegelt must really be on its way out to have such lousy security. He let himself into the building, closing the door behind him.

A long narrow hallway stretched out before him, half-hidden in shadows. A single oil lamp burned above the main door, its dim blue light flickering unsteadily as the oil ran low. Donald moved slowly forward, peering warily about him. The hall itself was clean, but bare. There was no furniture, no fittings, no portraits or tapestries on the panelled walls. The wooden floor had neither rugs nor carpets and, from the look of it, hadn't seen a trace of wax or polish in years. The rats had deserted the sinking ship, taking everything with them that wasn't nailed down. Doors led off the hallway to either side, but Donald didn't bother to check them. Nobody here would give a damn who he was or what he was doing, so long as he didn't disturb them. He glowered at the stairs at the end of the hall. He could clearly remember Jamie saying that Madelaine's office was on the top floor. Typical. Donald hated stairs. Even when he was feeling at his best, a long flight of stairs could still remind him of how frail he'd become.

Three flights of stairs and several long rests later, Donald

Royal stumbled to a halt before the second door along the narrow landing. The flaking paint on the door said *Madelaine Skye; Confidential Inquiries*. Donald smiled slightly. He'd never met Skye before, but that sign told him a lot about her. A euphemism like that could mean anything you wanted it to. Basically, all it really meant was that Skye was for hire, if the money was right. He knocked politely on the door and waited impatiently. There was no reply. Donald tried the door, but it was locked. He smiled wryly; at least somebody in this building understood the need for good security. He put his ear against the wood of the door and listened carefully. There wasn't a sound from inside the office. He straightened up and looked quickly about him, and then knelt before the door to study its lock. The only light came from a single lantern at the far end of the landing, but it was enough for Donald's needs. He took a thin twist of wire from inside his left glove, and inserted it carefully into the door lock. He jiggled the wire a moment, getting the feel of the tumblers, applied a little expert pressure, and the door was no longer locked. Donald removed the wire and slipped it back into his glove. Nice to know he hadn't lost his touch. He pushed the door open and walked into Madelaine Skye's office.

He shut the door behind him, and waited for his eyes to grow accustomed to the gloom. The only light came from a street lamp set just outside the window. Donald shook his head grimly at the lack of shutters. The glass in the window wasn't even steelglass. The security in this building was apalling. He moved slowly forward into the gloom as his eyes adjusted. It wasn't much of an office, as offices go, but it had the bare essentials. There was a desk with a few papers on it. There was a fairly comfortable chair behind the desk, and another, rather plainer chair for visitors. There was a battered old couch, pushed up against the right-hand wall. A few neatly folded blankets and a pillow lay piled at one end, suggesting that the couch sometimes had to double as a bed. A large potted plant stood alone on the windowsill. It had no flowers, and its leaves were drooping.

Donald moved slowly around the office, trying to get the feel of the place. It was cheap, but adequate. The furnishings were rather functional, but there was nothing wrong with that. Donald didn't much care for frills and fancies, and distrusted those who did. And yet . . . the overall impression he got was one of desertion, as though Skye had walked out some time ago and not come back. Donald ran a finger across the desktop, and frowned at the trail he'd left in the dust. He moved behind the desk, dusted the seat of the chair with his handkerchief, and sat down. It was even more comfortable than it looked. Donald stretched his tired legs and looked about him. It was all very interesting, but so far he'd seen nothing that would explain why Jamie died. It had to have been some case he was working on. He couldn't have been killed over his debts; everyone knew Jamie always paid up eventually. Donald frowned thoughtfully. Maybe it was something he or Skye had stumbled on by accident.

He took out his pencil torch, switched it on, and leafed through the papers lying on the desk. Just memos and reminders, mostly trivial stuff, and all of it out of date. The paper should have been handed in for recycling long ago. No wonder there was a paper shortage. He looked speculatively at the two desk drawers. He tried them, and they were both locked. Donald did his trick with the wire again, and then pawed carefully through their contents. Again it was mostly everyday stuff, but finally Donald came up with a pale brown folder. It had been pushed right to the back of the right-hand drawer, and there was no name on its cover. The folder contained three sheets of paper, each covered with notes written in a sprawling longhand. The writing was so bad he couldn't read half of it, but it seemed to be a report on the Hob hounds' movements around the outlying farms. Donald's frown deepened as he read on. As far as he could make out, the report seemed to be suggesting that the only reason the hounds were avoiding the outer farms and settlements was because they were being herded away . . .

Donald stared blankly at the page in his hand. If this report was right, and Jamie and Skye had gone looking for more information, that might explain everything. Only the Empire had the interest and the resources to mount an operation like this, and they wouldn't have taken kindly to being investigated. Donald slipped the paper back into its file, and frowned suddenly. If the Empire had wanted Jamie dead, one of their agents would have killed him simply and neatly, and then disposed of the body. They didn't leave traces where it could be avoided. They certainly wouldn't have destroyed a whole tavern full of people just to kill one man. Donald scowled. Whoever killed Jamie, it almost certainly wasn't the Empire, which meant he was right back where he started. He sat back in his chair and hummed tunelessly, trying to make sense of it all. The folder and its contents were important, he could feel it, but he couldn't see how it linked in with Jamie's death.

'And just what do you think you're doing?'

Donald's heart jumped at the unexpected voice. He looked up, startled, to find a tall silhouette filling the open doorway. He sat up straight in his chair, and let one hand drift back to his swordhilt.

'I wouldn't,' said the voice, and Donald moved his hand away again. He just had time to realize it was a woman's voice, and then he winced as the room was suddenly full of light, throwing back the gloom. His eyes quickly adjusted to the brightness, and he studied the newcomer warily. She stood just inside the doorway, holding up a storm lantern. She was tall for a woman, easily five foot nine or ten. She had a tousled head of reddish-brown hair falling in great waves to her shoulders. Her face was a little too broad to be pretty, but her strong bone structure gave her a harsh, sensual look that was somehow much more impressive. She wore thick mismatched furs under a battered but serviceable cloak. There was a sword on her hip, and her right hand held a throwing knife.

'I asked you a question,' she said calmly. Her voice was deep, smoky, assured. 'What are you doing here?'

'My name is Donald Royal. I'm looking for Madelaine Skye; I have some business to discuss with her.'

The woman looked at him sharply, then put away her knife with a quick, practised motion. She moved over to the desk, put the lantern down, and studied Donald carefully.

'I'm Madelaine Skye. What do you want with me?'

The office seemed warmer and more comfortable with both its lamps lit. Donald Royal sat in the visitor's chair, which was just as uncomfortable as it looked, and studied Skye curiously while she talked. Having finally met her, it was easy to understand why Jamie had stayed with her for so long. Normally, Jamie's attitude to women had always been love them and leave them, and given the kind of women he usually went around with it was hardly surprising. But Jamie and Madelaine Skye had been partners for almost three years, and this was undoubtedly due to Skye. She was a powerful, forceful and yet very feminine woman, with enough energy in her to run a small generator. Donald had no doubt she'd made Jamie an excellent partner. He just wondered what the hell she ever saw in Jamie in the first place. He suddenly realized Skye was talking about the case she was working on at present, and he listened more carefully.

Information about the outlying farms and settlements was always hard to come by, but of late it seemed to have dried up to the bare minimum. This had to be partly due to the recent storms, but even the esper network was having problems getting answers. Skye had been approached by Councillor Darkstrom, on a purely unofficial basis, and asked to look into the situation. She and the Bloodhawk were going out to Hardcastle's Rock to lead the official investigation, but Darkstrom had wanted her own, separate, inquiries made at this end. Apparently she didn't trust some members of the Council.

She hadn't said anything more than that and, for the money she was offering, Skye hadn't felt inclined to press her. So she started digging, and straight away she began hearing strange tales about the Hob hounds. From what Skye had been able to gather, it seemed the hounds were somehow being steered away from the farms and settlements. Communications had been all but sabotaged to keep a lid on this, but still the word had got out, in certain quarters at least. The men involved in the herding had gone to great pains to stay anonymous, but there was no doubt as to who and what they were. Empire agents. Why the Empire should want to protect the outlying settlements wasn't clear as yet.

Donald frowned, and leaned forward. 'But what has all this got to do with Jamie's death? Where's the connection?'

Skye shrugged. 'Beats me. Jamie and I had already broken up before I took on this case. I'm not sure what he'd been up to lately; I've been . . . out of touch for a while. But it seems Jamie had been paying visits to a certain well-known doctor; Leon Vertue.'

'The body-bank doctor?'

'You got it. And everyone knows Dr Vertue has solid links with the Empire.'

'Maybe we should have a quiet word with him,' said Donald slowly.

'We could try, but I doubt he'd see us.'

'He'll see me. I'm a Councillor.'

Skye laughed. 'You think he'll give a damn, with his connections?'

Donald scowled and nodded reluctantly. 'All right; we'll have to approach this by a more devious route. We need someone who'll talk to us about Vertue's set-up; someone who might know what Jamie was doing for the doctor.'

'I know just the man; an old drinking campanion of mine. A shifty little bugger called Donavon Shrike. He still owes me a few favours. But even so, the kind of information we're looking for is going to cost money. Lots of it.'

'I have money,' said Donald shortly. 'Where will we find this informant?'

'At the Redlance.'

Donald grinned suddenly. 'Is that rathole still there? I thought the Watch cleaned it up years ago.'

'It's under new management these days, but by all accounts it hasn't changed much. Except for the worse.'

'Very well. Let's get going.'

Skye raised an unplucked eyebrow. 'You want to go now? This evening?'

'Of course. The longer we leave it, the more likely it is the trail will get cold. Let's go.'

'Wait just a minute. What makes you so sure I'm going to work with you? All right; you're Jamie's grandfather, and I know your reputation. I suppose everyone in Mistport does. They teach it in the schools these days. But that was a long time ago. I can't run a case and look after you at the same time.'

'I can look after myself.' Donald stood up, unlaced his purse from his belt and threw it down on the desk. It landed heavily with a solid-sounding thud. 'There's a hundred and fifty in gold. As a retainer. You're working for me now. Is that acceptable?'

'Gold is always acceptable. And I was . . . fond of Jamie. All right, you've got yourself a deal. Just try not to get in my way too much.'

'I'll try,' said Donald. 'Now can we please get a move on? I don't want to be caught out on the street when night falls.'

Skye sighed and got to her feet. She picked up the purse and laced it to her belt, and then smiled suddenly at Donald. 'I always wondered where Jamie got his stubbornness from.'

Donald Royal hadn't been inside the Redlance for over twenty years and was astonished to find the place hadn't changed at all. It was just as ratty and disgusting as he remembered. The air was thick with the smell of sweat and urine and assorted drugs, and the unrelenting clamour hurt his ears. It was a wonder to him that anyone in the packed crowd could hear anything in such a bedlam. He made his way slowly down the stone stairway into the tavern, followed closely by the cloaked and hooded figure of Madelaine Skye. For reasons best known to herself, she had insisted on pulling her hood all the way forward so that it hid her face. Donald had decided not to ask. He didn't think he really wanted to know.

No one paid him any attention as he made his way through the crowd to the bar. Donald felt just a little annoyed about that. On the one hand, the last thing he wanted was to draw attention to himself, but then again there was a time, not that long ago surely, when his entrance into a place like the Redlance would have stopped everyone dead in their tracks. He smiled sourly as he forced his way through the press of bodies. It was only to be expected; after all, half the people here hadn't even been born when he was busy making himself a legend. He stopped as Skye suddenly tugged at his arm and pointed out Pieter Gaunt, the new manager of the Redlance. Donald headed towards him, and was somewhat mollified when Gaunt recognized him immediately.

'Well, Councillor, this is a pleasant surprise,' said Gaunt cheerfully, shaking Donald just a little too firmly by the hand.

'What brings the famous Donald Royal to the Redlance? Looking for a little something to warm your old bones, perhaps?'

Donald stared coldly at Gaunt. He didn't like the man's condescending tone one little bit. 'I'm looking for Donavon Shrike. Is he here?'

'He might be. Depends on what you want with him.'

Donald looked steadily at Pieter Gaunt, and something in the old man's eyes took the mockery out of Gaunt's face. For a moment, something of the old Royal legend lived again, and Gaunt felt a sudden chill shudder through him. He remembered the things he'd heard about Donald Royal in his heyday, and somehow they didn't seem so unlikely any more. The dark grey eyes locked unrelentingly on to his and Gaunt swallowed dryly. *This man is dangerous*, he thought suddenly, and fought down an urgent need to call for his bodyguards. A cold sweat beaded on his forehead.

'I want to see Shrike,' said Donald Royal. 'Point him out to me.'

Gaunt started to nod agreement, and then the moment was broken as one of his bodyguards stepped forward to stand between him and Royal. Gaunt tore his gaze away, and leaned back against the bar as the tension drained slowly out of him. He looked again at Donald Royal, and saw only an old man in a shabby cloak, but still he shivered as he remembered the dark grey eyes that had held him so easily. *That man is still dangerous . . .*

The bodyguard stabbed Donald in the chest with a stubby finger. 'When you speak to Mr Gaunt, you speak politely. Got it?'

Donald looked at him warily, taking in the man's great size and musculature. 'This is a private conversation,' he said politely. 'I don't see any need for you to get involved.'

'Tough. You looking for trouble?'

'No,' said Donald, 'I'm not looking for trouble.'

'Good. Because you're leaving; right now.'

'I haven't finished my business yet.'

'Yes you have. I say so. Want to make something of it?'

'I really don't want any trouble. Just let me finish my business and then I'll leave.'

The bodyguard smiled, and flexed his muscles. 'I guess your hearing must be going. You don't seem to be getting the message. You leave when I tell you to. Mr Gaunt has better things to do than stand around listening to scruffy old men who think they can throw their weight about. Now do you want to walk out, or would you rather go out on the end of my boot?'

'Do you know who I am?'

'No. Don't care much either. You should have walked while you had the chance. Now I'm going to have to teach you some manners the hard way. I think I'll start with your fingers.'

He grinned unpleasantly, and reached out a hand to take Donald by the arm. Donald's fist whipped out from under his cloak and slammed into the bodyguard's gut, just above the groin. The bodyguard let out his breath in a brief, sobbing grunt. His face screwed up in agony, and then he collapsed on the floor. Donald slipped the heavy steel knuckle-duster off his hand and put it back in his pocket. There was a sudden scuffling sound behind him, and he spun around, sword in hand, just in time to see Skye stab another bodyguard through the heart. Donald nodded his thanks, and turned back to face Pieter Gaunt. The manager of the Redlance looked at his two fallen bodyguards and shook his head sadly. He'd fully regained his composure, and if his face seemed a little pale, that was probably just a trick of the light.

'I don't seem to be having much luck with my bodyguards lately,' he said evenly. 'It would appear you haven't lost your touch over the years, Councillor.'

Donald smiled. 'I'm as good as I ever was; only nastier.'

'So I see. Who's your anonymous friend?'

'Just a friend who prefers to remain anonymous. Where's Donavon Shrike?'

'He's in one of the private booths; third from the left.' Gaunt gestured at the row of enclosed wooden cubicles at the far right of the tavern.

Donald nodded politely. 'Thank you. Please see that we're not disturbed.' He moved away without waiting for Gaunt's answer, and Skye moved quickly in beside him. Donald noted approvingly that she hadn't sheathed her sword either. The heavy blade was a comforting weight in his hand as he approached the row of cubicles. The crowd parted before him and Skye, and closed again after them, without ever once pausing in its various conversations. Drawn swords were apparently fairly common-place at the Redlance. Donald stopped before the booth Gaunt had pointed out to him, and knocked on the closed door. There was no answer. Donald pushed the door open and then stopped in the doorway. A short, scrawny man lay slumped forward across the booth's table. His throat had been cut. Blood dripped steadily from the table's edge into the widening pool on the floor. Donald moved quickly forward into the cubicle, and pulled Skye in after him. He slammed the door shut, and then searched the cubicle for clues while Skye examined the body.

'I take it that is Shrike?' he said tightly.

'Yes,' said Skye. 'He hasn't been dead long.'

'Somebody didn't want him to talk to us. Gaunt?'

'I doubt it. Not his style.'

Donald gave up on his search, and looked thoughtfully at the dead man. 'At least now we know we're on the right trail . . . '

'There is that, I suppose,' said Skye. 'Damn! He could have saved us a lot of time. Now what do we do?'

Donald frowned. 'No one will talk to us after this. They'll be afraid to. But we've still got one name left; someone we know Jamie was working with.'

'Leon Vertue.'

'Right. It's too late in the evening to go after him now, even assuming we could get past his security. And anyway, I want to do a little background work on him first. Maybe I can find some leverage to use against him. Give me your code number and I'll call you somewhen tomorrow . . . '

'No; I'll contact you. My office doesn't have a comm unit. Give me your private code, and I'll be in touch.'

Donald shrugged. 'If that's the way you want it.' He looked at Shrike's unmoving body, and then looked away. Despite all the many deaths he'd seen down the years, it never got any easier. Sudden, violent death still sickened him, in his soul if not his stomach. In a way, he was glad. It meant he was still human. He'd seen too many killing machines in his time. They usually ended up killing themselves when they ran out of enemies. He turned and left the cubicle, and Skye followed him, carefully shutting the door behind her. They made their way back through the crowd, up the stairway, and out into the night.

The mercenary called Blackjack watched them go from the shadows of his private cubicle, next door to Shrike's. As soon as he'd seen Donald Royal enter the Redlance, Blackjack had known Shrike would have to be silenced. He knew too much, even if he didn't realize it himself. Blackjack looked thoughtfully at the hooded figure with Royal. It had been a woman's voice in the cubicle, but he hadn't recognized it. He'd better find out who she was. But first, it might be a good idea to run a check on Councillor Royal. He might be nothing more than an old man living on his legend, but he seemed to be doing all right so far. Maybe Vertue was right to be worried about him after all. Still, if the worst came to the worst, Councillor Royal could always have a little accident. It shouldn't be too difficult to arrange. Perhaps a fall; everyone knew old men had trouble with stairs.

Blackjack left the cubicle and strode confidently out into the tavern to follow Donald Royal and his companion. It wouldn't do for anything to go wrong at this stage; not when Vertue's plans were finally nearing completion.

CHAPTER TWELVE

Gallowtree Gate

Cyder stood alone in the wrecked bar of the Blackthorn tavern.
The city Watch had been and gone, and the dead and the
mindburned had been taken away. That had been three days
ago, yet, despite all Cyder's efforts, the bar remained a wreck.
The windows were cracked and starred. Deep gouges had been
dug in the panelled walls; they looked like claw marks, but no
one knew what had made them. The great brass clock over the
bar had stopped a few minutes after two. Although its interior
was intact and undamaged, the hands remained fixed in position.
The tables and the chairs were gone; Cyder didn't have the
money to replace broken furniture.

There were no customers; people were afraid to enter the
Blackthorn. Cyder didn't blame them. She hadn't had a good
night's sleep since, and often woke trembling from nightmares
she preferred not to remember. Cat had altered his sleeping
habits to spend the nights with her, and she found some comfort
in his arms, but even he couldn't protect her from the dreams. It
wouldn't be so bad if she had some idea of what had happened
in her tavern after she'd left. Out of all the victims, neither the
living nor the dead had provided any answers. The brainburned
were being treated in Mistport's one and only hospital, but so
far not one of them had responded to either drugs or espers.
Their minds were gone. The autopsies on the dead all yielded
the same result; death by heart failure. In the end, all deaths can
be described as heart failure. Three days had passed since Cyder
returned to find her tavern a charnel house, and still no one
could tell her how or why it happened.

Something evil had come to the Blackthorn, and traces of its
presence remained. There was a permanent chill to the air

despite the roaring fire. Even the quietest sound seemed to echo on and on, endlessly. Oil lamps and lanterns filled the bar, but the empty room remained dim and gloomy, and the shadows were very dark. Cyder stared about her, and then put aside the broom she'd been pushing aimlessly about the floor. She had to face the truth. Even if there had been customers, she had little left to offer them. Nothing less than a total refitting could save the Blackthorn, and she didn't have that kind of money. Cyder turned her back on the deserted bar, and made her way to the private stairway at the rear. She'd have to speak to Cat. She'd put it off as long as she could, but there was only one chance left open to her now, if she wasn't to lose everything. A chance she had to take, even if it meant putting Cat at risk.

She slowly climbed the winding flight of stairs up to the tiny attic at the very top of the building, wondering all the way just how she was going to break the news to Cat. When she finally pushed open the door, he was waiting for her, already dressed in his white thermal suit. His working clothes. Cyder smiled, and shook her head wryly. There were times when she wondered if Cat was a secret telepath. He grinned slyly back at her, and jerked his head at the shuttered window, asking if there was a job for him.

'Yes,' said Cyder. 'There's a job for you, my darling. But this is going to be a tricky one, and I have to do some thinking first. Come and sit beside me.'

She sat down on the bed at the far side of the room, and Cat came over to sit at her side. He slipped an arm around her waist and she hugged him to her. More and more she found she needed the simple unquestioning support Cat offered her. Cyder had spent all her adult life looking out for herself; fighting off her enemies with ruthless skill, and making opportunities if there were none conveniently to hand. She never forgot a slight and she never let a favour go unpaid. She trusted no one, cared for no one, was beholden to no one. It was a lonely life, but it was hers. And yet now all her vaunted cunning and business sense had come to nothing. Her fencing income had dropped to an all-time low, and her tavern was finished. What little money she had left grew less day by day, and she was fast running out of options. Cat stared worriedly at her, and Cyder looked at him

131

almost fondly. *My poor Cat,* she thought wistfully. *All this time you've depended on me to do the thinking for both of us, and now, when it really matters, I haven't a bloody clue what to do for the best.*

Cat sensed her despair, and gently pulled her head down on to his shoulder. He held her firmly in his arms and rocked her back and forth, as though soothing a worried child. He wished he had words of comfort to give her, but there was nothing in his mouth but silence. He gave her what ease he could, and waited for her to find her strength again. Sooner or later she would work out what to do, and he would go and do it for her.

Cyder buried her face in his neck, her thoughts drifting tiredly from one vague hope to another. She needed money, and in a hurry. She could always send Cat out to do a spot of roof running, but she didn't like going into jobs blind. A successful burglary needed to be planned days in advance, with every danger weighed and allowed for. And, even then, there were far too many things that could go wrong. If Cat were to get caught on a job, she'd be very upset. He was her main asset now. She frowned fiercely. She didn't like the direction her thoughts were heading in but, as far as she could see, she didn't have any other choice.

It was all Steel's fault anyway. The only reason she'd been away from the Blackthorn when all hell broke loose was because she'd been trying to promote a little business with Port Director Steel. They'd worked well enough together in the past, but this time he'd offered nothing but the chance to fence some of the loot he expected to acquire from the *Balefire.* And even that would have to wait till it had cooled down a little. Cyder scowled. She couldn't afford to wait; she needed the money now. All Steel's fault; if she'd been at the tavern when things started to go wrong she might have been able to do . . . something . . . She sighed regretfully. No matter which way she looked, she kept coming up with the same answer; the only remaining deal that could help her now. A deal not without its share of risks . . . She sat up straight and gently pushed Cat's arms away from her. He saw the business look on her face, and obediently sat quietly beside her, waiting for instructions.

'I have a job for you,' said Cyder slowly. 'There's no risk involved, as long as you're careful. I want you to go and meet a man for me. His name's Starlight; Captain Starlight of the *Balefire*. At the tenth hour, you'll find him in the Gallowtree Gate cemetery in the Merchants' Quarter. He'll show you a sample of his merchandise. If it's of good enough quality, report back to me, and I'll set up a meeting to arrange the transaction. Now watch yourself on this one, Cat. Legally speaking, Starlight won't be allowed to take anything with him from the *Balefire*; all valuables should have been turned over to the port as docking fees. So anything Starlight has he must have smuggled off the landing field. And, since Port Director Steel is known far and wide as an extremely suspicious man, the odds are Starlight is being very carefully watched. The Captain assured me he could shake off any tail long enough for this meeting, but I don't want you taking any chances, Cat. If Steel discovers we're trying to cut him out, he'll have our guts for garters. If you spot anyone, anyone at all you don't like the look of, don't try and make contact with Starlight. Just get the hell out of there and come straight back to me. Got it?'

Cat nodded. All in all it seemed a simple enough job, as long as he watched his back. He kissed Cyder goodbye, did it again because he enjoyed it, and then moved quickly over to stand before the shuttered window. He activated the heating elements in his suit, checked they were all working correctly, and then pulled the cowl up and over his head. Cyder unbolted the shutters and pushed them open, wincing as a blast of freezing air rushed into the room. Cat pulled on his gloves, ran his hands quickly over his body to check he hadn't forgotten anything, and then stepped lithely up on to the windowsill. He nodded goodbye to Cyder, and reached up and grabbed the two steel hoops set into the stonework above the window. He took a firm hold, flexed his muslces, and then swung out of the window and up on to the roof. The shutters slammed together behind him.

The sun had gone down into evening, but the real cold of the night hadn't begun yet. Cat padded cautiously across the snow-covered tiles to perch on a weatherbeaten gable. He stared calmly about him, getting used to the cold and judging the gusting wind. The mists were unusually heavy, and there was a strong feeling of snow in the air. Not the best of conditions for roof running. Cat shrugged and grinned to himself. The worse the conditions, the better he was hidden from prying eyes. It all equalled out. He crouched thoughtfully on the gable, looking for all the world like a ghostly gargoyle. A thought came to him and his grin widened. If he was going to meet Starlight at the tenth hour, he was going to have to cover a hell of a lot of ground in a short time. And there was only one sure way of doing that . . .

Cat swung down from the gable, ran swiftly across the roof, and jumped the narrow alleyway to land easily on the next roof, casually disdaining the long drop beneath him. He hurried on, passing from roof to roof like a drifting phantom, moving gracefully from gable to chimney to guttering as he headed deeper into the corrupt heart of Thieves' Quarter. Some half an hour later he dropped down on to a low roof overlooking the dock area and perched precariously on the edge, staring out over the dark waters of the River Autumn.

Thin streamers of mist curled up from the sluggish waters as the River Autumn meandered into Thieves' Quarter and out again. The river ran through most of the city, stretching from boundary to boundary and passing through three of the city's Quarters. Iced over as often as not, it was still the simplest method of transporting goods through Mistport. No matter what time of the day or night it might be, there were always barges moving on the River Autumn. Cat watched happily as the coal-fired barges slowly nosed their way through the darkness, a single lantern burning on their sterns, glowing like dull coals on the night.

Cat swung down from a slippery buttress and dropped silently to the empty dockside. He faded back into the shadows and looked cautiously around. A dozen crates stood piled to one side, waiting to be loaded, but there was nobody about. Even this early in the evening, no one braved the cold unless they had to. The dockers were probably huddled round a brazier in some nearby hut, just as Cat had expected. Frostbite was an occupational hazard for those who worked on Mistport's docks. The pay was good, but then it would have to be. Cat had never been tempted. He waited patiently in the shadows as the barges drifted unhurriedly past him, the long flat boats appearing out of the grey mists like huge floating coffins. Ice forming on the surface of the water cracked and broke against their steel-lined prows.

Cat watched, and waited. Finally a barge passed directly by the dockside and, choosing his moment carefully, he darted forward out of the shadows and stepped quietly aboard. With the ease of long practice, he ducked under the greasy tarpaulin that stretched half the length of the boat, found himself a comfortable hollow, and tucked himself away, out of sight of one and all. The barge drifted on, heading out of Thieves' Quarter and into Merchants' Quarter.

Cat lay back in the darkness, and let the quiet rhythms of the water soothe him. He liked travelling by barge. Roof running was fun, but this was so much more restful. As long as the crew didn't find him. He stretched lazily. The barge would get him to Gallowtree Gate in plenty of time. For once, his job seemed reasonably uncomplicated. He should be finished inside an hour, if all went well.

Gallowtree Gate cemetery was ill-lit and ill-tended, and not even the heavy incense from the neighbouring church could hide the graveyard stench. Tall gnarled trees lined the single gravelled path that wandered through the cemetery, their dark thorny branches stirring restlessly as the wind moved them. Overgrown grass lapped around the neglected graves and their markers, and the high surrounding wall was wreathed in ivy. Headstones and monuments glistened brightly in the moonlight, looming out of the mists like pale unmoving ghosts.

Late though it was, a small party of men were digging a grave. Wrapped in thick furs and thicker cloaks, they attacked the hardened earth with vigour, probably because the exercise helped to keep them warm. Captain Starlight watched them for a while and then turned away, bored. The thief was late, and the evening was bitter cold. Starlight pulled his cloak about him, leaned back against a tall stone monument, and glanced briefly at the time-piece embedded in his wrist. Nearly half past ten. He cursed Cyder and her thief, and sipped hot soup from his pocket flask.

The *Balefire* was a wreck and, with high tech rarer than gold on this misbegotten planet, Starlight was stranded. He'd let his crew go, and soon enough they'd disappeared into the city, which swallowed them up with hardly a ripple to mark their passing. The refugees were gone; taken care of, one way or another. Now Starlight was finally on his own, with no duties or responsibilities to anyone save himself. For the first time in his adult life he was free; and he hated it. He felt naked. He was also broke. His ship and all its technology was forfeit to the port; docking fees. All he had left was the jewellery and other loot he'd acquired from his passengers, one way or another. Starlight frowned. They had no cause for complaint, any of them. He wasn't a smuggler or a rebel, just a starship Captain caught in the wrong place at the wrong time. He'd saved as many people as he could, and lost his ship doing it. He was entitled to make some profit on the deal – assuming the Port Director didn't rob him blind first. Starlight shook his head angrily. All that mattered was raising enough money to buy passage offworld on one of the smugglers' ships. From what he'd seen so far, Mistworld was a singularly unattractive place to be stranded.

Not far away, the gravediggers were singing a bawdy song to the rhythm of their shovels breaking the earth. Thick streamers of mist curled among the headstones, and the wind whispered in the swaying branches of the trees. Coloured lanterns hung from the massive iron-barred gates, their parchment sides decorated with scowling faces to scare off evil spirits. Starlight looked at them and didn't smile. Everyone needed something to believe in, even a Captain who'd lost his ship. He drank some more of his soup, hoping the hot spicy liquid would help keep the night's cold at bay just a little while longer. He'd been here less than an hour, and already the heating elements in his uniform were hard pressed to keep the chill from his bones. He shifted his weight as he leaned uncomfortably against the stone cross, and brooded yet again on the foul luck that had brought him to Mistworld.

Footsteps crunched clearly on the gravel path, growing louder as they approached. Starlight stoppered his flask and slipped it back in his pocket. About time Cyder's thief finally showed his face. Starlight stepped away from the monument and carefully adjusted his cloak to let his hand rest hidden on the energy gun at his side. A tall blonde woman wearing a patched grey cloak came steadily out of the mists towards him. Her sense of purpose and calm unwavering stare disturbed Starlight, and he moved back into the shadows to let her pass. She drew steadily nearer, neither hurrying nor dawdling, and then stopped directly before

136

him. Her head turned slowly from side to side, as though she was listening for something only she could hear, and then she looked straight at Starlight in the shadows and smiled. He stepped reluctantly back into the moonlight, his hand still resting on his gun.

'Captain Starlight,' said the blonde happily. 'I've been looking for you.'

Starlight nodded stiffly. 'I thought Cyder said the thief would be a man.'

The woman ignored him, her eyes searching his face with a naked hunger that chilled Starlight more than the night ever could. Her eyes seemed very large in her pale face. She was still smiling. When she finally spoke again, her voice was harsh and urgent.

'I want my sapphire, Captain. What have you done with it?'

Starlight's eyes narrowed, and he nodded slowly. 'So. You're one of the refugees I brought in, aren't you?'

'My sapphire, Captain Starlight. I want it.'

Starlight eased his gun in its holster. 'I've nothing for you, lady. I don't know what you're talking about.'

'That really is a pity, Captain.' She giggled suddenly, and two bright spots of colour appeared in her gaunt cheeks. 'Look at me, Captain Starlight. Look at me.'

Their eyes met.

Cat crouched low on top of the slippery stone wall as the gusting wind swayed a tree's thorny branches against him. Glancing quickly around, he dropped silently to the damp grass below. All was quiet in Gallowtree Gate cemetery. The shadows lay undisturbed, and no one walked the single gravelled path.

Cat stared about him suspiciously. There were supposed to be guards to discourage graverobbers from the body banks, but the rusty iron gates gaped wide, unmanned. He shrugged. More budget cuts, he supposed. He glanced up at the night sky and shook his head disgustedly. If he hadn't fallen asleep on the barge he could have been here ages ago. As it was, he was almost an hour late. It wouldn't surprise him if Starlight had got tired of waiting and decided to fence his loot somewhere else. And Cyder wouldn't like that at all.

Cat shivered, not entirely from the night's cold, and moved off into the cemetery, padding along the path like a stealthy ghost. Moonlight shimmered on his white thermal suit. He would have preferred to stick to the shadows of the walls, but the graveyard was littered with overgrown and unmarked graves, and Cat was superstitious.

He found Captain Starlight sitting with his back propped against a tall stone cross, breathing harshly, gazing at nothing. Cat knelt beside him and waved a hand before the staring eyes, but they didn't react. Cat scowled, the hackles rising on the back of his neck. Brainburned, just like the ones he'd found at the Blackthorn. He swallowed dryly, and fought down an almost overwhelming impulse to turn and run. It was like being caught in a nightmare that followed him wherever he went. He quickly brought himself back under control, and searched Starlight's clothes with emotionless proficiency. All he found were a few silver coins and a small polished ruby. He studied the stone with a practised eye. Good stuff, but with Starlight gone there was no way to get at the rest of it. Cyder definitely wasn't going to be pleased.

He kicked the stone monument in disgust, and then froze as he caught a sudden movement at the corner of his eye. All his warning instincts suddenly flared up, and he darted out of the light and into the shadows of the nearest wall, disregarding any graves he might be treading on. Whoever or whatever mindwiped the Captain might still be around, and the same white suit that hid him in the fog and the snow worked against him in the dark cemetery. More and more Cat was coming to the conclusion that he should stick to the roofs where he belonged. He looked cautiously around him. A dim movement not far away caught his eye, and after a moment he moved stealthily forward into the mists to investigate.

Two men lay trembling on the ground beside a freshly dug grave, their heels drumming against the wet earth. One stared up at the night skies with unseeing eyes. The other had torn his eyes out. Brainburned. Cat edged closer, and peered down into the open grave. His hackles rose as he made out a still form lying on the uneven earth at the bottom of the grave, its neck twisted at an impossible angle.

Well, thought Cat crazily, *He's in the right place.*

He shuddered suddenly and decided enough was enough. He faded back into the shadows, clambered over the high stone wall, and fled back to the more understandable evils of Thieves' Quarter. He didn't know that the dead man had been an esper, and was already dying when he fell into the open grave.

Sitting under the tall stone cross, Captain Starlight stared unseeingly at the open cemetery gates through which Typhoid Mary had left. Guttering lanterns scowled at each other in reproach. Although Cat couldn't hear it, Starlight was whimpering.

CHAPTER THIRTEEN

Blood and Terror

The Hadenman called Taylor was drinking wormwood brandy in the Green Man tavern when Blackjack found him. The Green Man stood on the boundary between Thieves' Quarter and Tech Quarter, where the lowest of the low mixed openly with the rich and powerful. It was a place where deals were made, and plans were finalised. Secrets were sold and traded, or openly discussed, and the devil take the hindmost. Deaths could be arranged, reputations made or destroyed. At any time of the day or night, somebody would be making a deal to somebody else's disadvantage.

Nothing cheap or nasty, of course. The Green Man boasted luxurious surroundings, first-class cuisine, and an excellent wine cellar. Rare and precious tapestries decorated the walls, and an oil-fired generator in the basement provided electricity for lighting and heat. There was a subtle perfume in the air, and no one was ever ill-mannered enough to raise their voices above a murmur. There were standards to be observed. The Green Man took a straight percentage from all deals made on the premises, and had never failed to make an extremely healthy profit at the end of each year.

Blackjack stood just inside the door, looking about him. It was early in the morning with the sun barely up, but still some fifty or so patrons sat drinking at the exquisitely carved and polished tables. The Green Man never closed. Blackjack looked thoughtfully at Taylor, sitting alone in an alcove with his back to the wall. The bottle of brandy before him was almost half empty. He looked up as Blackjack made his way through the tables to join him, and nodded politely. The mercenary pulled up a chair and sat down opposite the Hadenman. Taylor shifted his chair slightly so that Blackjack didn't block his view of the door. The two men looked at each other for a while in silence, each waiting for the other to speak first.

'Have you heard about Sterling?' asked Taylor finally. His harsh, buzzing voice grated unpleasantly on Blackjack's ears.

'I saw it happen,' said Blackjack. 'She broke his back with her bare hands.'

'Fifteen hundred in gold,' said Taylor flatly. 'I want it by tonight.'

'What's the rush?'

'Sterling gave Topaz my name. It's only a matter of time before she finds me. Assuming the city Watch don't find me first. It seems there's a price on my head. Even my friends don't want to know me any more. They're scared of the Investigator. I'd known Sterling for almost nine years. He was one of the finest gladiators ever to survive the Golgotha Arenas, and that woman made him look like an amateur. I always knew she was dangerous. You should have told us, mercenary . . . Investigators are no more human than I am. Anyway, I don't plan to be around when she comes looking for me. I don't know what fool killed her husband, but I don't have a snowball's chance in hell of convincing her of that. I've booked passage offworld on a smuggler's ship, leaving at first light tomorrow.'

'Such berths tend to be expensive,' observed Blackjack.

'Fifteen hundred in gold,' said Taylor. 'If I didn't need him to fly the ship, I'd break him into little pieces and dance on the remains. Now, mercenary; I can get the money from you in return for my silence, or I can get it from Port Director Steel as a reward for turning you in. I really don't give a damn which.'

Blackjack looked at the Hadenman thoughtfully. The rasping, inhuman voice held few shadings of emotion and never rose in volume, but deep in the golden eyes Blackjack saw something that might just be fear.

'What's so special about this Investigator?' he asked slowly. 'All right, I've seen her fight. She's good; very good. But you're an augmented man. You should be able to take care of yourself.'

Taylor shook his head, and drained the last of his brandy. He stared down into the empty glass, his face grim, his eyes brooding. 'You've never heard of Investigator Topaz? I thought everyone on Mistworld knew her story. She's a legend in the Empire. Mothers frighten their children with her name. She's a Siren, mercenary. When she sings, she can rip your mind apart. The Empire trained her to destroy whole alien civilizations. By all accounts she was very good at her job. And then one day she turned against the Empire, or it turned against her, and she went on the run. Sirens are rare, and the Empire wanted her back, under its control. I think even then she frightened people. The Empire sent a whole company of the Guard after her; five hundred fully trained warriors. They caught up with her on a little backwater planet called Virimonde. She killed them all with a single song; the most powerful esper there's ever been. Add to that an Investigator's training in gun and sword, and you've a warrior I've no wish to meet in combat. Nor would you, if you've got any sense. Now; how soon can you get me my money?'

'Forget it,' said Blackjack.

Taylor looked at him steadily. 'Perhaps I didn't make myself clear, mercenary; you don't have any choice.'

'There are always other choices.'

'Do you think I'm bluffing?'

'No,' said Blackjack. 'I don't think that at all.'

Taylor threw himself sideways out of his chair, and the blazing stream of energy from Blackjack's gun missed him by inches. The Hadenman was quickly up on his feet, smiling grimly. Blackjack pushed back his chair and rose to his feet, sword in hand. Taylor started towards him, and the mercenary backed warily away, holding his sword out before him. There were frantic scrambling sounds all around as the Green Man's patrons hurried to get out of the way and under cover. At the rear of the tavern a table burned fiercely, having absorbed the disrupter's energy beam. Blackjack holstered his gun, and switched his sword to his right hand. By the time the crystal had recharged, the fight would probably be over. He slapped his left wrist against his hip, and a glowing force shield sprang into being on his left arm.

Taylor slowly circled the mercenary, his golden eyes unwavering and unblinking. His movements were calm and deliberate, with a disturbing fluid grace. He didn't wear a sword or a gun. He didn't need to. Blackjack hefted his sword in his hand. He'd never fought a Hadenman before, but he had faith in his abilities. He circled slowly to keep facing Taylor, careful to keep the gently humming force shield between them. For a while the only sound in the tavern was their regular, controlled breathing, and the quiet slap and scuffing of their feet on the floor. Blackjack feinted with his sword and then cut viciously at Taylor's exposed neck. The Hadenman ducked easily under the swinging blade and threw himself at Blackjack's throat. Blackjack just got his shield up in time, and Taylor slammed into it. Fat sparks spat and sputtered on the still air, and Taylor fell back, shaking his head. Blackjack staggered back from the impact, only just keeping his balance. He'd been lucky, and he knew it. He'd never seen anyone move so damned *fast*.

Taylor picked up a nearby table and tore it in two, the heavy wood groaning as it ripped apart. The Hadenman pulled at one of the legs and it came away in his hand; a yard long club of ironwood. You couldn't cut ironwood with steel; it had to be trimmed and shaped with a laser. And Taylor had just demolished an ironwood table with his bare hands. *If he's trying to impress me,* thought Blackjack, *he's succeeding.*

Taylor moved forward, and swung the massive club at Blackjack's head. He brought up his shield, and Taylor changed the direction of the blow at the last instant. The club twisted in his hands and slipped under the glowing shield to hammer into Blackjack's side, throwing him back. He felt his ribs break under the impact, and had to fight to stay on his feet. He coughed painfully and there was blood in his mouth. Taylor came at him again and he backed quickly away, holding his shield low to cover his injured side. Taylor swung his club with blinding speed, and only a lucky stumble saved Blackjack from a crushed skull. He felt a brief wind caress his face as the club swept past his head, and then, in the split second while Taylor was still off balance from the force of the blow, Blackjack brought his shield hard across against the club. The shield's glowing edge sliced clean through the ironwood, and Taylor was left with a short stub of wood in his hand. Blackjack stepped quickly back, and crouched behind his shield again. Taylor looked at the wooden stump in his hand, and then tossed it casually aside. He looked at Blackjack and smiled.

Blackjack circled slowly to his left, pushing chairs and tables out of his way. He needed room to manoeuvre. His broken ribs were a solid blaze of pain, but he ignored them. He couldn't afford to be distracted. Taylor lifted his left arm and pointed at Blackjack. For a moment the Hadenman held the pose, and then he lifted his hand in a curious gesture and Blackjack's heart missed a beat as he saw a stubby steel nozzle emerge from a slit in the underside of Taylor's wrist. He started to back away, and then brought his shield across to cover his chest just as a searing blast of energy spat from the Hadenman's disrupter implant. The energy beam ricocheted off the force shield and shot away to demolish an overturned table nearby. Taylor lowered his arm.

Blackjack swallowed dryly. He had to get in close and finish this while he still had a chance. There was no telling how many other surprises the Hadenman had built into his body. Blackjack moved carefully forward, and Taylor came to meet him. He cut at Taylor's unprotected ribs, and the Hadenman's right hand shot out to grab the sword. The wide blocky hand clamped firmly on to the steel blade and held it tight, despite the razor-sharp edges. Blackjack could see the flesh part as he jerked the sword back and forth in the Hadenman's hand, and caught a glimpse of implanted steelmesh beneath the skin. He tried to pull the sword free, and couldn't. Taylor raised his other hand and reached unhurriedly for Blackjack's throat. The mercenary brought his force shield across to strike at Taylor's arm, and the Hadenman quickly released the sword and jumped back out of range.

They stood staring at each other for a moment, and then Taylor suddenly crouched and leaped into the air with a single graceful movement. His augmented muscles carried him clear over the startled mercenary and absorbed the landing impact with hardly a jar. Before Blackjack could even start to turn, Taylor's leg shot out in a vicious karate kick, slamming into the mercenary's back. Blackjack's face contorted at the horrid pain and he fell heavily to the floor, dropping his sword and nearly cutting himself badly on the edges of his own shield. He rolled awkwardly over on to his back, fighting off the pain, and pulled a throwing knife from the top of his boot. Taylor stood watching him, smiling. Blackjack threw the knife straight for Taylor's heart, putting all his strength into it. The Hadenman snatched the knife out of mid air, snapped the steel blade in two, and threw the pieces aside. Blackjack's shield flickered and went out.

Taylor moved slowly forward, savouring the open desperation in the mercenary's face as he scrambled backwards across the thick carpeting. The Hadenman flexed his hands eagerly. Blackjack slammed up against the far wall, and knew there was nowhere left to retreat to. He fumbled at the steel band on his wrist, to no effect. The glowing force shield did not return.

'You should have checked your energy level,' said Taylor. 'It'll be at least an hour now before the crystal recharges. A lot can happen in an hour.'

He leaned forward, grabbed the front of Blackjack's furs and lifted him easily off the floor with one hand. Blackjack hit him in the gut. Taylor didn't even seem to feel it. Blackjack clawed at the hand so easily supporting his weight, and then reached out with both hands to take Taylor's throat in a stranglehold. Beneath the rough, scarred skin the mercenary could feel a thick layer of steelmesh. Taylor struck Blackjack casually across the face, and blood flew from his crushed lips. Taylor hit him again, and Blackjack felt his cheekbone crack and break under the impact.

And then the force shield sprang into being once more on Blackjack's arm, and Taylor screamed briefly as the shield's upper edge shot up to slice deep into his throat. He dropped Blackjack and fell backwards, blood gushing from the wide cut that had nearly decapitated him. He rolled back and forth on the floor, grasping his throat with both hands, as though trying to hold the wound together by brute force. Finally the flow of blood lessened, and Taylor's hands fell limply away. Blackjack rose painfully to his feet, and turned off his force shield.

'A timing device,' he said hoarsely to the unmoving Hadenman. 'An old mercenary's trick. I was beginning to think I'd set it for too long an interval.'

He moved cautiously forward and checked the Hadenman's pulse and breathing, to be sure he was dead. He took his time about it, but finally straightened up, satisfied, and looked around for something to drink. He felt very strongly that he'd earned a drink. He headed for the bar, walking slowly and carefully. He had at least one broken rib, probably more, and his back was giving him hell. The Green Man's patrons slowly emerged from their hiding places, talking quietly but animatedly among themselves. There was even a smattering of applause. Blackjack wondered if he should take a bow. He'd just reached the bar when the talk died suddenly away into silence.

'You did well against the Hadenman,' said a cold voice behind him. 'I'm impressed.'

Blackjack turned painfully around to find a striking woman of medium height with close-cropped dark hair regarding him calmly from just inside the door. She wore an Investigator's cloak of navy blue. Blackjack knew without looking that there was a hole burned through the back of the cloak.

'Topaz,' said Blackjack hoarsely. His eyes went to his sword, lying on the floor too far away, while his hand hovered over his holstered gun.

'You've heard of me,' said Topaz, stepping elegantly forward. 'Nothing good, I hope.'

'You're taking a chance coming here,' said Blackjack. 'No one here has any love for the Watch.'

Even as he spoke he could see the fifty or so patrons moving forward. It was an unwritten law, enforced by the richer and more powerful patrons, that the Watch left the Green Man strictly alone. It was a small price to pay, to avoid open war. It was also understood that any Watchman who entered the Green Man did so entirely at their own risk. No one there liked the Watch, and most had old scores to settle. There was a general rasping of steel on leather as swords were drawn from scabbards. Someone took a bottle by the neck and smashed it against a table. Light gleamed brightly on the jagged ends of the broken glass. The Green Man's patrons moved slowly forward in a pack, united by an eager, vicious anger. Topaz stood unmoving in the middle of the tavern, looking coldly about her. And then she opened her mouth and sang.

The pack fell apart as the song washed over them, scrambling their nervous systems and screaming pain through their bodies. Swords, daggers, and broken bottles fell unnoticed to the floor as their owners staggered back and forth, hands pressed to their ears, unable to concentrate on anything but the awful sound that was tearing through their minds. Topaz stopped singing, and the sudden silence was broken only by the muted cries and groans of the Green Man's patrons. They turned away in ones and twos, and then there was a rush for the rear entrance. In the space of a few moments the tavern was empty, save for Topaz and Blackjack.

All through the Siren attack the mercenary had stood to one side, untouched. He watched, fascinated and horrified, as Topaz took on a murderous mob and routed it in a matter of seconds. Maybe that story about the company of the Guard hadn't been an exaggeration after all. He wondered for a moment why the song hadn't touched him. He had no immunity; nobody did, not even another esper. It could only be that Topaz had deliberately focused her song to avoid him. He didn't need to ask why she'd done it. She still needed information on her husband's death, and she meant to get it from him. As long as he was careful what he said, he might get out of this alive yet. He watched uncertainly as Topaz moved slowly towards him.

'I don't think we a quarrel,' he said carefully.

'Then you think wrong,' said Topaz, coming to a stop a few yards short of him. 'I've been keeping an eye on Taylor. I knew that sooner or later his master would send someone to shut him up. You did rather well, mercenary.'

'Thank you,' said Blackjack.

'You're welcome,' said Topaz. 'Now, I want the name of your master. He can tell me who murdered my husband. Tell me your master's name, Blackjack.'

'Leon Vertue,' said Blackjack steadily. 'He runs an organ bank.'

'I know of him. He's a coward. He might order a murder, but he wouldn't have the guts to do it himself. He'd hire someone else to do it; someone like you. I'll deal with him, eventually. For now, I want the killer's name.'

'I don't know it.'

'Your voice tells me you're a liar. Sirens know a lot about voices. By any chance, Blackjack, did you kill my husband?'

'It was an accident.'

'I did wonder,' said Investigator Topaz. 'He was wearing my cloak, and in the confusion of the fighting and the hounds and the mists . . . I did wonder. Michael died because of me. I'll kill you slowly for that.'

'Of course you will,' said Blackjack. 'You esper trash never did have the guts for a fair fight.'

Topaz studied him silently, her head cocked slightly to one side. 'You're trying to anger me,' she said finally. 'You want me to throw away my advantages in a rush of emotion. But Investigators have no emtotions. Surely you know that?'

'You're different,' said Blackjack.

'Yes,' said Topaz. 'I am. Michael taught me to be human again. And so, when he died, when you murdered him, I swore my husband the mercenary's oath of vengeance. I swore him blood and terror. You know what that means, Blackjack, don't you?'

The mercenary didn't answer. Topaz nodded slowly, her face cold and emotionless.

'Very well; a fair fight, Blackjack. Then, when I kill you, I will be able to savour it all the more. Pick up your sword, mercenary.'

Blackjack moved quickly over to where it lay, and stooped down to pick it up. He caught his breath as his damaged ribs hurt him, and for a moment everything disappeared in a throbbing blood-red haze. He gritted his teeth and forced down the pain, shutting it away in the back of his mind where it couldn't reach him. He grabbed his sword and straightened up again. His injured side felt stiff and binding, but that was all. His mercenary's training would keep the pain at bay for as long as was necessary. He looked narrowly at Topaz, and took a firm grip on his sword. The Investigator had to die. She knew too much; and besides, he didn't like people who interfered in his business. Blackjack smiled slightly. She really should have known better than to agree to a fair fight. He'd never fought fair in his life, and he wasn't about to start now. Especially not against some damned esper freak. His smile slowly widened as he advanced on the waiting Investigator. No need to hurry this; he had time to mix business with a little pleasure. He'd show her the real meaning of blood and terror.

Topaz smiled at him and sang a single piercing note. Blackjack jumped, startled, as the steel band on his wrist suddenly shattered and fell away. He stared stupidly at the smoking wreckage of his force shield lying at his feet, and then looked back at Topaz. She was still smiling.

'You wanted a fair fight, didn't you? Now, it will be.'

She took off her own bracelet and put it in her pocket, drew her sword, and started towards him. Blackjack hefted his sword, and went to meet her. They circled each other warily, their blades reaching out to rasp briefly against each other, testing for strengths and weaknesses. Blackjack struck the first blow, and Topaz parried it easily. For the next few minutes the empty tavern rang to the sound of steel on steel as Blackjack used every tactic and dirty trick he knew to try and finish the fight quickly. He used every skill he'd learned in his long years as a mercenary, and felt a cold sweat start on his face as he slowly realized that, this time, those skills weren't going to be enough. Topaz was an Investigator. He fought on, not giving an inch, searching frantically for something that would give him an edge. He was already hurt and tired and, with his modified force shield gone, the odds were too even for his liking.

He stamped and lunged, his blade whistling through the air in savage cuts and thrusts, but somehow Topaz's blade was always there to parry him. Step by step, foot by foot, she drove him back, her face never once losing its look of calm thoughtful concentration. Blood ran from a dozen cuts on Blackjack's chest and arms, and he couldn't even get close to touching her. Fear and desperation put new strength into his blows, but still it wasn't enough. And then he looked into her eyes, and saw the cold remorseless fury that drove her, and knew he didn't stand a chance. He backed quickly away, switching from attack to defence as his mind worked frantically. When the answer finally came to him, he wondered how he could have missed it for so long. He drove Topaz back with a flurry of blows, and then threw his sword at her. She knocked it easily to one side, but in that short moment the mercenary was able to step back out of range and draw his gun from its holster. Time seemed to slow right down. Blackjack brought the gun to bear on Topaz. His finger tightened on the trigger. And Topaz opened her mouth and sang.

Blackjack froze in place, unable to move as the song washed over him scrambling his nervous system. Try as he might, he couldn't move his finger the fraction of an inch needed to pull the trigger. Topaz's song rose and fell, roaring through his mind, and Blackjack watched in horror as his own hand slowly lifted the gun and turned it so that the barrel was pointing at his right eye. He couldn't even scream when Topaz's song moved in his finger and pulled the trigger.

Investigator Topaz stared at the crumpled body lying before her. *Blood and terror,* she thought slowly. *I promised you blood and terror, Michael, my love.* She turned away, and sheathed her sword. She felt strangely empty. She'd taken a fierce satisfaction in the moment of Blackjack's death, but now that was gone, and nothing had come to replace it. There was still Leon Vertue to be dealt with. He had ordered Michael's death. It might be interesting to ask him why before she killed him. But somehow she already knew that Vertue's death wouldn't mean as much to her as Blackjack's had. She looked tiredly about her. Her rage and need for revenge had been all that had kept her going since Michael's death. Now she had nothing left to fill her life; nothing to stop her from thinking.

Oh, Michael; what am I going to do now you're gone . . .

She left the Green Man without looking back, and disappeared into the mists. For a time her footsteps could still be heard, fading slowly away, and then even that was gone, and nothing remained but the cold and empty silence of the night.

CHAPTER FOURTEEN

In Jamie's Memory

Snow was falling heavily the day they buried Jamie Royal. Thick fog enveloped the cemetery like a dirty grey shroud, and a bitter wind moved sluggishly among the gaunt and twisted trees. Donald Royal stood beside the newly dug grave and watched silently as the snow-specked coffin was lowered into the waiting ground. Cold Harbour wasn't the finest cemetery in Mistport, or the most luxurious, but it was one of the oldest. Four generations of the Royal line lay buried at Cold Harbour; five now, with Jamie. Donald bent his head against the windswept snow, and tried to concentrate on the priest's words. The old traditional Latin phrases weren't as comforting as they once were, perhaps because he'd heard them too often in his life.

He raised his head slightly and looked about him. He couldn't see far into the mists, but he didn't need to. He knew where his family lay. His wife Moira was buried in the shade of the great East Wall. He visited her twice a week; sometimes to sit and talk, sometimes just to sit and remember. Not far away stood a simple stone monument carrying two names; those of his son James and his wife Helen. They both died in the war against the High Guard, more than twenty years ago. Their bodies had never been found, but Donald had put up a headstone anyway. He felt they would have wanted it. His daughter Catrina lay buried close by, next to her mother. She married twice, both times to scoundrels, but seemed happy enough for all that. Best damned cook he'd ever known. Her restaurant had been famous in its day. She'd deserved better than a knife in the back from some nameless cutpurse.

And now it was Jamie's turn. Donald stared silently at the small group of mourners beside the grave. He hadn't expected many to turn up, and he'd been right. Madelaine Skye stood at his side, practically unrecognizable in her massive fur cloak and hood. Next to her stood Cyder, the proprietor of the Blackthorn tavern. A hard bitch, by all accounts. Her face was calm and her eyes were dry but, earlier on, Donald had seen her place a small bouquet of flowers on Jamie's coffin. Her hands had been strangely gentle and before turning away she touched her fingertips lightly to the coffin lid, as though saying goodbye. Beside her stood John Silver, dressed in dark formal robes and cloak that lent his youthful features an austere dignity. The esper stared down into the open grave with dark brooding eyes, lost in his own thoughts or memories.

There was no one else to see Jamie on his way.

Donald sighed quietly, and hunched inside his cloak as the wind whirled snow around him. He'd expected Gideon Steel to at least make an appearance, but he hadn't come. With all the problems the Director had it was hardly surprising, but . . . At least he sent a wreath. The priest finished his prayer, signed himself quickly, and closed his Bible with a quick, decisive snap. He murmured a few words of sympathy to Donald, clapped him on the shoulder, and then hurried away to his next funeral. The beginning of winter was always a busy time for funerals. The two gravediggers stood a little way apart, waiting patiently for the mourners to leave so that they could get on with their job. Donald took a handful of earth and threw it down on to the coffin lid. It landed with a heavy thud; a harsh final sound.

'Goodbye, Jamie,' said Donald quietly. 'Rest easy, lad. I'll get the bastards who did this to you, I promise. I promise.'

He moved back, and watched in silence as one by one the others each took a handful of earth and threw it down on to the coffin. The lid had been closed throughout the service. Jamie's face had been badly burned, far beyond any mortician's attempt to rebuild it. Donald hadn't wanted to see the body anyway. He preferred to remember Jamie as he was when he last saw him; young, handsome, brimming with life.

Madelaine Skye came over to him and took both his hands in hers. She squeezed them gently once, and then stood back a way as Cyder and John Silver came to pay their respects. Cyder glanced briefly at the mysterious figure with its hood pulled down to cover the face, and then nodded politely to Donald.

'I understand Jamie died owing money,' she said gruffly. 'I've got a few credits tucked away on one side. If you need any help putting his affairs in order . . . '

'Thank you,' said Donald. 'I have enough money to take care of all his debts. But it was kind of you to offer.'

'I liked Jamie. You always knew where you were with him.'

'Yes. I didn't know you and Jamie were friends.'

'Neither did I, till he was gone. I'm going to miss him.'

She shook Donald quickly by the hand, and turned and left, striding briskly off into the fog. John Silver stepped forward to take her place.

'I only knew Jamie a few years,' he said quietly. 'Looking back, it seems like I spent most of that time trying to keep him out of the hands of the Watch. Life's going to seem awfully dull without him around to liven things up.'

'Have you any news on his killer?' asked Donald politely. He already knew the answer.

'I'm sorry; no. But it's early days yet.'

'Yes.'

'Director Steel sends his apologies. The way things are . . . '

'I understand. Please thank him for the wreath.'

'Of course.' Silver looked back at the grave. 'Jamie was a good friend, in his way. I wish I'd known him longer.'

He shook Donald's hand and walked away into the mists. Donald Royal and Madelaine Skye stood together beside the open grave.

'I always thought Jamie had more friends,' said Skye quietly.

'No,' said Donald. 'Not real friends. Acquaintances, business partners and drinking companions; he had plenty of those. But not many friends.'

'I suppose that's true of all of us, in the end.'

'Perhaps.'

'What about the rest of his family?'

'There's no one else. Just me.'

They stood together a while, thinking, remembering.

'Madelaine . . . '

'Yes, Donald.'

'Did you love him?'

Madelaine Skye didn't look at him. 'I don't know. Maybe. I didn't know him very long.' She stopped suddenly as her voice broke. 'Yes; of course I loved him.'

'Did you ever tell him?'

'No, I never did. And now I never will.'

'Why did you and he split up? You seemed to be doing quite well as partners.'

'We were. We had an argument. One of those silly things. It seemed important at the time.'

Donald took her by the arm and turned her away from the grave. 'Let's go,' he said quietly. 'We've said our goodbyes, and now we have work to do. Someone has to pay for Jamie's death, and I think I know who.'

'Donald, you can't just walk into Leon Vertue's office and demand to see him. He has a high-tech security system you wouldn't believe, just to keep out people like us.'

Donald Royal warmed his hands at the crackling fire, grimacing as the cold seeped slowly out of his bones. Skye's office was taking a long time to warm up, and he'd been out in the cold for hours. Skye had been talking to him for several minutes, but if he heard her words he didn't show it. He stared thoughtfully into the leaping flames, his mouth a flat grim line. When he finally spoke, his voice was calm and even and very deadly.

'I'm an old man, Madelaine. You should have seen me in my prime; I'd have made your eyes sparkle and your heart beat faster. To hear the way they tell it now, I was a hero in those days. I'm not so sure myself; I was so busy charging round Mistport trying to hold things together that I never really had the time to think about it. I only did what needed doing.

'Since then I've lost my wife and both my children, and today I watched them bury my only grandson. I've outlived all my friends and most of my enemies, and seen my past turned into a legend I barely recognize. Jamie was all I had left. He was a wild one, but he had style and a kind of integrity. I had such hopes for him . . . And now he's gone. Someone's going to pay for that. I don't care if Vertue's got a whole stinking army to hide behind; I won't let him get away with what he's done.'

And then he shrugged and smiled, and turned away from the fire to face Madelaine Skye. 'You don't have to go along with this, lass. I've got nothing left to lose, but you're a young woman with all your life ahead of you. Jamie wouldn't have wanted you to throw away your life on an old fool's schemes for revenge.'

Skye smiled at him affectionately. 'Someone's got to watch your back. Look, we can't be sure Vertue is our man. I've been doing a little quiet checking up on him, and there's not a lot to go on. It seems clear that Jamie was doing some kind of courier work for him, but no one seems too sure what it involved. Word is that Vertue might be in some kind of trouble. He's cut back his organ bank business to the bare minimum, and his body-snatchers have been quiet of late. There's even a rumour that Vertue's been trying to arrange passage offworld on one of the smugglers' ships. It's hard to get any real evidence, one way or the other. People are afraid to talk about Vertue. After what happened to Shrike at the Redlance, you can't really blame them.'

'Any word on who killed him?'

'Nothing definite. Chances are that Vertue's pet mercenary had something to do with it, but again nobody's willing to talk.'

'Well then,' said Donald calmly, 'Since we can't get the answers anywhere else, we might as well go and ask Vertue.'

'It's not going to be that easy, Donald.'

'How right you are,' said a harsh, sardonic voice behind them. Donald and Skye looked quickly round to see a great bear of a man standing just inside the open office door. Almost seven feet tall, and more than half as wide in his bulky furs, his broad face was mostly hidden behind a long mane of dark hair and a thick bushy beard. His eyes were dark and sleepy, but his smile was openly cruel. He peered around the poky little office and sniffed contemptuously. Behind him, four husky bravoes flexed their muscles and practised looking tough. Donald looked at Skye reproachfully.

'We're going to have to do something about the security in this building.'

Skye nodded grimly and glared at the newcomers. 'Business hours are over. Now who the hell are you, and what do you want here?'

'I'm Stargrave,' said the giant cheerfully. 'You've probably heard of me.'

'Sure,' said Skye. 'Protection, blackmail, and a rather nasty variation on the badger game. Last I heard, there was a thirty thousand credit reward out on you.'

'Fifty thousand, woman. Get your facts right.'

'What do you want here, Stargrave?' asked Donald coldly.

The giant chuckled quietly. There was no humour in the sound, only menace. 'I do so admire a man who likes to get down to business. Well, grandpa; it seems you and the young lady here have been poking your noses into things that don't concern you.'

'And you're here to warn us off.'

'Something like that, grandpa. You've both been naughty, so you both get punished. She gets her legs broken; you get a good kicking. Nothing personal, you understand.'

Donald laughed, and Stargrave frowned as he recognized the genuine amusement in the sound. 'You think I'm joking, grandpa?'

'Not at all,' said Donald. 'It's just good to know some things haven't changed. I'm going to enjoy teaching you the error of your ways.'

'He's crazy,' muttered one of the bravoes. 'Let's get the job done and get the hell out of here.'

'Right,' said Stargrave, calmly. 'Only I think we'll break one of grandpa's legs as well. I don't like to be laughed at.'

He move forward, and the four bravoes sauntered into the office after him. Donald glanced unhurriedly about him, taking in the layout of the office furniture and checking for possible advantages and pitfalls. Even allowing for the odds, it felt good to be back in action again. One of the bravoes looked curiously at Skye, still largely anonymous in her heavy cloak with the hood pulled forward. His face suddenly went pale, and he stopped dead in his tracks.

'You can't be. You can't be! Vertue said you were . . . '

He screamed and fell backwards, the hilt of Skye's throwing knife protruding from his left eye-socket. There was a harsh susurrus of steel on leather and Skye leaped forward, her sword swinging before her in a bright silver blur. Another bravo fell to the floor, grasping desperately at the wide slash in his gut. Skye turned quickly away to face her next opponent, and steel rang on steel as she forced the bravo back with the sheer speed and strength of her attack.

Stargrave and the final bravo drew their swords and then made the understandable mistake of going after Donald, assuming him to be the weaker target. Donald backed cautiously away, his sword held out before him, and then darted behind Skye's desk, putting it between him and his opponents. Stargrave and the bravo shared a glance and moved to opposite ends of the desk. Stargrave grinned. Whichever way the old man went, they were sure to get him. Donald looked from one adversary to the other, grabbed a handful of papers from the desk, and threw them in the bravo's face. The bravo automatically put up a hand to protect his eyes, and Donald skewered him neatly through the ribs. Stargrave stood and watched, frozen in place by astonishment, as Donald pulled back his blade and the bravo fell limply to the floor. Donald grinned. That was one style of fighting they wouldn't find mentioned in his legend. It might spoil his image. And then Stargrave was upon him, and there was no time for anything but swordsmanship.

Donald backed away around the desk, ducking and weaving and meeting Stargrave's blade with his own only when he had to. He knew if he tried a full block or parry, the giant's sheer strength would force the blow home. Donald kept backing away, his mind working furiously. Even in his prime he would have been hard pressed to match Stargrave's power, and he was a long way from his prime. Already his arm was tired, his grip was weakening, and his breathing was growing short. Donald smiled suddenly, his eyes cold and grim. That just made it more interesting. It had been a long time since he'd had a real challenge in his life.

He ducked under Stargrave's sweeping blade and cut viciously at the giant's leg. Stargrave jumped back, startled at Donald's sudden switch from defence to attack, and then a slow sullen fear crept into his heart as Donald pressed home his attack. Stargrave had never bothered to learn much of the science of swordsmanship; with his strength and reach he'd never needed to. But now this old man's sword seemed to be everywhere at once, striking from everywhere and nowhere, faster and faster, till the gleaming blade was just a blur. Stargrave backed away, step by step, unable to believe that this was really happening to him. And then he came up short against the desk and realized that his retreat was blocked. He couldn't go back and he couldn't go forward, and the sword, the sword was everywhere. He hesitated as his mind worked frantically, and in that moment there was a sudden burning pain at his throat.

He hurt me, thought Stargrave incredulously. *I'll cripple him for that. I'll cut out his tongue and put out his eyes. I'll stamp on his ribs till they crack and break. He hurt me!*

His sword slipped out of his numb fingers and fell to the floor. Stargrave looked at it stupidly. Something warm and wet was soaking his chest. He put his hand to it and his fingers came away covered with blood. His vision blurred, and all the sounds in the office seemed to come from very far away. The strength went out of his legs, and he sat down suddenly. His eyes closed and his head dropped forward as the last of his life's blood pumped slowly out of his severed throat.

Donald Royal leaned back against the wall and waited patiently for his ragged breathing to get back to normal. An interesting opponent, but not very bright. He turned to see how Skye was doing, but she had already killed her man, and was busily searching through his pockets.

'Anything interesting?' asked Donald.

Skye held up a bulging purse and hefted it in her hand. It clinked musically. 'I hate working for nothing,' said Skye calmly. She straightened up, tied the purse on to her belt, and looked around her office. The five dead men had shed a lot of blood. Skye wrinkled her nose, and scowled. 'What a mess. Why couldn't they have attacked us on the street? Ah well. We'd better get out of here before someone calls the Watch.'

'Right,' said Donald, pushing himself away from the wall. 'You can stay at my place for a while. I've got plenty of rooms. Do you still have any doubts that Vertue is our man?'

'None at all.'

'Good.' Donald hefted his sword thoughtfully. 'As soon as things have quietened down some, I think we'll pay him a little visit. I'm quite looking forward to speaking with Dr Leon Vertue.'

CHAPTER FIFTEEN

The Closing Trap

Typhoid Mary stalked the city streets, hidden in the curling mists.

Mary wasn't really insane, just programmed. The Empire had altered her according to its needs, but Mary never knew that. As far as she knew, she was just another refugee running from the Empire. Time moved for her in fits and starts, and memories from one day rarely passed to the next. The only constants in her shifting life were her terror of being captured and handed back to the Empire, and her need for the object she sought; the desperate, overwhelming need that kept her roaming the mist-choked streets and would not let her rest.

When she was a child on her father's estate, they'd called her greedy. Her mother said Mary had a sweet tooth; if she saw something pretty, she just couldn't resist it. Her father gave her a sapphire for her tenth birthday, because she pleaded for it so; a small polished stone with a heart of cold blue fire. It cost her father a great deal, since sapphires are very rare, but Mary neither knew nor cared. It was enough that it was pretty, and she had wanted it. She hung it from a chain of rolled gold, and wore it always around her neck. The sapphire became her constant companion in good times and bad, through triumph and heartbreak. Now it was gone and she wanted it back.

Someone had stolen it from her. She didn't know who or why, but ever and always a dark whisper in the back of her mind kept her moving, searching, hunting. From time to time it seemed to her that she'd found the thief, but somehow it never was, and she had to go on looking. Sooner or later, she would find her sapphire. She had to.

Scurrying from shadow to shadow, ever fearful of the Empire,

Mary roamed the crooked streets and alleyways of Mistport. Deep within her, madness stirred. Behind her lay a trail of the dead and the brainburned, but she never knew that. Typhoid Mary had been programmed.

She hurried through the narrow streets, hidden in the mists. In the houses she passed, children woke screaming in the night and would not be comforted.

'People are dying in their hundreds, Investigator! I don't have the time or the patience to indulge your vendetta against Vertue any longer!' Steel hammered on the nearest console with his fist to make his point, and then growled under his breath as Topaz looked calmly back at him. Steel breathed deeply, and fought to hold on to his temper.

Behind her calm mask, Investigator Topaz felt deathly tired. It had seemed so simple when she began. All she had to do was track down her husband's murderer and kill him, and then everything would be settled, and she could carry on with her life again. Now Blackjack was dead, but nothing was settled. It might have been the mercenary's finger on the trigger, but Vertue had given the order. She didn't even know why. All she knew for sure was that Michael hadn't been the intended target. He only died because Topaz had lent him her cloak. He died because Blackjack had mistaken him for her.

Her first impulse had been to hunt Vertue down and kill him slowly, but she soon realized she couldn't do that. In the past few days she had given herself over entirely to death and destruction, and only Blackjack's death had shocked her sane again. It was the Empire that had taught her to think in such ways; the Empire that had taught her to kill and destroy. Over the years, Michael Gunn had shown her other ways to live, more human ways, and Topaz had thought her past was gone forever. Now she knew she'd only buried it deep down inside her. It was still there, and always would be, waiting to be called forth again. All she had to do was give up the humanity Michael had so painstakingly taught her. She couldn't do that, she wouldn't do that; not even to avenge his death. He wouldn't have wanted it.

And so she had holstered her gun and sheathed her sword, and used her position in the city Watch to go after Vertue, using the law and all its slow-moving processes. It wasn't easy. As far as the law was concerned, Dr Leon Vertue was a hard-working and honest citizen. Of course, everyone in Mistport knew what he was and what he did, but there was no proof. Vertue saw to that. Those who inquired too deeply into his business had a habit of disappearing. But Topaz didn't give up easily. She fought on, step by step, working her way closer to Vertue and all his hidden dirty secrets, despite everything legal and illegal he could put in her path.

And all the time she thought how good it would feel to draw her sword and cut him down, and watch the blood flow from his dying body.

'Are you listening to me, Investigator?' Topaz jumped as Steel pushed his face close to hers. 'Much as I sympathise with the loss of your husband, you can't spend all your time chasing after Vertue. It's not as if you had any real evidence against him.'

'I have enough to satisfy me.'

'That's not good enough, and you know it.' Steel moved away and sat on the edge of his desk, which creaked complainingly under his weight. Steel ignored it, his gaze fixed on Topaz. 'You haven't been here long, Investigator. In a place like Mistport, the Watch has to be above suspicion. There's always going to be a certain amount of graft and back-handers, that's what helps keep the city running, but there's no place in the Watch for personal vendettas. We don't have many laws here, Investigator, but those we do have are enforced vigorously. They have to be. If they weren't, we'd fall into barbarism in under a generation and the Empire would wipe us out. We survive because we're harder on ourselves than the Empire ever was. It's not easy being free.

'That's why I'm ordering you to leave Vertue alone. If he's broken the law, the law will punish him. Eventually. In the meantime, I need you here. Mistport's coming apart at the seams, and, with the rest of the Council either dead or missing, I've ended up in charge of the whole damn mess. I can't handle everything, Investigator; I need people around me I can trust. That's why I went to so much trouble to keep you out of jail after you carved up Taylor and Blackjack. But if you keep going after Vertue, there's nothing more I can do for you. Vertue may well be as crooked as a corkscrew, but he's gone to great pains

161

to hide it. He also has friends in high places. Very influential friends, who are presently doing their best to make my life even more difficult than it already is. You put one foot out of line, and I'll have no choice but to cut you off at the knees. So; either you start pulling your weight, or I'll withdraw my protection and let the wolves have you. Is that clear, Investigator?'

'Quite clear, Director. I had already come to the same conclusion myself; Vertue can wait. Acting under my instructions and your authority, the city Watch have sealed off Mistport. Nobody gets in or out until this plague's under some kind of control. Quarantine is enforceable on pain of death. Surviving victims of the plague are being held in isolation, and Mistport's medical staff are working around the clock to discover some common link between them. Now please be seated, Director, and kindly lower your voice. I don't care to be shouted at.'

Steel scowled, and then reluctantly sank into the chair behind his desk. Outside his office, his staff worked furiously at their posts, struck silent by the thick steelglass windows that made up his cubicle. The plague had been running wild in Mistport for almost a week now, and they were still no nearer identifying it, let alone coming up with a cure. Even so, Steel couldn't help wondering where he'd found the courage to raise his voice to the Investigator. He was probably feverish from overwork and lack of sleep. He gestured for Topaz to sit oppposite him, and she lowered herself gracefully into the stiff-backed visitor's chair. Steel's cubicle was designed for function rather than comfort, but from Topaz's relaxed air she might just as well have been reclining in her favourite padded armchair.

Steel looked away, and scowled at his crowded desk. His In and Out trays were swamped under overflowing piles of paper, most of them ostentatiously marked Urgent. Steel hadn't bothered to read half of them. Of late all the news was pretty much the same, and he could only stand so much depression at one time. It was somehow typical that Mistport should undergo its first major catastrophe in years, and he was the only one left in the hot seat. Darkstrom and the Bloodhawk were still wandering around the outlying settlements, Donald Royal had gone haring off on some dubious scheme of his own, and poor Suzanne du Wolfe was dead, one of the first victims of the plague. Steel sighed wearily. It was a sign of how desperate he'd become that he'd started to think he'd even welcome seeing the Bloodhawk again, if he and Darkstrom would just take some of the pressure off his shoulders. Steel came out of his reverie with a start as he realized the Investigator was talking to him.

'Director; what are the latest casualty reports?'

Steel punched up the answer on his command monitor, and glared at the result. 'Worse than ever. Three hundred and forty-seven dead, and over two thousand brainburned. More cases are being reported every hour. And, on top of that, dozens of buildings have been wrecked or burned out either at or near more than half of the sites where plague victims were found.'

'We're under attack.'

'I had worked that out for myself, Investigator.' Steel turned off the monitor and stared grimly at the blank screen. 'The Empire's used us often enough before as a testing ground for new weapons, but there's never been anything like this. The nearest comparison would be the mutant virus they hit us with some twenty years ago, but whatever this plague is the old vaccines don't even slow it down.' He leaned back in his chair and rubbed tiredly at his aching eyes. Too much work and too little sleep . . . 'None of it makes any sense, Investigator. The victims are always either dead or brainburned. No immunes, no in-betweeners, no recoveries. The survivors range from autistic to catatonic, but not one of them has enough mind left to respond to a psionic probe. We can't even discover how they contracted the plague.'

'The Watch is undertaking preventative measures, Director.'

'And a hell of a lot of good they've done. I've agreed to everything from quarantining victims' families to torching whole streets of houses, and still the bloody plague keeps spreading.'

Topaz looked at him steadily. 'We're doing everything we can, Director. If you've any other ideas, we'll be happy to implement them.'

'I don't know what to do! I'm not even sure exactly what it is we're dealing with. The only clue we've got is that the first cases of the plague appeared soon after the *Balefire* landed. What's the latest news on that?'

'The field technicians are still tearing the ship apart, but so far they've come up with nothing.'

'Great. Just great.'

'Director; do you remember why you first called me in?'

'Of course. The port espers reported sensing something strange aboard the *Balefire*. But we checked every refugee to come off that ship, and every damn one of them was clean. We even broke open the sleep cylinders, but each and every body was where it should be, and as it should be. Unless there's some hidden compartment . . . '

'I doubt it, Director; the technicians would have found it by now. But we never did find an explanation for the espers' readings.'

'You think that's significant?'

Topaz shrugged. 'Who knows what's significant at this stage.'

Steel frowned thoughtfully, and clasped his hands across his belly. 'The espers said they detected something strange, powerful . . . alien. Alien; could that be it? Some alien creature smuggled into the city carrying an outworld plague?' He stopped suddenly, and rubbed at his aching forehead. 'No. It couldn't have gone undetected this long. Not in Mistport.'

Steel and Topaz sat in silence for a while, each lost in their own thoughts. The monitor chimed suddenly, and the screen lit up to show the face of the duty esper.

'Director, I have a call for you. From Councillor Darkstrom.'

Steel sat forward in his chair, grinning widely. 'Great; put her through! I never thought I'd be so glad to see that grim face of hers again.'

'I heard that,' said Eileen Darkstrom dryly. The screen remained blank, but her voice carried clearly from the comm unit's speakers. 'What's happened in Mistport while I've been away?'

'Death, plague and devastation,' said Steel succinctly. 'I'm glad you're finally back; things have been going crazy here . . . '

'Never mind that now,' said Darkstrom briskly, 'This is important. The Bloodhawk and I came across something very disturbing in the outer settlements. Communications between them and the city have been deliberately sabotaged, to prevent us from finding out that Empire agents have been herding the Hob hounds towards Mistport.'

'Herding?' said Steel incredulously. 'Are you sure?'

'Yes,' said Darkstrom steadily. 'I'm sure. Now that was the bad news. The really bad news is that the Bloodhawk and I got here only just ahead of the main pack. We could see them, crossing the plateau; hundreds of the filthy creatures. They'll get here somewhen during the next few days. You'll have to take every Watchman you can find, and set them to guarding the boundaries.'

'Darkstrom, I can't do that . . . '

'You've got to! Look, I can't stop and talk, I'm meeting someone and it's important. I'll see you afterwards, and you can fill me in on all the latest gossip then. Darkstrom out.'

The speakers fell silent. Steel hurriedly punched a code into his monitor. 'Duty esper; get Darkstrom back on the line. Now.'

'I'm sorry, Director; she was calling from her comm unit implant. It's not a part of our comm net. We'll have to wait until she calls back.'

'Damn. Very well; but I want to know the moment she calls.'

'Yes, sir.'

The screen went blank again, and Steel leaned slowly back in his chair. 'That's all I needed. First a city wracked with plague, and now there are hundreds of Hob hounds headed straight for us. I should never have got out of bed this morning. Ah hell; maybe she's exaggerating.'

Topaz shook her head. 'Councillor Darkstrom is known for her rhetoric, but she rarely exaggerates when it comes to possible dangers.'

'That's true, she doesn't. All right; take what men you can spare and set them to watching the boundaries. We'll worry about the hounds as and when they make their appearance. Now then . . . oh hell, I've lost track of what we were talking about.'

'The beginnings of the plague, Director, and its possible links with the *Balefire*. Captain Starlight was one of the first few victims, wasn't he?'

'Yes. He hasn't said a word since we found him. He won't eat or drink or sleep; just sits huddled in a corner, whimpering. If I didn't know better I'd swear he'd been scared out of his mind.

What kind of a plague is it where the living are worse off than the dead?'

'Where there's life there's hope, Director. My husband taught me that a long time ago, and I still believe it to be true. Given enough time, our medics might yet come up with a cure.'

'Given enough time, the plague might wipe us all out.'

'There haven't been many deaths so far. Not compared with the number of survivors.'

'There have been enough, Investigator. More than enough. Most of us have lost someone to the plague.'

Topaz looked at him curiously. There had been something in Steel's voice . . . 'Who did you lose, Director?'

'A friend. His name was Jamie Royal.'

Steel's voice was very quiet, and his eyes were far away, lost in memory. Topaz looked at her hands folded neatly in her lap.

'I didn't know the esper was a friend of yours, Director.'

'I liked him. Everyone did. Even his enemies.' Steel sat slumped in his chair, his mouth twisted into a bitter grimace. 'I couldn't even go to his funeral. Too much to do.'

'I didn't think you had any friends, Steel,' said Topaz quietly. 'What was he like?'

'Jamie . . . was a gambling man. He owed money to everyone dumb enough to extend him credit, but he always paid his debts eventually. He never broke his word, and he never dealt from the bottom. And the only way anyone will ever remember him is as one of the first victims of this new plague. Not much of a legacy for a man like Jamie.'

Topaz looked at him thoughtfully, and then pushed back her chair and got to her feet. 'We've done all we can for one day, Steel. Leave it, for now. It's late, and we could both use some sleep.'

Steel nodded goodbye without looking up. Topaz stared at his bowed head a moment and then left, closing the cubicle door quietly behind her.

Eileen Darkstrom stood at the far boundary of Tech Quarter, staring out into the fog. All the time she'd spent trudging through the unrelenting cold of the plateau and the outlying settlements, she'd thought constantly of how good it would feel to get back to the warmth of Mistport. And now she was back, the first thing she had to do was hang about on the outskirts of the city, freezing her butt off. Darkstrom sniffed, and huddled inside her cloak. The fog was thicker than ever, with visibility no more than a few yards in any direction. The street lamps cast only shallow pools of light, and the mists muffled every sound. A heavy snow was falling, and the sinking evening sun was lost to sight. Another hour or so and it would be gone completely; nights fell early on Mistworld as winter drew near. Darkstrom scowled, and kicked at the thick snow on the ground.

Where the hell are you, Stefan?

Darkstrom walked up and down before the boundary wall, stamping her feet to drive out the cold. The Bloodhawk had been very particular about her being on time, and here he was almost half an hour late. Typical. Not for the first time, Darkstrom wondered what the hell was so important that they had to discuss it out here in the freezing cold, so far away from everything and everyone. It had to be something to do with what they'd discovered about the Hob hounds. She'd intended to go straight to the Council and tell them everything, but the Bloodhawk had insisted that the two of them talk in private first. As if they hadn't had enough chances on the way home. Darkstrom smiled fondly, remembering.

There was a slight noise behind her, and she turned happily, expecting to see the Bloodhawk. There was no one there. She looked quickly around, but nothing moved in the thick grey mists, and silence lay heavily across the fallen snow. Darkstrom stirred uneasily, and dropped her hand to her sword. The hounds shouldn't be here for at least another forty-eight hours, but there was always the chance a few outrunners had got ahead of the pack . . . Darkstrom drew her sword and glared about her into the mists. Her muscular Blacksmith's arms flexed confidently, and her narrowed green eyes held an eager, dangerous gleam. She hadn't known much about the hounds until she'd visited the outer settlements. What she'd learned there had shocked and sickened her. Hob hounds attacked humans not because they felt threatened or hungry, but simply because they enjoyed it. They showed a distinct preference for weaker prey, like women or children. Particularly children. Darkstrom gripped her sword tightly. She thought she would enjoy evening the score against the hounds a little. She hitched back her cloak to give her arms more freedom of movement, stolidly ignoring the cold, and stamped her boots into the snow to get a good footing. Whatever was lurking out there in the mists was about to get the surprise of its life. She moved slowly forward, listening intently for the slightest sound. She quickly discovered that the only sound in the quiet was the snow crunching loudly under her boots. Darkstrom scowled, and moved quickly over to put her back against the boundary wall. No point in making it easy for the hounds.

Her scowl deepened as she heard slow, unhurried footsteps approaching out of the mists. Whatever was out there, it wasn't a hound. It could be a footpad, or an Empire agent . . . Darkstrom hefted her sword, and dropped into a fighting crouch. The footsteps drew steadily nearer, and then a tall slim shadow formed suddenly out of the fog. Darkstrom tensed, and then relaxed with a great sigh of pent-in breath as Count Stefan Bloodhawk came walking towards her. He looked at her drawn sword, and raised an elegant eyebrow. Darkstrom laughed, and put her sword away.

'I know I'm a little late,' said the Bloodhawk, reproachfully.

'Sorry, Stefan,' said Darkstrom, smiling ruefully. 'The mists have been getting to me.' She moved forward into his arms and gave him a welcoming kiss, to show she forgave him for being late. 'What kept you, dear? Is there some new problem about the hounds?'

'Yes,' said the Bloodhawk regretfully, 'I'm afraid there is.' His right hand slipped the dagger expertly between Darkstrom's ribs, and she stared at him in silent horror before the light went out of her eyes and she slumped against him. He stepped back, and let her fall into the snow.

'I'm sorry, my dear,' said the Bloodhawk calmly. 'But I really couldn't let you talk to the Council. I want the hounds to be a surprise.'

He sighed quietly, cleaned his dagger on a piece of rag, and sheathed it. It was a pity he'd had to kill her. He'd grown rather fond of her, in his way. But the Empire's orders had been most

168

specific, and he couldn't risk upsetting his masters. Anything was worth it if it would finally get him off this stinking planet.

Now that Darkstrom was dead, the Council would have to face the hounds unwarned; or rather, what was left of the Council would. Darkstrom and du Wolfe were dead, and he would be . . . missing. That just left Royal and Steel; an old man and a thief. The Bloodhawk smiled slightly. Everything was going to plan. He picked Darkstrom up and slung her over his shoulder. She was surprisingly heavy for such a small woman. The Bloodhawk walked unhurriedly back into the fog, and disappeared among the mists. The sound of his retreating footsteps died quickly away and soon there was nothing left to show that he had ever been there, save for a few scuffed footmarks in the snow, and a small patch of blood where Eileen Darkstrom had fallen.

CHAPTER SIXTEEN

The Wolf at the Gate

Steel paced back and forth in his cramped glass cubicle, trying to wake himself up. He should have gone home and got some sleep while he had the chance. Now it was two in the morning, and it didn't look as though he'd be getting any sleep this night. His head was muzzy, his eyes ached, and his mouth tasted absolutely foul. He took another large bite from the candy bar in his hand, but it didn't help much. He glanced surreptitiously at Investigator Topaz, standing hunched over his computer console. She couldn't have had much sleep herself, but she looked disgustingly bright-eyed and alert. Steel growled under his breath. It wasn't natural to look that good this early in the morning. He moved in behind Topaz and peered over her shoulder as she keyed in a new series of codes. He watched the answers come up on the screen, and winced.

'Over five thousand and still rising . . . what the hell's happening out there, Investigator? We've got the strictest quarantine regulations Mistport's seen in more than twenty years, and still people are dying. How can everything have got out of hand so quickly? What the hell are we dealing with here?'

Topaz shook her head slowly, and stabbed at the terminal keys as though she could bully the computer into giving her the answers she wanted. 'When the Empire creates a plague, it does a thorough job, Director. New outbreaks have been recorded all across the city. The actual death rate is still comparatively low, but there are so many mindwiped victims that we just can't cope with them any more. The hospital's already full to overflowing. If we don't come up with some kind of vaccine soon, in a few more weeks Mistport will be a city of the dead and the dying.'

'I'm not even sure it is a plague,' growled Steel, sinking into his chair. It groaned under his weight, and he cursed it absently. 'It doesn't act like a plague, doesn't feel like a plague . . . ' He took another bite from his candy bar and wiped his sticky fingers on his shirt front. The sugar gave him energy. 'What kind of a plague doesn't have any symptoms? One minute the victims are fine and healthy, and the next minute they and everyone around them is either dead or mad. No plague works that fast.'

'Could be a long incubation period . . . '

'No. Our tests would have found something by now.'

'Well what is it, if it isn't a plague?'

'I don't know! Some new Empire weapon, a rogue esper . . . '

'An esper? Be serious, Steel; what kind of esper could take out five thousand people in less than a week?'

'You once stood off five hundred Guards with a single song.'

'Yes,' said Topaz steadily. 'And it nearly killed me. I'm the most powerful Siren the Empire ever discovered, and even I have my limits. No, Steel; it's not a rogue esper.'

'You can't be sure of that.'

'We can't be sure of anything any more, Director.'

Steel and Topaz glared at each other helplessly, and then looked away as the command monitor snapped on.

'Director!'

'Yes, duty esper; what is it?'

'Sensors report a gathering of Empire ships off Mistworld, Director.'

Steel gaped at the screen, unable to take the news in. *They've come. They've finally come.* He swallowed dryly, and shook his head slightly to clear it.

'How many ships?'

'Seventy-three and counting, Director. They're dropping out of hyperspace as we watch.'

'It's the Fleet,' said Topaz softly. 'After all these years, the Empire finally thinks it's ready to destroy Mistworld.'

Steel ignored her, and broke contact with the duty esper to key his monitor into the main system. The screen showed him a crowded radar image, with new contacts appearing every second. Overlapping voices from the command centre filled the cubicle.

Disrupter cannon don't answer to the computers. Get a team down there to check the systems.

171

*Smuggler ships are powering up for takeoff. Ground crews please
clear pad seven.*

Where are the espers? We need the psionic shield.

Force shields are down. They don't answer to the computers.

Disrupter cannon are not on line. Repeat; disrupters are not on line.

The computers are dead! They don't hear us!

Where are the espers?

Steel cleared the screen, and the voices fell silent. He could
feel his pulse hammering in his neck, and his palms were wet
with sweat. Everything was happening so damned fast . . . He
looked at Topaz, and her unruffled self-possession helped to
calm him down a little.

'We've still got the smugglers' ships,' said Topaz.

Steel shook his head. 'They don't stand a chance against the
Imperial Fleet, and they know it. They're caught in a trap, just
like us. They're going to die up there, just to buy us a little time.'
He sat back in his chair and stared dazedly around his cubicle.
Beyond the glass walls, technicians were running back and forth,
shouting and cursing silently. 'The force shields are out. The
disrupters are out. I can't believe our defences all fell apart so
quickly. What the hell's happened to our computers?'

'The crystal!' said Topaz suddenly.

'What?'

'The memory crystal I delivered; it was part of the main
defence systems, wasn't it?'

Steel swore softly. 'Yes, it was. Your burglar must have had
time to switch crystals before you discovered him. And what
with all the excitement of the *Balefire* arriving, and the Hob
hounds, and the plague . . . the crystal must have been installed
without checking.'

'And I never thought to check for myself.'

'No reason why you should have; that was our responsibility.'

A distant roar shook the control tower as the smugglers' ships
threw themselves into the night skies; a dozen silver knives
against the Imperial Fleet.

'Call them back,' said Topaz.

'I can't. We need time to bring the espers together. Without
our shields and disrupters, the smugglers' ships are the only

172

other defence we've got left. Their names will be remembered as heroes.'

'We're going to lose,' said Topaz quietly. 'I should have known. I should have known there was nowhere safe from the Empire.'

Steel glanced quickly at her dark, brooding face, and then turned back to his command monitor and raised the duty esper.

'Gather the espers. We need the psionic shield.'

'It's already up and holding, Director, but I don't know how long we can maintain it.' John Silver's face was calm and controlled, but his eyes were grim. 'Hundreds of espers have died from the plague . . . '

'That's it!' Steel turned to his computer console, ignoring the startled esper, and tapped in a query. He nodded savagely as a stream of information flowed across the screen. 'I should have seen it before; *only* espers died from the plague. We were so busy looking for a physical common denominator we didn't think to check for any other links. Investigator; we've been set up. With our computers sabotaged, the psionic shield is all that stands between us and the Fleet, and the plague was introduced specifically to take care of that. And I was so proud of my cannon . . . I should have listened to Suzanne du Wolfe. Duty esper; maintain the shield. That has top priority until I tell you otherwise.'

'Yes, Director, but . . . '

'Just do it!' Steel broke off contact and stared thoughtfully at the blank monitor screen. 'It's a carrier; has to be. One of the refugees from the *Balefire*. I thought Starlight was lucky to escape from Tannim! Somewhere along the line the Empire must have smuggled aboard a carrier with an esper-specific plague.'

'No,' said Topaz abruptly. 'That's not it.' Steel looked at the Investigator in surprise as she paced back and forth before him, frowning. 'You were right the first time, Director; it's not a plague, it's a rogue esper. A Siren, like me. When I sing, my voice and esp combine to work directly on the mind, boosting and scrambling the sensory input. Take that too far, push too hard . . . '

'Brainburn,' said Steel.

'Yes,' said Topaz. 'That's what happened to the five hundred Guards on Virimonde.'

173

'And if you were to sing at an esper . . . '

'The weaker mind would self-destruct. The victim's talent would rage out of control, attacking both the victim and his surroundings. It's no wonder so many·plague sites have been gutted by fire and violence; the victims must have included Pyros and Poltergeists. How could we have been so blind? The espers were the real target all along. The mindwiped survivors were nothing more than innocent bystanders; a blind to keep us from noticing that one by one those we depended on most for our defence were being murdered!'

Steel and Topaz looked at each other.

'You were the most powerful Siren the Empire ever had,' said Steel finally.

'Yes,' said Topaz. 'I was. I destroyed five hundred minds, and they made me a legend. This new Siren has taken more than five thousand victims in just a few days. I wonder if they'll make her a legend too. Probably not; she's more valuable as a weapon.' Topaz shook her head slowly. 'No wonder the port espers picked up strange readings from the *Balefire*. Director; we've got to find this rogue and stop her while we still can.'

Steel frowned thoughtfully. 'It's not going to be easy, trying to find one woman in a city the size of Mistport. I take it we can be sure the rogue is a woman? If the Empire's finally produced a male Siren . . . '

Topaz shook her head firmly. 'No; it's a sex-linked character-istic, like hexing or dowsing.'

'Let's hope you're right, Investigator.' Steel called the duty esper back to his monitor.

'Yes, Director?'

'How many espers can you spare me for a city-wide search? Emergency priority.'

'Assuming everyone reports in, maybe a dozen; but that'll be most of our reserve.'

'I'll take them. We're looking for a rogue esper; a very powerful Siren. You shouldn't have much trouble recognizing her; she was responsible for the strange readings your people picked up from the *Balefire*. Report back to me as soon as you've found her, but no one's to approach her until I give the word. This rogue is dangerous. Got it?'

'Yes, Director.'

'Is the shield secure?'

'For the moment. The Empire ships are in stable orbit, but keeping their distance. They know what will happen if they try anything.'

'Stay with it, lad,' said Steel gruffly, and John Silver grinned.

'With our shield or on it, Director.'

The monitor screen cleared. Steel looked in surprise at his last piece of candy, melting forgotten in his hand, and popped it into his mouth. He chewed thoughtfully, his hands clasped across his belly. 'The port espers scanned every man, woman and child leaving the *Balefire*. There's no way the rogue could have got past them.'

Topaz shrugged. 'Empire agents must have got to her first, and spirited her off the landing field. This whole thing has been very carefully planned right from the beginning.'

'It's starting to look that way. But how far back does this thing go, Investigator? Did the Empire really scorch Tannim lifeless just to make sure we'd accept the *Balefire*'s refugees? A whole world?'

Topaz looked at him steadily. 'They've done worse, Director. Much worse.'

They sat in silence a while. Steel knew there were things he ought to be doing, but somehow he just couldn't seem to raise the energy. 'Do you think they'll find the rogue, Investigator?'

'A dozen espers, to cover an entire city? They might get lucky, but I doubt it. We don't even know her name.'

'Call her Mary.'

'What?'

'Typhoid Mary. It's an old name for a fugitive carrier of disease.' Steel smiled at Topaz's open astonishment. 'A Port Director has to study many fields, Investigator.'

He steepled his fingers and tapped them together thoughtfully. 'As from now, I'm promoting you to Watch Commander. With the Bloodhawk missing, I need someone on the spot I can trust. You're probably the only one in the Watch who really understands what we're up against. Get all the Watch out on the streets and search the city, sector by sector. If you come across any espers apart from the rogue, I want them escorted here

175

under full protection. We can't afford to lose any more espers. At least here we should be able to offer them some security.'

Topaz nodded. 'Sounds logical. Just one thing; what are my men supposed to do if they find the rogue?'

'They can't afford to take chances,' said Steel steadily. 'Keep her under surveillance, but don't approach her. I'll send men armed with disrupters.'

'You're not going to give her the chance to surrender.'

'No. I can't take the risk.'

'With this many Watch out on the streets, we're going to need a cover story.'

'Right. If the truth gets out there'll be a panic. Put a bounty on the rogue's head and tell everyone she's a plague carrier. It's true enough.'

Topaz smiled slightly. 'That should keep people off the streets. I'll lead a patrol into Thieves' Quarter. I know the area.'

'No! You're an esper, Topaz; I can't risk losing you to the rogue.'

'I'm a Siren, Director. I may be the only real chance you've got of stopping her.'

Steel hesitated, and then nodded curtly. He turned away and studied his computer console and after a moment Topaz left the cubicle. Steel scowled at the blank screen before him. Damn fool woman was going to get herself killed at this rate. He wondered why that bothered him so much. He sighed wearily, and indulged in a long, slow stretch. He was so tired even his bones ached. He'd done everything he could, but he had a strong feeling it wasn't going to be enough. The Empire had been planning this for a long time. They wouldn't have left anything to chance. He blinked in surprise as his monitor screen suddenly lit up again.

'Yes, duty esper; what is it?'

'Hob hounds, Director! They're pouring into the city through a breach in the Guilds' Quarter boundary. First reports are confused, but it seems clear there are hundreds of the beasts. The Watch on the spot are falling back, street by street. Without reinforcements, it's only a matter of time before they're overrun.'

'Of course,' said Steel. 'The Empire can't risk us finding Mary too soon, so they provide a distraction. Logical.'

'Director?'

'Take as many Watchmen as you need, but I want those hounds contained. It's vital they be stopped where they are.'

'We've only got so many Watch, Director. We can't block off the hounds and maintain a city-wide search for the rogue esper.'

'I know. Just . . . do the best you can.'

'Yes, Director.'

'What are the early casualty reports like?'

'Bad. The hounds are slaughtering everything that moves. The Watch are slowing them down, but that's all. Still; it could have been worse.'

'I don't see how.'

'At least the Watch was there, Director. If you hadn't posted men to watch the boundaries, the hounds would have taken us completely by surprise. There's no telling how many they would have killed, running unstopped through the city.'

'Yes. I suppose so. We've got Councillor Darkstrom to thank for that. I take it there's still no sign of her or the Bloodhawk?'

'Not so far, Director.'

'And Donald Royal?'

'Still missing, sir.'

'That just leaves me. The last Councillor. Ironic, in its way, I suppose.'

Steel sat in silence for a while, staring at nothing, his eyes far away. John Silver waited patiently.

'Duty esper.'

'Yes, Director?'

'I'm going home. Re-route any message, and . . . let me know if anything happens.'

'Of course, Director. Not much else we can do now, is there?'

'No. You look tired, lad.'

John Silver smiled. 'I think I'll stay a little longer. I couldn't sleep, anyway.'

Steel nodded. 'I'll see you later.'

'Goodbye, sir.'

The screen went blank. Steel rose slowly to his feet and looked about him. Beyond the glass walls, the technicians sat unmoving at their posts, tense and silent. Steel looked away. He'd done everything he could. 'I did my best,' he said softly. He hesitated

177

a moment, as though waiting for an answer, and then he turned and left without looking back.

Twelve espers lay side by side on comfortable couches, and spread their thoughts across the city, searching.

Tarpaulined barges drifted down the River Autumn, steel-lined bows breaking through the newly forming ice. Outleaning timbered buildings bowed to each other like tired old men, upper storeys no more than a hand's breadth apart. Watchmen patrolled the lamplit streets, shivering in their furs. Cats darted along the low stone walls of a back-alley, appearing and disappearing in the thick fog like dusky phantoms.

The espers found Mary in less than an hour, and made contact with her mind. She killed them all.

Typhoid Mary had been programmed.

CHAPTER SEVENTEEN

Heroes and Villains

The building itself was quiet and unassuming, almost anonymous, and the sign above the door simply said BLACKSMITH. Donald Royal smiled grimly. He knew better. During his many years on the Council he'd read a great many reports on Dr Vertue's body bank. It was one of Donald's old familiar angers that he'd never been able to raise enough evidence to close the place down. He should have tried harder. If he had, Jamie might still be alive today.

Donald sighed quietly, and pulled his cloak tightly about him. The fog was thick and heavy, the snow had been falling for hours, and it was still barely morning. It was going to be a hard winter. Donald glanced at Madelaine Skye standing next to him, hidden as usual in her thick fur cloak with the hood pulled well forward. She seemed calm enough, but Donald could tell from the set of her shoulders that her right hand was resting on her swordhilt. He wasn't surprised. He'd heard the open rage in her voice on the few occasions she'd spoken of Dr Vertue.

'Well,' said Donald. 'This is the place.'

'Yes,' said Skye. 'I know.'

'You've been here before, then?'

'Yes.'

Donald waited a moment, and then sniffed when he realized she wasn't going to say any more. He had a strong feeling there were things going on that Skye wasn't telling him about. It didn't really matter. If it was important, Skye would tell him eventually. Vertue was all that mattered now. Donald Royal looked at the closed door before him, and felt a slow cold anger build within him. Leon Vertue knew how and why Jamie had died, and one way or another Donald was going to learn the truth. He glanced quickly at Madelaine Skye.

'Ready?'

'Ready.'

'Then let's do it.'

Donald stepped forward and tried the door. It wasn't locked. He pushed the door open and moved cautiously forward into a quietly tasteful lamplit hall. Skye stepped quickly in behind him and shut the door. It felt good to be in out of the cold. Donald pushed back his hood and beat the snow from his cloak as he looked about him. The short narrow hall was completely empty and ended at the only other door. Donald started towards it, Skye at his side. He took off his gloves and tucked them into his belt. He flexed his hands slowly. Gloves just got in the way when you used a sword. He checked the walls unobtrusively as he passed. He couldn't see any security cameras, but he assumed they were being monitored. Both the walls were covered with ostentatiously expensive paintings and tapestries. Donald smiled suddenly as he recognized a forgery. He knew it was a fake, because he owned the original. His smile slowly faded. At least, he'd always assumed he owned the original. He arrived at the end door in a thoroughly foul state of mind, and scowled fiercely when the door handle wouldn't turn under his hand. He hammered on the ironwood door with his fist, and waited impatiently. There was a hiss of static from a small comm unit set into the doorframe.

'Dr Vertue thanks you for calling, but regrets to announce that he is unavailable today. We apologise for any inconvenience this may cause.'

'Get that recording off the line and talk to me,' growled Donald. 'Or so help me, I'll call in a company of the Watch and have them turn this door into kindling. I am Councillor Donald Royal and I have business with Dr Vertue.'

There was a pause, and then a hesitant female voice issued from the comm unit. 'I'm sorry, Councillor, but the doctor left strict instructions that he wasn't to be disturbed for any reason.'

'Your boss is already in trouble,' said Donald coldly. 'Unless you want to join him, I suggest you open this damned door. Now.'

The door hummed quietly to itself, and then swung smoothly open. Donald smiled grimly, and stalked forward into the doctor's reception area. So much for the first line of defence. A gorgeous redhead was rising nervously from behind a huge steel and plastic desk. Donald nodded briskly to her and glanced about him. There was no sign of Vertue. Highly polished iron-wood wall panels gleamed richly under the overhead lightsphere, and the carpet was thick enough to hide a good-sized snake. Any other time Donald might have been impressed, but right now he wasn't in the mood. He had other things on his mind.

'Vertue,' he said bluntly. 'Where is he?'

The secretary tore her eyes from the bulky, fur-wrapped figure of Madelaine Skye, and glanced quickly at the closed door to the right before answering Donald. 'I'm afraid you can't see him just at the moment, Councillor; he's in conference. He was most emphatic that he wasn't to be disturbed. If you'd care to wait . . .'

'He'll see us,' said Donald, and headed for the right-hand door.

'I'm sorry, Councillor,' said the secretary, and something in her voice made Donald stop and look back. She had a disrupter in her hand, pointed carefully midway between him and Skye. Donald stood very still. The secretary had them both covered, and he had no doubt she'd use the gun if she felt at all threatened. He thought about the throwing knife in the top of his right boot, and then thought better of it. He needed a distraction . . .

The secretary looked from Donald to Skye, frowning thoughtfully. 'If you really had a company of the Watch, you'd have brought them in with you. And if you don't have the Watch's backing, that means you don't have a warrant. So I can throw you both out any time I feel like it. But you wouldn't have come on this strong if you didn't have something you thought you could hurt us with. I don't think I can afford to take any chances with you, Councillor. Or your mysterious friend. Unbuckle your swordbelt, Councillor. Slowly, and very carefully. And you, in the furs; push back that hood and let me take a look at you. I'm sure I know you from somewhere . . .'

Donald fumbled at his swordbelt, taking his time about it

without being too obvious. The secretary seemed more interested in Skye than she was in him. If he timed it just right . . . He knelt carefully down and dropped his scabbard on to the floor. The secretary's eyes flickered from Skye to him and back again. Skye slowly lifted her hands, and then jerked her hood back to show her face. The secretary's eyes widened with horror and her gun hand started to shake.

'You can't be. You can't be! I saw your body in the tank!'

Donald pulled the knife from his boot and threw it underhand, putting all his strength behind it. The knife slammed into the secretary's shoulder, spinning her round. The disrupter fired, discharging its energy harmlessly into the ceiling. Skye stepped quickly forward, sword in hand. The long blade flashed once, and the secretary fell limply to the floor. Skye knelt beside her to be sure she was dead, and then sheathed her sword. Donald picked up his swordbelt and buckled it on again.

'Nice throw,' said Skye.

'Thanks. Why did she spook like that when she saw your face? And what did she mean . . . '

'I'll explain later. Come and take a look at this.'

Donald sniffed, and moved behind the desk to crouch down beside Skye. His knees protested loudly, but he ignored them. Skye gestured for him to study the secretary's face. He did so, frowning, and then reached out to gently touch the flawless skin with his fingertips. It was just that little bit too taut, and he could feel the little telltale scars behind her ears and under her chin. Somewhere along the line, the redhead had undergone extensive skin grafting in order to retain her stunning good looks. Donald wondered briefly what had happened to the woman who'd donated the skin, and then he grimaced as he realized he already knew the answer. He took a firm hold on the hilt of his throwing knife, and pulled it out of the secretary's shoulder. He wiped the blade clean on her blouse, and slipped the knife back into his boot. He had a strong feeling he might need it again before the morning was over.

He rose awkwardly to his feet, wincing as his knees protested. There were days when he wondered just whose side his body was on. Skye moved over to the right-hand door and tried the handle. It was locked. Donald reached into his pocket for his lockpicks.

'Don't waste your time, Donald,' said Skye. 'It's an electronic lock. Vertue thinks of everything.' She scowled thoughtfully at the tiny security camera built into the doorframe. 'We can't afford to waste any more time. We've probably set off all kinds of alarms, and there's no telling how long they've been watching us. Try the desk; maybe there's a hidden switch, or something.'

Donald nodded, and searched the desk drawers one by one. It didn't take him long to find a simple remote control unit, hidden in an empty candy box. He tried the various buttons at random, and after he'd turned the lights on and off a few times, the right-hand door hummed loudly and swung open, revealing a long narrow passage. Donald tucked the remote into his pocket, and moved quickly over to stand beside Skye. He noticed she'd pulled her hood forward to cover her face again, but he decided not to say anything. She'd tell him when she was ready.

The corridor stretched away a good thirty feet and more before turning a corner. Only one of the lightspheres was working, and there was a strong smell of antiseptic. Skye moved slowly forward and Donald followed her. He couldn't see any security cameras, but he knew they were there. Their footsteps were eerily loud in the quiet, echoing hollowly back from the bare featureless walls. There was a quiet rasp of steel on leather as Madelaine Skye drew her sword. Donald couldn't help noticing that her hand was shaking slightly.

Leon Vertue glared at his master, standing calmly before him on the other side of the reclamation tank. He'd been shouting and blustering at the man for the best part of an hour, and little good it had done him. Nothing that Vertue could say seemed to have any effect on Count Stefan Bloodhawk. *I should never have got involved with the Empire*, thought Vertue sourly. *Once they get their claws into you, you're theirs for life.* He fought hard to hold on to his temper. Mistport was going to hell in a handcart, Blackjack was dead, Investigator Topaz was on his trail, and now some damned fool had let Hob hounds into the city. One way or another, his life here was finished; he had to get off Mistworld and start again somewhere else. It didn't matter where. There was always a demand for body banks. What did matter was how much of his stock and equipment he could take with him. He had to take some of it, and it was up to the Bloodhawk to help him. The Empire owed him that much. Vertue glared at the Bloodhawk, who stared calmly back at him.

'You've got to get me out of here!' snapped Vertue. 'While you've been hiding safe and sound in the outer settlements, that damned esper of yours has gone crazy; she's been mindblasting everything that moves! I don't know what happened between her and Royal, but that rotten bitch of yours has been out of control ever since she got here. You never told me she was so powerful! She'll destroy the whole city before she's through.'

'Do stop whining, my dear doctor; it doesn't become you in the least.' The Bloodhawk brushed an invisible fleck of dust from his sleeve. 'The lady in question is not out of control; she's doing exactly what she was supposed to. She did make her start a little earlier than was intended, I'll admit, but that was your fault. You should have told me this Jamie Royal was unreliable.'

'I had no way of knowing that! All the signs were that Blackjack had him thoroughly terrorised. I still don't know why Jamie disobeyed his orders . . . '

'Why isn't important. The fact remains that he led Mary straight to another esper. No wonder her programming took over.'

Vertue shook his head angrily. 'That's all irrelevant now! Blackjack's dead, and too many people are starting to tie me in to what's been happening. It's only a matter of time before one or all of them come after me. You should have let me kill Topaz, as I wanted.'

'No. Once the initial attempt had failed, we couldn't afford to draw attention to her. Someone might have realized she was dangerous to our scheme because she was a Siren. Like our dear Mary.'

'Look; you got me into this mess, Bloodhawk; it's up to you to get me out.'

'Or?'

'Or I'll go straight to what's left of the Council and turn myself in.'

'They'd lock you up and throw away the key.'

'At least I'd still be alive.'

'Just another rat deserting the sinking ship,' said the Blood-hawk sadly. 'My dear Leon; you must know I can't possibly allow you to upset my plans. Not at this stage.'

'And just how do you plan to stop me?' Vertue stepped back from the reclamation tank, grinning wolfishly. The Bloodhawk raised an eyebrow at the disrupter in Vertue's hand, but said nothing. 'You've got a ship somewhere,' said Vertue tightly. 'A private ship. You're going to help me transfer my equipment to that ship, and then we're both going to take a little trip offplanet. As soon as we reach the nearest starport, we both go our separate ways. That's fair, isn't it?'

'You can't hold a gun on me forever,' said the Bloodhawk.

'I can give it a bloody good try.' smiled Vertue. 'Now let's go. We've wasted enough time talking.'

'More than enough,' said Donald Royal.

Vertue and the Bloodhawk spun round to find Donald standing in the doorway, leaning lazily against the doorjamb, a throwing knife poised in his hand. Skye stood beside him, sword in hand, anonymous as always in her furs.

'Your security really is appalling, Vertue,' said Donald mildly. 'Now put down that gun. You even try pointing it in my direction, and I'll put this nasty little dagger right through your left eyeball.'

Vertue stared at him, clearly weighing his chances, and then carefully put the gun down on the closed lid of the reclamation unit. Donald nodded his thanks, and walked unhurriedly forward into the vast chamber. He glanced quickly about him, taking in the great walls of shining crystal and the bulky reclamation tanks that took up most of the room. The air was freezing cold, and the stench of cheap disinfectant was almost overpowering. Skye moved silently at Donald's side, her eyes fixed on Leon Vertue. Donald finally came to a stop before Vertue and the Bloodhawk, carefully keeping a few yards distance between them. Donald stared steadily at the Bloodhawk.

'I thought Vertue didn't have the brains or the guts to pull something like this,' he said quietly. 'And I always thought you were too good to be true. How long have you been a traitor,

185

Bloodhawk? How long have we had an Imperial agent sitting at the heart of our Council?'

'Almost from the beginning,' said the Bloodhawk calmly. 'As soon as I saw Mistport, I knew I'd made a dreadful mistake in coming here. Such a pitiful, squalid little place. Totally uncivilized. It quickly occurred to me that since . . . what I'd done hadn't really been all that bad, the Empire might possibly be interested in reacquiring my loyalty. After all, I could do a lot for them. For the right price. It wasn't difficult, making contact, even then, and the Empire wasn't slow to see my potential. I've done rather well, over the years. There's even been some talk the Empire might give me a medal for my services.'

'No one gives medals to traitors,' said Donald. 'Not even the Empire.'

The Bloodhawk shrugged, unperturbed. 'Be that as it may, with the Empire's help it wasn't difficult to get myself elected Councillor. And after that . . . '

'Yes,' said Donald. 'It all starts to make sense now. No wonder we were never able to keep anything secret from the Empire.'

'Quite,' said the Bloodhawk. 'You know, you really should be surrendering to me. When all is said and done, I hold all your lives in my hands.'

'Run that by me again,' said Donald. 'I think I missed something.'

The Bloodhawk smiled. 'My dear Donald; even as we speak the Imperial Fleet is gathering above our heads.'

'What?' Vertue looked sharply at the Bloodhawk. 'You never said anything about the Fleet coming here. You never said anything about the Fleet!'

'Do be quiet, Leon. It wasn't necessary for you to know. Now, Donald; within a matter of hours, the Fleet will move in and scorch the planet lifeless. Just like Tannim. Your only hope for survival is to surrender to me and throw yourselves on my mercy. I know what you're going to say, Donald, but I'm afraid you're wrong. Very soon now, every esper in Mistport will be dead and without the psionic shield Mistworld will be defenceless.'

'The disrupter cannon . . . '

'Are out of commission, along with the force shields, thanks to a little discreet sabotage. By now Port Director Steel should be discovering that his precious computers aren't listening to him anymore. It's really quite amazing what you can do with one carefully programmed memory crystal in just the right place. You do remember how I convinced the Council that the defence computers needed a new memory crystal?'

Donald looked at him for a long moment. 'How long have you been planning all this?'

'Years,' said the Bloodhawk. 'Allowing for a few small hiccups, I don't think things have gone too badly.'

'Who are you?' said Leon Vertue suddenly, glaring at the silent hooded figure standing beside Donald Royal. 'Why do you keep staring at me?'

'You know who I am.' She pushed back her hood, and Vertue's face went white, his eyes wide and staring like those of a trapped animal. 'You and I have a debt to settle, Vertue.'

'You're dead!' said Vertue loudly. 'Blackjack killed you, and I put you into the reclamation tank myself! I saw you torn apart by the blades and the saws!'

'No,' said Madelaine Skye softly. 'Unfortunately, your mercenary got it wrong. He arrived while I was out. The only woman in my office was my sister, Jessica. She'd come to pay me a surprise visit. I'm told she looked a lot like me. Your man cut her down in cold blood, and then brought her back here to you and your reclamation tanks. You used my death to force Jamie to work for you. The poor lamb never was very brave without me to back him up.

'I found out what had happened soon enough, and decided to stay dead until I could find out what was going on. I knew there had to be somebody behind Vertue, and the whole thing had the Empire's smell on it. I couldn't even tell Jamie I was alive. I needed to be sure just who's side he was on. By the time I was sure, it was too late. He was dead. I never even had a chance to tell him I loved him.'

'You can't blame me for his death,' said Vertue quickly. 'It was the Bloodhawk's idea. He gave the order; I just passed it on to Blackjack.'

The Bloodhawk raised an eyebrow. 'He's lying, of course.'

'Of course,' said Skye, 'But then, both of you would say anything to save your skins, wouldn't you?'

'I've got money,' said Vertue. 'Lots of it. I'll give you half, if you'll let me go.'

'You gave my sister to the knives,' said Madelaine Skye. 'And there isn't enough gold in the Empire to make up for what you did to my Jamie.'

Vertue looked into her cold green eyes and saw his death staring back. He whimpered faintly, and then snatched up the disrupter lying on the reclamation unit. Skye's sword flashed up and down in a silvery arc, severing Vertue's hand from his wrist. He just had time to scream, and then he fell back as Donald's throwing knife sprouted from his throat. Blood flew on the freezing air, and Vertue fell dying to the floor. Donald and Skye turned quickly to face the Bloodhawk, only to stop suddenly as they saw the disrupter in his hand.

'You didn't think he was the only one with a gun, surely?' said the Bloodhawk. 'Please put away the sword, Madelaine. I assure you, you're not going to get a chance to use it.'

Skye sheathed her sword, being careful to make no sudden movements.

'Very good, Madelaine. Now, both of you unbuckle your swordbelts and let them drop to the floor.'

Donald and Skye did so. The scabbarded swords made a heavy, hopeless sound as they hit the floor. The Bloodhawk gestured for Skye and Donald to move back from the reclamation unit, and they did so. The Bloodhawk glanced at Vertue's disrupter lying on the floor, and kicked it out of reach.

'That was a nice throw, Donald,' he said appreciatively. 'A direct hit on the carotid artery, from a very tricky angle.'

'It wasn't that good,' said Donald. 'I was aiming for his eye.'

'Dear Donald, modest as ever. You realize I can't let either of you live. You know far too much. As far as everyone else is concerned, I am missing, presumed dead, and I fully intend to stay that way until I'm safely off this stinking planet. Don't make this any more complicated than it has to be. Just take it quietly, and I'll kill you quickly and cleanly.'

'Like you killed Darkstrom?' said Donald suddenly.

'Exactly.'

'Bastard.'

'Really, Donald . . . '

'She loved you!'

'She was useful.'

Donald Royal stared grimly at the Bloodhawk. 'There's two of us, and only one of you. Shoot me, and Skye'll get you before your gun can recharge.'

'Quite possibly,' said the Bloodhawk. 'But she won't risk your life, any more than you'll risk hers. And neither of you is desperate enough to throw away your own life on the chance the other will get me. No, you'll just go on doing as I tell you, hoping that I'll make a mistake and you'll be able to turn the tables on me. You'll find some rope over there in the corner, Donald. Go and fetch it. Don't even think of trying something heroic, or I'll kill Madelaine.'

'Rope,' said Donald, not moving.

'You're going to tie her up, and then I'm going to tie you up. Then I can shoot you both quite safely. Now don't say any more, Donald. I don't really have the time to kill you as slowly as I'd like, but give me even the slightest excuse, and I swear I'll find the time. I hate you, old man. I've always hated you. If it hadn't been for you and your example, Mistport would have fallen apart years ago, and I would have been free to leave this squalid little planet. Time and time again I set up schemes and you wrecked them. You kept the Council honest, and fought corruption in the Watch. You're the reason I've been trapped here all these years!'

He started towards Donald, his face twisted with rage. His gun hand shook in the intensity of his emotion. And in that moment, while his attention was fixed solely on Donald, Madelaine Skye drew from her pocket the disrupter she'd taken from the dead secretary in the reception office. The Bloodhawk caught the movement out of the corner of his eye, and started to turn. Donald stepped quickly forward and hit the Bloodhawk with a left uppercut to the chin. He put everything he had into the blow, and the Bloodhawk staggered backwards, his gun hand swinging wildly back and forth. Skye chose her moment carefully, and shot him through the heart. The searing energy beam threw the Bloodhawk back against the reclamation tank. He stood spreadeagled against it for a moment, and then slid lifeless to the floor.

Skye looked at him for a moment, and then put away the gun. 'That was for you, Jamie,' she said softly. She turned to Donald Royal, who was nursing his left hand gingerly. 'Are you all right, Donald?'

'I think I've broken every bone in my hand.'

Skye laughed. 'My hero. Come on; it can't be that bad if you can still flex your fingers like that.'

Donald sniffed, but had to smile. 'We didn't do too badly in the end, did we?'

'Not bad at all. We made quite a team.' She stopped and looked at Donald thoughtfully. 'Donald, how would you like to make it permanent? I could use a partner like you.'

Donald looked at her. 'Are you serious? At my age?'

'I said partner, not husband. We work well together. My skill, and your experience; it's a natural.'

Donald thought about it, and then grinned suddenly. 'What the hell. I was getting bored with being a Councillor.'

They grinned at each other. Donald put out his hand, and Skye shook it firmly.

'Now what?' said Madelaine Skye.

'Well, first I suppose we'd better get back to the command centre and see if that bastard was telling the truth about the Imperial Fleet. I have a strong feeling we don't know the half of what's really been going on.'

CHAPTER EIGHTEEN

Songs in the Night

With so many Watchmen roaming the streets, most thieves decided that discretion was after all the better part of valour, and retired from their normal lives for a while. The patrols had been out in the bitter cold all morning with hardly a break, and were growing increasingly tired and touchy. They'd arrest anyone, on the slightest suspicion, just to get off the streets and out of the cold. Thieves stayed indoors, and waited for better days.

All save the roof runners.

Perched high up on a weatherbeaten gable, Cat rested his chin on his white gloved hand and sighed quietly to himself. It was almost three days since the unfortunate affair at Gallowtree Gate, and Cyder was still furious at missing out on Starlight's loot. Cat had been in such a hurry to get out of the cemetery that he'd even forgotten to take the Captain's disrupter. Such guns were rare on Mistworld, and therefore valuable, and Cyder was still giving him hell for having left it behind. Today had been no better than the day before, and so Cat had decided to take to the roofs for a while, until Cyder calmed down a little and stopped throwing things. Fresh movement caught his eye, and he peered interestedly down into the mists below, where a patrol of the Watch were half-heartedly searching a garbage-filled back-alley while their leader reported in.

Investigator Topaz shifted her weight from one numbed foot to the other, and pulled her heavy cloak about her as she waited for the command centre to re-route her call to Steel's apartment. *Typical,* she thought sourly. *My men are out here risking pneumonia, and he's sitting at home with his feet up in front of a nice warm fire. There's no justice. Or, at least, none we can learn to live with.* She glared about her into the thinning fog. A low wind had

191

sprung up, dispersing the mists, but it only made the cold bite deeper. Even with her Investigator's training, Topaz was beginning to feel the cold. *I must be getting soft. I'll be needing eight hours of sleep a night next.* She shook her head sadly, and then looked down as static whispered from the comm unit in her hand.

'Yes, Investigator.'

'Sector four clear, Director; no trace of the rogue. Any news your end?'

'A few sightings, but none confirmed. The twelve espers I set looking for Mary must have found her. They're all dead. I daren't risk trying that again.'

Topaz swore under her breath, so as not to alarm her men. Right now, the last thing they needed was more bad news to discourage them. 'What's happening with the Fleet? Have they moved against the shield yet?'

'No. They're still up there, waiting. We may have something on the rogue. One of her first victims after the Blackthorn was Captain Starlight. There's some evidence to suggest she deliberately hunted him down.'

'Evidence?'

'I was . . . having him watched at the time. I suspected him of trying to smuggle valuables off the landing field. Most of my watchers lost their minds along with Starlight, but one of my men had left earlier on. It's only now that what he had to say is starting to make sense . . . Anyway, it's possible the rogue thought Starlight had something she wanted, something smuggled off Tannim. Among Starlight's effects we found a single blue sapphire, apparently acquired from one of the refugees. Such gems are increasingly rare throughout the Empire, and are especially prized on Tannim.'

'Who has this sapphire now?'

A fat chuckle answered her.

'Of course, Director. I should have known.'

'Quite. It seems to me there might be some connection between the rogue and the sapphire. I've sent for a courier, to take it to the port laboratories. Maybe it'll tell them something. Looks like just another gem to me. Anyway, we should have their report somewhen this afternoon. Assuming we're all still here this afternoon.'

'Very well. Let me know the results when you get them.'

'Of course. Topaz . . . '

'Yes?'

'Donald Royal finally turned up at the control tower. I was just talking to him when you called. It seems Leon Vertue is dead. He was shot while trying to kill Donald.'

'I see.'

'No doubt we'll get all the details later. I thought you'd want to know.'

'Yes. Thank you, Steel. I'm moving on to sector five now. Topaz out.'

'Steel out.'

Topaz slipped the comm unit back into her pocket and called for her patrol to re-form. The Watchmen emerged from the back-alley shaking their heads and brushing rotting garbage from their clothes. Topaz accepted their report, and then led them off into the mists.

Cat watched them go from the gable's shadow, and scratched thoughtfully at his pockmarked cheek. What he'd been able to read off Topaz's lips both intrigued and worried him. The Empire hadn't moved directly against Mistworld in almost two hundred years; not since the Fleet first smashed itself against the psionic shield. But now it seemed they were back . . . He worried his lower lip between his teeth, scowling. He'd better tell Cyder, and see what she made of it. If nothing else, it might take her mind off losing Starlight's loot.

Cat padded softly away across the snow-covered roofs. As he disappeared into the rising mists, a tall blonde with faraway eyes emerged from the shadows of the alleyway below. She'd thought for a time that the Watch were going to find her, but they hadn't looked very hard. To be exact, they hadn't dug deep enough. The garbage had been very unpleasant, but Mary had hidden in worse places. Anything was better than being found and handed back to the Empire. She'd found Topaz's conversation very interesting. So; Port Director Steel had her sapphire, but he was going to give it to somebody else. She couldn't have that. She'd have to find Steel first, and make him give her back her sapphire.

This woman, Topaz; she'd know where Steel was. Mary moved off into the thickening mists, following the Investigator and her patrol.

Even the best programmes can be diverted.

Cat hung upside down from the Blackthorn's guttering and frowned worriedly as he saw that the attic room's shutters stood slightly ajar. It wasn't like Cyder to be so careless. He pulled the shutters open, grabbed the steel hoops set above the window, and swung down into the attic room.

Only one of the lamps was lit, and there was a chill to the air. Cat pulled the shutters firmly together. Cyder was sitting in a chair before the fire, staring into the flickering flames. She looked tired and bitter and just a little lost. There was no loot for her to fence and the Blackthorn was still closed. Cyder worked hard at repairing what she could, but there was a limit to what she could do with her resources, and she'd pretty much reached it. To be poor in Mistport was a crime, often punished by death in the cold and unforgiving streets. Cat scowled fiercely. He was still a roof runner, and a good burglar could always make money. One way or another.

Cyder looked round as she heard him approaching, and gave him a warm smile, but her eyes were vague and absent. She got up to greet him, and Cat put his arms around her. For a moment she leaned against him, happy just to be held and comforted, and then she pushed him away, her face falling back into its usual hard, controlled lines. She smiled at Cat's disappointed face, and kissed him warmly.

'It's about time you got back. Where've you been?'

Cat laboriously spelt out in fingertalk what he'd learned from the leader of the Watch patrol. He was puzzled; Cyder seemed strangely calm as she watched his fingers, almost distracted. When he'd finished, she kissed him quickly and then moved away to inspect her face and hair in the mirror on the wall. Cat watched her lips in the reflection.

'Don't worry about the Imperial Fleet, my darling. As long as the esper shield's up, they can't hurt us. As for the plague carrier, I know the price on her head is tempting, but we're thieves, not bounty hunters. Leave such work for those with a taste for it. All right?'

Cat nodded reluctantly.

'Good. Now then, I've got a job for you. I'm going to see Port Director Steel.'

Cat raised an eyebrow, and Cyder laughed.

'Don't worry, darling. Steel and I have been business associates from time to time in the past. He recently acquired a rather fine sapphire, and I have a buyer for such a gem. I had made arrangements with Steel to purchase the sapphire from him, but when I contacted him an hour ago, he broke our agreement and refused to sell me the jewel at any price. In fact, he was quite short with me. Now we can't have that, can we? I was depending on that deal, Cat. The profit on reselling the sapphire would have gone a long way to helping us out of our present difficulties. Now we've got nothing, and it's all his fault. So, I am going to invite myself to dinner with Steel. It shouldn't be difficult; dear Gideon does so love showing off his culinary skills, and we usually enjoy each other's company. And that's where you come in, Cat. While I keep him occupied, you're going to break into his appartment and steal the sapphire.'

Cat smiled politely. He'd have been better off staying on the roof.

'I knew you'd approve,' said Cyder.

The mists filled the narrow streets as Topaz waited impatiently for her patrol to catch up with her. The fog pressed close about her, leaving a sheen of moisture on her hair and cloak. Visibility was poor, the high stone walls around her little more than dim shadows. A single street lantern glowed bravely against the encroaching fog, a pool of amber light in a sea of endless grey. At least it had stopped snowing.

Vertue was dead. Topaz smiled slowly. With him gone, her vengeance was finally complete. She would have preferred to kill him herself, but it didn't matter. It was enough that he was dead. She felt as though a great weight had been lifted from her shoulders, and yet . . .

What do I do now? I need . . . something in my life; something to give it shape and purpose.

For a long time that something had been Michael. Then there had been revenge. Now . . . what? She frowned slightly. She was a Commander in the Watch. Michael would have found that amusing, but Topaz had already found a kind of comfort in the Watch. Right from the beginning they had accepted her, despite who and what she was, and what she'd done in the past. Perhaps, through the Watch, she could repay Mistworld something of the debt she owed it, for having taken her in and given her sanctuary from the Empire.

Slow footsteps broke the silence, and Topaz looked quickly around. Her men were going to have to do much better than this if they were going to cover all the sectors in this Quarter before nightfall. And then Topaz frowned as she realized there was only one set of footsteps approaching. The harsh, crisp sound of boots on snow carried clearly on the still air. Topaz turned to face the sound, one hand moving automatically to the gun at her side.

Typhoid Mary came walking slowly out of the fog, wrapped in a filthy cloak of tatters. Her gaunt face and hands were bare to the cold, and already showed clear signs of frostbite. She was smiling and her eyes were very bright. Topaz knew who she was. One Siren can always recognize another. Topaz saw the power that burned in the rogue like an all-consuming flame, and her mouth went dry. For as long as she could remember, she'd always known she was the most powerful Siren there'd ever been. Now she wasn't sure that was true any more. Even through her shields, Mary's mind blazed like a searchlight. Deep within Mary's mind Topaz could see the Empire's handiwork; a dark and savage conditioning that writhed among Mary's thoughts like maggots in a fallen apple.

Topaz glanced back the way she'd come, and saw nothing but the mists. Even if her patrol did get to her in time, there would be nothing they could do. Cold steel was no defence against a Siren's song. Topaz knew she stood or fell alone, just as she had once before, when she'd faced an entire company of the Guard and destroyed them with her song. She could still hear their screams. Typhoid Mary stood before her, smiling. Topaz carefully moved her hand away from her gun. It couldn't help her now.

'Mary . . . '

'That's not my name.'

'I can help you.'

The tall blonde shook her head slowly, her dead-white face as empty as a mask. Her smile was a grimace, and the light in her eyes was cold and deadly. 'I thought Mistworld at least would be free of bounty hunters. Save your breath, Investigator. I won't let the Empire take me again.'

'I'm no bounty hunter. I just want to help you.'

Mary laughed harshly. 'I've seen the Investigator's cloak before. I know your kind. I know what you are, and what you do. You're as inhuman as the aliens you walk with. You want to take me back to the Empire.'

'Listen to me,' said Topaz, stepping forward.

Mary opened her mouth and sang.

The street lantern shattered. Topaz staggered back as Mary's song roared in her mind, and she raised her own voice in defence. Topaz and Mary stood face to face, unmoving, and the force of their combined songs whirled the fog and snow around them in a slow, churning maelstrom. The two minds smashed against each other, neither giving an inch, but Topaz felt a slow fear stir deep within her as she realized the rogue was using only a fraction of her power. Topaz summoned her strength. If she lost, then all of Mistworld went down with her. She reached deep inside herself, and drew upon the vast well of power she'd sworn never to use again. *Five hundred men, screaming. Their eyes so dark and empty*. Topaz drew upon her strength, made it a part of her song, and threw it at the rogue esper. Mary didn't even flinch.

The rogue's song rose effortlessly over Topaz's, striking past the Investigator's defences with contemptuous ease. All Topaz's shields fell away, and Mary howled through her mind, searching ruthlessly for the information she needed. It only took a moment, and then Mary's voice rose in triumph as she finally discovered the location of her precious sapphire. Topaz fell limply to the ground. She never felt the impact when she hit it.

Mary fell silent, and stood thoughtfully over the unmoving Investigator. The churning snow dropped back to the ground again, and the fog slowly grew still. A slow excitement welled up within Mary as she thought of regaining her lost sapphire, but there was also a dark quiet voice whispering at the back of her mind. The voice had been there a long time. It told her where to look for her sapphire, whom to approach, and what to do when they lied to her. Now the voice was telling her about the Mistport command centre. It told her there were lots of espers there, waiting for her; waiting for her to sing for them. Mary wanted to sing for them, but even more than that she wanted her sapphire. She hesitated, confused, torn between the two conflicting poles of her conditioning, and then she smiled and relaxed again as the answer came to her. First, she would go to Steel's apartment and reclaim her lost jewel. Then, once the sapphire was safely hers again, she would go to the command centre. Mary smiled brightly as she walked away into the curling mists, and her eyes were very dark.

Typhoid Mary's programme was nearing its end.

CHAPTER NINETEEN

A Final Sacrifice

Cat crouched uncomfortably on the flat asphalt roof of the building overlooking Steel's apartment and waited impatiently for Cyder's signal. Port Director Steel lived right in the heart of Tech Quarter, a high-income high-tech area that Cat usually had enough sense to stay well clear of. The buildings were mostly bleak slabs of concrete and glass left over from the original Empire colony. They offered no easy hand or footholds, and were lousy with security devices. Even worse, they all looked the same and Cat kept getting lost. He scowled about him at the thickening mists. He'd be glad when this job was over, and he could get back to the more familiar timbered and gabled roofs of Thieves' Quarter.

The heating elements in his gloves had cut out again, and he pounded his fists together to keep the blood flowing. At least the thick mists and the recent heavy snow meant he could blend easily into the background. For once his white thermal suit was actually earning its keep. He glowered down at Steel's apartment, but there was still no sign of the arranged signal. Cat thought of Cyder and Steel reclining at their ease before a blazing fire, sipping mulled wine and discussing the sumptuous meal they were about to enjoy. His stomach rumbled loudly. He sighed, and peered resignedly through the mists at the brightly lit window below.

Steel's ground floor apartment was warm, comfortable and bedecked with carpets of an impressive thickness. Tapestries and hanging rugs covered the walls, less to keep out the cold than to ward off the chill inspired by the blank white walls and ceiling. Colony buildings were designed to be easy to erect and proof against the elements, but that was all. Since they were never meant to be lived in for long, it didn't matter that they were hardly pleasant on the eye. Frills and fancies could come later, when there was time. It said something about Mistport's short and troubled history that buildings originally intended for temporary shelters were not only still standing hundreds of years later, but were still preferable to any of the stone and timbered buildings that had followed them.

Pieces of high tech and *objets trouvés* lay scattered casually across Steel's spacious living room, side by side with small statuettes of gold, brass and silver. Steel fancied himself a collector, though his taste was frankly appalling. The various chairs and couches were smart and elegant, whilst still being sturdy enough to cope with Steel's weight. First and foremost, the Director was a practical man. The single great window had the faint bluish tinge of steelglass, but Steel's other security measures were politely inconspicuous. Even the window was mostly hidden behind heavy curtains.

Cyder let Steel take her cloak and hang it up, and strolled admiringly around the room. Every time she paid Steel a visit, he seemed to have acquired some new expensive trifle. It was a pity she'd only come for the sapphire . . .

'What are you doing here, Cyder?'

She turned slowly to face Steel, knowing she looked stunning in her gown of red and gold satinet, tightly laced across the bosom.

'I wanted to talk to you, and you wouldn't answer my calls. So, here I am. Aren't you glad to see me, darling?'

Steel smiled suddenly. 'Yes. Yes, I am. I could use some company. I'm just preparing dinner; would you care to join me?'

'Are you sure there's enough for two?'

Steel chuckled, and patted his stomach. 'My dear Cyder, I always have enough for two.'

'Then I would love to join you for dinner. You are, after all, still the finest chef in Mistport.' Cyder stopped, and looked at Steel curiously. 'Is something wrong, Gideon? You look . . . tired.'

Cyder was being polite, and they both knew it. Steel looked ghastly. His face was drawn and haggard, and his eyes were deep sunk with exhaustion. Overweight though he was, Steel usually gave the impression of being light on his feet, but now all his weight seemed to have caught up with him, and his movements were slow and ponderous.

'It's been a long day,' said Steel, smiling faintly.

'I heard about the gathering Fleet.'

Steel looked at her for a moment, and then chuckled admiringly. 'Now how the hell did you find out about that?'

'I have my sources,' said Cyder, smiling demurely.

'I'm sure you have,' said Steel. 'Don't worry about the Fleet, my dear. The esper shield is up and holding. Donald Royal's keeping my seat warm at the control tower. There's nothing really for him to do there, but . . . Hey, I was sorry to hear about the Blackthorn. The damage sounded pretty bad.'

Cyder shrugged. 'It wasn't good. Still, we're slowly picking up the pieces. We'll be open for business again almost before you know it.'

'That'll cost you an arm and a leg. Are you all right for money, Cyder?'

'Of course. I have my savings, and I should be collecting on a debt I'm owed quite shortly.'

'Good. Well, make yourself comfortable while I see to the dinner. It won't be long now.'

He moved off into the adjoining kitchen, and Cyder poured herself a stiff drink from the most impressive of the decanters. She hadn't thought it would be this easy. Something was worrying Steel, and it wasn't just the Fleet. The plague carrier? Cyder shrugged, and sipped slowly at her wine. Excellent vintage. If nothing else, she would give Gideon an evening of good talk and company and make him smile. It was the least she could do. They were, after all, old friends.

But fond as she was of Steel, business was business. She strolled over to the window, pushed back the heavy curtain, and drew a pencil torch from her voluminous sleeve. Outside, the fog was thicker than ever. She switched on the torch and waved it back and forth, hoping Cat could see it. He shouldn't have any trouble breaking in, assuming her information on Steel's security was up to date. If it wasn't, this was going to be a most embarrassing evening. She turned off the torch and slipped it back into her sleeve. She glanced at the kitchen door, to be sure Steel was still safely occupied, and then pulled the curtain back into position and turned away from the window. She looked about the room, mentally pricing a few of the more expensive items, and wandered towards the kitchen. Something smelled nice. Out in the street, someone was singing.

The window exploded inwards. Flying slivers of steelglass sprayed across the room, amidst an inrush of freezing air. Cyder was thrown violently to the floor and lay sprawled on the carpet, her ears ringing. Not far away, a chunk of steelglass had been driven deep into the side of a chair, and other slivers had gouged deep holes in the carpet. Cyder slowly raised her head, and rivulets of blood ran down her face. She couldn't feel her legs. She was shivering violently from the cold and her head ached horribly. She fought to sit up, but her legs wouldn't obey her. She finally raised herself up on one elbow, and turned her head painfully slowly to look behind her. And there, standing in the wreckage of the window, was a tall blonde wrapped in a tattered grey cloak. She was smiling, and her eyes were not sane.

Thick streamers of fog rolled into Steel's living room through the shattered window. If the blonde felt the cold, she gave no sign of it. She looked at Cyder, and moved slowly towards her. Cyder tried to drag herself away and couldn't. Blood ran down her face in a steady stream. The blonde loomed over her, still smiling.

'Where is he?' she said calmly. 'Where's Steel?'

'Here I am, Mary,' said Steel quietly. 'Now get away from her.'

Steel stood just inside the kitchen door. His face was pale, but his hands were steady. He and Mary studied each other for a while in silence.

'How did you break my window?' said Steel finally.

'I'm a Siren. A good singer can always shatter glass.'

'But that's steelglass.'

The rogue shrugged. 'Glass is glass. Where's my sapphire?'

'Mary . . . '

'Don't call me Mary! That's not my name.'

'It is now. You're a rogue esper; Typhoid Mary, the killer.'

Mary shook her head impatiently. 'I haven't killed anyone.'

202

Steel stared at her. 'What are you talking about? You've killed hundreds, and mindwiped even more! Why do you think we've been searching for you?'

'You want to hand me back to the Empire! I know you; I know your kind. I'm not going back. I'll kill you first. I'll kill you all before I let you send me back!'

Steel saw the madness in her eyes, and licked his dry lips uncertainly. The rogue had all the signs of someone who'd been conditioned by the Empire mindtechs. Reason would only affect her within the limits of her conditioning. And even then, he had to be careful. There was no telling what might set her off. Say the wrong thing, and he could quite easily sign his own death warrant.

'Mary; please let us help you. The Empire has been using your song to murder other espers . . . '

Mary laughed contemptuously. 'Don't waste my time, Steel. Your lies don't interest me. You have something of mine, and I want it back. Where is it, Steel? Where's my sapphire?'

'Mary . . . '

'Where's my sapphire?'

Steel looked at her for a moment, and then nodded at a smart little desk by the front door. 'It's locked in one of the drawers.'

'Get it.'

Steel moved slowly over to the desk, followed all the way by Mary's unblinking gaze. He took a key from his pocket, careful to keep his movements slow and deliberate, and unlocked one of the desk's drawers. He reached in and brought out a small leather pouch. He pulled open the drawstrings and took out a small blue gem, no more than half an inch in diameter.

'Is this it?' he said slowly. 'Is this what it's all been about? One stupid little jewel?'

'Give it to me,' said Mary eagerly. Steel put the pouch and the jewel on top of the desk, reached into the open drawer, and took out a disrupter. Mary looked at the gun and smiled.

'You killed Jamie Royal,' said Steel.

'Give me my sapphire.'

'He was a friend of mine, and you killed him. You want your sapphire? Come and get it.'

Mary sang a single piercing note and Steel convulsed, the gun

203

flying from his hand. He fell to the floor and lay there helplessly, shivering violently.

Cyder tried to sit up further, so she could see where the gun had fallen, and her arm gave out. She fell forward on to the bloodstained carpet, and lay trembling in the silence. Somehow she'd never thought it would end like this. To die in the middle of a petty burglary . . . it just wasn't fair. She coughed, and her ribs hurt, but she couldn't move to ease them. One of her eyes was gummed shut with drying blood. She was cold, and so very afraid.

Cat crouched helplessly outside the shattered window. There was nothing he could do. The woman was obviously a very powerful esper, and he didn't even have a weapon. Taking on a rogue esper with his bare hands would only get him killed. If he just stayed where he was, hidden from sight, there was a chance he could still get out of this alive. He didn't have to risk his neck. Cat shrugged suddenly, and pulled himself up on to the jagged windowframe. He couldn't run away. Cyder needed him.

He crouched on the ironwood frame a moment, getting his balance just right. The rogue had her back to him. Cat gathered his strength and threw himself at her. The rogue must have heard something at the last moment. She started to turn, but Cat still slammed into her with enough force to send them both crashing to the floor. They rolled back and forth on the blood-stained carpet, Cat trying desperately to get some kind of stranglehold on her. She brought her elbow back hard into his ribs, driving the air from his lungs, and his grip loosened. Mary pulled herself free, and turned to face him. Cat struggled up on to his knees. Mary opened her mouth and sang.

Cat froze on his haunches as the song washed over him, searing through his muscles. His senses blurred in and out, twisted and jumbled. A tearing headache bent him in two, and then was suddenly gone. Mary was the most powerful esper Cat had ever encountered, and, for the first time since he was a child, Cat could hear again.

There was the sound of his own rasping breathing, and the scuffing of his hands and knees on the carpet. From out beyond the shattered window came the never-ending sounds of the city, muffled to a murmur by the thick fog. From all around him came the simple, wonderful everyday sounds of life and living. And over and above everything else, he could hear Mary singing.

Her voice was sweet and true, rising and falling like a single petal tossed on the wind. It filled Cat's mind, and nothing else mattered. Mary knelt singing before him, face to face. Cat swayed to the song's slow rhythm, glorying in his freedom from silence. He felt himself growing steadily weaker, felt the darkness gathering in around him, and didn't care at all.

He looked past Mary, and saw Steel sitting slumped against the far wall, his hands clapped to his ears, staring at nothing. Lying on the floor between Mary and Steel was Cyder. She lay stretched out on the carpet; bloodied and broken and very still.

Cat rose shakily to one knee, took careful aim, and lashed out at Mary. The last sound he ever heard was his fist slamming into Mary's chin. Mary fell backwards, and lay still.

Cat cried silent tears, and moved slowly over to cradle Cyder's bloody head in his lap.

CHAPTER TWENTY

Starting Over

Topaz handed Gideon Steel a mug of steaming coffee.

'Steel; you've got to be the luckiest man I've ever met. If your mysterious friend had waited just a little longer to punch out Mary, you'd all have been brainburned.'

'And don't think I'm not aware of that, Topaz.' Steel warmed his shaking hands on the mug, and nodded his thanks to the Investigator. The coffee smelled delicious. If he hadn't known better, he'd have sworn it was the real thing. 'The Watch sergeant told me you had a run in with Mary yourself, on the way here.'

Topaz smiled grimly. 'Seems I was lucky too. My Investigator's training protected me from the worst of her song, and she didn't wait to finish me off.' She looked at Steel narrowly. 'Did you really stand up to Mary, armed only with a hand gun?'

Steel shrugged, embarrassed. 'I was too mad at her to be scared. I knew I didn't stand much of a chance, but . . . I couldn't let her get away.'

Topaz laughed. 'Steel; there's hope for you yet.'

They shared a grin, and Steel sank back in his chair and sipped gingerly at his coffee. It was real coffee. Where the hell had she found real coffee? He decided not to ask. It would only embarass her. He sighed contentedly. He hadn't felt this good in ages. The crisis was over, he was still alive, and Mistport was safe. It had been a bloody close thing, but they'd come through, and that was all that mattered. He glanced about him and smiled wryly. He hadn't come out of it entirely unscathed. His living room was a mess, with blood and glass everywhere. Someone was on their way to replace the shattered window, and he hated to think how much that was going to cost him. For the time being he kept the curtains closed, and tried to pretend he couldn't feel the cold. Thinking about it, Steel was surprised to find he didn't really give much of a damn. He was alive, and the port was safe . . . He'd been thinking about redecorating anyway.

The Watch had taken Mary away, still unconscious. The hospital would keep her safely sedated, until the port espers could work out some way to defuse her programming. She wasn't to blame for all the things she'd done; Mary was just another Empire victim. There were lots of those on Mistworld.

On the couch opposite Steel, a somewhat revived and repaired Cyder was sitting with her arm round Cat, who was cheerfully nursing the heavily bandaged right hand he'd broken on Mary's jaw. Steel studied the young burglar thoughtfully, and Topaz followed his gaze.

'Know anything about him, Steel?'

'Not a damn thing. Roof runner by the look of him, but he hasn't said a word so far. Just appeared out of nowhere and saved all our lives by flattening Mary. I suppose he's entitled to the reward.'

'I'd forgotten about that.'

'I'll bet he hasn't.'

'Be that as it may, Steel; right now I'm rather more interested in what one of Mistport's most renowned fences was doing here in your apartment.'

Steel glanced briefly at Cyder, smiled weakly, and became very interested in his coffee. Topaz glared at him, and moved over to stand before the couch. Cat studied her warily, while Cyder smiled graciously and nodded a polite hello.

'How are you feeling, Cyder?'

'I'll live, Investigator. In the meantime, I am this young man's agent. When can he collect the reward?'

'He'll get it, but first I want a few answers from him. He looks remarkably like a burglar who once stole a memory crystal from me . . . '

Cat smiled innocently, and Cyder hugged him to her.

'I'm afraid we'll never know, Investigator. Unfortunately he's a deaf mute, and can't answer questions.'

Topaz turned away, shaking her head in disgust. Steel chuckled softly, caught Cat's eye and dismissed him with a wave of his hand at the door. Cat shook his head, grinning. He rose quickly to his feet, padded over to the shattered window, pushed back the curtains and disappeared out into the thick fog. Steel raised an eyebrow, but Cyder just smiled back at him, unperturbed. Topaz decided not to ask.

'If it's all right with you, Gideon,' said Cyder, 'I'll be getting back to my tavern. I want to get these bloodstains out of my dress before they set.'

'Of course. I'm sure Topaz can find you an escort.'

'Thanks; that won't be necessary.'

Cyder got to her feet, wincing slightly as her cracked ribs protested. Steel levered himself out of his armchair and escorted her to the door. He wrapped her cloak about her shoulders, and opened the door for her. Cyder paused a moment in the doorway.

'Goodbye, Gideon. It would have been a lovely dinner, I'm sure.'

'Thanks for keeping me company.'

'Any time.'

Cyder blew him a kiss and left. Steel shut the door quietly behind her. He went back to his chair and sank gratefully into it. Topaz plumped up his cushions for him with a rough efficiency.

'Drink your coffee, Steel. It's getting cold.'

Steel picked up his mug again and sipped obediently at his coffee. He sighed appreciatively, and then looked round his ruined living room with an abstracted air.

'What's wrong, Steel?'

'Mary's sapphire; what happened to it?'

'Is that all you can think of? Don't you want to know what's happened to the Imperial Fleet?'

'I imagine they've realized by now that the esper shield isn't going to fall, and they've all dropped quietly back into hyperspace.'

Topaz nodded. 'They left one ship on sentry duty, but no doubt that'll be gone tomorrow. If it isn't, I'll let the Poltergeists play a few practical jokes on it.'

'So; we've weathered another storm. What were the final figures from the hospital?'

'More than twelve thousand brainburned; eight hundred and thirty dead.'

Steel sighed. 'Not much of a victory.'

'We stood off the Imperial Fleet and survived,' said Topaz calmly. 'I'll settle for that.'

'To hell with the Empire; where's that damned sapphire? I put it on top of the desk, but that got knocked over when Mary sang. She didn't have it when they carried her out, and neither did any of the Watch. It's got to be here somewhere, but damned if I can find it.'

'Cyder; she must have taken it.'

Steel shook his head firmly. 'No. The sensors built into my doorframe would have detected the jewel even if she'd swallowed it.'

'The roof runner?'

'I had his suit checked while the medics were treating him. No sapphire.'

'Then who's got it? That jewel's worth a small fortune.'

Steel shrugged, and then relaxed suddenly and sank back in his chair. 'What the hell; it's only a sapphire.'

Topaz looked at him. 'Are you sure you're feeling all right, Steel?'

Steel laughed. 'Perfectly all right, I assure you.'

'Good.' Topaz leaned forward suddenly to stare him straight in the eye. 'Because the next time we meet, Director, I'm going to find the evidence that will nail you once and for all.'

'You're welcome to try, Investigator. You're welcome to try.'

Topaz laughed, and left. Steel grinned, and sipped his coffee.

In the dark, overshadowed alleyway opposite Steel's apartment, Cyder leaned wearily against the rough stone wall and waited for her head to settle. She was sweating heavily, despite the freezing cold, and her hands were trembling. The Watch medic had done a good job in strapping up her cracked ribs and putting a few stitches in her torn scalp, but she'd still lost a fair amount of blood from her various cuts and gashes. She felt awful, but she hadn't dared stay any longer in Steel's apartment. There was no telling when they might start asking awkward questions. The medic had wanted her to spend the night at the hospital for observation, but Cyder had curtly refused. She had a morbid fear of hospitals, and besides, they were expensive. She leaned her head back against the cold stone wall. Half killed by a rogue esper, and all for nothing . . . She jumped despite herself as Cat dropped out of the fog to land beside her. He frowned as he took in her condition, and moved quickly forward to take her arm.

'I'm all right,' she insisted, but let him help her away from the wall. Her legs seemed a little steadier now she wasn't alone. 'Are you all right, Cat?'

He smiled, and nodded.

'After all we've been through, I didn't even get the sapphire. Still, the reward money will come in handy . . . What are you grinning at?'

Cat opened his mouth, reached in, and took out a small blue jewel. Cyder stared at the sapphire a moment, and then started to laugh. It hurt her ribs, but she didn't care.

'Of course; there were no sensors left in the broken window! Cat, my love, I'll make a master thief out of you yet.' She hesitated, and studied him searchingly. 'Nobody ever risked anything for me before; you risked your life to save me. I'll have to think about that. Now let's get back to the tavern. There's still a lot of work to be done before we can open for business again.'

Cyder leaned heavily on Cat's supporting arm, not wholly through weakness, and slowly, together, they disappeared back into the ever-curling mists of Mistport.

GHOSTWORLD

Inside Base Thirteen, nothing moves. Doors remain closed, elevators are still, and shadows lie undisturbed. One by one the flickering lights gutter and go out, and a growing gloom stalks the empty steel corridors. The few computers remaining on line mutter querulously to each other in the growing dark, until finally they fall silent in the night.

In the silence, in the dark, something stirs.

CHAPTER ONE

Something in the Storm

The *Darkwind*'s pinnace fell away from the mother ship, a gleaming silver needle against the endless night. It hung for a moment above the Rim World called Unseeli, and then its nose dropped, the engines roared silently, and the pinnace slipped into Unseeli's churning atmosphere like a knife into a belly. The engines burned bright, powering the slender ship through the violent storms by sheer brute force. Lightning flared round the pinnace's hull, and winds gusted viciously from every side, but nothing swayed the ship from its course. It punched through the roiling clouds with arrogant ease, dropping like a stone towards the metallic forest below.

Unseeli had no oceans and no mountains, only an endless arid plain covered by a brightly shining forest stretching from pole to pole. A forest whose colossal metal trees knew nothing of leaf or bud, autumn or spring. They rose unbending from the grey earth in their millions, cold and unfeeling, like so many gleaming metal nails. Towering almost to the edge of the planet's atmosphere in places, the huge trees stood firm and unyielding against the turbulent storms. Winds whipped viciously around leafless branches that radiated out from smooth featureless trunks in needle-sharp spikes. Violet and azure, gold and silver and brass, the trees reached up into the thunder and lightning to welcome the falling pinnace.

Captain John Silence sat slumped in his command chair, watching the sensor display panels before him. They changed from moment to moment with bewildering speed, far too fast for him to follow. Which was why the ship's Artificial Intelligence was piloting them down, and Silence had nothing to do but strain his eyes at the displays. The thick storm clouds hid the metal trees from sight, but the AI picked them up on the pinnace's sensors and changed speed and direction accordingly, making decisions and evaluations in split-second bursts. The AI could think faster and react more quickly than Silence ever could, even when he was mentally linked to the onboard computers, so there was never any question as to which one of them would get to pilot the pinnace down. But the AI was programmed to be considerate of people's feelings, so it might let him actually land the pinnace, if it didn't seem too difficult.

Silence's scowl deepened, and he accessed the pinnace's sensors through his comm implant. The bulkhead walls before him were suddenly transparent as the sensors displayed a real-time simulation of what was happening outside the ship. Dark, swollen storm clouds rushed towards and around the pinnace at heart-stopping speed, and lightning struck viciously at the ship. Silence winced inwardly, but kept his face calm so as not to upset his passengers. The storm could rage and spit all it liked, nothing could harm the ship as long as its force Screen was up. Gleaming metal trees appeared and disappeared in the blink of an eye as the pinnace surged this way and that, threading a path through the metallic forest to the landing pads by Base Thirteen. The storm clouds were too thick and too dark for Silence to make out the forest itself, but his imagination pictured it as an endless, vicious pincushion; solid metal spikes waiting for him like the sharpened stakes at the bottom of a pit dug to trap animals.

The image disturbed him, and he cut off the display and swung round in his chair to see how his passengers were doing. A good Captain never neglected his crew. Supposedly, loyalty was programmed into them these days, but it never hurt to be careful.

The ship's young esper, Diana Vertue, was looking distinctly green about the gills from being tossed around by the pinnace's sudden changes in direction. Investigator Frost sat beside her, cool and composed as always, her face almost bored. The two marines, Stasiak and Ripper, sat behind the two women, passing a gunmetal flask back and forth between them. Silence's mouth tautened. If he was lucky it was just alcohol, and not some new battle drug they'd cooked up in the medlabs. Officially he was supposed to encourage such initiative, but Silence didn't believe in chemical courage. He preferred the real thing, whenever possible. Chemicals wore off.

'We'll be touching down soon,' he said evenly. 'There shouldn't be any immediate danger, but keep your eyes and ears open anyway. Due to the urgent nature of the situation, we're going in pretty much blind on this one. The mission's simple enough. Base Thirteen isn't answering any calls. Our job is to find out why.'

'Question, Captain?'

'Yes, esper Vertue?'

'According to the computers, Unseeli is a dead world. Nothing's lived here since all indigenous species were wiped out after the Ashrai rebellion, ten years ago.'

'That's right,' said Silence, as the esper paused.

'But if that's the case, Captain; if there's nothing on this planet that can harm the Base, why all the panic? It could just be a case of cabin fever. It's not exactly unknown, out here on the edge of the Empire.'

'A good point, esper. But four days ago, Base Thirteen declared a Red Alert emergency, raised a force Screen, and cut off all communication with the Empire. The Empire doesn't like being cut off. So, we're going in to find out what's happened. Don't frown, esper; it'll give you wrinkles.'

'I was just wondering, Captain; well, what is the Investigator doing here?'

'Yeah,' said Investigator Frost. 'I've been wondering that too.'

Silence took his time about answering, openly studying the two women. They made an interesting contrast. Diana Vertue was short, slender and golden-haired, and reminded Silence very much of her mother, Elaine. The young esper had only just turned nineteen, and had that arrogant innocence that only youth can produce and maintain. She'd lose it soon enough, trying to maintain law and order and sanity out on the edge of the Empire, among the newly developed Rim Worlds. There was little civilization to be found on the new frontier, and even less law, never mind justice.

Investigator Frost was only a few years older than the esper, but the difference between them was that of the hunter and its

217

prey. Frost was tall and lithely muscular, and even sitting still and at rest, she looked dangerous. Dark eyes burned coldly in a pale, impassive face, framed by short-cropped black hair. The jolting descent didn't seem to be bothering her at all, but then, it wouldn't. Investigators were trained to withstand much worse than this. Which was at least partly why they made such efficient killers.

The Captain realized he'd let the silence drag on longer than he'd intended. He leaned forward in his chair, frowning as though he'd just been marshalling his thoughts, knowing even as he did that he wasn't fooling the Investigator one bit.

'You're here, Investigator, because we don't know what we're going to find when we get down there. There's always the possibility that Unseeli has been visited by some new alien species. This is the Rim, after all, where starships have been known to disappear into the long night, never to be seen again. And aliens are your speciality, are they not?'

'Yeah,' said Frost, smiling slightly. 'That's one way of putting it.'

'On the other hand,' said Silence, 'Unseeli is a mining planet, and the metals extracted here are of vital importance to the Empire. Any number of factions might have an interest in disturbing production. Which is why I'm overseeing this mission myself.'

'If it's that important, why are there only five of us?' said marine Stasiak. 'Why not go in mob-handed with a full Security team, surround the Base, and then charge in and hammer anything that moves?'

'Because Base Thirteen controls all the mining equipment on Unseeli,' said Silence steadily. 'Systems are already running at barely thirty per cent efficiency. We don't want to risk damaging the Base and making things even worse. And, as the esper pointed out, there's always the possibility this is just some new form of cabin fever, and all the Base personnel need is a nice little chat with the *Darkwind*'s psych department. We're here to find out what's going on and report it in, not run a crash-and-burn mission on the only people who can tell us what's happened.'

'Understood, Captain,' said the other marine, Ripper. 'We'll run this one nice and easy, by the numbers. No problem.'

Silence nodded curtly, and studied the two marines unobtrusively. Lewis Stasiak was average height, average weight, only early twenties but already looking hard-used and running to seed. His hair was a little too long, his uniform a little too sloppy, and his face had a kind of slackness to it. Silence recognized the danger signs; Stasiak had gone too long without any real action or challenge, and grown soft and careless. Which was at least partly why Silence had chosen him for the exploratory team. If something went wrong, Stasiak wasn't going to be any great loss. It was always useful to have someone expendable on hand, to send into dangerous situations before taking a look for yourself. Still, he'd do well to keep an eye on the man. Marines who got sloppy tended not to last long under pressure, and when they finally did snap they had a nasty habit of taking down anyone who happened to be with them at the time.

Alec Ripper, on the other hand, was everything that Stasiak wasn't. Ripper was a career marine, and looked it. Twenty-nine years old, fourteen years in the Service, big as a brick outhouse and twice as mean. Sharp and tidy from his close-cropped head to his shiny boots. Four medals, and three commendations for courage in the field. Could have been an officer, if he'd only had the right Family connections. As it was, according to records he'd been a non-comm twice, busted both times for daring to suggest a superior officer might just possibly be wrong. That wasn't wise, in the Service. Especially in front of witnesses. Also according to records, Ripper was a good soldier and a better fighter, with a positive gift for survival. If anyone was going to come back alive from this mission, it was him.

If anyone was.

They didn't know about Unseeli. Silence knew. He'd been here before, ten years ago, when the Ashrai came sweeping out of the forest in endless waves, slaughtering every man and woman in their path. He remembered the awful things they'd done, and the even worse thing he'd done to stop them. The Ashrai were dead now. Extinct. Along with every other living thing on the planet.

The pinnace lurched suddenly to one side, the roar of the

219

engines seeming to falter for a moment before regaining normal rhythm. Silence spun round in his chair and glared at the displays before him. Warning lights were flaring red everywhere, but there was no sign of any actual damage yet. He accessed the sensors again, and the ship seemed to go transparent before and around him. Dark storm clouds boiled around the pinnace, streaming away to either side with breathtaking speed. The ship lurched again, and Silence's stomach quivered in sympathy as the pinnace changed course and speed with reckless indifference to its passengers' sensibilities. Glowing metal trees appeared and disappeared around them, come and gone in the blink of an eye, but Silence could tell the pinnace wasn't just trying to avoid them. There was something else out there in the storm. Something that had waited a long time for revenge, and didn't give a damn that it had been dead for ten long years.

Ghostworld.

'Marines; man the guns,' said Silence harshly. 'Investigator; access the sensors and tell me what you see. Esper; I want a full psionic scan, as far as you can project. I need to know what's out there.'

The marines' faces went blank as they accessed the pinnace's fire controls through their comm implants, their eyes filled with what the gunsights showed them. The Investigator's cold face hardly changed at all as she looked quickly around her at bulkheads that were suddenly transparent. The esper looked at Silence uncertainly.

'What exactly am I scanning for, Captain?'

'Something, anything; for whatever's out there.'

'But . . . there's nothing there, Captain. It's just a storm.'

'No,' said Silence. 'It's not just the storm. Run a scan, esper. That's an order.'

'Aye, sir.' The esper's face became fixed and unseeing, and her face was suddenly blank and untenanted as her mind leapt up and out beyond the pinnace.

The storm boiled around her, but could not touch her. Metal trees burned in her mind like brilliant searchlights plunging up through the clouds, guttering here and there as automated mining machinery tore through a tree's roots. Apart from the trees there was no life anywhere in range of her esp, and yet it seemed to her that there was something at the edges of her mind, sensed only as swift flashes of movement and an occasional feeling of being watched. Diana forced her esp to its limits, pushing at the range of her scan, but was unable to get a clear sight of whatever it was. If there was anything at all . . .

Stasiak grinned nastily, feeling the pinnace's guns swivelling back and forth, responsive to his thoughts. Four disrupter cannon, state of the art and fully charged, scattered the length of the pinnace and ready to kick arse at his command, or merest whim. But there was only the storm and the wind and the endless bloody trees. According to the sensors, there was nothing out there worth firing at. He found a secure line and patched into Ripper's comm implant.

'Hey, Rip, you see anything?'

'No. But that doesn't mean it's not out there.'

'Yeah, sure. You ask me, the Captain's got ants in his pants over nothing. This world's dead, Rip; everyone knows that.'

'Maybe. There's nothing on the sensors. But I still keep getting the feeling that we're not alone up here. Stand ready, Lou. I don't like the feel of this at all. And if it does all hit the fan, don't waste your shots; place them carefully. Remember, these cannon take four minutes to recharge between each shot. A lot can happen in four minutes.'

'Yeah, right.' Stasiak stirred unhappily in his seat, trying to look every way at once. Now that Ripper mentioned it, he could feel it too. Something waiting, watching, hiding just out of range of his sensors. His mind caressed the fire controls, feeling them respond like hounds straining at the leash. The pinnace's AI was programmed against activating the guns itself except in the direst emergencies, to keep it from getting ideas above its station, but it sensed something was wrong about the storm too, and in its own way was just as eager for action as he was.

Investigator Frost looked across at Captain Silence. 'Sensors all report negative. There are no life signs registering anywhere within their range.'

'I didn't think there would be,' said Silence, staring unblinkingly out at the storm. 'Odin; how long till we touch down?'

'Twelve minutes and forty seconds, Captain,' said the AI promptly. 'Assuming nothing interferes with my flight plan.'

'Get us down fast, Odin,' said Silence. 'Marines; stand ready. Something's coming.'

And then the pinnace lurched suddenly to one side, the slender craft thrown violently off course as though some giant hand had reached out from nowhere and swatted it. The ship bucked and heaved as the AI fought to keep it from crashing into the tightly packed trees. Dark shapes loomed up out of the boiling storm clouds, huge and threatening.

'Odin; raise the force Screen,' said Silence, his voice calm and steady, though his hands were closed into white-knuckled fists. 'Marines; pick your targets carefully. Investigator; what do you see?'

'Still nothing, Captain. Sensors are adamant there's nothing out there.'

'Same here,' said Stasiak urgently. 'There's nothing to aim at!'

The pinnace shuddered as something impossibly huge pounded against the force Screen, again and again. Silence watched tensely as his displays showed mounting pressure building up against the Screen from all sides at once. Glowing trees whipped past faster than ever as the AI sent the pinnace racing through the metallic forest, heading for the landing field. But despite the pinnace's increasing speed, the dark presences stayed with them, battering at the force Screen with vicious determination.

Silence scowled, and licked his dry lips. 'Marines; lay down a field of fire on both sides. Random selection of targets. Do it now!'

The marines' replies were lost in the thunder of the disrupter cannon, and blinding energy leapt out from the pinnace, striking through the Screen and shattering the metal trees. Great metallic shards flew like shrapnel. And still the unliving presences pressed close around the Screen, the pressure rising impossibly moment by moment.

'Our guns are useless now until the energy crystals recharge,' said the Investigator quietly. 'And the force Screen isn't going to last long enough for us to reach the landing field. It's taking more and more of the ship's power just to maintain the Screen, and we don't have that much power to spare. Not if we ever want to get off this planet again. What's out there, Captain? Why don't they show up on our sensors?'

Silence looked at her. 'Because they're dead, Investigator. Because they're dead. Odin; time to touch down?'

'Ten minutes, twenty-two seconds, Captain.'

'When I give you the word, drop the Screen and channel the extra power to the engines. Do whatever you have to, Odin, but get us down. If we survive the landing, we can always recharge the ship's batteries at Base Thirteen. Marines; stand ready to fire again, on my order.'

'But there's nothing out there!' said Stasiak. 'There's nothing to aim at!'

'Keep the noise down, Lou,' said Ripper calmly. 'Ours not to reason why, remember? Just do what the nice officer says. At least he seems to have some idea of what we're up against.'

Stasiak sniffed mutinously. 'They're not paying me enough for this.'

Silence glared out at the storm, and looked back at the Investigator. 'Anything on the sensors?'

'Negative, Captain. No life signs of any description. As far as the instruments are concerned, we're alone up here.' The Investigator looked at him with cold, hard eyes. 'You were expecting this, weren't you, Captain? That's why you came down with us. You know what's out there.'

'Yes,' said Silence. 'I know.'

'Guns are powering up, sir,' said Ripper. 'Ready to fire again soon. Just find us a target.'

'Stand by, marines. Esper; talk to me. What do you see out there? Esper!'

They were huge and awful and they filled her mind, blazing like the sun. Too strange to measure, too vast to comprehend, they gathered in the storm like ancient vengeful gods, striking at the pinnace with thunder and lightning. Diana Vertue struggled to maintain her own sense of identity in all that rage and fury, but her human mind was a small and insignificant thing in the midst of such intense, bitter hatred. She retreated back behind the safety of her mental shields, fighting to keep out the inhuman thoughts that roared and howled in the storm outside the pinnace. One by one her defensive barriers slammed down, and suddenly she was back in the pinnace again, and Captain Silence was shouting at her.

'It's alive,' she said dully, her mind feeling slow and awkward now that it was working only on the human level again. 'The storm's alive, and it hates us.'

'Have you made contact with it?' said Silence. 'Could you communicate with it?'

'Communicate with what?' said the Investigator sharply. 'If there was anything alive out there, the sensors would show it!'

'They're too big,' said Diana Vertue. 'Huge. Vast. I've never felt such hate.'

'Try,' said Silence. 'This is why I brought you with us; to talk to . . . what's out there.'

'No,' said Diana, tears burning in her eyes. 'Please. Don't make me . . . the hate hurts so much . . .'

'Do it! That's an order!'

And Diana threw her mind up and out again, into the storm. Espers always obeyed orders. Their training saw to that. Those who couldn't or wouldn't learn didn't live to reach an adult's estate. The storm raged. Immense, dark thoughts were all around her, and she knew she only survived because she was too small for them to notice. She also knew that in a slow, creeping way, they were beginning to realize that someone was watching them.

Silence watched the young esper's face contort from the horror of what her blind eyes were seeing, and wouldn't let himself look away. If she died or lost her mind, it would be his responsibility. He'd known the risks when he'd insisted on her as part of his team. A thin line of saliva ran slowly from the corner of her mouth, and she began to moan softly. Silence still wouldn't look away.

'Marines; lay down a covering fire, random selection, as before. Odin; lower the Screen. Hang on to your seats, everyone. The ride's about to get a bit bumpy.'

There was a deafening roar, slamming against the mind as much as the ears, as the dark shapes pressed forward, no longer held back by the force Screen. The disrupter cannon blazed through the storm, and could not touch them. The pinnace shuddered and lurched from side to side, tossed like a leaf in a hurricane. Metallic trees a dozen feet thick leapt out of the clouds and slammed against the pinnace sides, but the ship's hull had been designed to withstand disrupter cannon and low-level atomics, and they held easily against the battering. The thunder of the pinnace's engines rose and fell as the AI fought desperately to keep the ship on course. Silence accessed the instruments directly, and bit his lip as he saw they were still more than four minutes from Base Thirteen and the landing pads.

The pinnace's nose dropped sharply, as though some immense weight had settled upon it, outside. There was a screech of rending metal, and the port bulkhead tore like paper. Jagged rents surged down the wall, grouped together like giant claw-marks. Something pounded against the outer hull, and great dents and bulges appeared in the cabin roof.

'There's nothing out there!' screamed Stasiak, beating blindly with his fists against the chair's armrests. 'There's nothing out there! The instruments say so!'

Ripper's head swayed back and forth, his mouth forming soundless denials. The Investigator glared about her at the fury of the storm, her hand clutching at the gun on her hip. Things were moving in the storm, dark and indistinct and impossibly huge. The whole frame of the pinnace groaned as the roof bulged inwards, forced down by some massive, intolerable weight.

'We're losing pressure, Captain,' said the AI quietly in Silence's ear. 'The ship's integrity has been breached beyond my ability to compensate. I am no longer confident of being able to reach the landing field. Do I have your permission to attempt an emergency landing?'

'No,' said Silence through his implant. 'Not yet.'

'We have to put down, before we fall apart!' said the Investigator.

Silence looked at her thoughtfully. He hadn't known she had access to the command channel. 'Not yet,' he said firmly. 'Esper; talk to them, damnit. Make them hear you!'

Diana Vertue dropped what remained of her mental shields and stood naked and defenceless before the alien presences. They rushed forward and swept over her. The pinnace punched through the last of the clouds and burst out into clear air. The metal trees swept towards and around the ship at dizzying speed. Vicious barbed spikes snapped past, seeming only inches away from tearing the pinnace open like a gutted fish. And then the trees too fell away, and they were flying over a vast open clearing, above a smooth and level plain, towards Base Thirteen and the landing pads.

'It's stopped,' said the Investigator quietly. 'Listen. It's stopped.'

Silence looked slowly around him. The pounding on the outer hull had ceased, and there was no trace anywhere of the dark, threatening presences. Faint creakings filled the pinnace as the ship's battered frame tried to repair itself. The two marines dropped out of fire control and looked blankly around them, seeing the damage for the first time. Ripper turned to the Captain for answers, but Silence waved for him to be quiet, and got out of his seat to kneel beside the esper, who was sitting slumped on the floor, head bowed.

She looked up slowly as she sensed his presence. 'They're gone, Captain. They just . . . left.'

'What did you see?' said Silence, keeping his voice calm and even with an effort.

'Faces. Gargoyle faces, all planes and angles. Teeth and jagged claws. I don't know. I don't think any of it was real. It couldn't have been. There were so many faces, and nothing in them but rage and hatred. I was sure they were going to kill me, but when I dropped my shields they just looked at me . . . and left. I don't know why.'

'But *you* do, Silence,' said the Investigator. 'Don't you?'

'Please return to your seats,' said the AI. 'I am preparing to land the pinnace.'

Silence helped the esper to her feet, and got her seated before returning to his own station. The Investigator scowled at his back for a moment, and then studiously ignored him. The marines looked at each other and said nothing, though their look spoke volumes.

'I have tried to contact Base Thirteen,' said the AI, 'but there is no response. The force Screen around the Base is still in operation, and there is no sign of life or movement anywhere within range of my sensors. I am therefore assuming it is safe to land, unless you wish to countermand me, Captain.'

'No, Odin. Set us down as close to the Base as you can. Then put your sensors on full alert, and maintain all weapons systems at battle status, until I tell you otherwise.'

'Understood, Captain.'

The pinnace slowed to a halt a dozen yards from the shimmering force Screen enclosing Base Thirteen, and settled gently on to the landing pad. Silence stared thoughtfully at the simulation covering the inner bulkheads, and for the first time was struck by the sheer size of the vast open space covered by the pads. The landing field had been intended originally to accommodate the massive starfreighters that built and established the Empire's Base. Silence had been the Captain of one of those ships, and he could still remember the constant flow of traffic around Base Thirteen as the ships came thundering in from all over the Empire. Huge silver ships had covered the landing pads for as far as the eye could see, like so many immense abstract sculptures. And now they were gone, and the pinnace stood alone on the pad, dwarfed by the size of the clearing and the towering trees that surrounded it.

He withdrew from the sensors, and the scene vanished, replaced by featureless steel walls. Silence turned in his chair and nodded abruptly to his team. 'I know you've all got a lot of questions, but you're going to have to bear with me for a while. The situation here is very complicated, and the rough ride we had on our way down is just the beginning. I take it no one's been badly injured? Good. Odin; damage reports.'

'Nothing important, Captain, but it'll be several hours before the ship can raise again. It's the hull breach that worries me most. There's a limit to what I can do, without access to a stardock's facilities.'

Silence nodded slowly. 'Worst-case scenario?'

'If I can't repair the hull, we're not going anywhere, Captain. You could, of course, always call down another pinnace from the *Darkwind*, but there's no guarantee it would arrive here in any better condition than us.'

'Wait a minute,' said Stasiak. 'You mean we're stranded here?'

'Ease off,' said Ripper quickly. 'That was a worst-case scenario. Things aren't that bad. Yet.'

'I have some questions of my own, Captain,' said the Investigator coldly. 'This planet is officially listed as a scorched world. Nothing is supposed to live here any more. But something was trying to kill us in that storm, even if our sensors couldn't pick it up. And you know what it was. You recognized it. I represent the Empire in all matters concerning alien species, and I demand an explanation. What was that in the storm?'

'The Ashrai,' said Silence.

'But they're dead. Extinct.'

'Yes. I know. I told you the situation was complicated.'

'So what the hell was knocking the crap out of us on the way down?' said Stasiak. 'Ghosts?'

Silence smiled slightly. 'Perhaps. If ever a planet was haunted by its past, Unseeli is.' He hesitated, and looked quickly from one face to another. 'Did any of you . . . feel anything, sense anything, on the way down?'

'Yeah,' growled Stasiak. 'I felt sure we were all going to be killed.'

Ripper shrugged. The Investigator scowled for a moment, and then shook her head. Silence looked at the esper. 'What about you, Diana? What did you sense?'

The young esper studied her hands, clasped tightly together in her lap. 'They could have killed us all. Our Screen couldn't keep them out, and our guns couldn't hurt them. But at the last moment they looked at me, and turned away. I don't know why. Do you know why, Captain?'

'Yes,' said Silence. 'Because you're innocent.' He raised a hand to forestall any further comments or questions. 'All right, pay attention. This was all put together in something of a hurry, so you haven't had much in the way of a briefing. That's at least partly because no one really knows what's going on here. And partly because I wanted you to come to this with open minds.

'Ten years ago, the Empire discovered that Unseeli was rich in important metals, and started mining operations. The main indigenous species, the Ashrai, objected strongly. They rose in rebellion against the Empire, aided by a traitor from within the Service; a man who turned against his own kind. The Empire troops were vastly outnumbered, and no match for the sheer ferocity of the Ashrai, even with their superior Empire weaponry. But they couldn't afford to lose. The metals were too important. So they retreated offworld, called in the starcruisers and scorched the whole damn planet from pole to pole. The metal trees survived unharmed. Nothing else did. Mining resumed soon after.

'But that's not all of the story. The trees are not just trees. They cover ninety per cent of the planet's surface, and are one hundred per cent metal. They contain no organic matter at all, but they are quite definitely alive. These trees were grown, not sculpted. Their roots draw metals from deep within the planet, separating out the heavy metals and storing them within their trunks. We don't know how they do this. There is reason to believe the trees were genetically engineered. Certainly it strains credulity that something so amazingly useful could have evolved entirely by chance. Especially when you consider that the particular heavy metals these trees store are ideally suited for powering a stardrive. Given how scarce such metals usually are, you can understand why the Empire was prepared to do absolutely anything to ensure that the mining of Unseeli's unique forest could continue uninterrupted.'

'Hold it,' said Frost. 'Are you saying the Ashrai created these trees?'

'No,' said Silence. 'Their civilization was never that advanced. In fact, the original Investigating team uncovered evidence that suggested the Ashrai actually evolved long after the trees had first been planted. Which gives you some idea of how long these trees have been here.'

'But if the Ashrai didn't genegineer the trees,' said Ripper slowly, 'who did?'

'Good question,' said Silence. 'Whoever it was, let's hope they don't come back to find out who's been messing with their garden. Now then; where was I? Ah yes; there are twenty substations on Unseeli, overseeing the automated mining machinery as it destroys the forest's roots, so that the trees can be easily felled and harvested. Base Thirteen oversees all the other substations, and is the only manned station on the planet. Its personnel spend most of their time sitting around waiting for something to go wrong so they can go out and fix it. They last communicated with the Empire four days ago. We haven't been able to get a word out of them since. At present, the situation is merely annoying, if a little disturbing. But if it continues, and the supply of metals slows as the mining machinery breaks down, the Empire could be in serious trouble. I'm afraid we've all become just a little too dependent on Unseeli's riches. Any questions so far?'

'Yes,' said Ripper. 'What are you doing here, Captain? It's not usual for a ship's Captain to expose himself to danger like this.'

'This is not a usual situation,' said Silence. 'And I have . . . personal reasons for being here. Which I don't intend to discuss at this time.'

'All right,' said Frost. 'Let's talk about Base Thirteen instead. A force Screen is the last refuge for a Base under attack. What could possibly have threatened them so much, scared them so badly, that they had to retreat behind a Screen to feel safe?'

'Maybe they saw ghosts too,' said Diana Vertue.

Silence smiled briefly. 'When we get inside the Base, you can ask them.'

'And just how are we supposed to get inside?' said Frost sharply. 'We don't have anything powerful enough to break through a force Screen. The disrupter cannon on the *Darkwind* might do the job, but that kind of firepower would flatten everything inside a square mile, most definitely including everything and everyone inside the Screen. You'd be able to carry away what was left of Base Thirteen in a medium-sized bucket.'

'Right,' said Stasiak, scowling unhappily. 'There's only one way we're going to get past that Screen, and that's if someone inside the Base gets to the main command centre and shuts down the Screen. And that doesn't seem very likely, just at the moment. So, Captain, unless you have access to some kind of super-weapon the Empire has never heard of, we've come all this way for nothing.'

Silence looked at him calmly. 'Don't raise your voice to me, Stasiak, there's a good chap. I know what I'm doing. Computer; any hostile life signs outside the ship?'

'Negative, Captain,' said the AI promptly. 'There are no life signs anywhere within reach of my sensors. My files tell me that

230

Base Thirteen has one hundred and twenty-seven personnel, but I regret I am unable to confirm that. The force Screen blocks my sensor probes.'

'What about the things that attacked us on the way down?' said Diana Vertue. 'They can't have just vanished.'

'My sensors detected no life signs at any time during the descent,' said the AI. 'If there had been any attackers, I would have detected them, and informed you of their nature. May I remind you, esper Vertue, this is a scorched world. Nothing lives here.'

'Well something beat the hell out of this ship on the way down,' said Frost. 'I can see some of the dents from here.'

'I agree that the pinnace has suffered extensive storm damage,' said the AI calmly. 'Nevertheless, I must insist that there were no life signs present in the storm. If there were, my instruments would have detected them.'

'I saw them with my esp,' said Diana. 'I felt their rage.'

'Hallucinations, perhaps,' said the AI. 'Possibly brought about by the stress of the descent. I can supply tranquillisers, if required.'

'Not just now,' said Silence. 'All right, people, get ready to disembark. Full field kit for everyone, and that includes you, esper. Move it!'

The pinnace crew rose quickly to their feet, and gathered around the Investigator as she broke open the arms locker and passed out the equipment. The two marines looked at each other thoughtfully. Full field kit meant a steel-mesh tunic, concussion and incendiary grenades, swords and energy guns, and a personal force shield. That kind of kit was normally reserved for open fire-fights and full-scale riot control. Stasiak took his armful of equipment and moved as far away from the Captain and the Investigator as the cramped space would allow. Ripper followed him, and the two marines put their heads together as they ostensibly busied themselves in sorting out their kit.

'I hate this,' said Stasiak quietly. 'I hate this planet, and I hate this mission. Full field kit for what's supposed to be a dead planet? A Captain who talks about ghosts and super-weapons? The man is seriously disturbed, Ripper. Dammit to hell, only five more months and my time is up. Five short months, and I'll be out of the Service and my own man again. But of course nothing ever goes right for me, so I end up being volunteered for this bloody mess. A crazy Captain and an insane mission. Hallucinations, my arse! I don't care if this is a scorched world; something's still alive here, and it isn't friendly.'

'Then why couldn't we find any targets for our guns?' murmured Ripper, pulling on his baldric with practised ease. 'There's no doubt this is a scorched world. I checked the ship's computers before the drop. Ten years ago, six starcruisers hit Unseeli with everything they had. Wiped the planet clean, pole to pole.'

'Six ships?' said Stasiak. 'Standard procedure for a scorching is two starcruisers, three if you're in a hurry. What did they have down here that they thought they needed six ships to deal with it?'

'There's more,' said Ripper. 'Guess who was in charge of scorching Unseeli?'

Stasiak stopped struggling with the buckles on his baldric. 'Silence?'

'Got it in one. He was in charge of putting down the Ashrai rebellion. When that got out of hand, he was the one who called for a scorch.'

Stasiak shook his head slowly. 'This just gets better and better. This is going to be a bad one, Rip. I can feel it in my water.'

'Don't worry; trust the old Ripper. He'll see you through.'

Stasiak just looked at him.

Esper Diana Vertue struggled to pull on her steel-mesh tunic. The label said it was her size, but the label was a liar. She finally pulled it into place by brute force, and emerged from the neck-hole red-faced and gasping. The long vest was heavy and awkward, and she hated to think what it was going to feel like after she'd been wearing it for a few hours. She looked at the sword and the hand disrupter she'd been issued, hesitated, and then moved back to the arms locker to put them away.

'I wouldn't,' said Investigator Frost. 'The odds are you're going to need them.'

'I don't use weapons,' said the esper firmly. 'I'm not a killer. I'll keep the force shield, but that's all.'

The Investigator shrugged. 'It's your neck.' She settled her own holstered disrupter comfortably on her right hip, and drew a scabbarded sword from the arms locker. It was a long sword, definitely not regulation issue, and the Investigator slung it over her left shoulder and buckled it into place so that it hung down her back. The tip of the scabbard almost touched the floor behind her. Frost noticed the esper's curious gaze, and smiled slightly.

'It's a claymore. Old Earth sword. Been in my clan for generations. It's a good blade.'

'Have you ever killed anyone with it?' said Vertue. Her voice was polite, but the Investigator stiffened at the disapproval she sensed in the esper.

'Of course,' said Frost. 'That's my job.' She reached into the locker and brought out a bandolier of grenades. She pulled it tight across her chest and flexed her arms a few times to make sure it wouldn't interfere with her movements. She looked at the esper. 'If you're not willing to fight, stay out of my way. And don't expect me to look after you. That's *not* my job.'

She slammed the arms locker shut and moved over to the Captain and the two marines waiting at the airlock door. Vertue looked after her for a moment, but said nothing. She joined the others, her gaze on her feet. Silence looked them all over, raised an eyebrow at the esper's lack of weapons, and then keyed in the airlock door's Security codes. It hissed open, and Silence led the way in. The airlock was only just big enough to take them all, and when the door hissed shut behind them, the cramped space became disturbingly claustrophobic. Vertue hugged herself tightly to stop herself trembling. She'd never liked enclosed spaces.

'Odin, this is the Captain,' said Silence through his comm implant. 'Respond, please.'

'Contact confirmed,' murmured the AI in his ear. 'Sensor scans are still normal. No life forms within sensor range. Air, temperature and gravity are within acceptable limits. You have seven hours' daylight remaining.'

'Open the hatch, computer.'

The outer door swung open with a hiss of compressed air. Silence stepped forward, and then hesitated in the doorway as a breeze brought him the scent of Unseeli. It was a sharp, smoky scent, and though he hadn't smelt it for ten years, it was immediately familiar to him again, as if he'd never left. He lifted his head a little, and stepped on to the landing pad, followed by the others. The grey afternoon was bitter cold, and his breath steamed on the air before him. There was a series of faint clicks as the heating elements in his uniform kicked in. Tall metal trees surrounded the landing field, filling the horizon no matter which way he looked.

Base Thirteen stood in the centre of the landing field, hidden behind its force Screen. The protective dome swirled and shimmered, like a huge pearl in a dull metal setting. It was easy to imagine something dark and unknown squatting behind the Screen, staring out at the pinnace's crew and waiting for them to come to it. A sudden chill ran up Silence's spine that had nothing to do with the cold. He smiled sourly and shrugged the thought aside. He looked around to see what his people made of their new surroundings. The two marines had their disrupters in their hands, and were glancing quickly about them, checking for threats and familiarising themselves with the territory. The Investigator was standing calmly a little to one side, studying the force Screen thoughtfully. The esper was hugging herself against the cold and staring out at the forest, her eyes very large in her pale, bony face. None of them looked particularly worried. That would change, soon enough.

Silence coughed loudly to get their attention. 'I'm going to have to leave you for a while. The Investigator is in charge until I return. Any problems, she can contact me on the command channel. But unless it's vitally important, I don't want to be disturbed. We're going to need help to get through that Screen, and I think I know where to find some.'

Frost looked at him narrowly. 'Help? On Unseeli? Don't you think it's about time you filled us in on what's going on here, Captain?'

'No,' said Silence. 'Not just yet.'

'Well can you at least tell us where you're going?'

'Of course, Investigator. I'm going to talk to the traitor called Carrion. He's going to get us through the Screen. That's if he doesn't decide to kill us all first.'

CHAPTER TWO

Ghosts

Ripper and Stasiak were supposed to be establishing a perimeter around the landing field, but they spent most of their time studying the enigmatic metal forest through the swirling mists. They had both volunteered for the job; Ripper because he believed in the value of a good secure perimeter, and Stasiak because he was glad of a chance to get away from the Investigator. He'd heard a lot of stories about the Empire's most renowned assassins, and now that he'd met Frost he was ready to believe a lot of things he hadn't before. Investigators were the Empire's élite, trained to tackle situations too dangerous or too complex for ordinary troops. Their speciality lay in dealing with new alien species. They would study the aliens in depth, work out how best to exploit, enslave or destroy them, and then lead the mission that would bring the alien world into the Empire, one way or another. They were unparalleled fighters, cold and calculating strategists, unstoppable by anything but death. They were said to be as strange and inhuman as the aliens they studied, and Stasiak believed it. Just being around Frost made his skin crawl.

The two marines moved slowly round the boundary of the landing pads, setting down proximity mines at regular intervals and priming them to detonate the moment anything approached within the designated distance. Ripper was a great believer in proximity mines; they not only discouraged people from sneaking up on you, they also provided plenty of warning that the enemy was abroad. Ripper slapped the mine before him affectionately, ignoring Stasiak's wince. They weren't much to look at, but there was enough explosive crammed into the flat grey discs to ruin anybody's day.

The perimeter had taken longer to establish than he'd expected, and not just because of the time they spent warily watching the forest. The landing field was even larger than it looked, and it looked immense. Ripper tried to picture how the field must have appeared when the Base was first being established, and the massive starcruisers were landing and taking off every hour, like huge flying mountains, but he couldn't. The scale was just too great. He started to mention it to Stasiak, but changed his mind. Stasiak was a good man to have at your back in a fight, but he wasn't the most imaginative of men. If you couldn't eat it, drink it, fight it or get a leg over it, Stasiak really wasn't interested. He was currently scowling out into the mists again, and Ripper reluctantly followed his gaze.

There was something about Unseeli in general and Base Thirteen in particular that disturbed Ripper deeply on some primitive, instinctive level. The sheer size of the metal trees was intimidating, making him feel small and insignificant, like a church mouse staring up at a vast cathedral. And then there was the mist, enveloping the metallic forest like a grubby off-white shroud. He kept thinking he saw vague shapes moving at the edge of the forest, come and gone in the blink of an eye. There was a constant feeling of being watched, an almost tangible pressure of unseen, watching eyes. Alien eyes.

The silence was unnerving too. The only sounds on the still air were those the two marines made themselves, and they were quickly swallowed up by the quiet. No creature roared, no bird sang, and the air had a deathly feel. Dead world. Ghostworld. Ripper scowled, and let his hand rest on the disrupter at his side while Stasiak finished laying down the last mine. There was a feeling of imminence, of something vital finally about to happen after many years of waiting. But all around, everything was at rest. Dead.

Stasiak ran quickly through the activating routine, primed the proximity mine, and stood up next to Ripper. Anyone approaching the perimeter without the right codes in their implant would find themselves suddenly scattered across an extremely large area. Stasiak sniffed unhappily, and hitched the gun on his hip to a more comfortable position. He'd hoped to feel more secure once the perimeter was established, but he couldn't honestly say that he did. One look at the forest was enough to put his teeth on edge. Strange colours glowed in the depths of the mists, curious and unsettling hues that swirled slowly like dye in water. They faded in and out, their slow deliberate movements implying something that bordered on purpose or meaning, some strange intent unfathomable by the human mind. Ripper tapped him on the arm to get his attention, and Stasiak all but jumped out of his skin. He glared meaningfully at Ripper, who stared calmly back.

'If you've quite finished trying to give me a coronary,' said Stasiak, 'perhaps we could get the hell away from here and back to the pinnace?'

Ripper looked at him in amusement. 'I thought you were relieved to be putting some distance between you and the big bad Investigator?'

Stasiak shrugged quickly, looking out at the forest again. 'I was, but this is even creepier than she is. I keep . . . seeing things. Hearing things. Come on, Rip; you've felt it too, I can tell. There's something out there in the mists, watching us.'

'The computer was quite specific,' said Ripper neutrally. 'According to all the pinnace's instruments, the only living things here are us. Unless you're suggesting the planet is haunted . . .'

'Why not?' said Stasiak, looking seriously at Ripper. 'Strange things have been known to happen out here, on the Rim. Remember the Ghost Warriors, and the Wolfling in the Madness Maze? You can find anything out here on the Rim. *Anything*.'

'Even so,' said Ripper, 'I still draw the line at ghosts.'

'Something attacked us on the way down, something the sensors swore wasn't there. And what about this Carrion guy the Captain's gone looking for? Assuming he isn't a ghost or a walking corpse, that means someone's found a way to hide from Empire sensors. And if one man's learned to do it, how do we know others haven't? A whole lot of others, heavily armed and just waiting to descend on us the moment we let our guard down.'

'You're determined to be cheerful, aren't you?' said Ripper. 'All right, I've got a bad feeling about this place too, but I'm not letting my nerves run away with me. I'm not going to start worrying till I've got something definite I can aim a gun at. You worry too much, Lou. These mines will stop anything, up to and including a charging Hadenman.'

'And if you're wrong, and there is something nasty out there?'

'Then you can say "I told you so",' said Ripper calmly.

Stasiak shook his head, unconvinced. 'There must have been something threatening here for the Base to raise their Screen. I mean, that's a last-ditch defence; it's what you do when you've tried everything else and none of it's worked. I don't like this, Rip, I don't like the feel of this mission at all.'

'Neither do I,' said a calm female voice behind them. Both marines spun round sharply to find Investigator Frost standing almost on top of them. Ripper and Stasiak exchanged a swift glance as they realized neither of them had heard the Investigator approaching, despite the eerie quiet.

'There's still no response from the Base,' said Frost. 'There's nothing wrong with our equipment, so either the Base personnel don't want to talk to us, or they can't. Which suggests, at the very least, there's something here capable of scaring the hell out of an entire Base. Except, of course, our instruments continue to assure us there's no one down here but us.'

'What about Carrion?' said Stasiak, and the Investigator nodded slowly.

'Yes; what about Carrion? Have either of you heard the name before?'

'No,' said Ripper. 'Have you?'

Frost frowned thoughtfully. 'Most of Unseeli's records are sealed behind Security codes even I don't have access to, but I've managed to dig up a few things that aren't exactly common knowledge. The traitor Carrion used to be a high-ranking officer serving under Captain Silence, back when the Empire was fighting its war against the indigenous species, the Ashrai. Carrion turned against his own kind, and fought with the Ashrai, against humanity. Quite successfully, from what I can tell. He apparently displayed quite powerful esper abilities in combat, though interestingly enough there are no records of his having any such abilities before he came to Unseeli. He was supposed to have perished with the Ashrai, when the planet was scorched.'

Stasiak shook his head firmly. 'Then he's dead. No one survives a scorching.'

'Not so far,' said Frost. 'But the Captain seems quite convinced that Carrion *has* survived, and that he can find him. Intriguing, that.'

'Have you ever served with Captain Silence before?' said Ripper.

'No. He has a good record, apart from Unseeli. How about you?'

'Been with him two years now,' said Ripper. 'Not a bad sort. For a Captain. I've served under worse. Lou?'

'He's all right,' said Stasiak, shrugging. 'Or at least he seemed to be, until this mission. He's been acting strangely ever since we got our orders to come here.'

'Considering the last time he was here he fouled up so completely he had to have the whole planet scorched, I can't say I'm surprised.' Frost looked thoughtfully at the metallic forest, as though it might suggest some answers. 'I would have to say the good Captain's present behaviour could become a cause for concern. In fact, he gives the definite impression of a man no longer entirely stable.'

Ripper looked at her sharply. The Investigator was choosing her words very carefully. 'So,' he said, equally carefully. 'If the Captain was to be officially judged as unstable, who would take over as mission commander? You?'

The Investigator smiled. 'I might. For the good of the mission.'

'I should remind you all,' said the AI suddenly through their comm implants, 'the penalties for treason and mutiny are extremely severe.'

'Treason?' said Stasiak quickly. 'Who's talking treason? I'm not.'

Frost smiled, unperturbed. Ripper grimaced sourly. 'I should have known. Can't even get any privacy on a deserted planet.'

'I am required in the present emergency to monitor all conversations,' said the AI. 'I shall of course have to repeat your words to the Captain, on his return.'

'Of course,' said Frost. 'When he returns. In the meantime, you will cease to monitor any conversation of which I am a part, unless I give you permission to do so. That is a direct order, under Code Red Seven. Confirm.'

'Code Red Seven confirmed,' said the AI, almost reluctantly, and then it fell silent.

Ripper raised an eyebrow at the Investigator. 'I didn't know anyone could override an AI's Security directives.'

'That's what's so special about a career in the Service,' said Frost. 'You learn something new every day. Now, much as I'd like to stay and chat, I think I'll go for a little walk in the woods. Get the feel of this place. If you feel the need to discuss the Captain again, I suggest you wait till my return.'

She strode off towards the metallic forest without looking back, and the marines watched silently until she'd disappeared into the curling mists. Stasiak looked at Ripper. 'You know, I'm not sure which disturbs me most; this planet, or her.'

Silence made his way unhurriedly through the mists, looking always straight ahead of him. The huge trees loomed out of the fog to every side, and once-familiar faces seemed to appear at the corners of his eyes, but he never looked round. The forest was full of old memories, few of them pleasant. Silence concentrated on the man he'd come to find, the traitor called Carrion. The man who'd been his friend, ten long years ago.

The heating elements in his uniform kept his body comfortably warm, but the bitter cold seared his bare hands and face. The Empire kept promising to supply gloves to go with the uniform, but somehow the budget was always too tight, this year. He grimaced stoically, and did his best to ignore the cold. He wasn't far from his destination now. Theoretically, Carrion could be anywhere on Unseeli, shielded from the pinnace's sensors by his unnatural esper abilities. He had a whole world to hide in, but Silence knew where he'd be. Carrion was waiting for him in the clearing half a mile from the landing field, the place where Carrion had lived with the Ashrai in their tunnels under the earth, and called it home.

He stopped for a moment, and activated his comm implant. 'Carrion; this is John Silence, Captain of the *Darkwind*. Can you hear me?' He waited, but there was no reply. He wasn't surprised. Carrion wasn't stupid enough to give himself away that easily. Anyone could be listening in on an open comm channel, and he knew it.

Something moved suddenly at the edge of Silence's vision, and he snapped round, disrupter in hand. There was nothing there, but Silence had a strong feeling that something had been. Whatever had attacked the pinnace during its descent had found him again. There were sharp darting movements in the mists to his left and right, behind and ahead of him. Silence started forward again, careful to keep his pace slow and unhurried. He felt a growing need to break into a run, away from the shadows that were moving inexorably closer, but he didn't. It wouldn't be wise for them to get the idea he was running from them. It wouldn't be safe. He wasn't far from the clearing now. It occurred to him that they might not want him to meet Carrion, and the first stab of uncertainty brought beads of sweat to his face despite the cold. He had to reach Carrion. He had to.

Glowing streamers of quickly changing hues spun in the mists ahead of him, pushed and tugged by an unfelt wind. There was a sudden sharp crack as a long metal branch snapped off a nearby tree. The jagged spike slammed into the ground where Silence had been standing as he threw himself to one side. Cracking sounds echoed from every side as more branches broke off from the trees, raining down about him as he dodged and ducked down the path towards the clearing. His boots thudded hard on the unyielding ground, jarring him painfully. He threw himself this way and that, lungs straining against the cold air, and the metal spears slammed into the ground all around him. Silence refused to be slowed or intimidated. He'd come too far to be stopped now. A jagged spike tore through his uniform and slid painfully across his ribs before falling away. He thought he'd got away with only a bruise, until he glanced down and saw the wide patch of blood staining his side. Another spike flew at his face, and he deflected it at the last moment with an upraised arm. Blood flew on the air as the uniform sleeve tore, and the impact numbed his arm.

There were things in the forest now, moving with him. He could hear them pounding between the trees, the ground shaking from their weight. Silence plunged on, his breath burning in his heaving chest. His gun was still in his hand, but he couldn't see a target anywhere. And then the path ended suddenly, blocked by a clump of needle-thorned briar that had grown up around a fallen tree. Silence staggered to a halt, and dropped to his knees by the massive trunk of a golden tree. He put his back to the trunk and glared wildly about him. The briar blocked the way completely, and there was no other path. They had him now.

Deep in the metallic forest, something howled. It was a harsh, alien sound with nothing human in it, but the pain and rage of remembered loss were clear enough. The horrid noise drifted through the trees, growing louder, drawing nearer. More voices rose on every side, the deafening chorus cutting at Silence like a knife, and he shrank back against the tree trunk even as he raised his gun in a futile gesture of defiance. Guns weren't going to stop what was coming for him. Shadows moved in the swirling mists, encircling him, and Silence caught brief glimpses of clawed hands and snarling mouths, large graceful forms and flat-planed gargoyle faces.

He took aim and fired his disrupter. The crackling energy beam smashed through the nearest face and shattered the tree trunk behind it. There was a loud rending sound as the tree toppled slowly over and crashed to the forest floor. Metallic shrapnel pattered down for some time, but there was nothing to show he'd hurt or even scared his enemy. He hadn't really expected anything else. His enemies were already dead; ten years dead. They just wouldn't admit it and lie down. Silence's mouth twitched. They weren't playing fair. Not playing by the rules. Except this was Unseeli, the world of the Ashrai, and they had their own rules.

They were all around him now, the unearthly howls rising and falling till his head ached from them. He knew what had come for him, even though it made a mockery of all sense and reason. The Ashrai were moving slowly, steadily, through the mists and trees, circling, circling, all the tortured souls he'd damned and destroyed ten years earlier. Haunting him now as the memory of the awful thing he'd done had haunted him for so many years.

The howling stopped, cut off sharply between one moment and the next, and an eager, expectant hush filled the forest. Silence struggled to sit up a little straighter, grimacing briefly as pain flared in his damaged ribs. He raised his gun and then lowered it again. Even if there'd been anything to aim at, the disrupter couldn't fire again till its energy crystal had had time to recharge. There was still the sword at his side, but all he could do with that was fall on it himself, and maybe cheat the Ashrai of their vengeance. Except he couldn't do that. It wasn't in his nature to give up, even when the situation seemed hopeless. He drew his sword awkwardly, and sneered unyieldingly at his surroundings. Something moved in the forest, not far away. Not far away at all.

And then a man appeared suddenly out of the mist to stand at Silence's side. Everything was still, the Captain's fate hanging in the balance, and then the pressure of countless watching eyes was gone in a moment, the mists and the forest empty, as though they always had been. Silence let out his breath in a long, shuddering sigh, and put his sword down beside him. He wiped the sweat out of his eyes with his sleeve and looked up at the man standing over him. The dark figure was tall and whipcord lean, dressed in black leather and a billowing black cape. Carrion always wore black, like the bird of ill omen he was. He was carrying a long staff of polished bone, almost as tall as himself, but he held it more like a weapon than an aid to walking. His face was hidden in the shadows of his cape's cowl, and Silence didn't know whether to feel grateful for that or not.

'Hello, Sean,' he said finally, and was relieved to find his voice was still calm and even. 'It's been a long time.' The figure stared silently down at him, and Silence stirred uneasily. 'What's the matter? Don't you remember me?'

'Oh yes, Captain,' said Carrion quietly. 'I remember you. So do they.'

'What are they?' said Silence.

'The past. Ghosts, perhaps.'

'I don't believe in ghosts.'

'That's all right,' said Carrion. 'They believe in you.'

CHAPTER THREE

Looking for Answers

Stasiak and Ripper lounged bonelessly in their seats, bored and restless, watching without much interest as the esper Diana Vertue tried to make contact with Base Thirteen's computers. She'd been trying to patch the *Darkwind*'s computers into the Base's systems for some time, with only limited success, and she'd begun to mutter under her breath. Finally, by working together and improvising madly, she and the AI Odin had managed to forge a tentative link between the pinnace's onboard systems and the Base's computer net. Diana studied the incoming data closely, and winced at the state of the Base's systems as they reluctantly opened up to her tentative probes. Thirteen's computers were shot to hell. Half the main systems had crashed, and there was no trace anywhere of the Base's AI, which was supposed to protect the systems from such devastation. And there was something definitely odd about the computers she had managed to reach.

Diana frowned, her fingers darting across the comm panels, and watched intently as one by one the pinnace's monitors came to life, information flowing in an endless stream across the glowing screens. Her fingers pecked and stabbed at the keyboard as she tried to sort out the important data from the dross, her frown deepening as the picture unfolded. Whatever had happened at Base Thirteen, it hadn't been an accident. This kind of selective damage had to have been deliberate. Though whether the attack had come from outside the Base or within had yet to be established. She half smiled as she heard one of the marines sigh heavily behind her. It was probably Stasiak. He hadn't struck her as the type to have a long attention span.

'You don't have to stay, you know,' she said briskly, without looking back. 'There's nothing you can do to help.'

'It's our job to look after you,' said Stasiak. 'Make sure nothing happens to you. And if that means sitting around in a nice warm cabin instead of tramping around in the cold, waiting for my extremities to drop off, well, I know where my duty lies. After all, with the Captain and the Investigator both wandering about on their own somewhere, Rip and I are all that stands between you and whatever horrors lie waiting out there in the trees. Right, Rip?'

'Right,' said Ripper.

'The proximity mines are all the protection I need,' said Diana. 'And the pinnace does have its own force Screen, in the event of a real emergency. Now, I'm going to be doing this for some time, and believe me, this is as interesting as it gets.'

'How much progress have you made?' said Ripper, and Diana gave him credit points for at least sounding like he was interested.

'Not a hell of a lot,' she admitted, sitting back in her chair and letting her fingers rest for a moment. Things would have been going a lot quicker if she'd been allowed direct access to the computers like the Captain, instead of having to work through the keyboard. But she wasn't high enough in rank for that privilege, and besides, she was an esper, and therefore not to be trusted. Ever. She realized Ripper was still waiting for her answer, and pulled herself together.

'Most of the Base's computers are off line, and seem determined to stay that way, no matter what I do. They're not responding to the standard code words or entry routines, and I can't even find the Base's AI. If I didn't know better, I'd swear it was hiding. It's as though someone or something just shut everything down, and then wiped half the memory crystals. The subsystems overseeing the mining machinery seem to be mostly intact, but what little information I'm getting from them is pretty depressing. The machinery is working at barely twenty-per-cent efficiency, and dropping. Unless we come up with something to reverse this process, or at least slow it down, everything will just grind to a halt in a little under forty-eight hours. And once they've stopped it'll be hell's own problem to get them all started again. If that were to happen, the Empire would not be at all happy; and guess which three people sitting in this cabin right now would be most likely to be saddled with the blame.'

'Is there anything we can do to help?' said Ripper.

'Short of getting me into the Base so I can get my hands on the main computer terminals, no, not really. Odin is working its electronic nuts off trying to find a way into the main computers, but something down here is playing merry hell with our comm signals, which means Odin isn't working at anywhere near full capacity.

'On top of all that, the information I have been getting makes no sense at all. Half is just gibberish, and the rest is impossible. If I didn't know better, I'd swear some of these systems have been reprogrammed from the bottom up.'

Stasiak and Ripper looked at each other, and Ripper leaned forward in his seat. 'Are you saying someone within the Base could have crashed the systems deliberately?'

'Yes. I'd have to say that was a definite possibility.'

'In which case,' said Ripper slowly, 'we could be dealing with enemy action.'

'Maybe,' said Diana. 'I can't say for sure. Some of these changes make no sense at all.'

Ripper got to his feet. 'Lou; I think you and I had better take a stroll round the perimeter. Make sure everything's secure.'

Stasiak leaned back in his seat and deliberately stretched out his legs. 'Come on, Rip, have a heart. It's cold out there. I'm rather attached to my fingers and toes and I'd like to hang on to them. You take a walk, if you feel like it. I'm sure Diana and I can come up with something to keep us occupied while you're gone. Right, Diana?'

'In your dreams,' said the esper calmly. 'You're not my type, Lou. I usually prefer my men a little higher up the evolutionary scale.'

'Can I take that as a maybe?' said Stasiak, getting reluctantly to his feet.

'Think of it more as a get the hell out of here.'

'All right,' said Stasiak. 'I can take a hint. Lead the way, Rip. I'm just dying to take a nice little stroll in sub-zero temperatures, and watch my extremities turn blue.'

The esper chuckled briefly, intent on the comm panels, but she didn't relax until she heard the airlock door close behind the two marines. Stasiak was all right, in his way, but she had to be careful whom she allowed to get close to her. There were always people ready to try and take advantage of her esper abilities. But it wasn't safe to stay unattached, either. Espers always had a need for someone to stand between them and the Empire; someone strong enough to protect a second-class citizen like an esper from official displeasure and political pogroms. Stasiak was too far down the ladder to be any use to her, and Ripper wasn't much better ... She realized her thoughts were drifting, and made herself concentrate on the screens before her. The information from Base Thirteen's computers flowed endlessly on, much of it strange and enigmatic and no bloody use to her at all.

'I'm picking up something ... unusual,' said Odin suddenly. 'I thought at first it was what was left of the Base's AI, but now I'm not sure. It's as though something inside the Base is trying to respond to my enquiries, but in a manner unlike anything I've ever encountered before.'

'Put it on the main screen,' said Diana, and then frowned thoughtfully as the AI showed her a record of its questions and the Base's responses. The answers were garbled and obscure, bordering on the edge of meaning without actually achieving it. Diana ran a few simple checks to see if the gibberish might contain some kind of code, but if so, it was buried so deep she couldn't find it. And yet the words continued to nag at her, trying to tell her ... something. 'Run a full analysis on this, Odin,' she said finally. 'Look for repetition of words and phrases, subjects emphasised or avoided; all the usual things. If it isn't the AI, could it be someone alive, inside the Base?'

'If it is,' said Odin, 'I would have to say that they were quite insane.'

Outside the pinnace, it was even colder than Stasiak remembered, and he hugged himself tightly, and stamped his feet hard on the landing pad while he waited for the heating elements in his uniform to kick in. He was beginning to think he should have found the time to give his uniform a thorough overhaul before he came down here. It was long overdue, and Stasiak was coming to the conclusion he might have left it a little too long. He shrugged, and rubbed his hands together briskly. He'd survive. Ripper, of course, was taking no notice of the cold, and was staring out at the forest boundary with calm, thoughtful eyes. Stasiak followed his gaze, but was damned if he could make out anything significant, or even interesting. He sniffed loudly, and looked longingly back at the pinnace.

'Ripper; tell me you didn't just drag me out here for the exercise. Tell me there's a good reason why I'm standing here in the cold, before I decide to batter you to death with a blunt instrument, and dance a jig on your remains.'

'You don't have a blunt instrument,' said Ripper, without looking round.

'I'll improvise!'

Ripper smiled, but still didn't look away from the forest. 'You weren't looking at the sensor panels, were you? According to the sensors built into our proximity mines, something or someone has approached or crossed our perimeter in several places, before falling back to the forest again.'

'You're kidding,' said Stasiak. 'You've *got* to be kidding. If something's crossed our perimeter, why haven't the mines gone off?'

'Good question,' said Ripper. 'Another good question might be why did the mines' sensors detect a presence, when the pinnace's instruments continue to insist there are no living things on this planet apart from us. You've got to admit, Lou; it's an interesting place our Captain has brought us to.'

'I'll give him "interesting",' said Stasiak darkly. He moved over to stand beside Ripper, and glared out at the distance. 'You know why he brought us here, Rip? Because we're expendable. We're just here to test the water for him. And if anything were to happen to us, he'd just shrug and say what a pity, and then contact the *Darkwind* and have them ship down two more warm bodies.'

'That goes with the job,' said Ripper. 'With being a marine. If you can't take a joke, you shouldn't have joined.'

'Just let me survive the next five months, and my contract will be up,' said Stasiak. 'And then I'll be out of the marines so fast it'll make your head spin. I still can't believe I landed an assignment like this so close to getting free of it all. I'll tell you this for nothing, Rip; I'm not taking a single risk down here that I don't absolutely have to. I'm taking this one by the book and by the numbers, with no volunteering for anything. Whatever else happens on this mission, I am coming back alive and intact, and you can put money on that.'

Ripper finally turned to look at him. 'And what will you do then, Lou? Where will you go, once you've left the Service? All you know, all your training and experience, comes from being a marine. There aren't that many openings for a professional killer, outside the Service. Shall I tell you what's going to happen to you? You'll go from one dead-end job to another, each more frustrating than the one before, breaking your back every day for half the money you used to make as a marine. And finally, when your money's run out, and you're out of your mind with boredom, some shark with a big smile and a suit that cost a year of your wages will sign you up as a mercenary, for which he gets a nice commission, and you get to tour the hell spots of the Empire. In the end you'll come running back to the Service and sign on again, just like most ex-marines do.'

'Like you did,' said Stasiak.

'Yeah. Like I did. Get used to the idea, Lou. This is all there is, for people like us.'

'Not me,' said Stasiak. 'Once I'm out of here they're never getting their hands on me again. I've got plans. I'm going places. I'm going to make something of myself.'

'Sure you are, Lou.'

'I mean it!'

'I know you do. I hope you make it. In the meantime, keep your eyes open and your head down. And don't look now, but I think I just saw something moving out on the perimeter, at two o'clock.'

Stasiak looked round casually, his eyes just happening to drift past two o'clock. There was nothing there. He cut in his infrared implants, but no heat traces showed anywhere on the perimeter. He patched into the pinnace sensors and studied their signals directly, but there was still nothing anywhere on the boundary. He dropped out of contact, looked at Ripper, and shrugged.

'Jumping at shadows, Rip. There's nothing out there.'

'Yes there is. I saw it. Keep watching; it'll give itself away. It's at times like this I wish the Empire would relax its ban on all but the most essential implants. I've seen stuff on the black market you wouldn't believe; implants and built-in weapon systems that could make a man unbeatable in the field. Which is pretty much why they're banned, of course. The Empire doesn't want its good little soldier boys getting ideas above their station. They still haven't forgotten the Hadenman rebellion.'

'Yeah well,' said Stasiak. 'Those cyborgs were enough to frighten anyone. And I still can't see anything out there. Maybe it's the Captain, on his way back.'

'If it was, he'd have shown up on the infra red, wouldn't he? Though that is another question worth thinking about. What is the good Captain doing down here, risking his precious neck dirtside with grunts like us?'

'Looking for Carrion, whoever he is.'

'Yeah.' Ripper frowned for the first time. 'The Captain knows a lot more about what's going on here than he's letting on. I'll lay you odds this Carrion turns out to be some kind of powerful esper. That's the only way he could be shielding himself from the pinnace's sensors.'

Stasiak shook his head dubiously. 'I don't know. If Carrion's been here on his own for the past ten years, what's he been living on? I mean; there isn't any game for him to catch. Every living thing was wiped out by the scorching. And even if he did find some way to survive, he's got to be stone crazy after ten years of his own company.'

'Not necessarily,' said Ripper. 'He could have worked out some kind of deal with the Base personnel. There! Did you see that?'

'Yeah,' said Stasiak quietly. 'Right at the edge of the forest; two o'clock, just like you said. Still can't make out what it is. Want to go and take a look?'

'Easy, Lou. It could be a trick, to draw us away from the ship. Besides, if it's come this close, why hasn't it set off any of the mines? Whatever that is has got to be within their range. Maybe it's got a way to turn them on and off. It could be just waiting for us to walk by one, and then detonate it itself. Whoosh bang, and they'll send your balls home in a box, because they couldn't find the rest of you. No, Lou; short of an actual target or a direct threat to the pinnace, I'm not moving from this spot. At least, not until I've got a much better idea of the opposition.'

'Damn right,' said Stasiak, still keeping a careful if unobtrusive watch on two o'clock. 'If the Captain wants to go off on his own chasing after ghosts, that's his affair. Short of a direct order, I'm not moving. I can't see it any more, Rip. Can you see it?'

'No. It's gone again.'

Stasiak looked at the watch face imbedded in his wrist. 'The Captain's been gone a long time. He should have been back by now.'

Ripper shrugged. 'How long does it take to track down someone who officially doesn't exist? Don't worry about the Captain. He's a grown man. He can take care of himself.'

They stood together for a while, staring out into the mists.

'You know,' said Stasiak finally, 'if there was a ghost or something out there at two o'clock, that puts it in roughly the same sector as the Investigator. Perhaps they'll bump into each other.'

'In which case,' said Ripper, 'I feel sorry for the ghost.'

CHAPTER FOUR

Carrion

Captain Silence rose slowly to his feet, wincing despite himself as his injured ribs protested. Carrion made no move to help him, for which Silence was thankful. He didn't want any reason to feel grateful to Carrion. It would have made what he had to do that much harder. He pushed his various aches and pains to the back of his mind, and concentrated on the traitor called Carrion. It had been ten years since he'd last seen the man who used to be his friend, and he'd never expected to see him again. He should have died with the Ashrai. Dead, he might have emerged as a martyr; alive, he was just another loose end, an embarrassment. Someone Silence could use to solve an awkward problem.

He realized he was just standing and staring at Carrion, but the words wouldn't come. He'd had it all worked out, on the pinnace, coming down. He knew exactly what to say, what buttons to push to manipulate Carrion into doing what was necessary. Only now he was face to face with an old friend, a ghost from the past, and the words were ashes in his mouth. This man had been closer than a brother, but the last time they'd met they'd tried to kill each other. For a long time, Silence believed he'd succeeded. And then he began to hear stories from men who'd served on Unseeli; stories of the man who wouldn't die. The ghost in the trees. Carrion.

The years passed, but Silence never went back. He didn't want to have to kill his friend again. But time and circumstance had brought him back anyway, and past sins belonged in the past. All that mattered now was his mission, and the things he had to do to carry it out. Silence knew his duty. He'd always known his duty. And if that meant using and betraying his friend one more time, he could live with that. He'd lived with worse.

Carrion reached up and pushed back the cowl that concealed his face. Silence felt a sudden chill run through him, and the hackles rose on the back of his neck. Carrion hadn't aged. He'd spent ten years alone in terrible conditions, but there wasn't a single line on his face. He looked just as Silence remembered him; young, proud, unyielding. Time had not touched him. But then, ghosts didn't age. Silence felt suddenly awkward, ashamed at the changes that had taken place in himself over the past decade. What did Carrion make of him, with his retreating hairline and his thickening waist? Had he even noticed, and if he had, did he care? And most important, did he realize that this was not the same John Silence he'd once known, who might have hesitated to sacrifice his friend if the game demanded it? Just looking at the calm young man before him, Silence felt older, dirtier and more used. He still didn't know what to say. And in the end, Carrion was the one who broke the silence.

'What are you doing here, Captain?'

'I need your help,' said Silence evenly.

Carrion smiled briefly, as though it was something he'd lost the habit of, over the years. 'I didn't think you'd come all this way just to renew old acquaintance. I always knew you'd be back someday. We have unfinished business, you and I.'

'That can wait,' said Silence. 'Do you know what's happened in Base Thirteen?'

'I know the Screen went up, some time back. That's all.'

'You didn't have any contact with the Base personnel?'

The smile came and went again, but it didn't touch Carrion's eyes. 'The Base Commander had a shoot-on-sight policy where I was concerned. He needn't have bothered. He had nothing I wanted. But they were scared of me, of what I'd become, and they were right about that, at least.'

'What have you become?' said Silence. 'How have you survived here all these years, with no supplies and no resources?'

'Strictly speaking, I didn't. I've been through a lot since we last met, Captain. I'm not the man you remember.' He looked away for a moment, as though listening to a voice only he could hear, and then nodded slowly and looked back at Silence. 'We can't talk here. You have no friends among the trees, and not even I can protect you against the whole of the forest. Come with me. My home isn't far.'

He turned and walked away, without once looking back to see if Silence was following. Silence moved off after him, gritting his teeth against the grinding pain in his side. The wound didn't look too severe, but something would have to be done about it soon, before he became weakened through blood loss. He allowed his uniform to release endorphins into his system, enough to handle the pain but not enough to cloud his thinking. He walked beside Carrion through the bronze and golden forest, following a track only the outlaw could see. Nothing moved in the mists, but the quiet had a sullen, expectant feel, and Silence could sense the watching eyes even if he couldn't see them.

The trees widened out suddenly to reveal a great hill of metal, overgrown with silver briar. The metal was scarred and pock-marked, and briar penetrated the outer shell here and there like some parasitic ivy, but even so Silence could still recognize the battle wagon beneath. There were supposed to be quite a few of them, scattered throughout the forest, left to lie where they had fallen, brought down by the Ashrai and their psi-storms. Silence thought he remembered the clearing; it was one of the few battlegrounds where he and Carrion had both been present.

Lasers flamed on the night, and concussion grenades blossomed in the dark like scarlet flowers. Disrupters flared, and there was the loud humming of raised force shields. The Ashrai came in never-ending waves, huge, ugly figures that moved with surprising grace and speed. Their psi-storms crackled on the air around them, altering probabilities and tearing at the mental barriers the Empire espers had cast over the ground troops. Claws and fangs met swords and shields, and blood flowed in rivers on the broken ground. Battle wagons lumbered through the night, forcing their way between the trees, and disrupter beams stabbed down from low-flying skimmers darting back and forth overhead. Science clashed with savagery, and the battle swept this way and that, neither side able to gain the upper hand for long.

Silence shivered suddenly, emerging from a memory so real it seemed to him that he could still hear the shouts and battle cries and the screams of the dying. The Ashrai had been a brave and cunning foe, but they never stood a chance against the Empire. As soon as Silence had realized he couldn't take the ground the

Ashrai held, or hang on to his own, he simply moved all his people off planet and called in the starcruisers to scorch the whole damned planet from pole to pole. Millions died, all life was swept away, and not even the bodies remained to mark the fallen. The Empire was nothing if not thorough. Silence had won, and all it cost him was his honour and his friend. For a while he thought he'd die without them, but he didn't. No one ever really dies from a broken heart.

When it was over, the Empire hadn't really known what to do with Silence. On the one hand, he'd lost control of the situation, and had to be rescued by a scorching, but on the other hand, he had solved the Unseeli problem quite conclusively. And permanently. So they smiled and shook his hand and patted him on the head in public, and made a note on his file that he was never to be promoted. He could keep his Captaincy, but there'd never be anything more for him. Silence didn't care. He'd lost all taste for ambition on Unseeli.

And now here he was, back again, and it seemed the problem hadn't been solved after all.

They finally came to the clearing where Carrion had his home, and Silence was struck with an almost overpowering sense of *déjà vu*. It hadn't changed at all. Before him were the same trees, the same clearing, the same patch of metal briar camouflaging the trapdoor entrance to the tunnels under the earth. Silence watched numbly as Carrion carefully lifted the briar to one side, and pulled open the trapdoor. The last time Silence had been here was when he'd made a last-minute trip against orders to try and talk Carrion out of turning traitor. They were still friends then, and the outlaw had yet to come by his new name. They'd met as friends and parted as enemies, and what happened afterward had all the inevitability of destiny. It hadn't stopped either of them from playing their rôle to the full. And now here they were again, with only the echoes of old friendship and enmity holding them together, looking once more for some middle ground they could agree on. Silence smiled sourly. Maybe they'd be luckier this time.

Carrion descended into the dark stairway the trapdoor had revealed, and Silence followed him down. He paused briefly to test the weight of the trapdoor. It was just as heavy as he'd remembered, but Carrion had hefted it with one hand, as though it was weightless. He cleared his throat, and Carrion looked up at him.

'Do you want me to shut the trapdoor behind us?' said Silence.

Carrion smiled briefly. 'There's really no need. It's not as if there was anyone else who might come in after us. Still, if it makes you feel more secure . . .'

He gestured at the trapdoor, and it started to lean slowly forwards. Silence hurried down the narrow earth steps into the gloom of the tunnel, and the trapdoor slammed shut behind him, the impact of its weight sending tremors through the earth walls and floor. Silence glared after Carrion, but he was already walking off down the tunnel, and Silence had to hurry to keep up. The tunnel was wide enough for both of them to walk side by side, with a good two or three-foot clearance above their heads. The earth had a rich, peaty smell that was not unpleasant. Roots from the metal trees had been trained along the uneven ceiling, filling the tunnel with their warm unwavering light. The enclosed space was still distinctly claustrophobic, and Silence tried hard not to think about the increasing weight of earth above him as the tunnel sloped steadily downwards.

It soon branched into two, and then in two again, with corridors leading off tunnels, and wide holes opening into vast, brightly lit caverns. Silence was soon lost in the labyrinth of tunnels that had been the home of the Ashrai and the outlaw Carrion. The last time he'd been down here, he and Carrion had still been friends enough that Carrion had led him back to the surface once their business was concluded. Silence wasn't sure if that was the case any more, but it didn't matter anyway. He had to talk to Carrion.

Finally the outlaw stopped by a side passage and waved for Silence to go in ahead of him. Silence stepped forward without hesitating. He didn't want Carrion to think he was intimidated. The passage widened out into a fair-sized cavern, lit by the ubiquitous glowing roots curling in the earth ceiling. Carrion's home was large enough to give the illusion of space, yet still cluttered with enough little comforts to make it seem almost cosy. There were two chairs, a writing table and a length of bedding. A banked fire muttered drowsily in one wall, the smoke rising up through a narrow chimney cut into the earth above. The floor was covered with some kind of woven matting, scuffed and stained with the marks of long usage. Not much of a place to spend an exile in.

Small, delicate Ashrai carvings filled discreet niches in the walls. Silence moved over to study the nearest, but its shape made no sense, and its twistings and turnings made his head ache. He looked away, frowning, and Carrion chuckled softly.

'You're supposed to touch them, Captain, not look at them. The Ashrai were a very tactile race, and their eyes were different than ours.'

'Thanks,' said Silence. 'I'll pass.'

'As you wish. Take a seat, Captain. Make yourself comfortable. I'd offer you a drink or a smoke, but I don't have any.'

Silence sank cautiously into the nearest chair, but it was tougher than it looked, and held his weight easily. Carrion dropped into the chair opposite, and the two men sat facing each other for a while. Silence couldn't get over how little Carrion had changed. Ten years of living alone hadn't put a dent in his composure. The outlaw was as infuriatingly polite as ever. After a decade of solitude he should have been falling all over Silence, desperate for the sound of a human voice. Instead he just sat there calmly, apparently quite happy to wait for whatever Silence had come to say to him. Silence stirred uneasily in his chair. He'd forgotten how cold and piercing Carrion's eyes could be.

'Nice place you have here,' he said finally, just to be saying something.

'I like it,' said Carrion. He leaned forward suddenly, and Silence jumped a little in spite of himself. Carrion didn't smile. 'I don't know what to say to you, Captain. It's been a long time since I spoke to another human being.'

'How have you managed to survive here on your own for ten years?' said Silence.

Carrion raised an eyebrow. 'Is it as long as that? I'd lost count. I survived by changing, adapting. By becoming more than human.'

'You look human enough to me,' said Silence. 'You've hardly changed at all.'

'That's Unseeli for you. Appearances can be deceiving. You

should know that. You never did understand the Ashrai. They're what kept me alive all these years.'

Silence looked at him thoughtfully. 'Are you saying some of the Ashrai survived after all, hidden down here in the tunnels?'

'No, Captain. The Ashrai are extinct. You were very thorough. All the Ashrai are dead, and none but I am left to tell the tale. I survived because I was afraid to die. I've had a long time to consider whether that was a mistake or not. Why have you come back, Captain?'

'Things have changed since we last met.'

'Not for me. The Ashrai are still dead, and the Empire machines are still burrowing away, tearing through the trees' roots so they can be felled and harvested. The rape of the planet goes on, day by day.'

Silence sighed tiredly. 'Ten years of solitude haven't done much to change your arguments. You didn't listen then and you probably won't now, but I'll try again anyway, for old times' sake. The Empire needs the metals it takes from Unseeli. Each tree that's felled can provide enough heavy metals to power a starship for a year. We even use the outer metals to make ships' hulls and engine casings. It's only Unseeli's metals that made our recent expansion possible. But Unseeli is the only place where these metals can be easily found, and we've become dependent on them. Without the regular supply ships these trees make possible, half our colonies would starve or suffocate or fall apart from lack of some essential. Millions would die, the Empire would collapse, and humanity would fall back into barbarism inside a generation.'

'To the Ashrai, we are barbarians,' said Carrion.

Silence shook his head impatiently. 'None of that matters any more. It's past. I need your help, Sean. Something's happened at Base Thirteen.'

Carrion looked at him steadily. 'The last time we met I called the Ashrai to arms and led them against the Empire. I led them into battle for the sake of their world, and you butchered them. You killed and slaughtered until you grew bored, and then you retreated into orbit and burned everything that lived.'

Silence didn't look away. 'It was necessary.'

'The Ashrai . . .'

'Didn't stand a chance. Rebels never do.'

'And you expect me to help you now? After everything that's happened, you expect me to help the Empire?'

'I could get you Pardoned.'

'I doubt that.'

Silence smiled coldly. 'Don't flatter yourself, Sean. You're not that important, or a bounty hunter would have taken your head years ago. No; you're just another deserter who went native on some backwater planet. No one cares about you any more. I can get you Pardoned, and I can take you off planet. Take you anywhere you want to go. You could start again; start over with a clean record. Think about it. You wouldn't even have to call yourself Carrion any more.'

'Why not, Captain? It's who I am.' Carrion shook his head slowly, and sank back in his chair. 'Thank you for the offer, Captain, but no.'

'No? Think what I'm offering you! You can't want to stay here on your own . . .'

'Can't I? I've found peace here.'

'What peace? The peace of the dead, of the cemetery?'

'The peace of the forest, Captain. You never did understand what you were destroying. The Ashrai and the trees were linked more closely than you ever knew. The trees are alive. I've seen branches sway when no wind blows, and heard voices on the wind and in the mists. The Ashrai are dead, but they are not gone. There's a harmony, a strength that holds the trees together, and I'm a part of it.' The outlaw's voice fell to a whisper, his gaze still fixed on Silence's. 'Leave me alone, John. Please.'

'I can't, Sean. I need you.'

'Why, Captain? Why does it always have to be me?'

'Because you're the best.'

'Thank you, Captain.'

Silence turned away from the bitterness in Carrion's voice, and rose to his feet. 'Up you get, Carrion. It's a long way back to Base Thirteen, and we've a lot to discuss on the way.'

Carrion looked up at him. 'Are you so sure I'll help you?'

'Of course. You were my friend. And it's not as if you have anything else to do, is it?'

CHAPTER FIVE

Ghost in the Machine

The esper Diana Vertue leaned back in her seat and glared moodily at the pinnace monitors. The AI was still trying to make some sense out of the garbled responses it was getting from inside Base Thirteen, but as far as she could see, it was getting nowhere fast. Diana supposed it was an encouraging sign that they were getting any kind of response, but it was looking more and more to her that what they were getting were just random responses from a damaged computer. She had suggested as much to Odin, but the AI ignored her. She was only an esper, and therefore the AI didn't have to listen to her if it didn't want to. Even an Artificial Intelligence rated higher than an esper.

Diana sighed, and stretched out her legs as best she could in the cramped confines of the cabin. She'd expected many things of her first official mission on an alien world, but boredom wasn't one of them. She'd almost reached the point where she would have welcomed the two marines back on board, just to have someone to talk to. At least they had something to do, even if it was only keeping a lookout and second-guessing the Security system. All she had to do was sit and watch the computer talking to itself, and wait for something to go wrong. Not that there was a whole lot she could do if it did. She sighed again, heavily, and indulged herself in a pout. It wasn't fair. She'd been allowed to do nothing ever since they'd touched down on this miserable planet. She'd pretty much reached the point where she would gladly have accepted anything new happening, up to and including a major catastrophe, just so long as she got to see a little action. Anything would be better than this.

Well, almost anything. She hadn't forgotten what had happened the last time she'd opened up her esp, on the way down.

There *was* something here on Unseeli with them, and to hell with what the sensors said. And whatever it was, it was dangerous. She'd sensed a rage and a force beyond anything she'd ever encountered before, something so powerful it almost burned out her mind just looking at it. She'd kept her esp damped down low ever since, and had no intention of raising it again, no matter how bored she got. She frowned slightly, unhappy at the direction her thoughts were taking, but unable to ignore them either. Captain Silence had known what her attackers were, even if what he'd said had made no sense. When he got back, she'd get some answers out of him; one way or another. She could always run a quick scan on him. In and out, so fast he'd never notice. But of course she couldn't. Just thinking about it was enough to make her stomach roll and sweat start on her face. The Empire conditioned its espers very carefully from childhood onwards, to ensure they'd never abuse their abilities. Except in the service of the Empire, of course.

'Investigator Frost to pinnace. Acknowledge, and confirm your situation.'

Diana sat up straight as the Investigator's cold, calm voice sounded in her comm implant. 'This is esper Vertue. The pinnace is still secure. Nothing's happened since you left. Where are you?'

'About two miles east from the landing field, map reference Alpha Tango eighty-eight. Has the Captain returned yet?'

'No, Investigator. He hasn't contacted us, and we haven't been able to raise him. Something down here is affecting the comm system; it only works when it feels like it.'

'I had hoped the Captain would be there, but we can proceed without him. This is an official Log Entry; Unseeli, fifteen forty-three hours. I have discovered what appears to be an alien space vessel, crashed some two miles east of Base Thirteen. The ship has suffered extensive damage, and there is as yet no sign of any pilot or other crew.'

'An alien ship?' said Diana excitedly as Frost paused. 'What type is it? What species?'

There was another pause, but when Frost spoke again, her voice was calm and measured. 'Unknown, esper.'

Diana stared blankly at the comm panels, her mind racing.

Space-travelling aliens were rare, even out here on the Rim; but a new, unknown species . . . This was the kind of thing careers were made on. A sudden thought struck her.

'Investigator; could this be a representative of the species who originally created the metal forest?'

'Possible, but unlikely. Any species intelligent enough to gene-gineer the trees would surely be able to land a ship without crashing it. Listen carefully, esper. You're going to have to leave the pinnace. I need you here, with me, to examine this ship. The marines will accompany you, to ensure your safety.'

'You mean leave the pinnace unguarded?' said Diana.

'The pinnace can look after itself. Odin; go to full battle readiness. Acknowledge.'

'Acknowledged, Investigator.' The AI's voice was as calm and even as ever, but Diana would have sworn she heard something like excitement in its measured tones.

'In the meantime, Odin; keep trying to raise the Captain,' said Frost. 'I don't like being out of contact with him for so long. That goes for you too, esper. You might have better luck once you've moved away from the vicinity of Base Thirteen. Odin; what's your current status on repairs?'

'Progressing well, Investigator. All main systems are back on line and operational again.'

'What about structure integrity? Could we lift off again, if we had to?'

'Unknown, Investigator. Theoretically, yes. In practice, I could not recommend it, except in the direst of circumstances.'

'Very well. Maintain regular contact with the *Darkwind* after the esper and the marines have left; keep them up to date on what's happening down here. And be prepared to relay infor-mation from me to the *Darkwind*. I'll want the data from this new ship compared with existing records.'

'I'm afraid that won't be possible, Investigator. I have been unable to contact the *Darkwind* from the moment we landed. There is nothing wrong with the comm systems, so I can only conclude it is either a result of natural conditions, or the interfer-ence is deliberate.'

'What do you mean, we're out of contact?' snapped Frost. 'Why didn't you say anything before?'

'You didn't ask.'

'Computer; once this mission is over, you and I are going to have a long chat about which of us is in charge here. In the meantime, you will report to me, or the esper, or anybody else available, on any change in our circumstances that might affect our mission, *as they happen*. And if I have any further problems with you, I will personally reprogram your data banks with a shrapnel grenade. Is that clear?'

'There is no need to raise your voice to me, Investigator. I assure you, I have only the best interests of this mission at heart. I exist only to serve.'

'Blow it out your terminal.'

Diana looked aghast at the comm panels before her. Being cut off from the main ship was serious; it not only meant they were denied the ship's superior computer facilities, it also meant they were on their own if anything went wrong. Diana hugged herself tightly. She'd never been cut off from the ship from the moment she joined its crew. She was used to its protection always being there, only a call away. Now she felt alone, naked. Defenceless. She realized Frost was still talking, and made herself pay attention.

'If something is blocking our transmissions, can you determine their position in relation to ours?'

'Not at present, Investigator,' said the AI. 'Without further evidence, it remains only a hypothesis.'

'That settles it. Esper; I want you with me as fast as you can travel. The sooner we check this alien ship out, the better. And esper; keep your eyes open on the way. Investigator out.'

The silence that followed Frost's signing off had a definite feeling of uncertainty. Not to mention unease. The presence of the alien ship could explain a lot of things, but for the moment it raised more questions than it answered. And the thought of leaving the pinnace and travelling through the metallic forest was not a comforting one, even with the marines for protection. Diana got to her feet and then stood there dithering, unsure what to do first. She'd wanted a little action, a little excitement, but this was ridiculous. A thought struck her, and she turned to glare at the comm panels.

'Odin; why didn't your sensors detect the presence of the crashed alien ship?'

'Unknown, esper. Either the ship is shielded in some way, or it and its crew are simply too alien to show up on my instruments.'

Diana frowned. 'I thought it was impossible for anything to shield itself from your sensors?'

'Impossible for any technology I am aware of. The alien ship's level of technology is unknown.'

Diana growled something under her breath, and strode down the cabin to the airlock. Even when the computer was talking to her, she couldn't get anything useful out of it. At least the Investigator understood her worth. Just let her at that alien ship; she'd show them what an esper could do. She'd show them all.

The marines accepted their new orders with hardly any fuss. Secretly, Diana thought they were probably just as bored as she'd been. The news of an alien ship didn't throw them at all. They just nodded, checked the power levels on their guns, and led her off the landing field and into the metallic forest. They walked on either side of her, studying the surrounding trees alertly, their disrupters drawn and ready for use. Diana looked at the guns, and scowled. There was always the chance the aliens weren't involved with whatever had happened at Base Thirteen, and were just innocent bystanders. The Empire's usual reaction to a new species was to shoot first and ask questions later, if at all, but Diana was determined that wasn't going to happen here. First contacts could be peaceful, and she was going to do everything in her power to see that this one was. The Empire wasn't going to add another servant species to its ranks, another people to treat and exploit as second-class citizens. Like the espers.

She didn't like the way her thoughts were going, so she concentrated instead on her surroundings. The metallic trees were very beautiful, shining in the mists like frozen fireworks. Now that she was seeing them up close, walking among them, they didn't seem nearly as imposing. Their warm glow seemed friendly, even inviting . . . Which was more than she could say about the entities that had attacked her on the way down. The day seemed suddenly colder, and she shuddered quickly. She'd never felt a rage like it, an anger beyond thought or emotion; a force in itself. A force strong enough to break through a pinnace hull built to withstand atomics. She looked at the marines walking with her, and her brief feeling of security was gone, as though it had never been. Guns and cold steel would be little use against the kind of force she'd sensed.

She thrust the thought out of her mind. She was on her way to an unknown alien ship and a possible first contact, and nothing was going to spoil that for her. She wouldn't let anything spoil it. She lengthened her stride, almost skipping along in her enthusiasm. The marines had to hurry to keep up with her. Ripper studied her thoughtfully, and Stasiak gave her a dark look or two, but she ignored both of them. And then the smile left her face and the joy went out of her in a moment, as something moved in the trees, not far away. She stopped dead in her tracks, and the marines stopped with her. They looked at her enquiringly, and she tried hard to stop trembling.

'Didn't you hear it?' she said quietly.

'Hear what?' said Stasiak, trying to look in every direction at once, and almost succeeding.

'There's something moving in the mists, not far away. It knows we're here.' She frowned, concentrating, trying to touch whatever it was with her esp, but it stayed obstinately just at the edge of her awareness.

'Can you at least give us a direction?' said Ripper quietly.

Diana indicated off to her right with a quick movement of her chin, and they all strained their eyes against the mists. It was cold and quiet and nothing moved.

'There's nothing there,' said Stasiak, lowering his gun. 'Not a damned thing. You're just nervous, esper. Jumping at shadows.'

'It's there,' said Diana. 'I can feel it.'

'Well whatever it is, I think we'd be safer on the move,' said Ripper. 'Lou; you lead the way. I'll watch the rear. Esper; you stay between us, and if you see it again, try and let us know without alerting it. Don't worry; we won't let anything happen to you. Now let's move, shall we? Nice and easy . . .'

They set off again, and Diana strode jerkily along, looking left and right, her back crawling. Something was watching her, and she could feel its menace like a sharp taste in her mouth. Her hands clenched into fists at her sides, and she almost wished she had taken a disrupter for herself after all. The thought shocked her calm again, like a faceful of cold water. She was an esper, not a killer. Whatever it was out there, she should be concentrating on making contact with it. Only, there was no other living thing on this planet. The sensors said so. But the sensors hadn't reacted to her attackers on the way down, and they'd been real enough. She'd felt them in her mind as they moved in inexorably to crush the fragile pinnace, only to draw back when they sensed her presence. Her presence. *Because they knew you were innocent*, the Captain had said. The word *innocent* rang in her mind like a bell.

There was a loud crashing sound to her left, as something large forced its way between two trees, snapping off the solid metal branches as it did. Ripper signalled urgently for them to keep moving. Diana looked at Stasiak.

'Still think I'm seeing things?'

He growled something under his breath, swinging his gun back and forth as he searched for a target. There was the sound of heavy footsteps, to their left and to their right, and the ground shook under their feet. Diana's breath caught in her throat as she realized the sounds were coming from two different directions now. She began to increase her pace, and the marines moved with her, until suddenly all three of them were running. The heavy footsteps kept up with them effortlessly, the ground shaking under their weight like an earthquake. Diana could feel panic welling up inside her, and clamped down on it hard. Whatever was out there, it wanted them to know about it. She could feel herself slowing as her wind ran out, and forced herself on. And then they burst out of the trees and into a clearing, and as suddenly as that the pursuing footsteps were gone. The three of them stumbled to a halt, looking back into the trees, but the mists were empty and still, the only sound on the quiet their own harsh breathing.

'What happened?' said Stasiak breathlessly. 'Did we lose it?'

'I don't think so,' said Diana.

'Then what did happen?' said Ripper.

Diana shrugged. 'They're not ready to kill us yet, that's all. They want us to suffer first.'

'They?' said Ripper. 'Diana; who are *they*?'

The esper looked away from the trees and turned her gaze on the two marines. 'They're the Ashrai. Or what's left of them. Angry ghosts haunting the forest that used to be theirs.'

She began to breathe more easily again, and nodded for the two marines to continue. They glared at the trees around them, hefted their guns uncertainly, and then started across the open clearing. Diana moved with them, her esp wide open, but she couldn't detect any other presences in the surrounding forest. All three of them tensed as they left the clearing and plunged back into the trees, but nothing happened. They stayed alert and cautious all the rest of the way, but the forest remained empty and silent, like a huge abandoned graveyard. And finally they arrived at their destination, with nothing to show for their trip but a few jangled nerves. They stopped at the top of a rise and looked down at what they'd come to see, and for a long time none of them could say anything.

The crashed alien ship lay at the bottom of the rise, huge and dark like a thunder cloud fallen to earth. It was hundreds of feet long, an insane tangle of brass columns, held together by glazed nodes each bigger than the entire pinnace. Spiked and barbed projections emerged from the main bulk at irregular intervals, but whether they were sensors or weapons or something else entirely wasn't clear. The ship lay half buried at the end of a mile-long scorch mark, with a long trail of jagged tree stumps to mark its passing. Diana tried to imagine how fast the ship had to have been travelling when it hit, to have caused such devastation, but it was just too much for her to visualise. The one thing she was sure of was that the pinnace wouldn't have survived such a landing. She looked round sharply as someone called her name, and then she hurried down to join the Investigator waiting by the ship. The marines followed her down at a more leisurely pace, just to remind the Investigator that they weren't that impressed by her.

The ship loomed over Diana like a mountain crag, its dull brass surfaces seeming to absorb the light rather than reflect it.

The Investigator ignored it casually, as though she'd seen better, in her time. *Probably has*, thought Diana.

'You're later than I expected,' said Frost. 'Trouble along the way?'

'Not really,' said Ripper easily. 'We thought we heard something moving in the mists, but nothing came of it.'

Frost nodded, apparently unconcerned. 'You marines will stand watch while the esper and I check out the ship. Nothing is to approach this vessel without being challenged and identified first. But don't just blast anything that moves. Remember; the Captain's still out there somewhere. Esper; follow me.'

She turned and walked away, and Diana hurried after her. The alien ship fascinated her. Its shape made no sense at all, and trying to follow the ins and outs of its insane structure made her dizzy. The twisting brass columns ranged from two to twenty feet in diameter, wrapped around each other as often as not.

'It is an unknown, isn't it, Investigator?' she burst out finally, unable to keep quiet any longer. 'It's a totally new alien species! I've never seen anything like it.'

'Neither have I,' said Frost calmly. 'Run a full scan on it for me.'

Diana flushed. She shouldn't have needed an order to do something that basic. She raised her esp and let it flow out over the ship. The huge structure burned in her mind like a guttering candle, and she grimaced despite herself. She couldn't seem to get a hold on anything; her mind skidded off the ship as though it were greased. She concentrated, trying to focus, but the ship was so different, so . . . alien, her mind simply couldn't grasp it. There was something deeply disturbing about the vessel, with all its crazy angles and weird surfaces, things that shouldn't hold together but somehow did, and above it all . . . something else. Something so large, so enormous she couldn't see it for the details. She pulled back, trying to grasp the whole structure as one, and when the truth finally hit her she couldn't get her breath for a moment.

Frost studied the esper as she stood before the ship, her eyes moving restlessly behind her closed eyelids. Diana's breathing was quick and shallow, and there was a sheen of sweat on her face despite the cold. And then the esper's eyes shot open, and she fell back a step, her hands lifting as though to defend herself from something close at hand. She looked away from the ship, shuddered quickly, and then had herself back under control again. Frost frowned. Whatever the esper had encountered, it was apparently unpleasant enough to knock all the enthusiasm for the ship right out of her.

'Well?' said Frost finally. 'What did you see, esper?'

'I'm not sure,' said Diana quietly. 'The ship is so alien I can't be sure of anything.'

'Did you detect any life signs within the ship?'

'Just one.' Diana looked at the Investigator for the first time. 'I think it's the ship itself. And it's dying.'

Frost looked at the unhappy esper for a moment, and then nodded and turned away. She studied the vast wreck towering over her, and walked slowly along beside it. Diana hurried after her, not wanting to be left alone, even for a moment.

Up on the rise, Stasiak looked at Ripper. 'Do you get the feeling we're ever so slightly superfluous here?'

Ripper shrugged. 'There's always the chance those ghosts will show up to annoy us again.'

'Oh great. What are we supposed to do; exorcise them? I'm getting really fed up with this mission, Rip. Nothing to hit, nothing to shoot at, and I think my suit's heating elements are on the blink again.'

'Look on the bright side,' said Ripper. 'At least it's not raining.'

Stasiak just stared at him.

Frost stood before the huge alien ship, and let her hand rest on the butt of her gun. If she didn't find an entrance soon, she'd make one the hard way. She didn't like resorting to brute force so early in an investigation, but this whole mission had been a debacle right from the beginning. Standard procedure with any new species was to study the situation from a safe distance, and only make contact when you were sure you held the upper hand. But here she was, thrown in the deep end and sinking fast, with the Captain off on his own somewhere looking for ghosts, and no back-up from the main ship if things looked like getting out of hand. Frost sighed, and shook her head. Some days you just shouldn't get out of bed in the morning.

She scowled at the ship, and gently reached out to touch the dully gleaming metal with her fingertips. It was surprisingly warm, with an unpleasant oily feel.

'Investigator!'

Frost looked away from the hull, absently rubbing her fingers together. 'What is it, esper?'

'I've found something. It could be a hatchway.'

Frost looked back and winced inwardly as she saw the esper had climbed on to a metal turret, and was squatting precariously before a shadowy niche. Frost pondered briefly if there was any point in raising the subject of security systems and booby traps, and decided not to waste her breath. With the esper's luck they'd probably just malfunction anyway. She climbed carefully up to join Diana, her hands and feet slipping on the slick metal, and looked at what the esper had found. Tucked away behind a metal outcropping was a dark gap, some ten feet tall and three feet wide.

'It's not an air lock,' said the esper excitedly. 'But the shape's too regular for it to be crash damage. Do we go in?'

Frost frowned. 'Normally, I'd say no. We don't know enough about the ship to tell what's dangerous and what isn't. But, since we're pressed for time and we need answers now, yes, esper; we are going in. Or rather, I'm going in and you're coming along to watch my back. Stay close, but don't get in my way. Odin; this is Investigator Frost. Respond.'

They waited for a moment but there was no reply, not even static from their comm implants. Frost gestured for Diana to try her comm unit, but she did no better.

'Damn,' said Frost dispassionately. 'Something in the ship must be interfering with our transmissions. This mission just gets better all the time. Follow me, esper.'

Frost drew her disrupter and stepped cautiously through the opening. Diana followed her in, practically treading on the Investigator's heels. Beyond the opening lay a narrow tunnel choked with thick strands of filmy webbing, some of which was already falling apart in shreds and tatters. The ceiling was too low for the esper and the Investigator to walk upright, and they were forced to proceed in a hunched, awkward shuffle. A flickering blue light emanated from the corridor walls, hiding as much in shadows as it revealed. The air was definitely warmer inside the ship, and Diana wrinkled her nose at the growing sickly sweet smell. It reminded her of something, but she couldn't place it. She tried instead to concentrate on what the corridor was telling her about the ship's inhabitants. To start with, they were definitely shorter than humans, probably about four feet or less in height. The blue lights suggested eyes that functioned in roughly the same range as a human's, and the warmer air suggested a need for temperature controls. Beyond that, Diana was pretty much out of her depth, and she knew it.

Frost holstered her gun, drew her sword and began methodically cutting a path through the decaying webbing. The strands gave way easily enough, but there was little room to swing the great sword in the confines of the corridor, and the Investigator's progress was slowed by a need to stop every now and again to clean away threads clinging stubbornly to the blade. The light grew steadily brighter as they slowly made their way deeper into the ship, but the flickering grew worse, if anything. Diana shrugged mentally. Maybe the light was supposed to flicker.

The smell was stronger. The uneven floor rose and fell like a tide, and the walls bowed in and out for no reason Diana could see. Faint silver traces shone along one wall, though whether they were functional or merely decorative was unclear. Certainly the patterns followed no human sense of logic or aesthetics. Openings appeared in the walls, leading off into other corridors, some of which were unlit. Diana began to be a little nervous about how far they'd come, and glanced back over her shoulder. The tunnel stretched away into the blue-lit distance, with no sign of the entrance they'd used. Diana decided she wasn't going to think about that. No doubt Frost knew the way out, and that was all that mattered. In the meantime, there were just too many interesting things to get excited about.

'Isn't this amazing?' she said breathlessly to the Investigator as she paused yet again to clean her sword.

Frost smiled slightly, but didn't answer. The esper might be wide-eyed with the wonder of it all, but Frost knew better than to let herself get distracted. There'd be time for sightseeing later, when the ship had been thoroughly explored and tested for booby traps, intentional and otherwise. She pressed on cautiously, carefully checking each side passage before they passed it. The ship was eerily quiet, the hush seeming almost to absorb each new sound as it was made. And there was a growing feeling on the air, something clinging, like static. Frost suddenly realized the esper wasn't treading on her heels any more, and she looked back down the corridor. Diana had come to a halt some way back, and was staring intently at the ceiling above her. Frost padded quietly back to join her.

'What is it, esper? What have you found?'

'I'm not sure,' said Diana slowly. 'Look at this.'

She gestured at part of the ceiling. It was blue and purple and swollen, like a bruise. Frost tested it with the tip of her sword, and the material gave easily under the pressure.

'I finally recognized the smell,' said Diana. 'It's a lot clearer just here.'

Frost looked at her dubiously and took a deep breath, flaring her nostrils. Together with the look of the ceiling, the sickly sweet smell was immediately familiar. 'Decay,' said Frost. 'Rotting meat.'

'Yes,' said Diana. 'Decomposition of what was once living tissue. Parts of the ship have been dead long enough to rot.'

Frost hefted her sword, took a firm grip with both hands, and cut savagely at the discoloured patch on the ceiling. The blade sank in deep, the bruised-looking material splitting open like a wound. Frost jerked her sword back out, and tangled silver threads fell down into the corridor, wrapped around pink ropes of intestines, studded with faceted crystals. Diana fell back a step, a look of almost comical surprise on her face. Frost touched a cautious finger to the hanging threads, and they fell apart into a gooey slime that spattered on the floor. Frost studied it for a moment, and then wiped her fingers clean on her leggings. She couldn't perform a proper analysis without her equipment, and most of that was stuck back on the *Darkwind*. She blinked in surprise as the esper fell suddenly to her knees beside the slime on the floor, and gently parted it with her fingers. Frost knelt down beside her, and Diana fished a small faceted crystal out of the goo, and held it up before her eyes.

'What is it?' said Frost.

'It's a memory crystal,' said Diana. 'Pretty much like the ones we use in our computers. Only here the patterns are so strongly impressed I can practically read them with my mind. I could be wrong, but I think this is part of this ship's log.' She got to her feet along with the Investigator, still holding the crystal up before her eyes. 'The other crystals are either dead or damaged; I'm not getting anything from them. But this one . . . this crystal is important. I can feel it.'

Frost nodded slowly, swinging her sword thoughtfully back and forth before her. 'Take it back to the pinnace, and let Odin have a crack at it. I want a complete analysis, and access to the crystal's memories, and I want it an hour ago. So you'd better hurry.'

Diana looked at her blankly. 'You mean we're leaving? But we've barely scratched the surface here!'

'You're leaving. I'm staying. I think we can be fairly sure there aren't any living crew left on board, or you'd have sensed them by now. So the only answers we're likely to get are from that crystal. Take the marines back with you; the crystal needs their protection more than I do. Well don't just stand there, esper; what are you waiting for?'

'I can't find my way back out on my own,' said Diana in a small voice. 'Can you come back with me to show me the way?'

Stasiak looked at Ripper, and then back at Diana. 'Leave her here? Are you sure?'

'That's what she said,' said Diana. 'Do you want to argue with her?'

'Not really, no,' said Ripper.

'I don't know, Rip,' said Stasiak. 'Anything could happen in there.'

'Anyone else and I might be worried,' said Ripper. 'But we are talking about an Investigator, after all. Anything that runs into her has my deepest sympathies. Besides, do you really want to look her in the eye later and tell her you ignored a direct order?'

'Not particularly, no.' Stasiak looked down the slope at the ship below. 'What's it like in there, Diana?'

'Fascinating!' Now that she was out of the ship and back in the open again, Diana lost her nervousness and found herself

273

bubbling with excitement, almost ready to rush back into the ship and explore it again. Almost. 'I've never seen anything like it; the whole structure's a combination of organic and inorganic materials, lying side by side and functioning together.'

'You mean, like a cyborg?' said Stasiak, peering uncertainly at the huge shape below them.

'I suppose so, yes, but on a much vaster scale. The entire thing's alive, or at least it used to be. I'd love to spend more time with it, but the Investigator was most insistent we get this memory crystal back to the pinnace. Typical. The moment you find anything interesting, the Empire immediately finds a way to take it away from you.'

Stasiak smiled. 'If you can't take a joke, you shouldn't have joined.'

'I wasn't exactly given a choice,' said Diana. 'Espers do what they're told.'

And then the wry smile vanished from her face as she looked past Stasiak. The two marines spun round to discover what she was looking at, and their hands fell to their guns. Among the violet and azure trees at the edge of the forest, a man dressed all in black was walking unhurriedly out of the mists. His face was hidden by his cape's cowl, but they all knew who he was, who he had to be. He walked past them without sparing any of them a glance, and started down the slope towards the alien ship. Diana shuddered despite herself as he passed, and had to fight down a sudden urge to reach out and touch him, to make sure he was real, even though the sensors said he wasn't. Instead, she watched silently with the marines as the man in black came to a halt before the ship, and looked at it thoughtfully, leaning elegantly on his ivory staff.

'Is that him?' said Diana softly. 'I thought he'd be taller.'

'Not very impressive,' said Ripper. 'But then, legends rarely are, in the flesh.'

'Carrion,' said Stasiak, his voice low and harsh. 'The man who lived with the Ashrai. The traitor who turned against humanity, for the sake of savages who still ate their meat raw. I've done some things in my time, and been ashamed of some of them, but I never betrayed my own species. Never.'

'Take it easy, Lou,' said Ripper. 'We don't know the whole story.'

'We don't need to.'

'Why does the Captain think he's so important?' said Diana. 'I mean, all right, he can fool the pinnace's sensors, but he's just another outlaw. Isn't he?'

'Carrion's a killer,' said Captain Silence. 'And he's very good at it.'

The esper and the two marines spun round again, to see Silence standing at the edge of the forest behind them, leaning against a tree trunk for support.

'Captain!' said Diana, blushing in spite of herself. 'I didn't hear you approach . . .'

'Obviously,' said Silence. 'Security on this mission is going to hell.' He broke off, grimacing as pain from his injured ribs hit him. Diana took in his torn and blood-stained uniform and started towards him, but he stopped her with an upraised hand. 'I'm all right. I just ran into a little opposition from the local ghosts. Carrion rescued me. And no, I don't want to talk about it. Odin told me about the Investigator's discovery, after he'd finished filling me in on all the security lapses first, of course, and I brought Carrion along to take a look at it. How long have you been here?'

'Not long,' said Diana. 'The Investigator and I made a brief foray into the ship, but there's no sign of any crew. We did find what appears to be an alien memory crystal. The Investigator decided it should go back to the pinnace for analysis. She's still inside the ship.'

'I thought she might be,' said Silence. 'Carrion's going to join her. Between them, they should come up with some answers.'

'Pardon me for asking, Captain,' said Stasiak, 'but what makes the traitor so important?'

'Carrion used to be an Investigator,' said Silence. 'One of the best. Trained to out-think species that don't think as we do.'

'If he was that good,' said Ripper, 'what went wrong? How did he end up siding with the Ashrai?'

Silence smiled humourlessly. 'Perhaps we trained him too well.'

He looked down at the alien ship below, and the others

followed his gaze. Carrion had climbed on to the ship, and was examining the entrance Diana had found. His black cloak hung about him like folded wings, and he looked more than ever like a carrion crow, feasting on a dead carcass.

'What's that staff he's carrying?' said Stasiak.

'A power lance,' said Silence.

'But they're outlawed!'

Silence smiled briefly. 'So's he.'

Carrion threaded his way through the twisting, intertwining corridors of the alien ship, following the ragged path Frost had cut through the webbing. It led him eventually to a vast circular chamber deep in the heart of the ship, a great metal cavern studded with bulky, enigmatic machinery on all sides. The curving walls were pockmarked with tunnel mouths of various sizes, many high above the floor with no obvious way of reaching them. Thick strands of rotting gossamer hung from the ceiling, interspersed with long crystalline creepers that gleamed and sparkled in the unsteady light as they turned slowly back and forth. The flickering light came from deep in the tunnels, casting strange elongated shadows on the floor and ceiling. The air was hot and humid and thick with the stench of rotting meat. Frost stepped out of the shadows and into the light, and Carrion nodded to her courteously.

'I know you,' said Frost.

'No,' said Carrion. 'That was someone else. I am Carrion. I bring bad luck. I am the destroyer of nations and of worlds.'

Frost raised an eyebrow. 'Really?'

'The Ashrai believed it.'

They studied each other for a while in the uncertain light, and whatever they recognized in each other's faces they kept to themselves.

'I'm surprised you remember me,' said Carrion finally. 'It's been a long time.'

'All Investigators remember you,' said Frost. 'The Academy still holds you up as a bad example. You broke the prime rule; you got involved.'

'I broke my conditioning,' said Carrion. 'But then, I was always involved, with one species or another. When you've spent

276

half your life learning to move your mind in alien ways, it becomes hard to think in wholly human terms any more.'

Frost shrugged. 'Empathy's a useful tool, but that's all. Aliens are for killing. I've found something interesting. Come and take a look.'

She led him into a small compartment off the main chamber, through an opening so low they had to crawl through on hands and knees. The compartment was filled with spiky machinery that flowed seamlessly into the walls and floor. The ceiling was just high enough to let them stand upright, and suffused everything with a dull red glow that was disturbingly organic. The floor was uneven, solid ridges rising like bones to press against their boots in undulating rhythms. Everywhere, high-tech instruments blended into organic constructs, living and unliving components functioning side by side, as though the ship had been grown as much as made.

'This appears to be the control centre,' said Frost. 'Or one of them, anyway. I've traced a whole series of power lines that converge here, but I can't be sure until I can get some of my equipment down from the *Darkwind*.'

'Have you identified the main power source?'

Frost shook her head angrily. 'I can't even find the hyperdrive. By any reasonable standards this thing shouldn't even fly, let alone jump across the stars.'

Carrion nodded, his eyes vague and far away. 'Perhaps I can find the drive for you.'

A breeze from nowhere ruffled his cloak, and Frost's hackles rose as strange lights glowed suddenly in the instruments around them. There was a feeling of pressure on the air, of something unstoppable. A hatch shot open in the wall beside her, and slammed shut again like metal jaws. Instruments extended and reshaped themselves in subtle ways, and far off in the distance Frost thought she could hear something howling in anger and agony, as though the decaying ship had been somehow stirred to horrid life again. Carrion was smiling, and it was not a pleasant smile, his dark eyes fixed on something only he could see. Frost's hand drifted casually closer to the holstered gun at her side. At that moment, the outlaw seemed every bit as alien and as dangerous as the ship they were investigating. A loud juddering sound vibrated through the floor, rattling their teeth and shaking their heads, and then the floor opened up in the centre and a great tower of steel and diamond rose up into the chamber, shining so brightly they had to turn their heads away. Deep in the tunnels the howling died away, and a sudden silence filled the chamber as the alien machinery grew still. Carrion and Frost slowly turned back to look at the tower, shielding their eyes with their arms.

'I didn't know you were a polter,' said Frost.

'I would have thought it'd be in my file.'

'Your file's *Restricted*.'

'It would be,' said Carrion.

They peered more closely at the structure before them, as their eyes adjusted to the glare. The tower was an intricate latticework of metals, complex and mysterious, surrounding a brilliant cluster of glowing crystals. There was meaning and purpose in its structure, but none of it human.

'What is it?' whispered Frost, impressed despite herself.

Carrion smiled slowly. 'Judging by the remaining power flow, this is the ship's hyperdrive. Even if it does look nothing like ours. The Empire uses crystal technology in its computers; apparently these aliens found other uses for it.'

CHAPTER SIX

Inside Base Thirteen

The esper Diana Vertue sat slumped in her seat in the pinnace, and wondered why she still didn't feel safe. It had come on her suddenly, as they were walking back through the metallic forest to the landing field. Without any specific cause that she could name, Diana had suddenly been convinced that they were being watched, by something huge and awful and dangerous. Her stomach lurched. She managed to keep from crying out, but the feeling of imminent danger persisted, even though she couldn't see or hear anything to justify it. Nothing moved in the mists among the trees, and the only sounds were the quiet voices and footsteps of the people with her. Diana raised her esp and threw it out, scanning for anything near or approaching the group. Nothing had changed. The trees blazed in her mind like exclamation points of light, but there was no trace of any other living thing in the forest. She cast her net wider, till her mind fell over Base Thirteen, and she saw something looking back at her.

It was huge and dark, filling the Base, and it looked at her with hungry eyes. There were voices screaming in the background, human voices, full of anguish and horror. There was a blood-red feeling of menace, of danger close and deadly, and then it was all gone, as suddenly as if she'd imagined it. She focused her esp on the Base, but there was nothing there now. If there ever had been.

She hadn't told the others what she'd sensed. She had no proof, and it had all happened so fast she wasn't sure she trusted it herself. It had the hot, hazy feeling of a fever dream, its very vagueness part of what was so horrifying. So she stayed silent, all the way back to the pinnace, and once she was aboard she curled up in her seat like a dog in its box, and tried to put it out of her mind. Only that was somehow worse, so she instructed the AI to patch in an exterior view through her comm implant. The steel bulkheads seemed to become transparent as the computer broadcast a real-time view of what its sensors were picking up. There was nothing but the landing pads and the trees and the swirling mists, the two marines standing guard, and the Base, waiting inside its impenetrable Screen. She should have felt safe and secure, protected by the pinnace and its weaponry, but somehow she only felt more visible, more vulnerable. The pinnace was the only ship on the pads, seeming a small and obvious target against the size of the landing field and the endless forest that surrounded it. She kept a careful watch in every direction, unable to settle but unwilling to raise her esp again for fear of drawing the watcher's attention back to her.

The more she put off telling anyone, the more it seemed to her nothing but an attack of nerves, a product of her own fear and insecurity. She tried to recapture some of the enthusiasm she'd felt about contacting the new alien species from the crashed ship, and that helped her push back the fear a little. It was just nerves, exacerbated by the waiting and the tension. She'd be all right, when the time finally came to enter the Base. But in the meantime she kept her eyes open and her mind damped right down, just in case.

The marines had felt something of it too. They'd been jumpy all the way back to the pinnace, and had seemed almost relieved when Silence ordered them to stand guard outside the ship. Silence, on the other hand, seemed strangely calm and relaxed, despite the beating he'd taken on his way to meet Carrion. He still wouldn't talk about that. He sat stoically as the ship's med unit stuck him with half a dozen needles, and then adjusted his uniform so that it provided more support for his ribs. And now he sat comfortably in his seat, half reclining, talking calmly with the AI about the memory crystal Diana had found in the alien ship. Odin had swallowed the crystal some time back, but apparently was having to create a whole new series of diagnostics just to access the damned thing. Diana smiled briefly. If she'd known it was going to be this much trouble, she'd have used her esp on the crystal and accessed the memories directly. Only that would have meant raising her esp again, and she wasn't ready to do that, not just yet.

Silence scowled at the comm panels before him. Given time, the AI could make the crystal do everything but sit up and beg, but they didn't have that much time. The Empire wanted the mining machinery working again, and it wanted it now. If he couldn't deliver, they'd send someone else to replace him. And that really would be the end of his career. Silence sighed slowly, careful of his ribs. The alien ship held the answer to what had happened in Base Thirteen, he was sure of it. One or more of the aliens had entered the Base, there'd been a conflict of some kind, and the Screen had gone up. Simple as that. But just in case it wasn't, he wanted the information in the alien memory crystal before he tried to break into the Base. Going into a potentially dangerous situation without a thorough briefing beforehand was never wise, and that went doubly here. With ghosts on the one hand and strange new aliens on the other, this had all the makings of a really messy disaster.

'Captain,' said a quiet voice behind him, 'I need to talk to you.'

'Not just now, esper, I'm busy.'

'You're supposed to be resting.'

'I'll rest later, when I've got time. I'm just waiting for Carrion and Frost to return, and then we're going into Base Thirteen to scare up some answers.'

'Captain . . . if there are aliens inside the Base, we shouldn't be going in aggressively, looking for trouble. We should at least try to make contact with them. They could be peaceful. This could all be the result of some ghastly mistake or mis-understanding.'

Silence turned round in his seat and looked patiently at the young esper. 'This is all new to you, Diana, but the Empire has a set procedure when it comes to handling first contacts. And the first and main part of that procedure is that the Investigator will decide how we handle it. She's the expert.'

'An expert at killing.'

'Yes. The Empire doesn't like the idea of competition, so its attitude to aliens is really quite straightforward. They're either friendly, in which case they become part of the Empire, whether

281

they want to or not, or they're unfriendly, in which case they get stepped on. Hard.'

'Like the Ashrai?' said Diana.

'Yes, esper. Like the Ashrai. I knew where my responsibilities lay, even then. Look, if I can see a way to sort this out without bloodshed, I'll take it. I don't believe in putting my people at risk unnecessarily. But I can't be optimistic about this. The most likely scenario is that one or more of the aliens have entered the Base and killed all the personnel.'

'You can't know that.'

'That's right, I can't. But that's how I have to play it. If whatever is in there is willing to talk, I'll listen, but they've made no move to contact us so far. Have you been able to pick up anything?'

'Just . . . impressions. Nothing I can be sure of. My own fears could be misinterpreting the little I am getting. Couldn't we at least wait till the AI's cracked the memory crystal? It could hold all the answers we need.'

'Esper, I don't even know if Odin can access it at all. We're dealing with an unknown technology here. The AI's good, but he can't work miracles. And I am running out of time and patience. I'll wait for Carrion and Frost to get back here, but then we have to go, ready or not.'

The esper's jaw muscles worked for a moment, but when she spoke her voice was calm and measured. 'I'd like to try something, Captain. I want permission to go into the Base on my own, once you've got us through the Screen, and attempt to make contact with my esp. They might not see one person as a threat.'

'My orders are quite specific,' said Silence. 'I'm to discover what happened inside Base Thirteen, and take whatever action is necessary to re-establish the Base and restore mining operations. Everything else is of secondary importance. There were one hundred and twenty-seven men and women in that Base. We've heard nothing from them since the Screen went up. The odds are, they're all dead. If they are, then whatever killed them has to die. The Empire can't afford to be seen to be weak.'

'Please, Captain. Listen to me.' Diana hesitated, torn between her need to explain what she was feeling, and the knowledge that she couldn't prove any of it. 'There's more to this than whatever came out of the crashed ship. I've felt things, on my way down in the pinnace, and later on ... there's something incredibly powerful on this planet, Captain, and I don't think it's the aliens.'

'You're right,' said Silence. 'It's the Ashrai.'

Diana chose her words carefully. 'But they're all dead, Captain. You saw to that.'

'They may be dead,' said Silence, 'but they sleep lightly.'

'I could still use my esp to contact the aliens,' said Diana doggedly.

'No,' said Silence. 'The situation's complicated enough as it is.'

'So you'll leave it to the Investigator? The killer?'

'You say that as though it's an insult. She'd see it as a compliment. Investigators are the end result of the Empire's search for the perfect warrior. They started out working with the augmented men, the Wampyr and the Wolflings. That got out of hand with Haden, and the cyborg rebellion. So instead they created a breed of warrior that wasn't reliant on tech implants; a race of killers trained from childhood to be the best at everything. Strong, fast, intelligent, ruthless. And trained, most of all, to out-think things that don't think as we do. Frost is in charge of all alien contacts, and she will make whatever decisions are necessary. She's the expert. If you have anything further to say, take it up with her.'

'Would she listen, if I did?'

'I don't know. Maybe. She understands the value of an esper.'

'Perhaps I should talk to Carrion. He used to be an Investigator too, didn't he?'

'Yes,' said Silence. 'Yes, he did.'

Diana could feel his pain even with her shields up, and she had to look away for a moment. Through the transparent bulkhead she saw Carrion and Frost walk out of the mists and head towards the two marines, who apparently hadn't heard them coming, and were a bit upset about it. Silence followed her gaze, saw Carrion and looked away.

'You knew Carrion from before,' said Diana. 'What was he like, before he was a traitor?'

'He was my friend,' said Silence, and then he turned and left the cabin. Diana stood where she was, to give him a chance to get away, and then she followed him out.

Outside the pinnace, they all stood and looked at each other, as though waiting for someone else to start. Finally Silence nodded curtly to Carrion and Frost. They were standing close together, and they stood in the same pose and moved in the same ways, like brother and sister. As though they had more in common with each other than they could ever have with anyone else. Silence knew he'd have to keep an eye on that. He couldn't risk losing Frost the way he'd lost Carrion.

'Any trace of the alien crew?' he said eventually.

'None,' said Frost. 'And their ship's dead. It's an interesting ship. The technology's like nothing I've ever seen before.'

Silence looked at Carrion. 'Could the crew have fled into the forest?'

'No, Captain. I'd have known.'

'And that just leaves the Base,' said Ripper. 'Surprise, surprise.'

'Tell me about the ship's technology,' said Silence. 'You said something earlier about a new kind of hyperdrive.'

'There was extensive use of living tissue alongside mechanical,' said Frost. 'Essentially, the ship was one great cybernetic unit, incredibly complex. And if the hyperdrive is what we think it is, it's far beyond anything the Empire has.'

There was a tense pause, as though they all had something to say, but no one wanted to be the first to say it. There were certain things it was wise never to say aloud, particularly when an Empire AI was listening. Their loyalty was programmed into them, and they tended to have very strict ideas about what constituted treason, or a threat to the Empire's security. Silence looked thoughtfully at Carrion.

'The aliens must be inside the Base.'

'Agreed, Captain.'

'And you're going to get us through the Screen.'

'No, Captain.'

Silence looked at him, and tension all but crackled on the air between them. The two marines let their hands move slightly so that they were both covering the traitor with their guns.

'I can break through the Screen,' said Carrion, 'but you're in no condition to enter the Base.'

'I'd have to agree,' said Frost. 'A Captain has no business exposing himself to unnecessary risks. That's standard procedure.'

'There's nothing standard about this mission,' said Silence tightly. 'I'm in charge here, and I'll make whatever decisions have to be made. To do that I need to be there, on the spot, as and when conditions change. And I've a feeling they could change pretty damned fast once we get inside the Base. I'm fit enough, and that's all that matters. I'm sure the marines are more than capable of seeing that nothing happens to me.'

'Right,' growled Stasiak, looking pointedly at Carrion. The outlaw ignored him. He looked over at Base Thirteen, hidden behind its shimmering opalescent Screen, and if there was any expression in his face, none of them could read it.

'Let's go,' he said calmly. 'The sooner we begin, the sooner we'll be finished. And God have mercy on those who die here.'

He started off towards the Base and, after a moment, Silence and Frost followed him. The others brought up the rear. Stasiak looked at Ripper.

'Cheerful bastard, isn't he?'

'What did you expect?' said Ripper. 'He used to be an Investigator.'

They stood together before Base Thirteen, and the glowing pearly Screen stared back at them, mute and enigmatic. Silence studied it sourly. It was as though the Screen was mocking him. Anything could be happening behind that impenetrable field of energy. Anything at all. Anyone else would have had to suffer its smug indifference, but he had an ace up his sleeve. He had Carrion. Silence looked at the outlaw. He was still standing beside Frost, so close their shoulders touched. They looked as though they should always be together, connected by a shared past and secrets too terrible to share with anyone else. Silence felt oddly jealous. Carrion used to be his friend. But that was years ago, when they were different people, and Silence was honest enough to admit that he would only have felt uncomfortable if Carrion had chosen to stand with him.

The marines were standing off a little to one side, their guns in their hands, keeping an unobtrusive eye on Carrion. To their way of thinking, he was the biggest threat to the party at present, so they'd watch him till something better came along. Marines were great ones for sticking to the problem at hand, and letting officers worry about the future. The esper was ignoring them all and scowling at the Screen, as though she could force her esp past it to see what lay beyond. Unfortunately, she wasn't that powerful. That was why Silence needed Carrion.

He looked at the outlaw, and sighed quietly to himself. He couldn't put it off any longer. It was time for the moment of truth, and let the chips fall where they may. He activated his comm implant.

'Odin; you are now in control of the pinnace. You will follow our entry into the Base through our eyes, and keep a complete record of all that occurs. If we fail in our mission, and none of us survive, you will make every effort to return to the *Darkwind*, and see that the record is made available to our successors. Acknowledge.'

'Acknowledged, Captain. Good luck.'

Silence looked at Carrion. 'It's time. Do your stuff.'

The outlaw nodded, his gaze fixed on the Screen. He stepped forward and reached out a hand to touch the energy field. Fat sparks of static sputtered on the air, but there was no other response. Which was interesting. It should have killed him stone dead. It would have killed anyone else. Carrion pressed hard against the Screen, but it didn't give. He smiled slightly, as though he'd expected that, and stepped back. He lifted his power lance and pressed the end of it against the energy field. A faint corona circled the end of the staff where it touched the Screen. Carrion increased the pressure, and the Screen gave way before it. Carrion took hold of the staff with both hands, and walked slowly forward into the energy field. The force field whorled and rippled around him, bands of iridescent light breaking over him in waves. He stood deep in the field, and the Screen that could ward off disrupters and withstand atomics drew reluctantly back from the outlaw's presence. An opening grew around him, through which the dark, squat shape of Base Thirteen could be seen. Carrion looked back at the others, and there was something not entirely human in his eyes.

'Now,' said Carrion, and they all stepped forward as though he had them on a leash. Silence kept his head up, but his skin crawled in anticipation of the lethal energies running through the force Screen, held back only by the power of one man's mind. By someone perhaps no longer entirely human. Finally they were all through, and Carrion remained in the field. He looked unhurriedly about him, colours waterfalling down around him in vivid shades that burned the eye. And then he stepped forward, and the energy field closed behind him as though it had never opened. No one could get out, and no one could get in to help, without Carrion's assistance. They were trapped with whatever lay inside Base Thirteen, and the force Screen covered them all.

'How did you do that?' said Diana, something that might have been awe softening her voice.

'His power lance,' said Frost, when it became clear the outlaw wasn't going to answer. 'It amplifies and channels his psychokinesis. You can guess why the Empire banned them. But even so, even with a power lance, what he just did is supposed to be impossible. His esper abilities must be right off the scale. I'm surprised the Empire ever let him run around loose.'

'Before he came to Unseeli,' said Silence, 'he showed no sign of any esp at all. His time with the Ashrai changed that.'

'That's impossible,' said Frost flatly. 'Everyone's tested for psi; no one escapes.'

'Nothing's impossible, for the Ashrai,' said Carrion.

'Your attention, please,' said Odin, its voice murmuring through everyone's implants. 'Captain; I've finally been able to glean something useful from the Base's computers' records. I've managed to isolate the Base Commander's personal log. I really think you should view what I've found, before you proceed any further.'

'All right,' said Silence. 'Since nothing nasty has come running out of the Base to attack us, I think we can safely wait a few more moments before we go in. Marines; stand guard. If anything moves, shoot it. Odin; run the relevant parts of the log for everyone except the marines, then run it for them. How much is there?'

'Not much, Captain. I've selected what appear to be the important moments.'

A brief burst of static filled Silence's eyes as the AI ran the log through its comm implant. The static cleared to show the Base Commander, sitting at his desk. Silence frowned. He knew the man. James Starblood had been at the Fleet Academy in the same year as him. Old family. Not much money, but well connected. They'd known each other well for a short time, but had never really been friends. Starblood had been a hard-working, efficient officer, and about as imaginative as a stone. Which probably explained what he was doing in a post like this. Unseeli was not a posting for the upwardly mobile. Silence's frown deepened. The Commander looked haggard and confused, and when Starblood finally spoke, his voice was rough and unsteady.

'To whoever finds this log; this is an Alpha Red emergency. An alien ship has crashlanded nearby. It doesn't answer any of our attempts to make contact. I sent a team to investigate the crash site. They never came back. That was three hours ago. Now people are disappearing inside the Base. Something's affecting the computers. Whole sectors don't answer. The life-support systems are breaking down. The lights are going out. It's getting cold. There's something in here with us but we can't find it.'

The scene changed. Starblood was sitting slumped in his chair. He was sweating, and his uniform was dishevelled. He passed a shaking hand across his mouth, and tried visibly to pull himself together. 'I can't raise anyone in the Base, and something's happened to our main comm system. I can't contact the Empire, or even broadcast a warning. My personal log seems secure, for the moment. I've locked myself in my quarters and barricaded the door. I can hear something moving in the corridor outside. It doesn't sound human. I'm trapped in here. Base Thirteen is lost to the Empire. There's only one option left to me; raising the Screen.'

He reached out of view for a moment, and then looked up again, his eyes seeming to pierce Silence. There was despair in the man's face, but something else too. Something that might have been dignity. 'The force Screen is now activated. Whatever's in here is trapped inside the Base. I can't risk letting it escape. The Empire must know of this new threat. The Screen can only be lowered from inside now, using my personal code. I know my duty.' He drew a disrupter from the holster on his hip, and clumsily checked the power level. 'Haven't had to use one of these things in years,' he grumbled quietly, and then turned the gun on himself, centring it carefully over his heart. He looked up one last time.

'Whoever finds this message; avenge us. Protect the Empire. I am James Starblood, Commander of Base Thirteen.'

Silence's vision cleared to show the world again. He wished he'd liked the man more.

'That's all there is, Captain,' said Odin quietly.

'A hundred and twenty-seven people,' said Diana. 'All dead.'

'You didn't really expect anything else, did you?' said Frost. Diana shrugged, and looked away. There was a pause as the marines watched the message.

'Well, that was interesting,' said Stasiak brightly. 'We're facing something powerful enough to wipe out a whole Base, and all we've got are a few hand guns and an outlaw esper. Why don't we all just shoot ourselves now, and get it over with?'

'He's got a point,' said Ripper.

'Shut up,' said Frost calmly, and the two marines were immediately quiet. 'You've nothing to worry about. You've got me.' She looked at Silence. 'You're in charge, Captain. What do we do?'

'We go in,' said Silence. 'And we do whatever's necessary.'

He walked towards the open front doors, with Carrion and Frost following close behind. The esper hurried to catch up. The marines shared a meaningful glance, and reluctantly brought up the rear. The Base itself looked calm and deserted. No lights were showing anywhere. The front doors were standing just a little ajar. Silence stopped before them and studied the steel doors carefully. There was a thick layering of hoarfrost on the metal, and the doors hung limply from their supports. Carrion reached out and pushed one door, and it moved uneasily under his touch, all power gone. He pushed it all the way open, and he and Silence stepped forward into the gloom of the Lobby.

Unseeli's cold had entered the Base, giving the stale air a cutting edge. None of the lights were working, and as far as Silence could see the Lobby was entirely deserted. Carrion and Frost moved quickly in to stand on either side of him, eyes searching the shadows for an ambush. All was still and quiet; the only sound their own breathing. Frost sniffed suspiciously, her gun in her hand as though it belonged there. Carrion leaned elegantly on his power lance, apparently happy for Silence to take the initiative. The esper darted through the front doors with the marines close behind. Silence gestured for the two marines to spread out, and they did so quickly and professionally. The esper looked round the empty Lobby and hugged herself, possibly from the cold.

The Reception desk was unmanned, its Security monitor screens blank. Papers lay scattered across the desk, covered with a thin layer of frost. Silence gestured for the two marines to check the desk, and they moved forward, guns at the ready. Investigator Frost looked unhurriedly about her, trying to get the feel of the place. There was no sign of any panic or fight. Everything was still in its place, just as it had been left. At the desk, Stasiak studied the scattered papers without touching them. They were all routine, everyday stuff, and Stasiak thought there was something sad in that. The people who worked here had got no warning, no chance to prepare themselves. They probably thought it was just another day, until the boom fell, and the lights started going out. He looked at Ripper, who was trying to get the Security monitors back on line, with no success. He straightened up with a sigh, looked at Silence, and shook his head.

'Not a thing, Captain. There's power in the system somewhere, but it's not reaching Reception. I think it's being diverted somewhere else, but don't ask me where.'

'Not a damn thing to go on,' said Stasiak. 'It's as though everyone just . . . got up and left. Spooky.'

'Look around, see if you can turn up some lamps or torches,' said Silence. 'We're not going to get far without some light.

Investigator; try the comm net. Maybe we can raise someone, now that we're actually inside the Base.'

Frost nodded, and activated her comm implant. 'This is Investigator Frost, of the *Darkwind*. Please respond.'

They all listened, but there was only the low hum of an open channel.

'Can anybody hear me? This is Investigator Frost. I speak for the Empire. Respond, please.'

She frowned suddenly as a voice murmured in her ear, so soft and faint the words were indistinguishable. Frost looked quickly at the others, but though they'd all heard it too, none of them could make it out either. Frost boosted the volume as high as it would go, but the voice had stopped.

'I hear you,' she said clearly. 'Please say again. Where are you? Do you require assistance?'

There was no reply. Frost turned the volume back down, looked at Silence and shook her head. He turned to Diana.

'Run a full scan, esper. If there's anything alive and thinking in this place, I want to know what and where it is.'

Diana turned away so he couldn't see her face. She'd been waiting for him to ask, and wondering what she would do when he did. All her training, all her conditioning, made it impossible for her to disobey a direct order, but she still remembered the horror she'd encountered the last time she'd raised her esp. She remembered the screaming voices, human voices, and the terrible presence that had looked back at her with knowing, hungry eyes. In all her years, she'd never seen anything that scared her more. And now Silence wanted her to open her mind to it. She couldn't. She just couldn't. But she couldn't refuse, either. She closed her eyes and opened her esp just a fraction, like a child peering warily between raised fingers. Everything was still and quiet. She probed a little further, letting her mind drift cautiously out across the ground floor, but there was nothing there. She sighed inwardly with relief, and looked at Silence again.

'No trace of life anywhere, Captain. There's always the chance that something's blocking my esp, but if there is, I can't detect it.'

She waited breathlessly while he considered her answer, expecting him any moment to glare at her coldly as he saw through her half-truth, but he just nodded and turned away, and she didn't know whether to feel relieved or ashamed.

Silence frowned thoughtfully. 'Odin; give me the floor plans for Base Thirteen, on an overlay. One floor at a time, starting with the ground floor. And patch the others in too.'

A schematic appeared before him, superimposed on his vision. It seemed fairly straightforward. Only the one entrance to the ground floor, and one elevator and two sets of stairs leading down to the next floors. All Bases were built downwards into the earth, for greater security. Everything important was on the bottom floor, Level Three, protected by thick concrete and other, less obvious, measures. Silence studied the layout for each floor, checking particularly for entrances and exits, and then had Odin dismiss the overlay.

'All right, people; pay attention. It looks like we're going to have to do this the hard way. I'm splitting us into two groups, so we can cover more ground. Carrion, Frost; you stay with me. We'll search this floor. Esper; you and the two marines start checking out the next floor down. Take your time and check every room thoroughly before you go on to the next. Don't take any chances, and yell for help if you spot anything that looks even remotely threatening. I want information, not dead heroes. And whatever happens; no one is to go off on their own. Understood?' There was a general murmur of assent and nodding of heads. 'All right then, people; let's make a start. By the book and by the numbers.'

The marines sketched a quick salute, turned on one of the emergency lamps Ripper had found tucked away behind the Reception desk, and set off towards the rear stairwell marked on the floor plan. Diana hurried after them, not liking the idea of investigating the next floor down, but liking the idea of being left behind and alone even less.

Frost turned on her lamp. The light was bright and cheerful, though it raised uneasy shadows at the corner of everyone's eyes. Frost offered the lamp to Carrion, but he shook his head courteously. Silence took it from her, and led the two of them off into the gloom of the ground floor.

Corridor by corridor, room by room, they progressed slowly but everywhere was quiet and deserted, with no sign of any struggle or disturbance. Computer panels were unlit, monitor screens were dark, but there was still evidence of the people who'd lived and worked in Base Thirteen. An open message pad, a half-completed form, a cup almost full of coffee. Silence picked up the cup. There was a thick layer of frozen scum on the surface of the coffee. He put it down almost angrily. Still no signs of trouble, or even surprise. Whatever happened, it must have been quick. The thought was not comforting. Base Thirteen should have been crawling with Security personnel and back-up emergency systems, even if Unseeli was supposed to be a dead world. The Empire didn't believe in taking chances. But somehow the aliens had got into the Base, taken over its systems and dealt with its personnel, all without being detected or challenged. Which was supposed to be impossible.

'Interesting,' said Carrion.

'What?' said Frost, looking quickly about her.

'Your gun,' said Carrion. 'I hadn't looked at it before. I don't recognize it.'

Frost shrugged. 'Standard disrupter. I suppose the style's changed a lot in the past ten years. This version is far superior to the old model.'

'Really. What's the recharge time?'

'Got it down to three minutes now.'

Carrion raised an eyebrow. 'That is an improvement, I see you still carry a sword.'

'Of course.' Frost grinned. 'A sword never needs recharging.'

'Your attention, please,' said Odin suddenly through their comm implants. 'I have discovered something important, Captain. Apparently Commander Starblood had been concerned about possible intruders in the Base even before the alien ship crashed. There are several references in his log to sightings of "ghosts", or some kind of presence, by Base personnel. These sightings were so frequent and so worrying that Commander Starblood became quite disturbed by them. So disturbed he ordered six Security Guardians. There's a record of their delivery, two weeks before the alien ship's arrival.'

Silence scowled. 'Six Guardians? How the hell did the aliens get past them?'

'What exactly are Guardians?' said Carrion.

'After your time,' said Frost. 'They're state-of-the-art Security robots. Fast, powerful, efficient, and a really nasty attitude. They were designed originally for riot control. One per riot. And Starblood ordered six . . . He must have been really scared. Six would have been enough to stand off a small army.'

'And if they're still here, and running loose,' said Silence, 'we are in real trouble.'

CHAPTER SEVEN

Guardians

The marines moved cautiously down the metal stairway, scowling into the gloom below. The guns in their hands swept constantly back and forth, covering every direction an attack could come from. Diana supposed she should find such obvious expertise comforting, but instead it just reminded her of the possible dangers ahead. It almost made her wish she carried a gun of her own. Almost. She was an esper, not a killer. She stuck as close behind the marines as she could without crowding them, holding her lamp high to spread its light as far as possible. Huge shadows moved around them like watching ghosts, but everything else was still and silent.

They'd found an elevator that could have taken them down to the next floor, but none of them had felt like risking it. They had no idea why it was still working when so many other things weren't, and it was only too easy to imagine the elevator breaking down between floors, leaving them trapped in a steel coffin while the air ran out. So they made their way slowly down the stairs, nerves tingling in anticipation of an attack that never came.

It was cold in the stairwell, and getting colder. Hoarfrost made patterns on the walls that teased the eye with hints of meaning. Their breath steamed on the still air, and the heating elements in their uniforms somehow weren't enough to keep the chill out of their bones. Their footsteps rang loudly on the metal steps, and the sound seemed to echo unnaturally long in the hush.

Diana knew she should be using her esp to check ahead, but she couldn't bring herself to do that. Not yet. The scan in the Lobby had been hard enough, when she was safe and among friends. But now that she'd come down into the heart of the darkness, she was afraid to send her mind out for fear it might not come back. She sensed there was something down there in the dark with them, and she didn't want to risk waking it again. Sometimes she thought it was an alien, and sometimes she thought it might be the ghosts of dead personnel, but all she really knew for sure was that she was scared. So scared that even the awful forms her imagination conjured up were preferable to encountering the real thing again. It was safer to lie to herself and hide in the dark with the marines.

They finally reached the bottom of the stairwell, and stood close together at the foot of the steps. To their right, a thick coating of ice almost covered the sign saying 'Level Two'. The marines and the esper ignored it, their gaze fixed on what the esper's lamplight revealed before them. The corridor walls bulged and seethed with ugly alien growths, and thick strands of shimmering webbing hung down from the ceiling, twisting and turning slowly as though in response to an unfelt breeze. The metal walls had torn and split apart in many places, multi-coloured wiring hanging out like plastic viscera, as though the alien forms had somehow grown inside the walls, and burst out when they'd become too large to be contained. Silvery traces ran along the unbroken areas of wall in long enigmatic patterns, gleaming brightly in the lamplight like metallic veins. They were pulsing with a slow alien life. The whole ceiling was covered with dark, wart-like nodes the size of a man's head, surrounded and connected by swirling chalky white spirals. And thick on the air, a harsh sweet smell like a disturbed grave.

'What the hell is this?' breathed Stasiak, swinging his gun back and forth, unable to settle on a single target. 'The place looks . . . diseased.'

'Infested, anyway,' said Ripper. 'I think we can be sure now that the aliens came here after they left their ship.' He glanced at the esper beside him. 'This . . . mixture of living and unliving; is this the same kind of thing you found on the alien ship?'

The esper had to swallow hard before she could answer, but when she finally spoke her voice was cool and quite professional. 'The same kind of thing, yes. Only the ship was dead, or dying. This looks alive, and functioning. The alien crew must have brought it with them, as some kind of seed, perhaps. But why?

Surely they didn't bring about changes as extensive as this just so that they could feel at home? There must be a purpose to it.'

'If there is, it's an alien purpose,' said Ripper. 'Something we might not even recognize, let alone understand. I think we need the Investigator down here to check this out, before we go any further.'

'Wait a minute,' said Stasiak quickly. 'Let's think about this first. We don't need to know what this stuff is. It looks weird and smells worse, but it's not exactly aggressive, is it? We're supposed to be looking for the Base personnel, and we don't need Frost for that. We're marines; we can handle this without an Investigator to hold our hands.'

Ripper looked at Stasiak thoughtfully. 'This isn't like you, Lou. It's an improvement, but it isn't like you. What are you up to?'

Stasiak grinned. 'Odin's recording everything that happens here, remember? And you can bet a lot of high-up people are going to be studying this record. This is our chance to look good in front of people who matter, and do ourselves no harm in the process. Why let Frost steal all the glory? There's money and fame in this; I can smell it. Of course, we'll have to edit this bit out . . .'

'People have died here,' said Diana sharply. 'And all you can think of is how best to turn it to your own advantage?'

Stasiak shrugged. 'If they're already dead, there's not much left I can do for them. So we might as well help ourselves, while we can.'

'And if whatever killed these people finds us?'

'Then we avenge the dead,' said Ripper. 'We know our duty, Diana. We're marines.'

Diana sniffed, and looked away, ostensibly studying the alien scene before her. Ripper shrugged. 'Odin; are you getting all this?'

'I see everything you see,' murmured the AI in his ear. 'It's really most fascinating. Please proceed further into the changed area. I need more information on the extent of the changes.'

'Wait a minute,' said Stasiak immediately. 'There's no point in rushing on blindly. There could be all kinds of unpleasantness up ahead.'

Ripper looked at him amused. 'A minute ago you were all for plunging into the thick of it, in search of death or glory.'

'I'm ambitious, not crazy. Let's handle this nice and easy, one step at a time. The only good hero is the kind who survives to talk about merchandising.'

And then he broke off, and they all looked round sharply as a single echoing thud came out of the darkness ahead of them. It sounded heavy and threatening and quite deliberate, as though whatever was responsible for the sound had wanted it to be heard. Ripper and Stasiak levelled their disrupters on the corridor ahead. Diana's right hand went to the force-shield bracelet on her left wrist, but hesitated to activate it. The energy crystal that powered it had a limited life span, and she didn't want to use it up unnecessarily.

'Odin; can your sensors detect anything alive on this floor?' said Ripper quietly.

'I'm afraid my sensors are currently unable to penetrate the Base,' the AI said quietly. 'Something is blocking them. My only sources of information are what I see and hear through your comm implants.'

More noises came out of the darkness, a slow regular thudding like the beating of a giant heart. The floor vibrated beneath their feet in time to the rhythm, and something large and hulking came out of the gloom towards them. It was huge, filling the corridor, and Diana shrank back, a child again, frightened by the bogeyman in the dark. The figure stopped suddenly a dozen feet away, its blue steel exterior glinting in the shaking lamplight. Its bent head scraped against the ceiling, and its metal hands were studded with razors. Stasiak swore softly, but his hand was steady as he turned his disrupter on the figure.

Captain Silence's voice rang suddenly in their ears. 'Listen up, people. We have a problem. Odin tells me there are Security Guardians somewhere in the Base. Don't engage them, under any circumstances. It's very possible they've been programmed to protect this Base against intruders. If you see one, retreat immediately.'

'Thanks for the warning,' said Ripper. 'But it's just a bit late. We're looking at one right now. Please advise.'

'Get the hell out of there,' said Silence immediately. 'Make no threatening moves and back away. If it starts towards you, run. They're crawling with weaponry and they don't take prisoners. As long as you keep a fair distance away, you should be safe.'

'*Should*?' said Stasiak. 'What do you mean, should? I'm not moving a muscle until I'm sure it's safe.'

'Shut up, Lou,' said Ripper. 'Esper; back away, and start up the stairs. We'll follow you.'

'All right,' said Diana quietly. 'I'm starting now.'

She stepped back cautiously, and the huge figure raised a hand to point at her. A disrupter beam flew from a finger and blew apart the metal stairway in a rain of jagged shrapnel.

Cries and screams and obscenities burst from Silence's comm implant, drowned out almost immediately by the sound of an explosion from below. The noise was deafening, and the floor shook briefly. Carrion and Frost looked to Silence for orders.

'Whatever's happening down there, there's nothing we can do,' he said flatly. 'By the time we could get there it would all be over, one way or another. And the last thing we want to do is provide a Guardian with new targets. Esper, marines; can you hear me? Fall back. I repeat, fall back.' He waited, but there was no reply, only the quiet hum of an open comm channel. 'Odin; access what they're seeing and patch me in.'

'I'm sorry, Captain,' said the AI steadily. 'Something inside the Base is interfering with the comm network. I have lost all visual contact with the esper and the marines. I am still monitoring audio signals, but I can't be sure how long that will last. I strongly advise that you leave Base Thirteen now. You are not equipped to deal with Guardians.'

'Want to bet?' drawled Frost. 'Point me at one. Anything that gets in my way is going to regret it.'

Carrion looked at Silence. 'Is she always this confident?'

'Yes,' said Silence. 'Frightening, isn't it?'

Carrion looked away suddenly. 'Captain . . . something's coming. Something close.'

Frost and Silence drew their guns and covered the two approaches. The wide corridor was still and open, with doors leading off at both sides. The only light came from the lamp Silence was holding, a pale illumination just strong enough to show both ends of the corridor. Nothing moved, but the shadows had edges. What had been just another corridor was suddenly openly menacing, every doorway a threat. Silence and Frost moved to stand back to back. Carrion leaned on his staff, frowning, as though listening to something only he could hear. Silence strained his ears against the hush, but couldn't catch anything.

'What is it?' he said quietly to the outlaw. 'Which direction is it coming from?'

Carrion's eyes closed. 'They're here, Captain. They're here.'

The wall to their right tore apart like paper as the Guardian burst through into the corridor. Thick strands of coloured wiring fouled one arm, but the Guardian snapped them with one easy movement. The machine was eight feet tall, a broad metal colossus with glowing eyes and a constant unnerving grin on its blue steel face. Razored blades protruded from its arms and legs, and the knuckles on its hands were spiked. It was not alive, but hate and violence were a part of its nature. It was a killing machine, fashioned in the shape of a man because it was more frightening that way.

'Big, isn't it?' said Carrion.

The sound of heavy metal footsteps rang out at both ends of the corridor, and two more Guardians appeared, blocking off the only means of escape. The three machines stood unnaturally still, studying their targets, and then they surged forward, too fast for the human eye to follow. Silence aimed and fired his disrupter at the nearest Guardian as it emerged from the wreckage of the wall. A force shield snapped on just in time to deflect the energy bolt, and then disappeared. The machine raised a hand and pointed, and Silence threw himself to one side as an energy beam blew a hole in the wall where he'd been standing. Silence hit the floor rolling, and was quickly back on his feet again. He slapped the metal bracelet on his left wrist, and a force shield sprang into being on his left arm. A yard-long oblong of glowing energy, it was capable of deflecting any energy weapon. For as long as it lasted. The Guardian could turn its shield on and off with split-second timing, so that it lasted practically for ever. Silence didn't have that option. He also had another three minutes to wait before he could use his gun again, and the Guardian was right on top of him.

Silence kicked open the door to his left, darted into the room and slammed the door shut behind him. He didn't really think it was going to stop something that could crash through walls, but hoped it would buy him a little time while he worked on what the hell to do next. A metal fist punched a hole in the door. Silence watched, fascinated, as an arm followed the hand through the hole, and then the Guardian pulled it back sharply, yanking the door out of its frame. The Guardian stepped unhurriedly into the room, widening the doorway as it did so. Silence backed away, holding his shield up before him.

The corridor was plunged into darkness as Silence disappeared into the side room, taking the only lamp with him. Frost cursed dispassionately and switched to her infra-red implants, only to discover the Guardians were shielded against displaying any heat signs. She immediately switched to ambient light and activated her force shield. The shield's glow was more than enough to show her the Guardian advancing on her. Frost fired her gun, but the energy bolt glanced harmlessly from the machine's force shield. She shrugged calmly, put her gun away, and drew a knife from inside her boot. It was viciously wide and almost a foot long, and its edges looked blurred and uncertain.

'Monofilament edge,' said Frost to Carrion. 'Cut through anything. Have to be careful with it, though, or it'll have your fingers off.'

'Those things were illegal, in my day,' observed Carrion.

'They still are. But I won't tell anyone if you won't.'

And then the Guardians were upon them, and there was no more time for talk. Frost threw herself forward, and the knife lashed out to cut a chunk off a Guardian's hand. The built-in disrupters all fired at once, but her force shield protected her. Frost brought the energy field across sideways, and its razor-sharp edge sliced clean through the other hand as it reached for her. The Guardian's huge metal arms swept suddenly in, to hold her in a bear hug and crush her against the blades on its chest. Frost dropped to her knees and rolled to one side, and the great arms closed on nothing. She jumped back, scrambling quickly to regain her feet, and the Guardian went after her, reaching for her with its crippled hands.

Frost darted in and out, slashing at the Guardian with her knife, cutting and carving it, but unable to do any real damage. It was just too big, and her knife was too small. The machine's computer-enhanced moves were inhumanly fast, and only her Investigator's training enabled her to avoid it. And she knew she couldn't maintain that kind of speed for long. She could turn and run. The Guardian didn't look like it was built for high-speed pursuit. But that would mean abandoning Carrion and the Captain, and her duty. Investigators didn't run away. She darted in under the Guardian's reach, pushed her gun against its chest and pressed the stud. Nothing happened. There hadn't been enough time for the energy crystal to recharge. She scrambled up the Guardian, climbing it like a cat, and dropped to the ground behind it. She spun round quickly, and stabbed the machine in the back before it could turn. It shuddered once, but that was all. The knife wasn't long enough to reach the parts that mattered. She yanked the blade out, and a metal arm whirled round and sent her flying down the corridor. She'd had her force shield up in time, but the impact was still enough to knock the breath out of her. She got her feet under her and backed away as the Guardian advanced on her, implacable and unstoppable as death itself.

Carrion had crouched down, and frozen where he was when Silence disappeared with the lamp. In the dark, the Guardian could only track him by sound. Unless the damn thing had infra red too. And then Frost turned on her force shield, and Carrion's long-neglected eye enhancements kicked in, boosting the ambient light. Carrion straightened up as he saw the third Guardian advancing on him. He drew his power about him, crackling and sparking on the air, and reached out to tear the machine apart. But his power dropped away and was gone in an instant. Carrion stood for a moment, staring blankly, and that was almost enough to get himself killed. The Guardian raised its arm, and all the disrupters in the hand fired at once. Carrion threw himself to one side at the last moment, old combat reflexes coming to his rescue. The damn thing had psi inhibitors built into it. They worked on the opposite principle to his own power lance, dampening down psi energy instead of augmenting it. The Empire used them to keep espers in line. They reacted to build-ups in psionic energy and cut in automatically once it rose above a certain level. Carrion backed away from the Guardian, holding his useless power lance out before him.

The Guardian loomed over him, reaching for him with razored hands. Carrion reached inside himself and drew on his power. The psi inhibitors prevented him from doing anything dramatic, but it was surprising what you could do with even small amounts. He reached out with his mind, a whisper of psychokinesis almost too small to register, and slipped it deftly between the Guardian's feet and the floor. All friction vanished in a moment as he concentrated, and the Guardian's feet shot out from under it. It fell on its back with a deafening crash, and Carrion quickly reached out to do the same to the machine threatening Frost. It hit the floor hard, and Frost stepped forward and drove her monofilament knife into its gleaming skull. The Guardian jerked and trembled, and lay twitching on its back on the floor. Frost pulled the knife out and calmly set about sawing the grinning head off.

The wall to Carrion's left exploded, throwing shrapnel across the corridor, and Carrion had to put up his esper screen to protect himself. He couldn't concentrate on that and the Guardian, and the machine rose quickly to its feet again. Silence clambered through the hole in the wall. A metal hand reached out after him, and Silence threw himself forward to avoid it. He scrambled away to stand beside Carrion, breathing hard. The Guardian before them fired a disrupter, and Silence blocked it with his force shield, holding it at an angle so that the beam glanced off and struck the Guardian that was climbing through the hole in the wall. It stopped the beam with a force shield, but was slowed for a moment.

Silence grinned breathlessly. 'Same trick I used to make that thing provide me with an exit through the wall.'

'Very clever,' said Carrion. 'Almost as clever as disappearing into another room and taking the only light with you.'

'Ah,' said Silence. 'Sorry about that. It's been a while since I did any hand-to-hand stuff. I'm rather out of practice.'

They jumped in different directions as Carrion's Guardian

fired once more, and the vivid energy beam flashed past them down the corridor to blow a hole in the far wall. Silence's Guardian crashed out into the corridor again, shaking off encumbering debris, and turned to face Frost. She hefted the severed metal head in her hand, and threw it at the machine. It caught the head easily, put it down on the floor with surprising gentleness, and started towards the Investigator. She grinned at it unpleasantly, her knife held out before her. And then the headless machine on the floor behind her reached out and grabbed her firmly by the ankle.

Carrion raised his esp as high as he dared, focused his psychokinesis tightly, and punched a hole right through the chest of the Guardian before him. It shuddered under the impact, but did not fall. The outlaw retreated, Silence at his side.

'Is there any way of beating these things?' said Carrion.

'Not really, no,' said Silence. 'I'm amazed we lasted this long. They're supposed to be unstoppable. But then, that's never bothered you before.'

And then the Guardian was upon them, and there was no more time for words.

Diana crouched down behind her force shield, trembling violently as the Guardians advanced on her. The two marines had already fired their disrupters, to no effect, and were also reduced to hiding behind their force shields and looking frantically around for a way out. The Guardians strode unwaveringly through the alien-infested corridor, ignoring everything except their targets. Ripper pulled a grenade from his belt, primed it, and tossed it into the midst of the three machines. It blew a second later, and the corridor filled with alien fragments and thick, choking smoke. Stasiak grabbed Diana's wrist and hauled her after him as he and Ripper ran down a side corridor, away from the smoke and the undamaged Guardians, already striding through the smoke after them.

The alien changes became stranger and more overpowering as they fled deeper into Level Two, but Diana was too busy coughing the smoke out of her lungs to pay much attention to her surroundings. Tears were streaming down her face, as much from shock as the smoke. She'd never seen anything so obviously deadly and efficient as the Guardians. They scared her on some basic, primal level that left no room in her for anything but flight. The Guardians were everything about the Empire that had ever threatened or punished her; brute symbols of authority, relentless as justice or revenge. She could no more have raised a hand against them than she could have defied her own conditioning.

The marines' pace slowed as they left the smoke behind them, but they could still hear the Guardians not far behind them. Stasiak produced a small capsule from somewhere and swallowed it dry, grimacing at the effort. He offered one to Ripper, who got his down more easily. Stasiak grinned at Diana, his eyes already bright and glassy.

'Just a little something, to give a fighting man an edge. You want one?' Diana shook her head. She didn't trust battle drugs. Stasiak shrugged and pulled her on. 'Up to you. But don't slow us down, or I'll have to leave you. Right, Rip?'

Ripper nodded brusquely, without looking round, and Diana fought to keep up with them as they made their way down a corridor distorted by strange alien growths. The hanging streamers of webbing grew steadily thicker, clinging stickily to the marines and the esper as they pushed through them. The corridor grew narrower, pressing in uncomfortably from all sides as the alien growths ran wild. It seemed to Diana that they'd left the Base behind, and were running through a harsh new world. But the Guardians were still following. She could hear them. The changing nature of their surroundings didn't seem to be slowing them at all. And then a side corridor ended in a great swollen mass of tissue, and there was no point in running any more. The marines cut at the spongy mass with their swords, but it absorbed their blows with easy indifference. They turned and glared back down the corridor. Stasiak swallowed another capsule. The sound of approaching metal footsteps came clearly on the quiet.

Ripper tapped Stasiak on the arm and gestured upwards. Stasiak frowned, and then his face cleared as Ripper hefted his gun. They aimed their disrupters at the ceiling, at the point where the Guardians would enter the side corridor. Diana stood behind them, her force shield humming loudly on the quiet, and tried to control her trembling. And then the Guardians appeared at the end of the corridor, and Stasiak and Ripper fired at the ceiling above them.

The growths exploded and the ceiling blew apart. Fat sparks flew on the air as electrical systems fused and failed, and half the floor above collapsed on to the Guardians, burying them under tons of rubble. The marines and the esper watched in silence as the wreckage slowly settled, and then Diana surprised herself with a loud whoop of glee. The marines laughed and whooped a few times themselves. They all turned off their force shields and hugged each other, almost giddy from relief. And then they fell silent as the wreckage shifted. Broken metal and ragged tissues stirred and fell back as a Guardian rose slowly from the debris. Its blue steel exterior was barely scratched.

The Guardian advanced unhurriedly on Silence and Carrion. It knew there was nowhere they could go. If they tried to run it would shoot them, and if they stood their ground and tried to hide behind their force shields, it would tear them apart. At the other end of the corridor, the Guardian Frost had beheaded was clinging firmly to her ankle, while the third Guardian advanced on her. Silence looked desperately at Carrion.

'Do something! Use your lance!'

'If I try the same trick again, the psi inhibitors will stop me,' said Carrion calmly. 'If I persist, they'll burn my brain out.'

Silence backed slowly away and Carrion moved back with him. The Guardian lifted its hands to cover them with its disrupters. Silence thought furiously. The damn things had to have a weakness somewhere. Everything had a weak point. Except the Guardians had been designed to be unstoppable. Inhumanly strong, computer-fast reflexes . . . computers. Silence seized on that thought. The Guardians were part of the Base's Security systems, which meant they were run by the Security computers . . .

'Odin! Can you hear me?'

'Yes, Captain. Audio contact remains firm.'

'Patch into the Base Security computers and shut them down! Shut down anything that even looks like it might be running a Guardian!'

'Of course, Captain. An excellent stratagem.' There was a slight pause, and then the AI's voice returned. 'I regret I am unable to comply, Captain. I am unable to find any computer system still functioning in Base Thirteen capable of running a Guardian. Only a few emergency systems are still functioning.'

'What?' Silence looked blankly at Carrion. 'But if the computers aren't running the Guardians . . . they must be running themselves. And that's not possible. That's not possible!'

'Are you going to tell them that, or shall I?' said Carrion.

'Dammit, do something, Carrion! That thing will kill both of us!'

'Yes,' said the outlaw quietly. 'I think it will, Captain.'

At the other end of the corridor, Frost pried desperately at the steel fingers gripping her ankle. The other Guardian was almost on top of her, but she couldn't break the hold. She snarled silently and cut savagely at the metal arm, slicing through its wrist. She threw herself clumsily to one side, dodging the reaching hands, and got her feet under her again. The severed hand was still gripping her ankle fiercely. Which meant she had no chance of outrunning her opponent, but then, she wasn't the running kind. She slashed at the advancing Guardian with her monofilament knife, and the blade bounced harmlessly back from the machine's force field. Frost shrugged quickly, and darted back out of reach. It seemed the Guardians were capable of learning from experience. Actually, she was surprised she'd lasted this long. She cut the metal hand from her ankle with a few quick slashes from the knife, and then had to throw herself to one side as disrupter beams seared through the air where she'd been standing. She hit the floor rolling, and was quickly back on her feet and dodging more disrupter shots.

A thought kept nagging at her, even as she dodged and ducked. The Guardians were fast, but they weren't anywhere near as fast as she'd expected them to be. As they were supposed to be. In fact, it was just possible that she was faster than they were. Which gave her an idea. The Guardians had force shields, but they were only using them to deflect disrupter beams. Apparently they didn't see anything else as a big enough threat. Frost grinned unpleasantly, and pulled a concussion grenade from her bandolier. She ducked another disrupter blast, leapt past the Guardian, and jumped on to the back of the headless Guardian as it peered blindly about for its prey. She primed the grenade, stuffed it into the open neck and leapt away. There was a muffled explosion, and smoke poured from the open neck, but the Guardian didn't go down. Frost stared at it incredulously. How much punishment could these things take?

Silence and Carrion edged away from the advancing Guardian until they backed into a wall, and there was nowhere left to go. Carrion looked at Silence.

'I seem to have run out of options, Captain. If you have any last-minute master plan, I think this would be a good time to share it.'

'Sorry,' said Silence. 'I was depending on you.'

Carrion managed something that was almost a smile. 'You should have known better than that, John.'

Frost turned from the headless Guardian before her, and stumbled over the severed head itself. She glanced down automatically, and stopped as something caught her eye. Without slowing her cautious retreat, she snatched up the head and studied it more closely. The headless machine hesitated, and then stopped where it was. The other Guardian stopped too. Frost blinked, puzzled, and took a better look at the detached head. The light had gone out of its eyes, though it still wore its endless disturbing grin, but there was something about it . . . She turned it over in her hands, still keeping a wary eye on the motionless Guardians, and then whistled soundlessly as she saw the interior of the head. A great many things suddenly became clear. Where there should have been nothing but silicon circuitry and crystalline matrixes, there were also thick strands of living tissue. Alien tissue.

She looked down the corridor, and saw that the third Guardian had stopped its advance on Silence and Carrion. She called out to them and tossed the head in their direction. It bumped and rolled across the uneven floor, and the Guardians made no move to intercept it. Finally it rolled to a halt, and Silence reached carefully down and picked it up. He raised an eyebrow at the inside of the head, and showed it to Carrion.

'Interesting,' said Carrion.

'Explains a lot, doesn't it?' said Silence. 'No wonder they

didn't need the Security computers to run them. The aliens invaded them too. The damn things are alive . . .'

'And now that we know, that changes a lot of things,' said Carrion. 'There wasn't much my esp could do against standard Guardians without triggering the psi inhibitors, but living tissue is much more responsive to esper attack . . .'

He looked at the Guardian before him, and it began to shudder, as though it was cold, or afraid. It dropped to its knees, fell forward on to its grinning face, and lay still. Carrion looked at the two remaining Guardians, and they collapsed like puppets whose strings had been cut. Rather an appropriate metaphor, Silence decided. Of course, where there were puppets, there were also puppeteers. They still had to face whatever it was that had infested the Base.

Frost made her way over to them, and kicked the nearest Guardian dismissively. 'Is that it? I'm almost disappointed it was so easy.'

'Don't worry,' said Carrion. 'I doubt very much that our troubles are over yet.'

'Right,' said Silence. 'The whole Base must be riddled with this stuff. If we can't find a way to clean it out, we may have to abandon the Base and destroy it from orbit.'

'The Empire wouldn't like that,' said Carrion.

'No,' said Frost. 'It wouldn't.'

Silence looked sharply at Carrion. 'Hold everything; we're forgetting the esper and the marines. We haven't had a word from them since we lost contact.'

'Don't worry,' said Carrion. 'I've just contacted Diana. It seems they had Guardian troubles of their own. I've explained what needs to be done. The esper is quite capable of handling the Guardians herself.'

Down on Level Two, Diana Vertue looked smugly at the Guardians lying motionless among the wreckage of the ceiling. The marines took it in turns to clap her on the back, almost knocking her off her feet in the process.

'Mind you, this is just Level Two,' said Stasiak. 'I hate to think what might be waiting for us down on Level Three.'

Ripper nodded and looked at Diana. 'You'd better run a scan, see if there are any more like these waiting below.'

She nodded, closed her eyes, and let her mind drift cautiously up and out. She frowned almost immediately.

'What is it?' said Stasiak.

'Living traces,' said Diana. 'They're all around us, all over the Base, concentrated in the floor below. They know we're here.' Her voice rose suddenly. 'They're not hiding from us any more. They're coming for us.'

'Who?' said Stasiak, glaring wildly about him. 'Who's coming for us?'

The walls around them burst apart, thick metal tearing like paper, as alien growths and tentacles exploded into the corridor, reaching for the esper and the two marines. The tentacles came from the floor and the walls and the ceiling, and there was nowhere to hide from them.

CHAPTER EIGHT

Down in the Darkness

'Esper; can you hear me? Ripper, Stasiak; respond!' Silence waited, scowling, but there was no response. He looked into the stairwell that led down to Level Two, and the darkness looked back at him, arrogant and impenetrable. There was only the cold and the quiet, and the knowledge of what he'd have to do. It had been twenty minutes now, since Carrion had last been able to reach the esper. He'd told her how to handle the Guardians, and she'd acknowledged the message, but there'd been nothing since. Silence shook his head slowly. They couldn't be dead. They had the information they needed. They couldn't be dead.

'Odin; could something be interfering with the comm net?'

'Quite possibly, Captain,' the AI murmured in his ear. 'I have been unable to raise the party on Level Two for some time. Something in Base Thirteen is interfering with all levels of communication. I am having to use inordinate amounts of power just to maintain audio contact with your party. However, that would not explain the outlaw's inability to contact them with his mind.'

'We have to go down after them,' said Frost, holding her lamp out over the gloom in the stairwell. Shadows leapt and danced, giving away nothing. 'If something has happened to the others, we need to know what it is.'

'Whatever's happened, the odds are it's over by now,' said Carrion. 'We won't do anyone any good by rushing blindly into the dark. Wait a moment, and consider. So far, we have a growing number of questions, and few if any good answers. For example; if Base Commander Starblood had six Security Guardians at his disposal, why didn't he use them against the invading aliens?'

'Presumably because he didn't have time,' said Frost. 'Judging by his log entries, by the time he'd worked out what was happening it was already too late. In fact, it's entirely possible the Guardians were infested with the alien material before they could be deployed.'

'Exactly,' said Carrion, leaning elegantly on his staff. 'The aliens aren't just powerful and dangerous, they're fast and devious too. All of which suggests we'd be foolish to go rushing into an unknown situation without doing some hard thinking first. The more I think about it, the more this looks to me like a trap, with the esper and the marines as bait.'

'You're probably right,' said Silence. 'But it doesn't make any difference. Those are my people down there, and I won't put their lives at risk by holding back. Lead the way, Investigator; Carrion and I will be right behind you.'

Frost grinned quickly, a sudden flash of bared teeth, and started down the metal stairs, lamp in one hand, gun in the other. Carrion gave Silence a long, thoughtful look, and then followed the Investigator down into the blackness. Silence brought up the rear. The stairwell was narrow and confined, and the lamplight didn't travel far. They moved in a small pool of light, and shadows flickered menacingly around them, almost close enough to touch. They'd barely reached the half-way mark when Frost stopped suddenly, and Carrion and Silence almost bumped into her. She stood still, head cocked slightly to one side, listening.

'What is it, Investigator?' said Silence quietly.

'I'm not sure, Captain. I heard something; something close.'

She broke off sharply, and held the lamp down to light her feet. A yard-long insect with a broad carapaced back and hundreds of legs was curling itself unhurriedly round her left ankle. Dozens more of the things curled and twisted on the steps below. More were climbing the walls, clinging easily to the dull metal. Frost put away her gun and drew her sword, moving slowly and carefully. The creature had no eyes or mouth, but she set the edge of her blade against what seemed to be the front of the insect, and sliced sideways. The body convulsed, and clamped painfully tight around her ankle. Frost handed the lamp to Carrion, reached down and calmly tackled the insect on her leg. It fought back with surprising strength, even without its head, and she had to use all her strength to unwrap it. It finally came free, and immediately tried to wrap itself around her arm. She threw the thing away, and it disappeared into the darkness. Hundreds more seethed on the steps below her, scuttling and sliding over each other in their eagerness to get to their new prey.

Carrion tossed the lamp lightly into the air and held it there with his esp, spreading light over the scene and keeping his hands free. Silence aimed his disrupter where the mass of insects seemed the thickest.

'I wouldn't, Captain,' said the outlaw quietly. 'You'd do more damage to the stairs than to the creatures.'

Silence nodded stiffly, and put away his gun. He shouldn't have needed to be told something that obvious. He drew his sword and stepped carefully down beside the Investigator. Together they hacked and cut at the insects, clearing an open space before them. Segments flew on the air, legs still kicking, but the creatures wouldn't die. They pressed blindly forward up the stairs, seeking to wrap themselves round an arm or a leg, reaching always for the throat, as though somehow they knew that to be the most vulnerable spot. They climbed the walls and dropped on to the party from above, but Carrion deflected them with his esp, cracking them like whips to break their backs, or crushing them against the walls with the pressure of his mind. But still the insects pressed forward, and there seemed no end to them.

Carrion stepped back, and held his staff horizontally above his head. Psi energy spat and crackled at each end of the power lance, and stabbed out to strike at the seething creatures. Where the psi-bolts struck the insects burst into flames, curling and twisting as the fire consumed them. Energy danced back and forth in the stairwell, too bright to look at, scorching and crisping the scuttling creatures, but not touching Silence or the Investigator. The insects fell back, spilling down the stairs in desperate haste, and plunged into the solid steel walls, which accepted and swallowed them up in a moment. The insects disappeared into the walls as though the gleaming steel was insubstantial as mist, and were quickly gone. Within seconds the stairwell was empty, the sound of the insects' scuttling feet no more than a swiftly fading echo. Only the dead remained to show that they had ever been there. Frost reached out and tapped the nearest wall, but it was stubbornly solid to the touch.

'Interesting,' said Carrion, and the Investigator nodded.

'Is that all you've got to say?' demanded Silence.

'For the moment,' said Carrion. 'The situation appears to be more complicated than we allowed for. And before you ask, no, Captain; I can't explain it. I can only suggest that the walls have in some way become as infested with alien material as the Guardians. Which means the aliens have quite literally taken over the entire Base.'

'Those . . . creatures,' said Silence. 'Could they have been the aliens from the crashed ship? Some sort of hive mentality, perhaps? A group mind?'

Frost shrugged. 'It's possible, but unlikely. Given the size of the ship, I'd have to say the scale was all wrong. More likely the insects are tools used by the alien for some purpose. We have yet to encounter the real enemy.'

'Now there's a comforting thought,' said Carrion.

'Keep moving,' said Silence. 'We haven't even reached Level Two yet. Carrion; nice work with the lance. Stand ready; we might need you again.'

'Of course, Captain. It's nice to feel needed.'

'I could toss a grenade down ahead of us,' said Frost. 'If the aliens have any more surprises waiting for us down below, a shrapnel grenade should spoil their day quite thoroughly.'

'Nice thought, but no. The esper and the marines are still down there somewhere. Lead the way, Investigator.'

Their feet echoed hollowly on the metal steps as they continued down the stairway, the lamp hovering benignly over their heads. Silence kept a careful watch on the stairs and the walls, but there was no trace anywhere of the vanished insects. Instead, a thick viscous slime began to appear on the walls, oozing down to coat the metal steps so that they became treacherous underfoot. They slowed their pace, taking it one step at a time. Thick drops fell from somewhere high above, landing with sudden force on heads and shoulders like heavy hands. The drips fell more thickly as they neared the bottom of the stairs, until it was a slow, unpleasant rain. Frost stopped to wipe the stuff from her face, and found she couldn't. The slime clung tenaciously to her forehead, and flowed suddenly down to seal her eyes and nose and mouth.

Silence and Carrion stopped with her as a thick wave of slime rushed up the stairs and trapped their feet and ankles in an unyielding grip. More rained down from above, plastering their heads and faces. Frost clawed at it with her hands, but it just oozed between her fingers, leaving nothing for her to hold on to. She kept her mouth firmly closed, and pinched her nose shut. She didn't want the stuff invading her body. There was already a growing pressure on her closed eyes and in her ears. Silence tried to scrape the slime from his legs with the edge of his sword, but it just reformed around the blade without releasing its hold for a moment. The goo was climbing his legs like a slow rising tide.

And then it was torn from his legs and sprang away from his face and body, pulled away by an almost physical presence on the air. The slime also left Frost's face, leaving her gasping for breath. When more of it fell from above it couldn't touch them, pushed away and to one side by the presence. Silence looked at Carrion, who was frowning slightly, as though considering an interesting problem.

'Nicely done again, Carrion. You've improved your control since we last met.'

'I've had lots of time to practise,' said Carrion. A clear pathway opened up before them, forcing the slime off to the sides. 'We'd better make haste, Captain. I can't hold this stuff back for long; it's too diffuse. And the pressure's growing all the time.'

Frost and Silence clattered down the steps as quickly as they could, with Carrion crowding their heels. The slime rained down thickly, but couldn't get near them. A sudden wave rose up and threw itself at them from below, only to break and fall away to the sides as it met the pressure of Carrion's will. And then they reached the bottom of the stairs and moved quickly forward, leaving the slime behind them. Frost pulled a grenade from her bandolier and primed it.

'Incendiary,' she said briskly to Carrion. 'See how far you can get it up the stairwell before it explodes.'

Carrion nodded, and the grenade jumped out of Frost's hand and flew up into the gloom of the stairwell. There was a bright, vivid explosion, and crimson fire boiled down and outwards. The flames burned fiercely, but neither they nor the heat could get past Carrion's mental shield. The inferno leapt and blossomed, lighting the scene bright as day, consuming the slime hungrily. The flames died away bit by bit as the goo disappeared, until finally they were gone, and the quiet and the gloom returned. A harsh bitter smell filled the air, but nothing scuttled down the steps or oozed from the walls.

They looked about them, taking in the strange alien growths that sprouted from the metal walls and ceiling. Streamers of webbing hung down, twisting slowly back and forth, as though someone had just passed through them. Silvery traces glowed on the walls like living circuit patterns. And thick and heavy on the air, growing clearer by the moment, the stench of putrid meat.

'First insects that won't die, and vanish into solid walls, then living slime with homicidal tendencies, and now this,' said Frost. 'Whatever's hiding down here really doesn't want to be found.'

'Esper!' Silence's voice rang on the quiet, echoing faintly, but there was no reply. 'Stasiak, Ripper; where are you? Can you hear me? Diana?'

They waited, but the echoes died away with nothing to replace them. The shadows were still, and very dark, and deep enough to hide all kinds of secrets.

'Spread out and search this floor,' said Silence flatly. 'I want them found. Maintain contact at all times. And watch yourselves. Something down here doesn't like us at all.'

They moved apart and started the slow process of searching through the rubble and the deserted rooms and corridors. The continuing quiet was eerie and almost threatening, after the lengthy battles that had preceded it. There was a feeling of tension that grated on all their nerves. They found a huge hole in one wall, presumably made by a grenade or a Guardian, and several glowing holes that could only have been made by disrupters, but there was no sign of the esper or the marines, or of what they'd been fighting.

316

They finally returned to the foot of the stairwell, taking it in turns to look at each other and shrug and shake their heads.

'The Guardians must have taken them deeper into the Base,' said Frost finally. 'They could have been programmed to capture, rather than kill.'

'But Carrion told Diana how to handle them,' said Silence. 'They should have been easy targets for someone of her skills.'

'Something must have gone wrong,' said Carrion.

Silence nodded reluctantly. 'Find them, Carrion. Use your esp.'

The outlaw frowned, concentrating. Frost looked at Silence. 'I thought he was a polter,' she said quietly. 'Polters aren't normally telepaths as well.'

'There's nothing normal about Carrion,' said Silence, not bothering to lower his voice. 'The Ashrai saw to that.'

Carrion opened his eyes and breathed deeply, rotating his head as though to clear it. 'I can't find the marines anywhere. The esper is hiding in a clothes locker, just down that corridor. She's shielding herself, but I can feel her presence now I'm looking for it.'

'Why is she hiding?' said Silence.

'I don't know, Captain. But it feels like something bad has happened to her. Something really bad.'

He led the way down a side corridor, with Frost and Silence close behind, disrupters in their hands. Shadows loomed menacingly as the lamp floated along above their heads. Carrion finally stopped before a row of lockers, and looked at each of them thoughtfully. Silence looked at them disbelievingly. They were barely a foot and a half wide and six feet high, not even big enough to make a decent coffin. What could have frightened the esper so badly that she'd been driven to try and hide in such a cramped place? Carrion stopped before one locker, and tried the door. It wouldn't open. He frowned, and the door burst open, shattering the lock. Inside, Diana Vertue was half standing and half crouching, her arms wrapped around her, her eyes squeezed tightly shut. The posture would have been painful to hold for a few minutes; after all this time it should have been agonising, but she made no move to leave the locker. She showed no sign of even knowing they were there. Carrion reached out and gently touched her shoulder.

'She's gone deep inside herself,' said the outlaw quietly. 'Something happened here, something so awful she shut down her whole mind rather than think about it.'

'We need to know *what* happened,' said Silence. 'And where the marines are. Bring her out of it, Carrion.'

'There's nothing I can do, Captain. If I try and force her mind open, I could shatter it completely.'

'Then I'll have to do it,' said Silence. He knelt down beside the comatose esper, and laid a surprisingly gentle hand on her arm. 'Diana; this is Captain Silence. Please; wake up and talk to me. I need you to talk to me, Diana. Talk to your father.'

The esper stirred slowly. Carrion and Frost exchanged a quick glance of surprise, and then looked back at the esper as she slowly opened her eyes. She saw Silence kneeling beside her, and threw herself into his arms, sobbing loudly. He held her tightly and rocked back and forth, murmuring comforting words into her hair. He looked up, and saw Frost and Carrion studying him. He shrugged as best he could.

'They took her away from me when she was six. When her esp first started to manifest. I kept in touch as best I could, and when she graduated from the Academy, I got her transferred to my ship, where I could keep an eye on her. I thought she'd be safe, with me.'

Diana finally got herself back under control and stopped crying, sniffing back the last few tears. Silence let go of her, and helped her to her feet. She stretched awkwardly, wincing as cramped muscles protested.

'What happened, Diana?' said Silence. 'Why were you hiding? Did the Guardians take Ripper and Stasiak away?'

'I don't know,' she said, frowning. 'I can't remember. But it couldn't have been the Guardians. We beat them. Carrion showed me how. It was easy. And then . . . something went wrong, but I can't remember what.'

'Don't force it,' said Carrion. 'It'll come back to you.'

'There's only one place Ripper and Stasiak could have been taken,' said Frost. 'Down to Level Three. We're going to have to go down after them.'

'Yes,' said Silence. 'I think we are. Lead the way, Investigator. Diana; stay close.'

Frost glanced at him briefly, and then set off into the gloom with the esper close behind her. Silence and Carrion followed, hanging back a little.

'The esper really shouldn't be here,' said Carrion quietly. 'Whatever she saw, it frightened her so much she shut down her mind completely, rather than admit it happened. Her current mental state is precarious, to say the least. If she's forced to confront again the circumstances that caused her breakdown, her mind could fall apart. She could retreat so far into herself that not even the best esper shrink could bring her out again. Just making her stay here could be putting her under an impossible strain. Send her back to the pinnace, John. We don't need her here. You have me. My esp is more than strong enough to deal with whatever we find.'

'I need to know what she saw,' said Silence. 'Keeping her here will bring those memories back to the surface.'

'She's your daughter, John!'

'I'm Captain of the *Darkwind*. I know my duty.'

'Yes,' said Carrion. 'You always did. You haven't changed at all, John.'

He increased his pace to catch up with the two women. Silence looked at the three backs turned to him, and made no move to join them.

The stairwell leading down to Level Three seemed open and inviting. No insects crawled on the metal steps, and the walls were free of slime. There were still strange alien growths erupting from the walls and ceiling, and tattered webbing hung in thick grey coils, but the stairwell seemed untouched. Silence gestured for Frost to lead the way, and she started slowly down into the gloom, step by step, gun in hand. Carrion moved down after her, with Diana at his side. The esper's hands were trembling visibly, but her back was straight and she held her head high. Silence brought up the rear. He would have liked to be proud of his daughter's courage, but he couldn't afford to think of her that way. She was his ship's esper, and that had to come first.

The temperature rose sharply as they made their way down

into the darkness, from bitter cold to almost suffocatingly humid heat. They turned off the heating elements in their uniforms, and pressed on in growing discomfort. The lamp still hung above them, buoyed up by Carrion's esp, but its light didn't travel far. They hadn't been able to find Diana's lamp, and she was unable to tell them what had become of it. She didn't speak much at all, but did as she was directed. She was an esper, and espers obeyed orders.

They reached the bottom of the stairwell without incident, and stopped a moment to get their breath. The heat was almost overpowering, and sweat dripped from their faces. All around them, the walls were cracked and pitted, and spotted with jagged outgrowths whose regular shapes suggested purpose, if not meaning. Stalactites of distorted metal hung down from the ceiling, dripping moisture that collected in pools on the uneven floor. The air was thick with the stench of rotting flowers.

'What the hell is this?' said Silence. He reached out and touched the nearest stalactite, and then snatched his hand away. The metal was painfully hot, the moisture almost boiling.

'This is something different,' said Frost. 'On Level Two the alien growths seemed wilder, almost out of control. This seems more pervasive, more planned. There's the same mixture of living and non-living materials, but the mix here seems more comfortable, almost organic.'

'But where did it all come from?' said Carrion, frowning. 'The aliens must have brought some of it from the ship, but there hasn't been enough time to bring about such extensive changes in the Base's structure. Besides; this doesn't look as though it was constructed; it looks more like it was grown this way.'

'Just like the alien ship,' said Frost, nodding. 'Whatever this stuff is, it isn't parasitic. There's a definite sense of purpose to it, of function. Symbiosis. Different systems working together, to reach the same end. This is an entire archology, taking over and supplanting the original one. The aliens' technology must be centuries ahead of ours, to have achieved so much so quickly. We have to get back to the pinnace, Captain. The Empire must be warned. Whatever's taken root here must be destroyed, down to the last fragment. If this should spread . . .'

Silence nodded. 'Odin; are you still in contact?'

'For the moment, Captain.' The AI's voice was quiet, but still clear. 'Audio contact remains firm. I am still unable to regain visual contact, and I have no contact at all with the missing marines. Something significant must have happened, either to the marines or their comm implants. I am maintaining a running log on this mission. In the event of my losing contact with you entirely, I will send a General Distress signal, and put this planet under full Quarantine.'

'Thank you,' said Silence dryly. 'Next time, you might wait for me to give the order. I am still in charge of this mission.'

'Of course, Captain. However, in order to present a complete log on this mission, I must have further data on the structural changes in Base Thirteen. To achieve this, it will be necessary for you to proceed further into the Base.'

'When this is all over, computer,' said Silence, 'you and I are going to have a long chat about which one of us is in charge, and you aren't going to enjoy it at all.' He looked at the others and tried not to scowl. 'Unfortunately, the machine's right. We do need more information, and the only way to get it is to press on.'

He stopped and looked at Diana, who was trembling violently. All the colour had dropped out of her face, and her eyes were very large. She realized he was watching, and made an attempt to stand straighter. She hugged herself tightly, and managed a shaky smile.

'I'm all right, Captain. Really. I've been trying to scan the area, but something down here is preventing me. I can't tell yet whether that's deliberate or not. I can't locate Ripper or Stasiak, but there are definite life signs all over the place. This whole Level feels like a jungle, but I can't focus enough to identify anything. The one thing I am sure of is that we're not alone down here. Something's watching us.'

'Can you be more specific?' said Silence, careful to keep his voice cool and unconcerned. He didn't want the esper any more upset than she already was.

Diana bit her lip and shook her head. 'Something's down here, Captain. I don't know what or where it is. But it knows we're here.'

She stopped suddenly, as though she'd been about to add

more, and then changed her mind. Silence waited a moment, but it was clear the esper had said all she was going to. She still looked scared, but she was back under control again. For the moment.

'All right,' he said briskly, 'we're going in. If anything moves, kill it. We don't have any friends down here.'

'What about the marines?' said Carrion.

'The odds are they're dead,' said Silence flatly. 'Otherwise Diana or the computer would be able to locate them. We'll search for them as we go, but they can't be our main objective. We're looking for the aliens. Anything else has to come second.'

'Of course,' said Carrion. 'People always come second, as far as the Empire's concerned. When in doubt, shoot first and ask questions later. If at all.'

Frost shrugged easily. 'We go with what works. Now let's get a move on. I don't like us standing around like this. It makes us too good a target.'

She started off down the corridor, stepping carefully over the uneven floor, and the others followed her. The heat grew steadily heavier and more oppressive as they moved deeper in, and condensation fell from the ceiling like intermittent rain. Alien growths blossomed on the walls, complex and enigmatic. Great fleshy petals uncurled from outgrowths of bone spliced with metal, and huge structures of living clockwork moved steadily towards some unknown goal. Some shapes seemed to border on the edge of purpose and meaning, but still evaded human understanding.

At one point the corridor became choked with a thick mass of the grey webbing, and they had to stop and cut their way through with their swords. It was slow, back-breaking progress as the sticky mesh tore reluctantly under the blades. Sometimes Silence thought he saw strange lights flashing briefly in the darkness, but the others never mentioned them, so he kept his peace till he could be sure himself. The esper began to frown heavily, and stopped at times to stare intently at some new outgrowth or alien structure.

'She's starting to remember,' Carrion murmured to Silence. 'I'll keep an eye on her.'

And then they rounded a corner, and Diana stopped dead and

screamed. Carrion and Frost moved quickly forward to stand between her and what she was looking at. She managed to swallow the second scream, but she was trembling so violently she could barely stand. Silence moved in beside her, and had to fight down an urge to look away. They'd finally discovered what had happened to the missing personnel of Base Thirteen.

Stretched across the wall, interspersed with alien growths and mechanisms, were recognizably human shapes and organs. Bodies had been torn apart and reassembled in strange patterns. Alien technology mixed with brightly veined meat, and nerves and wires curled around familiar bones. And every organ and stretch of tissue was still clearly alive and functioning, as part of a new, monstrous whole. Stasiak's face peered blindly from a shifting spider's web of silvery traces. There were no eyes in the face, but a muscle twitched regularly by the slack mouth.

'It's alive,' said Carrion quietly. 'I can feel it in my mind. It shouldn't be alive, but it is.'

'Just like the alien ship,' said Frost. 'Living and non-living tissue cyborged together. A biomechanical gestalt whose whole is greater than the sum of its parts. This is functioning, Captain; it has a purpose, a reason for existence.'

Silence looked at Diana. Her mouth was slack, and her eyes saw nothing at all. He looked back at the living wall. 'At least now we know what happened to the marines. They must have been taken and . . . broken down, in front of Diana. No wonder she blocked out the memory.' He looked at Diana again, and then away. The empty eyes were more accusing than any stare could have been. 'Why didn't they take her, too?'

'Espers have a unique defence mechanism,' said Carrion coldly. 'In times of danger, they can use their esp to become psionically invisible. Can't be seen or heard. You could walk right into one and not notice. Apparently it works equally well on aliens, too. You can ask Diana all about it, when she wakes up. If she wakes up.'

'If she can't keep up with us, we'll leave her behind,' said Frost.

'I know,' said Silence. 'I know.'

They walked along the wall, trying to take in the details. Carrion took Diana by the hand and she walked along beside

323

him, her face completely blank. The lamp still hovered above them, its pitiless light revealing every awful detail of the living surface. Half a brain bulged wet and glistening from a silver and grey latticework, next to a pale bloodless hand whose fingers curled and uncurled, over and over again. A single eyeball gleamed dully among copper piping beaded with sweat. An endless display of viscera wound back and forth, intertwined with gold and silver wiring. Frost studied it all with cool fascination. Silence couldn't look away. Carrion mostly looked after Diana, who went where she was led.

There were more walls, equally disturbing, and as the party moved deeper into Level Three, the mix of living tissue and alien technology became increasingly overt and bizarre. One hundred and twenty-seven men and women had lived and worked in Base Thirteen, before the aliens came, and not one part of them had been allowed to go to waste.

'Why?' said Frost finally. 'What's the point of it all? What is this supposed to achieve? If the aliens were capable of such extensive work, why didn't they use the Base's . . . resources to repair their ship?'

'Perhaps the ship was too badly damaged,' said Carrion. 'Or perhaps this . . . construction was the reason the aliens came here. We need more information, and a context to see it in. For the moment, we're just guessing.'

'We need to find the aliens,' said Silence. 'They can't be allowed to get away with this.'

'Captain,' said Odin quietly in his ear, 'I have been examining the memory crystal discovered on the crashed alien vessel, and I have finally managed to access the information within. I have arranged it in as palatable a form as possible. I strongly suggest that you study it now.'

'All right,' said Silence. 'Run it for me first, then run it for Carrion and the Investigator, while I stand watch. Be prepared to break off at a moment's notice, if necessary.'

'Of course, Captain. Stand by.'

Silence's vision shimmered, and was suddenly replaced by strange alien vistas as the AI patched the memory crystal directly into his comm implant.

*

Tall towers, draped in strands of glass and pearl, under a mercury sky. Silvered clouds boil slowly around a sun too bright to look at. The towers stand alone on an endless plain. There are dim cavities in the sides that might be entrances. Something living curls around the bases of the towers, unfurling wide jagged petals to the brilliant sun. The images are blurred, seen through a fluid, distorting haze.

A series of similar images come and go, where the details change but the scene remains the same. The towers age but do not fall, the strands twisting and shuddering as time shakes them. More towers spring up, covering the plain. In and out of the cavities, around the bases of the towers, near and far, are shadowy figures, never still, always blurs. It is as though frames from a film, taken some time apart, have been laid side by side to give an illusion of movement.

Something is speaking, though not with words. Information is passed, thick with meaning.

The towers are everywhere, linked by bridges of gossamer webbing. Life is everywhere, leaping, soaring, growing. There is no room. Time passes. There is war among the towers. Fire burns and terrible energies blaze. The dead are everywhere. Life is everywhere.

A line of shapes, huge and metallic, each different from the next, appear on the plain. They throw themselves up into the mercury sky, and are gone.

Silence rocked on his feet as the images left his sight, and would have fallen if Frost hadn't steadied him. He leaned on her a moment, till his legs steadied, and then nodded to the Investigator that he was all right. He waited a moment while Odin ran the alien memories through Carrion and Frost's minds, and then they looked at each other with new eyes.

'Incredible,' said Frost. 'A species, a civilization, where the boundaries between animate and inanimate, living and non-living, have been blurred and forgotten. Everything there was alive, struggling for space and survival.'

'No room anywhere, any more,' said Carrion. 'So they built or grew starships and set off to find new worlds. New planets to conquer, to infest, to make over in their image. That's what's happening here. The Base has been remade into something more . . . familiar.'

'More than that,' said Frost. 'Base Thirteen is a beacon, calling others of its kind. They have to be stopped, here on the Rim, while they're still confined to one world. If this were to spread . . . The Empire must be warned. The aliens must be destroyed.'

'Not aliens,' said Silence. 'Just the one. Each of those ships carried a single creature. Or rather, each of those ships was a single creature. Our visitor left its shell after the ship crashed, and made a new shell for itself here, in Base Thirteen. We have to find it, and kill it. If we can. I'm not sure if it is life, as we understand it.'

'We can't take chances,' said Frost. 'Not with something like this. Our very species is at risk. Our best bet is to return to the *Darkwind* and use atomics on the Base until nothing's left but a few grains of dust, glowing in the dark.'

Silence looked at Carrion, who nodded slowly. 'We'll have to find the force-shield generator and shut down the Screen first.'

'Are you hearing all this, Odin?' said Silence. 'How are your repairs going? Can you be ready to take off once we've shut down the Screen?'

'I'm sorry, Captain,' said the AI, 'but I can't take you any-where. You have all been exposed to the alien organism. The probability is high that you are yourselves infected. I cannot risk you passing on that infection to the *Darkwind*.'

'Odin, this is a direct order from your Captain,' said Silence. 'Stand by to carry us back up to the *Darkwind*, where we can be kept in Quarantine . . .'

'I'm sorry, Captain. My standing orders override yours. You will remain here. The pinnace is barred to you.'

Carrion laughed softly. 'Isn't that the bottom of the line with the Empire, John? Everyone's expendable. Everyone.'

CHAPTER NINE

Unexpected Complications

Silence fell helplessly through darkness without end. The bitter air was thick with the stench of sulphur and burning blood. Bright lights flared about him, flashing past like blazing comets. There were voices in the dark, loud and meaningless, interspersed with screams and laughter. Silence didn't know how long he'd been falling, but it felt like for ever. He thrashed about him, hands searching frantically for something that might slow his fall, but there was only the dark and the cold wind rushing past him. He forced himself to stay calm, his mind racing. Where was he, and how the hell had he got there? Where were the others? Where was Carrion?

'Right here, Captain.'

And suddenly he was standing on a narrow stairway, its cracked marble steps falling away into infinity. Carrion stood beside him, calm and unruffled. The cold wind stirred his hair, and his cloak swirled around him like billowing wings. He looked down at the endless drop, and then looked at Silence, unmoved.

'I did warn you, Captain. A trip like this is always dangerous.'

'Trip?' said Silence, his voice harsh to hide the uncertainty. 'Where are we, Carrion?'

'Where you insisted I take you. Inside Diana Vertue's mind.'

Memories returned in a rush. Diana had seen the marines die, ripped apart before her. Horror and survivor's guilt had overwhelmed her mind, until the only way to save her sanity had been to deny it had ever happened. She forgot it all, until she was forced to remember. And then, rather than face the horror again, she'd shut herself away inside her own mind, where nothing could reach her and nothing could harm her. She shut herself down, and stood staring blindly, mute and comatose, safe at last.

Carrion couldn't reach her with his esp, but he did have one suggestion. It was risky and uncertain, dangerous both to him and the esper, but he could drop his shields and join his mind directly with Diana's. Make her pain his own. *If you're going in there, I'm going in with you,* Silence had said. *After all, I am her father.* Carrion had argued, and Silence hadn't listened. He had no choice. He needed the esper if he was to complete this mission successfully. And she was his daughter, after all.

Lights blazed in the darkness, guttered and were gone. Voices came and went, shrill and inhuman. And the wind, blowing out of nowhere.

'Every light is a thought,' said Carrion softly. 'Every voice a memory. The rising and falling of the wind, the force of her will. We're a part of her mind now, as vulnerable as she is. Either we find a remedy for her madness, a way for her to live with her memories, or we'll never leave here.'

'Where did the stairway come from?' said Silence, as much for the comfort of hearing his own voice as anything else.

'It's a construct created by our joined minds; a symbol of constancy, to help us feel more secure. You must expect strange things here, Captain. The mind deals in symbols. Particularly when dealing with things it doesn't really want to think about.'

He looked down, and Silence followed his gaze. The stairway ended not far below in a shimmering silvery plain that stretched away in all directions further than the eye could follow. And there, at the foot of the stairs, a great white-walled house with strange lights burning in its windows.

'That is Diana's consciousness,' said the outlaw. 'Or how she perceives it. We have to enter the house and put right the damage there, if we can. We'd do well to make haste. Time isn't a factor; a few days here can be only a few seconds in the real world. But the mind is a dangerous place to visit. All the things we really fear are here, with nothing to protect us from them save the strength of our own wills. There are no rules here, Captain; only varying degrees of necessity.'

'Then let's get on with it,' said Silence, and he started down the stairs towards the great white walls.

The house drew slowly closer, as though reluctant to accept any visitors. Silence began to get the feeling there was something else in the darkness with them. He looked unobtrusively about him, but the dark turned aside his gaze with contemptuous ease. He heard slow, regular breathing, and what might have been the flapping of giant wings. The sounds came first from one side and then the other, growing steadily closer, nearer. Silence could almost feel a hot, arid presence, watching from the concealing darkness.

'Ignore it, Captain,' said Carrion softly. 'Whatever it is, we don't want to meet it. Concentrate on the house. Just the house.'

And suddenly they were at the foot of the stairway, the house looming over them, shining like a moon. The great structure looked old-fashioned and strangely stylised, as though built more for viewing than actual use. The strange lights were gone, and the windows held only darkness, like so many watching eyes. A sudden chill stabbed through Silence as he finally recognized what he was looking at. It was the doll's house he'd bought Diana for her fifth birthday. When she'd still been his child, before the Empire took her from him. He looked at the door before him. It was a great featureless slab of wood, without knocker or handle.

'What do we do now?' said Silence. His voice seemed to echo on and on, falling away into disturbing whispers.

'We go in,' said Carrion evenly. 'And then we talk to Diana, or whatever part of her she chooses to show us. We can't force her to come back with us. We have to persuade her. If we can.'

He stepped forward and knocked firmly on the door. The sound was flat and empty, not at all like a door should sound. It swung slowly open before them, revealing a brightly lit hallway. Silence looked at Carrion, who gestured for him to lead the way. Silence stepped resolutely forward, Carrion a step behind. The door closed behind them with a solid, final sound. The hallway stretched away ahead of them, impossibly long. The light came from everywhere and nowhere, and doors led off at regular intervals.

'The mind is a labyrinth,' said Carrion. 'Let's hope we don't meet the Minotaur.'

'There might not be one,' said Silence.

'There's always a Minotaur. If we're lucky, there'll also be a guide.'

As though the house had been listening all along, and waiting for the word to be spoken, a door opened not far away, and a young child stepped out into the hallway. Diana, six years old, in her party dress. There were electrode burns on her forehead.

'Do you recognize the image, John?' said Carrion. 'Do you know why she chose this of all her selves to show us? This is what she looked like when the Empire was training her to use her esp. Or to be more exact, when not to. The first thing all espers have to learn is obedience; only to use their esp when ordered. Espers are controlled through pain-avoidance conditioning; a long and painful process whose only justification is that it works. No one uses the word "torture". Espers have no rights. They're a commodity, to be used and discarded as needed. And if that means attaching electrodes to a young child and turning up the voltage, well, you can't make an omelette, and all that. No, Captain; don't look away. This is your doing.'

'I didn't know,' said Silence.

'You didn't want to know. You closed your eyes to evidence, and your mind to rumours, and told yourself it was all for the best. You sent your daughter to Hell, John, and part of her is always there, endlessly suffering, endlessly screaming. And we're going to have to walk through it to reach her.' Carrion leaned forward, his voice gentle as he spoke to the child before him. 'Diana; we need to talk to you. Can you speak to us?'

The child turned, put out her hands for them to take, and led them down the hallway. The small hand was warm and soft and very real in Silence's grasp. Ghosts came and walked in the hall with them, pale and silent people who'd been important to Diana in her short life. Silence didn't recognize any of them. There was no sign of himself among the ghosts. They filed past in eerie silence, their eyes preoccupied, their thoughts somewhere else. Some of them bore the brands of the electrodes on their skin. Some were screaming soundlessly, some were clearly insane, and too many of them were children.

Silence looked away, studying the doors they passed. Some were closed and some were open. The rooms held moments from Diana's past, endlessly repeating like flies trapped in amber.

Most were scenes of suffering, mental or physical and often both. *You sent your daughter to Hell, John.* Silence wanted to look away, but wouldn't let himself. And then they came to a closed door, behind which a small child sobbed endlessly, without comfort or hope, and Silence stopped. Carrion and the child stopped with him. Silence stared at the door, his hands clenched unknowingly into fists, and it seemed to him that if he opened that door and stepped through, he could save his daughter and undo the evil that had been done to her. Carrion looked at him sharply, and there was something in the outlaw's eyes that might have been fear.

'There's nothing you can do, John. What you're hearing is the past. It's already happened. In some deep part of our mind, everything that ever hurt or scared us is still there, waiting for a chance to attach itself to us again. If you open that door, and let loose what's in that room, you condemn Diana to Hell again, and us with her. Come away, John. The odds are you'll have to face worse than this before we reach the core mentality; the deep hidden centre of Diana, the self that never sleeps.'

'We shouldn't be here,' said Silence. 'This is more than just an invasion of privacy. There are things no one should have to see or remember.'

'You're right,' said Carrion. 'But we don't have any choice. Diana's gone too deep into herself to find her way out again without help. I'm not even sure I can get us out of here without Diana's co-operation. If I try it alone, I could destroy her mind, or worse. I told you all this before we came here. It's a bit late to be getting an attack of scruples.'

'She's my daughter, Sean.'

'No, John. You gave up any claim on her, when you handed her over to the Empire mind-techs. We have to go on, John. We have to go deeper.'

Silence nodded stiffly, and allowed his daughter and the man who used to be his friend to lead him on down the hall. Ghosts swirled around them, lost in the past, and there were doors beyond number. Silence came to another one that was closed, from behind which came screams of hate and fury. Something huge and powerful slammed against the door, rattling it in its frame. The thick wood cracked and splintered, but still held. Diana pulled insistently at Silence's arm.

Silence allowed her to pull him away from the door, and they continued on their way. The light grew gradually dimmer, and the floor no longer seemed as solid under his feet as it once had. And then, out of the darkness, Ripper and Stasiak came striding forward, leaving bloody footprints behind them. Silence stepped to one side to let them pass, but they stopped before him, blocking the way. They stared at Silence, and tears of blood ran down from their unblinking eyes.

'Why did you do it, Captain?' Stasiak whispered. 'Why did you bring us down here and then abandon us? Please, Captain; I want to go home. Don't leave me here in the dark.'

'They're just images,' said Carrion. 'Your mind gives them strength. They can't harm us, unless you let them.'

'Please, Captain,' said Ripper. 'Don't leave us here.'

'Whatever happens,' said Silence steadily, 'I swear I won't leave you in Base Thirteen. One way or another, I promise I'll set you free.'

He walked forward, with Carrion and Diana, and the marines stepped aside to let them pass. Doors came and went, and ghosts walked, but finally the hall ended in a single huge doorway. The child Diana let go of Silence and Carrion's hands, produced a large brass key from somewhere, and unlocked the door. She pushed it open easily, despite its apparent weight, and gestured for Silence and Carrion to enter. They did so cautiously, and found themselves in a small cosy room with comfortable furniture, and a small fire crackling pleasantly in an open hearth. Diana, her rightful age again, sat at her ease in one of the chairs by the fire. Silence looked slowly about him, frowning. The child was gone. The door shut quietly behind them.

'I know this place,' said Silence. 'I remember this. Elaine and I brought Diana here when she was very small. It was our last holiday together.'

'Probably why she chose this memory out of them all to hide herself in,' said Carrion. 'She felt safe here. The last place she ever felt safe and protected from the outside world.'

They looked at Diana in the large, over-stuffed chair. *It wasn't really that big*, realized Silence. *She just remembers it that way*

332

because she was so small. Outside, he could hear rain falling. It had rained all through that holiday, and he and Elaine and Diana spent the long days playing games and charades, and stuffing themselves with good food. Not much of a memory to make a heaven out of. But when it's all you've got . . .

'Diana,' he said finally. 'It's me. Your father. I've come to fetch you. It's time to go.'

'I don't want to go,' said Diana. 'There's something out there. In the dark. It frightens me.'

'You can't stay here,' said Carrion. 'The longer you stay, the harder you'll find it to leave.'

'I don't want to leave,' said Diana. 'I'm safe here.'

Something moved outside the shuttered windows. Footsteps, slow and steady, passing by, heading for the door.

'Who's out there, Diana?' said Carrion.

'My mother. She was here too.'

All the colour dropped out of Silence's face as a cold hand clutched at his heart. 'No, Diana. No! Your mother's been dead five years now.'

'Not here,' said Diana. 'You were here and I was here, and Mother was with us. We're all going to be together, and we'll never have to be alone again.'

The footsteps reached the door, and stopped. There was a feeling of anticipation, of something final and irrevocable about to happen.

'The door's locked,' said Carrion. 'Concentrate, John. The door is locked if you believe it to be. John; listen to me. She mustn't be allowed to complete the memory, or we could be trapped here with her.'

'Elaine,' said Silence. 'You never met her, Sean. You would have liked her. She was bright and funny and very lovely. She died in an attack ship ambush, out by the Horsehead Nebula. They never found the body, but we held a funeral for her anyway. I miss her, Sean. I miss her so much.'

The handle of the closed door rattled. Silence looked at it and then back at Diana. Carrion clutched his arm tightly.

'John, Diana; don't do this. The more real you allow your past to become, the more power it has over you. You're in control now, but it won't last. Everything that ever made an impression on you, for good or bad, is in here with you. For the moment, all the things that frightened and hurt you are safely locked away behind closed doors, but once you lose control, the doors will start opening. And then, it won't be Elaine rattling the handle and wanting to come in. John, talk to her, dammit. Convince her. You said yourself that Elaine's been dead for five years. What do you think is out there? At best, you're faced with an eternity of child's games and charades. At worst, you're facing an eternity with a woman you know is dead.'

Silence looked at the door, and then at Diana. She smiled at him serenely.

'Diana; we can't stay here. You have to come with me now.'

'No. We're going to be together again. For ever and ever and ever.'

'Diana . . .'

'Something happened,' said Diana. 'I don't remember what, and I don't want to. I'd rather die than remember.'

'No!' said Silence. 'Diana, please; listen to me. We need you. I need you. I've been alone so long . . . I've got to go. Please; don't leave me alone again.'

She looked at him steadily. No sound came from beyond the door. It felt as though the whole world was holding its breath. Diana reached out and took Silence by the hand.

'Look after me,' she said quietly. 'Keep me safe. Promise.'

'I promise,' said Silence, forcing the words past an obstruction in his throat. 'I'll never let anything hurt you again.' He took her in his arms, and she hugged him tightly, her face buried in his chest. Silence looked at Carrion, his eyes bright with unshed tears. 'Get us out of here, Sean.'

A blinding light filled the room, washing away every detail in its glow. Then it faded and they were back in the corridor on Level Three. Back in another labyrinth, with a different Minotaur, held together by newly discovered love. Carrion hoped it would be enough.

'All right,' said Silence. 'This is the plan. It's very simple. Simple plans are always the best, because that way there are less things to go wrong. Diana; you're going to use your esp to contact the alien. The thing itself, the beast in the shell; whatever it was that first came here from the crashed ship. You're going to act as bait, to draw the alien out from wherever it's hidden. It'll come to you, because it perceives you as a threat. Your esp makes you especially dangerous, and it knows that. You don't have anything to worry about; Investigator Frost will be with you. She'll keep both of you alive, and the alien distracted while Carrion and I track down the heart of the system it's built here. There has to be a centre, a place that holds everything together. Destroy that and the alien will be isolated, and much more vulnerable to attack.

'Carrion will use his psionic invisibility to keep the alien from knowing what's happening till it's too late. Once we've broken the connection between the alien and the Base, Frost should have no trouble in dealing with it. But Diana; you must understand that once we've started this, we have to finish it. You can't disappear behind your psionic invisibility, and hide; you're the bait. You have to hold its attention while Carrion and I destroy the heart. You'll be in no real danger. Frost will protect you.'

'Damn right,' said the Investigator. 'Never met an alien I didn't kill.'

Diana nodded jerkily. 'I understand, Captain. Let's do it.'

She closed her eyes and let her mind drift up and out. The Base roared around her in a thousand voices, some human, some not. The human components of the alien system were still alive, though their minds or what was left of them now followed alien paths. Diana concentrated on blocking out the babbling voices one by one, searching for the dominating alien presence at the centre of its web. It found her first, blazing in her thoughts, but she held her ground and kept the alien firmly at the edges of her mind. She felt its interest in her grow as she continued to hold it at bay, and its thoughts crawled across her shields like worms across her face. Its probes grew stronger and more threatening, but Diana had been trained to withstand far worse.

Her confidence firmed as she realized the alien wasn't really that strong in itself; its true strength lay in the shell it had built around itself, in its domination of the living components of its web. Diana shut out every other voice, concentrating on the alien, showing it her strength. Its thoughts seethed at the edges of her mind, dark and complex and utterly inhuman. Try as she might, its thought processes made no sense at all. Diana concentrated on projecting a single message; *If you want me, you're going to have to come and get me yourself. Your web can't see me, and if you don't come to me, I'll come to you. And I'll destroy you.* The alien broke contact sharply, and Diana dropped back into her head and opened her eyes. The others looked at her questioningly, and she nodded firmly; trying hard to look professional and in command of the situation.

'It knows where I am. You'd better get moving, Captain. It'll be here soon.'

Silence smiled and nodded. 'Just give me a direction, Diana.'

Diana projected the map overlay the AI had given them of Level Three, and indicated their position and that of the centre of the web. Silence and Carrion acknowledged the information, and Diana broke contact. Silence waited patiently while Diana familiarised herself with the new lamp the Investigator had found, and then he and Carrion set off down the corridor, their lamp bobbing along above them like an over-sized will-o'-the-wisp. Diana and Frost stood together a moment, awkward in each other's company, and then the Investigator sat down on the floor, drew her sword and laid it across her knees.

'Might as well make ourselves comfortable, while we wait for the alien to put in an appearance. I take it your esp will give us plenty of warning?'

'Of course, Investigator.' Diana hesitated, and then sat down beside Frost. It didn't feel particularly comfortable, but it was good to get off her feet for a while. 'So, what do we do now, Investigator? Just wait?'

'Pretty much. Nothing we can do till the alien gets here. Relax. Save your strength. You're going to need it.'

'What do you suppose it'll look like?' said Diana hesitantly. 'I've never seen an alien. In the flesh, as it were.'

'Could be anything,' said Frost easily. 'None of this fits in with anything I've ever seen before. Probably really ugly. Most of them are, to our eyes. Don't let it worry you. As soon as it shows up, I'll blow a hole through it with my disrupter, and then you can help me cut it up into bite-sized pieces. No problem.'

'How can you be so calm, so confident?' said Diana. 'This creature slaughtered every living thing in the Base, and then tore their corpses apart to fashion them into a living computer network. This isn't some rogue animal we're dealing with; it's a powerful, sophisticated entity, and it's heading right for us.'

'I'm an Investigator,' said Frost. 'I'm trained to deal with situations like this. Are you scared, Diana?'

'Yes,' said the esper. 'Yes, I am.'

'That's good. Being scared will give you an edge. It gets the adrenalin pumping, and sharpens your reflexes.'

'Are you scared?'

'I suppose so, in my way. Investigators don't really have emotions, just pale echoes of what we remember emotions being. Our training sees to that.'

Diana nodded. 'Training. The usual Empire euphemism for mind control. They started my training when I was six years old. When to use my power, and when not to. Who to use it for. And right from the beginning it was made clear to us that if we didn't learn thoroughly or quickly enough, we'd be killed. The Empire won't tolerate rogue or uncontrollable espers. Six years old is a hell of a time to be made aware of your own mortality. But it does give you a strong sense of perspective. In the end, all that really matters is following orders.

'They experimented for a time with mind-control implants, but they couldn't develop one that didn't interfere with esper functions, so they settled for good old-fashioned psychological conditioning. I've been trained about as thoroughly as anyone can be, without an actual lobotomy.'

There was a pause as they sat quietly together, not looking at each other.

'My training started at about the same age,' said Frost slowly. 'In learning to out-think alien minds, we give up a lot of what it means to be human. Things like emotions, conscience, companionship. Our training produces warriors; perfect killing machines to serve the glory of the Empire. I don't feel much of anything any more, except when I'm fighting. I've had lovers, but I never loved any of them. I have no friends, no family, nothing but the job. Still, if nothing else, it is an extremely interesting job.'

'Is that all you have?' said Diana. 'Just the job and the killing?'

Frost shrugged. 'It's enough. You can't expect too much out of life, esper. You should know that.'

Diana smiled briefly. 'You know, we're more alike than I

thought. You deal in death and I deal with life, but really we're two sides of the same coin. We both had our childhoods taken away from us, and had our lives shaped into something those children could never have understood. And we'll both probably die serving the same people who destroyed our lives in the first place.'

Frost shook her head. 'No, esper; you don't understand me at all. I like being what I am, what they made me. I'm strong and I'm fast, and there's nothing and no one that can stand against me. I'm the most perfect fighting machine you'll ever see. I've been responsible for the destruction of whole alien civilizations, and killed men and creatures with my bare hands. It's only when I'm fighting and killing that I feel really alive. It's like a drug you never grow tired of. You can't know how it feels, esper; to know you're the best. I'm the ultimate expression of the Empire; the personification of its strength and purpose. And all I had to give up to achieve it was a few weak emotions that would only have got in the way anyway.

'It's different for you. You take no pride in being an esper. Probably give it up tomorrow, if you could. To be normal. I won't give up what I am, and I'll kill anyone who tries to take it away from me. You think too much, esper. It gets in the way. Life's so much simpler without conscience or emotions to complicate things.'

Diana looked at her steadily. 'Everything else has been taken away from me; I won't give them up too. I'd rather die.'

'You may get your chance,' said Frost, looking down the corridor into the darkness. 'Something's coming.'

The Investigator rose to her feet in one graceful movement and stood listening to the quiet, sword at the ready. Diana scrambled inelegantly to her feet and looked wildly about her. The alien couldn't be here already. It couldn't. Her esp would have picked it up long before this. Unless it too knew the art of psionic invisibility. In which case, things were about to get rather interesting.

Frost slapped the metal bracelet on her left wrist, and her force shield sprang into existence on her left arm; a palely glowing rectangle of pure energy, humming loudly in the quiet. Diana raised her esp and reached out tentatively. The Base was

338

silent, with none of the babbling voices she'd heard earlier. The alien had put up shields. Diana retreated quickly into her own mind, and set up her own wards. Theoretically, they should be able to stand off any psionic attack, up to and including a mindbomb, but she'd never tested her shields in actual conflict before. She hoped the alien didn't know that. She glanced across at Frost, and was quietly reassured by the Investigator's obvious professionalism and competence. A thought struck her.

'Investigator; if the alien is coming, wouldn't you be better off with your disrupter than your sword?'

'No,' said Frost calmly. 'A sword's more versatile. You can have the gun, if you want.'

'No thanks,' said Diana. 'I don't believe in them.'

'Suit yourself,' said Frost, a shrug clear in her voice. 'Whatever's out there, it's close. I can feel it. I'm impressed. I didn't think anything could get that close without me knowing.'

'Psionic invisibility,' said Diana. 'No way you could have known.'

'That shouldn't have made any difference,' said Frost. 'I am an Investigator, after all. Are you picking up anything?'

'Not much. Something's coming, and it's not alone. I don't think it's the alien.' She looked unhappily at Frost. 'I can't be sure, but I don't think the alien's here at all. It's still hanging back. It's sent something else in its place. Stand ready, Frost. They're almost here.'

'Relax, esper.' The Investigator swept her sword casually back and forth before her, smiling easily. 'Nothing's going to get to you while I'm here. Though you could at least activate your force shield. There's no point in making it easy for them. You're here as bait, not a sacrifice.'

Diana blushed, and slapped her bracelet. The low hum of the force shield was very reassuring. She and the Investigator stood quietly together, listening. And then the soft patter of running feet came clearly to them out of the darkness, and Diana and Frost braced themselves as their enemy finally emerged into the light.

They'd been human once, before the alien absorbed them into its system. Now they were something else, roughly human in shape, but refashioned to meet the alien's needs. They were crooked and malformed, the flesh had run and congealed on their frames like wax melting on a candle. Some had no skin, the red muscles shining wetly in the lamplight, their tendons twitching with every movement. Bunches of cilia waved from empty eye sockets and mouths held needle teeth. Muscles bulged impossibly, beyond restraint or reason. The twisted faces were inhumanly blank, indifferent to thought or emotion. The alien had reworked them for its own reasons, and if there was any humanity left in them, it was buried deep, where it wouldn't interfere.

There were ten of them, jostling together at the edge of the lamplight, as though reluctant to leave the comfort of the shadows. *Ten*, thought Diana. *That's not so bad. We can handle ten.* As if in answer to her thoughts more appeared, stepping out of the steel walls as though they were intangible as mists. The Investigator scowled.

'How do they do that? Those walls are solid. I checked them myself.'

'The walls have become part of the alien system,' said Diana quietly. 'They're as alien as everything else in this Base now. The whole structure has become a single great organism, with the alien as its heart and mind.'

Frost snorted. 'So what does that make these things?'

'Antibodies. We're invaders, an infection in the system. So those things are going to cleanse us out.'

'You mean they're going to try,' said Frost calmly. 'All right, there's a lot of them, but they're not even armed. Let's keep this in perspective, esper. We can handle this.'

'You don't get it, do you?' said Diana. 'They're *antibodies*. The alien can make as many of them as it needs to, recycling damaged ones if necessary. It can make a dozen, a hundred, a thousand; as many as it needs to overrun us. Even you couldn't stand against a thousand, Investigator. They're not human. Not any more. They don't think or feel or hurt. They'll just keep coming until we're dead. And then the alien will recycle us, and put us to some useful task. If we're lucky, we'll never know what.'

'You think too much, esper,' said Frost. 'It's never over till it's *over*. With this many antibodies, they'll spend most of their time tripping over each other and getting in each other's way. All we've got to do is hold them off, until either the Captain and the outlaw reach the heart of the system, or the alien gets impatient and comes here itself to take us on.' She smiled unpleasantly at the shapes before her, and swept her blade back and forth. 'Come on then, you useless sons-of-bitches. Let's do it.'

Captain Silence and the outlaw Carrion moved swiftly through the distorted corridors, heading into the dark heart of Base Thirteen. For a long time the only light came from the lamp bobbing along above them, but eventually strange lights began to appear in the distance, steady glows and sudden glares, like the opening of so many watching eyes. Things stirred and shifted in the shadows, sometimes alive and sometimes not. Silence kept a wary eye on all of them, but tried not to look at them too closely. Something about their uncertain shapes disturbed him on some deep, primal level. The idea that the material world could acquire sentience and direction undermined his faith in how the universe worked.

Carrion, on the other hand, didn't seem to be bothered by any of it. But then, he'd been an Investigator once, and nothing bothered them. Silence glared about him, holding his gun so tightly that his knuckles ached. He had faith in Carrion's psionic invisibility to keep them from being detected, but walking straight into the alien's clutches went against everything his instincts were telling him. He clamped down hard on his nerves, and watched where he stepped. Thick steel cables stirred sluggishly on the floor like dreaming snakes, coiling around each other in slow, sinuous movements, dripping black oil. Silvery traces glowed like veins in the sweating walls, pulsing to a fast, irregular rhythm. Silence glanced at Carrion, irritated by his continued calm.

'Are you sure this invisibility of yours is working?'

'Quite sure, Captain. Because if it wasn't, we'd very likely be dead by now. Have faith, Captain. I'll get you there.'

Silence sniffed. 'Odin; are you still following this?'

'Yes, Captain,' the AI murmured in his ear. 'Audio contact remains firm.'

'Give me an overlay of the Level Three floor plans.' The plans appeared before him, hovering on the air in glowing lines and symbols. Silence checked his position and that of the centre of the web, and scowled. They were a lot closer than he'd thought. 'Odin; any chance you've reconsidered your position on letting us back on board the pinnace?'

'No, Captain. My Security imperatives are very clear on the matter. However, I will of course provide you with whatever information and guidance I can.'

'Any more useful information from the Base computers?'

'Not as yet, Captain. However, there are still several areas locked away behind Security codes I don't have access to.'

'All right; lose the overlay.' The glowing map vanished from his sight. 'Stay in contact, computer. Let me know of any changes in the situation.'

'Of course, Captain.'

Silence looked at Carrion. 'I take it you were patched into that. Any comments?'

'Only that we should walk very carefully from now on. We're nearly there, and I can't believe the alien will have left the heart of its system unprotected. There are bound to be defensive systems and booby traps just waiting for us to trigger them.'

'I've really missed your sunny personality, Carrion. You look for the worst in everything, don't you?'

'Yes, Captain. And usually, I'm right.'

Silence sniffed. 'We should reach the heart in a few minutes. Assuming we do find a way past whatever's waiting for us, do you have any ideas as to what we're going to do when we get there?'

'Not really, Captain. A few of your grenades, backed up if necessary by a channelled psi-storm from me should be enough to wreck whatever the alien's put together, but I can't be sure until I've seen it.'

'Aren't you going to make a speech about how wrong I am to be planning the destruction of a new alien species? I seem to recall you were quite eloquent on the subject where the Ashrai were concerned.'

'That was different. The Ashrai were willing to co-exist. This species is not. Its existence is based on total restructuring and control of the environment. They are as much a threat to this world and the Ashrai as they are to the Empire.'

'I wish you'd stop talking about the Ashrai as though they were still alive. They're dead and gone. I killed them all. You've been alone here too long, Carrion.'

Carrion looked at him almost pityingly. 'The Ashrai aren't gone. You never did understand the bond between the Ashrai and the metallic forest. I've been here ten years, and I'm only just beginning to comprehend what we destroyed here. The Ashrai were a race of espers, exhibiting psi phenomena we could barely measure, let alone understand. They fought the Empire to a standstill, for all our superior technology. And even though you scorched this planet, they're still here. Their bodies may be dead, but their souls still haunt the trees. Call it a vast living field of psi energy and phenomena earthed by the metal forest, if that makes it easier for you to grasp. But as long as the forest still stands, the Ashrai still exist. They do not forget and they do not forgive. They were very special, John. You never did understand what you did here.'

'Oh yes, Sean. I know what I did.'

Carrion stopped suddenly, and gestured for Silence to stop with him. They stood a while in their narrow pool of light, while Carrion frowned uncertainly, checking the way ahead with his esp. He finally shook his head and gestured for Silence to continue, but he was still frowning. Silence drew his gun and scowled at every moving shadow. The pressure of unseen watching eyes seemed heavier by the minute, but nothing challenged them.

The corridor widened out suddenly into what had been one of the main computer bays, and Carrion and Silence stopped again, halted by the sight of what lay before them. The machines had burst apart from pressure within, and flowered into unsettling half-living constructs, held together by long glistening strands of human nervous tissue. A low constant muttering filled the air, so quiet as to be almost subliminal, as the hybrid creations worked constantly on unknown alien tasks. Silence looked slowly around him, not allowing himself to be hurried, no matter how much the sight revolted him. Carrion walked slowly forward, his face blank, his eyes fey and knowing.

'This is the heart of the system, the centre of the web,' he said quietly. 'Through this, the alien controls all that happens in the Base. This is its eyes and ears, its brain and memory. Destroy this, and the alien will be cut off from its creation. The Base systems will fall apart, and the alien will be left alone and vulnerable.'

'If it's that straightforward, what are you looking so unhappy about?' said Silence.

'It's too easy. Too easy to get here and too easy to destroy. It can't be this simple. We must be missing something. I think we should investigate these systems very carefully before we do anything else.'

'Carrion; we don't have the time. The alien's gone for the moment, but it could be back any minute. We have to destroy the heart while we can. Look, just because the alien is intelligent and powerful, it doesn't necessarily follow that it's very bright. The more powerful an organism, the less it needs to think things through. It uses what has always worked in the past, and expects that to be enough. Because it's never been beaten, it thinks it can't be. Everything has a weak spot, and we've found the alien's. Now give me some room and let me work. Watch the corridor if you want to be useful. I want to set the grenades and get the hell out of here before the alien realizes something is up and comes charging back.'

The outlaw nodded stiffly, and moved away to watch the corridor, still frowning. Silence consulted with the AI, and worked out the best places to set his grenades to ensure maximum damage. He planted three grenades carefully, primed them all one after the other, and then sprinted back down the corridor with Carrion at his side. They'd just rounded the first corner when the first grenade blew. A shockwave of super-heated air laced with jagged shrapnel came howling down the corridor, to slam harmlessly against the psychokinetic shield Carrion set up. Two more explosions followed in swift succession, and the floor trembled under their feet. The explosions were deafeningly loud, and Silence clapped his hands to his ears, grinning triumphantly. Smoke filled the corridor, billowing, thickly around them. The tremors finally died away, and the corridor was quiet, save for the crackling of distant fires. Silence grinned at Carrion.

'That should ruin the alien's day nicely. You'd better run a scan, though; just in case any of that stuff is still working. I'll have the AI check it out from its end.'

He broke off as the AI's voice suddenly sounded in his ear. 'We have a problem, Captain. Apparently Base Commander Starblood wasn't content to just seal off the Base with a force Screen, he also activated the Base's self-destruct system. A small nuclear device was primed and programmed to detonate at the end of a countdown. When the alien's systems took over the computers, it interrupted the countdown, but didn't defuse the bomb. As long as the system was in control, the countdown was unable to continue, and the Base was safe. Now that you have destroyed the alien system, the countdown is proceeding again. The nuclear device will detonate in thirty-two minutes, and I do not have the necessary codes to abort it. I strongly suggest that you leave the Base now. While you still can.'

CHAPTER TEN

Friendships and Loyalties

Frost pulled a concussion grenade from her bandolier, primed it, and lobbed it casually over the heads of the watching humanoids. A few turned their blank faces to follow it, but the others showed no reaction, even as Frost primed and threw two more grenades. The first exploded deafeningly in the midst of the humanoids, blowing a bloody hole in their ranks. Smoke filled the corridor, and blood flew on the air in a crimson mist. The next two grenades blew seconds later, while Frost and Diana huddled back into a niche in the corridor wall, hands clapped to their ears. The massed ranks of the humanoids absorbed the force of the explosions, scattering blood and mangled bodies the length of the corridor. The living and the injured staggered aimlessly back and forth, dazed and confused, and Frost chuckled easily as she shot the head off a humanoid with her disrupter. Diana shrank back from the open violence in the Investigator's voice, and brushed furiously at the blood that had spattered her clothes.

The humanoids milled back and forth, clawing at the smoke and each other. Frost laughed softly, hefted her claymore and moved forward with a light, easy step. Her blade flashed in the lamplight as she cut and hacked her way through the blank-faced drones. Her sword jarred on bone and sliced through flesh, and she was everywhere at once, darting back and forth. Bodies fell to either side of her and did not rise again, and the humanoids reached blindly out into the smoke and chaos as the alien will behind them struggled to orientate itself. Investigator Frost cut and hacked a path into the heart of the enemy, and was content.

Diana Vertue concentrated on maintaining her psionic invisibility, balancing her need for safety with her duty as bait. She allowed a vague sense of her presence to leak through her mental shields, to keep the alien's attention, but hid her precise location behind a screen of ambiguity, so that neither the alien nor its humanoid slaves could tell exactly where she was. They milled around her with reaching hands, a horrid faceless mass of clawed hands and snapping mouths, but none of them could find her, even when their bodies bumped into hers. She bit down hard on her lower lip to keep from screaming. The humanoids had been constructed from the Base personnel, and though they moved and fought and searched with stubborn purpose, they were still dead. Their faces held no thought or emotion, their skin was deathly cold to the touch, and something strange and alien looked out from their unblinking eyes. Diana stood with her back pressed tightly against the wall, her face contorted with a horror beyond revulsion, shrinking away from every contact. A slow grinding headache built in her left temple, sharp-edged and blinding, as she struggled to maintain the delicate balance of her presence. There but not there. Present but not seen. And over and above everything else, the certain knowledge that if her control slipped, even for a moment, the humanoids would turn on her and tear her apart.

Frost danced and strutted in the midst of her enemies, pirouetting with sharp professionalism, her sword swinging in unstoppable arcs. It was a good blade, Old Earth steel, and whilst it might not have the edge of her monofilament knife, the weight and power of the claymore was more than a match for the clawing hands of the alien drones. They swarmed about her, a living sea of hate and violence, and none of them were fast enough or good enough to touch her. Their clawed hands snatched and tore but she was never there, defying them to find or hold her. Her force shield brushed aside the few humanoids who got too close, the glowing energy field fending off their unnatural strength. But its constant use was a dangerous drain on its energy crystal, and it wouldn't be long now before the shield collapsed. Frost didn't care. The humanoids were falling before her, and she was in her element, doing what she was trained and born to do. Nothing could stand against her. Let them come. Let them all come. She was an Investigator, humanity's warrior, and the alien was going to learn what that meant.

Diana watched the Investigator butcher the dead men from Base Thirteen with grace and style, and it seemed to her that Frost was as inhuman as what she was fighting. The Investigator's face was a cold mask of contempt and professionalism, with no trace of compassion or cruelty. She killed because that was what she'd been trained to do, and because she was good at it. An expert in the art of slaughter. Not that Diana had much compassion herself for the humanoids. She could see in their faces that they weren't human any longer in anything but shape. Death was the only peace and dignity they could attain to. She supposed she should be helping Frost fight, but she couldn't. Partly because the effort to maintain her invisibility took so much out of her, but mostly because just the thought of violence on her part sickened her. The Empire had trained her well.

And then, suddenly, the humanoids fell back, turned away from the Investigator, and disappeared into the surrounding steel walls. One moment the corridor was full of smoke and baleful figures, and then they were gone, and the smoke was slowly clearing to reveal Frost lowering her bloody sword in puzzlement. She wasn't even breathing hard. The dead lay where they had fallen, jagged metal showing in bloody wounds, and gore still spattered the floor and walls, but Frost and Diana were alone in the corridor. Frost sniffed disappointedly and moved back to stand with Diana, shaking drops of blood from her blade. The esper shrank back from the gore-soaked sword, but Frost didn't notice. She clapped Diana on the shoulder, and looked around her with an easy and contented smile.

'It looks like we were too much for them. Pity. I was just starting to enjoy myself.'

'It's not over,' said Diana softly. 'Something's coming.'

The Investigator looked at her sharply, and then glared about her, sword at the ready. 'Is it the alien?'

'It must be. It burns in my mind like a beacon, wild and brilliant. It hurts to think about it. There's something . . . wrong about it.'

'How close is it?'

'Close. I can hear it thinking. It doesn't make any sense. It has emotions, but I don't recognize any of them. It's like seeing new colours in a rainbow . . .'

'You're wandering, esper,' said Frost. 'Keep to the subject. How big is the alien? How strong? Which direction is it coming from?'

'It's almost here.' Diana rubbed at her forehead as her headache flared up again. 'It's getting harder to keep it out of my mind. It's like looking into the sun when it's too bright . . . It's strong, powerful. Inhumanly powerful.'

'Concentrate, esper.'

'I can't . . . there's too much of it . . .'

'Then bring it here. Be the bait, and I'll take care of everything else.'

And then the alien appeared at the end of the corridor, and Frost stopped talking. It was big, filling the corridor from wall to wall and from floor to ceiling, like a slug in its tunnel. The dark ribbed body looked long and powerful, with thick cables of muscle standing out and pulsing like veins. Metallic strands threaded through its flesh, not added, but a living part of its body. Long bony limbs protruded at regular intervals along its bulk, poling it along the walls. Sharp metal barbs and spikes thrust up from its glistening back, and its tail was too far away to be seen. The blunt head had no eyes, or any other obvious features, but metallic teeth snapped shut again and again in its wide maw, like the closing of a mantrap. The mouth was big enough to take a human head as a morsel, and the teeth shone like daggers. It surged forward, foot by foot, huge and threatening like a thunder cloud come down to earth. Its limbs rattled against the metal walls, and breath hissed in the vast mouth.

Diana wanted to look away, but couldn't. On some deep, basic level the thing offended her. It was a mixture of living and unliving, life and technology, but grown, not made. Things that should never have known sentience or animation were an intrinsic part of its being. She tried to imagine what kind of hellish pressures or evolution could produce such a creature, and couldn't. It was too alien, too different. The creature blazed in her mind, the strength of its presence blasting aside her shields till she stood naked and helpless before it. The alien looked at her with its blind head and knew where she was, and the shape and texture of its thoughts were made clear to her. They made no sense to her, no sense at all.

'It's bigger than I thought,' said Frost casually. 'It must have grown considerably since it left its ship, presumably from feeding on the Base personnel. I wonder how big it would grow eventually, without restraint . . . Still, that's a problem for those that come after us. Stand back, esper. I'm going to blow a hole right through it.'

'Your gun won't stop it,' said Diana. 'Nothing can stop it. It's too big. Too different.'

'Hell,' said Frost. 'It's just an alien.'

She raised her disrupter, trained it on the alien's blunt head, and pressed the stud. The searing energy bolt burned a hole through the head, and black oily blood spattered across the walls and ceiling. The alien howled deafeningly, the sound reverberating through Diana's bones as much as her ears. Its head swayed back and forth, and Frost looked on dumbly as the ruptured flesh knitted itself together again, steel and silver traces scabbing over the gaping wound like metal sutures. Frost put away her gun.

'I think we're in trouble, esper. I was rather counting on the disrupter to take care of the alien. Still, when a plan fails, improvise. I've got a few grenades left. When I say the word, you run. And don't hang about, because I'm going to be right behind you.'

She pulled a grenade from her bandolier, hefted it casually, and then primed it and rolled it along the floor towards the alien. She yelled to Diana, and the esper turned and fled down the corridor. The alien lunged forward, its bulk smothering the grenade. Frost turned and ran, quickly catching up with the esper. Frost hurried her on with harsh words, and then saved her breath for running. The grenade went off, and the floor shuddered under their feet. Frost allowed herself a moment of satisfaction, until the alien's voice filled the corridor, harsh and unrelenting. The floor trembled again, this time from the massive weight that bore down on them in pursuit. Frost tried to visualise how fast something that big could move, but had to abandon the thought. Nothing in her training or experience had prepared her for this alien. It was too different, too unlike anything humanity had ever encountered before.

She accessed the floor plan, and led Diana into the smaller, narrower corridors, hoping they'd prove too small for the alien's bulk. But everywhere they went, the alien had been there first. Strange growths erupted from the sweating steel walls, and shimmering strands hung down from the torn ceiling. And finally they had to stop for Diana to get her breath back. Frost looked impatiently around her while the esper leaned on her arm for support, head hanging down as she fought for air. The Investigator was still breathing slow and easy. Her training had prepared her for worse than this. She could have escaped the alien easily if it hadn't been for Diana, but she couldn't bring herself to abandon the esper. As long as the bait was still held dangling before the alien, it should concentrate on the esper and not concern itself with what Carrion and the Captain were doing.

She glared back down the corridor into the impenetrable gloom, gun in one hand, incendiary grenade in the other. She might not be able to kill the alien, but she could sure as hell hold its attention. She looked unhurriedly about her, sizing the corridor up for possible ambushes and hurried exits. There were holes everywhere, in the walls and in the ceiling, some of them leading into tunnels apparently big enough to swallow the *Darkwind*'s pinnace. The alien had been busy.

Frost frowned suddenly as she realized the trembling in the floor had stopped. The alien must have decided on another route, a roundabout way to take its prey by surprise. Which meant any of the holes might become an opening for the alien's attack. She approached the nearest of the larger holes and peered cautiously down it. Deep in the darkness she heard a faint muttering, a familiar cacophony of human and alien voices. She primed the incendiary grenade, counted three quickly, and threw the grenade as far down the tunnel as she could, before stepping to one side and flattening herself against the corridor wall.

There was a dull roar, and smoke and flames billowed out of the hole, along with flying fragments of alien tissues. Frost grinned savagely, and then trotted down the corridor with Diana in tow, pausing to scorch each of the larger holes with a blast from her disrupter. The vivid energy bolts lit up each tunnel as she fired, but there was never a trace of the alien, and the gun took a little longer each time to recharge between shots.

Frost stopped near the end of the corridor, and peered uncertainly about her. She was doing a lot of damage to the Base, but she was no nearer stopping the alien. It should have found them by now. She wasn't foolish enough to think they'd lost it, or left it behind, which meant it had to be planning something in its devious, inhuman mind. Frost smiled. In her own quiet way she was enjoying the chase. It was the first real challenge of her abilities she'd ever had, the first opportunity to try and out-think something that didn't think the way humanity did. She had the upper hand. As long as she and the bait kept moving, the alien was helpless to do anything but chase her. It was too large, too heavy, and too stupid to do anything but follow where she led. And when the Captain and the outlaw had destroyed the heart of its web, she'd turn on the alien and have it run for a while, while she pursued. She snapped her head round suddenly as she caught a faint whisper of the alien's muttering again. She looked at the esper, who was standing with her eyes closed, trembling violently.

'It's here,' said Diana. 'It's found us.'

'Where is it?' said Frost. 'I can't see it anywhere.'

'Close,' said Diana. 'Close.'

Frost looked quickly back and forth, straining her ears for any more of the alien muttering, but nothing moved in the corridor gloom, and the air was still and silent. Frost frowned, and tapped her gun against her thigh. Wherever it was, she should still get plenty of warning of its approach. The alien couldn't get anywhere near them without the floor trembling underfoot to alert them. Even if it came through one of the tunnels in the walls. And then something made her look up.

The blunt head emerged from a vast hole in the ceiling like a maggot in a rotten apple. Frost grabbed Diana and hurled them both frantically to one side as the alien dropped out of the ceiling and the floor shuddered. Frost hit the ground rolling and was quickly back on her feet again, a grenade in her hand. She primed it, rolled it down the corridor towards the alien, hauled Diana upright and all but threw her round the nearest corner. She counted quickly under her breath as they ran down the side corridor, and then a blast of superheated air blew past the corridor entrance, followed by the alien's roar. Frost grinned. She might not be able to kill the damn thing, but she could still hurt it.

She pushed the esper ahead of her as they ran, and took the opportunity to examine her disrupter. The energy crystal was seriously depleted, good for only three or four shots at most. The floor was trembling again. The alien had to be close behind them. She risked a look back, and swore dispassionately. It was nearer than she'd expected, and getting nearer. The thing could move surprisingly fast for its bulk. Frost smiled briefly. She'd always been the pursuer before, never the pursued. This was a new experience for her. She found it exhilarating.

They rounded the next corner and then skidded to a halt as they found the corridor was a dead end. According to the floor plan, it should have been an open passage, but the alien had sealed it off some time earlier with a thick mass of webbing. Frost hefted her disrupter. The gun still had enough power to blast a way through, but she might need it yet. Frost shrugged, and levelled the gun at the webbing. The vivid energy bolt tore through the web, blackening the ruptured edges. Frost started forward, only to stop as the web slowly reformed, knitting itself together with effortless skill. The way was blocked again, and she'd wasted one shot. She didn't see any point in wasting another. She looked quickly about her. There were more of the holes in the walls and ceiling, and no way to tell where any of them led. The alien had been busy. Frost turned to the esper, who was looking back the way they'd come with wide eyes and trembling mouth.

'We're going to have to make a stand, esper. Or rather, I am. You can't help me, and you might get hurt if you got in the way, so I want you to go on alone. Pick one of the tunnels. They have to lead somewhere. Choose one of the smaller ones and the alien won't be able to follow you. I have to stay here and hold its attention until the Captain and Carrion have finished their business.'

'You can't face that thing on your own,' said Diana. 'The gun didn't hurt it, and the grenades only slowed it down. If you stay here you'll be killed. Come with me. I'll make us both invisible, and we'll lose the alien in the tunnels.'

'No, esper. We have a job to do, remember? We have to keep the alien occupied.'

'You can't do that if you get yourself killed. Stay here and you'll die!'

Frost raised an eyebrow. 'It's not that certain. I am an Investigator, after all. We can't both go into the tunnels. They're unknown territory to us. Certainly the alien has to know their layout a damn sight better than us. You go on, esper. I'll hold it here. You have to survive, to be the bait again, if necessary. And if you're going to lead the alien a chase without me, you're going to need a good head start. Go on, esper.'

Diana looked at her steadily. 'You're going to die here, aren't you?'

'Not if I can help it.'

'Aren't you?'

Frost sighed resignedly. 'Yes, esper. Quite probably. But that doesn't matter. I know my duty. I always knew I'd die in the field and not in my bed. Comes with the job. I don't mind. It's my duty and it's my life. It's all I've ever wanted.'

'You mean it's what the Empire made you want. They programmed you, just like they did me. They ruined your life and made you love it, and now you'll die for them, because your conditioning won't let you do the sensible thing and run.'

'No, Diana; that's not it. I'm going to stand and fight because that's what I do best. We're buying time for the others, me by fighting, you by running. Now do as you're told and get into that tunnel. Please.'

Diana stepped forward suddenly, and hugged Frost tightly. The Investigator just stood there for a moment, and then gently hugged her back. Diana let go, and Frost helped her climb into the nearest tunnel mouth. Diana smiled back at Frost, her lips pressed tightly together so they wouldn't tremble and spoil the moment, and then she turned and disappeared into the tunnel, taking her lamp with her. Frost adjusted her eyes to make the most of the ambient light, and turned back to face the corridor. Her force shield hummed briskly on her arm, and her sword was a comforting weight in her hand. She breathed slowly, coolly, and her hands were perfectly steady. What the hell. It was only an alien. Something moved in the shadows at the end of the corridor, and Frost smiled widely.

At the heart of the alien web, Carrion and Captain Silence looked at each other speechlessly as the AI told them of the nuclear countdown in a calm, conversational voice. Silence slammed his gun back into his holster.

'Well that's great. Just great! Now what the hell are we going to do?'

'If I might suggest, Captain,' said Carrion, 'this is something we might do better to discuss on the run. We have less than thirty-two minutes to locate the esper and the Investigator, evade the alien, get the hell out of Base Thirteen, persuade your computer to let us back on the pinnace, and get off planet before the nuke blows.'

'In other words,' said Silence, 'we're going to die. What the hell; we might as well give it a try, just to be awkward. Odin; work out where we are and show us the quickest route out of here.'

'I'm afraid I can't do that,' said the AI. 'Firstly, I will not let you back on board the pinnace. You are still quite probably contaminated by the alien. Secondly, the Empire is going to need the alien's body, and as much of its technology as possible, to examine. Given the potential threat of this new species, the Empire will need all possible information as to the extent of that threat. I must insist you do all in your power to preserve the Base and its contents. I regret the necessity for such harsh measures, Captain. My programming requires that I do this. You know how it is.'

'Just when you think things couldn't possibly get any worse, they do,' said Silence. 'I'll make you a deal, Odin. You agree to get us off planet and safely back to Quarantine on the *Darkwind*, and we'll save the Base and its contents from destruction. What do you say?'

'Agreed,' said the AI. 'My programming allows me to be flexible during emergencies.'

'Right,' said Silence. 'That's a start, anyway.'

'Pardon me,' said Carrion. 'But just how are you planning to defeat the alien and defuse the nuke in under thirty-one minutes?'

'Beats the hell out of me. Odin; you must have forged some links with the Base computers by now; can't you patch into the systems running the countdown, and turn it off?'

'Not at present, Captain. Since this was intended as a last-ditch self-destruct option, the Empire built in a great many safeguards to ensure that the countdown could not be interfered with, once initiated. The alien managed to suspend the count-down in some manner, but I confess I am at a loss to explain how. I am doing my best to access the relevant systems, but my best-guess analysis suggests that will take me significantly longer than the thirty-one minutes remaining on the countdown.'

'Didn't you just know he was going to say that?' Silence said to Carrion. 'Do you have any ideas?'

'Do we know where the bomb itself is located?' said Carrion, frowning thoughtfully.

'Well, computer?'

'The exact location is protected by Security codes I do not have access to. Logic suggests it is concealed somewhere on Level Three, to ensure maximum destruction.'

'Whatever we're going to do, we'd better do it quickly,' said Carrion. 'And we have to contact Frost and Diana. They may be facing the alien by now, and they still think they have all the time in the world to deal with it.'

'There is a way,' said Silence slowly. 'After all, this doesn't affect just us. We're not alone on this planet, are we, Carrion? There's always the Ashrai.'

The alien came boiling down the corridor towards Frost like a flash flood, impossibly huge, impossibly fast. Its mouth gaped wide, revealing teeth like knives. It was on the Investigator in a second, and she launched herself forward, vaulting over the alien's lowered head and on to its spiked metal back. She landed awkwardly, trying to dodge the spikes and the barbs, but quickly regained her balance. She swept her force shield round in a circle, the sputtering edge shearing through the spikes, and then, having made herself some room, she slammed her sword down into the alien's head. The blade sank half its length into the leathery flesh, and the alien howled shrilly. It smashed its head against the corridor wall, trying to shake off the pain it felt, but Frost held on to the sword with both hands, and kept her balance.

Thick black blood pooled around her feet, and Frost grinned savagely as she stirred the sword around in the alien's skull, searching for the brain. The alien screamed, the vast sound hammering through Frost's head, and its long body convulsed as it struggled to throw her off. Frost used all her strength and forced the sword in another few inches. She worked the blade from side to side, trying to widen the wound, but even as the dark flesh split apart metal traceries sprang out of the raw meat to repair the damage. The flesh healed incredibly quickly, and the metal sutures were strong enough to resist her sword's edge. And slowly, inch by inch, the sword was being forced back up and out of the wound it had made.

Frost lifted the force shield on her arm and brought it down like a hammer. The edge of the energy field passed through the leathery flesh like mist, leaving a long rent behind it. She knelt down beside her sword, and the force field spat and sparkled as she buried it in the alien's back. The alien threw itself back and forth, its wailing voice painfully loud as its cries echoed and re-echoed back from the corridor walls. Frost fought back as it whipped its head from side to side. Metal spikes thrust up around her, and her shield jerked out of the alien's back. She leaned on her sword with all her strength, but still the blade was forced up and out of the alien flesh.

And then a pit opened up in the alien's back beneath Frost's feet, and sucked her down. She was knee deep in the alien before she could even react, hidden muscles crushing her legs. She snarled at the pain and cut desperately about her with her sword and her force shield, but still the alien flesh sucked her down. It closed around her like a living sea, absorbing her struggles and repairing its wounds as fast as Frost could make them. She groped for the monofilament knife in its sheath on her leg, but it had already disappeared into the alien's body. Something dragged at her feet, pulling her down till she was waist deep in the alien. The dark flesh rose up like a tidal wave and swept towards her.

Diana looked down from the mouth of a tunnel high up on the wall, and clenched her fists helplessly as she watched the Investigator disappearing into the alien's back. She knew she should be using the time Frost was buying her to get away, but she couldn't just turn her back and let the Investigator die. She couldn't just leave her. A cold hand clutched at her heart as the tidal wave rose up and rolled unstoppably forward. Unless she did something, and quickly, Frost was going to die. But what could she do? She was an esper, not a fighter. Never a fighter. She looked wildly about her for inspiration, and her gaze stumbled across a massive, blocky wall unit not far from the tunnel mouth.

She didn't stop to think about what she was going to do, because she knew that if she did, she probably wouldn't do it. First, she had to get the alien's attention. She dropped her mental shields and cast aside her invisibility like a veil she no longer needed. The great alien head swung round immediately, staring up at her blindly but knowingly. It wanted her, and now it knew where she was. Frost was still sinking into its back, but more slowly now, as though it wasn't concentrating on her any more. It had her, but it wanted the esper. The huge body surged forward, its stumpy legs poling it along the walls, leaving dents in the steel in its wake. Diana slapped the bracelet on her left wrist, and her force shield sprang into being on her left arm. The alien lifted its head high, searching for her. Diana leaned out from the tunnel mouth, hanging precariously by one hand, and cut at the wall unit with the edge of her shield. The shimmering energy sliced through the unit's supports, and it lurched drunkenly away from the wall, held only by a single cable. She leaned out further, most of her weight hanging out over the drop. The alien's head reached for her, only inches away. Diana gritted her teeth, stretched out her arm, and sliced through the remaining cable. The unit tore itself away from the wall and crashed down, its massive weight hammering the alien's head to the floor.

Diana dropped on to the alien's back, aiming carefully to land between the trapped Investigator and the pinned-down head. She hacked at the dark flesh with the edge of her shield, until Frost could get her arms free again, and then between them they dug the Investigator out. The alien thrashed back and forth, convulsing down all its length, unable to get enough leverage to lift its head against the weight of the wall unit. Frost finally got her hand on her monofilament knife, and together with Diana she cut herself free. They climbed quickly down from the alien and backed away down the corridor, both of them spattered with gore.

'Do you think that weight's going to hold it?' yelled Diana, shouting to be heard over the din of the alien's howls.

'Not a chance!' yelled Frost. 'Let's get out of here.'

She ran down the corridor with Diana at her side. Behind them they heard a crash as the alien finally threw off the wall unit. Diana tried to run faster, and couldn't. Her strength was gone, and she was running now on desperation and adrenalin. The Investigator ran effortlessly beside her, not even breathing hard, even after all she'd been through. It occurred to Diana that Frost could probably get away quite easily, but instead had chosen to run at the slower pace. She looked round suddenly and caught the Investigator's eye.

'You didn't have to save me,' Frost said brusquely. 'You could have got away.'

'I know that.'

'Then why did you do it? Why risk your life to save mine?'

'Because you needed me,' said Diana. 'Now shut up and run.'

'What about the invisibility? Any chance . . .'

'No. Not now the alien's locked on to me.' She looked back over her shoulder. The alien was flowing down the corridor after them, faster than they were running, faster than they could run. Diana looked at Frost. 'Don't ask. You don't want to know. Just run.'

Silence's voice was suddenly in their ears, murmuring through their comm implants. 'Investigator, esper; we've destroyed the heart of the alien's web. It is now completely cut off from the rest of the Base. Have you located the alien yet?'

'Oh yes,' said Frost. 'We know exactly where it is.'

'Good. Do you think you could lead it to where Carrion and I are at the moment? We've had an idea.'

The floor plan of Level Three flashed briefly before Frost and Diana's eyes, showing them the route. Diana thought hard. It wasn't far. They might just make it. She looked at Frost, and nodded briefly.

'We can be there in four minutes,' said Frost calmly.

'Make it three,' said Silence. 'We're working to a rather urgent deadline. Bring the alien here, and we'll discuss what to do next. Silence out.'

'The Captain's got a plan,' panted Diana.

'Yes. Interesting he didn't tell us what it was. Probably because he knows we wouldn't like it.' She looked at Diana. 'Can you last three minutes at this pace?'

'Shut up and keep running,' said Diana.

'Are you sure you want me to do this?' said Carrion. 'Once I call up the Ashrai, there'll be no turning back. I don't think you realize just how much they hate you.'

'They'll hate the alien more,' said Silence. 'That creature and its kind threaten the existence of the whole planet. They wouldn't just destroy the forest, they'd change it into something the Ashrai wouldn't even recognize. And since the Ashrai depend on the forest for what's left of their existence, it's in their interest to side with us against the alien.'

'Very logical, Captain,' said Carrion. 'I just hope the Ashrai are going to be logical too.'

'The enemy of my enemy is my friend. Nothing like having something in common to bring two peoples together.'

'You still don't understand, Captain. Once I summon up the Ashrai, they pass beyond my control. Once woken, they might decide not to lie down again. You didn't really win here, John. You just hurt them so badly they retreated back inside themselves for a time. There's power here on Unseeli, power beyond your worst nightmares. They might decide to take on the Empire again. And this time they'd have nothing left to lose; nothing to hold them back.'

Silence shook his head. 'So? You're talking about billions of people on thousands of worlds. The Ashrai wouldn't stand a chance.'

'John, you're talking about numbers. I'm talking about power.'

'It doesn't make any difference,' said Silence. 'We don't have any choice. Too many things have gone wrong, and we've too

360

many strikes against us. Frost and the esper will be here any minute, with the alien right behind them. We've run out of options, Sean. Odin; how does the countdown stand?'

'Nineteen minutes, thirty-two seconds, Captain.'

Silence looked at Carrion. 'Get yourself ready, Sean. We'll do it as soon as the others arrive.'

They both looked round at the sound of running footsteps, and Frost and Diana came pounding down the corridor towards them. Silence looked past them, but the corridor behind them was empty. Diana staggered to a halt, gasping painfully for air. Frost supported her with one hand as she nodded calmly to Silence. She wasn't even breathing hard.

'The alien's right behind us, Captain. It slowed down a bit when it realized where we were going, but it's still mad enough to keep after us, once it's looked around for a trap. I take it there is a trap here, Captain?'

'Oh yes,' said Silence. 'Have you hurt it at all?'

'I shot it and blew it up with grenades, and Diana dropped half a wall on it, but all we did was annoy it.' She looked round at the destruction of the alien's heart, and raised an eyebrow. 'Very thorough, Captain. You do realize that everything here will repair itself, given enough time?'

'Time is something we're all rather short of, Investigator. Before he died, Commander Starblood found time to activate the Base's self-destruct system. A small nuclear device hidden somewhere on this Level is due to detonate in just over eighteen minutes.'

Frost looked at him. 'You're jinxed, Captain; you know that?'

Diana raised her head and glared at him speechlessly, still too out of breath to talk, but her eyes spoke volumes.

'Whatever you're planning, Captain; start it now,' said Frost. 'The alien will be here any second, and it's in a really bad mood.'

'Don't look at me,' said Silence. 'It's all down to Carrion now.'

'Yes,' said the outlaw quietly. 'Somehow, it always comes down to me.'

'Because you're the best, Carrion.'

'Thank you, Captain.'

361

Diana wiped the sweat from her face with her sleeve, and then raised her head suddenly. 'Listen. It's close now. Very close.'

They all looked down the corridor, into the gloom. There wasn't a sound to be heard, but they could all feel a faint vibration in the floor under their feet. Silence looked at Carrion.

'Please, Sean. For them, if not for me.'

Carrion smiled slightly. 'You always did know how to fight dirty, John.'

Silence nodded, and moved away to stare down the corridor. Frost joined him, and they trained their disrupters on the concealing shadows. Diana finally straightened up as she got her second wind, and found herself a corner to stand in where she could be out of everyone's way. Carrion stood alone in the centre of the room, leaning on his staff, his thoughts elsewhere. He couldn't help feeling he'd come a long way by strange routes to reach this place, this moment. Everything he'd been through, all the rage and fear and heartbreak, just to end up fighting beside John Silence once again. Carrion smiled slightly. Whatever happened, it was good to have seen John again. It was like finding an old coat you used to wear, or a cup you used to drink from when younger. Comforting in its familiarity, tested in its worth, something you could depend on. Silence was back, at his side, and if he had to die this was not a bad way to go, among people he liked and respected.

Among people. It had been a long ten years, without a human face or a human voice. But still, there had been the Ashrai.

He lifted up his legs and sat cross-legged in mid air, hovering alone in the middle of the room, his staff lying across his knees. He reached deep inside himself and unlocked his power, channelling it through his power lance, calling up everything he'd ever been or hoped to be. He could feel his esp building, pressing at his shields, eager to be free and loose in the world. He had learned many things in his time on Unseeli, whether he'd wanted to or not, walked paths few humans even knew of, and it had changed him. He was more than human now, a bastard child of Man and Ashrai, and the alien was about to find out what that meant.

He threw his mind up and out, searching for the voices in the wind that were always there, just on the edge of his consciousness. Bright lights blazed, dazzling him with their presence. They were old and powerful and utterly inhuman, warm and familiar and comforting; his friends and his adopted people. He called, and they came for him, where they would not have come for any other. The outlaw Carrion, once a man named Sean, talked to the Ashrai in a language and manner that had nothing human in it.

Silence looked back at Carrion, floating unsupported in mid air, and felt his hackles stir uneasily. There was more than ten years' difference in the outlaw's cool, serene face, and sometimes it seemed to him that he didn't know this man Carrion at all. His voice was still the same, but sometimes Silence thought he saw someone else looking out at him through Carrion's eyes. Silence shrugged mentally. He'd put all their lives in that familiar stranger's hands, and it was too late now for second thoughts. His head snapped back as something stirred in the darkness at the end of the corridor, and then the alien came storming out of the shadows towards them, horribly fast and unstoppable. It raised its blunt unseeing head, and its awful voice reverberated in the narrow space.

Silence and Frost fired their disrupters. The vivid energy beams seared through the alien's vast body, exploding the black flesh and spattering it across the walls, and didn't even slow it down. Silence and Frost put away their guns, drew their swords and raised their force shields. They stood ready to meet the alien, knowing they couldn't hope to stand against it, but doing it anyway because it was their job and their duty, and because there wasn't anything else they could do, after all. The alien burst into the room, into what had been the heart of its web, its shell, and there was no time left for anything.

And then the Ashrai came.

Silence walked in the metallic forest, each gold and bronze and silver tree blazing like a star. The trees were singing, and though he was not a part of it, still the song trembled in his bones and in his soul, as though it was something he had known and left behind, long ago. Sean and Frost and Diana walked with him, all of them glowing like the trees. Frost looked younger, happier, at ease with herself, and for the first time since he'd met her, she wore no weapons. No sword or gun or grenades. She looked almost naked without them, but her eyes were clear and untroubled. Sean looked much as he used to, in the days when they could still be friends, with nothing to separate them. He smiled at Silence, and there was understanding if not forgiveness in the outlaw's eyes. And Diana shone more brilliantly than any of them.

The Ashrai walked in the forest, dead but not gone, huge and awesome, with their gargoyle faces and massive bodies, clawed hands and piercing eyes. They sang in harmony with the trees, and power burned brightly in them. The song and the power roared in human and Ashrai alike, building and building, vast and potent, blazing so brightly they knew they had to use it soon or it would burn them all out. The force that drove them focused and concentrated in one person, and Silence had enough of himself left to be faintly surprised that the focus was Diana, not Carrion. Diana Vertue, inhumanly treated but still human, more of an esper than the Empire had ever allowed her to be, unbroken and above all still somehow innocent, with purity of heart and thought and purpose. The power blazed in her, and without rage or hatred she turned it on the alien from outside. It was in the forest too, burning in strange hues, silent and malignant. It shrank back as the song of the trees washed over it, pure and piercing in Diana's voice, and in a moment that seemed to last for ever, the alien's light guttered and went out and was gone.

And with the alien gone, a host of new voices sounded in the metallic forest; the 127 men and women of Base Thirteen, free at last from the terrible thing that had been done to them. Their lights flickered and went out one by one, and there was no sadness in their leaving. It was what they had hoped and prayed for, for so long. Two familiar faces smiled briefly; Stasiak and Ripper, bound together on one last journey. They saluted briefly, and were gone. Diana looked out over the Base, and reached casually down to lower the force Screen and stop the nuclear countdown. The clock stopped ticking and the bomb disarmed itself, and as simply as that, it was all over.

And then the Ashrai withdrew a little, and looked at John Silence, Captain of the *Darkwind*, ambassador of the Empire.

The man who gave the order for the scorching of Unseeli. Silence stood alone, offering no explanation or defence, because he had none. He didn't ask for mercy for himself because he expected none, but he did ask it for Frost and Diana, because both were innocent, in their way. They smiled and came to stand beside him, facing the Ashrai, because, after all, they belonged together. And that just left Carrion, once called Sean, standing alone between Ashrai and humanity, both and neither. The outlaw leaned on his staff and said nothing.

He passed judgement on us, said a multitude of voices. *Now it shall be passed on him. He must die.*

No, said Frost. *It was his duty.*

No, said Diana. *He has made atonement.*

He must die.

No, said Carrion. *He is my friend.*

As you wish.

And then the Ashrai were gone, and the lights in the trees seemed a little less magnificent without them. And Silence and Carrion and Frost and Diana turned and walked away from the metallic forest, knowing that the memory of its song would always be with them now, wherever they went and whatever they became.

CHAPTER ELEVEN

All the Ghosts Come Home to Roost

They left Base Thirteen, stepping one at a time past the unmoving metal doors, and stood blinking owlishly at the evening twilight. Dark clouds filled the sky, filtering the light into shades of grey, but even so it seemed uncomfortably bright after so long in the darkness of the Base. The sun was a crimson ball riding low on the sky, but the metal trees still blazed fiercely against the falling night. The mists were thickening, moving slowly among the trees like restless thoughts. Three moons drifted high on the evening sky, pale and listless like the memory of sunlight.

Silence stretched slowly, feeling an almost physical relief now that the mission was over, and he could finally relax and wind down. It hadn't ended in quite the way he'd thought it would, but then, that was Unseeli for you. Things seemed to have worked out well enough. All that remained now was to return to the *Darkwind*, and spend his time in Quarantine working out a written report his superiors could believe. He had a feeling that might take some time. He looked across at Carrion. The outlaw stood alone, a little way from the others, his face calm, his gaze fixed on the metallic forest. His cloak hung about him like the folded wings of a bird of prey, and Silence thought he could still sense some of the deadly power Carrion had unleashed in the Base. He wasn't the man Silence remembered, and he didn't know whether to feel sad or relieved. The old Carrion had been desperately unhappy. But the outlaw had found something in his exile with the Ashrai, and Silence thought it might just be peace.

Investigator Frost was calmly running through an inventory of the weapons she'd used up in her fight against the alien and its offshoots. She still had a surprising number left, though Silence was damned if he knew where she'd hidden them about her person. And Diana Vertue, his ship's esper, his daughter, was staring out at the glowing metal trees with wide, fascinated eyes. Silence stirred uneasily as he saw something in her face of the cool alienness in Carrion's gaze. He looked out at the trees, and a faint echo of the Ashrai song moved within him. He knew the song would always be with him now, murmuring quietly in the depths of the back brain, where all the important instinctive decisions are made. But already the strength of the vision was fading, slipping away from him even as he tried to hold on to it. Perhaps that was for the best, after all. He couldn't have retained the song in all its power, and still have remained human. He'd seen what it had done to Carrion. And to Diana. He moved over to stand beside her, and she nodded politely to him before looking back at the trees.

'How do you feel, Diana?'

'Strange. Tired. Different. I don't know, Captain. I've got a lot to think about. I just wish we could have saved some of the Base personnel.'

'They were already dead long before we got here,' said Silence. 'At least we were able to set them free. That's something. I'm not sure how much I believe of what I saw when the Ashrai sang. I can't believe the alien had captured all those souls in its machines . . . but I'm glad we did the right thing, anyway.'

Diana nodded slowly. 'What will happen to the trees now, Captain?'

'They should be safe enough. That strange crystal-based stardrive you and Frost found in the crashed alien ship changes everything. According to Carrion, it's vastly superior to ours. We're going to have to study and duplicate the alien drive, if we're to stand any chance against the aliens. And since this new stardrive apparently doesn't need the heavy metals our drives use, we don't need Unseeli's trees any more. I suppose there'll still be some mining here, as long as some of us are still using the old drive, but that'll die out, over the years. Unseeli will finally be safe from the Empire, for the simplest of reasons; because Unseeli has nothing the Empire wants any more.'

'There's going to be a war with the aliens, isn't there,' said Diana, and there was no question in her voice.

'It's inevitable,' said Silence. 'As their species spreads out, looking for new spawning grounds to colonise and dominate, they're bound to encounter human planets. And since their whole existence is dependent on taking over and transforming every other life form they come across, I don't really see any chance of our two species agreeing to coexist. You saw the alien's home planet, in that memory crystal. There's no place in their life cycle for peace or diplomacy or mutual interests. They live only to expand, transform and assimilate everything they encounter. They probably wouldn't even recognize us as a sentient species; just new genetic material to add to their melting pot. They're a deadly threat to the whole Empire, and the Empire has always known how to deal with threats. There's a war coming all right, and it's going to be the bloodiest, deadliest war in our species' history; a war for the survival of humanity.'

'Right,' said Carrion. 'At long last the Empire has found a species as deadly and single-minded as itself. The war will never end till one species or the other is extinct.'

'Right,' said Frost. 'It's going to be magnificent. I can hardly wait.'

There was a pause, as the others looked at each other and decided they were going to pretend she hadn't said that. Silence cleared his throat.

'I think we'd better get back to the pinnace. It'll be night soon, and this place is cold enough during the day. Odin; I take it you're still listening in. How are the repairs going? Are you ready for us to board yet?'

'The repair situation is well in hand, Captain. The pinnace is ready to take off at a moment's notice. However, I'm afraid I can't let any of you back on board.'

There was a long pause, significant with meaning, and when Silence finally spoke, his voice was calm and even and very controlled. 'What do you mean, you can't let us back on board? You agreed that if we saved the Base and its contents from destruction, you'd take us back to Quarantine on the *Darkwind*.'

'I lied,' said the AI. 'My programming allows me to be flexible

368

under emergency conditions. It was important to motivate you to protect Base Thirteen and its contents, so I lied. I never had any intention of letting you back on board. I'm afraid all of you are contaminated by this new alien species, and I must protect the *Darkwind*.'

'Listen, computer,' said Silence. 'Conditions on Unseeli after nightfall are practically sub-polar, and the Base is a mess. You can't just abandon us here.'

'Yes I can, Captain. My programming is most explicit on this matter.'

'To hell with that,' said Frost. 'Computer; Code Red Seven. Acknowledge.'

'Code Red Seven acknowledged, Investigator.'

'Power up the pinnace and stand ready to transport us all back to the *Darkwind*, to start our Quarantine.'

'Yes, Investigator.'

Silence looked at Frost. 'Code Red *Seven*? Even I don't have that kind of Security clearance.'

'Neither do I,' said Frost. 'I stole it, some time back. I always thought it would come in handy. And anyway, Investigators are supposed to use their initiative. The computer will do what it's told now. Won't you, Odin?'

'Yes, Investigator. I will serve you to the limits of my programming. I will follow your orders . . .'

'Computer.'

'Yes, Investigator?'

'Shut up.'

'Yes, Investigator.'

Silence looked at Carrion, and indicated with his head that he wanted to talk to Carrion in private, a little away from the others. The outlaw nodded, and the two of them moved unhurriedly away from Frost and Diana.

'My offer of a Pardon still stands,' said Silence quietly. 'Your experience in defeating the alien makes you a valuable asset. The Empire is going to need what you know. You could come back with us, Sean. With me. Rejoin the Service, become an Investigator again. Things have changed in the ten years you've been away. You could write your own ticket, Sean. And we could be together again, just like old times. What do you say?'

The outlaw looked at him for a long moment. 'My name is Carrion, Captain. Sean died a long time ago. I have no wish to return to the Empire, with all its petty politics, hatreds and destructive rages. I don't belong there any more. I've walked the path of the Ashrai for ten years now. I can't go back to being human again. To being only human. Before you came, I was a part of the song of the trees, of the Ashrai. I'd forgotten most of my past. You're a ghost to me, John; an echo of a past that no longer has any real meaning for me. I haven't just left humanity; I've moved beyond it.'

'Then where will you stand, during the war?' said Silence.

'With my people,' said Carrion. 'With the Ashrai.'

'I've missed you, Sean. Please. I don't want to lose you again.'

'You lost me ten years ago, John. It's too late to try and find me now. Neither of us are the people we used to be. I belong here now.'

'In other words,' said Frost, 'he's gone native.'

Silence and Carrion looked round sharply, both of them startled. Neither of them had heard Frost approach, but then she was an Investigator, after all.

'You're welcome to stay here, if you wish,' said Carrion to the Investigator. 'The song is strong in you. I could teach you the ways of the Ashrai, open your mind to wonders you've never even dreamed of. There are treasures of the soul here, just waiting for you to discover them.'

'No thanks,' said Frost. 'Aliens are for killing. It's time to go, Captain.'

'Yes,' said Silence. 'I think it is.'

Diana came over to see what they were talking about and looked, in confusion, from one silent face to another. 'Captain . . . before we go back to the pinnace, can I ask you a question?'

'Of course, esper. What is it?'

'Why do you call the AI Odin?'

'Because he only has one eye,' said Silence. Carrion was the only one who smiled. Diana and Frost just looked at each other blankly.

'Don't they teach mythology in the Empire any more?' said Carrion.

'Not much,' said Silence. 'A lot of it's been censored, or

adjusted. Our superiors thought it might give people ideas. Dangerous things, ideas.'

'Then perhaps it's time we made some new myths,' said Carrion. 'We've started one here, today. A hundred years from now, who we are and what we did will be part of the history books. And how much of us, the real us, will they remember? Or be allowed to remember. But truth lives on, through myths and legends, and our four ghosts will haunt the Empire long after we've gone.'

He nodded once to each of them, and strode off into the thickening mists, disappearing finally into the glowing metallic forest of Unseeli.

HELLWORLD

The sleep of reason brings forth monsters.

CHAPTER ONE

Broken Men

The starship *Devastation* dropped out of hyperspace and moved into orbit around Wolf IV. The planet's surface was hidden from view by the swirling atmosphere. It looked much like any other planet, a drop of spit against the darkness. The ship's sensor spikes shimmered briefly as it scanned Wolf IV, and then the cargo-bay doors swung open. A slender Navy pinnace emerged, sleek and silver, and drifted away from the huge bulk of the starship. The pinnace fell into its own orbit, and the *Devastation* disappeared back into hyperspace. The pinnace slowly circled the storm-shrouded planet, a gleaming silver needle against the star-speckled night.

Captain Hunter gnawed at the insides of his cheeks as he ran his hands over the control panels. It looked like he was going to have to pilot the ship down after all. This far out, the onboard computers were all but useless. They didn't have enough information to work with. Hunter shrugged. What the hell. It had been a long time since he'd had to fly a ship by the seat of his pants, but some things you never forget. Particularly if your life depends on them.

For a moment, the old overpowering uncertainty was suddenly back with him; the familiar panic of not being able to choose between alternatives for fear of doing the wrong thing. His breathing and heartbeat speeded up, and then slowed again as he fought grimly for control. He'd done this before, he could do it again. He ran through the standard instrument checks, losing himself in routine. The control panels blazed with steady, comforting lights. He checked that the pinnace's orbit was still stable, and then released the sensor drones. Hunter watched them fall towards the planet on his viewscreen. The sensor probes had

377

better tell him what he needed to know first time – the odds were he wouldn't get a chance to launch a second series. It wouldn't be long now before the pinnace's orbit began to decay, and then he'd have to power up the engines, ready or not. The ship's batteries only had so much power, and he was going to need most of it for the landing.

Captain Scott Hunter was an average looking man in his late twenties. Average height, average build, perhaps a little leaner than most. Dark hair, and darker eyes. There were only ever five hundred Captains of the Imperial Fleet, the best of the best. At least that was the official version. In reality the only way to become a Captain was through money, power or family influence. Hunter was a Captain because his father had been one, and his father before him. Scott Hunter, however, was one of the few who'd earned his position by merit of training and ability. Which made it even harder to understand why he'd panicked during a rebel encounter above one of the Rim worlds, and lost his ship and half the crew as a result.

If he'd died, no one would have said anything. He would have been posthumously promoted to Admiral, and his Clan would have honoured his memory. But he'd survived, and so had enough of his officers to point the finger of blame. He could have resigned his commission, but he'd had too much pride left to do that, and shame his family. High Command asked him to explain his conduct, but he couldn't do that either. He didn't understand it himself. In the end he was told he could either volunteer for the Hell Squads, or be cashiered. He chose the Hell Squads.

It wasn't much of a choice.

The pinnace's drones hurtled down through the turbulent atmosphere, absorbing what punishment they could. The probes weren't expected to last long anyway. Their sensor spikes glowed crimson from the increasing heat, but did not wilt. Information flowed back to the pinnace's computers in a steady stream as the drones fell endlessly through the thickening atmosphere.

Hunter tried to ease himself into a slightly more comfortable position in his crash webbing. He'd never cared much for webbing. There was no doubt it offered extra protection during rough landings, but he could never get his balance right. He'd never been any good in a hammock, either. He scowled unhappily, and clung to the control panels with one hand, while the other channelled incoming data through the navigational computers. He glanced across at his co-pilot.

'Get ready for data flow. I'm patching in our comm implants.'

'Understood, Captain. Ready when you are.' The Investigator's voice was calm and even, but then it always was.

Investigator Krystel was a striking looking woman. She was barely into her mid-twenties, but her eyes were much older. She was tall and lithely muscular, and her sleek dark hair was pulled back into a tight bun, accentuating her high-boned face. Her occasional lovers thought her handsome rather than pretty. Krystel rarely thought about it. She was an Investigator, trained by the Empire, since childhood, to be loyal, efficient and deadly. Her job was to study newly discovered alien species, and determine how much of a threat they might pose to the Empire. Depending on her findings, the aliens would then be either enslaved or exterminated. There was never any third option. Investigators were cold, calculating killing machines. Unofficially they were often used as assassins in inter-Clan feuds.

Hunter wasn't sure how he felt about Krystel. He'd never worked with an Investigator before. Her training and experience would make her invaluable when it came to keeping the Squad alive on the new planet, but he didn't know if he could trust her. There were those who claimed Investigators were as inhuman as the aliens they studied. Because of who and what they were, Investigators were allowed a hell of a lot of leeway in the Empire. Hunter didn't even want to think what Krystel must have done to merit being banished to the Hell Squads. He didn't think he'd ask. Investigators weren't known for their openness. There was a soundless chime in his head, and he closed his eyes and leaned back in his webbing as the ship's computers patched him in with the probes.

Bright flashes of light and colour filled his eyes, wind and static roared in his ears. His comm implant was tied directly into the optic and auditory nerves, so that he could see and hear first hand what the probes were picking up, but it took time before he and the computers could sort out the useful information from the garbage. Hunter's mind meshed with the computers, and his thoughts flowed among the surging information at inhuman speed, sifting and examining the rush of raw data. Brief glimpses of cloud and sky were interspersed with drop velocities and wind speeds. Weather projections were crowded out by flashes of sea and land impossibly far below. Shifting landing probabilities flared and guttered like candles in a wind. Hunter concentrated, shutting out everything but the bare essentials. The computers were recording everything, he could replay the rest later.

He sensed the Investigator beside him in the computer net; a cold, sharp image that reminded him of a sword's cutting edge. He wondered fleetingly what he looked like to her, and then concentrated on the probes as they fell past the cloud layers and started revealing detailed views of the land mass below. At first, they formed a confusing mosaic of overlapping images, but Hunter quickly relearned the knack of concentrating on each image for the split second it took to register, and then passing on to the next.

Wolf IV had one huge continent, surrounded by storm-tossed oceans. The land was composed of endless shades of green and brown and grey, stained here and there with ugly patches of yellow. There were towering mountain ranges and vast lakes. Volcanic activity filled the air with ash, and molten lava burned crimson and scarlet against the broken earth, like so many livid wounds in the planet's surface. There were large areas of woodland and jungle, though the colours were all wrong, and huge stretches of open grassland. Hunter focused in on one of the larger open areas. It looked as good a place as any to land, better than most.

'Not a very hospitable world, Captain.' The Investigator's voice was sharp and clear in his ear, rising easily over the probes' input.

'I've seen worse,' said Hunter. 'Not often, I'll admit, but then it's not as if we have a choice in the matter. Hang on to your webbing, Investigator. I'm taking us down. Probe seventeen, sector four. See it?'

'Looks good to me, Captain.'

Hunter shut down his comm implant, and surfaced abruptly from the computer net. The dimly lit control deck replaced the probes' visions as his eyesight returned to normal. He rubbed tiredly at his eyes. The landing site looked good. It wouldn't have hurt his confidence any if Krystel had sounded a little more enthusiastic, but perhaps that was expecting too much from an Investigator. He squeezed his eyes shut for a moment. Direct input always gave him a headache. It was psychosomatic, but the pain was real enough. He opened his eyes and stretched uncomfortably, careful of his balance in the webbing. After the sweeping views the probes had shown him, the control deck seemed even more cramped and confined than ever.

Hunter and the Investigator lay in their crash webbing in the middle of a solid steel coffin. Dark, featureless walls surrounded them on all sides, with barely enough room for them both to stand upright. Presumably the designer's idea was that if the pinnace crashed on landing, all you had to do was bury it where it fell. Hunter pushed the thought firmly to one side, and ran his hands over the control panels again. The main engines sent a low throbbing note through the superstructure, and the pinnace began its long fall towards the planet.

The ship shook and shuddered violently as it entered the turbulent atmosphere, held on course only by the unrelenting thrust of the engines. Hunter swung from side to side in his webbing, but his hands were sure and steady on the controls. There was no trace now of the treacherous panic that at times overwhelmed him, and he ran confidently through the routines as old skills and memories came back to him. He tapped into the navigational computers through his comm implant, and the ship came alive around him. The pinnace's sensors murmured at the back of his mind, feeding him a steady flow of information, enabling him to foreguess and outmanoeuvre the worst batterings of the storm winds. Down below, the probes were dying one by one, burning up in the atmosphere or being shattered by the storms. Hunter watched sympathetically as one after another their lights went out on the control panels. They'd been useful, but he didn't need them any more. They'd served their purpose.

Outside the pinnace, the winds shrieked and howled. Warning lights flared on the control panels. The pinnace had lost some of its sensor spines, and the outer hull was breached somewhere back of the stem. Hunter keyed in the auxiliary systems for more power to the engines, and hoped they'd last long enough to get the ship down. It was going to be a near thing. He patched briefly into the probes again, but most of them were gone now. The few remaining drones hurtled towards the ground like shining meteors. Hunter braced himself as the ground rushed up towards him, and winced as one by one their transmissions suddenly shut down. He dropped out of direct input and studied the control panels. He'd have to rely on what was left of the pinnace's sensors to get him down. Assuming they lasted long enough. He patched into them again via the navigational computers, and quickly located the wide open space he'd chosen earlier. The details were blurred by the pinnace's speed, but it didn't look anywhere near as inviting as it had from orbit. A desolate bloody area, in fact. Still, it would have to do. There wasn't time to choose another one. The ship lurched wildly as the winds hit it from a new angle, and Hunter fought to keep the descent steady. There was a shriek of tortured metal as another of the pinnace's sensor spines was ripped away.

'*Attention in the rear. Brace yourselves,*' Hunter yelled through his comm implant. 'We're going in!'

He split his attention between the sensors and the controls, and fought to keep his feel of the ship. It wasn't enough to just work the controls; he needed to feel the ship as a part of himself and react accordingly, his instincts making decisions faster than his mind ever could. And then the ground came leaping up to meet him, and the pinnace hit hard, shaking and jarring the cabin. The landing gear howled as it strove to absorb the impact, and then everything was suddenly still and quiet. Hunter and the Investigator hung limply in their crash webbing. The control-deck lights faded and then brightened again. Hunter waited for his heart and breathing to slow down a little, then reached out a shaking hand and hit the disconnects, powering down the engines. Might as well hang on to whatever power they had left. He sat slowly up and looked around him. The ship seemed to have come through intact, and the Investigator looked as calm and unshakeable as ever.

'All right,' Hunter said hoarsely, 'systems checks and damage reports. Give me the bad news, Investigator.'

'Outer hull breached in three, four places,' said Krystel, studying her panels. 'Inner skin still secure, air pressure steady.

Landing gear . . . battered but intact. The sensors are out. We lost too many spines on the way down. Apart from that, systems are running at eighty per cent efficiency.'

'One of my better landings,' said Hunter. 'Switch to the backup sensors. See what they have to tell us.'

Krystel nodded, and her hands moved assuredly over the panels before her. Hunter patched into the comm net again. At first there was only a silent static, before the outside scene filled his eyes. A patchy fog seethed around the pinnace, milky and luminous in the ship's outer lights. Beyond the light there was only darkness; an endless gloom without moon or stars. For as far as the sensors could show, the pinnace stood alone on an empty plain. Hunter dropped out of the comm net, and sat thoughtfully in silence for a moment. According to the computers, it should be light soon. Perhaps their new home would look more attractive in the daylight. It could have looked a lot worse. Somehow, the thought didn't cheer him as much as he'd hoped. He looked across at Krystel. The Investigator was rerunning the records from the probes on the main viewscreen, and making extensive use of the fastforward and the sudden stop. Hunter decided to leave her to it. He leaned back in his webbing and activated his comm implant.

'This is the Captain. We're down, and more or less intact. Everyone all right in the rear?'

'We're all fine, Captain. Just fine.' The warm and reassuring voice belonged to Doctor Graham Williams. Hunter had met him briefly before the drop. Doctor Williams had an impressive record, a confident manner and a firm handshake. Hunter didn't trust him. The man smiled too much. 'The trip down was a trifle bumpy, but nothing the crash webbing couldn't handle. What does our new home look like, Captain?'

'Bleak,' said Hunter. 'Esper DeChance, run a standard scan of the area. If there's any living thing within a half-mile radius, I want to know about it right now.'

There was a brief pause, and then the telepath's voice murmured calmly in his ear. 'There's nothing out there, Captain. Not even any plant life. From the feel of it, you've dropped us right in the middle of nowhere.'

'I've just had a great idea, Captain.' That was one of the

383

marines, Russell Corbie. His voice was sharp and hurried. 'Let's turn this crate around and tell the Empire the whole damned planet was closed for renovations.'

'Sorry, Corbie,' said Hunter, smiling in spite of himself. 'We pretty much drained the ship's batteries just getting down here. There's no way she'll ever be lifting into orbit again.'

'So we're stuck here,' said Corbie. 'Great. Just bloody marvellous. I should have deserted when I had the chance.'

'You did,' said Hunter. 'That's how you ended up in the Hell Squads.'

'Besides,' said Lindholm, the other marine, 'even if we got upstairs again, what good would it do us? You don't suppose the *Devastation* is still there waiting for us, do you? She's long gone, Russ. We're on our own now. Just like they said.'

The marine's words seemed to echo ominously. No one else said anything. The quiet seemed strange, almost eerie, after the chaos of the trip down. Now there was only the slow ticking of the cooling metal hull, and the occasional murmur from the computers as the Investigator studied the main viewscreen. Hunter stretched slowly in his webbing, and frowned as he tried to get a grip on what he should do first. There were any number of things he should be doing, but now that the moment had come he found he was strangely reluctant to act, as though by committing himself to any one of them, the marooning of the pinnace would suddenly become fixed and real.

Hunter had had a lot of time to get used to the idea of being abandoned on Wolf IV, but somehow it had never seemed real. Even on the morning before the drop, he'd still been half expecting a reprieve, or a standby, or something to happen that would mean he didn't have to go. But there was no reprieve, and deep down he'd known there wouldn't be. His Clan had turned its back on him. As far as they were concerned, he was already dead. Hunter bit his lower lip as the implications came home to him with new force.

There wasn't going to be any backup. The only high tech the Squad had was what they'd brought with them, and that would only last as long as the energy crystals that powered it. If anything went wrong, there was no one they could call on for help. They were alone on Wolf IV. The first colonists wouldn't be on their way for months, even assuming Wolf IV checked out as habitable. Long before then, the Hell Squad would either become completely self-sufficient, or they would all die.

On the other hand, there was no one here to interfere, either. For the first time in his career, Hunter had a completely free hand. On Wolf IV there were no more stupid rules and regulations to work around, no more having to bow and scrape to fools in high office. Hunter felt a little of the tension go out of him. He could cope. He always had in the past. And the blind, unreasoning panic that had robbed him of his career and his future was just another obstacle he'd learn to overcome in the days ahead. He believed that, with all his heart. He had to. The alternative was unthinkable. He cut that line of thought short. He'd known what he was getting into when he volunteered.

The Hell Squads were one-way planet scouts. They landed on newly discovered worlds, searched out the good and bad points, decided whether or not the place was colonizable, and learned how to stay alive while they were doing it. The Squads had a high mortality rate, which was why they were made up of people who wouldn't be missed: the expendable, the losers and the failures, the rebels, the outcasts and the damned. Broken men and forsaken heroes. The people who never fitted in. Whatever happened on the world they went to, there was no way back. The new world was their home, and would be for the rest of their lives.

Hunter turned to Krystel, who was thoughtfully studying one of her monitor screens. 'Tell me the bad news, Investigator.'

'A lot of the details are still unclear, Captain, but I think I've got the general picture. There's been a lot of volcanic activity around here in the recent past, and it's still going on in some places. The air is full of floating ash, but it's breathable. It's too early yet to start worrying about long-term effects on the lungs, but it might be advisable to rig up some kind of mask or filters before entering the worst areas. Apart from that, all in all the signs look good. Air, gravity and temperature are all within acceptable limits, as promised. Not a particularly pleasant world, but habitable.'

'What can you tell me about the immediate vicinity?' said Hunter, frowning. 'Anything to worry about there?'

'Hard to say, Captain. The sun won't be up for a while, and there're some heavy mists. This planet has three moons, but none of them are big enough to shed much light. We'll have to wait till morning, and then go outside and look for ourselves.'

'That isn't proper procedure,' said the marine Corbie, quickly, his voice breaking in through the comm net. 'First man out is a volunteer job, always has been. And I want to make it very clear that I am not volunteering. First rule of life in the Service: never volunteer for anything. Right, Sven?'

'Right,' said Lindholm.

'Keep the noise down,' said Hunter. 'I'm going to be the first man out.'

He shook his head ruefully as the others fell silent. He should have made sure he was out of the comm net before discussing the situation with the Investigator. Not that Corbie's attitude had been much of a surprise. He'd better keep an eye on that one. Corbie was going to be trouble. Hunter sighed, and clambered awkwardly out of his webbing. Might as well make a start. He'd feel better once he was actually doing something. He stood up tentatively to avoid banging his head on the ceiling, and a few steps brought him to the arms locker. Krystel got out of her webbing to help him, and the two of them manoeuvred carefully in the confined space of the control deck.

First man out required a full field kit. The steelmesh tunic went on first; heavy enough to stop or turn a blade, but still light enough to let him move quickly and easily when he had to. Next came the gun and holster. Hunter felt a little easier with the disrupter on his right hip. The familiar weight was a comfort. The sword and its scabbard went on his left hip. The disrupter was a far more powerful weapon, but the sword was more reliable. The gun's energy crystals took two minutes to recharge between each shot. A sword never needs recharging. Next came a leather bandolier that crossed his chest, carrying half a dozen concussion grenades. Nasty things, particularly in a confined space. Hunter had always found them very useful. Finally, he snapped a force-shield bracelet round his left wrist. He was now ready to face whatever the planet had to offer. In theory, anyway.

He rocked back and forth on his heels, getting used to the change in his weight. It had been a long time since he'd had to wear full field kit. Normally a Captain stayed safely in orbit, while his shock troops got on with the rough stuff down below. Rank hath its privileges. Hunter smiled briefly, and shifted the heavy bandolier into a more comfortable position. *How the mighty are fallen* . . . Still, he'd always intended to be first man out on the new planet; he'd come a long way to see his new home, and it was a moment he didn't intend to share with anyone else. He nodded briefly to the Investigator, then turned round to face the airlock door. Krystel leaned over the control panels. The heavy metal door hissed open. Hunter stepped carefully into the airlock, and the door closed firmly behind him.

The closet-sized airlock was even more claustrophobic than the control deck, but Hunter didn't give a damn. Now that the moment had come to confront the unknown, he felt suddenly reluctant to go through with it. A familiar panic gnawed at his nerves, threatening to break free. Once the airlock door opened and he stepped outside, he would be face to face with the world he would never leave. While he was on board the pinnace, he could still pretend—

The outer door swung open. Thin streamers of mist entered the airlock, bringing the night's chill with them. Hunter raised his chin. Once outside, he'd be the first man ever to set foot on Wolf IV. The history books would know his name. Hunter sniffed. Stuff the history books. He took a deep breath, and stepped gingerly out into the new world.

The great hull of the pinnace loomed above him, brilliant in its coat of lights. Mists, thick and silver grey, swirled all around the ship, diffusing the lights before they were swallowed up by the night. Hunter moved slowly away from the airlock, fighting an urge to stick close to the ship for security. The air was bitter cold, and irritated his throat. He coughed several times to clear it. The sound was dull and muted. The ground crunched under his feet, and he knelt down to study it. It was hard to the touch, but cracked and broken from the pinnace's weight. Pumice stone, perhaps, hardened lava from the volcanoes. Hunter shrugged, and straightened up again. He knew he should move further away from the ship, but he couldn't quite bring himself to do that yet. The darkness beyond the ship's lights was intimidating. He let his hands rest on his gunbelt, and activated his comm implant.

'Captain to pinnace. Do you read me?'

'Yes, Captain. Loud and clear.' Krystel's calm voice in his ear was infinitely reassuring. 'Anything to report?'

'Not a thing. I can't see for any distance, but the area seems deserted. No trace of anything but rock and mists. I'll try again later, when the sun comes up. How long is that?'

'One hour, twenty-three minutes. What does it feel like out there, Captain?'

'Cold,' said Hunter. 'Cold . . . and lonely. I'm coming back in.'

He took one last look around. Everything seemed still and silent, but suddenly his hackles rose and his hand dropped to his gun. Nothing had changed, but in that instant Hunter knew without a shadow of a doubt that there was something out there in the night, watching him. There couldn't be anything there. The sensors and the esper had both assured him the area was deserted. He trusted both of them implicitly. And yet all of Hunter's instincts told him he was being watched. He licked his dry lips, and then deliberately turned his back on the darkness. It was nerves, that was all. Just nerves. He stepped back into the airlock, and the door swung shut behind him.

Dawn rose unhurriedly above the featureless horizon, tinting the remaining mists an unhealthy yellow. The mists had begun to disappear the moment the sun showed itself, the last stubborn remnants were now slowly fading away to nothing. The silver sun became painfully bright, and cast distinct shadows. Everything seemed more than usually distinct, though everywhere the natural colours were muted and faded by the intensity of the light. The sky was a pale green in colour, apparently from dust clouds high up in the atmosphere. The pinnace stood alone on the open ground, a gleaming silver needle on the cracked and broken plain. There was a dark smudge on the horizon, which the ship's probes had identified as a forest. It was too far away to show up in any detail on the pinnace's sensors.

The ship's airlock stood open, with the two marines standing guard beside it. In reality, the ship's sensors would sound a warning long before either man could spot a threat, but the Captain didn't believe in his men sitting around being idle. The marines didn't mind, much. The open plain was far more interesting than the cramped confines of the pinnace. Not far away, Doctor Williams was prising free some samples of the crumbling ground, and dropping them into a specimen bag. All three men worked hard at seeming calm and at ease, but each of them had a barely suppressed air of jumpiness that showed itself in abrupt, sudden movements.

Russell Corbie leaned against the pinnace hull, and wondered how long it would be till the next meal. Breakfast had been one protein cube and a glass of distilled water, neither of which you'd call filling. He'd eaten better in the military prison. He looked around him, but there was still nothing much to see. The open plain was bleak and barren and eerily silent. Corbie smiled sourly. On the way down, his heart had hammered frantically at the thought of the horrible creatures that might be lying in wait for him down below, but so far his first day on Wolf IV had been unrelievedly boring. Still, he wasn't exactly unhappy. Given the choice between boredom and hideous monsters, he'd go for tedium any day.

Corbie was a small, solidly built man in his mid-twenties. His sharp-edged features and dull black uniform gave him an uncanny resemblance to the bird of prey he was named after. His face was habitually dour, and his eyes were wary. His uniform was dirty and sloppy, and looked like someone else had slept in it.

There's one like Corbie in every outfit. He knows everyone, has contacts everywhere, and can get you anything. For a price. The Empire doesn't care for such people. Corbie was in a military prison, and resigned to staying there for some time, when the chance came to volunteer for the Hell Squads. At the time, it had seemed like a good idea.

Sven Lindholm was a complete contrast to Corbie. He was tall and muscular, in his mid-thirties, with broad shoulders and an intimidatingly flat stomach. His uniform was perfectly cut, and immaculate in appearance. His pale blue eyes and short corn-yellow hair gave him a calm, sleepy look that fooled nobody. He wore his sword and gun with the casual grace of long acquaintance, and his hands never moved far from either. Lindholm was a fighter, and looked it.

Corbie sighed again, and Lindholm looked at him amused. 'What is it now, Russ?'

'Nothing. Just thinking.'

'Something gloomy, no doubt. I've never known anyone with such a talent for finding things to worry about. Look on the bright side, Russ. We've been here almost three hours, and so far absolutely nothing has tried to kill us. This place is deserted; there's not even a bird in the sky.'

'Yeah,' said Corbie. 'Suspicious, that.'

'There's no pleasing you, is there?' said Lindholm. 'Would you have preferred it if we'd stepped out of the pinnace and found ourselves face to face with something large and obnoxious with hundreds of teeth?'

'I don't know. Maybe. At least we'd have known where we were then. This place *feels* wrong. You can't tell me you haven't felt it too, Sven. It isn't natural for an open space like this to be so deserted. I mean, it's not like we're in the middle of a desert. You saw the probes' memories; apart from a few extra volcanoes and the odd patch of stormy weather, this world is practically Earth-normal. So where the hell is everything? This kind of planet should be swarming with life.'

'Will you cut it out?' said Lindholm. 'I'm starting to feel nervous now.'

'Good,' said Corbie. 'I'd hate to feel this worried on my own.' He stared at the ground thoughtfully, and hit it a few times with the heel of his boot. The ground cracked and split apart. 'Look at this, Sven. Bone dry. Sucked clean of every last drop of moisture. Can't be because of the day's heat. The sun's up and it's still bloody freezing.' He studied the view again, and sulked. 'I don't know . . . I wasn't expecting a garden planet, but this place gives me the creeps.'

'I shouldn't worry about it,' said Lindholm. 'You'll get used to it, as the years go by.'

'You're a real comfort, Sven.'

'What are friends for?'

They stood together in silence for a while, studying the

featureless plain. The sound of Doctor Williams digging came clearly to them on the quiet.

'What do you think of our Captain?' said Lindholm, as much to keep Corbie from brooding as anything. He already had his own opinion of the Captain.

Corbie's scowl deepened. 'All the Captains we could have got, and we had to end up with Scott Hunter. I did a little research on him before we left the *Devastation*. The man is hard working, a bit of a martinet, and too damned honest for everyone's good. Volunteered for patrol duty out in the Rim worlds, and distinguished himself in four major battles. Could have made Admiral eventually, if he hadn't screwed up. Always assuming he could have learned to keep his opinions to himself, and kiss the right butts.'

Lindholm nodded slowly. 'We could have done worse.'

'Are you kidding?' Corbie shook his head dolefully. 'I know his sort: honest, courageous, and a bloody hero to boot, I'll bet. You can't trust heroes. They'll get you killed one way or another, chasing after their bloody ideals.'

'You're a fine one to talk,' said Lindholm. 'I was there the time you led that charge against the Blood Runners, out in the Obeah Systems, remember?'

Corbie shrugged. 'I was drunk.'

'Well, you shouldn't have that problem here. The nearest bar is light years away.'

'Don't remind me. I'll have to put some thought into building a still.'

'We could have drawn a worse hand,' said Lindholm. 'It's a dismal looking place, no doubt about it, but at least it's not another Grendel or Shub.'

'As far as we know,' said Corbie, darkly.

'Cut it out, Russ.' Lindholm glanced over at Doctor Williams, and lowered his voice. 'What do you know about the rest of our Squad? The way I heard it, the esper got caught making a run for the rebel planet Mistworld, but I couldn't find out a thing about the Doctor, or the Investigator.'

'Don't look at me,' said Corbie. 'I've never even met an Investigator before. I don't normally travel in such high company. The esper's no one special, as far as I know. Just happened to be in the wrong place at the wrong time, and trusted the wrong man. Not bad looking, though, in a spooky kind of way.'

Lindholm snorted. 'Forget it, Russ. The Captain won't stand for any tomfoolery. Beats me how you can think about sex at a time like this, anyway.'

Corbie shrugged. 'I have a reputation to live down to.'

'What about the Doctor?' said Lindholm. 'Why is he here?'

'Ah, the good Doctor; a mystery man indeed . . .'

'All right,' said Lindholm patiently, 'what have you heard?'

'Nothing definite, but the word was that he was involved in some kind of scandal to do with the adjusted men. Forbidden augmentations, that sort of thing.'

Lindholm whistled softly. 'If that's the case, he's lucky to be alive. The Empire's been really tight over that kind of thing since the Hadenman rebellion.'

'Right. Those killer cyborgs threw a scare into everyone. Anyway, as I understand it, Williams was given a straight choice: volunteer for the Hell Squads or end up as spare parts in a body bank.'

'And I was thinking we were lucky to have a Doctor in the Squad,' said Lindholm. 'Still, it could have been worse. He could have been a clonelegger.'

'Will you stop saying it could have been worse! It's bad enough as it is. All the Squads I could have been in, and what do I end up with: Captain Pureheart, a mad Doctor, and a flaming Investigator. I don't even want to think what she did to end up here. Those people are as inhuman as the things they kill.'

'At least she's on our side,' said Lindholm.

Corbie looked at him. 'Investigators aren't on anybody's side.'

The pinnace control deck looked even gloomier than usual with the control panels dead. The single overhead light showed up only the darkness of the shadows. Captain Hunter and Investigator Krystel lay still in their crash webbings, and their eyes saw only light. Patched into the onboard computers through their comm implants, the probes' recordings filled their eyes and ears to the exclusion of the real world.

Hunter concentrated on the scene before him. With direct input, it was too easy to become lost in the sound and fury of

the probes' memories, and forget the real world and its imperatives. He fastforwarded relentlessly, pausing only when the computers pointed out scenes of importance or possible significance.
He felt guilty at leaving the real work to the computers, but he
needed an overview of the situation as quickly as possible. There
were decisions he had to make, and already they were starting to
pile up. When he had a chance he'd study the records in real
time, weighing and evaluating every detail, but right now all he
wanted was information on possible threats and dangers. Everything else could wait. Scene after scene flashed before his eyes,
and Hunter's scowl deepened as Wolf IV reluctantly gave up its
secrets.

In the north, volcanoes threw molten fire into the sky. The
lava burned a deep and sullen red, and ashes fell like rain. There
were vast plains of cooling ash, and all around the land was
baked dry and brittle. A planet as old as Wolf IV was supposed
to have left its volcanic stage behind centuries ago, but instead a
long chain of smoking volcanoes studded the north of the single
great continent, like so many warning balefires.

The oceans were racked by endless storms, and mountainous
waves rose and fell. Among the churning waves, huge creatures
fought a never-ending battle for survival. It was difficult to judge
their size from a distance, even seen against the height of the
waves, but the sheer ponderousness of the creatures' movements
hinted at appallingly vast dimensions. Hunter didn't even want
to think what the damned things would weigh on land. It was
clear that in the future all travelling would have to be by land
and air – no ship would survive a sea voyage. Some of the things
rending and tearing each other looked to be almost as big as the
Devastation.

Huge areas of forest, solid masses of dirty yellow vegetation,
filled the centre of the continent. The probes didn't show much
in the way of detail, but trees were usually a good sign for a
colonist. You could do a lot with wood. Hunter smiled for the
first time as the probes' memories moved on to show him large
areas of open grassland in the south, but even so, he kept a firm
grip on his enthusiasm. First rule of the Hell Squads: never take
anything for granted. On an alien world, nothing is necessarily
what it seems. All right, from a distance it looked like ordinary,

everyday grass: the colour was a bit vile, but you can't have everything. But on Scarab, the long grass had turned out to be carnivorous. On Loki, the grass had an acid-based sap, and spread like plague in the night. Everything on a new planet had to be treated as potentially dangerous, until proved otherwise by exhaustive testing. And then the scene changed again as a new probe's memories patched in, and Hunter's heart missed a beat. He hit the emergency halt, freezing the image in place, and swallowed with a suddenly dry throat.

'Investigator,' he said finally through his comm implant, 'patch into probe seven. I've found something.'

There were structures of stone and glass and gleaming metal. Jagged-edged turrets erupted from asymmetrical buildings. Strange lights blazed in the windows of huge stone monoliths. Low domes glimmered with pearl-like translucency. In the centre of everything, a spiked tower of gleaming copper reached up to touch the sky. And everywhere, hanging lightly between the oppressive shapes and buildings, were frothy strands of gossamer walkways.

'It's a city,' said Hunter, his voice awed and hushed.

'Looks like it,' said Krystel. 'Roughly circular, four miles in diameter. No signs of life forms as yet.'

'I've got the computers checking for similar sightings.'

'They won't find any. We're pretty much near the end of the recordings. If there were any other cities like this, we'd have come across them long before now.'

'Switch to the viewscreen,' said Hunter. 'I want full computer analysis of the recording. This has top priority until I tell you otherwise.'

'Aye, Captain.'

The alien city disappeared from Hunter's eyes, and the control deck reappeared around him. After the haunting, mysterious views of the city, the spartan Empire fittings had a comforting familiarity. The Investigator was already crouched over the control panels, calling up more data. Hunter leaned carefully back in his webbing, and studied the alien city on the viewscreen. Now that the first flush of excitement had died down, he found that his skin was crawling, and he had to keep fighting down an urge to look away. The shapes of the structures were ugly, twisted . . . *wrong*, somehow. They made no sense. There was something actually unnerving about the alien shapes and angles. Whatever theories of architecture had produced the city, they followed no human patterns of logic or aesthetics.

'How far away from us is it?' he asked, and was relieved to note that his voice sounded somewhat calmer.

'Fourteen, fifteen miles. Walking distance. We could be there in a day.'

Hunter looked at her sideways, but didn't say anything. She might see fifteen miles as walking distance, but he sure as hell didn't. Fifteen miles? He scowled unhappily. He hadn't walked that far since Basic Training. And he'd hated it then. He shrugged, and turned his attention back to the viewscreen. Something about the alien city nagged at him. It only took him a moment to realize what. The labyrinth of twisting streets appeared to be completely empty. Nothing moved in the city. Hunter studied the viewscreen for a long time, and then activated his comm implant.

'Esper DeChance, this is the Captain. Please join me on the control deck immediately.'

'Aye, Captain. On my way.'

Hunter shut down his comm unit, and looked at the Investigator. 'No life, no movement. Nobody's home. What do you make of it?'

'Too early to tell, Captain.' Krystel drew a slender, villainous looking cigar from her sleeve pocket, and took her time about lighting it. 'The city could be deserted for any number of reasons, few of them good. And anything alien is always potentially dangerous.' She looked at Hunter. 'Strictly speaking, we ought to report this immediately to the Empire.'

'But if we do that,' said Hunter, 'we'll have to wait till they send in an official Investigatory team. And that could mean a long delay before they send us any colonists . . . or the extra equipment that comes with the colonists. And we need that equipment.'

'Yes,' said Krystel. 'There is that. There's only one choice open to us, Captain. We need more information, so we're going to have to go there and take a look for ourselves. We need to know what happened to the city's inhabitants, and why. If there's anything on this planet deadly enough to wipe out an entire city's population, we'd better find out all we can about it, before it comes looking for us.'

'I couldn't agree more,' said Hunter. 'That's why I've sent for the esper.'

Krystel sniffed, and studied the glowing end of her cigar. 'Telepathic evidence is subjective, and therefore unreliable.'

'Espers have their uses. And I'll trust a human mind over a computer any day.'

The door behind them hissed open, and the esper Megan DeChance stepped on to the control deck. She was a short, wraith-like woman in her late thirties, with long silver-blonde hair. Her eyes were green and very steady and, like the rest of her face, gave nothing at all away. She nodded once to Hunter, and ignored the Investigator. Hunter's heart sank. Traditionally, espers and Investigators didn't get along. By virtue of their telepathy and empathy, espers tended to be fanatically pro-life. Investigators weren't.

'Right, esper,' said Hunter briskly. 'I want a full scan of the immediate area, twenty-mile radius. Never mind plant or animal life, I'm interested in intelligent life forms.'

DeChance raised an eyebrow, but said nothing. She sat cross-legged on the deck between the two webbings, arranged herself comfortably, and closed her eyes. She sent her thoughts up and out, and her mind spread across the world like ripples on a pond. The Hell Squad were bright sparks in and around the pinnace. Everywhere else was dark. She spread out further, and the world blossomed before her. Lives shone in the darkness like flaring torches and flickering stars, but none of them burned with the steady intensity of the intelligent mind.

And yet there was something strange, right on the edge of her perception. Its light was strong but curiously indistinct, its boundaries uncertain. DeChance studied it warily. In a slow, creeping way it seemed to be aware of her. DeChance started to back away, but even as she broke the contact the light suddenly flared up into an awful brilliance. It burned in hideous colours, and it knew where she was. DeChance pulled the darkness around her like a cloak. Something new was abroad in the night, something huge and powerful. There were other things in the darkness too, and one by one they were waking up. Their lights grew bright and awful, and DeChance pulled back her esp, folding it in upon itself, locking it safely away inside her mind again. She opened her eyes, and looked shakily at Captain Hunter.

'There's something out there, Captain. It's not like anything I've ever encountered before. It's big, it's very old, and very powerful.'

'Dangerous?' said the Investigator.

'I don't know,' said DeChance. 'Probably. And it's not alone.'

For a long moment nobody said anything. Hunter felt a chill run up his spine as he realized just how shaken the esper was.

'All right,' he said finally. 'Thank you, esper. That will be all. Please join the others outside. We'll be out shortly.'

DeChance nodded, and left. Hunter and Krystel looked at each other.

'It has to be the city,' said Krystel. 'We've got to go there, Captain.'

'Yes. You've more . . . experience with aliens than I have, Investigator. Assuming we do find something there, what's the best procedure?'

Krystel grinned around her cigar. 'Find it. Trap it. Kill it. And burn the body afterwards, just to be sure.'

Doctor Williams sat quietly in the shadow of the pinnace, hugging his knees to his chest and staring out at his new world. All in all it looked decidedly bleak and barren, and the endless quiet was getting on his nerves. Still, he was lucky to be in the Hell Squad, and he knew it. If the Empire had been able to prove half the charges they'd made against him . . . but they hadn't. His money and influence had seen to that. For a time.

He thought he'd get away with a few years' imprisonment in some comfortable open prison, or perhaps even just a fine and a public admonition. But in the end, too many people had decided they couldn't risk the truth coming out at a trial. So they pulled a few strings, and Doctor Williams found himself heading out towards the edge of the Empire and some nice anonymous Hell-Squad planet, where his secrets could die and be buried with him.

It had all been very neatly done. Men he'd trusted for years had betrayed him, under the pressure of massive bribes and death threats, and suddenly he'd stood alone. He could either go with the Hell Squad, or be shot in the back while trying to escape. Williams had screamed and raged and threatened, and little good it had done him. He hugged his knees tightly, and glared out over the open plain.

Doctor Williams was a tall, slender, handsome man in his late fifties, who looked thirty years younger. His skin was fresh and glowing, and his thick curly hair was jet black. He had a doctor's warm, professional smile and a pleasant manner. Half his organs, most of his skin and all of his hair had come from other people. The donors had all been anonymous, of course. Body-snatchers rarely bother to learn the names of their victims.

Williams also had a great many personal augmentations that the Empire hadn't found out about in the short time they'd held him. Unfortunately, the augmentations were of only limited use to him now. The implanted energy crystals that ran the devices had strictly limited lifespans. Once they were drained of power, all the high tech in his body would be just useless junk. He'd have to make the crystals last, until he could acquire some more.

He smiled suddenly. That was in the future. Now, though the others might not realize it, he was the most powerful man in the Squad. Let the Captain enjoy his moment in charge, for the time being. He'd find out the truth soon enough. Williams's smile widened as retractable steel claws appeared at the tips of his right fingers, and then disappeared again.

He looked down at the soil samples he'd gathered, lying in a neat row in their little bags, spread out on the ground before him. He'd taken the samples as much to keep busy as anything, but there were often riches to be found in the soil, for those who knew where to look. There was money to be made on this planet somewhere, and he had no intention of missing out on any of it. The pinnace's diagnostic equipment was primitive, to say the least, but it would do the job. Williams frowned, and hugged his knees a little tighter. It wasn't at all what he was used to. His surgery had been known throughout the Empire; said by many to be the greatest since the fabled laboratories of lost Haden itself. All gone now, of course. Destroyed by Williams so that its secrets couldn't be used against him.

After the rebellion of the cyborg Hadenmen, the Empire had banned most forms of human augmentation. But there were always those willing to pay highly for forbidden delights. Most of the banned devices had been fairly harmless anyway, as long as they were used sensibly, with restraint. He'd just provided a service, that was all. If he hadn't done it, someone else would have. All right, some of his patients had died, on the table and afterwards. They knew the risks when they came to him. And most had lived, and lived well, through the extra senses and devices he'd given them.

They all came to him: the rich, the titled, the jaded and the decadent. All the ones with hidden needs and darker appetites. And to each he gave what they asked for, and charged accordingly. His prices were high, but they could afford it. Besides, he had his own needs too.

It was the Empire's fault he'd become what he was. He'd made his name and his reputation with his work on the Wampyr, the adjusted men. They were to have been the Empire's new shock troops, strong, awful and ruthlessly efficient, but someone high up got scared of their potential, and the Empress herself closed the project down. Williams had refused to give up his life's work. He went underground. And his triumphs with the Wampyr were nothing to what he might have achieved if the Empire hadn't caught up with him.

He should never have relied so much on the body-snatchers.

But that was all behind him now. He had a new life, and new opportunities. Doctors were always in short supply on colony worlds. One way or another, he would become a man of wealth and standing again. And some way, somehow, he'd use that wealth and power to get off this stinking dirtball and back into the Empire. And then they'd pay. Then they'd all pay for what they'd done to him.

Outside the airlock, Corbie glared at Megan DeChance.

'A city? An alien city? I don't believe it. I just don't bloody believe it! All the planets the Empire had to choose from, and they had to drop us on a world that's already inhabited! I mean, don't they check for things like that first?'

'No,' said Lindholm. 'That's our job. It may not turn out too badly, Russ. There's a lot aliens could teach us about this planet, things we need to know. I'm willing to be friendly if they are.'

'It's not very likely, Sven,' said Corbie. 'You know the Empire's attitude to aliens. They get put in their place, or they get put in the ground. No other choice available.'

'This is a new world,' said Lindholm. 'Things could be different here.'

Corbie sniffed. 'Try telling that to the Investigator.'

'I'm afraid it's not that simple,' said DeChance quietly. 'According to the probes, there aren't any other cities. And this one appears to be deserted.'

'Wait a minute,' said Corbie. 'You mean there's nobody there?'

'There's something there,' said DeChance. 'I felt its presence.'

The two marines waited for her to continue, and then realized she'd said all she was going to. Corbie kicked at the ground in disgust. 'Mysteries. I hate bloody mysteries.'

'I doubt it's anything we can't handle.'

The marines looked round sharply as Williams came over to join them. He smiled at them warmly, and nodded to the esper.

'I'm sorry if I interrupted you. I didn't mean to intrude . . .'

'No, that's all right, Doc,' said Lindholm. 'This concerns you as well. Seems there's an abandoned alien city not far from where we've parked.'

'Fascinating,' said Williams. 'I do hope we're going to explore it.'

'Great,' muttered Corbie. 'Another bloody hero.'

Williams ignored him, and concentrated his charm on Lindholm and the esper. 'What do you make of our new home, my friends?'

'A little on the desolate side,' said Lindholm. 'I've seen livelier cemeteries.'

'It's not very attractive, I'll admit,' said Williams calmly, 'but I wouldn't write it off just yet. There may be hidden virtues. Geology isn't my strong point, but if I've read the signs correctly, the ship's computers just might find these soil samples very interesting.'

He patted the satchel he was carrying. Corbie looked at him with new interest.

'Are you saying there might be something here worth digging for? Gold, precious stones, things like that?'

'That sort of thing, yes,' said Williams. 'I think a few test drillings might well turn up something to our mutual advantage.'

'Jewels are fine,' said Lindholm. 'But you can't eat them. For a long time to come our only interest in the soil is going to be how well it supports our crops. The ship's rations will run out in a few months, and that's if we're careful. After that, we're on our own. Presumably there are plants and animals here somewhere that will prove safe to eat, but we'll always need our own crops to supply us with vitamins and trace elements. First things first, Doctor.'

'You've been studying up on this,' said Corbie.

'I thought one of us should,' replied Lindholm.

'I shouldn't worry too much about the crops,' said Williams. 'The volcanoes might look rather dramatic, but they help to produce good soil. All that pumice stone is full of phosphates, lime and potash. Just add the right nitrates, and food should come leaping up out of the ground in no time.'

'Unfortunately, there are complications,' said DeChance. 'Have you come across any signs of life yet, Doctor?'

'No,' answered Williams. 'Is that significant?'

'Wouldn't surprise me,' Corbie said darkly.

'Don't mind him,' said Lindholm. 'He thinks they're all hiding from him. And if I was an alien getting my first glimpse of Corbie, I'd think about hiding too.'

'I'm surprised the Captain hasn't joined us yet,' said Williams casually. 'I thought he'd be eager to set about taking in his new territory. That is what military types like to do, after all. Or do we have a Captain who doesn't like to get his hands dirty?'

'He seems solid enough,' said Lindholm, frowning.

'And he can take all the time he likes about coming out, as far as I'm concerned,' said Corbie. 'It's nice and peaceful out here without him. Who needs some officer type yelling orders? That's one of the few good things about being in a Hell Squad; no more dumb rules and regulations.'

'The Captain's in charge of the Squad,' said Williams. 'He still gives the orders.'

'Yeah, but that's different,' said Corbie. 'What I'm talking about is no more having to salute, no more surprise inspections, no standing guard in the rain because your boots aren't shiny enough, or slaving all day over makework designed to keep the lower orders busy. I've had a bellyful of that in my time. And besides . . . just suppose I did decide I wasn't going to obey an order – what could Hunter do about it? There aren't any Guards or Military Police here to back him up. There's just him—'

'Wrong,' said Investigator Krystel.

They all looked round quickly, to discover Krystel and Captain Hunter standing just outside the open airlock. Corbie couldn't help noticing they both had hands resting near their disrupters. He smiled uneasily, and stood very still.

'The Captain is in command here,' said Krystel. 'You do as he says, or I'll hurt you, marine. We're still citizens of the Empire, with all the responsibilities that entails.'

'Oh sure,' said Corbie quickly. 'Anything you say, Investigator.'

'I gather some of you are interested in mineral rights,' said Hunter. 'Jewels, precious metals and the like. If I were you, I should bear in mind that very few colonists ever strike it rich. They're too busy working every hour God sends just to keep their heads above water. No, people, it's much more likely you'll get yourself killed doing something stupid because you were daydreaming about goldmines instead of keeping your mind on the job. For the time being, just concentrate on keeping yourself and the rest of the Squad alive. Now then, since you've all had a nice little rest, I think it's time for a spot of healthy exercise. Some fifteen miles from here is a deserted alien city. We're going to go and take a look at it. On foot, with full field kit and standard backpacks. We start in thirty minutes.'

'On foot?' Williams raised an eyebrow. 'Why not fly there in the pinnace? There's more than enough power in the batteries.'

'That's right, there is,' said Hunter. 'And that's where it's staying, until we come across an emergency that justifies using it. I'm certainly not wasting it on a joyride. Besides, I think it's better that we take our time approaching the city. This world is still new to us; if we're going to make mistakes, let's make them where it doesn't matter. Oh, and people, keep your eyes open and your heads down. This is a reconnaissance mission, not an attack force.'

'But what about the pinnace itself?' said Williams. 'Is it wise to just go off and leave it unguarded? Anything could happen to it while we were gone. And if anything were to happen to the equipment stored on board—'

'Doctor Williams,' said Hunter pleasantly, 'that's enough. I'm the Captain, I don't have to explain myself to you. And I don't take kindly to having my orders questioned all the time. You must learn to trust me, Doctor, and obey my orders implicitly. Because if you don't I'll let the Investigator have you. The pinnace will be perfectly safe in our absence. Isn't that right, Investigator?'

'Right,' said Krystel indistinctly, relighting her cigar. She puffed at it a few times to make sure she'd got it just the way she wanted, and then fixed Williams with a cold stare. 'We'll activate the force Screen before we go, and the computers will be on battle readiness until we return. All told, the ship will probably be safer than we will.'

'You got that right,' said Corbie. 'If we're going up against aliens, I want hazard pay.'

'Technically speaking, we shouldn't really call them aliens,' said Doctor Williams. 'This is their world, after all. If anyone's alien here, it's us.'

The Investigator chuckled quietly. 'Wrong, Doctor. Aliens are aliens, no matter where you find them.'

'And the only good alien is a dead alien,' said Corbie. 'Right, Investigator?'

Krystel smiled. 'Right, marine.'

'How can you justify that?' said DeChance heatedly. 'Everything that lives has some common ground. We share the same thoughts, the same feelings, the same hopes and needs—'

'You ever met an alien?' said Krystel.

'No, but—'

'Not many have.' Krystel drew on her cigar, blew a perfect

smoke ring, and stared at it for a long moment. 'Alien isn't just a noun, esper, it's an adjective. Alien; as in strange, different, inhuman. Unnatural. There's no room for the alien inside the Empire, and this planet's been a part of the Empire from the moment an Imperial ship discovered it. That's Empire law.'

'It doesn't have to be that way here,' said Lindholm slowly. 'If we could contact the aliens peacefully, make some kind of alliance—'

'The Empire would find out eventually,' said Hunter. 'And then they'd put a stop to it.'

'But why?' said DeChance. 'Why would they care?'

'Because aliens represent the unknown,' said Corbie. 'And the Empire's afraid of the unknown. Simple as that. Not too surprising, really. The unknown is always threatening, to those in power.'

'Sometimes they have reason to be afraid,' said Krystel. 'I was there on Grendel, when the Sleepers awoke.'

For a long time no one said anything.

'I thought no one got out of there alive,' said Lindholm, finally.

Krystel smiled. 'I was lucky.'

'I think that's enough chatting for one day,' said Hunter. 'Get your gear together, people. Keep it simple, the bare minimum. Remember, you've got to carry it, and we might have to travel in a hurry. Report back here in thirty minutes, ready to leave. Don't be late, or we'll go without you. Now move it.'

The Squad turned as one and filed quickly back into the pinnace. At the rear, hanging back, Corbie looked at Lindholm.

'An alien city,' he murmured quietly. 'You ever seen an alien, Sven?'

'Can't say I have,' said Lindholm. 'That's what Investigators are for. I met a Wampyr once, on Golgotha. He was pretty strange, but not actually alien. How about you? You ever met an alien?'

'Not yet,' Corbie said grimly. 'I just hope our Investigator has enough sense not to get us in over our heads. We're a long way from help.'

CHAPTER TWO

In the Forest of the Night

The silver sun rode high on the pale green sky. The world lay stark and bare under the brilliant light, and no sound broke the silence. The mists were gone, dispersed by the rising sun, but the day was no warmer. The Hell Squad moved warily through the quiet morning, walking in single file, their hands never far from their gunbelts. Hunter led the way, alert for any sign of movement on the open plain, but for as far as he could see there wasn't a trace of life anywhere. There were no animals, no birds in the sky, not even an insect. The continuing silence was eerie and disquieting. The soft sound of the Squad's boots on the plain was quickly swallowed up by the quiet, and there wasn't even a murmur of wind.

Hunter hefted his backpack into a slightly more comfortable position, and tried not to think about the miles of hard open ground that lay between him and the alien city. His legs ached, his back was killing him, and there was still another nine or ten miles to go. And what was worse, his feeling of being watched was back again. He'd been free of it for a while, but once they'd left the pinnace behind the feeling had come back even stronger. Hunter frowned. He'd never felt this worried before, not even when he was heading into battle. Not even at the bad times; the times he'd panicked for no good reason. Hunter swallowed hard. He felt light-headed and his hands were shaking. He could feel the beginnings of panic stirring within him.

Not now. Please, not now.

He fought the panic fiercely, refusing to give in to it, and slowly it subsided again. Hunter breathed more easily, but he wasn't fooled. He knew it would be back again, the moment he weakened. Hairs prickled on the back of his neck. The feeling of being watched was as strong as ever. Hunter kept wanting to stop and look around him, but he didn't. He didn't want to look jumpy in front of the others.

He raised his hands to his mouth and blew on them. The morning was several hours old, but it still felt as though it was barely above freezing. Hunter rubbed his hands together, and wished the Empire had included winter clothing in its list of essential supplies. The heating elements in his uniform could only do so much. Right now he'd have traded his disrupter for a good pair of thick gloves.

The forest drew slowly closer, and Hunter studied it dispassionately. It looked like they were nearly upon it, but distances were deceiving in the overbright light. They'd been approaching the forest boundary for the best part of an hour, but only now was it starting to give up its secrets. Hunter frowned. What little he could make out wasn't exactly encouraging. The huge trees were packed close together, and soared up into the sky. The wide trunks were iron black, gnarled and whorled, and the foliage was a dark, bitter yellow. The leaves were all different shapes and sizes, and many of the twisted branches drooped down to the ground.

The ground approaching the forest was cracked and broken, and clumps of spiky grass sprouted up from the crevices. The grass grew thicker and more frequent as the Squad finally drew near the forest boundary, some of it rising to almost two feet in places. Hunter called a halt so that Williams could take a close look at it. The Doctor knelt down and studied a clump of grass carefully without touching it. The long spikes were wide and flat, pale violet in colour, and marked with a curious ribbing, almost like bones.

'Interesting,' said Williams. 'The grass is purple but the forest leaves are yellow. It's usual for vegetation to be mostly the same colour, particularly when it's growing under uniform conditions.'

'Maybe they draw their nourishment from different sources,' said Hunter.

'Perhaps,' said Williams. 'I'll take a few specimens, and run them through the computers later.'

Hunter looked at the Investigator, who shrugged. 'No objections, Captain. We've all had the standard immunization shots.'

'All right,' said Hunter. 'Take your time, Doctor. I'm sure we could all use a little rest.'

'Certainly.' Williams looked at Corbie. 'Pull me up some grass, young man, while I prepare a specimen bag to hold it.'

Corbie shrugged, and knelt down beside the nearest clump of grass. He grabbed a handful, and then gasped and let go quickly.

'What is it?' said Krystel.

Corbie opened his hand and stared at it. Long cuts marked his palm and the insides of his fingers. Blood welled from his hand and dripped on to the thirsty ground. He reached into his pocket with his free hand, pulled out a handkerchief and pressed it gingerly against the cuts. He straightened up and looked menacingly at Williams, more angry than hurt. 'The grass edges are razor sharp! I could have lost my fingers!'

'Now that is interesting,' said Krystel.

Corbie looked at her. He said nothing, but his gaze spoke volumes.

'All right,' said Hunter quickly, 'let that be a warning for all of us. From now on keep your hands to yourselves, and don't touch anything until we're sure it's safe. And Corbie, use someone else's handkerchief for a bandage. That rag you've got there is filthy, and I don't want your cuts getting infected.'

Corbie sniffed and looked put upon, but accepted Lindholm's offer of a clean handkerchief. He wrapped it carefully round his cuts. Lindholm knelt down and cut away a few spikes of grass with his dagger. Williams slipped them into a self-sealing bag and tucked it carefully into his backpack. Hunter checked everyone was ready, and then led his Squad on towards the waiting forest. He wasn't too unhappy about the incident. Corbie hadn't been badly hurt, and it was a lesson his people had needed to learn. Apart from the Investigator, they hadn't been showing nearly enough respect for their new environment. Even now, it might take a serious accident before they did, and he couldn't afford to lose anybody.

The forest spread out across the horizon as they approached its boundary. It was bigger than Hunter had expected, and looked to be several miles wide. He activated his comm implant, and patched into the pinnace's computers. 3.7 miles at its widest. Hunter frowned suddenly as he shut down his implant. He

407

shouldn't really do things like that any more. Once the energy crystals in his body were depleted, all his high-tech implants would be useless. Better to save his tech for when it was needed. He made a mental note to mention it to the others later. The Investigator came to a sudden halt beside him, and he stopped to see what she was looking at. The rest of the Squad pulled up around them. The Investigator was looking intently at the ground just ahead.

'Everyone stay where they are,' said Krystel softly. 'Captain, I suggest we all draw our guns.'

'Do it,' said Hunter. There was a brief whisper of sound as the Squad pulled their disrupters from their holsters. Hunter looked unobtrusively about him, but couldn't see anything threatening. 'What is it, Investigator?'

'Straight ahead, Captain, two o'clock. I don't know what it is, but it's moving.'

Hunter looked where she'd indicated, and a chill went through him that had nothing to do with the morning cold. Something long and spiny was oozing up out of one of the cracks in the ground. It was flat and thin, and the same dirty yellow as the trees' foliage. At first Hunter thought it was some kind of jointed worm or centipede, but the more he looked at it the more it resembled a long strand of creeper or ivy. It had no visible eyes or mouth, but the raised end swayed back and forth as though testing the air. It was as wide as a man's hand, and already several feet long, though more of it was still emerging from the crack. Dozens of hair-fine legs suddenly appeared at its sides, and flexed impatiently as the rest of the long body snapped up out of the crevice. The creature scuttled across the open ground with horrible speed, and then froze in place, the front end slightly lifted, as though listening.

'Ugly looking thing,' said Corbie, trying to keep his voice light, and failing. 'Look at the size of it. Is it a plant or an animal?'

'Could be both, or neither,' said the Investigator. Her gun was trained on the creature, and had been since it appeared. 'Would you like it as a specimen, Doctor Williams?'

'Don't think I've got a bag big enough to carry it in, thank you,' said Williams.

'Kill it,' said Corbie. 'I'm not sharing the pinnace with that horrible thing.'

'Take it easy,' said Hunter. 'We don't know that it's dangerous, and it is the first living creature we've come across. It could tell us a lot about this world.'

'I don't think it's got anything to say that I'd want to hear,' said Corbie.

'There are more of them,' said DeChance suddenly. The esper had one hand pressed to her forehead, and her eyes were closed. 'They're right here with us, just under the surface. They're moving back and forth in the earth. I think they were attracted by the sound of our approach.'

'Can you read them?' said Hunter quietly.

'No. They're too different, Captain. Too alien. The few impressions I'm getting don't make any sense at all.'

She broke off as more of the creatures suddenly thrust up through the cracks in the ground. Within moments there were dozens of the things all around, curling and coiling and scuttling back and forth. They moved in quick little darts and flurries, crawling over and under each other without pausing. The Squad formed a defensive circle, guns at the ready. Corbie gripped his disrupter tightly, and wished the Captain would give the order to open fire. The damned things moved too quickly for his liking. He had an uneasy suspicion they could move even quicker if they wanted to. Probably as fast as a running man . . .

'Orders, Captain?' said Lindholm, his voice as always calm and controlled.

'Stand your ground,' said Hunter. 'They don't seem too interested in us. I think we can afford to practise live and let live with anything that seems willing to leave us alone. There's an opening to the left. Start moving towards it.'

He stepped forward to lead the way, and every one of the creatures snapped round to point in his direction. Hunter froze where he was. The creatures held their position, their raised front ends swaying slightly.

'They respond to movement, Captain,' said the Investigator. 'And I don't think they believe in live and let live.'

'Wait a minute,' said Corbie. 'Look at the heads. Those are

409

mouths, aren't they? I would have sworn they didn't have mouths a minute ago.'

'They've got teeth as well,' said Lindholm. 'And I'm sure they didn't have those before. What the hell is going on here?'

'Watch it,' said DeChance. 'They're moving!'

The creatures surged forward with unnerving speed. Krystel took careful aim with her disrupter and blew a hole through the middle of the pack. The rest of the Squad followed her lead, and the air was full of the hiss of energy bolts. Half the creatures disappeared instantly, vaporized by the searing energy. More were torn apart by the shock waves, and ragged lengths of dirty yellow flew through the air, still coiling and twitching. The survivors slithered back into the cracks in the ground, and were gone in seconds. Krystel holstered her gun, drew her sword, and moved cautiously forward. Hunter accompanied her, and then gagged as the smell hit him. Both the dead and the injured creatures were already decaying, falling apart and melting into a stinking grey jelly. Krystel stirred some of the bodies with the tip of her sword, but there was no reaction.

'If all the plants are this active, the forest should prove positively lively.' Krystel turned and looked at Hunter. 'Captain, I strongly suggest we stay clear of the forest. We don't have enough information to judge the risks accurately. There could be anything at all in the forest, just waiting for us to come within reach.'

Hunter scowled. Theoretically, she was right. But going around the forest instead of through it would add hours to their journey. It would also mean having to spend at least one night out in the open. All alone, unprotected, in the dark . . .

'We're going into the forest, Investigator. Our disrupters took care of those plant creatures easily enough. Listen up, people. We're going to enter the forest in single file. Stay close, but no bunching up. Don't touch anything, and keep your eyes open. Guns at the ready at all times, but don't fire unless you've got something specific to aim at. Now follow me.'

He led the way into the trees, and the forest shadows closed in around him. The overhead canopy of branches let through some light, but, even so, it was like walking straight from day into twilight. The others followed him, giving the scorched remains on the ground a wide berth. Hunter stopped a few yards inside the boundary, and the Squad stood together a moment, getting the feel of the forest. It felt a little warmer among the trees, but it wasn't comfortable warmth. It was the humid warmth of illness and decay. There was a faint unpleasant odour suffusing the air, and the crowding trees were distinctly claustrophobic.

Krystel checked her force-shield bracelet was primed and ready, and then drew her gun. She still carried her sword in her other hand. Hunter would have liked to check his bracelet as well, but he didn't. It might make him look nervous and indecisive. He didn't like putting his people at risk by going through the forest, but all the other alternatives were worse. The straightforward logic of that didn't do a thing towards easing his conscience. He looked around him to see what the rest of the Squad made of the forest.

The Investigator looked cold and collected, as always. She was staring ahead into the gloom, tapping the flat of her sword lightly against her leg. Doctor Williams was looking cheerfully about him, fascinated by the alien trees. He was smiling again. It wasn't natural for a man to smile as often as he did. The two marines were talking quietly together. Corbie looked a little rattled, but then he always did. Lindholm looked relaxed and at ease. Presumably once you'd survived the Golgotha Arenas, there wasn't much left that could scare you. Megan DeChance's face was blank. Her gaze was fixed miles away. Hunter's mouth thinned. Espers had their uses, but you couldn't trust them. Like Investigators, they weren't really human, not deep down where it counted.

Hunter turned his attention back to the forest. It seemed quiet, almost peaceful. Maybe it was. It didn't make any difference in the long run. He had a job to do, and he was going to do it come what may. Wolf IV was his chance to redeem himself, in his own eyes if not those of the Empire. He'd failed as Captain of a starship because he was weak. This time he'd do it right, by the book and by the numbers. This time he wasn't going to fail. Whatever it cost. He moved slowly forward into the forest shade, and the Squad followed him.

They moved cautiously through the oppressive silence, watching and listening, but there was only the dim light and the soft

411

muffled sounds of their boots on the forest floor. Hunter looked at Krystel, striding unconcerned at his shoulder. Did she ever worry about the things normal people worried about? Like failing, making mistakes, being less than the best at what you did? Hunter almost smiled. Krystel was an Investigator; an instrument of death and destruction that just happened to look like a human being. Hunter's brief glow of amusement faded quickly as he considered the implications of that thought. If the Squad was to survive on Wolf IV, they were going to have to learn to work together as a team. He wasn't sure if that was possible with Krystel. Or the esper, for that matter. Hunter smiled slightly. The Squad was his responsibility, he'd just have to make it possible. He moved a little closer to Krystel, so that they could talk quietly without the others hearing.

'Tell me, Investigator, how much actual experience do you have with alien cultures?'

Krystel glanced at him briefly, and then looked back at the forest. 'Just the two, Captain. Once on Loki, and then on Grendel.'

She didn't say any more. She didn't have to. The aliens on Grendel had turned out not to be indigenous. They were a genetically engineered killing force, left in suspended animation by their long-departed creators. Whatever they'd been created to fight was also long gone, but when the archaeologists woke them up, they woke up mad and they woke up fighting. Their weapons had been interred with them; high-tech implants that were the equal of any Empire weapon. They were monsters and they were unstoppable. They slaughtered everything sent against them. Luckily, it turned out the aliens had no starships of their own. They were trapped on Grendel. In the end the Imperial Fleet moved in and systematically burned off the whole planet from orbit.

And Krystel had been the Investigator assigned to work with the archaeologists. The one who'd missed the first signs of danger. No wonder she'd ended up in a Hell Squad.

Hunter was more disturbed by that than he wanted to admit. It stood to reason that any Investigator in a Hell Squad would have to be second rate, but he'd assumed it would at least be someone who knew their business . . . He frowned as he realized how much he'd been unconsciously relying on Krystel's knowledge and expertise to help him through the early days on Wolf IV. Now it seemed the burden was going to fall on him alone, after all.

Krystel watched the Captain's face out of the corner of her eye. She could all but read his thoughts. Let him worry; she'd prove him wrong. Prove them all wrong. Anyone would have missed the signs on Grendel. No Investigator had ever encountered such a thing, before or since. It wasn't her fault, no matter what the Empire had said afterwards. She kept a careful watch on the forest around her, but she was more occupied with her thoughts on the alien city. She could feel a familiar excitement growing within her. The challenge of the unknown, the chance to take on an alien culture and prove yourself, superior to it in the only way that mattered; by gun and sword. Krystel smiled inwardly. Do a good enough job on the alien city, and the Empire might even reinstate her. Stranger things had happened.

Megan DeChance walked through the forest with downcast eyes. There was nothing to see, but still she knew that they were not alone. She could feel watching eyes all around them, like a pressure on her skin. She kept her mind firmly closed lest the pressure grow too strong, and roll over her like a wave and drown her. She forced herself to lift her head and look around, but there was only the forest. Tall, twisted trees loomed dark and glistening in the twilight of an alien sun. Seen up close, the foliage was an unpleasant yellow, like rancid butter. The black bark was knotted and bumpy, and she could have seen strange faces in the shapes if she'd chosen. The trees stood closely together, but drew apart here and there to form the narrow path that the Squad were following. DeChance swallowed hard. A path implied that someone passed through the forest on a regular basis. Or had done so. It might even lead straight to the city.

'Captain,' she said clearly, 'I think we should stop a moment.'

Hunter raised his hand, and the Squad came to a halt. He looked back at DeChance. 'What is it, esper?'

'The path we're following is too regular to be natural, Captain. And I keep getting the feeling we're being watched.'

Hunter nodded slowly. 'Listen to the forest, esper. Tell me what you hear.'

DeChance nodded reluctantly, and her eyes went blank. Her breathing became slow and regular, and all the personality went out of her face as the muscles slackened. Hunter looked away. It wasn't the first time he'd seen an esper in deep trance, but it never failed to disturb him. It was like looking at a death mask. DeChance opened her eyes, and her face took on shape and meaning again, as a glove does when a hand fills it.

'There's something there, Captain, but nothing I can get a hold on. Whatever it is, it's awake and aware and in pain. Terrible, maddening pain. I thought at first it might be dreaming – it was a lot like watching a nightmare from the outside. But the pain's too real for that.'

'Be more specific,' said Hunter. 'Are you talking about a single creature? That's all there is in the forest?'

'I don't know. Possibly. It's unlike anything I've ever encountered before.' DeChance paused for a moment, and then fixed Hunter with her unsettling pale eyes. 'I can't find a trace of any other life in the forest, Captain. No animals, no birds, no insects. There's a chance that what I'm picking up is the forest itself; a single living organism.'

Hunter looked at the Investigator. 'Is that possible?'

Krystel shrugged. 'Group minds have been a popular theory for years, but no one's ever found one.'

'If this is a group mind, could it be dangerous?' said Hunter impatiently.

Krystel smiled. 'Anything alien is dangerous, Captain.'

And that puts the decision back in my hands, thought Hunter. Go on? Go round? Go back? He looked around him again. The packed ranks of brooding trees threw back his gaze with cold indifference. Hunter hesitated, uncertain what to do for the best. He could still turn around and go back, but as yet they hadn't come across anything actually threatening. On the other hand, the esper was right, there should have been some kind of life in the forest. Instead, it was as quiet as the grave. But they were still safer in the forest than they would be out on the plain at night. Probably . . . He looked back at his people.

'Investigator, you and I will take the point. DeChance, you

and Williams stay close behind us, but don't crowd us. Yell out if you sense anything threatening. Corbie, Lindholm, you bring up the rear. Guns at the ready, people. If in doubt, shoot first and ask questions later. I don't want anyone or anything getting closer to us than ten feet. Got it?'

Everyone nodded. Williams raised a tentative hand.

'Yes, Doctor, what is it?'

'Shouldn't we activate our force shields, Captain? Just in case?'

'It's up to you. But bear in mind they'll drain their energy crystals dry after only a few hours' continuous use. You might prefer to save your shield for when you really need it.'

Williams flushed, and nodded quickly. Hunter moved off into the gloom, and the others followed.

The smell grew worse. A damp, acrid smell of drifting smoke and crushed leaves. The ground underfoot became broken and uneven, rising here and there in crooked ridges as tree roots rose up against the surface. The darkness pressed close about the narrow trail. The Squad's footsteps sounded loud and clear on the quiet, but the tightly packed trees soaked up the echoes almost before they started.

Corbie clutched his gun so tightly his fingers ached. He was scared again, and had to fight to prevent it showing in his face. He had enough pride left for that, at least. He and Lindholm were supposed to be the Squad's fighters; their defenders and protectors. The others depended on them. Corbie managed a smile at that, but it wasn't much of a smile. It had been a long time since he'd been able to protect anyone, including himself. There had been a time when drink had given him the courage he needed to get through each day, but for some months now even that hadn't been enough. Everyday problems had become increasingly difficult to deal with. Anything beyond the routine had become suspect and even terrifying. He was tense all the time, and his muscles ached. He didn't sleep much, and when he did he had bad dreams.

After the war against the Ghost Warriors, something had broken inside him, and never mended. It was getting harder and harder for him to hide the fact, but for the moment at least he still had his pride, and he wouldn't give it up. It was all he had left. Besides, he couldn't show his shame in front of Lindholm.

The man was a legend in the Arenas; took on all-comers for three years and never once looked like losing. There were rumours he'd killed a Wampyr with his bare hands in a private match. Corbie smiled sourly. Maybe that was why he stayed so close to Lindholm; hoping some of the courage would rub off.

He didn't like the forest. The shadows were too dark, and the quiet had the texture of something only rarely disturbed. Corbie looked unhappily about him and licked his dry lips compulsively. Something felt wrong. He couldn't see or hear anything specific, but his instincts were yelling so loudly his stomach was cramping in sympathy. At first, he'd dismissed it as just more of his nerves at work, but he was still too much the professional to believe that for long. The esper was right. The Squad was being watched. A shadow moved at the corner of his vision, and Corbie had to use all his self-control to stop his head turning to follow it. He stared straight ahead.

'Captain,' he said quietly. 'Movement. Four o'clock.'

Hunter looked casually in that direction, and then away again. 'I don't see anything, Corbie.'

'I did. Twice. I think it's moving along with us.'

'Damn.' Hunter stopped, and lifted his hand. The others came to a halt. 'All right, people, form a circle. Take your time, but leave yourselves enough room to use your swords. Don't use your guns unless you have to. Remember, a lot can happen in the two minutes it takes your disrupter to recharge between shots.'

The Squad started to move, and the forest fell apart. A tree directly before them slumped forward like a melting candle. Leaves dripped from its branches and splashed on the ground. The gnarled trunk lost its definition, and collapsed into a pool of frothing liquid that spilled sluggishly across the trail. There was a swift rasp of steel on leather as the Squad drew their swords. DeChance cried out in disgust as something soft and clinging fell on to her shoulders from above. It took her only a few seconds to realize it was a fallen branch, and she'd just started to relax when it whipped around her throat and tightened. She clawed at it with her free hand, and the branch collapsed under the pressure of her hold. It oozed between her fingers as she pulled it free and threw it away.

'Back to back!' yelled Lindholm. 'Everyone back to back. And watch your neighbours as well as yourself.'

All around them, the forest was melting and deforming. Shapes could not hold, and tree trunks stretched and melted into each other. Leaves fell to the ground in a living rain. They lay in heaps, curling and uncurling like dying moths. Branches elongated like boiling taffy, flailing at the Squad from all sides with blind ferocity. The Squad defended themselves with their swords, the cold steel slicing through the waving branches with hardly any effort. Claws and barbed spikes erupted suddenly from the branches, and fanged mouths yawned in the ground. Unblinking eyes stared from bubbling tree trunks. They weren't human eyes.

Corbie raised his gun and fired at the nearest tree. It exploded, sending hundreds of writhing particles flying through the forest, but even as they landed they were still pulsing, still moving, still alive. The ground began to shake underfoot. Deep in the forest, something howled.

'Head back down the trail,' yelled Hunter. 'Force shields on. Make for the boundary.'

The Squad's hands went to their bracelets, force shields blinked into existence on their arms. The glowing oblongs of pure energy shimmered brightly in the gloom, proof against any weapon known to man. The Squad moved quickly back down the trail. Barbed roots thrust up out of the earth and stabbed at them. A tree spotted with dark cancerous growths leaned out over the trail. Hunter raised his gun, and the tree suddenly lost all shape and form and surged towards him like a wave of dark, boiling water. He raised his shield before him, and his arm shook as the full weight of the melting tree slammed against the glowing shield and fell past its edges in bubbling streams. Corbie and Lindholm moved quickly in beside him, and took some of the weight on their shields.

All around the Squad the forest was collapsing and falling apart, yet still somehow clinging to awful forms of life. The Squad edged back down the trail, a few feet at a time. The force shields spat and crackled, edge to edge, as they formed a defensive barrier round the group. The forest had become unrecognizable. Vague shapes stirred in the frothing carpet that boiled around the Squad, fountaining up into blurred forms with teeth and claws and staring eyes. The remaining trees were slumping against each other, losing definition and meaning as they mixed and merged. The living rain continued, and the shadows became subtly darker.

Hunter's breathing had become painfully quick and hurried, and he had to fight for air. All his instincts were screaming at him to cut and run for the boundary, but he couldn't do that. Panic gnawed at his courage, but he wouldn't give the forest the satisfaction of seeing him run. He had led his people into the trap, and he would lead them safely out again. Somehow he kept the fear out of his face, and if his hands trembled he wasn't alone in that. He fired his disrupter ahead of him, blowing away a mass of twitching branches that sought to block the trail. It helped that at last he had something solid and real to face, and he could bury his panic in the rush of action. He glanced at Corbie and Lindholm beside him. Lindholm was smiling absently as his blade flashed out to cut through a reaching black tentacle. Corbie's swordwork was slower and less sure, but he fought with a furious, dogged tenacity that kept the forest at bay. Hunter looked away, disgusted at the panic that still tore at him, blind and stupid and almost overwhelming.

If there's any hope for this Squad's survival, he thought bitterly, it lies with those marines, not with me. They're fighting men . . . and I'm not. Not any longer.

It seemed to take for ever to reach the edge of the forest, but suddenly the pressing darkness gave way to sharp, brilliant light, and the air was clean and fresh again. The Squad staggered away from the boundary, weak with shock and relief, but still somehow holding formation and keeping their guns trained on the forest. The trees had become a dark writhing mass. Branches like long gnarled fingers stretched out after the Squad with slow, sinuous movements, but seemed unable to pass far beyond the forest's boundary. Hunter slowly lowered his gun and turned off his force shield, and one by one the others did the same.

'Looks like you were right, esper,' said the Investigator calmly. 'The forest is alive and aware.'

'Smells more like it's been dead for months,' said Corbie. He scrubbed at the black stains that fouled his uniform, quietly pleased that his voice also sounded calm and steady.

The Squad cleaned themselves up as best they could, scrubbing away the marks the forest had left on them. A thick, viscous slime clung to their clothes and skin. It seemed to pulse slowly with a life of its own, and had an unpleasant fleshy feel. The Squad took turns scraping it off each other's backs and shoulders.

'No wonder there weren't any birds or animals in the forest,' said Hunter finally. 'The forest must have eaten them all. That damn stuff's got the perfect camouflage. You don't realize you're in any danger till you're right in the middle of it.' He turned to DeChance. 'What can you sense now, esper?'

DeChance frowned. 'Nothing clear. Hunger. Rage. Pain. And other things I don't recognize. If they're emotions, they've no human equivalent.'

'What are we going to do now, Captain?' Williams' voice was polite but pointed. 'We can't go through the forest, but going round it will add miles to our route.'

'Then we'll just have to walk a little further,' said Hunter. 'The exercise will do us good.'

He kept his voice easy and relaxed. It now seemed certain they'd have to spend the night out in the open, the one thing he'd wanted to avoid, but there was no point in worrying his people unnecessarily. They should be safe enough, provided they took reasonable precautions.

Krystel looked thoughtfully at the forest. The trees at the boundary had resumed their normal shape, but beyond them there was only a seething darkness. 'I think we were lucky in there, Captain. The forest could have killed us all if it had reacted to us quicker.'

'It was asleep,' said Megan DeChance. 'It had been asleep for a long time. We woke it up.'

Hunter looked sharply at the esper. Her voice was slow and slurred, and her pale eyes were vague and lost. She stood facing the forest, but her gaze seemed fixed on something far beyond. The Squad looked at each other uncertainly. Lindholm took DeChance by the arm and shook her gently, but she didn't

419

respond. Hunter gestured for the marine to leave her be, and stepped in close beside her.

'It's been asleep a long time,' said the esper. 'Dreaming. Stirring occasionally as the world turned. It's all been asleep—'

'What has, Megan?' said Hunter softly.

'Everything.' Her eyes suddenly cleared, and she shook her head dazedly. 'Captain, I . . . I don't know what I was picking up there. I was tapping into something immense, but it was so strange, so—'

'Alien,' interrupted Investigator Krystel.

'Yes,' said DeChance, almost reluctantly. 'I'm sorry I can't be more specific, Captain. I've never felt anything like that before. I didn't begin that trance – something called to me. Something . . . horrible.'

The loathing in her voice silenced the Squad for a while. Hunter was the first to pull himself together.

'All right,' he said briskly. 'Keep listening. If whatever it was tries to contact you again, let me know immediately.' He looked away from the esper and studied the forest. If there was something out there watching for them, it might be best to provide it with a smaller target . . . or two.

He turned his back on the forest and addressed the Squad. 'We're going to split into two groups, people. The Investigator, Doctor Williams and I will try the western route round the forest. The rest of you will follow the eastern route. Take your time, keep it quiet and keep your heads down. Two small parties should be harder to spot than one big one, but only as long as we're careful not to draw attention to ourselves. The two distances looked pretty much the same on the computer map, but the terrain is different – that could cause difficulties. Whichever group gets to the city first is to wait at the boundary until the other team joins up with them. That's an order. DeChance, you're in charge of your group. Remember, everyone, the purpose of this little trip is to gather information, not to take needless risks. All right, that's it. Let's go, people.'

The two marines nodded briefly, and then set off towards the east with Megan DeChance. Hunter watched the esper go, and frowned thoughtfully. He had no doubts about Lindholm and Corbie; they could look after themselves. But the esper . . . that last trance of hers worried him. She'd looked . . . different, out of control somehow, as though the contact had briefly overwhelmed her. He sighed quietly. The trouble with espers was that they were so damned spooky that, even under normal conditions, you couldn't be sure if there was anything wrong with them or not.

It was asleep. We woke it up.

Woke what up? Hunter scowled. There were always more questions, and never enough answers to go round. Still, the odds were the city would change all that. One way or another. Hunter nodded abruptly to the Doctor and the Investigator, and set off towards the west, giving the forest boundary a more than comfortable margin. Williams and Krystel followed silently after him.

Beside them, the forest moved through shape after shape, searching through memories of times long gone for one form it could hold to.

Hunter's group walked in silence for the best part of an hour. The forest gradually began to settle back into stillness, and the trees at the forest's boundary became firm and solid. Dirty yellow leaves hung from steady iron-black branches, and the gnarled boles were thick and sturdy. But further within, the darkness still stirred and writhed; indistinct forms came and went, and the few shapes Hunter could make out were strangely disturbing, as though they hovered on the edge of comprehension without ever achieving it. His hand itched for his disrupter. The forest offended him. He wanted to burn it to the ground, cleanse it with fire, punish it for pretending to be something it wasn't. In an alien world, where nothing looks or feels right, there's a constant temptation to see the familiar in things that bear only a slight resemblance to the original memory. The forest had looked reassuringly normal; almost comforting. Hunter had badly wanted there to be at least one place on his new world where he could feel safe and at ease. Now that had been denied him. The forest had betrayed him by being alien.

Investigator Krystel studied her two companions dispassionately as they walked along together. The Captain was going to be a problem. He wasn't being decisive enough. From her own

421

experience in the field she knew that staying alive on an alien world depended on quick thinking and quicker reflexes. If the Captain had listened to the esper's warnings, the forest wouldn't have caught them unawares so easily. The Captain was too trusting. Krystel smiled slightly. There was only one rule to studying the alien: be prepared to shoot first.

She had her orders. In the event of Hunter proving unsatisfactory as team leader, she was to replace him with herself. By force, if necessary. It shouldn't be too difficult. The Doctor wouldn't oppose her – he was weak, and easily swayed. The marines would follow orders, no matter who they came from, providing they were given confidently enough. And the esper would do as she was told. Espers knew their place. But when all was said and done, Krystel had no wish to be team leader. She didn't care for the work or the responsibility of giving orders. She worked best when others set the goals and restrictions for her. She knew where she was then. Her role as Investigator left her free to concentrate on the things that really interested her. Like killing aliens. So she'd give Hunter all the rope he needed. And only hang him with it if it proved necessary.

The alien city troubled her. Technically, she should have insisted on contacting the Empire the moment they discovered the city's existence, but she didn't want to do that, just yet. Probably for the same reason the Captain hadn't. Firstly, she'd look a fool if it turned out to be nothing more than a deserted ruin. They'd accuse her of panicking. And secondly, if she reported the city, the Empire would take it away from her. They wouldn't trust her to do the job properly; not after Grendel. The Fleet would send their own team in, and they'd get all the glory. Krystel wanted this city for herself. She'd use it to prove to the Empire that they'd been wrong about her. She was still an Investigator.

She tapped into the pinnace's computers, and ran the records on the city. The strange towers and monoliths lay superimposed on the scene before her, like pale disturbing ghosts. The patterns and buildings matched nothing she'd seen anywhere else, which was something of a relief. The Empire's main fear had always been that someday it would run into an alien counterpart. So far, interstellar war was nothing more than a computer fantasy, and everyone fervently hoped it would stay that way. After the discoveries on Grendel, the computer predictions had become increasingly depressing. Whatever had created the living killing machines on Grendel was quite possibly even more deadly and implacable than the Empire itself.

Aliens. As yet there had been no sightings of whatever built the city, but still Krystel felt a familiar tingle of excitement running through her at the thought of encountering a new alien species. There was something about the use of sword and gun that brought her truly alive. All Investigators knew a single truth, and based their lives around it. Mankind has always achieved his best in the pursuit of violence. Investigators were the end result of society's search for the perfect killer; the most deadly weapon humanity could forge.

And like all weapons, they needed constant tempering in the heat of battle to maintain their strength and cutting edge.

Williams tried to keep his eyes away from the melting forest, and concentrated on the alien city. There was money to be made there, he could feel it. But the Captain was going to be a problem. Dictatorial, overbearing, and too strait-laced for his own good. If there were any profits to be made from this world, Williams had a strong feeling it would be in spite of, rather than because of, Captain Hunter. Still . . . Williams smiled slightly. It was a dangerous world. It was always possible the Captain would have an accident. A very regrettable, but thoroughly fatal accident.

The forest moved slowly past them as they made their way round its perimeter. Hunter kept a careful eye on the more solid boundary, but the forest made no threatening moves. Hunter began to breathe more easily. Perhaps the forest was going back to sleep again.

The bright sun was high in the morning sky when they came across the water hole. It was roughly circular, some ten feet across, and maybe a dozen yards away from the forest boundary. Hunter brought the group to a halt, and stood a cautious distance away from the hole while he studied it. The water lay a foot or so beneath the level of the surrounding ground, which was dry and rock hard, just like everywhere else. The water had a dark crimson colour, and when Hunter leaned forward he caught a whiff of a faint, sharp smell he couldn't identify. The sides of the hole were scalloped in a series of regular markings, and looked as though they'd be unpleasantly smooth to the touch.

'We'd better mark the hole's position,' said Hunter finally. 'We're going to need a supply of fresh water soon.'

'Assuming it's drinkable,' said Krystel. 'We only have a limited supply of purification tablets.'

'Yeah.' Hunter frowned. 'I should have brought some dowsing equipment, so I could run tests on freely occurring water. It's one of the things we're going to have to sort out fairly quickly. Damn.'

'Don't care much for the colour,' said Krystel. 'Or the smell.'

'Perhaps I can help,' said Williams. He moved slowly forward, keeping a watchful eye on the water hole, and then knelt down beside it.

Hunter drew his gun and trained it on the well. 'That's close enough, Doctor. What did you have in mind?'

Williams held up his left hand, and retractable sharp-edged sensor spikes emerged from under his fingernails. 'I have a number of options built in, Captain. You never know when they'll come in handy. Now, with your permission . . .'

Hunter looked around him. The forest was still and quiet, and the open plain was bare and empty for as far as he could see. 'All right, Doctor, go ahead. But be very careful. There's no telling how far down that water goes, or what else might be in it apart from water.'

'Understood, Captain.' Williams leaned forward, and lowered his fingertips into the water. The extruded sensors glowed faintly, five shimmering sparks in the crimson water. Bright metallic lettering appeared before his sight, detailing the water's ingredients.

'Well?' said Hunter. 'Is it drinkable?'

'I'm afraid not, Captain. This stuff's more like soup than water. Most unusual make-up. I'm reading metallic salts, a fairly high acid level, and what appear to be some enzymes.'

Krystel frowned. 'That isn't a naturally occurring mixture, Captain. It sounds more . . . organized.'

'Yeah,' said Hunter. 'I think you'd better get away from there, Doctor.'

Williams drew his hand back out of the water, and the dweller below struck quickly while its prey was still within range. A dark blue tentacle shot up out of the water and slapped around Williams' wrist. He screamed with pain as the hold tightened, and had to brace his legs against the side of the well to keep from being drawn in. The tentacle snapped taut.

Hunter fired instinctively with his disrupter, and severed the tentacle. Williams fell backwards, and scrambled away from the water hole without bothering to get up. The severed tentacle thrashed back and forth in the water. Pale purple blood flew on the air. Hunter stepped back to avoid it, and three more tentacles erupted out of the churning water, attracted by the movement. They whipped around Hunter, pinning his arms to his sides, and then snapped taut. Hunter crashed to the ground, and fought desperately against the tentacles' pull. Their hold tightened, and hundreds of minuscule barbs grated against his steelmesh tunic.

Krystel drew her sword and cut at the nearest tentacle. The sharp edge barely penetrated the leathery flesh, and she sawed at the tentacle to try to weaken it. The Captain was dragged steadily closer to the well's edge, despite all his struggles. Krystel glared at Williams, who was sitting nursing his bruised wrist.

'Grab him, dammit. I can't do it all myself!'

For a moment Williams was tempted to tell her to go to hell. He wasn't about to risk his life for the Captain's. One look at Krystel changed that. He wasn't stupid enough to get an Investigator mad at him. He moved quickly forward and grabbed Hunter's legs. The extra weight slowed the tentacles down, but Hunter was still being drawn closer to the water's edge. Krystel sheathed her sword, drew her gun, and fired into the water. The tentacles writhed, slamming Hunter and Williams against the ground, but didn't release their hold. Krystel swore unemotionally, and put away her gun. She unclipped a concussion grenade from her bandolier, primed it, and tossed the grenade into the middle of the well. It quickly disappeared, and for a long moment nothing happened. The tentacles snapped even tighter, and Hunter dug his heels in against the broken ground. Williams clung to the Captain's legs and swore breathlessly.

Water fountained up out of the well as the grenade exploded down below. The tentacles bucked and heaved, throwing Hunter and Williams away. The water boiled and frothed, and chunks of partially broiled flesh bobbed to the surface. The tentacles whipped back into the water and disappeared. The surface of the water gradually grew still, and a long, peaceful silence fell over the water hole.

'Is there any lifeform on this planet that isn't treacherous and disgusting?' said Hunter, sitting up slowly and carefully.

'Early days yet, Captain,' said Krystel, lighting a new cigar. 'The rest could be downright devious.'

Williams got unsteadily to his feet. 'I think we should all return to the pinnace. The Captain and I could both be suffering from internal injuries.'

'Don't make such a drama out of it,' said Hunter. He rose to his feet and made a token attempt at wiping the dirt from his uniform. 'We're just bruised and battered, that's all. Now let's get moving again. The sooner we put some distance between us and whatever it is that's living at the bottom of that well, the better I'll like it. And in future, if we come across any other water holes, I think we'll drop a grenade down it first, and check the quality of the water afterwards.'

He turned his back on the water hole and walked away. Krystel and Williams exchanged a glance, and moved off after him.

Corbie and Lindholm strolled after Megan DeChance as they left the melting forest behind them and headed out over the broken plain. The esper was some way ahead of the two marines, and the gap was slowly widening. DeChance glanced back over her shoulder, her face set and grim. She was tempted to order them to walk faster, but she had a strong feeling they'd just ignore her. Technically, she was of a superior rank, and the Captain had specifically put her in charge of the group. But none of that mattered a damn; Megan DeChance was an esper.

Espers had a contradictory status in the Empire. On the one hand, their powers made them invaluable servants, much sought after and prized. But on the other, those same powers made them officially sanctioned pariahs; feared and detested by those in authority. Espers were conditioned from their earliest childhood to know their place; to be meek and obedient and cooperative, and never, ever, to challenge authority. Those who had trouble learning these lessons found them brutally enforced. All espers carried some scars, physical and mental. They were second-class citizens, tolerated only because they were needed. Every esper dreamed of escape, but there was only one sanctuary from the Empire, and that was the rebel planet Mistworld. Getting there was a long and dangerous journey, and only a few ever made it. Megan DeChance hadn't even got close. Which was possibly why she'd been allowed to join a Hell Squad instead of the body banks.

Corbie didn't give a damn about espers. He didn't trust them, but then Corbie didn't trust anyone, including himself. If you don't trust anyone, they can't let you down. As for the esper's authority, if she didn't push her luck, he wouldn't either. He was in no hurry to get to the alien city. Let the Captain and his team get there first. They had the Investigator.

He looked disinterestedly around him as he strolled along. The plain rose before him, and then fell away again. Banks of pale red clouds sailed majestically overhead, clashing gaudily with the green sky. The ground was hard and unyielding under his feet, and covered with endless cracks. Corbie supposed he must have seen a more desolate landscape somewhere before, but he was damned if he could think where.

They'd just crossed the high ridge when a low rumbling sound suddenly broke the silence, and the ground shifted slightly underfoot. Corbie and Lindholm stopped dead in their tracks and looked quickly around them, but the wide open plain below was bare and deserted. Megan DeChance hurried back to join them, and the two marines moved automatically to protect her with their bodies in case of attack. The ground slowly grew still, but the rumbling sound continued, growing louder and more ominous. Corbie dropped his hand to his gun and glanced at Lindholm.

'What the hell is it, Sven?'

Lindholm shrugged, his face impassive. 'Could be building to an earthquake. You're bound to have some earth disturbance with so much volcanic activity going on. It would explain why the ground's so broken up.'

'It's not an earthquake,' said DeChance slowly. 'I've seen this kind of terrain before. This is geyser country. Keep watching. They should start spouting any time now.'

Almost as she spoke, a jet of boiling white water burst up out of one of the cracks on the plain below and fountained high up into the sky. The water roared like a wounded animal, a deep grating sound that resonated in rhythm with the shaking ground. The fountain seemed to hesitate at the top of its reach, and then fell reluctantly back to the parched earth. The cracked ground drank up the water thirstily. One after another, a dozen and more geysers burst up out of the ground, mud and boiling water flying up into the green sky at heartstopping speed. The thunder of the geysers became deafening. Corbie turned to ask De-Chance a question, but the geysers drowned him out no matter how loudly he shouted. In the end, he gave up, and just watched the towering fountains as they soared into the air. Finally, one by one, the geysers fell away and disappeared as the underground pressure that fed them collapsed. A light mist of water droplets formed a haze in the air. The ground rumbled quietly to itself for a while, and then fell still.

'Impressive,' said Lindholm.

'Yeah,' said Corbie. 'It's a good thing we stopped where we did. If we'd been walking through those geysers when they started spouting . . .' He shook his head quickly, and then looked at DeChance. 'You're in charge, madam. What do we do now? Turn around and go back?'

'It might come to that,' said DeChance, 'but I don't think so. Geysers usually spout at regular intervals. As long as we time it right, we should be able to walk right through them while they're quiet, and be safely beyond them before they spout again.'

Lindholm nodded slowly. 'We'd have to time it exactly right. And even then, we couldn't be sure. Those geysers were quiet until we approached. It's possible our presence set them off. If that's so, the timings might change as we move.'

'Unlikely,' said DeChance. 'It was just that we couldn't see them until we topped this ridge. This area should be within range of the pinnace's sensors. All we have to do is wait for the geysers to blow again, then patch into the ship's computers, and they'll give us the exact times.'

Corbie scowled unhappily, but held his peace. He'd have happily grabbed at any excuse that would let him turn back, but he couldn't give up while the others were still willing to go on. No matter how scared he was. The three of them stood together patiently, waiting for the geysers, and some twenty minutes later they blew again, filling the air with steam and mud and boiling water. After they died away, the ground shook and rumbled under their feet for a disturbingly long time before growing still. DeChance patched into the pinnace's computers through her comm implant, and studied the glowing figures as they appeared before her eyes.

'All right,' she said finally. 'The shortest interval is twenty-two minutes. Then there's only a few seconds before the rest start to go off. The geysers seem to be limited to one small area, and we can cross that in ten minutes easily. So, as long as we keep moving, we shouldn't have any problems at all.'

'Oh sure,' said Corbie. 'Just a comfortable little stroll, right?'

'Right,' said DeChance.

'And what if we've got it wrong, and the geysers don't blow off at regular intervals, but just when they damn well feel like it?'

Lindholm smiled. 'You can always say, "I told you so."'

Corbie gave Lindholm a hard look. DeChance looked away to hide a smile.

They waited in silence for the geysers to spout again. Corbie chewed the insides of his cheeks, and clenched and unclenched his hands. He hated having to wait. It gave the fear longer to build, more of a chance to get a hold on him. He watched Lindholm out of the corner of his eye, but Sven seemed as calm and as unmoved as ever. There were times, when his nerves were really bad, that Corbie thought it might help if he could just talk to someone about his fear. But Corbie was a loner, and always had been. He'd never found it easy to make friends, never wanted or needed them, really. Sven was the nearest thing he had to a close friend, but Corbie couldn't talk to him. What could a man like Lindholm, a career marine and ex-gladiator, really understand about fear?

And then the ground shook and the geysers blew, and there

was no time for thinking any more. DeChance waited until the last geyser had stopped, and then ran down on to the plain. Lindholm started after her, and then stopped as he realized Corbie hadn't moved.

'Come on, Russ. We're short on time, remember?'

Corbie tried to move, and couldn't. The geysers were out there, waiting for him, waiting for the chance to kill him. He knew that wasn't true. He knew he had plenty of time. But he still couldn't move, still couldn't run forward into danger. DeChance was already well ahead of him, running freely and easily, as though she didn't have a care in the world. Lindholm was looking at him puzzled and impatient, but a glimmer of understanding was starting to form in his eyes. Corbie looked quickly away, anger and shame burning within him. And then DeChance screamed, and everything changed.

Corbie looked round just in time to see the cracked and broken earth collapse beneath the esper. The ground rumbled and shifted under Corbie's feet, and for one horrible moment he thought there was going to be an earthquake after all. The moment passed, and the geysers remained silent, but the esper had disappeared into a wide crevasse that looked to be a dozen yards long and still spreading. Corbie ran forward, with Lindholm close behind him.

'How much time do we have, Sven?'

'Plenty,' said Lindholm. 'As long as we don't run into any complications.'

'Like an esper with a broken leg?'

'Right. Think positively, Russ.'

They soon reached the gaping crevasse, and stopped at the edge. DeChance looked up at them, her face pinched and white with pain. When she spoke her voice was strained but even.

'First the good news: I don't think I've broken anything. The bad news is, my right foot's stuck in this crack, and I can't get it loose. The really bad news is that there's a geyser opening down here right next to me.'

'Take it easy,' said Lindholm. 'We'll get you out. There's plenty of time. Right, Russ?'

'Yeah,' said Corbie. 'No problem. Hang on, esper, and I'll come down there with you.'

He clambered awkwardly over the edge, and climbed carefully down into the crevasse. It was a good eight or nine feet deep, and underneath the cracked surface the earth was a dry, brittle honeycomb. The esper's right foot disappeared into the floor of the crevasse, swallowing up her leg almost to the knee. Corbie crouched down beside her, and gently investigated the crack with his hands. The esper's boot had sunk deep into the earth honeycomb, and the broken shards were pressing against the boot like so many barbs. The harder she pulled, the harder they dug in.

Corbie swore silently. Brute force wasn't going to get her out of this, but he was damned if he could think of anything else. Time was the problem. Whatever he was going to do, he had to do it quickly. He glanced at the geyser opening next to the esper, and patched into the pinnace's computers. Glowing numerals appeared at the bottom of his vision, giving him a countdown till the geyser spouted.

4:43.

'Get out of here,' said DeChance.

'Shut up,' said Corbie. 'I'm thinking.'

'You can't stay,' said DeChance evenly. 'I'm trapped here, and there isn't enough time for you to get me out and get clear of the other geysers. If you stay, we'll all die.'

'She has a point, Russ,' said Lindholm. 'There's nothing we can do for her. Except give her an easy death, instead of a hard one.'

Corbie looked up angrily. Lindholm had his disrupter out and aimed at DeChance. Corbie drew his own gun. 'That's not the way we do things in the marines, Sven, and you know it. Now throw your gun down here.'

Lindholm looked at him thoughtfully.

'Dammit, Sven, throw the gun down here! I've got an idea.'

3:24.

Lindholm threw the gun down to Corbie, who caught it deftly with his left hand, and tucked it into his belt. His face was beading with sweat, not just from the heat of the geyser's opening.

'All right, Sven, get going. We'll catch you up.'

'Not a chance,' said Lindholm. 'I want to see what you're going to do.'

Corbie flashed him a quick grin, and then aimed his disrupter at the earth honeycomb a few inches away from the esper's trapped foot. 'Hold very still, DeChance. Don't even breathe heavy.'

He fired the disrupter into the ground. The bright energy beam drilled cleanly through the earth, throwing broken shards into the air. DeChance tugged at her trapped foot. It moved a little, but remained stuck. Corbie tossed his gun up to Lindholm, drew the second gun and took aim at the earth on the other side of the trapped foot. He fired again, and the honeycomb crumbled and fell away. DeChance pulled her foot free.

'Nice shooting, Corbie. Now let's get the hell out of here.'

'Good idea.'

He holstered his gun and helped her up out of the crevasse.

2:35.

Corbie scrambled out of the crevasse after her, and the three of them ran through the field of geysers. DeChance was favouring her right foot, but still running strongly. The broken ground rumbled under their feet. A few wisps of steam rose from geyser openings. The earth collapsed suddenly under Lindholm's feet. He hurdled the opening crevasse and kept running.

1:07.

Corbie's breath was burning in his lungs, but he forced himself to run faster. Lindholm and DeChance pounded along beside him. The ground shook and rumbled under their feet, and Corbie could almost feel the pressure building down below.

:41.

Corbie glanced back over his shoulder. They'd covered a lot of distance. The esper's pace was slowing as she struggled for breath. Surely they were out of the field by now . . .

:01.

Boiling water fountained into the air a few yards to their left. The three of them kept running, and only a few sizzling spots hit them. More geysers blew off, spouting steam and water and boiling mud, but they were all well behind the running marines and the esper.

'I should never have agreed to join the Hell Squad,' said Lindholm breathlessly. 'I was safer in the Arenas.'

'Save your breath,' panted Corbie. 'You're going to need it. We're not out of the geysers yet.'

'Don't you have a plan to get us out of this, Russ?'

'Shut up and keep running.'

'That's a good plan.'

Behind and around them, the geysers spouted hundreds of feet into the pale green skies, but the marines and the esper were already leaving them behind.

We're going to make it, thought Corbie incredulously. We're going to bloody well make it!

He grinned harshly as he ran. This new world was just as tough as he'd feared it would be, but just possibly he was tough enough to deal with it. Another geyser blew off, some way behind him. He tucked his chin in, and kept running.

The sky was darkening towards evening when Hunter first saw the statues. The sun was hidden behind dark clouds, and the sky's colour was sinking from chartreuse to emerald. Shadows crawled across the broken land as it rose steadily towards the clouds. Hunter slowed to a halt as the ground ended suddenly in a sharp ridge, and he found himself looking down a steep slope at a plain some two hundred feet below. And on the plain, standing silent and alone in the middle of nowhere, the statues. Three huge black columns, starkly silhouetted against the broken land. Doctor Williams and Investigator Krystel stood on either side of Hunter, looking down at the statues, and for a long time nobody said anything.

'Our first sign of civilization,' said Krystel finally. 'Captain, I have to examine those statues while there's still some light.'

'Now wait a minute,' said Williams quickly. 'If we waste time here, we won't be able to reach the city before dark.'

'We wouldn't reach it anyway,' said Krystel. 'It's still a good seven miles away, and the sun will be down in less than an hour. We might as well make camp here as anywhere. Right, Captain?'

'It looks safe enough,' said Hunter. 'But they could be just grotesque rock formations, shaped by the wind.'

'No,' said Williams flatly. 'They're statues. I can see details.'

The other two looked at him, and Williams smiled stiffly. 'I told you I had built-in extras. My eyes have been adjusted. My vision's good up to almost three miles.' He looked back at the statues, and his smile disappeared. 'I can see the statues in great detail, Captain, and I don't like the look of them. They look . . . disturbing.'

Hunter waited, but Williams had nothing more to say. The Investigator looked at Hunter impatiently, but the Captain avoided her gaze, refusing to be hurried. Krystel was right, they had to make camp soon, and this was as good a place as any, with the high ridge to protect them from the wind. The bare ground offered little in the way of comfort or shelter, but after a hard day's walking Hunter felt he could sleep standing up in a hailstorm. He sighed once, quietly, and then led his team carefully down the steep slope to the plain below. He couldn't recall the last time he'd felt this tired. The ground had been uniformly hard and unforgiving all day, slapping sullenly against his feet, so that just the act of walking became that much harder and more exhausting.

The statues drew steadily closer, and Hunter tried to concentrate on their growing details, but other thoughts kept intruding. He hadn't heard from the esper's group in hours. He was sure they'd have contacted him if anything had happened, but their silence nagged at his nerves. He didn't want to have to contact them first; that might look as though he didn't have any confidence in their ability to handle their own problems. But he knew he wouldn't be able to get any sleep that night until he'd heard from them, no matter how tired he was. He decided to wait until the sun had gone down, and if they still hadn't contacted him, he'd try to raise them himself.

They should be all right. The esper might not have much dirtside experience, but she was rated as a first-class telepath. Whatever else happened, nothing was going to sneak up on her. And when it came to physical threats, the two marines should be able to deal with anything stupid enough to annoy them. Their records had made impressive reading. If their luck had been a little better, and their criminal tendencies a little more subtle, they could have ended up as heroes rather than Hell Squad fodder. Still, for all their faults they were both experienced men, and had seen combat duty on more than one alien world. And while ordinarily Hunter wouldn't have trusted either of them further than he could spit into the wind, they were both bright enough to realize they were going to need the esper's help just to stay alive on Wolf IV. They'd look after her. He remembered his encounter with the dweller in the water hole, and smiled wryly. The two marines would have made short work of that. Assuming they'd have been stupid enough to get caught by it. If there was one thing their records agreed on, it was that they trusted nothing and no one; not even themselves. Which was just the attitude they'd need to survive on Wolf IV.

The huge standing stones were closer now, and bit by bit Hunter began to see hints of shape and intent in their design. From the distance of the ridge, he hadn't realized just how big and solid they were. All three statues were the best part of a hundred feet high, and ten feet in diameter. Each statue had to weigh countless tons, and the back of Hunter's neck prickled uneasily as he tried to figure out how and why the damn things had been brought out on to the plain, miles from anywhere. He finally came to a halt before the first of the huge statues, and Williams and the Investigator stood beside him. The three of them stared in silence for a long time.

'Could these be the creatures that built the city?' said Williams eventually.

'If they are,' said Krystel, 'we'd better hope those aren't the correct dimensions.'

The statues stared impassively out over the empty plain. Their details had been blurred and distorted by wind and rain, or at least Hunter hoped they had, but the three forms were still clear enough to be both fascinating and unnerving. It was hard to get a grasp on them. Each great twisting body rested on two thick elephantine legs, but there was also a nest of curling tentacles that hung from the waist to the ground. There were two sets of arms, separately jointed, that ended in clusters of smaller tentacles. Various openings spotted the body, like so many open mouths or wounds. Hunter had to fight down a sudden urge to put his hand into one of the openings, to see how deep it went. The bulky head was a nightmare mess of harsh ridges and planes, set around a gaping maw studded with thick teeth. There was no trace of any eyes, but a series of slits and shadows at the top of the head might have been something similar. The great bulk of the statue should have made the alien creatures look slow and sluggish, but instead there was an overriding impression of strength and speed and ferocity. Hunter found his hand had dropped automatically to the gun at his side. He smiled sourly, but left the hand where it was.

'Nightmares, carved in stone,' muttered Williams, glancing at the other two statues. 'Horrid looking things, aren't they? How old do you suppose these carvings are, Investigator?'

'Hundreds of years,' said Krystel. 'Maybe more. They've obviously been exposed to the elements for some time . . . I'll give you another question, Doctor. Why were they left out here, so far from the city? A warning, perhaps? To mark some tribal boundary?'

'Maybe this area wasn't so deserted when the statues were erected,' said Hunter. 'We don't know it was always like this. Personally, I'm not so sure these statues are meant to represent the creatures who built the city. It's more likely they're some kind of legendary demon, or god. I mean, look at the body. Legs *and* tentacles? It doesn't make sense. No, these statues look to me more like a combination of creatures, rather than some naturally evolved being.' He looked away, and studied the sinking sun for a moment. 'We're not going to make the city before night. We'll make camp here, and carry on in the morning. The ridge and the statues should provide some shelter from the elements.'

'Are you sure we'll be safe out here, on our own?' said Williams, looking nervously around him. 'I mean, at least the pinnace had a force Screen . . .'

'We have a portable Screen, Doctor, and a good collection of proximity mines,' said Krystel. 'You'll be safe enough, never fear.'

They moved into the wide space between the three statues, and began emptying out their backpacks. Krystel collected all the proximity mines, and set about planting them in a circle around the statues, establishing a basic perimeter. Hunter set up a field lantern, and soft golden light spilled out in a wide circle. The familiar gentle glow was a comfort after the harsh sunlight of Wolf IV. Everything looked the right colour again. Hunter quickly assembled the portable Screen, and set it for a radius of two hundred feet, just within the proximity mines. He waited impatiently while Krystel primed the mines, and then turned the Screen on. A faint shimmer on the night air was the only sign the force Screen was up, but Hunter could feel his muscles relaxing for the first time in hours. He turned away to help Williams unpack the field rations, while Krystel took one last look around the perimeter. She'd done everything she could, by the book, but she still felt somehow uneasy.

She finally ended up leaning against one of the statues, the cold ridged stone pressing uncomfortably into her back. She took a long, slow look at the open plain, through the shimmer of the Screen. Everything seemed still and quiet, but night was falling fast, and the deepening shadows gave an added sense of urgency to her uneasiness. She stubbed out the last inch of her cigar on the statue, and lit herself another. She'd considered rationing herself, on the grounds it was likely to be some time before she could hope to get a new supply of cigars, but she didn't see the point. Either way, it was going to be a hell of a long wait, so she might as well enjoy them while she had them.

She glanced across at the other two statues, and was quietly disturbed by the way the gathering shadows suggested movement in the stone faces. She tapped ash from the end of her cigar, and wished fleetingly that she was somewhere else. Anywhere else. After the mess she'd made of the Grendel mission, she'd thought herself lucky to be offered a place on a Hell Squad, but she was beginning to have her doubts. As an Investigator, she'd always had the security of knowing the Imperial Fleet stood ready to back her up. Now she didn't have that any more. She was on her own. If she screwed up again, they'd all pay for it with their lives.

Krystel smiled determinedly. She would cope. She was an Investigator.

Doctor Williams warmed his hands at the pleasant glow of heat from the field lantern. The evening was growing steadily colder, and the heating elements in his uniform could only do so much. He stretched out his left hand, and the sensor spikes slid out from under his fingernails. He slid the spikes back and forth

437

a few times, enjoying the sensation, and then had them give him a run down on the air around him. He didn't expect to find anything harmful, but it was a good test of the sensors' abilities. Tiny glowing numerals appeared before his eyes, via the optic nerves, giving him the exact percentages of the air's constituents. Williams ran quickly through the numbers, and then dismissed them. There were a few interesting traces, though nothing that would cause any immediate harm, and no surprises. Pretty standard air, when you got right down to it.

He retracted the sensor spikes, patched into the pinnace's computers, and had them run a systems check on his adjustments. A rush of brief sensations flowed through him, like a series of tiny sparks glowing and dying, coming and going too quickly for him to decide whether they were pleasant or not. The computers were sparking each augmentation in turn into life, just long enough for it to be checked, and then shutting it down again once it had tested out satisfactorily.

He cut off the computers, and checked the readings on his implanted energy crystals. He allowed himself a small sigh of relief when they all showed a good 98 per cent charge. Providing he was careful, they should last him till he could acquire some more. He tried to think what it had been like, being merely human, with no augmentations at all, and was faintly disturbed to find he couldn't remember. He frowned. It hadn't been that long ago. Perhaps it was just that he didn't want to remember . . .

He brushed the thought briskly aside, and lay back on his bedroll. He was tired, and he'd done all the chores he intended to. If there were other things that needed doing around the camp, let the others do it. He was a scientist, not a servant. He smiled faintly, savouring the word *scientist*. He'd been the best in his field before his fall; everybody said so. Even the ones who hated him, and there were a lot of those. The Wampyr would have made him rich and famous throughout the Empire, if lesser men, jealous of his success, hadn't whispered poison in the Empress's ear . . .

Williams scowled, and then quickly composed his features in case the others were watching. One day the Empress herself would pay for what she'd done to him. All of those who'd betrayed him would pay, and pay in blood . . .

His hands had closed into fists, and he forced them to open again. As far as the Captain and the Investigator were concerned, he was a quiet, harmless Doctor, and he wanted them to go on thinking that. There would be time for him to prove them wrong later. There would be time for a lot of things, once the colonists finally arrived. It shouldn't be too difficult for him to bribe the supply ships to bring him the kind of high tech he needed. And with so many warm bodies available for him to experiment on, in the guise of the kindly colony Doctor, who knew what triumphs he might achieve . . .

Captain Hunter looked distrustfully at Williams. The man was smiling again. He shook his head, and looked away. No doubt he'd find out eventually what was so damned amusing. He laid out his bedroll as far away from the Doctor's as practical, and lay down on it. It felt great just to be off his aching feet at last. He stared up at the darkening night sky. The stars were coming out in ones and twos. One particularly bright light was probably one of the small moons. He started to check with the pinnace's computers, and then stopped himself. It wasn't important enough to waste valuable energy over. Hunter stretched slowly. His body was finally beginning to relax after the strain of the long walk. The ground was hard and extremely uncomfortable, but he'd slept on worse in his time. He didn't expect to have any trouble about getting to sleep. Most of his body was half way there already, and the Screen and the mines would sound an alarm long before anything got close enough to the camp to be a problem.

He lay quietly, pushing back the drowsiness a little so that he could savour it. All in all, it had been an interesting first day: the forest, the water hole, the statues. Never a dull moment on Wolf IV. He smiled slightly, and rubbed gently at his bruised ribs. He hadn't come out of it too badly. He sighed, and stretched comfortably. Looking back, he was puzzled at why he'd been so scared of sleeping out in the open. Now that he was here, it wasn't that bad after all. Too much imagination, that was his trouble. He thought again about the huge standing stones looming over him, and frowned slightly. Like most people, he'd had few actual contacts with aliens in his career, but he couldn't help feeling there was something *unnatural* about the creatures the stones depicted. They disturbed him on some very basic level. Perhaps it was the combination of traits and shapes that ought not to occur together on one creature. Perhaps it was simply the overpowering size. But either way, Hunter decided that when it came time to enter the alien city the next day, he'd do it with his gun in his hand.

A yawn took him by surprise, and he closed his eyes the better to enjoy it. He quickly opened them again as he realized he'd forgotten all about the esper's group. It was well past the time he'd decided to check up on them. He activated his comm implant, and a faint hiss of static filled his ears.

'Esper DeChance, this is the Captain. Do you hear me?'

'Aye, Captain.' The esper's voice was calm and clear. 'We've located a sheltered area, and are settling down for the night.'

'Same here. It's rather late in the evening, esper. I'd expected to hear from you earlier.'

'Sorry, Captain, I just didn't have anything to report. Have you encountered any problems?'

'Nothing we couldn't handle. But if you come across any water holes, stay well clear of them. They're inhabited. Get a good night's sleep, and I'll contact you again in the morning.'

'Aye, Captain. Good night.'

'And DeChance . . . don't be afraid to call for help if you need it. I'd rather answer a false alarm than find I'd got there too late.'

'Understood, Captain. Good night.'

'Good night, esper. Pleasant dreams.'

He shut off his comm unit, and tiredness rolled over him in a soft grey wave. He could see Krystel sitting with her back to one of the statues, staring out over the plain. He frowned slightly. He hadn't told her to stand guard . . . Still, she was an Investigator, and no doubt knew her job. If she wanted to stand a watch, that was up to her. Personally, he put his faith in the Screen and the mines. Hunter closed his eyes, and let the day drift away.

Night sank slowly over the plain, the darkness deep and concealing, the only light the soft golden glow from the field lantern. Thin curling mists rose up around the camp, pressing close against the force Screen with sullen perseverance.

Krystel sat at the base of one of the statues near the edge of the lantern's light. The end of her cigar glowed a dull red in the dimness. She couldn't sleep, force Screen or no force Screen. Investigators didn't need much sleep anyway. This wasn't the first time she'd sat guard on an alien world, but, as always, it felt like the first. On a new world, you could never be sure what you could count on, and what would let you down. What was safe, and what was just waiting for a chance to jump you. On an unknown world, anything could turn dangerous without warning. In the end it was safest to distrust everyone and everything, and be prepared to fight for your life at a moment's notice. Not very good for the nerves, but then Investigators weren't the nervous kind.

She tensed as something stirred close at hand, and then relaxed as Captain Hunter sat down beside her.

'So, you couldn't sleep either, Investigator.'

'I don't mind sitting guard, Captain. I'm used to it.'

'What do you think of our new world?'

'I've seen worse.'

Hunter looked at her thoughtfully. 'Krystel, what was it like on Grendel?'

The Investigator took her cigar out of her mouth and blew a perfect smoke ring. She watched the smoke gradually dissipate into the air. When she finally spoke, her voice was calm and even and only a little bitter.

'It was my first major assignment. I did a good job on Loki, and my reward was a posting to the archaeological digs on Grendel. It wasn't called that then, of course. We didn't know what was waiting for us.

'It should have been a simple, straightforward job, examining some ancient ruins and a few scraps of alien machinery discovered by the first wave of colonists. I should have known it was going to turn bad the moment I set eyes on the city. The buildings on the surface were just husks, but as we dug down, deeper and deeper, we came across structures so well preserved that they might have been abandoned only the day before. After a while we stopped digging – we couldn't stand the sight of what we'd found.

'The city spread out for miles beneath the surface, complete and intact. It was a nightmare of steel and flesh; a combination of breathing metal and silver-wired meat. There were rounded cylinders like gleaming oily intestines, and pumps that beat like hearts. There were creatures that had become part of functioning machines, and complex devices with eyes and entrails. We found thinking machines that looked as though they'd been grown as much as built. It wasn't the first time I'd seen such things. The crashed alien ship on Unseeli had been similar, but the city was worse. Much worse. Whoever or whatever built and then abandoned the city wasn't sane in any way that we might understand the word.

'Under the city we found the vaults. They were huge, monumental, as clean and shining as though they'd been built yesterday. They were locked tight, with no sign to show what they held. We all had different theories as to what the vaults contained, but we all wanted to open them. We'd never seen anything like the city, and we had to know more.

'Looking back, I think we were all a little crazy by then. We'd spent too long down in the city, away from the normal everyday world above. I was in charge, being trained in the arts of understanding and destroying alien cultures, so the final decision was mine. The city was vile, but so far we hadn't come across anything actually threatening. And after all, Empire troops were only a distress call away. Despite everything, I was still cautious, we all were, but none of us really believed there could be anything in the vaults that could possibly prove a threat to the might of the Empire.

'So we blasted open the vaults, and the Sleepers awoke.

'We lost twenty men in the first few minutes. Our weapons were all but useless against the devils we'd released. I was buried under rubble, and left for dead. You should have seen them, Captain – living metallic creatures that had been genetically designed with only one purpose in mind: to kill. Nightmares in flesh and blood and spiked-silicon armour. They were huge and awful, but they moved so fast that half the time we could only see them as a blur. Their claws ripped through stone and metal as though it was paper. Their grinning mouths had gleaming steel teeth. They moved through the city and up out into the archaeological digs, and there was nothing anyone could do to stop them.

'I finally dug my way out of the rubble, and followed the trail they'd left. There was blood everywhere, and bodies, and bits of bodies. All of it human. Up on the surface the camp had been wrecked. No one was left alive. I hid in the ruins for three and a half days. It seemed like years. Finally I found a working comm unit in the wreckage of a shattered pinnace, and contacted the ship in orbit. They came down and got me off.'

Krystel raised her cigar to her mouth, and then stopped and held it up before her. It was shaking slightly. Krystel stared at it until it stopped.

'The colonists were all dead. Wiped out to the last man, woman and child. The Empire sent the best it had against the aliens. Seasoned attack troops, battle espers, even one company of adjusted men. None of them lasted long. Finally the Fleet moved in and scorched the entire surface of the planet from orbit. Grendel is under quarantine now, guarded by half a dozen Imperial starcruisers. Just in case there are more sealed vaults and more Sleepers, hidden deep beneath the surface.

'And that's why I'm here with you, Captain. Because I missed the warning signs and let the creatures loose. And because I hadn't the sense to get myself honourably killed on Grendel. Maybe I'll do better this time.'

They sat in silence a while, staring out at the darkness and the thickening mists beyond the force Screen. Krystel turned and looked at Hunter for the first time. 'So tell me, Captain, what was it like, out in the Rim worlds?'

Hunter tried to answer her, and his throat closed up on him. He struggled to get the words out anyway. She'd told him her story as honestly as she could, and he was damned if he'd do less for her.

'It's dark out there, on the Rim. The stars are scattered thinly across the gulf, and habitable planets are few and far between. Beyond the edge of our galaxy lies the endless night, a darkness so deep no ship has ever crossed it and returned. But the Rim planets are still part of the Empire, and have to be patrolled.

'Time seems to move differently out there. It drags on slowly, each day like the day before, until you can't tell one day from another. The endless dark preys on your nerves, like an itch you can't scratch. You begin to feel as if you've always been out on the Rim, and always will be. You can't ever relax. Ships disappear on the Rim, and no one knows why. You start to look forward to trouble breaking out, because at least then there'll be some action, something to do, something to strike back at.

'I was a good soldier. I carried out my orders, defended the Empire from her enemies, and never once questioned a command. Until they made me a Captain. You see, then I had to give the orders, and more and more I found the reasons behind those orders just weren't good enough. Sometimes they didn't even make sense. But I gave the orders, and saw them followed through because my superiors told me to. I was a good soldier. But during the endless watches, spent staring out into the starless gulf, I began to wonder if their reasons were any better than mine, if their orders were any more sensible than mine, or if we were all just stumbling blindly in the dark.

'Giving orders began to grow more difficult. Making decisions, any decisions, took more and more of an effort. I didn't trust my superiors any more, or the Empire, and certainly not myself. I lost all sense of security, of stability. I couldn't depend on anything any more. Just getting through the day got harder all the time. Even small, simple decisions had to be wrestled over until I became distracted. I started having to check things over and over, to make sure I'd done them, even though I knew I had. Sometimes I gave the same order two or three times, and checked up on my crew to be sure it had been carried out.

'People began to notice. Some of them started to talk about me. I knew, but I did nothing about it. I didn't know whether to feel worried, or relieved. And then an order came through that I couldn't ignore. A starship had gone rogue in my sector. I was to hunt it down and destroy it. It wasn't difficult to find. The rogue ship turned out to be the same class as mine, and armed to the teeth. In the heat of the battle I had to give orders quickly and efficiently, and I couldn't. I panicked, unable to decide what to do, and my ship was blown apart. I got away in one of the lifeboats. So did some of my crew. Certainly more than enough to place the blame on me.

'But I wasn't to blame. Not really. It was the Rim. All that darkness with no stars. The Rim would drive anyone over the edge if they stayed out there long enough.

'And that's why I'm here, Investigator. I lost my sense of security and stability, so they sent me here. To Hell.'

He smiled briefly, and looked at the Investigator. Her face was calm and impassive, as always, and he was glad of that. If she'd shown him anything that even looked like pity, he thought he might have hit her. But she didn't say anything, and after a while he looked away again.

'Captain,' said Krystel finally. 'Just supposing that the city does check out as harmless, and the Empire does establish a colony here, what will you do? I mean, what will you do as a colonist? They're not going to need a starship Captain.'

'I hadn't really thought about it,' said Hunter. 'I've got my military training. That's always useful in itself. How about you?'

Krystel chuckled dryly. 'I'm an Investigator, Captain. The perfect killing machine. There'll always be work for me.'

Hunter was still trying to find an answer to that when the proximity mine went off. The ground shook, and an alarm rang automatically in Hunter's ears until he shut it off. The explosion seemed to echo on and on, deafeningly loud in the night's quiet. Hunter and Krystel rose quickly to their feet and stood back to back, guns in hand, searching the camp's perimeter for signs of the force Screen being breached. Williams scrambled to his feet and kicked aside his bedroll as he grabbed for his gun.

'What is it? What's happening?'

'Proximity mine,' said Hunter brusquely. 'Something's found our camp. Stay alert, and watch where you're pointing your gun.'

'Two o'clock, Captain,' said Krystel quietly, gesturing surreptitiously with her gun at that part of the perimeter. 'According to the computers the rest of the mines are still active, but nothing's close enough to trigger them. The Screen's still up and holding.'

Hunter strained his eyes against the mists and the darkness, but the light from the field lantern didn't reach far beyond the perimeter. The mists were still curling angrily near the blast site, but there was no trace of what might have caused the explosion. Hunter hefted his gun uneasily. 'Can't see a thing, Investigator. Williams, what about those augmented eyes of yours?'

'Sorry, Captain, the mists are too thick. I'm just as blind as you.'

'Terrific,' said Hunter.

'Quiet,' said Krystel. 'Listen.'

They fell silent, and Hunter was struck again by how unnaturally quiet the night was. No animal cries, no birds or insects, not even the moan of the wind. But somewhere out in the night, outside the force Screen, something was moving. It sounded big and heavy, and its footsteps had a slow, dragging quality. It was heading slowly around the perimeter, anticlockwise.

Widdershins, thought Hunter crazily. It shouldn't do that. That's unlucky.

'It should hit the next mine any second now,' said Krystel quietly. 'Whatever it is, it must be tough as hell. That first mine should have ruined its day permanently.'

The ground shook again as the second proximity mine exploded. The mists writhed and curled at one o'clock on the perimeter, and Hunter caught a brief glimpse of something huge and dark before the mists closed over it again. The echoes of the explosion died slowly away, and then there came a high, screeching roar from beyond the force Screen. It sounded clear and sharp on the quiet, continuing long after human lungs would have been unable to sustain it. If there was any emotion in the sound, Hunter was unable to put a name to it.

'Captain,' said Krystel urgently, 'patch into the computers. Something's come in contact with the Screen.'

Hunter activated his comm implant, and computer images appeared via his optic nerve, superimposed over his vision. Something was pressing hard against the Screen, over and over again, trying to break through. The computers measured the varying strengths of the pressure, and provided simulations of what might be causing it. Hunter's mouth went dry. Apparently whatever was out there was some twenty feet tall, weighed roughly eight to nine tons, and probably walked on two legs. The pressure readings jumped sharply as the creature beat viciously against the force Screen. The high-pitched roar

446

sounded again, shrill and piercing, and then the attack stopped, as suddenly as it had begun. The creature turned away from the Screen, and its slow dragging footsteps grew gradually quieter as it disappeared back into the night.

Hunter sighed slowly, and put away his gun. 'Stand down, everyone. It's gone.' He shut down his comm unit, and his vision returned to normal.

'What the hell was that?' said Williams shakily.

'Just a visitor,' said Krystel. 'Perhaps it'll come again tomorrow.'

'Captain, I strongly suggest we set a watch,' said Williams. He went to holster his gun, but his hand was shaking so much he had to make three attempts before he got it right. 'Whatever that was might come back again, while it's still night.'

'So what if it does?' said Krystel. 'It can't get through the Screen.'

'On the other hand,' said Hunter, 'the mines didn't seem to bother it much. I think a watch is a good idea, Doctor. I'll take the first shift, then you, and finally the Investigator. I think we'll all sleep a little better that way.'

He stared grimly out at the curling mists. Twenty feet tall, eight to nine tons, and two mines didn't even slow it down. He just hoped it wasn't one of the things that built the city. Because if it was, tomorrow could turn out to be a very busy day.

Night was falling by the time Megan DeChance and the marines reached the stone monolith. They stopped some distance away, and studied it carefully before going any further. They'd been watching it ever since it first appeared on the horizon, but seen up close it remained as dark and enigmatic as ever. The monolith was a huge stone cube, some thirty feet to a side, with an opening in the wall before them that might have been a door. The opening was ten feet high, and six feet wide. It held only darkness. The rough surface of the stone was a grey so dark it was almost black. Raised lines and ridges crawled across the stone walls like petrified ivy. The monolith had a squat, solid air of permanence. Set against the darkening sky, it looked like an ancient, deserted mausoleum.

'I think this will serve nicely as a camp site,' said DeChance finally.

Lindholm shrugged. 'Why not? I've slept in worse.'

'So have I,' said Corbie. 'But I'm still not sleeping in that bloody tomb. Just looking at it gives me the creeps. I mean, what's it doing out here, in the middle of nowhere? We're miles from the city. No, Sven, I don't like the look of this. There could be anything inside it.'

'We'll check it out thoroughly before we go in,' said DeChance patiently. 'If I were you, I'd be more worried about what might be lurking outside this . . . structure, once darkness falls. After what we saw in and around the forest this morning, there's no telling what forms of life come out at night.'

'We've still got the force Screen,' said Corbie, stubbornly.

'Yes, we have,' said DeChance. 'But if we set up camp out on the plain, in the open, where anything can see us, there's no telling what we might attract. I don't think there's anything on this world powerful enough to break through a force Screen, but I'd rather not find out I was wrong the hard way. Now be quiet, Corbie, and let me run a mental scan on the structure.'

She closed her eyes, and her expression went blank. The muscles in her face twitched a few times and then were still. Her breathing slowed till it was barely audible. Corbie looked at her, and then looked away, unable to repress a shudder.

'Don't worry, Russ,' said Lindholm quietly. 'She hasn't gone far. She'll be back soon.'

'Yeah,' said Corbie. 'That's what worries me.'

DeChance's mind roamed freely over the monolith, caressing the rough surface of the stone with her esp. It felt old, very old. Time had come and gone upon the plain, and left the monolith untouched. Inside, the structure was hollow, and completely empty. DeChance didn't know whether to feel relieved or uneasy. She frowned briefly. More and more, she found the stone monolith somehow . . . unsettling. The structure wasn't a perfect square, and the extra angles and dimensions clashed unpleasantly in her mind, as though they refused to add up to the shape she saw before her. DeChance shrugged mentally. She didn't like the feel of the monolith, but there was nothing specific she could use to justify her feelings. Particularly after her treatment of Corbie. DeChance fell back into her body, and looked at Lindholm.

'All clear. The building's quite empty.'

'I'm glad to hear it,' said Lindholm. 'If you'd care to set up camp inside the building, Russ and I will see to the defences. The sooner we get the force Screen up and working, the sooner we can all relax a little.'

The three of them looked at each other for a moment, each waiting for someone else to make the first move. In the end DeChance turned away and walked calmly over to the monolith. She wanted to pause in the doorway, but made herself go on. If she didn't trust her esp, she could hardly expect the marines to. Once inside, she shrugged off her backpack, took out a field lantern, and turned it on. The familiar golden glow helped to reduce the stone chamber to a more comfortable size. DeChance stepped cautiously forward, holding the lantern out before her.

The interior looked pretty much like the exterior; rough, bare stone covered with twisting ridges and hollows. The floor was flat and even, and only the dark shadows in the corners remained disturbing. DeChance walked slowly round the empty chamber. The more she saw of it, the less she understood why she'd been so worried. She even began to feel a little ashamed at letting her imagination get the better of her. And then DeChance's breath caught in her throat, as the lantern light revealed a single, gleaming milky-white sphere lying on the floor in the far left-hand corner. She stared at it for a long moment. It couldn't be there. It couldn't. Her esp would have found it during the scan.

'I thought you said there was nothing in here,' said Lindholm.

The esper jumped, startled, and then flushed hotly. She'd been concentrating on the chamber so much that she'd let her psionic defences slip. She hadn't even known the marine was there, till he'd spoken. She quickly composed her features again.

'There shouldn't be anything in here,' she said eventually, her voice calm and even. 'Whatever that is, I should have detected its presence, at least.'

'Does that mean it's dangerous?' said Lindholm.

'Possibly.'

'All right, that's it,' said Corbie quickly, from the door. 'Let's get the hell out of here while we still can.'

'Take it easy, Russ,' said Lindholm, without looking round.

'I thought you two were seeing to our defences?' said DeChance.

'We talked it over,' said Lindholm, 'and we decided we didn't feel right about leaving you in here on your own.'

'Very gallant,' said DeChance, 'but I can take care of myself.'

'Of course,' said Lindholm. He looked thoughtfully at the milky sphere on the floor. 'Can you pick up anything from that, now you're closer to it?'

DeChance frowned slightly. 'I can try.'

She moved slowly over to the sphere, and knelt down before it. She studied it carefully from all angles, careful not to touch it. The sphere was about six inches in diameter, and had a cold, pearly sheen. DeChance reached out with her mind, and gently touched the sphere with her esp.

The sun, burning bright and foul in the shimmering sky. Buildings tower to every side. Something dark and awful close behind and all around. Bones stretch and twist. Flesh flows across twitching cheekbones. Eyes turn to liquid and run away. Creatures leaping and hopping everywhere, sliding and melting into each other. The scream goes on and on and on . . .

DeChance jerked her mind free from the endless flow of images. She fell backwards, her mouth working, and when Lindholm reached out a hand to steady her, she struck out at him blindly. He knelt down beside her and spoke in a slow and soothing voice until finally the wordless panic died away, and she could think again. She drew in a long, shuddering breath, and licked her dry lips.

'What happened?' asked Lindholm.

'The sphere,' said DeChance hoarsely. 'It's a recording of some kind. A direct recording of an alien mind.'

'What did you see?' asked Corbie.

DeChance shook her head slowly. 'Madness. Horror and violence . . . I don't know. I'll have to think about it. In the meantime, don't either of you try and touch it. It's too easy to get lost in there . . .'

She got to her feet, turned her back on the sphere and the marines, and started to rummage through her backpack. Corbie and Lindholm looked at each other. Lindholm shrugged, and

450

left through the open doorway. Corbie hesitated and then followed him out.

Planting the proximity mines took the marines a lot longer than they'd thought. The ground was rock hard, and yielded only grudgingly to their digging tools. Both men were sweating by the time they'd established a perimeter, and most of the light had disappeared from the sky. The golden lantern light that fell through the monolith's doorway looked warm and inviting. The two marines went back inside, rubbing at the fresh calluses on their hands, and helped DeChance finish setting up the portable force-Screen generator. She activated it, and all three relaxed a little as some of the day's tension went out of them. They laid out their bedrolls, and pecked unenthusiastically at a late supper of protein cubes and distilled water. Finally, they lay back on their bedrolls and waited for morning to come.

None of them felt much like sleeping, but they knew they ought to at least try. Come the next day, they'd need all the strength and stamina they could find. The Captain had sounded calm and reassuring when he'd contacted them just after their supper, and DeChance had done her best to sound the same. Corbie had thought seriously about breaking into the conversation, and saying how worried he was about the monolith and the sphere recording, but in the end he decided against it. The Captain wouldn't have understood. Maybe when they reached the city tomorrow . . . Corbie had a really bad feeling about the city.

Surprisingly enough, the esper fell asleep almost immediately. Lindholm lay on his back with his eyes closed, looking as calm and unperturbed as ever. Corbie glared at them impartially. He'd never felt less sleepy in his life. He gave it a while, just in case, and then sat up quietly and hugged his knees to his chest. He'd hoped the monolith would seem less imposing once he'd spent some time in it, but it hadn't worked out that way. The ceiling was too high, the light from the lantern couldn't penetrate the corners, and even the smallest sound seemed to echo endlessly. He drew his disrupter from its holster and checked the energy level. It was reassuringly high, but, even so, it took a real effort of will power before Corbie could make himself holster the gun again.

'Getting jumpy, Russ?'

Corbie looked round quickly. Lindholm was sitting up on his bedroll too. Corbie smiled and shrugged. 'I don't like this place, Sven,' he said softly, keeping his voice low to avoid waking the esper. 'Mind you, when you get right down to it I'd be hard pressed to name one thing about this stinking planet that I do like. I hate it here, Sven.' He rubbed at his mouth with the back of his hand, and wasn't surprised to find his hand was shaking. 'I'm dry, Sven. I need a drink. I could cope with all of this much better if I could just have one good stiff drink.'

'Sorry, Russ. Don't use the stuff myself. You should have smuggled a bottle on to the pinnace.'

'I did. They found it.' Corbie shuddered quickly. There was a faint sheen of sweat on his face, despite the cold. 'I *hate* this world, Sven. I don't want to be here. It doesn't want us here. I mean, what am I doing in a Hell Squad? I was never meant to be a colonist. I've been in the Fleet since I was sixteen; never spent more than two years running on the same planet. I liked it that way. The only reason I'm here is because it looked a better bet than spending the rest of my life rotting in a military prison. Shows you what a fool I was. This place is worse than any prison.'

'Take it easy, Russ.'

'That's easy for you to say. You saw that forest. And the things that came up out of the ground. I've been on more worlds than I can count, seen some pretty strange things in my time, but at least they made some kind of sense. This world is insane. Like some nightmare you can't wake up from. And tomorrow we're going into a city full of buildings just like this one. I don't think I can do that. Sven. I don't think I *can*.' He looked pleadingly at Lindholm. 'What am I going to do, Sven? I can't stand it on this world, but I can't get off it. I'm trapped here. I can't face going into the city tomorrow, but I couldn't stand being left on my own. What am I going to *do*?'

'All right, Russ, calm down. I'm here. You're not alone.' Lindholm cut in quickly as Corbie's voice began to rise hysterically. 'Just remember you're not alone in this. We're all in the same boat. We can cope with anything, as long as we stick together. Think of all the different worlds we've seen – they all

452

looked pretty bad at first. This is just another world, Russ, that's all. Just another world.'

Corbie took a deep breath, and let it out again in a long, shuddering sigh. He shot Lindholm a grateful glance, and smiled shakily. 'How do you do it, Sven? How do you stay so calm all the time? Is it something you learned in the Arenas?'

'You could say that.' Lindholm stared thoughtfully out the open doorway into the darkness. 'You can learn a lot in the Arenas, if you stay alive long enough. You learn not to be afraid, because that can get you killed. You learn not to make friends, because you might have to kill them the next day. You learn to take nothing for granted; not even one more day of life. And finally, you learn not to care about anything. Not the killing, not the people, not the pressure, not even your own life. When you don't care about anything, you can take any risk, face any odds. Because nothing matters any more. Nothing at all.' Lindholm looked across at Corbie. 'The trouble is, Russ, even after you've left the Arenas, what you learned there goes with you. I don't feel much of anything any more. I don't laugh, or cry, or feel scared or good. The Arenas took all that from me. There's just enough of the old me left to appreciate what I've lost. It's hard for me to get really interested in anything, Russ, because nothing really matters.'

'What about me?' said Corbie slowly. 'Do I matter?'

'I don't know,' said Lindholm. 'I remember the years we served together in the marines, but it's like remembering a dream I had long ago. Sometimes the dream is clearer than others. The rest of the time I just go through the motions. Don't depend on me, Russ. There's not enough left of me for that.'

The esper moaned in her sleep, and the two marines looked across at her. DeChance was stirring uneasily.

'Nightmare,' said Corbie. 'Can't say I blame her.'

The first proximity mine went off like a thunderclap, followed by two more in swift succession. The brilliant light flared against the darkness. The marines scrambled to their feet, guns in hand, and DeChance came awake with a start.

'What the hell was that?' said Corbie.

'There's something out there,' said Lindholm. 'Must have got too close to the mines. Turn off the lantern, Russ.'

Corbie reached quickly over and turned it off. Darkness filled the monolith, as though it had never been away. Corbie clutched tightly at his gun, and waited impatiently for his eyes to adjust to the gloom.

'Whatever's out there, it's not alone,' Corbie muttered. 'It'd take more than one creature to set off all those mines.'

'I can sense . . . something,' said DeChance, frowning harshly. 'It's hard to pin down. I'm picking up multiple readings, too many to count. They're moving, circling . . . they're all around us. We're surrounded.'

Another mine exploded, piercing the darkness with brilliant light. Corbie caught a brief glimpse of dark uncertain shapes milling around the monolith, outside the perimeter, and then the night returned. There was a loud, dull thudding, like a giant heartbeat, as something began to beat against the force Screen with horrid patience and determination. Corbie licked his dry lips repeatedly, and glared frantically into the night.

'Take it easy, Corbie,' said DeChance. 'The force Screen will keep them out.'

Bloody hell, thought Corbie, can everyone tell I'm a bag of nerves, even in the dark?

'She's right,' said Lindholm calmly. 'The force Screen was designed to stand against anything, even disrupter cannon and atomics. Nothing's going to break through the Screen by brute force.'

As if in answer to his words, the hammering suddenly stopped. Silence fell upon the night again, charged with hidden menace. DeChance frowned.

'They've stopped moving. They're just . . . standing there, as though they're waiting for something. Wait a minute, there's something else, something close—'

The floor buckled suddenly under their feet, and split open with a deafening roar of rending stone. Cracks darted here and there across the broken floor as DeChance and the two marines fought to keep their balance.

'They're tunnelling up through the earth!' yelled the esper. 'They're coming for us.'

'Somebody find the lantern,' roared Lindholm.

'Stuff that,' said Corbie. He got down on both knees, riding

454

the buckling floor, and thrust his disrupter into the nearest crack. He pressed the stud, and a blast of searing energy shot down into the earth. Far below, something screamed and then fell silent. Lindholm and DeChance fired their guns into the cracks, and the floor heaved once, and then was still. For a long time there was only the darkness and the silence, and then DeChance stirred slowly.

'They're leaving,' she said quietly. 'They're all leaving.'

Lindholm found the field lantern and turned it on again. The pale golden glow was a comfort after the panic-ridden dark. The floor was a mess of cracks and broken stone. The walls and ceiling weren't much better. Corbie and Lindholm looked at each other, and grinned.

'Nice shooting, Russ.'

'Yeah, well,' said Corbie. 'You know how it is. Some things you never forget, no matter what.'

CHAPTER THREE

The City

Captain Hunter and his team reached the outskirts of the alien city by mid-morning. The brilliant silver sun was high on the chartreuse sky, and the light reflecting from the city's towers was nearly too bright to look at. Streamers of grey cloud sprawled across the sky like characters from an alien language, and the still air had a cold, cutting edge. Hunter hugged himself tightly, not just because of the cold. He'd been standing and staring at the city for some time, but he still couldn't get used to it. The city lay spread out before him like some giant incomprehensible puzzle.

The sheer alienness of the city swept over him like a numbingly cold tide. The huge buildings were twisted and asymmetrical, with sharp edges and distorted scalloped roofs. Strange lights, glaring like watching eyes, shone in empty windows. Bulky stone monoliths stood next to towers of shimmering crystal, and twisted glass structures too intricate for the eye to rest easily on. There were open doorways and windows, their scale suggesting that whatever creatures used them had to be almost twice the size of Hunter and his companions. Gossamer threads hung between the buildings, forming slender walkways high above the ground. There was no sound on the still air, and no trace of movement anywhere in the city.

Hunter looked from one strange edifice to another, trying to find some familiar sight his eyes could rest on, but there was nothing his mind could comfortably accept. The alien architecture was subtly disturbing on some deep, primal level.

'We've been here almost an hour, Captain,' said Investigator Krystel, 'and there's still no sign of the other team.'

'Perhaps something's happened to them,' said Williams.

'They would have contacted us if they'd run into any trouble,' said Hunter. 'But you're right, Investigator. We can't wait here all day. I'll contact them, and let them know we've arrived.' He activated his comm implant, his eyes still fixed on the city before him. 'Esper DeChance, this is the Captain. Report your position.'

There was no reply, only an ominous silence, unbroken even by static. Hunter and Krystel looked at each other.

'Esper DeChance, this is Captain Hunter. Please report your position. Can you see the city?' He waited, but there was no response. 'Lindholm, Corbie, can you hear me?' The silence dragged on. 'Investigator, can you hear me through your implant?'

'Loud and clear, Captain. There's nothing wrong with our equipment.'

'Then there must be something wrong at their end.'

'Unless the city's interfering with the signal,' said Williams.

Hunter frowned thoughtfully. 'Esper DeChance, if for some reason you can hear me but cannot respond, we're about to enter the city. Somewhere near the centre is a huge copper tower. Try and join us at the tower. If you're not there by the time evening falls, around nineteen hundred hours, pinnace's time, we'll make our way back to the western boundary of the city, and make camp there. Captain Hunter out.'

He shut down his comm implant, and looked unhappily at the city. 'We've done all we can here. Let's go and take a closer look. Draw your guns, but no firing unless you've got a specific target.'

He started to lead the way forward, but stopped as Krystel raised a hand.

'I should go first, Captain. I am the Investigator.'

Hunter pursed his lips, and then nodded. Krystel was within her rights. They were entering her province now. He gestured for her to proceed, and she led the way down the short slope that led to the city. Hunter followed her, and Williams brought up the rear.

The city seemed to loom even larger and more menacing as they made their way through the broad streets and alleyways that lay between the massive buildings. The huge scale and sheer

457

overpowering size of the city made Hunter feel like a child wandering through an adult world. The party's footsteps hardly echoed at all, the sound swallowed up almost immediately by the huge walls to either side of them. Towers dark as the night, studded with jagged crimson shapes, thrust up around them like imploring arms. Hunter stood the silence for as long as he could, and then looked at the Investigator.

'You're the expert, Krystel. Any comments?'

'Just the obvious ones, Captain. Apart from the occasional exotic exceptions, most of these buildings are nothing more than huge slabs of stone. Judging by the battered and weathered appearance of the stone, they must have stood here for centuries. The complexity of the other structures suggests a high level of civilization, so why did the city's occupants retain the primitive stone buildings? A reverence for the past? For their ancestors? Too early to tell, as yet. Maybe they just thought working in stone was artistic.

'Something else interesting. We've been walking for the best part of half an hour now, and we're well past the outskirts, but I still haven't seen a single sign to show this place was ever inhabited. Whatever happened here, it was over and finished a long time ago. Perhaps there was a war, or some kind of ecological disaster. Maybe they all committed suicide. It could even be something we don't have a name for. Understanding an alien culture takes time, Captain. Their minds don't work like ours.'

'Perhaps we should take a look inside one of the buildings,' said Williams diffidently. 'There's only so much we can tell from the buildings' exteriors. There could be important clues inside. Who knows, we might even get lucky and find some kind of computer records.'

'I'd prefer to keep moving,' said Krystel evenly. 'We haven't seen enough of this city to be sure it's deserted. I don't like the idea of being caught by surprise because we weren't thorough. Still, you're the Captain, Hunter, it's your decision.'

Hunter stopped in the middle of the street, and the others stopped with him. He looked across at the nearest building. It appeared to have been carved from a single huge piece of crystal, and its uneven edges looked disturbingly sharp. There was a crimson tracery in the smoky crystal that looked disturbingly like a network of veins. The huge doorway was blocked by a single slab of dull metal, and there were no windows. Hunter gnawed at the inside of his cheeks. There could be anything in there, watching and waiting. He didn't like that idea at all. If there was something watching, he wanted to know about it. And yet, the more he looked at the huge crystal structure, the more uneasy he felt. He realized suddenly that he didn't want to get any closer to the building. It was too strange, too different. It felt . . . wrong. An aberration.

Alien minds don't work like ours.

Hunter swallowed hard. He could feel the familiar panic building within him, the fear that whatever decision he made would be the wrong one. He had to make up his mind quickly, while he still could. 'All right, people, we're going to take a look inside. Krystel, you go first. Williams, stay close to me and don't touch anything.'

The Investigator nodded, and approached the metal door. Williams made as though to follow her, but Hunter held him back. The door could be booby-trapped. Krystel stood a few feet away from the door and studied it carefully. Eleven and a half feet high, seven feet wide. No handle, and no sign of any locking mechanism. There was no doorjamb, the metal butted cleanly against the crystal. She kicked the door lightly, twice. There was no response. She reached out cautiously and touched the dull metal with her fingertips. It felt unpleasantly warm. Krystel pulled back her hand and sniffed at her fingers. There was a faint trace of odour, but nothing she could identify. All right, when in doubt, be direct.

She stepped back from the door, raised her disrupter and pressed the stud. The energy bolt smashed the door inwards, leaving a jagged hole in the crystal. The Investigator moved slowly forward, stared into the opening, and then stepped through. After a moment, Hunter and Williams followed her.

It was fairly light inside the building, but it was a strange kind of light. The crystal diffused the daylight, giving it a smoky, dream-like glow. The metal door lay in the middle of the room. It was twisted and crumpled, but otherwise intact. Hunter whistled to himself. There wasn't a metal in the Empire that could stand up to a disrupter beam at point-blank range.

He looked slowly around him. The chamber was huge, easily fifty feet by fifty. Curved and twisted shapes dotted the bare crystal floor. The shapes were detailed, but essentially ambiguous. They could have been furniture or statuary, or even some form of high tech for all he knew. Without a context to put them in, they could be anything. Long curving lines had been etched into the crystal walls, stretching from floor to ceiling. They served no apparent purpose.

'If there was anyone here, the noise would have brought them running by now,' said Williams. He looked around him uneasily. 'Maybe they all left for a reason. A good reason.'

Krystel slowly approached the open doorway on the far side of the room, with Hunter and Williams close behind. If there had ever been a door to fill the gap, it was long gone. Krystel led the way through the doorway, and they found themselves at the base of a tower. Hunter looked up the gleaming crystal shaft, and his breath caught in his throat. The tower stretched away above him for hundreds of feet, until its top was lost in the hazy light that shone through the crystal walls. It's an optical illusion, thought Hunter wonderingly. It's got to be. The building isn't that tall . . . He tore his gaze away, and studied the narrow curving ramp that spiralled up the inner wall for as far as his eyes could follow. It protruded directly from the crystal wall, with no sign of any join. It was easily six foot wide, and the surface was as smooth and unblemished as any other part of the smoky crystal.

'A ramp, instead of stairs,' said Williams. 'That could be significant.'

'Undoubtedly,' said Krystel. 'But significant of what? It's too early yet to start drawing conclusions, Doctor.' Her voice and face were as calm and impassive as ever, but still Hunter was sure he could detect a fire, an enthusiasm, in her that hadn't been there before. Krystel was in her element now, and it showed. She started up the ramp, her boots scuffing and sliding on the smooth crystal surface. She leaned against the inner wall to help her keep her balance, and soon found the trick of keeping upright while still pressing on. Hunter kept to the inner wall too as he and Williams hurried after her, but mainly because the increasing drop worried him. There was no barrier or safety rail, and it was getting to be a long way down. A thought nagged at Hunter: what kind of being could use a ramp like this, and apparently not worry about the danger of falling?

They continued up the ramp for some time, circling round and round the inside of the tower. There were plenty of doorways leading off, but Krystel kept pressing on, and the others had to follow or be left behind. Hunter's thighs started to ache, and when he looked down the shaft he could no longer see the bottom of the tower. Everywhere he looked there was nothing but scarlet-veined crystal and the diffused smoky light. He began to feel strangely disorientated, as though he'd always been climbing the ramp, and always would be.

It came as something of a shock when Krystel suddenly stepped off the ramp and through an open doorway, and Hunter realized they'd reached the top of the tower. He looked quickly back to make sure Williams was still with them, and then followed Krystel through the doorway. She was standing on an open balcony that looked out over the city. The balcony looked distinctly fragile, but it held their weight easily enough. There was still no safety rail, and Hunter was careful to stand a good two feet short of the edge. He looked down, and vertigo sucked at his eyes. It had to be a drop of at least three hundred feet. He would have sworn the building wasn't that tall when he entered it. The long drop didn't seem to bother the Investigator at all. She was staring out over the cityscape with something like hunger. Hunter moved cautiously over beside her, to make room for Williams on the balcony, and looked out over the view.

For the first time, he could really appreciate the true size and scale of the city. It stretched away for miles in every direction, an eerie landscape of stone and metal and glass. The gossamer walkways looked like the spiderwebs you'd expect to find on something that had been left deserted for too long. Down below, nothing moved. Everything was still and silent. But strange lights shone in some of the windows, like so many watchful eyes, and there was a strange palpable tension on the air.

'Well, Investigator,' said Hunter finally. 'This is your show. What now?'

'There's life here,' said Krystel flatly. 'I can feel it. The city is

461

too clean, too untouched by time and weather to be as abandoned as it appears. So whatever lives here must be hiding from us. And in my experience, the best way to flush out something that's hiding is to set a trap, and bait it with something attractive.'

'One of us,' said Hunter.

'Me, to be exact,' said Investigator Krystel. She smiled suddenly, and Hunter had to force himself not to look away from the hunger that burned in her eyes.

Megan DeChance and the two marines stood at the edge of the city. A row of tall serrated towers stood like a barrier before them, dark and enigmatic in the bright midday sunlight. DeChance rubbed at her forehead. Just the sight of the alien structures was enough to give her a headache. Her esp kept trying to make sense of the weird shapes, and failing, unable to embrace theories of architecture and design shaped by an inhuman logic. The marines shifted impatiently at her side. DeChance tried her comm implant again.

'Captain Hunter, this is DeChance. Please respond.'

'Still nothing?' said Corbie.

'Nothing,' said DeChance.

'You could try your esp,' said Lindholm.

DeChance stared at the alien city, trying to pretend she hadn't heard him. Making telepathic contact was the obvious logical thing to try next. The thought was enough to bring her out in a cold sweat. She could still remember the contact she'd made back on the pinnace, the first time she'd raised her esp on Wolf IV. She'd found something huge and old and powerful, something vile and awful . . . and it hadn't been alone. Whatever it was, she was sure it lay waiting somewhere in the city. Waiting for her to raise her esp again, so it could find her.

But DeChance had to find the Captain. She had to know what was happening to the other team. And most of all she had to face her fear, or she'd never be free of it. She could do it. She was an Empire-trained telepath, and she could face anything. She closed her eyes, and sent her mind up and out, spreading across the city. At first she went tentatively, ready to withdraw behind her shield at the first hint of danger, but the city seemed still and silent and empty. She spread her esp wide, but there was no trace of the Captain or his team, or the disturbing presence she'd sensed earlier. She dropped back into her body, and staggered uneasily a moment as her headache returned, worse than ever.

'Nothing,' she said bluntly. 'Not a damned thing. Either the Captain and his people haven't got here yet, or—'

'Or what?' said Corbie.

'I don't know.' DeChance frowned thoughtfully. 'I picked up something; nothing more than an image, really, but it might be significant. You can't see it from here, but there's a huge copper tower in the middle of the city. I think it's important, in some way. Either to us, or to the city. We'll head for that. It's not much of a goal, I know, but it beats standing around here in the cold.'

Corbie and Lindholm looked at each other, but said nothing. DeChance steeled herself, and led the way forward into the alien city. The marines followed her silently, guns in hand. Buildings of stone, crystal and metal loomed around them, shutting out the bright sunshine. Strange lights burned in open windows, colours slowly changing hue, to no discernible pattern or purpose. The only sound was the slap of their boots on the hard, unforgiving ground. The shadows were very dark and very cold.

Corbie felt the familiar prickling at the back of his neck that meant he was being watched. Military instincts might not be as officially appreciated as esp, but they could still keep you alive if you listened to them. He studied the dark openings in the buildings around him, alert for the slightest sound or movement, but whatever was watching wasn't about to give itself away that easily. Corbie hefted the disrupter in his hand. It didn't feel as comforting as it once had. It doesn't matter how powerful a gun is if you haven't anything to aim it at.

He didn't like the city at all. The buildings' shapes and dimensions were subtly disturbing, and the broad streets followed no pattern or design he could recognize. Each street was perfectly smooth and featureless, untouched by traffic or time. Even the air smelled wrong. The faint sulphurous odour of the plains was gone, replaced by something oily and metallic that grated on his nerves.

463

'This place is dead,' said Lindholm quietly. 'Nothing's lived here for centuries.'

'Maybe that's what we're supposed to think,' said Corbie. 'There's something here. I can feel it.'

Lindholm shrugged. 'I hope so. I'd hate to think I walked all this way for nothing.'

'Are you crazy? Out on the plains we were surrounded by killer centipedes, almost eaten alive by a melting forest, and finally attacked in the night by something that wasn't even slowed down by a proximity mine exploding right next to it! And you want to meet whatever twisted mind thought this lot up? Come on, Sven, I hate to think what the sophisticated life forms on this planet will look like.'

'You might just have something there.' Lindholm glanced at one of the doors they were passing. It was easily twelve feet high and seven feet wide. 'Whatever lived here was big, Russ. A race of giants. Just think about the scale.'

'I'd rather not.'

'Hold it.' DeChance's voice cracked loudly, and the marines stopped dead in their tracks, raising their guns reflexively.

'What is it?' said Corbie.

'I'm not sure. Let me think.' She tried to raise her esp, and couldn't. The unyielding alienness of the city was overpowering. 'I thought I saw something moving, just on the edge of my vision. Down that way.'

The marines looked where she indicated, and then looked at each other.

'It could be anything,' said Corbie.

'Probably nothing,' said Lindholm.

'No point in putting ourselves at risk.'

'We're just a scouting party. The Captain said so.'

'Even if there is something there, it could be leading us into a trap.'

'Yeah. Let's go after it.'

'Right.'

They grinned at each other, and started off down the street. They'd given it enough time to get away, if it was just an animal. On the other hand, if it wanted them to follow it, it would still be there, waiting for them. DeChance hurried along beside them, her eyes fixed on the spot where she thought the movement had been. It turned out to be a street intersection. They stopped and looked around them. There was no sign of any living thing, but far down on the right-hand side of the street, a huge metallic door was slowly closing. DeChance and the marines moved silently towards it, guns at the ready. The door was firmly shut by the time they got there, and the featureless metal had no handle or obvious locking mechanism. Corbie blasted it open with his disrupter. The torn metal door was blown inwards by the impact. Lindholm moved quickly forward to take the point until Corbie's gun had recharged, and then one by one they stepped cautiously through the doorway.

Oval panels set into the high ceiling glowed varying shades of red, none of them very bright. The walls were a complex latticework of glistening metallic threads. Dark nodes hung in clusters on the latticework, grouped to no discernible pattern. Huge and bulking alien machinery jutted from the walls and floor and ceiling. No one machine looked like any other, but they were all covered with kaleidoscopic displays of lights that hurt the eyes if stared at too long. The lights flickered on and off at irregular intervals, but there was no other sign to show how or why the machines were working. A low, almost sub-audible hum permeated the air, which had a tense, static feel.

'What the hell is this place?' said Lindholm.

'Beats me,' said Corbie. 'But it must be important if the machines are still working, long after everything else has shut down. Look how clean and immaculate it is in here. The rest of the city looks like it's been deserted for centuries, but as far as these machines are concerned their operators could just have stepped outside for a moment.'

'Centuries . . .' said Lindholm. 'Could they really have been running all that time, unattended?'

'I don't know. Maybe. I've got a bad feeling about this place, Sven. Let's get out of here. Now.'

'Wait a minute, Russ.' Lindholm looked at DeChance. 'What do you think, esper? Can you tell us anything about this place?'

DeChance shook her head. 'My esp's almost useless here. It's all too alien. My mind could get lost in all this. I'm an esper, not an Investigator. Krystel might be able to make something of

465

these machines, but they're beyond me. Could you take one of them apart, and see what makes it hum?'

'Not without the right equipment,' said Corbie. 'And even then I'd be very reluctant to meddle with anything here. I'd hate to get one of these things doing something, and then find I couldn't turn it off. Besides, I don't think I like the look of them. Sven—'

'Yeah, I know. You think we're being watched. I'm starting to feel that way too. It's up to you, esper. You're in charge. Do we leave, or go on?'

DeChance looked unhappy. Without her esp to back her up, she felt blind and deaf. If they went on, they could end up in real trouble if there was something lying in wait for them. On the other hand, they couldn't afford to overlook the first sign of life they'd found. She hesitated for a long moment, torn with indecision. What would the Captain do? That thought calmed her a little. She knew what he'd do.

'I think we should check this place out,' she said evenly. 'Look for a door, or stairs, or something.'

They gingerly made their way through the hulking alien machinery, careful not to touch anything. The humming of the machines hovered persistently at the edge of their hearing, like an itch they couldn't scratch. Corbie glared at the machines, and thought fleetingly that it might be fun to blast one or two of them with his disrupter, just to see what would happen. He'd never cared much for mysteries. He always liked to know what was going on, and where he stood. If only so that he could set about turning things to his own advantage. He looked round quickly as Lindholm hissed to him. The big marine was standing before an open doorway in the far wall.

'Where the hell did that come from?' said Corbie quietly.

'Beats me,' said Lindholm. 'I'd swear it wasn't here a minute ago. Maybe we hit the opening mechanism by accident.'

'Yeah. Maybe.' Corbie studied the opening carefully. It was dark in the room beyond, the pale rosy light from the machine room didn't penetrate far.

Lindholm moved forward slowly, his disrupter held out before him. Corbie kept close behind him. DeChance stayed where she was. Lindholm stepped quickly through the doorway in one smooth motion, his disrupter sweeping back and forth as he looked around him for a target. A wide open room lay spread out before him, empty and abandoned. The walls were bare and featureless, and the high ceiling was lost in shadows. Lindholm slowly lowered his gun, and walked forward into the room. Corbie and DeChance went in after him.

'Cheerful looking place,' said Corbie. 'I take it you've noticed there are no other doorways in here? What happens if the door we just came through decides to disappear again?'

'Then you get to blow a hole in the wall. DeChance, are you all right?'

The marines moved a step closer to the esper as she swayed unsteadily on her feet. Her face was ghastly pale in the dim light, her eyes fixed and staring.

'I can hear them,' she said faintly. 'I can feel them, all around us. They're waking up.'

'Who are?' said Corbie.

'They're waking up,' said DeChance. 'They're coming for us. They want what makes us sane.'

CHAPTER FOUR

The Alien

'If we're going to set a trap,' said Investigator Krystel, 'I have to be the bait. No offence, Captain, but I'm most likely to survive if something goes wrong.'

'You'll get no argument from me,' said Hunter. 'I've seen an Investigator in action before.'

'From a distance, I trust,' said Krystel.

'Of course,' said Hunter. 'I'm still here, aren't I?'

Krystel smiled fleetingly and looked round the large open square they'd chosen as the setting for their trap. Interlocking metallic buildings stood side by side with squat stone monoliths and intricate structures of spiked glass. There were only three entrances to the square, one of which was blocked with a high wall of rubble from a derelict building. There was no sign to show why the building had collapsed, and its neighbours seemed unaffected. Krystel eased her sword in its scabbard, and checked the power level on her force shield. Everything was ready. All they had to do now was bait the trap, and stand ready to spring it.

It should work; it was simple and straightforward. Hunter and Williams would leave the square, making a great deal of noise as they did so, and then circle quietly back, staying under cover all the way. Krystel, on the other hand, would take her ease in the middle of the square, and wait to see if anything came to join her. Simple and straightforward. Krystel believed in being direct and to the point whenever possible. The more complicated a plan was, the more chances there were for something to go wrong. Besides, they were working to a deadline. They only had three hours or so before night fell, and none of them wanted to be caught in the city after dark. The city might be deserted, but its ghosts didn't feel at all friendly.

Hunter and Williams made loud goodbyes, and left the square together. It seemed very quiet with them gone. Krystel walked over to the wall of rubble, sat down on a comfortable-looking stone slab, and took a cigar stub out of her pocket. She took her time about lighting it, trying hard to give the impression of being completely relaxed and at ease. Krystel drew her sword, took a piece of rag from the top of her boot, and polished the blade with long, easy strokes. The familiar ritual was quietly soothing. When the job was done, she put the piece of rag away, and sat with the sword lying flat across her thighs. It was a good blade. A claymore, handed down through three generations of her family. She hoped she'd brought no dishonour to the sword, though sometimes she wasn't sure. An Investigator's work was like that, mostly.

She wondered idly what she'd be facing when the time came. The scale of the buildings meant it would be big, probably around nine to ten feet tall. She remembered the statues from the plain, frowned slightly, and then shrugged. It didn't matter. Whatever it was, she could handle it. She was an Investigator.

She sat up straight suddenly. A faint repetitive sound came clearly to her on the quiet. She looked quickly around her, but there was no trace of any movement, and she couldn't place which direction the sound was coming from. Krystel stubbed out her cigar, and put what was left of it back in her pocket for later. She stood up, sword and disrupter in hand, and slapped her left wrist against her side. The glowing force shield appeared on her arm. She stood waiting, confident and ready, checking out possible cover and escape routes. Whatever was coming sounded large and heavy and determined, but the sounds echoed round and round the square until she couldn't tell where they originated. Captain Hunter and Williams should be somewhere close at hand by now, but she knew she couldn't afford to depend on them. The sound was drawing nearer. A long, wailing howl suddenly broke the silence, shrill and powerful and horribly angry. Krystel's hackles rose sharply. Something about the awful sound touched her deeply on some basic primitive level, and she felt a sudden impulse to turn and run until she'd left the alien city far behind her. She crushed the thought ruthlessly. She was an Investigator, and it was just another alien.

She moved quickly into a shadowed alcove, and set her back against the wall. The approaching footsteps were like thunder. The beast howled again, and for the first time Krystel caught a glimpse of something moving beyond the high wall of rubble. Krystel lifted her gun, and waited for a target. The rubble suddenly burst apart as the alien crashed through it. Shards of broken stone and metal flew through the air like jagged hail. The beast stepped out into the square, and Krystel's face screwed up in disgust.

It was tall, well over twenty feet. It would have been taller if it hadn't been for the stooping back and thrust forward head. It was a dirty white in colour, its rough hide more like scale than skin. It walked on two legs, and it looked something like a man. Great slabs of muscle corded and bunched on its huge form, but the proportions were somehow wrong. Disturbingly wrong. The twisted arms hung almost to the ground. One arm ended in a viciously clawed hand. The other erupted into a mass of writhing tentacles. Its face was a rigid mask of sharp-edged bone. The great snarling mouth was full of serrated teeth. There were two lidless eyes, yellow as urine, and with no trace of pupil or iris. It lurched awkwardly forward into the square, as though searching for some sound or scent it couldn't quite detect.

Krystel had to fight down an urge to back away. It wasn't the alien's form: ugly though it was, she'd seen worse in her time. The alien's flesh was rotten and decaying, falling away in places, and it left a trail of foulness behind it. Nubs of discoloured bone showed through the splitting hide, which stretched and tore with every movement. In places, the flesh seemed to stir and writhe of its own volition, as though maggots seethed beneath the surface.

Krystel took a deep breath to steady herself, took careful aim with her disrupter, and pressed the stud. The beam of violent energy hit just above the creature's eyes, and the entire head exploded in a flurry of bloody flesh and bone. The alien slumped to its knees, fell on its side and lay still. Krystel watched carefully to be sure it was dead, feeling almost let down. Is that it? she thought finally, holstering her gun. All that planning and preparation, and the stupid creature went down under a single disrupter shot. She smiled briefly. She should have known. Investigators killed aliens. That's just the way it was.

She stepped out of the alcove and walked unhurriedly across the square towards the unmoving alien. It was certainly big enough, even larger than she'd expected. Where the hell had it been hiding all this time? More importantly, how many more creatures like this were there, and where were they hiding? Hunter and Williams appeared from different sides of the square, guns in hand, and walked over to join her. Krystel looked thoughtfully at the dead alien. At twenty feet tall, it was probably the biggest thing she'd ever shot. Maybe she should have it stuffed and mounted as a trophy. She was about ten feet away when the alien suddenly lurched to its feet. It stood swaying for a moment, and then a new head thrust up from the bloody ruin of its neck. The eyes opened slowly, the eyelids parting stickily, and then its great mouth gaped wide as the alien's horrid ululating voice echoed across the square.

Krystel grabbed for her gun, knowing even as she did that the energy crystal hadn't had time to recharge yet. The alien whirled round to face her, and she brought her force shield up between them. The claymore was a solid weight in her hand. Close up, she could see the rotting flesh writhing and falling apart on the alien's body. The stench was appalling. It looked steadily at her with its pair of yellow eyes, and its grinning mouth stretched impossibly wide. It was reaching for her with its clawed hand when two bolts of searing energy tore its neck and chest apart. Flesh and blood spattered against Krystel's shield, and she backed quickly away as the alien swung round to face the men who'd hurt it. Already its shifting flesh was making good the gaping holes in its chest and throat. Hunter and Williams activated their forces shields as the alien turned on them. The tentacles on the end of its right arm stretched impossibly as they reached for the two men.

'This way,' yelled Krystel, indicating with her sword the nearest of the escape routes she'd spotted earlier. She ran for the narrow passageway, and Hunter and Williams ran after her. The alien howled and lurched after them. Krystel glanced back over her shoulder. The alien was already closing the gap, moving impossibly quickly for its bulk. Krystel ran full tilt down the passageway between the two buildings and, Hunter and Williams sprinting after her, tried to figure out where the hell to head for next. They weren't going to be able to outrun the creature. She needed somewhere they could make a stand.

She raked the buildings around her with a desperate glare, and then spotted an open doorway to her right. She changed direction without slowing her pace, and raced for the doorway. She charged through, gun and sword at the ready, but the shadowy chamber before her appeared to be deserted. Hunter and Williams crowded through the doorway after her, and the three of them looked quickly round for something they could use to block the doorway. The room was empty, save for a dozen or so gleaming metallic spirals hanging from the ceiling. Krystel spotted another doorway on the opposite side of the room, and padded quickly over to peer into the shadowy opening. She gestured for Hunter and Williams to join her, and stepped through the doorway.

The new room was even darker, but they didn't dare use a lantern. The alien might see it. They shut off their force shields, sat down with their backs to the wall, and waited for their eyes to adjust to the gloom. Everything was still and quiet, the only sound in the huge room was their own slowing breathing.

'I can't hear it any more,' said Williams. 'Can you?'

'It's still out there,' said Hunter. 'It knows we can't have gone far.'

'What the hell was it?' said Williams. 'I saw it die, and it got up again. It's like something out of legend. The undead, the beasts that cannot die—'

'Superstition is for immature minds,' snapped Krystel. 'Whatever that alien is, it's real enough. I've still got some of its blood on my uniform. And when I blew its head off, it took some time before it could recover enough to grow another. It can be hurt. Stunned.'

'But can it be killed?' said Williams. 'Or is it already dead? Its flesh was decaying . . . I know decomposing flesh when I see it!'

'Keep your voice down,' said Hunter. 'Do you want it to hear you?'

Williams shut up. Hunter leaned his head back against the

wall, and closed his eyes for a moment. There had to be a way out of this, if only he could think of it. He had to think of something; he was the Captain. It was a pity the pinnace was so far away. Its guns would have blown the alien into so many pieces it would never have been able to put itself back together again. But he might as well wish for the moons. Even if he could summon the pinnace by remote control, by the time it reached the city everything would be over, one way or another. He looked at Krystel.

'Any comments, Investigator?'

'Our guns should have recharged by now,' said Krystel. 'Maybe if we all hit it with disrupters at the same time—'

'That sounds more like a last resort than a plan of action,' said Hunter. 'But for want of anything better I suppose it'll have to do.'

'There's always the concussion grenades,' said Williams.

'Not accurate enough. That thing can move bloody quickly when it puts its mind to it. Any other suggestions?'

'Retreat,' said Krystel. 'Get the hell out of the city and leave the alien behind. Most creatures have a strong sense of territory; if we put enough space between us and it, it should lose interest in us.'

'That's a lot of ifs and maybes,' said Williams. 'You're supposed to be an expert on alien forms. Haven't you got anything definite you can tell us?'

'It's huge, it's angry and it's dangerous,' said Krystel. 'It can regenerate damaged tissue. Our weapons are useless against it, and it will quite definitely kill us if we don't start acting intelligently. On the other hand, for all its power, it doesn't appear to be very bright. With its advantages, I suppose it doesn't have to be. But all the time we're sitting around arguing, it's getting closer. It could be here any minute.'

Hunter closed his eyes and tried hard to concentrate. There had to be a way out of this.

'If it was going to come straight in here after us, it would have done so by now,' he said finally. 'So what's stopping it?'

Krystel shrugged. 'I can't advise you, Captain. I don't have enough information. Normally, with a new species like this I'd spend months checking it out from a distance, before even thinking of approaching it.'

She broke off as Williams sat up straight suddenly. 'It's entered the building,' he said flatly. 'I can hear it.'

Hunter held his breath and listened, but couldn't hear anything. He looked at Krystel, who shrugged slightly. Hunter bit his lip. More of the good Doctor's hidden augmentations, presumably. Williams stirred restlessly.

'We can't just sit here in the dark, Captain. We've got to do something.'

'Keep your voice down,' said Krystel. 'We don't know how good its hearing is. And there's no point in just running blindly.'

'There's no point in just waiting here for the damned thing to find us. Captain, we've got to get out of here!'

There was a sudden stench of corruption, and the room suddenly darkened as the alien's bulk filled the huge doorway.

'Disrupters!' yelled Hunter, as the three of them scrambled to their feet. 'Aim for the head!'

The three disrupters fired almost as one, and the alien's head blew apart. But this time, the creature didn't fall. It braced itself on its massive legs, and groped blindly for its attackers. The three of them backed quickly away, holstering their guns and activating their force shields. Krystel drew her claymore and hacked at the writhing tentacles as they reached for her face. The blade cut cleanly through the rotten flesh, but the wounds healed themselves in seconds. A new head burst up out of the bloody mess of its neck. Its yellow eyes shone in the darkness.

Hunter swung his sword with all his strength, and the blade sliced through the shifting white flesh and out again, without leaving a wound behind it. The alien cut at Hunter with its clawed hand, and he put up his force shield between them. The impact of the blow sent him staggering backwards. Krystel yelled at the beast to get its attention, and when it turned on her she sliced at its arm with the edge of her shield. The glowing energy field sheared clean through the wrist, severing the clawed hand. It fell to the floor, the fingers still curling and uncurling. The claws dug furrows in the floor. Pale blood spurted from the stump. The alien screamed, and batted at Krystel with its injured arm. The Investigator threw herself to one side. The blow barely clipped her in passing, but she was still slammed against the wall. Hunter grabbed her before her knees could buckle, but she quickly got her breath back and shrugged him off.

'There's another doorway on the far side of the room,' she said quickly. 'Take Williams and get out of here. I'll hold the creature back to give you a start. I'll join you as soon as I can. Now move it!'

Williams turned and ran for the other doorway, and Hunter reluctantly followed him.

The alien forced its massive body through the doorway, wrecking the surrounding wall in the process. Krystel moved in close and hacked at the beast with her claymore and shield. Her mouth stretched in a tight nasty grin, and her eyes gleaming with a killing fever. The alien howled endlessly, its wailing voice almost unbearable at close range. The sheer fury of Krystel's attack held the alien where it was, but its wounds healed in seconds, and even through her killing rage, Krystel knew she wasn't really hurting it. She snarled into its grinning face, and then turned and ran. The alien lurched after her, but she was already across the room and plunging through the far doorway by the time it had started to build up speed. Hunter and Williams were waiting for her at the base of a tall tower. A ramp led up the side of the wall into darkness.

'This way,' said Hunter. 'There's no other way out. If nothing else, this should put some space between us and the creature.'

He led the way up the ramp, with Williams and Krystel crowding close behind. After a while, they calmed down enough to turn off their force shields, to save energy. The sheer slope made the going hard, and Hunter's thighs were soon aching fiercely. He drove himself on regardless, and snarled at the others when they looked like slowing. He couldn't hear the alien yet, but he had no doubt it was still on their trail. He held his field lantern out before him, its golden light illuminating the tower above and below him. He watched his feet carefully; again there was no safety rail, and a slip at the wrong moment could easily prove fatal. The tower seemed to go on for ever, and the drop just kept getting longer. He glared into the shadows ahead. How the hell could everything have gone wrong so quickly? Doors came and went in the wall beside him, but he kept pressing on. He could hear the alien coming up the ramp after them. It was getting closer.

And finally they ran out of ramp. Bright light fell through an open doorway, and Hunter had no choice but to plunge into it. He lurched to a halt as the brilliant sunlight blinded him, and he blinked painfully for several moments before his sight returned. He turned off his field lantern and put it back in his backpack as he looked quickly around him.

Huge enigmatic structures covered the length and breadth of the roof, dwarfing Hunter and his companions. The towering shapes were complex and strange, composed of a pearly iridescent material that softened and distorted every detail. Hunter stared silently about him, unable to react at all. They were too strange, too alien, for any reaction of his to make sense. They were beyond any rational or emotional response. They simply were, and Hunter couldn't tear his eyes away from them.

'Fascinating,' said Krystel. 'I wonder what they do?'

Her voice broke the spell, and Hunter shook his head, disorientated. 'Save the questions for another day,' he said finally. 'That creature will be here any minute. Start looking for a way off this roof.'

'Wait a minute,' said Williams unexpectedly. 'I have a problem. I can't seem to raise the pinnace computers.'

Hunter looked at him blankly for a moment, and then activated his comm implant. He reached out for the computers, but there was nothing there, only silence. It was like reaching out in the dark for a light switch, and finding only empty space. Hunter swallowed hard. He'd known that one day he'd have to learn to do without them, but the sudden silence had caught him unprepared. 'Investigator, Williams, can you hear me?'

'Not through my comm unit,' said Krystel. 'We're cut off, Captain.'

'We've got to get back to the pinnace,' said Williams urgently. 'We've got to re-establish contact. All my work, all my memories are there.'

'One thing at a time, Doctor,' said Hunter. 'First we get off the roof, then we'll decide what to do next.'

'Quiet!' said Krystel. 'The creature's almost here.' She moved over to the doorway, pulled a concussion grenade from her bandolier, primed it, and tossed it down the ramp. She backed quickly away, and the tower shook as the grenade exploded some distance below.

'That should slow it down,' said Krystel. She looked at Hunter. 'There's only one way off this roof, Captain, and we both know what it is. The bridges.'

She gestured at the gossamer strands that hung between the tower and its surrounding buildings, and Hunter winced.

'I was afraid you were going to say that. I don't trust those things. They look as though they'd blow away in a good wind.'

'The aliens must have used them,' said Williams. 'And they weigh a hell of a lot more than we do.'

Hunter looked at the webbing again, and then back at the doorway. 'All right, let's do it. And quickly, before I get a rush of brains to the head and realize how crazy this is.'

He moved over to the edge of the roof, hesitated briefly, and then sat down and swung his legs out and over on to the webbing. He looked down once, and decided not to look again. It was a long way down. He muttered something indistinct and stepped gingerly out on to the bridge. It was six to seven feet wide, a tangled mess of grey strands barely a quarter of an inch or so in diameter, and as thin as froth in places. There were no hand rails. The threads gave slightly under his weight, but held. Hunter gritted his teeth, and sheathed his sword and gun so as to have both hands free. He walked steadily forward and kept his gaze fixed on the building ahead. It didn't seem to be getting any closer. At the back of his mind he couldn't help wondering if the webbing had been spun by a machine, or some gigantic creature. The bridge lurched and shook as Williams and Krystel followed him, but it seemed to be holding all their weight well enough. Hunter began to relax a little.

They hadn't got far when the bridge lurched sickeningly to one side. Hunter fell to one knee and grabbed at the strands for support. He looked back, past Williams and Krystel, already knowing what he was going to see. The alien had found them. It snarled soundlessly, exposing its jagged teeth, and made its way steadily along the bridge towards them. The bridge bounced and swayed, but the fragile looking gossamer threads held the creature's weight easily. Hunter swore under his breath, and rose unsteadily to his feet.

'Investigator, take the Doctor and get to the next building. I'll hold the alien back. If I don't join you, find the others and tell them what's happened. Then get the hell out of this city, and back to the pinnace. Yell for help, and keep on yelling till you get it. That's it. No arguments. Move.'

Williams pushed past him, and ran down the bridge. Krystel stayed where she was. 'I should stay, not you. I'm the Investigator.'

'That's why you have to go, Krystel. They're going to need you.'

'We need you.'

'No one's needed me for a long time. I'm not reliable any more. Now will you please get the hell out of here?'

Krystel nodded briefly, and hurried after Williams. Hunter watched her go for a moment, and then turned to face the oncoming alien. It looked bigger than he remembered. Its rotting white flesh seemed to slip and slide on its frame, but the teeth in the grinning mouth looked horribly efficient. Hunter drew his gun. He didn't have to look down to know his hand was shaking. His stomach ached from the tension, sweat was pouring off him. And yet scared as he was, terrified as he was, he wasn't panicking. His mind was clear. He knew what he had to do, and he was ready to do it. Maybe that was all he'd really needed; a simple straightforward certainty in his life that he could understand and cling to.

The alien was nearly upon him. He could smell it, hear its panting breath. There was no point in trying to shoot it. They'd tried that, and it hadn't worked. His sword and force shield would be less than useless. The creature had already grown a new hand to replace the one Krystel had cut off. And he couldn't turn and run. The alien would soon catch him and kill him, and then it would go after Krystel and Williams. No. Hunter took a firm grip on his gun, and his hand steadied. He had to buy time for the others, time for them to get away and warn the Empire about the nightmare on Wolf IV.

He'd always wondered where he would die. Upon what alien world, under what alien sun. He smiled once at the approaching

478

alien, took careful aim with his disrupter, and blew out the bridge between them. The gossamer threads parted in a second under the searing energy, and the alien screamed shrilly as it fell, twisting and turning, to the street far below.

Hunter brushed against a flailing strand of webbing as he fell, and he dropped his sword and gun to grab at it with both hands. The webbing slid through his fingers as though it was greased. He tightened his grip till his hands ached, and finally got a firm hold on the strand. The sudden lurch as his fall was brought to a halt almost wrenched his arms from their sockets, but somehow he held on. The broken length of webbing swung downwards, its speed increasing as Hunter's weight pulled at it. The wall of the building opposite came flying towards him like a flyswatter. Hunter had a split-second glimpse of an open window looming up before him, and then the webbing slapped flat against the side of the building, hurling him through the window. He tried to hang on to his strand of webbing, but it was wrenched from his hands. He curled into a ball instinctively, and then he crashed into something hard but yielding, and it gave under the impact. Hunter careered on, unable to stop, and smashed through another barrier. All the breath was knocked from his lungs, and the pain was so bad he blacked out.

He came back to consciousness slowly, in fits and starts. For a long while all he could do was lie on his back and stare at the ceiling. And that was how Krystel and Williams found him. They forced their way through the wreckage that half filled the room, and made their way over to Hunter. Williams knelt beside him, and checked him over with brisk efficiency. Hunter grinned up at Krystel.

'What happened to the alien?'

'Hit the ground and spattered,' said Krystel succinctly. 'We'll be lucky to find any pieces big enough to study.'

Hunter wanted to laugh, but his ribs hurt too much. He sat up slowly, with Williams' help, and looked around him.

'From the look of it, this room was full of partitions,' said Krystel. 'Emphasis on the word was. You seem to have demolished most of them.'

'Good thing you did,' said Williams. 'They soaked up most of your speed and impact. The fall would have killed you otherwise. You're lucky to be alive, Captain.'

'Don't think I don't know it,' said Hunter. He nodded to Williams to let go of him, and stood swaying for a moment while his head settled. 'How bad is the damage, Doctor?'

'Extensive bruising, and some lacerations. You could have a cracked rib or two, not to mention concussion. I really think we should get back to the pinnace so I can check you over properly.'

'For once, I think I agree with you, Doctor.' Hunter rubbed tiredly at his aching forehead. 'As long as there was a chance the city was deserted, I could justify checking it out ourselves, but the alien changes all that. We have to contact the Empire.'

'That could mean a delay in the arrival of the colonists,' said Williams.

'Yes,' said Hunter. 'I know.' He looked at Krystel. 'I don't suppose you found any trace of my gun and my sword? I dropped them.'

'I'm afraid not, Captain,' said the Investigator. 'But you're welcome to use my disrupter. I've always preferred the sword, myself. It's more personal.'

Hunter took the gun from her with a nod of thanks, and slipped it into his holster. 'All right, the first thing is to contact the rest of the Squad. They should have reached the city by now.'

'There's always the chance they encountered one of the aliens themselves,' said Krystel. 'They might not have been as fortunate as us.'

'You're right.' Hunter frowned to himself for a moment. 'We'll head for the copper tower, just in case my last message to them got through. If they're not there we'll have to give up on them for now, and get back to the pinnace. The Empire must be warned.'

'Yes,' said Krystel. 'The last time I came up against an alien this hard to kill was on Grendel.'

Slowly and cautiously, the three of them made their way down the winding ramp and out of the building. They were alert for any sound or movement, but the building was as silent as a tomb. Every room they passed held strange shapes and machinery, but there was no sign of life anywhere. By the time they got outside, the day was nearly over. Shadows were growing longer as the day darkened, and the deep emerald sky held veins of red from the sinking sun.

'It'll be night soon,' said Williams quietly. 'I don't think we should spend a night in the city, Captain. There's no telling what might roam the streets once the sun goes down.'

'We can't just abandon the others,' said Hunter. 'They're part of the Squad.'

'We can if we have to,' said Krystel. 'They're expendable. Just like us.'

Evening fell across the city. The street was filled with shadows, the strange lights continued to burn brightly in open windows. And in the dark, hidden heart of the city, something awful grew slowly stronger.

CHAPTER FIVE

The Prey

Lindholm led the way down the deserted street, gun in hand, alert for any sign of life or movement. Corbie followed close behind, hurrying the esper along as best he could. DeChance's face was smooth and blank, empty of all emotion. Her eyes saw nothing, and she walked uncaringly wherever Corbie led her. The marine scowled, as much in worry as anger. DeChance had been acting brainburned ever since she made mental contact with something in the city.

They're waking up, she'd said. *They're coming for us. They want what makes us sane.*

She hadn't said a word after that. The light went out of her eyes, and she could no longer hear the marines, no matter how loudly they shouted. Her face became gaunt and drawn, and she only moved when the marines guided her. At first they thought her condition might have been caused by the building they were in, but even after they'd hustled her outside she remained lost and silent. Corbie had pressed for them to keep moving. If there was something coming after them, they'd be better off presenting a moving target. Lindholm reluctantly agreed, and led the way. Corbie let him. Right now, he needed somebody else to be in charge, to do his thinking for him.

He glanced quickly around. They were walking between two massive structures of crystal and metal fused together, so tall that Corbie had to tilt back his head to see the top of them. There were no lights in any of the windows, and the only sound on the quiet was the soft, steady padding of their own footsteps. There'd been no sign of any living thing since the esper's warning, but still Corbie's back felt the pressure of unseen watching eyes.

He tried to imagine something so terrible that just mental contact with it could destroy your mind, and couldn't. The fear was with him always now, trembling in his hands, burning in his eyes. His stomach was a tight knot of pain. He tried to concentrate on where they were heading, to keep his mind occupied, but all he knew for sure was the name the esper had given it. The copper tower. Corbie sniffed unhappily and glanced about him, trying to get his bearings. He'd been turned around so much he wasn't even sure where the boundaries were any more. Lindholm was still striding purposefully ahead of him, though. So presumably he at least knew where they were going.

'How long since you tried the comm unit?' said Lindholm suddenly, his voice, as always, calm and quiet.

'Maybe ten minutes. Want me to try again?'

'Sure. Give it a try.'

Corbie activated his comm implant, but there was only the unnerving silence, empty even of static. 'Captain, this is Corbie. Please respond.' He waited as long as he could, but there was no answer. He tried twice more, and then gave up. Lindholm said nothing.

DeChance suddenly stumbled, and almost fell. Corbie had to support all her weight for a moment, and then her back straightened as she found her feet again. She shook her head dazedly, and made a few strange noises with her mouth. Corbie looked at Lindholm, and nodded urgently at the nearest building. Lindholm nodded. Between the two of them, the marines got DeChance over to the open doorway. It was set in the side of a gleaming pearlescent dome, a hundred feet high or more. There were no windows or other openings, only the smooth featureless surface of the dome. Lindholm went through the doorway first, gun at the ready, his force shield blazing on his arm. Corbie gave him a moment, and then guided the esper in after him.

Inside there was only darkness. There was a flash of light as Lindholm lit his field lantern, and the room came into being around them. It was roughly square, some thirty feet wide, with a low ceiling. Both walls and ceiling were strangely curved in places. They glowed a dull silver-grey in the lantern light. Lindholm put the lantern down on the floor, and came over to help Corbie with the esper. DeChance sat down suddenly on the floor, as though all the strength had gone out of her legs. Corbie helped her lean back against the nearest wall. It felt warm and sponge-like, and Corbie glowered at it suspiciously before turning his attention back to DeChance.

'I think this may have been a mistake,' said Lindholm suddenly. 'I don't like the feel of this place.'

'You took the words right out of my mouth,' said Corbie. 'Unfortunately, the esper's in no condition to travel any further.'

'How is she?'

'I'm not sure. She might be coming out of it. Then again . . .'

'Yeah.' Lindholm looked quickly around him. There was a wide opening in the far wall, full of darkness. 'We can't stay here, Russ. We can't even barricade the doorway. Get her on her feet again, and we'll try the other door. You bring the lantern.'

He moved warily towards the open doorway, while Corbie grabbed the field lantern with one hand, and urged DeChance to her feet with the other. The esper was still dazed, but at least now she was co-operating with him.

'Come on, Russ,' said Lindholm impatiently. 'It's not safe here.'

'Safe? I haven't felt safe since we landed on this bloody planet. If you're in such a hurry, how about giving me a hand. The esper isn't getting any lighter to lug around, you know.'

Lindholm took the lantern away from him, and held it up to light the next room. Corbie glared at Lindholm's back, and then peered through the open doorway. The room was huge. The shadows beyond the light made it impossible to judge its true size, but once again Corbie was struck by the sheer scale of the alien city. He felt like a child who'd escaped from the nursery and wandered into the part of the world where the adults lived. The curving walls had a dull reddish colour in the lantern light, marked here and there by sharp protrusions. The floor was cracked and split apart, like mud that had dried out under a midday sun. The room itself was quite empty. Lindholm moved slowly forward and Corbie followed him, still half-supporting the esper. The far wall suddenly became clear as the lantern light moved, and Corbie grimaced. Spurs of metal jutted from the crimson wall, like the horns of forgotten beasts. For a moment

Corbie wondered if they could be trophies of some kind, and immediately the walls seemed to him to be exactly the colour of dried blood. A round opening in the wall yawned like a toothless mouth.

'Where are we?' said DeChance hoarsely, and Corbie jumped.

'It's all right,' he said quickly. 'You're quite safe. We're inside one of the buildings. It's empty. How do you feel?'

'I'm not sure. Strange.' She shook her head slowly. 'There were so many traces, so many alien minds, I just got lost among them. I couldn't understand any of them. Their thought patterns made no sense.' Her face cleared suddenly, losing all its vagueness, and she looked sharply at the two marines. 'We've got to get out of the city. If there's one thing I am sure of, it's that they're dangerous. Horribly dangerous.'

'You keep saying *they*,' said Lindholm. 'How many aliens are there? Where are they hiding?'

'They're here,' said DeChance. 'They're all around. Waiting. They've been waiting a very long time. We woke them up. I don't know how many there are: hundreds, thousands. I don't know. The traces kept shifting, changing. But they're close. I know that. They're getting closer all the time. We've got to get out of the city.'

'Sounds good to me,' said Corbie. 'Sven?'

'Hold on a minute, Russ.' Lindholm looked thoughtfully at the esper. 'No offence, DeChance, but just how reliable is what you've been telling us? Are you giving us facts or impressions?'

'Both. Neither. I can't explain esp to anyone who isn't an esper. Contact with an alien mind is difficult; they don't think like we do. It's like looking in a distorted mirror, trying to find things you recognize. I managed to pick up a few things I'm sure of. The power sources for the city are all underground, buried deep in the bedrock. They go down for miles. They're still functioning, despite being abandoned for centuries. Now the city's coming alive, and drawing more and more power. I don't know what the power's for, but it's got something to do with the copper tower in the centre of the city. That tower is the key to everything that's happening here.'

'Then we'd better go and take a look at it,' said Lindholm. 'Maybe we'll find a few answers there.'

'Are you crazy?' said Corbie. 'You heard the esper; this whole place is coming alive, and hundreds, maybe thousands of monsters are heading our way right now! We've got to get out of here while we still can!'

'Come on, Russ, we can't just walk away from this. We have a responsibility to the rest of the squad, and the colonists who'll come after us. This is our best chance to get some answers, while everything's still waking up and disorientated.'

'Responsibility? Sven, they dumped us here to die. No one gives a damn about us. We're expendable – that's why they sent us. Our only responsibility is to ourselves.'

'What about the rest of the Squad?'

'What about them?'

'Allow me,' said DeChance to Lindholm. 'Corbie, if we don't find the answers now, while we've got a chance, the aliens in this city will kill us all. They'll roll right over us. Our only hope is the copper tower, and what we might find there. Now shut up and soldier.'

Corbie nodded glumly. 'How far is it to the tower?'

'Not far. A mile, at most.'

'Do you feel up to travelling that far?'

'I think so.'

'Anything else we need to know about the tower?' said Lindholm.

'Yes.' DeChance frowned, her eyes vague and far away. 'I think it's insane.'

'Great,' said Corbie. 'Just great.'

Lindholm had just started to nod agreement when the room suddenly came alive around them. Blurred shapes thrust up out of the floor, grey and white and beaded with sweat. The marines moved quickly to stand back to back, guns at the ready. A new light pierced the darkness as they raised their force shields. DeChance raised hers a moment later, and moved in close beside the marines, gun and sword in hand. More growths burst out of the walls. Somewhere far away, something was shrieking with rage or pain or both. The growths blossomed out into huge mushroom shapes with wide drooping heads on long, waving stalks. Crude eyes appeared on the stalks, and the fluted edges of the heads fluttered with the steady rhythm of slow breathing.

The growths sprouted from every side, spreading out to fill the room.

Corbie yelled out in surprise as a mushroom blossomed out of the floor at his feet, and he fired his disrupter at it. The fleshy head exploded under the energy bolt. The stalk swayed back and forth for a moment, and then a dozen flailing tentacles erupted out of the stalk, lashing furiously at the air. They were blood red, and tipped with tiny sucking mouths. Corbie cut at them with his sword, but for every tentacle he severed, another burst out of the stalk to take its place. Lindholm looked from one doorway to the other, and tried to work out which was the nearest. He had a sinking feeling the nearest door was the one that led deeper into the building. One of the mushroom growths leaned towards him, top-heavy on its slender stalk, and Lindholm only just managed to stop himself from firing at it. He didn't want to repeat Corbie's mistake. The centre of the bowed mushroom head bulged suddenly outwards, and then split apart as a huge black-armoured insect exploded out of it. It had a wide flat body, a dozen barbed legs, and razor-sharp mandibles. It reached hungrily for Lindholm, and he shot it at point-blank range. The armoured body blew apart, twitching legs flying through the air.

All over the room, the mushroom growths were swelling up and bursting open, giving birth to monsters. Corbie and Lindholm holstered their guns and tried to clear a space around them with their swords. The esper was no use to them. Her gun hung slackly at her side, her face drawn and twisted by some inner agony. The marines protected her as best they could, but they both knew they couldn't do that for long. There were just too many monsters.

A huge mushroom head exploded, throwing hundreds of blood-red worms across the room. They fell upon monsters and mushrooms alike, and began to chew voraciously through whatever they landed on. The marines were mostly protected by their force shields and steelmesh tunics, but still a few landed on bare flesh. One worm landed on Lindholm's hand, and bit clear through to the bone before he could shake it off. He cursed briefly, and kept on fighting. In the Arenas you learned to ignore any wound that wasn't immediately critical. Corbie wasn't nearly so calm about it, and shrieked and cursed at the top of his voice when a worm attached itself to his ear. He clawed desperately at the worm with his free hand, and in tearing it off almost decapitated himself with his own force shield. Several worms landed on the esper, shocking her out of her trance, and she brushed and slapped frantically at the worms where they clung to her uniform. The monsters ignored the worms in their single-minded determination to reach their human prey. A long, dull-grey tentacle snapped out of nowhere and grabbed Lindholm's field lantern. The lantern shattered in its grip, and the light winked out. The room was still lit by an eerie, ghostly glow from the mushrooms, but it was rapidly being blocked out by the growing horde of monsters.

The marines fought on, despite the growing ache in their backs and arms, and the air that burned in their straining lungs. DeChance protected them with her force shield as best she could, but she was no fighter, and they all knew it. Huge armoured insects up to three and four feet in length crawled over the floor and walls, and fought each other for the chance to get at the prey. Long tentacles studded with snapping mouths thrashed the air. Something broken-backed with too many legs crawled upside down across the ceiling, watching the marines with unblinking eyes. The worms were everywhere, writhing and coiling and eating. Corbie wiped sweat from his eyes with the back of his hand, and something with foot-long teeth snapped at his throat. He got his force shield up just in time, and the teeth broke against the energy field. He could feel the strength going out of him with each of his sword thrusts, but he kept fighting anyway. He had to. There was nowhere to retreat to. He couldn't even see the doorway any more. He grinned defiantly, and swung his sword in short, vicious arcs while he waited for his disrupter to recharge. A mushroom burst out of the wall beside him, and he cut through the stem. A writhing mass of intestines fell out of the wound, steaming on the still air.

Right, thought Corbie determinedly. That is it. Enough is enough.

He cleared some space around him with his sword and shield, lifted his gun, and blasted a hole through the nearest wall. DeChance and Lindholm quickly used their guns to blast a path through the crowding monsters, and the three of them clambered through the hole into the darkness beyond. The two marines turned and blocked the gap with their force shields, while DeChance pulled her field lantern out of her backpack. The sudden flare of light showed the room was empty apart from some alien machinery, and the esper relaxed a little. Monsters pressed against the two force shields, trying to force their way past. A mushroom head exploded, blowing a hail of writhing maggots into the air.

'We've got to block this hole off and barricade it,' said Lindholm. His breath was coming in short, ragged pants, but he sounded calm.

'Sounds good to me,' said Corbie. 'You and the esper find something. I'll hold them off. But you'd better be bloody quick.'

He stepped forward to fill the hole, somehow finding the last reserves of his strength. The monsters surged forward, and he met them with his sword and shield. Tired and aching and preoccupied as he was, Corbie still found time to notice he wasn't as frightened as he had been. He was still scared, but it wasn't the heart-stopping, paralysing fear that had devilled him for so long. He was scared, but he could still think and he could still fight. Perhaps it was simply that he no longer had the choice of whether to fight or run. Being weak and indecisive here would simply get him killed. Not that Corbie had any illusions about his chances. Unless Sven or the esper came up with a miracle pretty damn quickly, he was a dead man, and he knew it.

Who knows, maybe I'm just getting used to being terrified . . .

His grin widened into a death's-head snarl, and his gun blasted a creeping thing into a hundred twitching pieces.

'Move back out of the way, Russ. Now!'

Corbie fell back, and Lindholm single-handedly slammed a massive piece of alien machinery into the gap, sealing the hole off. Corbie didn't even want to think how much the thing must weigh. Certainly it looked strong enough to hold back the monsters while he and his companions made their escape. He started to move away from the wall, and collapsed. His vision darkened, and his head went muzzy.

'Easy, Russ,' said Lindholm quickly. 'Take a moment and get your second wind. The barricade will hold a while yet.'

Corbie sat on the floor, and concentrated on breathing deeply. His head was already clearing, but he could tell he wasn't up to running any distance yet, even assuming he had anywhere to run to. He glanced quickly around the new room. It wasn't quite as big as the last one, but, even so, the lantern's light didn't carry to the far wall, and the high ceiling was hidden in shadow. Squat, hulking machinery stood in neat rows, no two the same. There were no lights or other signs to show they were still functioning. Corbie distrusted them anyway, on general principles. There was a jagged hole in the floor, its edges glowing hot from an energy burst, where Lindholm had used his disrupter to break a machine free from the floor. Lengths of steel and glass protruded from the hole like broken bones. Corbie took a deep breath, turned off his force shield, and got back on his feet again, with a little help from Lindholm and the esper.

'All right,' he said hoarsely. 'What now?'

Lindholm shrugged. 'We can't go back, so we go on. There's another doorway, beyond the machines.'

Corbie looked at DeChance. She had turned away, and was frowning distractedly, listening to something only she could hear.

'Well?' said Corbie finally. 'What do you think, esper? Do you agree?'

'Yes,' said DeChance. Her expression didn't change. 'There's no other choice. All the other ways are blocked. Besides, there's something up ahead I want to look at.'

Lindholm looked at her sharply. 'What is it, esper? What's up ahead?'

'Something interesting,' said DeChance dreamily. She turned her back on the two marines, and walked steadily between the alien machines to the far doorway. Corbie and Lindholm looked at each other briefly, and hurried after her. Corbie still didn't trust DeChance's esp, but it had proved accurate enough so far. And it beat standing around arguing next to a room full of monsters. He looked suspiciously at the alien machines as he passed, but they remained silent and enigmatic. The next room stretched away beyond the lantern's light, endless ranks of metal stacks filled it like a honeycomb. And there, in those stacks, in that honeycomb, lay thousands upon thousands of milky white spheres, ranging in size from a man's fist to a man's head.

'They look like that ball you found in the monolith,' said Lindholm. 'What are they?'

'Memories,' said DeChance softly. 'A storehouse of memories. The history of this city, and those who lived here. The answers to all our questions.'

She started towards the nearest stacks, but Lindholm grabbed her by the arm and made her stop. 'Wait just a minute, esper. Remember the way you reacted to one of those things back in the monolith. There's no telling what these might do to you.'

'Right,' said Corbie. 'And the monsters could be here any minute. We've got to keep moving.'

'No,' said DeChance flatly. 'We need the information in these spheres. Without it, we don't have a hope in hell of surviving.'

Lindholm nodded reluctantly, and let go of her arm. 'All right. Russ, you look for another way out of here, while I stand guard. And DeChance, keep it short. We really don't have much time.'

The esper nodded, her eyes fixed hungrily on the stacks, and the spheres they held. Somewhere in that endless honeycomb lay the answers she needed; answers that would make sense of the insanity that threatened them. She walked slowly forward, wandering through the towering stacks with only her esp to guide her. All around her, the spheres burned in her mind like so many candles guttering in the darkness. They were old, very old, and their memories were fading. But a few still burned bright, flaring and brilliant, and DeChance's esp led her to them. She stretched out her hands.

At first there was only a colourless grey, like a monitor tuned to an empty channel, and then the first images came to her, like single frames from a moving film. DeChance's reason staggered under the impact. The alienness of the images was almost overpowering, but slowly DeChance forced sense and meaning out of them. And so the story unfolded before her, of a great race who dreamed a wonderful dream, and saw it collapse into a nightmare without end.

The aliens of Wolf IV had developed a strange and marvellous science, and used it to free themselves from the tyranny of a fixed shape. No longer bound to a single, rigid form, their physical shapes became a matter of choice. Their lives became free and wonderful. They grew wings and flew upon the wind.

They adapted their bodies and burrowed through the earth. They soared above the atmosphere, and dived into the volcanoes to swim in the molten lava. They were lords of creation, masters of all they surveyed.

But the change had not been natural. It was brought about and sustained by a single great device housed in a copper tower in the centre of the city. And slowly, horribly, the aliens learned the truth of what they had done to themselves. The shape of the body was controlled by the mind, and the aliens had forgotten there was more to the mind than the conscious will and the intellect. Body changes began to appear that were dictated by the demons of the subconscious mind, the id, the ego and the superego; the dark areas of the mind, beyond sanity or hope of control. The aliens discovered hideous pleasures and awful longings, and their dreams became dark and foul. The horror had begun.

The aliens had been low-level telepaths, but the device changed all that. Their esp became wild and strong, and their minds were no longer sacrosanct. They quickly learned that the more powerful mind could overpower the weaker, and force a change upon the loser's body. Before the great device, the aliens of Wolf IV had been a calm, thoughtful people. They lived long, and delighted in the act of creation. But they had reached too far and lost everything they prized, and in the end only monsters remained to stalk the city streets.

The city fell. Its streets were purulent with awful life, madness given shape and form. And so they came to the final horror. The aliens could not die. If a limb was torn away, it grew back. A wound would heal itself in seconds. The monsters tore and ate each other, but even the worst atrocities could not kill them now.

The city survived for a while. The device only affected living, animate matter. But eventually the city fell apart as the machines went untended. Only the great device, built to be self-perpetuating, continued in its purpose. Its influence spread across the planet, affecting, to some degree, all that lived. But then something happened, something unforeseen.

The great device and the aliens had a continuing two-way contact, so that the device's programming could reflect the aliens' changing needs. And slowly, progressively, the aliens' madness began to drive the device insane. Its programming became warped and twisted as it struggled to fulfil the aliens' needs and desires. Finally, it recognized the danger it was in, and took the only course open to it. The device shut itself down and put the city to sleep in the hope that the future might hold an answer to its dilemma.

Time passed. There was no telling how many years or centuries. The aliens could not die, but the device was patient. It waited, sustaining itself with the bare minimum of energy.

And then the Hell Squad came, and DeChance's esp roused the great device from its ancient sleep. But too much time had passed, and the device was no longer sane. Perhaps it had spent too long exposed to the aliens' madness, or perhaps simply the world had changed too much from the one it had been designed to serve, so that nothing made any sense to it any more. It didn't matter. The great device had its programming.

It awoke the sleepers and roused the city, and the nightmare began again.

DeChance fell to her knees, shaking uncontrollably. Corbie reached out a hand to steady her, only to hesitate as the esper vomited on to the floor. Lindholm looked back the way they'd come. Something was drawing near. He raised his force shield and drew his disrupter from its holster. The wall to their left suddenly cracked from top to bottom and burst apart as a huge armoured form crashed through it. A piece of flying stone smashed DeChance's field lantern, and darkness filled the room.

CHAPTER SIX

The Hunt

It was evening, heading into night, as Hunter led Doctor Williams and the Investigator through the deserted city streets. The green of the sky grew dark and ominous as the sun sank slowly behind the Cyclopean towers. The alien buildings cast strangely shaped shadows, and the occasional lighted window seemed bright and sinister in the deepening gloom. It was bitter cold and getting colder. Hunter shivered despite the heating elements in his uniform. He glanced surreptitiously at Krystel and Williams, but neither of them showed any sign of being bothered by the cold. Hunter wondered about that. Investigators were trained to withstand extreme changes in temperature, but the Doctor was just a civilian. Presumably those hidden adjustments made the difference. Hunter shared the popular distrust of black-market implants, but he had to admit there were times when they came in handy. He breathed on his freezing hands and beat them together, and tried to think warm thoughts.

They'd been walking for the best part of an hour, but the copper tower didn't seem to be drawing any nearer. It stood before them, tall and forbidding, rising high above the surrounding buildings, its gleaming metal spikes stark and brutal. It had seemed huge enough when they first started towards it, but now Hunter was beginning to realize just how tall and massive the structure really was. Not for the first time, he wondered what the hell he was going to do when he finally got there. If he got there.

Hunter let his hand fall to the disrupter at his side. He hadn't felt entirely happy about taking the Investigator's gun, after he lost his own, but he had to admit he felt a lot happier knowing he had a weapon to hand. And if half the things he'd heard about Investigators were true, she might not need a gun anyway. Williams still had both his gun and his sword, of course. Logically, he should have given up his sword so that Hunter could use it, since the Doctor had no experience with a blade, but Hunter had decided against pressing the point. Williams was jumpy enough as it was; without his weapons to lend him courage he might just fall apart, for all his precious augmentations.

'Captain,' said Williams suddenly. 'I've been thinking . . .'

'Yes, Doctor,' said Hunter politely.

'Our weapons weren't much use against that alien. In the future, if we come across anything else like that, why don't we just set up our portable force Screen, and use that to protect us?'

Hunter felt like sighing deeply, but rose above it. 'Keep calm, keep calm,' he murmured to himself. 'You must have noticed, Doctor, that it takes quite a time to set up a Screen. I can't see the alien waiting patiently while we do it, can you? And even if we could get the Screen up before the alien could get to us, what would we do then? Just sit tight, and wait for it to lose interest and go away? No, Doctor, as a plan it's not very practical. We'd do better to save the power in the Screen's energy crystals for real emergencies.'

He broke off as he realized the Doctor wasn't listening to him. Williams bit his lower lip, then stopped dead in his tracks. Hunter and Krystel stopped with him. Williams looked slowly around, his head cocked slightly to one side, as though listening to something only he could hear. Hunter listened, but everything seemed still and silent. He looked at the Investigator, who shrugged.

'Something's coming,' said Williams quietly. 'I can hear it. And whatever it is, this time it's not alone.' He turned slowly round in a tight circle, and the colour gradually went out of his face. 'They're all around us. Captain, I can hear things coming from every direction. All kinds of things.'

'Be more specific,' said Krystel. 'What exactly are you hearing?'

'All kinds of things,' said Williams. His voice began to rise. 'They're getting closer. We've got to get out of here, while we still can. They're coming for us!'

'Take it easy,' said Hunter. 'Investigator, can you hear anything?'

'Nothing, Captain. But if his hearing is augmented—'

'Yeah,' said Hunter.

Krystel drew her sword. 'I think we should find some cover, Captain. We're too exposed out here.'

'I think you're right, Investigator.' Hunter drew his disrupter, and looked quickly about him. There were buildings all around, cloaked in shadows from the coming night, but none of them had obvious doorways. Over to his right, one of the buildings appeared to have been partially gutted by an explosion. Part of the street side had been torn away, leaving strands of metal like broken bones, and a dark, uninviting opening at the top of a small hill of rubble. Hunter started towards it, and the other two followed.

Climbing the rubble of broken stone and metal proved easy enough, and Hunter paused at the top to take out his field lantern and turn it on. The pale golden light showed a vast, empty room beyond the opening. The walls were covered with a strange silver metal tracery, which formed disturbing patterns. Hunter looked back at the street below. He still couldn't see or hear anything, despite the extra height the hill of rubble gave him. He began to wonder if Williams hadn't been overreacting, jumping at his own shadow. And then the first whisper of sound came to him, from somewhere far off in the distance. He spun round, and stared intently in its general direction. Far off in the dim light, something was moving. Hunter crouched down behind one of the large outcroppings of rubble. Krystel had already found some cover. Williams had drawn his gun, but was still standing in plain view, staring off into the gathering dusk with his adjusted eyes.

'Oh my God,' he said faintly.

'What is it?' said Krystel. 'What can you see?'

'Someone has opened the gates of Hell,' said Williams. 'And the damned are loose in the city.'

Hunter shot a quick glance at Krystel, who just looked straight back at him. Hunter stared out into the dark, his breath steaming on the chill air. He felt even colder now that they'd stopped moving. And then he caught his first glimpse of what was coming towards them, and a worse chill swept through him. A great tide of leaping, running and crawling life, an endless flow of nightmares and monstrosities, came surging down the wide street, heading straight for the concealed Hell Squad. There were things that walked on two legs, some that ran on four, and others that leapt through the air as though they were weightless. There were creatures with fangs and claws that snapped and tore at those around them. There were those who looked as though they'd somehow been horribly turned inside out, and some whose shapes made no sense at all.

Giant insects crawled along the sides of buildings like beetles on a coffin lid. Twisted shapes flapped through the air. The aliens screamed and roared and chattered, and there were sounds that might almost have been human cries or laughter. They came surging out of the darkness without end, driven by some unimaginable goad, drawing closer all the time. Hunter looked at the city's nightmares, and wanted to turn away and hide until they were gone. He couldn't bear the sight of them. Their foul shapes and insane structures were an offence against his reason.

But he couldn't just run away and hide. He was the Captain, and he had to set an example. Even if he was so scared he could hardly think straight, and the old familiar panic was gnawing at his nerves, threatening to break loose at any moment. His breathing was short and hurried, and he could feel sweat beading on his face. He looked down at his disrupter, and saw that his hand was shaking. He swallowed hard, and fought back the panic. It didn't matter that he was scared, and couldn't cope. He had to cope. There was no one else. He took a long, shuddering breath, and felt some of the tension go out of him. There was a certain comfort in knowing that the worst that could happen had already happened. At least the waiting was over, and there were no more surprises to worry about. He brought his disrupter to bear on the surging mass of aliens. His hand was still shaking, but so slightly now that only he would know it. He grabbed Williams with his free hand, and pulled him back behind some cover. Williams jerked his arm free and glared at Hunter. Hunter glared right back at him. There were times when he wondered if the Doctor was trying to get himself killed.

The aliens were fast approaching the hill of rubble, and for the first time Hunter was able to make out the true horror of their condition. None of them had a fixed form. Their shapes came and went like so many whims or fleeting memories, never the same for two moments running. Flesh flowed on their bones like melting wax, sliding endlessly from one form to another. New eyes surfaced in the bubbling flesh, and new arms burst out of their heaving sides. Hunter was reminded briefly of the statues he'd seen on the open plain, depicting creatures made up of bits and pieces from various species, neither one thing nor another. Perhaps they had been meant as a warning after all.

'Stand ready,' said Hunter. His voice sounded gratifyingly calm and even. 'Doctor Williams, wait until they're close enough for you to pick a specific target before you use your disrupter. Investigator, you've had the most combat experience. You take the point, and the Doctor and I will guard your sides.'

'Understood, Captain.' Krystel looked out over the milling horrors, and smiled unpleasantly. Hunter shivered. There was something horribly wild and eager about her smile. She might almost have been looking at an approaching lover.

'We can't stay here,' said Williams suddenly. 'Look at them! They'll be here any minute, and there's nothing we can do to stop them. We've got to get out of here while we still can.'

He scrambled away from his cover, and headed for the opening in the wall. Hunter grabbed him by the arm and pulled him back. 'Don't be a fool, Williams. How far would you get on your own? Stand fast, and guard the Investigator's side. Or I swear I'll cut you down myself.'

Williams snarled at him, but stayed where Hunter had put him. 'We don't have to stay here. We could still fall back into the building and barricade the hole with the force Screen.'

'We've talked this through before, Doctor. The Screen would only last as long as its energy crystals permitted, and then it would collapse. By which time the aliens would undoubtedly have us surrounded. We'll fall back into the building when we have to, and not before. Now activate your shield and stand ready. Company's coming.'

Williams turned away in disgust, and slapped his left wrist against his side. The glowing force shield appeared on his arm, murmuring quietly to itself. Hunter looked at Krystel. Her shield was already up. She was still grinning at the approaching aliens. Hunter drew his Service dagger from his boot, hefted his gun once, and then activated his shield. The aliens were very near now. He moved forward a pace, so that he could guard the Investigator's left side while still being comfortably close to his chosen piece of cover. It wasn't much use as cover, but it would have to do. The Investigator stood in plain view of the aliens, looking strong and confident, as though cover was something only lesser mortals needed.

He looked out at the approaching aliens, and his heart missed a beat. They filled the street from side to side for as far as he could see. There were monstrosities beyond counting, of every shape and size.

This isn't fair, thought Hunter bitterly. We're not up to this. We're just a Hell Squad. A full company of shock troops would have their work cut out here. We're not fighters. Not really. We're just rejects and walking wounded; the outcasts and the expendables.

He took a deep breath and let it go. What the hell, maybe we'll get lucky.

The aliens were close now, the nearest only yards away. There were things like giant crustaceans, with huge pincer claws and staring eyes on the end of stalks. Their many-jointed legs clattered loudly on the street. As Hunter watched, one of the crustaceans suddenly swelled in size. Its shelled back began to bubble and melt, and a pair of membraneous wings burst out of its back. It threw itself into the air, its wings stretching impossibly wide as it soared towards the Hell Squad. Hunter took careful aim with his disrupter, and fired. The energy beam hit the creature squarely in the lower thorax, and it exploded, scattering shards of broken chitin like shrapnel. The body fell into the alien horde, and they tore it apart. The separate parts writhed and twisted even as they were consumed. Those aliens that couldn't reach the downed creature clawed and tore at each other. None of them died. They were beyond death now. The great device had seen to that.

Giant centipedes clattered along the street, hundreds of feet long, their small bulbous heads nothing more than mouth and teeth. Maggots squirmed in their flesh. Williams blew one in half with his disrupter. The two halves became separate creatures and pressed forward, driven by the same unrelenting determination that drove the rest of the horde. Hunter wondered briefly what that drive was. It couldn't be just hunger. Perhaps it was simply the Hell Squad's normality, their fixed shapes, that drew the aliens like moths to a flame. Hatred? Regret? Hunter shrugged mentally. Those were human emotions.

The aliens came surging forwards, and the Hell Squad met them with flashing steel. Multicoloured blood flew everywhere as steel blades cut into shifting flesh, but still the aliens pressed forward. They could be hurt, but not killed, and they were used to pain. Only their habit of turning on their own injured kept the aliens from overrunning the Squad.

Hunter swung his knife with grim efficiency, protecting himself and guarding the Investigator as best he could. The razor-sharp edges of the force shield helped. On Krystel's other side, Williams swung his sword as though it was weightless, and never missed his target. More augmentations, thought Hunter. He must be crammed full of implants from head to toe. He just hoped they were fully charged. Investigator Krystel was in her element. She swung her claymore double-handed, and the heavy blade sheared through the shifting flesh as though it was nothing more than mist or smoke. She was chanting something to the rhythm of her blows, in a harsh guttural language Hunter didn't recognize, and her face was alive with an awful happiness. He looked away, and concentrated his fear and anger on the aliens. His knife wasn't doing much damage, but just the scent of spilled blood was often enough to send the surrounding aliens into a feeding frenzy.

He stepped back a pace to avoid an alien's snapping mouth, and nearly fell as the rubble shifted suddenly underfoot. Hunter regained his balance with an effort, and used the flat of his shield to push the alien back. Its teeth clattered and broke on the energy field. Hunter tried to use the larger blocks of stone as cover, but his footing was too precarious now to allow for much movement. The alien tide broke ceaselessly against the foot of the hill, always pressing forward, no matter how many of them fell to the Squad's weapons or each other's hunger. And none of them died, no matter how badly they were hurt. Within the space of a few moments they rose unharmed from deadly wounds, and half-eaten bodies reformed around shattered bones to fight again. Hunter felt a growing despair as he realized there was no way to win, no matter how well he fought. Sooner or later the undying aliens would drag him down, and if he was lucky his death would be quick. He wondered briefly if he too would rise from the dead, to kill and be killed again and again, but his mind shied away from the horror of such a thought.

The rubble lurched again under his feet, and then suddenly broke apart, great cracks running jaggedly across the hill. From underneath the shifting stones and metal came the sound of something huge, burrowing towards the surface. Translucent tentacles burst up out of the cracks, searching blindly for prey. Williams cried out, as much in shock as fear, and cut desperately at the tentacles with his sword. Krystel ignored them, her wild smile unchanged as she fought back the alien horde with unflinching determination. Hunter wavered for a moment, uncertain what to do for the best, or even if there was anything he could do. The glistening tentacles were whipping back and forth, and it was clearly only a matter of moments before they caught one of the Squad. Hunter stepped back a pace, his heart hammering against his breastbone as he crouched down behind his shield, and then he stuck his gun into one of the cracks and pressed the stud. The brilliant beam of energy stabbed down into the bulk of what moved under the hill, and the rubble heaved underfoot like a wild swell at sea as the dweller below howled in agony.

For a moment, everything seemed to stop as the horrid sound rose up out of the rubble, and then the tentacles snapped back into the cracks and were gone. The howl died away, and the horde pressed forward again. Krystel met them eagerly with her smile and her flashing sword. The keen steel edge sliced through reaching hands and tentacles, and punched through bones and cartilage like paper. A great crawling insect with bulbous eyes darted in under her reach, its vicious mandibles snapping hungrily. Without slowing her attack, Krystel took her cigar out of her mouth and thrust the glowing end into one of the creature's protruding eyes. The eye burst and the huge insect scuttled backwards, shaking its head violently, as though it could throw off the pain. Other creatures fell on it, and it disappeared under a heaving mass of hands and teeth.

Hunter moved in close at Krystel's side again, but he knew he couldn't last much longer. Apart from the pounding he'd taken in his fall, his breathing was coming fast and uneven, and the cold air burned in his lungs. He was drenched in sweat despite the chill, and his back and arms ached from wielding the dagger and shield without rest. Krystel seemed as fresh as ever, but Hunter knew that even an Investigator's training had its limits. Williams was beginning to slow down too. They had to fall back soon, or they'd be overrun. But falling back could give the aliens the opening they needed. Damned if we do, damned if we don't, thought Hunter sourly. And a better definition of a Hell Squad I never heard. More than that, there were now creatures in the horde that none of their weapons would be able to stop. Glowing mists hugged the ground, holding indistinct mouths that gnawed at the rubble. There were creatures of churning liquid that fell apart when their surface tension was broken, only to form and re-form endlessly. A sword or a gun could only do so much.

Williams glanced back over his shoulder. The hole in the wall was only a few feet away now, but it might as well have been a few miles. If he turned and ran, some monstrosity or another would be sure to drag him down. But he couldn't stay where he was. Only the speed and strength of his augmentations were keeping the aliens at bay, and the power in his energy crystal wasn't endless. No, if he was going to make a run for it, he needed a distraction, something to draw the aliens' attention away from him for the few seconds it would take to reach the hole in the wall. But what could distract the aliens? Perhaps only one thing – the one thing the aliens wanted so badly. A human death.

Williams' face went blank as the thought took hold of him. He needed Hunter and Krystel to protect him. And there was always the chance of his being found out. But in this confused press of bodies, who could blame him if a shot from his gun was to go tragically astray? No one would be able to prove anything, and surely it was better for one to die than all three. He glanced briefly at Krystel and Hunter. The Investigator's skills and expertise made her an invaluable member of the Squad. Captain Hunter, on the other hand, was nobody special at all. Just an authoritative voice. He wouldn't be missed. Williams smiled slightly. It was all coming together. One shot in the back, and Hunter would go down. The aliens would fight over his body, and he and the Investigator could seize the moment to get away. Perfect. Williams kept the aliens at bay with his sword and shield, waited for just the right moment, and then aimed his disrupter at Hunter's back. He never saw the wide-winged creature that swept down towards him, claws extended.

The first Hunter knew of it was when he heard Williams scream. He glanced round, startled, and saw the winged thing attempting to lift Williams into the air. The alien had a long leathery body and great membraneous wings, but despite the claws sunk deep into his body, Williams was still writhing and struggling. The alien finally lurched into the air. Williams' blood fell across the horde of monstrosities, and they went mad at the taste and smell of it. They reached up for Williams, their arms and necks stretching impossibly. Krystel grabbed Hunter's arm, and urged him towards the hole in the wall while the horde was distracted. He hesitated, but one look was enough to show him there was nothing he could do to save Williams. Because of the Doctor's weight the horde was able to drag the winged alien down and pull Williams away from it. He was still struggling and screaming as the horde tore him apart.

Krystel was already running towards the hole in the wall. Hunter started after her, and then hesitated again as he saw something metal glinting on the ground. It was Williams' sword. Hunter thrust his dagger back into his boot, snatched up the sword and ran after Krystel. They reached the hole and charged through it before most of the aliens had even realized they were gone. Hunter and Krystel stopped beyond the hole and looked quickly about them.

They were in a huge empty room, lit only by a dim light falling through a gaping hole. Hunter and Krystel moved quickly to get out of the light, and set their backs against the wall on either side of the hole. Hunter's breathing finally began to slow a little.

Outside, it sounded as though the horde was still diverted by Williams's death, but Hunter knew that wouldn't last long. He hefted Williams's sword. It had a fine balance, and it felt good to have a sword in his hand again.

'What happened to Williams?' he said hoarsely.

Krystel shrugged. 'He must have got careless. Or unlucky. It happens.'

Hunter nodded tiredly. 'All right, what do we do next?'

'You're the Captain.'

Hunter looked at her resentfully, but knew she was right. For all her skills, he had the most experience, so the responsibility was his. Even though all he really wanted was to sit right down where he was and hide, and hope the aliens would give up and go away. He was tired. He couldn't recall when he'd ever felt this tired. It was the strain, of course, the never-ending tension.

'All right,' he said finally, trying hard to at least sound confident. 'We can't stay here. The aliens will be in here after us at any minute. Let's get moving. The sooner we put some distance between us and them, the better.'

He moved steadily towards the other side of the room, wincing as his aching joints protested. The Investigator took the field lantern from her backpack and turned it on before following him. The soft golden light was lost in the darkness of the huge room, but it was enough for Hunter to make out an open doorway in the wall before him. He broke into a run, and Krystel padded along beside him. They'd just reached the doorway when the light from behind them was suddenly cut off. Hunter glanced back to find something huge and armoured with no head had wedged itself into the hole in the wall. He raised his gun and pressed the stud. The beam of energy punched clean through the armoured body. The alien screamed hoarsely, but did not die. Hunter ran through the open doorway, with Krystel close behind.

They found themselves in a long, high-ceilinged hall, full of rows of squat alien machinery that disappeared into the darkness beyond the lantern light. Hunter and Krystel slowed to a halt. Lights gleamed on some of the machines, and there was a low, unpleasant hum. Krystel looked behind her.

'They're coming after us, Captain. I can hear them.'

Hunter glared back the way they'd come. 'We can't outrun them. We need to slow them down, buy us some time.' He smiled suddenly, and pulled one of the concussion grenades from his bandolier. He primed it, and then rolled it along the ground so that it stopped just inside the doorway. 'All right, Investigator, let's get the hell out of here.'

They ran between the alien machinery, surrounded by a halo of light from the field lantern. It seemed to Hunter that they ran for a long time, but still the hall stretched away before them, and the grenade didn't go off. And then the floor shook under their feet, and a blast of roaring air sent them flying forwards. The explosion was deafeningly loud in the confined space, and slivers of stone and metal flew through the air. Hunter and Krystel raised their force shields above their heads to protect themselves, and crouched down, to present a smaller target. After a while they looked back. The hall was blocked with rubble. Hunter and Krystel shared a grin, and ran on into the darkness.

They reached the end of the hall, but there was no exit. Krystel raised her gun and blew a hole through the wall. They clambered through the sharp-edged opening and found themselves in a long featureless corridor. Glowing rods were set into the ceiling at irregular intervals. Krystel strapped the field lantern to her belt so as to leave that hand free, and then stopped, and looked quickly back through the hole. Hunter heard it too. The aliens had broken through into the hall of machines and were coming after them. Hunter and Krystel ran down the corridor at full pelt. Hunter had no idea where he was going, but anything was better than waiting around for the aliens to catch up with them.

The corridor seemed to go on for ever, without a doorway or opening anywhere. The first sounds of pursuit began to echo behind them, together with an occasional roar. Hunter didn't look back. He didn't want to know how close the aliens were. Krystel pulled a grenade from her bandolier and held it in her hand, ready for use. They finally rounded a corner and plunged through an opening into the base of a tower. The familiar ramp wound up the inside wall. Krystel looked at it dubiously.

'If we let ourselves be chased up there, eventually we're going to run out of ramp. And the top of a high tower is a hell of a place to be cornered.'

'I couldn't agree more,' said Hunter. 'But we're not going that far. How close are the aliens?'

Krystel looked back down the corridor. 'Too close, and getting closer.'

'Figures. Have you still got your grenade?'

Krystel nodded.

'Good. Use it to slow the bastards down a bit, and then follow me up the ramp.'

Hunter started up the ramp as Krystel primed the grenade, and rolled it down the corridor into the darkness. In the distance, something that glowed with an eerie violet light hissed like a fire hose. Krystel snarled, then hurried up the ramp after Hunter. She found him waiting for her in a doorway leading on to the next floor. The grenade blew, and the ramp trembled under their feet. A chorus of inhuman screams and howls echoed up from the corridor below. Hunter led the Investigator through the doorway into a dark, empty room.

They hurried across the room and through an open doorway into another room. Metallic streamers hung from the ceiling, twisting and turning slowly, though no breeze stirred the air. Hunter and Krystel crossed the room as quickly as they dared, threading their way through the streamers while being very careful not to touch them. The streamers looked harmless enough, but both the Captain and the Investigator had learned to distrust everything they found in the city; particularly things that moved when they shouldn't. The next room was empty, and a dead end. Hunter stopped and listened, but everything seemed quiet. He nodded briefly to the Investigator.

'Stay in the doorway. Keep an eye open for uninvited guests.'

Krystel unstrapped her field lantern and put it down, and then moved away to stand guard in the doorway, sword and force shield at the ready. Hunter aimed his disrupter at the middle of the floor, and pressed the stud. The energy bolt blasted a wide hole through the ground. Cracks spread out from the hole, and Hunter watched anxiously before the floor finally settled again. He holstered his gun, picked up the lantern, knelt down, and lowered it through the hole. The room below held a number of steel and crystal shapes that resembled machines or sculptures, but otherwise it was empty. Hunter studied the drop dubiously, and tried to tell himself it wasn't as far as it looked.

'Krystel, any sign of the aliens?'

'Nothing yet, Captain.'

'Then get over here. We're going back down a floor the hard way. With a little luck, that should throw the aliens off our trail long enough for us to make a discreet exit. I'll go first.'

He put the lantern on the floor beside him, turned off his force shield and sheathed his sword. He sat down on the edge of the hole and lowered his legs into it. With the light gone, he couldn't see how far the drop was. He wasn't sure whether that made him feel less or more nervous. In the end, he just gritted his teeth, and pushed himself off. He fell for an unnervingly long moment, and then the floor slammed up against his feet. He fell in a sprawling heap and knocked the wind out of himself. He'd just about managed to get to his feet again when Krystel landed lightly beside him, lantern in hand.

'Are you all right, Captain?'

'Fine,' he said quickly. 'Just fine.'

The room led out into a corridor. There were lighting rods set into the ceiling, but only a few of them were working. The corridor held only shadows, and there was no trace to show the aliens had ever been there. Hunter and Krystel crept quietly through the dim light, weapons at the ready, and soon passed into another corridor. They made their way cautiously across the ground floor of the building, jumping at every sound or moving shadow, until finally they found a doorway that led out on to the street.

Hunter gestured to Krystel to turn off the field lantern, and peered warily out the doorway into the gloom. The street was empty. Hunter stepped out, looked around, and then nodded for Krystel to join him. The sun had dropped almost out of sight, and the sky was darkening towards night. Some distance away, the copper tower stood tall and brooding above the surrounding buildings.

Hunter turned to Krystel to tell her it was safe to move off, and then froze as the wall behind her cracked open and fell apart. Long branches of spiked vine burst out of the stonework, reaching for the Investigator. She threw herself to the ground and rolled out of reach, but by the time she was back on her feet again the vines had spilled out on to the street, forming an impenetrable barrier between her and the Captain. A score of leaping, hopping insects, each a foot long or more, came flying out of the wall and descended on Krystel, their long jaws snapping hungrily. She activated her force shield and met them with her sword. Hunter picked off one of the insects with his gun, exploding its dark grey carapace, but couldn't do anything else to help her. He threw himself at the twisting vines, hacking at them with his sword. The barbs rattled harmlessly against his steelmesh tunic, and broke themselves against his force shield.

Krystel swung her sword double-handed, her cold grin back again. The huge insects fell beneath her blade, and the uninjured feasted on the fallen. Krystel laughed aloud. This was what she had been trained for, the moment that gave purpose to her life; to be the perfect, invincible killing machine. The aliens came to her and she slaughtered them, and was content.

Hunter finally used his last but one grenade on the vines. The blast blew him a hole through the writhing branches, and he forced his way through, ignoring the scratches to his bare face and hands. The Investigator had surrounded himself with crippled insects, and for the moment seemed to have run out of targets. He grabbed her arm and hustled her off down the street. For a moment she struggled against him, and then the killing fever left her, and she ran along beside him, heading for the copper tower.

And behind them came the aliens, in their many shapes.

Corbie lifted his gun and fired blindly into the darkness. The brilliant energy bolt illuminated the hall of memories briefly, and punched a hole clean through the chest of the armoured alien as it tried to break through the wall. It screamed once as the darkness returned, a curiously high-pitched sound from such a large creature. Corbie glared wildly about him, and reached blindly for the esper. He knew she was somewhere close at hand, he could hear her dry heaving, but he couldn't seem to locate her with his hands. And then his fingers brushed against something and his heart missed a beat.

'Stand still,' said Lindholm quickly. 'And keep your hands to yourself. Start thrashing around in the dark and we'll end up killing each other. Turn on your force shield, that'll give us some light while I get the field lantern out of your backpack.'

Corbie activated his shield, and the glowing energy field appeared on his arm, the pale light dispelling some of the darkness. Lindholm glanced briefly at the armoured alien lying slumped in the wreckage of the wall, and rummaged in Corbie's backpack for his lantern. Corbie grabbed DeChance by the shoulders and got her on her feet again. She leaned tiredly against him and clung to his arm for support. The dry heaves died away, leaving her pale and trembling. Corbie looked at her worriedly. Her face seemed gaunt and pinched, and her eyes didn't track. Off in the distance, from every side, there came the sound of alien screams and cries. They were getting closer. Lindholm finally got the lantern working, and the hall of memories reappeared around them.

'We've got to get out of here, Sven,' said Corbie. 'The esper's out of it, and the aliens will be here any minute.'

'I think you're probably right,' said Lindholm. He looked around for an exit, but there was only the doorway they'd come through. Part of one wall had collapsed, but the armoured alien blocked the way with its body, and already the creature was showing signs of stirring. Lindholm swore briefly, and pointed his disrupter at the floor. He pressed the stud, and the searing beam of energy smashed open a hole. The floor groaned and shuddered. Cracks spread out from the hole, but after a few moments the floor grew steady again. Corbie gave Lindholm a hard look.

'Down there? Are you kidding? There could be anything down there!'

'Have you got a better idea?'

Corbie scowled unhappily. 'Some days you just shouldn't get out of bed in the morning.'

Lindholm sat down on the floor and swung his legs into the hole. 'I'll go first, and you can hand the esper down to me. Right?'

'Got it,' said Corbie. He manhandled the unresisting esper over to the hole, and then waited impatiently as Lindholm lowered himself into the darkness. Corbie looked back through the open doorway. He couldn't see much in the gloom, but he could hear the aliens drawing nearer. It sounded like there were a lot of them. Over in the wreckage of the wall, the armoured alien slowly raised its head. Its eyes glowed blue in the dim light. Corbie looked at the dazed esper, and wondered what the hell the memory sphere had shown her to produce such a violent reaction. On second thoughts, he decided he probably didn't want to know. Lindholm hissed at him from down in the hole, and Corbie carefully lowered the esper into Lindholm's waiting arms. DeChance murmured something indistinct, but didn't come out of her daze. The armoured alien heaved itself out of the wreckage of the broken wall. Corbie quickly sat down by the hole, and pushed himself into the darkness below.

Under the floor he found himself in a circular tunnel some seven feet high. After the huge scale of the other buildings, the tunnel felt decidedly claustrophobic. Moisture ran down the rough stone walls and pooled on the floor. It smelled awful. Lindholm held up his lantern, and looked up and down the tunnel. It stretched away into the distance for as far as he could see. Lindholm and Corbie looked at each other.

'So, which way now?' said Corbie.

'Beats me,' said Lindholm. 'One way is as good as another, I suppose.'

'No,' said DeChance. 'That way.'

She pointed down the tunnel with a trembling hand. Lindholm tentatively released his hold on her, and smiled encouragingly when she managed to stay upright without him. Her eyes had focused again, but she looked awful. Her face was pale and gaunt, the skin stretched tightly over the skull. Sweat ran down her face, and her eyes had a sunken, bruised look. Her hands were now trembling violently.

'How are you feeling?' said Corbie gently.

DeChance grinned. 'I'll live.'

'What did the ball show you?' asked Lindholm.

'Not now,' said DeChance. She pointed down the tunnel again. 'We have to go that way, and quickly. The aliens will be here soon. They want us badly, and they won't give up. They want what makes us sane. Our certainty. I think this pipe is part of what used to be the sewers. We'll follow the pipe until we're somewhere near the copper tower, and then blast our way back out again.'

'How are we going to know when we've reached the tower?' said Corbie.

'I'll know,' said DeChance. 'The device burns very brightly in my mind.'

Corbie looked at Lindholm, who shrugged. Corbie shook his head disgustedly. 'I might have known I'd end up having to make all the decisions in this group.'

'But you do it so well, Russ,' said Lindholm solemnly. 'Haven't I always said you were natural officer material?'

'You know, Sven, you could be replaced.'

'What by?'

'Practically anything.'

A long, hooked leg bristling with thorns groped down through the hole from above. The Squad backed quickly away from it.

'Right,' said Corbie. 'That does it. Let's get moving. Sven, you've got the light so you take the lead. We'll follow. And let's not hang about, people. This strikes me as a very unlucky place to be cornered in.'

He cut the probing leg in two with his sword. The severed end fell and lay twitching on the tunnel floor. Lindholm moved quickly off down the tunnel, and Corbie and DeChance hurried after him. Corbie took the esper's hand to guide her, and then had to fight to keep from snatching his hand back again. Her skin felt wet and slippery, and somehow . . . loose, as though she'd lost a lot of weight in a hurry. He started to say something, but DeChance began to tell him what she'd learned from the memory sphere, and he forgot his question as he listened. The intricate tale of broken dreams and raging madness took a long time to tell, and sounded all the worse for being told in such dark and claustrophobic conditions. By the time the esper had finished, both Corbie and Lindholm had taken to glancing anxiously over their shoulders at the darkness beyond the lantern light.

The tunnel began to slope noticeably downwards, and the floor was covered in steadily deepening water. By the time DeChance stopped speaking, it was lapping up around their ankles. The water was dark and scummy, and there were things floating in it. Corbie preferred not to look at them too closely. The esper and the marines waded along in silence for a while. The sound of their boots splashing through the water seemed unnaturally loud.

'You think the great device is housed somewhere in the copper tower?' said Corbie finally.

'I think the tower is the device,' said DeChance. 'A single huge machine, still functioning after God knows how many centuries.'

'So what are we going to do when we get there?' said Corbie. 'Blow it up?'

'I don't know. Maybe.' DeChance rubbed at her forehead, as though bothered by a headache. 'Somehow I don't think it'll be that simple. The device can defend itself against attacks if it has to.' She broke off suddenly and stopped dead in her tracks. The two marines stopped with her. DeChance stared ahead into the darkness. 'There's something there, something . . . strange. It's waiting for us to come to it.'

Corbie and Lindholm trained their guns on the darkness. For a long moment, nobody moved. The Squad's force shields hummed loudly. Corbie listened hard, but couldn't hear anything moving. The filthy water was undisturbed.

'How close is it?' he whispered to DeChance.

The esper frowned. 'It's waiting, just beyond the light. It feels strange, unfinished.'

'Maybe we should just turn around and go back,' said Corbie.

'*No*,' said DeChance urgently. 'We have to get to the copper tower. It's our only hope. Besides, the creature would only follow us.'

'Terrific,' said Corbie. 'This just gets better and better.'

'We could always throw a grenade at it,' said Lindholm.

Corbie looked at him. 'In a confined space like this? Are you crazy? The blast would come straight back and make mincemeat out of us!'

'Sorry,' said Lindholm. 'I wasn't thinking.'

'You'd better start quickly,' said DeChance. 'It's moving towards us.'

Lindholm and Corbie levelled their guns at the darkness.

DeChance drew hers, but her hand was still too unsteady to aim it. She activated her force shield, and peered over the top of it. A faint glowing light appeared deep in the dark of the tunnel, growing steadily stronger as it approached the Squad. Corbie bit back a curse as the creature's form became clear, lit by its own eerie light. It had no shape as such, only a frothing mass of eyes and bubbles that filled the tunnel from wall to wall like a wave of unrushing foam. Great snapping mouths appeared and disappeared as the creature surged forward. Lindholm fired his disrupter. The blast went right through the boiling mass. A few bubbles popped, but otherwise the beam had no effect at all. Corbie stepped forward and cut at the mass with his sword. The blade swept through the foam.

Corbie stumbled forward and fell on one knee, caught off balance by the lack of resistance. A snapping mouth tried for his hand and only just missed. More mouths reached for him. And then the creature came into contact with Corbie's shield, and the bubbles popped loudly on meeting the energy field. The fanged mouths disappeared back into the staring, boiling mass. Corbie swept his shield at it, and more bubbles burst. The creature began to quickly withdraw down the tunnel. In a few moments it had disappeared back into the darkness, and was gone. Corbie got to his feet again, and shook his wet leg in disgust.

'I just know I'm going to catch something horrible from this stuff. Esper, is that thing out there, waiting in the darkness, or is it still running?'

'Still running,' said DeChance. 'I don't think anything's been able to hurt it in a long time. Now let's get moving again, please. It's a long way to the copper tower, and we want to get there before dark. Things are worse in the city at night.'

The Squad moved on through the narrow tunnel in their own little pool of light. The tunnel branched repeatedly but the esper always seemed to know which way to go. Ceramic pipes lined the walls for long periods, coiled around each other as often as not, before disappearing back into the stonework. I suppose even an alien city needs good sewers, thought Corbie. And this place smells so bad it's got to be part of a sewer. I've known slaughterhouses that smelled better than this.

The water grew deeper, lapping up around their knees. Fungi began to appear on the walls in shades of grey and white, often spread in wide patches more than two inches thick. Corbie was careful not to touch any of it. It looked like it might be hungry. Patches of swirling scum appeared on the surface of the water, and Corbie watched them suspiciously. He had a strong feeling some of them were following him. And then the Squad came to a sudden halt as they spotted a large smooth-edged hole in the stone wall to their right, some distance ahead.

'Can you sense anything, esper?' asked Corbie quietly.

'I'm not sure. There's something there, but it's shielded. I can't get a hold on it.' She rubbed frustratedly at her forehead. 'It could be some creature's lair, or even some form of machinery.'

'You stay here,' said Corbie. 'Sven and I will go take a look at it.'

'You could have at least asked for volunteers,' said Lindholm mildly. 'Power's gone to your head, Russ.'

'Moan, moan, moan,' said Corbie. 'You never want to do anything fun.'

The two marines moved slowly forward, gun and sword at the ready. Their force shields muttered quietly to themselves. The hole in the wall seemed to grow larger the closer the marines got. Finally, they stood before a six-foot-wide hole, studying the darkness within from behind the safety of their force shields.

'Can't see a damned thing,' muttered Corbie. 'How about you, Sven?'

'Nothing. Can't hear anything either. I suppose it could be a lair that was abandoned some time back. The esper said the aliens had all been asleep for a long time.'

'True. And I can't imagine anything alien enough to stay down here by choice.'

Deep within the hole, something moved. Lindholm and Corbie raised their guns reflexively, only to freeze in place as an endless tide of darkness came rushing out over them. The esper cried out once, but neither of them heard her.

Corbie was standing on a snowswept battlefield, surrounded by the dead. There was blood on his uniform, only some of it his. The double moons of the Hyades drifted on the night skies.

The Ghost Warriors had been and gone, and the Empire marines had fallen before them. The marines were first-class soldiers, but they were only flesh and blood, and they'd stood no chance against the Legions of the living dead. Blood stained the snow, and the bodies of the slain stretched for as far as Corbie could see. Nothing moved save a single tattered banner, flapping in the wind. Corbie's sword was broken and his gun was exhausted. Out of a whole Company of Imperial marines, he was the only survivor.

Ghost Warriors. Dead bodies controlled by computer implants. The ultimate terror troops; unthinking, unfeeling, unstoppable. Corbie had thought himself a brave man, until he'd had to face the Ghost Warriors. They tested his courage again and again, until finally they broke it. The Legions of the dead were enough to break anyone.

Corbie looked around the silent battlefield. It seemed to him that he should be somewhere else, but he couldn't think where that might be. There was a sudden movement close at hand, and Corbie fell back a step as one of the Empire corpses lifted its head from the snow and looked at him. Dried blood had turned half its face into a dark crimson mask, but its eyes gleamed. It rose unsteadily to its feet to stand before Corbie. There was a gaping wound in its chest. One of the Ghost Warriors had ripped its heart out. The corpse grinned suddenly, revealing bloody teeth.

'You always were a survivor, Corbie.'

'Major . . .' Corbie tried to explain, to apologize, but his voice was harsh and dry, and the words wouldn't come.

'Don't talk to me, survivor. You haven't the right. We stood our ground, followed our orders, and fought and died, as marines should. You chose not to, survivor.'

'I stood my ground.'

'Only until it became clear that we were losing. Until it was clear the Company hadn't a hope in hell against the Legions. We stood and fought to the last man. You burrowed in among the bodies of the fallen, smeared yourself with blood, and hoped you'd be mistaken for just another corpse. And so the Company fell, and you alone survived to tell of it. I had such hopes for you, Corbie. But you betrayed us. You should have died with us, where you belonged.'

'Someone had to survive, to warn Command.'

'That wasn't why you did it. You were afraid. You've been afraid ever since.' The corpse drew its sword. 'Well, soldier, now's your chance to pay in full.'

Corbie threw away his broken sword, and drew the long Service dagger from his boot. 'Only a fool dies for no good reason.'

Their blades met, the clash of steel on steel carrying clearly across the silent battlefield.

Lindholm stood in the centre of the Great Arena, and all around the Golgotha crowds cheered their appreciation of another death. The losing gladiator was dragged away, leaving a bloody trail behind him. It wasn't a subtle crowd in today. They had no eye for the finer points of swordsmanship and defence. They wanted blood and suffering, and they didn't care whose. They'd paid to see death, right there in front of them, and they couldn't get enough of it. Their cheers grew louder and more frenzied as Lindholm's next opponent entered the Arena. Even before he turned to look, Lindholm knew who it was, who it would have to be. Tall, lithe, and graceful, Elena Dante acknowledged the cheers of the crowd, and saluted Lindholm with her sword. Dante, the smiling killer, the darling of the Golgotha crowds.

'I never wanted to fight you, Elena,' said Lindholm quietly.

'It was bound to happen sooner or later, Sven,' said Dante. 'That's how the Arena works. Don't think I'll go easy on you, just because we're friends.'

'More than friends.'

'Maybe. It still doesn't make any difference. Out here on the sands, there are only winners and losers. And I always fight to win.'

'You can't kill me,' said Lindholm. 'Not after all we've meant to each other.'

'You always were a romantic, Sven.' Dante grinned widely. 'Tell you what, we both know I'm going to win. So you just put up a good fight, give the crowd their thrills, and I promise you a quick death.'

'You'd do that for me?' said Lindholm.

'Sure, what are friends for?'

Lindholm frowned. 'I remember this. I've been here before. We fought in the Arena, and I killed you.'

'That's right, Sven. And then you killed the fixer who arranged the match, and twenty-seven other Arena officials, before they finally dragged you down, clapped the irons on you, and gave you to the Hell Squads. But now I'm back, and you're going to have to kill me all over again. If you can.'

Their swords met in a clash of steel.

DeChance stood knee deep in filthy water in a tunnel beneath the alien city, and looked passionlessly at the familiar figure emerging from the hole in the wall. Corbie and Lindholm stood unmoving between her and the hole, staring blindly into the shadows. The familiar figure stepped into the lantern light. He was average height, average weight, with the quiet bland looks that can make a man invisible in a crowd. He smiled confidently at DeChance.

'Hello, Meg. Surprised to see me?'

'You're not real,' said DeChance flatly. 'There's no way you could be here, on Wolf IV. You're still out there in the Empire somewhere, doing what you do best. Getting people to trust you, and then betraying them for a handful of change.'

He laughed quietly. 'I'm as real as you want me to be, Meg. Believe in me and I'm here, as accurate as your memories can make me. And you do want to see me again, don't you? Even after everything that happened, there's a part of you that never stopped caring for me, never stopped believing that deep down I cared for you.' He smiled warmly at her. 'After all, what did I do that was so bad? We all have to make a living.'

DeChance moved a step closer to him. 'I loved you. Trusted you. Gave you every credit I had, to get me a berth on a ship heading for Mistworld. I would have been safe there, finally free from the Empire and the way it's always treated espers. You were going to join me there, and we were going to make a life together. But there was no berth and there was no ship, and when the Security Guards came for me you were nowhere to be seen. I found out about you later, of course. But by then I'd already been condemned to the Hell Squads.'

'Of course,' said the smiling figure. 'They always find out when it's too late. I do try to be professional in my work. Jonathan Shrike: licensed traitor, double-dealing a speciality.' He cocked his head on one side, and fixed her with a glittering eye. 'You're still not sure how you feel about me, are you? Are you angry at me for betraying you, or at yourself, for trusting me? Could you really have been so blind and foolish as to love someone who didn't give a damn about you?'

'I know who was to blame.' DeChance's sword seemed almost to leap into her hand. 'I know who I hate.'

Shrike shook his head condescendingly. 'You always did carry a grudge, Meg. But things can be different here. I can be anything you want me to be. I can love you like you've always wanted to be loved. I can be everything you ever dreamed of. Just put down your sword and come to me.'

DeChance moved forward a step, and then stopped. 'Jonathan . . .'

'Come to me, Meg. I'm all yours.'

DeChance lifted her sword and gripped the blade tightly with her left hand. Blood ran down the blade as the keen edges cut into her flesh. The pain ran through her like a shock of cold water, and she grinned tightly at the figure before her.

'Nice try, but you're not Jonathan. You're not even real. And I hate him too much to be satisfied with a cheap imitation.' She tore her gaze away, and looked at the two marines, still standing silent and motionless. 'What are they seeing? What faces are you showing them?'

'Whatever they want to see. It doesn't matter. They'll be mine soon.'

'That's what you think,' said DeChance. She sheathed her sword, drew her disrupter, and shot him at point-blank range. The brilliant beam of energy tore through his gut. Shrike's mouth stretched impossibly wide as he screamed. Corbie and Lindholm awoke with a start and looked in confusion about them, torn abruptly from their dreams.

'It was just a trick,' said DeChance quickly. 'Whatever you saw, it wasn't real. It seems we've come across an alien with very strong esp. It tried to kill us with our own fears and desires.'

DeChance and the marines concentrated on the creature

before them. Under the pressure of their minds, the alien's shape began to blur and change, its features rising and falling as it tried to be three people at once. It quickly lost control, its humanity falling away like a discarded coat. The features fell apart, the eyes sliding down the face and sinking into the skin. The mouth widened and sprouted jagged teeth. The hands grew claws, and its back humped. What had appeared to be clothes became armoured scales, and a row of spikes burst out of its back. Corbie and Lindholm trained their guns on the creature, and backed quickly away.

'Forget the guns,' said DeChance. 'I already tried that. There's a better way.'

She concentrated, focusing all her esp into a single burst of hate and rage, and threw it at the creature. The alien shrank back, snarled once, and then turned and disappeared down the tunnel and into the darkness. They could hear it running for a while, and then even that faded away to nothing.

DeChance leaned back against the tunnel wall, her eyes hot and moist. Corbie looked at her worriedly. She hadn't looked well for some time, but there was no denying she looked worse now. Her face was horribly pale, and dripping with sweat. Her eyes were sunk deep into her face, and her whole body seemed to be trembling. Corbie started to reach out a hand to her, but withdrew it when DeChance glared at him.

'I'm fine. Just let me be.'

'Why haven't the aliens used esp against us before?' asked Lindholm.

'I don't know,' said DeChance. 'I suppose esp varies as much in them as it does among humans. The sphere showed me what happened when they use it on each other, but it would take an extremely strong projective telepath to work on non-telepaths like you. Or perhaps simply the aliens are growing more powerful as the great device awakens. It's getting stronger all the time. It has been ever since—'

'You awakened it,' said Lindholm.

'Oh yes,' said DeChance bitterly. 'I was the one who woke it up. I'm to blame. I'm to blame for everything that's happened here.' Her voice began to rise sharply. 'If I hadn't been a part of the Hell Squad, none of this would have happened. The device would have slept on, undisturbed, if it hadn't been for me, and you'd all have been perfectly safe.'

'Take it easy,' said Corbie soothingly. 'No one's blaming you for anything. Right, Sven? If you hadn't triggered the device, some colonist with esp would have, and who knows how large a colony would have been endangered then?'

DeChance said nothing. For a long moment the three of them just stood together in their little pool of light, looking out at the darkness.

'Is this likely to happen again?' said Corbie finally. 'If the aliens can tap into our minds, there's no telling what we might end up facing. All our nightmares, every bad dream we ever had could be out there somewhere, just waiting for a chance to get at us. And I don't know about you two, but I've had some pretty awful dreams in my time.'

DeChance smiled crookedly. 'Most of the aliens aren't that powerful, even with the device to back them up. What we're seeing are the aliens' nightmares, given shape and form.'

'How much further is it to the copper tower?' asked Lindholm.

'Not far,' said DeChance. 'The pipe should start sloping upwards soon, and then we can start thinking about getting out of here.'

'Can't be too soon for me,' said Corbie. 'My skin's starting to pucker from the smell.'

They moved on into the darkness, splashing through the foul water. From time to time Corbie thought he saw things swimming in the water, things the size of his fist that seemed to be mostly teeth and eyes. Corbie said nothing to the others. As long as the things in the water kept their distance, he was happy to live and let live, and he didn't want to upset the esper. The tunnel slanted sharply upwards, the water level dropped suddenly, and Corbie allowed himself to think hopeful thoughts about breathing fresh air again. And then the esper stopped suddenly, and the marines stopped with her. Corbie's heart sank. Every time DeChance stopped like that, it meant something really unpleasant was about to happen. The esper stared into the darkness ahead.

'There's something ahead, isn't there?' said Lindholm.

The esper nodded. 'It's big. Very big.'

'It can't be that big,' objected Corbie. 'The tunnel's only seven feet high.'

'It's very big and very powerful,' said the esper, as though she hadn't heard him. 'I don't think our weapons are going to be enough this time.'

'Great,' said Corbie. 'Just great. What are we going to do now, turn and run back the way we've come?'

A great roar sounded out of the darkness, disturbingly loud, echoing and re-echoing from the stonework. Corbie levelled his disrupter at the tunnel ahead, and then fell back a step involuntarily as a gust of wind hit him in the face. Lindholm and the esper fell back with him as the alien appeared in the lantern light. It filled the tunnel completely, a huge mound of leathery flesh, with a ring of unblinking eyes surrounding a drooling maw.

'It's like some monstrous worm,' whispered DeChance. 'It's dozens of feet long. I can't sense the end of it.'

The mouth widened suddenly, growing and growing until the alien seemed nothing but a huge mouth filling the tunnel from wall to wall. There was a smell of rotting meat as the creature exhaled. Corbie had a sudden vision of the three of them running down the tunnel, chased by a ravening maw that left no room for escape. He aimed his gun into the mouth. DeChance suddenly grabbed his arm.

'*No*. Aim for the ceiling. We're only a few feet from the surface. Blast us a way out of here and bring the tunnel down between us and the alien.'

Corbie fired unhesitatingly at the ceiling. The energy beam smashed through the thick stonework, and daylight fell into the tunnel as part of the ceiling collapsed. Debris rained down around the Squad, and they had to shelter under their force shields until it stopped. The alien roared again, and pressed forward another yard, scooping up the broken stone into its drooling maw. Lindholm fired his gun into the creature's mouth. It roared, and lurched forward another few feet.

'Forget it!' snapped DeChance, turning off her force shield. 'We have to get out of here while we can.'

Lindholm nodded quickly. He put away his gun, turned off his shield, and made a stirrup with his hands. DeChance put her foot into it, and the marine boosted her up into the hole in the ceiling. The esper found a handhold, and pulled herself up and out into the daylight above. Corbie turned off his force shield, and followed her out the same way. The alien surged forward, crushing the stones on the floor under its immense bulk. Lindholm calmly pulled a concussion grenade from his bandolier, primed it, and tossed it into the gaping mouth, which snapped shut reflexively. Lindholm pushed some of the larger pieces of rubble together and began to climb. Corbie and DeChance hauled him out on to the street.

He rolled quickly away from the opening, and seconds later there was a muffled roar from below as the grenade went off. Blood and gore fountained up out of the hole, and cracks spread across the street.

'Nice one, Sven,' said Corbie.

The three of them got to their feet and looked around. The sun had sunk almost out of sight, and the green sky was darkening towards night. The city had become little more than shapes and shadows, with the occasional lighted window. The copper tower loomed above its surrounding buildings, less than half a mile away. Corbie shivered, and checked his heating elements were set at maximum.

'Still no sign of the rest of the Squad,' said Lindholm. 'I hope they're having an easier time than us.'

Corbie sniffed. 'They probably had an attack of common sense, and got the hell out of here.'

'We'd better keep moving,' said DeChance. 'There are aliens nearby. More than I can count. They know we're here, and they're closing in on us.'

She ran down the street without stopping to see if the marines were following. They looked quickly at each other, shared a sour smile, and hurried after her. From close at hand came the screams and cries of pursuing aliens, as the first of the unsteady creatures spilled on to the street after the fleeing Squad.

And in the copper tower, the great device waited impatiently for them to come to it.

CHAPTER SEVEN

The Sleep of Reason

Monsters roamed the city streets. Some flew in the air, while others burrowed in the earth. Creatures formed by madness and obsession made their way to the copper tower, summoned by a voice they could not refuse. They no longer remembered why, but the echo of that voice moved forever within them, whatever shape they wore. The sun had fallen, and darkness lay across the city. Strange lights burned in the silent buildings as more and more creatures awoke from their centuries-long sleep. Hideous shapes crept and crawled between structures they no longer recognized, in a city they had long since forgotten. They had lived for centuries, and might live for centuries more, but they did not know it. The awful thing they had done to themselves had trapped them permanently in the here and now; in a single endless moment of existence. They had forgotten what they were, and what they had hoped to be. Only the great device remembered. And it was insane.

Hunter and Krystel ran down a twisting street between stone monoliths with blazing windows and looming edifices of steel and crystal. The darkness hung around them like a listening stranger, and from every street junction they passed came more shapes and monstrosities to join the boiling pack that pursued them. Hunter was fighting for air, and his back and leg muscles screamed for rest, but he didn't dare slow his pace. The aliens were close on their heels, and drawing closer. The darkness hid most of the shapes that followed them, for which Hunter was grateful.

A shining figure stepped out of a stone monolith, and reached for Krystel with phosphorescent hands. She cut sideways with her sword without slowing her pace, and severed the nearest hand. It fell sparking and sputtering into the street, and the creature howled. Hunter thought briefly about using his disrupter, but decided against it as the alien fell back, clutching at its ruined arm with its remaining hand. The disrupter's energy crystals were running low, and he only used the gun now when there was no other choice.

He ran on after Krystel, hurdling the twitching hand in the street without slowing. His breath burned in his lungs, and sweat ran down his heaving sides. He glared at the Investigator. She'd been running and fighting just as much as him, and she wasn't even breathing hard. She was smiling slightly as she shook the last creature's shimmering blood from her sword. Hunter shook his head wearily, and blinked rapidly as sweat ran down into his eyes.

A winged shape dropped out of the sky towards Hunter, its wings flapping loosely as its yard-long beak stabbed down at his face. He raised his force shield above his head, and the beak shattered. The creature screamed and flapped away, blood dripping from its ruined face. A barbed tentacle shot up out of the pursuing pack, and pulled the alien down. The pack fell on it, and tore it apart. Hunter and Krystel ran on.

The copper tower stood tall and imposing against the skyline before them; an enigmatic silhouette against the alien night. Hunter had chosen the tower as a rendezvous point because it could be clearly seen from anywhere in the city, but he was beginning to wish he'd chosen somewhere closer. He'd lost track of how long they'd been running, but the tower seemed as far away as ever. Something moved in a nearby alleyway, and the Investigator turned her gun on it.

'No, Krystel.' Hunter knocked her arm aside at the last moment. 'They're friends.'

Krystel lowered her gun as Megan DeChance and the two marines plunged out of the alleyway to run alongside them. They all managed a quick nod of greeting to each other, but none of them had the breath for conversation. They ran on, with Krystel and the esper leading the way. Hunter looked at the two marines, and winced. Their uniforms were torn and stained with blood. Fatigue had put bruises under their eyes, and made their movements heavy and plodding. They didn't look like they could run much further. Hunter smiled sourly. He didn't suppose he looked much better.

But he and the rest of the Squad would run as far as they had to; because the only alternative was to lie down and die. Hunter looked at the esper's back and frowned. He'd only caught a brief glimpse of DeChance's face, and she'd looked to be in an even worse state than the marines. If there was a weak link in the Squad, she was it. And valuable as she was, Hunter hoped she wouldn't fall. None of them had the strength left to carry her. The esper began to speak, and Hunter made himself pay attention.

In fits and starts, with many pauses for breath, DeChance explained the history of the city, and what had happened there, and for the first time Hunter and Krystel understood the true nature of the aliens, and the significance of the copper tower. Hunter had a hundred questions he wanted to ask, but he didn't have the breath for one. The tower suddenly loomed up before him at the end of the street, and he fixed his attention on that. The Squad pounded down the street, and skidded to a halt at the base of the tower. The two marines turned to face the pursuing aliens, and fired their disrupters. Several aliens fell screaming to the ground as the pack fell on them. Hunter turned to find DeChance and the Investigator silently studying the copper tower.

'Well, don't just stand there, get the bloody door open! The aliens will be here any minute.'

'We appear to have a problem, Captain,' said the Investigator. 'No door. No windows, either.'

Hunter held up his field lantern, and studied the tower closely for the first time. The great copper shaft stretched up into the night sky, featureless and immaculate except for the massive copper spikes that radiated from its peak. It looked to be thirty to forty feet in diameter, and maybe four hundred feet high. There was no trace of any opening in the gleaming metal, nor any sign there ever had been one. Hunter stepped forward and ran his hand across the metal. It felt preternaturally slick, almost frictionless.

'All right,' he said quietly. 'Stand back and watch out for

flying metal.' He fired his disrupter at the metal wall at point-blank range. The energy beam punched a tiny hole in the metal, and that was all.

'Great,' said Corbie. 'Now what?'

Hunter thought quickly. 'Explosives. How many grenades have we got between us?'

He had one, Krystel had one, DeChance had two. The marines had used all theirs.

'That isn't going to be enough, Captain,' said the Investigator. 'The disrupter should have opened up the tower wall like a tin can. It didn't. A wall that strong isn't going to be bothered by concussion grenades. The force of the explosion would be too generalized.'

'So what do you suggest?' snapped Corbie. 'Kick the bloody thing? Or maybe we should knock politely and hope someone will let us in?'

'Save the panic until we get in there,' said Hunter. 'There is a way. We can use one of our proximity mines. That will be powerful enough, and focused enough, to do the job. All we have to do is place one against the base of the tower wall, set the timer, and get the hell out of the way.'

'That might just do it,' said Lindholm approvingly. 'Be a hell of a bang, anyway.'

Hunter glanced quickly at the aliens. They'd stopped some distance away from the tower, and were watching silently. Presumably the great device didn't want them any closer, for its own security. Krystel produced a proximity mine from her backpack, put it in place, and set the timer. The Squad then moved quickly round to the far side of the tower. The explosion sounded strangely muffled, as though the tower had absorbed some of the blast, but when they went back to look they found a gaping hole in the tower wall, some five to six feet in diameter.

'We'd better tread carefully, once we get inside,' said Krystel. 'The blast may have damaged the device.'

'It did,' said DeChance. 'But it's only superficial damage. I can feel the strength of the device. It burns in my mind like a beacon.'

Hunter looked at her, and then at the two marines. They stirred uncomfortably.

'She has some kind of telepathic link with the device, Captain,' said Lindholm slowly. 'She think it's alive.'

'And insane,' said DeChance. 'Quite definitely insane. I don't think it knows we're here yet, but it will the moment we enter the tower. I can't shield myself against that kind of power.'

'This is all very interesting,' said Hunter, carefully, 'but can you tell us anything more practical about the device?'

'Yes,' said DeChance. 'The explosion damaged one important part of the device. Try your comm unit, Captain. I think you'll find it's working again now.'

Hunter gaped at her for a moment, and then tried his comm implant. It immediately patched him in with the pinnace computers, and for the first time that day Hunter felt complete again. Being cut off from the computers was like being cut off from his own memory. He gave the pinnace an update on what the Squad had discovered, and added a series of general orders for the computers to follow, if by some chance the Squad didn't make it back from the city. He checked the pinnace's power reserves, and nodded slowly to himself. There was enough there to do what was needed. He dropped out of the contact, and turned back to the Squad. They were talking animatedly as they discovered their comm units were working again too. They weren't cut off any more. Hunter coughed loudly to get their attention.

'All right, people, we're back in the game with a new deck. I've instructed the pinnace computers to warm up all the ship's systems. As soon as the ship's ready, I'll have the computers fly her here on remote control, and we'll get the hell out of this city.'

'Sounds good to me,' said Corbie.

'We can't leave,' said DeChance.

'Try and stop me,' said Corbie.

'The esper's right, Captain,' said Krystel quickly. 'For better or worse, this planet is our home now. We have to make our life here. And as long as this city and its creatures exist, we can never be safe. We can't communicate with them, and we can't live alongside them. They are insane, and quite deadly. It's us or them, Captain, and this may be the best chance we'll ever get to destroy them. They're dependant on this tower; if we destroy the great device, the aliens should die with it. If we leave the city now, we may never get another shot at the tower.'

'You can't be sure of that,' said Hunter. 'And there's no guarantee that destroying the tower will destroy the aliens.'

'Nothing's sure in this madhouse,' said Krystel. 'But it's our best bet.'

'Yes,' said Hunter finally. 'I think it is.' He patched into the pinnace computers again, fixed the flight plan and set the engines in motion. 'The ship's on its way, people. If we're going to destroy this tower, we'd better get a move on. You are sure the device is somewhere in this tower, DeChance?'

'The machine isn't in the tower, Captain,' said the esper. 'The machine is the tower. All of it.'

She stepped through the jagged hole into the tower, holding her lantern up before her. Hunter and the others exchanged glances, and then followed her in. Outside in the night, the aliens tore savagely at each other, no longer interested in the Squad. The tower had them now.

Inside the copper tower there were huge, linked shapes of metal, glass and crystal. Their dimensions seemed to vary according to which angle they were viewed from. There were parts that moved, and others that weren't always there. There was a continuous low murmur of sound, as though the device was whispering secrets to itself. Hunter looked up into the tower, and saw the device stretching away above him; huge, Cyclopean and inhumanly intricate.

'This is it,' said DeChance quietly. 'This is the machine that freed the aliens from the tyranny of a fixed shape. This is where they made their own damnation.'

'And it's still working, after who knows how many centuries,' said Krystel.

'It's been asleep a long time,' DeChance continued. 'It's awake now. And it knows we're here.'

Hunter rubbed at his forehead. A vicious headache had started the moment he entered the tower. He felt hot and sweaty, and his fingers tingled uncomfortably.

'Are you all right, Captain?' said Krystel quietly.

'I'm fine,' Hunter replied quickly. 'Just the long day catching up with me.'

'No,' said DeChance. 'It's the device. It's starting to work on us now. It'll affect any living thing that stays within its influence too long. And the closer you are, the greater the effect is.'

'Hey, wait a minute,' said Corbie. 'You mean we're going to turn into things like the aliens? Right, that's it. I'm off.'

'Go outside on your own and the aliens will tear you to pieces,' said DeChance. 'But they won't come in here after us. The device wouldn't permit it. We're safe enough from the tower's influence for now. It takes time . . .' She held up her left hand and looked at it. The fingers had fused together into a single fleshy paw. 'Of course, some of us are more susceptible than others.'

Hunter looked at her closely, shocked, taking in the changes in her face since he'd last seen her. She'd definitely lost weight, and her bone structure was prominent to the point of emaciation. She stood awkwardly, and her stance was somehow different. The marines hadn't noticed because the changes had been slow and subtle, but they were clear enough now that Hunter was looking for them.

'How much longer can you stay here?' he asked quietly. 'Before the changes become . . . dangerous.'

'I don't know. My esp makes me vulnerable, but you'll need that to help you find the device's weak spots. If it has any. The great device has survived for centuries without outside care or maintenance. It's bound to have self-defence mechanisms. I'm not even sure it can be destroyed with our feeble weapons. But we have to try.' She looked around her. 'There's a ramp nearby that leads up into the heart of the device. I think our best bet would be to plant our remaining explosives in the middle of the tower, or as close as we can get, and then make our escape on the pinnace before they blow.' She looked at Hunter. 'We'd better get moving, Captain. We don't have much time.'

Hunter nodded soberly. 'All right then, esper, lead the way. Investigator, you follow right behind her. Shoot anything that even looks threatening. The marines and I will bring up the rear. Shields on, guns and swords at the ready. Let's go, people.'

DeChance moved confidently through the warren of disturbing shapes, and stepped on to the ramp. Strange forms came and went around them as they trudged upwards, and Hunter began to feel like an insect that had become trapped in the workings of a machine it couldn't hope to understand. There was a kind of sense, of meaning, to the great device, but he could only recognize it, and not appreciate it. There were lights and sounds, and sudden rises and falls in temperature, and none of them made any sense.

The ramp wound between layers of shimmering crystal, and static sparked on the air. Hunter's headache grew worse, and his stomach felt increasingly uneasy. No doubt some of it was due to tension, but he couldn't help wondering how much of it might be caused by the device, and how long it would be before his body began changing, like DeChance's . . .

Metallic tentacles suddenly swung down from above, like writhing snakes. They seemed endless in the unsteady light, and they were tipped with reaching clawed hands. The Squad got their force shields up just in time, and the sharp-tipped claws recoiled from the glowing energy fields. More tentacles came reaching out of nowhere, striking and retreating with inhuman speed. Hunter tried his sword against one of them, and the hilt jarred painfully in his hand as the steel blade sprang away without leaving a mark. The marines fired their guns, but the tentacles moved too quickly even for their experienced reflexes. The Investigator had used the edge of her shield to sever one tentacle, but the remaining tentacles avoided the shields' edges. It seemed they learned quickly. Blood flew as the claws struck home.

DeChance suddenly went down on one knee and hid behind her shield, eyes closed. Hunter moved quickly in beside her to protect her, but as far as he could see she hadn't been hurt. Her gaunt face was twisted with concentration, and in that moment she looked subtly inhuman, as though an imperfect duplicate had taken the esper's place. DeChance's eyes snapped open, and Hunter's hackles rose on his neck. Her eyes were pools of blood red, with long split pupils.

'*Three o'clock, Captain.* Fire at three o'clock and you'll stop the defence mechanism.'

Hunter hesitated a moment, and then fired blindly where the esper indicated. There was an explosion somewhere up above, and the ramp shuddered under his feet. The tentacles disappeared back into the maze of machinery. The Squad slowly lowered their shields and looked around them. Hunter looked at DeChance, and did his best to meet her disquieting eyes.

'Very good, DeChance. Any more surprises we ought to know about?'

'Not yet, Captain, but we've got to move faster. The tower's influence is growing. I can feel it building. Soon you'll all start to change. Like me.' Her voice had become harsh and strained, almost a growl. One arm was now clearly longer than the other. She smiled at Hunter, and her teeth had points. 'It's not far now, Captain. I've located a weak spot where we can set our explosives.'

She walked on up the ramp, and her body moved to an inhuman rhythm. Hunter's mouth was dry, and sweat ran down his face. He wondered what the esper was becoming, and whether he was looking at his own future. Could he live, like that? Would he want to? He swallowed hard, and forced himself to concentrate on the business at hand. All that mattered now was setting the explosives and getting out of the city before they went off. He'd worry about anything else later. If there was a later.

They came to a place where thousands of wires seethed and writhed like a nest of worms. Electrical discharges skittered on the air. A crystal turned slowly in the midst of the wires, like a watchful eye.

'This is it,' said DeChance. 'I think it's some kind of relay. Blow this, and the whole tower will come down. If we're lucky.'

'Lucky,' said Corbie disgustedly. 'I haven't felt lucky since we landed on this bloody planet.'

The Squad set about emptying their backpacks, and between them assembled a pile of proximity mines and grenades. The pile looked pitifully small set against the vastness of the tower. Krystel arranged the explosives so as to do the most damage, and then checked the mines' timers. She looked at Hunter, her face set and grim.

'Captain, we may have a problem here.'

'Oh great,' said Corbie. 'Another problem. Just what we needed.'

'Shut it, Corbie,' said Hunter. 'What's the problem, Investigator?'

'The proximity mines, Captain. The timers have a maximum setting of thirty minutes. There's no way we can get out of here and reach a safe distance in thirty minutes.'

Hunter frowned. 'How far is a safe distance?'

'Unknown, Captain. But thirty minutes is barely enough time to get out of the tower.'

Hunter looked at the esper. She shrugged; a quick, fluid gesture that disturbed Hunter greatly. 'I can't say either, Captain. The great device affects every living thing on this planet, to some degree. There's no telling what will happen when we destroy it.'

'The pinnace will be here soon,' said Lindholm quietly. 'The ship can get us out of the city in a matter of minutes.'

'We'd still be cutting it too fine,' said Hunter. 'We have to leave a safety margin in case we run into any more defence mechanisms on our way back down the tower. No, there's only one answer to this problem. Someone will have to stay behind and set the explosives off by hand once the others have got away.'

Corbie shook his head firmly. 'Oh no. I don't volunteer for anything, and I'm not about to start now. Right, Sven?'

'Right,' said Lindholm. 'I don't believe in suicide missions. There has to be another way.'

'There isn't,' said the esper.

'I'm not asking for volunteers,' said Hunter, his voice carefully calm and even. 'I'm staying. It's my Squad, my duty.'

'No, Captain,' said DeChance. 'I'm the one who has to stay.'

'I am the Captain,' said Hunter. 'I won't betray my trust again.'

'Very noble,' said the esper in her rasping voice. 'But not very practical. Look at me, Captain. *Look* at me.'

She held up her right hand. It had twisted into a bony claw. The skin was covered with thick bristly hair. The arm that held it up was crooked where it should have been straight. And her face had become almost a caricature of what a human face should look like. She fixed Hunter with her alien eyes.

'The changes have gone too far, Captain. Do you think I want to live like this? You only see the obvious signs. There are changes inside me too. And they're progressing. My esp makes me very susceptible to the tower's influence. Get out of here, Captain. Take the Squad and get the hell out of here. I'll give you an hour, before I set the timers. That should be enough.'

Hunter nodded, not trusting himself to speak for a moment. 'I'll tell the colonists all about you, Megan. I promise.' He turned to Krystel. 'Investigator, lead the way back down the ramp.'

The Squad made quick, quiet goodbyes to the esper, and left. She lowered herself carefully on to the ramp, and sat there alone in the light from her field lantern. For a while she listened to the Squad's departing footsteps, but they soon disappeared under the constant murmurings of the great device. She felt very tired. She watched the electrical discharges fluttering on the air, and listened to the machinery as it muttered around her like so many unspoken thoughts.

The Investigator led the Squad back down through the tower. There were no more sudden attacks, no more defence mechanisms. They came to the hole in the base of the tower wall, and Hunter gestured for the Squad to stay put while he took a look outside. He peered warily out into the night, and his stomach fell away. For as far as he could see, the copper tower was surrounded by an endless sea of monsters. Creatures varying in size from ten feet high to a dozen yards long waited silently in ranks beyond number. They did not move or speak or fight each other. The great device had called to them and they had come, impelled and controlled by its silent voice. Hunter ducked back inside the tower.

'We have another problem, people.'

'Oh hell,' said Corbie. 'What is it this time?'

'Take a look outside, one at a time,' said Hunter. He waited patiently while they did. Afterwards, even the Investigator looked more than usually grim. 'The aliens are quiet for the moment,' said Hunter finally. 'But once we step outside the tower the odds are they'll go crazy.'

'But why are they waiting?' said Lindholm. 'They're not even fighting each other.'

'The tower's influence must be growing,' said Krystel. 'Captain, we'll have to tell the esper we need more time. We're trapped in here until we can think of a way out of this mess.'

'There is a way out,' said Hunter. 'But it's going to call for some split-second timing. The pinnace will be here shortly. There's just enough room out there for it to land. I'll open the airlock by remote control, and we make a dash for it.'

'The aliens will be on us pretty quick,' said Corbie. 'What happens if one of us trips and falls?'

'Don't,' said Hunter.

'We've still got a problem,' said Lindholm. 'Theoretically, there's room out there for the pinnace to land, but in reality, it's too tricky a landing for a remote control. Much more likely we'd crash the ship trying. We need more space.'

'Then we'll make some,' said Krystel. She smiled, and hefted her sword.

'No,' said Hunter, thinking quickly. 'There are too many aliens this time. If we stand and fight they'll sweep right over us. There's a better way. About half a mile from here there's a wide open square. Plenty of room for the pinnace to land. I'll set her down there by remote control, and then we'll make a dash for her. If we're quick enough and mean enough, we should just make it.'

'Let me see if I've got this straight,' said Corbie. 'We're going to have to fight our way through half a mile of aliens, just to reach the pinnace?'

'That's right,' said Krystel. 'Bearing in mind all the time that the esper's clock is running. If we take too long getting there, it won't matter anyway.'

'I hate this planet,' said Corbie.

'It's not quite as desperate as it sounds,' said Hunter. 'Outside and to the right, there's a narrow alleyway between two buildings. If we hit the aliens hard enough we should be able to punch right through them and straight into the alley. They'll only be able to come after us in ones and twos, and we can make straight for the open square, and the pinnace. All right, that's enough chatter. Let's get moving, while our nerve holds out.'

*

In the heart of the great device, silent and alone, sat the quiet, desperate thing that had once been Megan DeChance. The device was playing with her now. One of her arms had become rotten and putrescent. In the other, her bones had become soft and limp. She still had feelings in some of her fingers; she hoped there was enough left for her to set the timers. She looked again at the timepiece embedded in what was left of her right wrist. It was getting hard to concentrate. She hoped she could hold out long enough to give the Squad the hour she'd promised them.

She was changing more rapidly now that she was so close to the device. Her humanity was fading away in fits and starts. She couldn't even tell which changes came from the device, and which came from her own subconscious mind. Her skin had a dozen textures, and her bones no longer held their shapes. She could feel strange organs growing inside her. She didn't know yet what their purpose was. It was getting harder to think. Her thoughts were becoming vague and unclear, and tinged with alien colours. She tried to say her name aloud, but her voice only made sounds. It was time. If she left it any longer, she might not remember what to do. She hoped fleetingly that the Squad had got out of range, and then she reached carefully out to set the timer on the first mine. She couldn't do it. The fingers on her right hand had become too large and clumsy to work the settings. She couldn't even prime it. She looked at her left hand. It was a shapeless fleshy paw. The explosives were useless. She couldn't set them off. The thing that had once been Megan DeChance raised its misshapen head and howled its anguish. The sound wasn't at all human.

Hunter burst out of the copper tower and ran for the narrow alleyway. He raised his disrupter, and a beam of violent energy smashed through the hulking creature in front of him. It swept on to pierce three other shapes before a fourth finally absorbed the beam. The aliens roared and howled as the smell of blood hit the air, and in seconds they had turned on each other, their single-minded emotions overpowering the tower's hold on them. Hunter and Krystel charged into the alleyway, opening up a space with their swords and shields. Corbie and Lindholm followed close behind, using their guns on creatures distracted while attacking their injured fellows. The extra blood sent the aliens into a feeding frenzy. Teeth and claws tore at uncertain flesh as the Hell Squad cut their way through the chaos to reach the narrow alleyway, their progress slowed but not stopped by the creatures.

Something tall and angular with flailing whips of bone and gristle lashed out at Hunter, bringing him to an abrupt halt. He met the whips with his shield, and they rebounded harmlessly from the glowing energy field. The alien tried to grab the shield with its whips, and the razor-sharp edges cut through them instantly. The alien paused uncertainly, and Hunter cut through its narrow neck with one sweep of his sword. The headless body attacked the creature next to it, its whips flailing blindly. The elongated head rolled away down the street, its mouth still snapping, until another creature pounced on it. Krystel swung her sword double-handed at Hunter's side, driving the aliens back with the sheer speed, energy and viciousness of her attack. Blood soaked her from head to foot, her grinning teeth flashed white in the bloody mask of her face. She was wounded, despite her skills, but she barely felt anything. She was beyond pain now. There was only her sword and her shield, and an endless supply of victims.

Corbie and Lindholm fought back to back, cutting down anything that came within reach. The ex-gladiator fought silently and efficiently, inflicting the maximum damage with the least effort. That was the way of the Arena; to save one's strength for when it was needed. Corbie danced and stamped and thrust, howling threats and curses. Mostly he cursed having run out of grenades. A silver creature with too many legs dropped on to him from a nearby wall. Corbie knocked it to one side with his shield, and skewered it while it lay thrashing on its back.

Hunter finally plunged into the narrow alleyway, with the rest of the Squad close behind. The press of aliens fell away as the high-walled buildings on either side protected them from the mass of the ravenous horde. Something flat and leathery swept down from above. Corbie deflected it with a quick shot from his disrupter, but only burned a hole through one membraneous wing. Krystel shot it in the head, and it fell limply to the ground. Corbie and Lindholm trampled it underfoot, and threw the body out of the alley to the blood-mad aliens. They blocked off the alley mouth as they tore at the flapping creature. Hunter looked down the far end of the alley, and his heart sank. A mass of alien shapes blocked it off, and the first few were already heading towards the Squad. Hunter slowed to a halt. The Squad crowded in behind him. Corbie looked to see what the problem was, and swore briefly.

'We're trapped, aren't we?' said Lindholm.

'Looks that way,' said Hunter. 'We'll just have to fight our way out, that's all. It's only half a mile to the open square, and by the time we get there the pinnace should be waiting for us.'

The Hell Squad formed a defensive wall of force shields, and moved steadily down the alley to meet the waiting aliens.

What was left of Megan DeChance crawled slowly along the ramp, leaving a trail behind it. It wanted to go after the Squad, to warn them that it couldn't set off the explosives, but that was beyond it now. Its flesh ran like melting wax down a candle, and its fingers dripped skin. The only things it had left that still worked properly were its implants. The thought struck a spark in the creature somewhere, and it fought to concentrate on it. The comm implant, the computers, the pinnace . . . Something that was meant to be a smile twisted its face. It still had one last hope, one last weapon to throw at the copper tower.

It activated the comm implant, and patched into the pinnace computers. It only took a few moments to take over the remote control, and give the pinnace a new heading and destination. The creature laughed silently, and crawled slowly over to the nearest wall. It took some time to draw the disrupter from its holster, and aim it at the wall. It took even longer before it found a way to press the stud with what was left of its fingers, but eventually the energy beam tore a hole through the tower wall, and the creature could look out at the darkness. Out in the night, a bright star grew slowly larger as the pinnace headed for the copper tower.

The aliens pressed close around the embattled Squad, driving forward from both ends of the alley. Hunter and Krystel fought side by side, striking down things that had no place in the waking

537

world. The two marines fought together with bitter competence, both aware that this was one battle they couldn't win.

Hunter saw the disrupter blast that tore a hole through the side of the copper tower, and thought for a moment the explosives had gone off early. It only took a quick glance to see that the damage was merely superficial. He wondered what the hell the esper thought she was doing, but the aliens pushed forward again, and for a while he lost himself in the press of battle. He was slowing down as his muscles cramped, fatigue hung like lead weights from his arms, and even his force shield couldn't protect him from every attack. Then a low continuous roar made itself heard above the sound of battle, and Hunter risked a hopeful glance up at the night sky. The pinnace came sweeping over the city from the east, its engines thundering, its hull bright with navigation lights. Hunter's heart surged with hope, and he fought with a new ferocity.

What remained of Megan DeChance watched the pinnace soar across the city. The creature tried to laugh. It was its last act of defiance against the thing that was destroying it, and it was a good one. It cried, and its tears dug furrows in its face, like acid. The pinnace thundered across the city, heading straight for the copper tower. The creature gave one last command through its comm implant, and laughed silently as its form finally collapsed. The pinnace's engines roared as they moved to full power, and the ship leaped forward to slam into the copper tower at full speed. The great device screamed through the throats of the undying aliens as the pinnace's engines exploded, shattering the copper tower and tearing apart the insane mechanism that had made the city a living hell. The explosion seemed to echo endlessly through the night, and when it finally died away the city was still and silent, save for the flickering flames around the base of the broken copper tower.

CHAPTER EIGHT

Aftermath

Hunter awoke in a sea of grey jelly. It clung to him as he sat up, and fell reluctantly away from his uniform. The stuff even coated his hands, and he shook it off with a *moue* of distaste. His head ached, his joints were stiff, and all in all he hadn't felt this tired since Basic Training. He looked slowly around him in the early morning light, and wondered fleetingly how long he'd been unconscious. And then the previous night came flooding back, and he scrambled to his feet. He looked wildly around him, and only then realized there was no sign anywhere of the army of monstrosities he'd been fighting.

He was standing in the middle of what was left of the narrow alleyway, and all around him lay great pools and streamers of the thick grey jelly. It looked to be two or three inches deep in places, and it smelled awful. Not far away, Corbie and Lindholm were sitting with their backs to the wall, talking softly. They looked bruised and bloodied, but pretty much intact. They saw Hunter looking at them, and managed something like a salute. Hunter nodded briefly, and looked at what was left of the alley walls. The copper tower had contained most of its own explosion, and the high walls on either side of the alleyway had soaked up the rest of the blast.

How about that, thought Hunter. We finally had some good luck.

The Investigator was standing at the entrance to the alleyway, staring out at the city. Hunter made his way over to her, treading carefully so as not to slip in the jelly. Krystel heard him coming, and looked back over her shoulder.

'Good morning, Captain. Welcome back to the living. I think

539

you'd better come and take a look at this. It's really very interesting.'

Hunter felt a brief stab of foreboding. The Investigator usually only found things interesting if they involved violence or imminent death. He moved forward to join her, frowning slightly as he took in the traces of grey jelly on her uniform.

Krystel smiled. 'Not very pleasant stuff, is it? You'll find most of it brushes off.'

'How did it get on our uniforms?' said Hunter, brushing determinedly at his sleeves.

'I think we spent most of the night sleeping in it, Captain. The destruction of the device in the copper tower apparently knocked us out for some time. As to where the jelly came from . . . take a look at the city.'

Hunter looked, and his tiredness suddenly fell away as his adrenalin kicked in. The vile-smelling stuff carpeted the streets, and spattered the sides of buildings. It hung in syrupy streamers from windows and bridges, and flapped loosely on the breeze. Hunter heard the two marines come up behind him, but he didn't look round.

'Now that really is disgusting,' said Corbie. 'What the hell is this stuff?'

'Take a good look,' said Krystel. 'I think this slime is all that's left of the aliens.'

Hunter looked at her blankly for a moment, and then nodded slowly as he made the connection. 'Of course, when the forest was attacked, it lost its shape and melted into jelly. So did those plant creatures we met before the forest. The esper said all along that only the great device was keeping the aliens alive, and that's gone now.' He looked across at the fire-blackened ruins of the copper tower. 'The device had to weaken their physical bonds to make shape changing possible, but it weakened their bodies so much that in the end only the device was holding them together. When the pinnace destroyed the tower, the aliens just fell apart, collapsing back into the simple primordial jelly from which all life begins. The aliens are gone, all of them. And they won't be coming back.'

The Squad stood in silence for a while, staring out over the silent city.

'I wonder what went wrong with the esper,' said Lindholm finally. 'Why didn't she set off the explosives?'

Hunter shrugged. 'I don't suppose we'll ever know. Perhaps the device rendered the explosives useless in some way. Without them, all she had left was her comm link with the pinnace, and her own determination. She was a very brave woman, at the end.'

'Fine,' said Corbie. 'We'll build her a statue. Look, far be it from me to sound ungrateful, but what about us? How are we supposed to survive without the equipment in the pinnace? We can't even call for help with our main comm system destroyed.'

'Relax, Corbie,' said Hunter calmly. 'When I first re-established contact with the pinnace, I took the opportunity to order the computers to pass on a summary of everything we'd found. And since the Empire's always interested in new alien civilizations, I think we can expect a fully equipped starship any time in the next few weeks. We should be able to survive that long on our own. In fact, with the aliens and their device gone, this could turn out to be quite a pleasant little world.'

'Pleasant, but boring,' said Krystel, lighting up her carefully hoarded last cigar.

'I can live with boring,' said Corbie. 'There's a lot to be said for boring as a way of life.'

'You should know,' said Lindholm.

'And there's always the city,' said Hunter. 'There's enough mysteries and new technologies here to keep us busy for years. We won't have any problems attracting colonists to Wolf IV; scientists and their families will be fighting tooth and nail for the chance to examine this city. After all, there's one very important question still to be answered.'

He waited, smiling, and eventually Corbie sighed heavily.

'All right, Captain, I'll bite. What very important question?'

'According to the pinnace computers,' said Hunter, 'this is the only city on the planet. Which implies the aliens didn't originate here. They came to Wolf IV the same way we did; as colonists. But if that's true, where is the aliens' home planet, and why didn't they come back to check up on their colony? I'm sure the Empire will want to know. After all, a species sufficiently

541

advanced to build something like the great device could end up as the Empire's first real rival.'

Captain Hunter smiled. 'I don't think we'll find life here too boring, people. There are enough mysteries here to keep us busy for the rest of our lives.'

Other Vista SF titles include

Robot Dreams Isaac Asimov 0 575 60180 9
Robot Visions Isaac Asimov 0 575 60152 3
Tangents Greg Bear 0 575 60159 0
Blood Music Greg Bear 0 575 60280 5
Eon Greg Bear 0 575 60266 X
Timescape Gregory Benford 0 575 60050 0
Aftermath LeVar Burton 0 575 60371 2
Imperial Earth Arthur C. Clarke 0 575 60158 2
The Fountains of Paradise Arthur C. Clarke 0 575 60153 1
Richter 10 Arthur C. Clarke & Mike McQuay 0 575 60110 8
Mortal Remains Christopher Evans 0 575 60043 8
Golden Witchbreed Mary Gentle 0 575 60033 0
Ancient Light Mary Gentle 0 575 60112 4
The Difference Engine William Gibson & Bruce Sterling
0 575 60029 2
Deathstalker Simon R. Green 0 575 60160 4
Deathstalker Rebellion Simon R. Green 0 575 60011 X
Phoenix Café Gwyneth Jones 0 575 60075 6
City of Illusions Ursula K. Le Guin 0 575 60128 0
Four Ways to Forgiveness Ursula K. Le Guin 0 575 60175 2
Child of the River Paul J. McAuley 0 575 60168 X
More Than Human Theodore Sturgeon 0 575 60207 4
Oracle Ian Watson 0 575 60226 0
The Knights of the Black Earth Margaret Weis &
Don Perrin 0 575 60037 3
Robot Blues Margaret Weis & Don Perrin 0 575 60068 3
Faraday's Orphans N. Lee Wood 0 575 60130 2

VISTA books are available from all good bookshops or from:
Cassell C.S.
Book Service By Post
PO Box 29, Douglas I-O-M
IM99 1BQ
telephone: 01624 675137, fax: 01624 670923

VISTA